KISS

— OF THE —

BASILISK

LINDSAY STRAUBE

Bloom books

Published by Bloom Books, an imprint of Sourcebooks
P.O. Box 4410, Naperville, Illinois 60567-4410
(630) 961-3900
sourcebooks.com

Cataloging-in-Publication data is on file with the Library of Congress.

Printed and bound in the United States of America.
LSC 10 9 8 7 6 5 4 3 2 1

This book is for anyone who has ever wanted more.

ABOUT THIS BOOK

I'm told it's best to go into this book with absolutely no knowledge of its contents. As such, you'll find no blurb or summary here. Instead, I will leave you with some sincere advice: buckle up. The Split or Swallow series is unlike anything you've ever read before, and you may not read anything like it ever again.

Say goodbye to the person you were before this book. And once you've read it, hand it to your friend so they can read it too.

PART
ONE

CHAPTER ONE

Y OU'LL NEVER GUESS WHAT HAPPENED TO ME LAST NIGHT," VERA WHISPERED.

Tem sighed. She had come to the bakery to deliver eggs and had gotten gossip instead. It was always that way with Vera.

"What happened?" she asked.

Vera leaned over the counter so only Tem could hear. "Jonathan took me under the bridge."

Tem's mouth fell open. Everyone knew what happened when a boy took you under the bridge. "Are you serious?"

"Yes." Vera smirked. "I saw his"—she glanced over her shoulder, then back at Tem—"*cock.*"

Tem blushed at the word.

"You've never seen one?" giggled Vera, tossing her blond curls over her shoulder in haughty satisfaction.

"No," Tem muttered. Vera knew quite well that she had never seen one, at least not in person. There were plenty depicted on the marble statues that lined the steps leading up to the church, but those were nothing to write home about. They looked like baby carrots. "What was it like?"

Vera leaned in, pursing her lips in a conspiratorial triangle. "It was firm," she whispered. "Like a cucumber. But warm, and it fit perfectly in my hand."

"You *held* it?"

Vera laughed.

Tem resisted the urge to hurl an egg at her.

"You don't just hold it. You *play* with it. You stroke it up and down." Vera moved her hand to mimic the motion, and Tem memorized it instantly. "Until he finishes."

Vera giggled cruelly at the look on Tem's face. "Oh, Tem," she whimpered, her condescending tone unbearable. "Don't worry. You'll learn tomorrow night. That's what the basilisk is for."

Everyone knew what the basilisk was for.

"Of course," Vera continued. "It doesn't hurt to have an advantage. After all, the prince is going to pick the most skillful girl. I intend to get as much practice as possible."

Only Tem knew the painful truth, which was that there was no one she could practice with. The boys her age didn't talk to her, and if they did, it was only to inquire whether her mother's farm had any spare roosters available. Gabriel was her only friend, and he wasn't interested in girls at all. But it didn't matter anyway. Tem had always known she wouldn't have a chance with the prince, regardless of what the basilisk taught her. The prince was far more likely to choose an experienced girl like Vera to be his wife.

It was as if Vera knew what Tem was thinking, because she said, "You could always practice at home."

Tem looked up. "How?"

"Touch yourself. If you know how to do that, you can better understand how to touch someone else."

For once, Tem felt a small surge of victory.

She had already touched herself plenty of times in the privacy of her own room. She'd done it for as long as she could remember, and she knew exactly how to bring herself pleasure. Those solitary moments were important to her; they made her feel sexual and alive. She loved the euphoric weakness she felt after her orgasm, and she wondered if men felt a similar way when they finished.

"I'll try that tonight," Tem said, keeping her secret to herself.

Her superiority disappeared immediately at Vera's next words. "Of course, I was *so* pleased when Jonathan returned the favor."

Tem's jaw dropped. "He touched you too?"

Vera smiled widely, eager to perform for her audience. "He didn't just touch me. He *tasted* me."

Tem frowned. "I don't understand."

Vera laughed, the sound cutting Tem to her core. "No, you wouldn't, would you? You've never even been kissed."

Tem's embarrassment only deepened. If Vera wasn't referring to kissing, she must mean the other, more intimate act—the one Tem had only ever imagined and never expected to experience. Blush rose once again on her cheeks, dovetailing perfectly with her shame.

"What was it like?" Tem asked despite herself. She loathed giving Vera a platform but desperately needed to know the answer.

"Oh, Tem," Vera giggled again. "You'll find out eventually." She paused, and her mouth twisted cruelly. "Or maybe you won't. After all, who would want a girl who tastes like chicken shit?"

The insult was too great for Tem to bear. It hit her right in her insecurities, confirming every dark, horrible thing she had ever thought about herself—that she was nothing but a farm girl, that she was dirty and unlovable, that no man would ever look at her the way she dearly wished to be looked at. It took enormous effort to keep those thoughts at bay, and just when she'd managed to do so, girls like Vera reinforced them.

Tem had had enough of this stupid conversation. "Do you want these or not?" She brandished the carton of eggs in her arms.

"Yes," Vera sighed, clearly disappointed they were no longer talking about her. "One moment." She grabbed the eggs and flounced away.

Tem used the time to gather herself. She felt ridiculous and pathetic every time she let Vera get the best of her. But it was impossible not to feel inferior when she'd never even kissed a boy. She would never be like Vera with her silky pink ribbons, dangled teasingly in front of the boys at the market. She would always be the girl who tasted like chicken shit.

When Vera returned with Tem's payment, she sneered one last time.

"Get some rest, Tem. You're going to need it."

On the walk home, Tem allowed herself to cry.

She took the roundabout way through the woods so nobody would see her tears, walking along the edge of the wall that encircled the entire village. Twelve feet tall and made of wood, the wall looked nondescript from the inside. But on the outside, it was sheathed in mirrors.

Centuries ago, when humans had arrived in this part of the world, they hadn't known that the basilisks were already here. The monsters weren't a problem at first; when they wore their human forms, they looked just like humans—*attractive* humans. Their sexual influence was undeniable, and it was the main reason the villagers were able to coexist with them for so long.

But when they wore their *true* form—when they turned into huge, ruthless snakes—they became a threat. The resulting war was bloody. The basilisks had magic that the villagers couldn't defend themselves against. That is, until they learned that the basilisks had weaknesses: the crowing of a rooster, the smell of a weasel. It wasn't until a snake dropped dead after looking at itself in a puddle of water that the villagers realized they were also a threat to themselves. They'd won the war with mirrored shields. In exchange for the territory outside the wall, the basilisks agreed to use their seductive talents to train the prince's future wife to ensure she would bear him an heir. A tentative truce was formed, and the two groups had lived in relative peace ever since.

The small cottage Tem shared with her mother was nestled on the edge of the forest, and Tem felt a wave of warmth when she saw it. It had always been home to her, no matter what awaited her outside its walls.

Her mother looked up from the kitchen table when she walked in. "How did it go at the bakery, my dear?"

"Terrible," Tem said.

"With the eggs or with Vera?"

"With Vera."

"I told you to ignore that girl."

"She's like a gnat. Gnats are hard to ignore."

Tem's mother sighed, wiping her hands on her apron. "You must learn to shut out the noise, Tem."

"Like you do?"

It was a low blow, and Tem knew it. Her mother was the only person more affected by the town gossip than Tem was. Raising a child on her own in a village that revered fatherhood and idolized male heirs hadn't been easy. Add to that her occupation as a chicken farmer, and Tem's mother was a pariah. Which made Tem the daughter of one.

"I'm sorry, Mother," Tem said preemptively.

Her mother pursed her lips, clearly suppressing her hurt. "Think nothing of it, my dear. I know you're nervous for tomorrow."

Nervous didn't even begin to cover it.

Before she could put her foot in her mouth again, Tem retreated to her bedroom. It was her sanctuary in more ways than one: every time the world seemed too large, she knew she could end the day alone in her bed.

Tem hung her cloak in her wardrobe before lying down and staring blankly at the ceiling. She felt endlessly tired, like the weight of the entire world was on her shoulders. And it might as well have been. If she didn't do well tomorrow, she would let her mother down. They were humble farmers, and people like Vera looked down on them. They had nothing. If Tem were to win the prince's hand in marriage, their entire reputation could change.

Tem wanted nothing more than to make her mother proud, which entailed getting as far along in the training process as possible. She stood no chance of winning. But if she could make it past the first elimination round at least—maybe even the second, Kora willing—then maybe her mother would forgive her when the prince didn't choose her. There were matches available for girls who ranked highly in the training but didn't marry the prince. She could marry a duke or a lord of some sort. But even if the prince was impressed with her—an impossibility—she wouldn't have a true chance with him unless she was one of the final three girls. Those three girls would sleep with the prince, showing off everything they'd learned during the training. The prince would choose his wife after that.

Tem rolled onto her side with a sigh. She stared at the palms of her hands, which were sprinkled with freckles. The tiny dots of pigment trailed from the end of one palm to the other, forming a pattern across her skin not unlike a constellation.

"You hold the stars in your hands," her mother had always said, rubbing Tem's fingers between hers. "Just like your father."

But when Tem had asked to know more, her mother had grown quiet, and Tem had learned quickly not to dig any deeper. She knew her father was a sore subject. Her mother had left him before she was born, and that was the extent of her knowledge. Tem had often wondered what he could have done to make her mother leave, especially given how difficult it was to run the farm without a man shouldering some of the burden. But it was useless to wonder. And Tem didn't care to know anyway. It wouldn't change the way the villagers whispered about them or the way Vera looked at her like she was some disgusting bug she needed to squash. Things were never to be fair for them. Tem had accepted that long ago.

The only thing that mattered was what would happen in the caves tomorrow.

Vera's words replayed in her mind: *Get some rest, Tem. You're going to need it.* Tem closed her eyes. By the time she woke, it was dinnertime.

Her mother was at the stove, tending a pot of stew. Tem pulled a loaf of bread from the cupboard and had barely begun to slice it when there was a knock on the door. Tem knew from the sound of it—five short, sharp *braps*—that it was Gabriel.

Her mother's head popped up from the pot.

"*Don't* let that infernal boy in."

Tem rolled her eyes. The last time Gabriel came in, he'd accidentally knocked over the drying rack, shattering several of her mother's favorite serving platters. Tem had spent hours trying to glue the ceramic back together, to no avail. Gabriel couldn't help it; his limbs moved almost of their own accord, with utter disregard for inanimate objects—or people for that matter.

"I won't," Tem said, already gathering her cloak. She'd forgotten Gabriel had wanted to drink tonight, and now that she had remembered, it sounded like the best thing in the world.

"And don't stay out too late," her mother insisted.

"I won't."

"And don't—"

"I *won't*." Tem placed her hands on her mother's shoulders.

Her mother looked up at her. "Tomorrow is important, Tem. I just want you to—"

"Make an impression. I know. And I will."

"I want you to make a *good* impression."

"I *will*."

Her mother didn't look convinced. Tem wasn't really convinced either.

Brap brap brap brap brap.

Tem glanced at the door. "I have to go. I'll be back early, I promise."

She pressed a quick kiss to her mother's temple before throwing on her cloak and opening the door. There stood Gabriel, all six chaotic feet of him. He wore a long leather jacket, his caramel hair lightly tousled from the walk over.

"Leather?" Tem said. "Really? You said you weren't trying to take someone home tonight."

"I'm always trying to take someone home." Gabriel stuck his head through the doorframe to give Tem's mother a jaunty wave. "Hello, Mrs. Verus. You're looking lovely this evening."

Tem's mother gave him a scalding glare.

Gabriel was unfazed. "What's cooking? Smells delightful," he crooned.

"We'll be back soon," Tem said hurriedly, pushing Gabriel onto the porch.

He threw his arm around her as they stepped into the garden. "Your mother doesn't seem to like me anymore."

"You terrorized her serving platters. The woman holds a grudge."

"*Pah.*" Gabriel flicked his fingers as if that was of no concern to him. "Give me a week. I'll be back in her good graces."

Knowing Gabriel, he would be.

"But enough about me." His arm tightened around her. "Can you smell that, Tem?"

"Smell what?"

He made an exaggerated show of sniffing the air. "*That* is the smell of your virginity disappearing into the wind."

She shoved him as hard as she could, with little effect.

"Are you sure we shouldn't be trying to get *you* laid tonight?" he continued without missing a beat. "It couldn't hurt to get you some practice before tomorrow."

"With who?" Tem asked bitterly.

"I'm sure we can find a lively bartender who would delight in your company."

"The only bartender at the Horseman is Old Steve. You want me to fuck Old Steve?"

"No. But I'm sure Old Steve wouldn't mind fucking a pretty young thing like—"

She smacked his arm. "Why don't *you* fuck Old Steve?"

Gabriel gasped dramatically. "Please, Tem. I have standards."

"Not that I can see."

"Bit feisty tonight, are we?"

She smacked him again, and this time he threw his hands up in surrender.

"*Fine*, neither of us will fuck Old Steve. His loss. *I*, on the other hand"—he grasped the lapels of his leather jacket, snapping it down smartly against his shoulders—"am on a mission to get the stable boy to notice me."

Tem frowned. "From what I saw last night, Henry already noticed you."

"No, not Henry. Peter."

"What's wrong with Henry?"

"Nothing. He's been commissioned for a travel assignment. He'll be gone for the next two weeks."

"What travel assignment?"

"He's helping ferry people in for the eliminations."

It was customary for the prince's extended family to congregate for the duration of the training. Those with a high enough ranking would stay in the castle, while the rest would infiltrate the village's inns. It was a notoriously fruitful time for the village economy. Even the homeliest bed-and-breakfast would experience a boost from the uptick in wealthy patrons.

"You seriously can't go two weeks without kissing a stable boy?" Tem said.

Gabriel laughed. "I *could*. But why would I want to?"

She had no answer to that.

By the time they got to the Horseman, Tem was aching for a drink. The bar was busier than usual, which wasn't a surprise. The entire village was on edge, anticipating the events of the next several weeks.

"Beers?" Gabriel said.

"You're buying."

"Anything for you, dearest."

Tem slid into their usual booth and looked around the room. There was Vera, sequestered in a corner with Jonathan. She was sitting aggressively close to him, practically on his lap, with her breasts pushed together. Two tables over was a group of girls talking excitedly. Tem recognized them; they would be going through the training with her. She wondered if they were as nervous as she was. If the way they were laughing was any indication, she doubted it.

By the time Gabriel returned with the beers, Tem's stomach had worked itself into a fiddly knot.

"To Kora," Gabriel said, raising his glass to hers. It was the traditional toast.

"To Kora." Tem downed half her beer in one gulp.

Gabriel raised an eyebrow. "Thirsty?"

"Very."

He followed her gaze to Jonathan and Vera, who were kissing each other like it was their last night alive. He raised an eyebrow. "Don't they know they're in public?"

"True love waits for no one," Tem said bitterly.

Gabriel snorted. "That's not true love. *That's* an unplanned pregnancy waiting to happen."

Tem had to laugh at that. She doubted Vera was stupid enough not to take the infertility herb, considering how much sex she had on a weekly basis. All the girls took it, including Tem, although it wouldn't matter during the training; it wasn't possible to become pregnant by a basilisk. At least that's what everyone said. But the same stories had circulated the village for years that, in extremely rare cases, it *was* possible. And if it were to happen, the baby would be an abomination of nature: half human, half basilisk, forever caught between the two species, never fully fitting in with either. But that was nonsense. Nobody Tem knew had ever met such a creature, and there was no reason to believe the rumors.

Gabriel's voice pulled her from her musings: "Who do you think will win?"

Tem looked up at him. "Win what?"

"The prince's hand in marriage, of course. Who will be the lucky lady?"

Tem found it telling that he didn't automatically assume it would be her. Even her best friend had no faith in her abilities. She could only answer with the truth. "Vera. She doesn't even *need* the training."

"Hm," Gabriel said thoughtfully, taking a sip of his beer. "She's too easy. Men don't like that."

Tem cocked an eyebrow at Jonathan, whose hands were unashamedly down the front of Vera's dress. "It would seem that men do."

"That's not a *man*, Tem. That's a boy."

Tem could hardly tell the difference. "Who do *you* think will win?"

Gabriel shrugged. "You, of course."

Tem blinked. Maybe he did believe in her after all. "You must be joking."

"I'm not. Why shouldn't the prince choose you?"

"I can think of a hundred reasons."

"Name one."

Tem could've listed them all, but she chose the most obvious. "I'm inexperienced."

"That's what the basilisk is for."

It was the conversation at the bakery all over again.

Tem bristled. "I *know* what the basilisk is for. But even if I learn everything there is to learn, I'll never look like *that*." She jerked her head at Vera, who was barely distinguishable from Jonathan.

Gabriel scoffed. "If you ever look like that, I'm never hanging out with you again."

She shot him a glare. "Be serious, Gabriel."

"I *am* serious, Tem. You're too hard on yourself. You're a catch."

"It doesn't count when you say it."

"Does it count when Old Steve says it? Because I'm sure he would if we asked him."

Tem resisted the urge to pour her beer on his lap. "The *prince* has to think I'm a catch. And I can assure you, he won't."

Gabriel tapped her twice on the nose. "You'll never land a man with that attitude."

"The prince is hardly a man," she grumbled, swatting his hand away.

The prince was twenty years old, just like Tem. Only girls born in the same year as the prince were eligible for the training. She'd never seen the prince up close, although if Vera's bullshit story about running into him in the town square was to be believed, his eyes were green. Tem didn't believe the story, and she definitely didn't care what color his eyes were.

"It could be worse, you know," Gabriel said.

"What could?"

"The training. At least the prince will make his choice based on who he likes in bed. If it were based on other skills, you'd have no chance at all."

Tem frowned. "What other skills?"

"Oh, I don't know. Cooking, for example."

"*Cooking?*"

"I've had your shepherd's pie, Tem." He wrinkled his nose. "Gamey."

Thankfully, at that moment, Peter walked through the door.

Gabriel leaped to his feet, adjusting his jacket and running a hand through his hair. "Duty calls," he said before making a beeline for the stable boy.

After that, there was nothing left for Tem to do but watch Vera and Jonathan test the bounds of what was appropriate to do in public. Two beers later, Tem was ready to go.

True to her word, she wasn't home late. But the cottage was quiet when she arrived, her mother already in her room, probably asleep in anticipation of an early morning on the farm. Tem washed her face in the bathroom before crawling into her bed and staring once more at the ceiling. Usually, she would touch herself before falling asleep, but the thought of meeting the basilisk tomorrow was so intimidating that she couldn't even do that. She tossed and turned violently, unable to settle.

When she finally slept, she dreamed of fire.

It didn't burn her. Rather, it warmed her gently, from the tips of her toes to the base of her skull. The fire felt familiar somehow, as if it were sent by someone she had known a long time ago. Flames licked her fingers, her palms, her arms. A single breath brushed her cheek. Then it was over.

The next morning dawned like any other. Tem went about her chores, delivering her eggs and helping her mother in the kitchen just as she always did. But in the back of her mind was the constant knowledge that in less than twelve hours, she would be face-to-face with a basilisk.

By the time evening arrived, she was taking her angst out on the potatoes.

"*Careful*, Tem," her mother said. "You're going to cut yourself."

A cut was the least of Tem's problems. She threw down the knife in exasperation. "I'm not ready, Mother," she said. "How will I know what to do?"

Her mother sighed, brushing her hair from her face.

"You will learn what to do. The basilisk will teach you."

"What if I'm inadequate?"

"All girls are inadequate when they go into the caves."

"Not all girls," Tem muttered, thinking of Vera with Jonathan.

"Trust me, my dear. You will do just fine."

Tem sighed. It was no use—her mother simply didn't understand. Tem had absolutely everything to fear. Inadequacy was but a single feather on the wing of her insecurities. Tem couldn't imagine a scarier scenario than the one she was about to experience.

And yet the dream ran through her mind.

If what awaited her in the caves was anything like what had happened in the dream, she knew she had no reason to fear.

"It's nearly nightfall. Why don't you go get ready?"

Tem nodded. Anything was better than chopping potatoes.

She retreated to the bathroom, drawing a bath and washing quickly, trying not to think about every inch of her naked body. When she returned to the kitchen, her mother gestured to the bench.

"Sit."

Tem sat.

Her mother tapped her on the knees. "Pull up your skirt, my dear."

"Why?"

Her mother held up two amber glass vials. "We must apply oils to your thighs."

Tem frowned. She didn't want to go into the caves with oily thighs. "What for?"

"Ylang-ylang is for bravery. Sandalwood for heat. They will give you courage and capture the eye of the basilisk."

"Hopefully not literally," Tem muttered as she pulled up her skirt.

"Of course not, my dear. You know what I mean."

Tem sighed, watching as her mother took the stoppers from the vials and spread the oils on her thighs. She rubbed them in with warm fingers, leaving the skin shiny and bright. The rich, woodland softness of the sandalwood was an appropriate mate for the floral depth of the ylang-ylang. Tem could imagine how the scents would entice a man.

But was it truly a man she was to entice?

"Mother," Tem said tentatively as her mother resealed the vials. "What will it be like?"

She'd never asked her mother about her own time in the caves. But her mother had been just like Tem, born in the same year as a prince, and she had participated in the same training. The current king hadn't chosen Tem's mother as his wife, but Tem often wondered what her life would have been like if he had.

Her mother sighed deeply, and for the first time that evening, her brow softened. She looked like she was remembering something significant.

"It will be…transformative. You will take the first step to becoming a woman."

"I thought I was one already."

"Not nearly, my dear. You have barely begun to live. You cannot possibly fathom the journey you are about to embark on." Her mother tugged Tem's dress down, stepping back to look at her fully. "Now remember, this is but the first of many nights. Do not offend him, or else he may not allow you to come back."

"How would I offend him?"

"Kora willing, you won't. But knowing you, you'll find a way."

Tem sighed. Her mom wasn't exactly wrong.

"You must remember to be polite," her mother continued. "And to defer to him completely. You are the student, and he is the teacher. This is not the time for your headstrong nonsense. You will do as he says and try to learn something."

Tem nodded, although her stomach had turned into a tangled mess. She was no good at following instructions—she never had been. Why would she be good at this most important, fundamental thing?

"I'm hopeless, Mother," she whispered, her eyes on the ground.

"No, my dear," her mother said kindly, placing her palms on Tem's shoulders. "No girl is hopeless."

Her words were of no comfort to Tem. She craved specificity from her mother—she wanted to hear that she, herself, wasn't hopeless. But that was not what she expected, and it was not what her mother provided. There would be no specificity; there would be no coddling for Tem tonight or any night. There was only the task at hand and her willingness to complete it.

"It is nearly time," her mother said. "Come."

Tem nodded, following her mother out the front door and along the cobblestone path to the street. She could see Vera ahead of her, following her own mother out of their cottage. By the time they reached the edge of the trees, Tem was last in the line of fourteen girls and their mothers.

They walked as if in a trance, nobody speaking as they followed the long dirt path into the woods. It was a chilly night—one of the first nights of autumn. Tem tried to calm herself down, but it was no use. Her thighs were oily and her head was light; she felt as if she might be sick. She was seriously considering turning around and sprinting home when suddenly the wall loomed in front of them.

Tem had never been beyond it. She knew there were doors at various points along it but had never gone through one. They weren't even locked—locks were unnecessary when the mirrored exterior was protection enough. But the thought of running into a basilisk in its true form—and risk being turned to stone by its deadly gaze—was plenty of motivation to stay within the wall.

Tem said a silent prayer to Kora as they passed through the door.

As soon as they were outside the wall, Tem saw that they were at the base of the mountain. The line of girls stopped before a long row of caves, each entrance a gaping mouth in the moonlight. For a long moment, nothing happened. And then, through the haze of the evening gloom, a figure emerged from the shadows.

Tem's heart caught in her throat. She was too far away to see it clearly but close enough to know that it was wearing its human form, as expected. That was part of the deal: none of the girls vying for the prince's hand would die in the caves. It would violate the truce. Of course, Tem found it hard to trust an agreement that was made hundreds of years ago. But she had no choice.

Beside her, Tem's mother grasped her wrist. "Be brave, child."

Tem didn't have to turn around to know she was gone. All the other mothers were leaving too, kissing and embracing their daughters before disappearing back down the path until only the girls were left standing alone in the cold.

Nobody said a word.

Tem realized that despite being told about the training nearly every day for the better part of her life, she had no idea what actually happened next. How would she know which basilisk she would be paired with? Would she be the one to choose, or would they?

Before she could ask the girl next to her, the basilisk stepped forward.

"You have come here to learn," he said, his voice echoing against the rocks. "At the end of the training, the prince will select one of you as his wife."

Silence.

It wasn't exactly new information. Still, it was jarring to hear it now, moments before it was about to begin.

"It is our job to prepare you for that honor." His eyes flicked over them, and Tem flinched when they landed on her. "Proceed to your caves."

Nobody moved.

How were they supposed to know which cave was theirs? They awaited further instruction, but the basilisk didn't speak again. To Tem's satisfaction, even Vera looked nervous.

Suddenly, the girl in front of her gave a short, garbled scream before turning and running back toward the wall. She disappeared through the door a moment later.

One down, thirteen to go.

Somehow, the deserter gave Tem strength. She was no coward; she would not run. She had come here to make her mother proud and, more importantly, to make herself proud. She may not care about the prince, but she *did* care about a life beyond the chicken coop. She owed it to herself to find it.

Before she could talk herself out of it, Tem stepped forward.

Everyone looked at her, but she ignored them. Instead she concentrated on the caves, staring at each of them in turn. Fourteen caves. Fourteen basilisks. It was no use. She closed her eyes. The second she did so, something came to her, unbidden. The sensation was like a light in the darkness, calling to her. She moved to follow it, walking toward the farthest cave, feeling a shadow of what she had felt in the dream—a soothing warmth that drew her in. She knew, somehow, that she was heading in the right direction.

She didn't see whether the other girls followed her lead. Instead she clambered over the rocks to reach the entrance of the cave before slipping into the pitch-black. It was warm. Almost uncomfortably so. It took her eyes a moment to adjust, but once they did, she saw there was a dim light in the distance. She walked toward it, eventually finding herself in a room lit by firelight.

In front of her stood her basilisk.

CHAPTER TWO

•••✦•••

H E WASN'T AT ALL WHAT SHE HAD PICTURED.

Somehow, in her imagination, he never had a face. Tem's version of the basilisk was always mysterious—a featureless creature with nothing distinguishable about it, a blank canvas that couldn't be identified as anything remotely close to human. But the real thing was completely different. The real thing looked like the most searingly attractive man Tem had ever seen. He was an amalgamation of every feature she'd ever found beautiful—so much so that Tem wondered briefly whether it was on purpose. Basilisks were known for their powers of seduction after all. Had he tailored himself to look like this knowing it would appeal to her?

He was tall—so much taller than her—with broad, proud shoulders and rigid posture. The firelight flickering over his face accentuated his features, which were a mesmerizing sculpture of sharp, unforgiving angles that made him seem like he was carved from stone. His dark hair was longer than the current style, but somehow it suited him. He was wearing a light linen shirt and trousers, both of which did absolutely nothing to hide the hard outline of his body. Warmth. It was all she felt.

When the basilisk stepped forward, Tem's mind went completely blank.

"What is your name?" he asked, his voice a deep, glowing murmur.

Tem's voice seemed to have stopped working. "Temperance," she managed to whisper. "But I go by Tem."

There was a fireplace set into the stone wall, its flames reflecting in his golden eyes. Eyes that, if he were wearing his true form, she knew would kill her. The basilisk tilted his head, appraising her. His gaze made her feel so *exposed*.

"My name is Caspenon. But I go by Caspen."

"Caspen," she repeated, his name a rock in her throat.

There was a long silence, and in it, he studied her. Tem had a sudden fear that he would reject her right then. Was it possible to be expelled from the training before it even began? She had never heard of that happening, but she wouldn't be surprised if it happened to her. Before she could truly panic, he spoke again.

"You are afraid," he said.

Tem nodded, because of course it was the truth. He stepped closer, and her throat closed completely.

"There is no need to be afraid of me."

"I'm not afraid of *you*."

His head tilted the other direction. "Then what are you afraid of?"

Tem didn't know how to put it into words. So she simply said, "Failing."

The basilisk frowned. "At what?"

"At..." she started but didn't know how to finish.

"Sex," he finished for her.

Tem wasn't used to that word—her mother certainly never said it out loud, and Vera always called it *making love*, which was objectively atrocious. Tem herself had never heard it from a man's mouth. Whenever she had been taught about the training in school, the lessons were taught by women. But those lessons were years ago now, and Tem rather wished she'd paid more attention during them.

"I suppose," she whispered.

"Do you consider me an incapable teacher?" the basilisk asked.

"I don't know the first thing about you."

Caspen smiled a little at that. Something inside her untangled.

"The princes have chosen my students for generations. Rest assured, I will not allow you to fail."

Tem's mouth dropped open at the revelation. If what he said was true, it meant that Caspen was the Serpent King: the legendary basilisk whose power was far superior to all the others. His reputation was exemplary in the village; people talked about him like he was a god. Tem had the most coveted teacher.

Rather than easing her mind, this information did the exact opposite. Now she felt even more pressure than before. If she failed to win the prince despite being trained by the Serpent King, it would be beyond humiliating. Her mother would never forgive her.

Caspen was still considering her. "You do not seem desperate to be here," he said presently. His wording was odd. *Desperate?*

Tem frowned. "Should I be?"

Caspen shrugged. "Most girls are. It is an honor to be chosen by the prince. An even higher honor to eventually be crowned queen. Do you not desire those things?"

Tem thought about the question. Her mother certainly desired those things. It was the pinnacle of societal achievement and the ultimate way to transcend their simple life on the farm. She knew how badly her mother wanted her to succeed—*needed* her to succeed. But the truth was that it wasn't Tem's desire. She stood no chance with the prince. Schoolyard bullies had drilled that into her every single day since she was old enough to comprehend her place in the village hierarchy. So *was* she desperate to be here?

Tem found that she was.

Perhaps she wasn't desperate in the way the other girls were—perhaps she didn't crave the crown as Vera did—but she *was* desperate to be here in her own way. She wanted nothing more than to know what all the fuss was about—to touch a man and to have him touch her, to desire and be desired. The basilisk's voice cut through her thoughts.

"You are free to leave at any time."

Tem snorted and immediately regretted it.

Caspen seemed amused by her reaction. "Do you not believe me?"

"I'm not exactly in a position to leave."

He cocked his head. "It is not possible to effectively teach an unwilling student."

Tem supposed that was true.

"Has anyone ever left the training?" she asked.

"Once," Caspen said. For some reason, it looked like it pained him to say it. A second later, the discomfort vanished. "But she was not my student."

Tem considered that. If it was true, it was unheard of. The training was portrayed as an honor for any girl born in the same year as the prince. Tem wondered why this particular information had been left out of the school curriculum. She thought of the girl who had sprinted back behind the wall and wondered if she would one day regret it.

"Well," Tem said, jutting her lip. "I'm not leaving."

Caspen's mouth twitched once more in amusement. He stepped closer, and every single cell inside Tem lit on fire.

"Tell me, Tem. Have you ever been kissed?"

Tem blushed. She'd never even come close to being kissed. She realized suddenly that she might have asked Gabriel to kiss her. He was her best friend—surely he would've kissed her, especially if he knew it would have settled her nerves. But it was far too late for that now. Now she was standing in front of Caspen, the Serpent King, and he expected her to be so much more than she was.

"No," she whispered, the word a pebble in a pond.

Caspen smiled fully, baring his teeth. "That is good," he said. "It means there are no bad habits to unlearn."

Tem nodded, although she didn't quite believe him. She couldn't imagine it was better to have no experience at all. And yet basilisks couldn't lie—they were fundamentally incapable of it. At least that was what all the legends said. So he must be telling the truth, and if he was telling the truth, it meant Tem was better off than Vera. The thought cheered her immensely.

"Is that what we're doing tonight?" she asked with sudden courage. "Kissing?"

"No." Caspen shook his head. "I will not touch you tonight."

"Oh."

He seemed to sense her surprise, because he continued. "Before we touch, I need to see you."

She frowned. "You're seeing me right now."

He smiled. "Not all of you."

Anticipation curled in her stomach. She remembered the dream, the warm darkness surrounding her. She remembered the feel of breath against her bare skin. She wondered if somehow, it was Caspen's breath she had felt, if the dream was foreshadowing this.

He stepped back, splaying his hands palm up. "Please. Whenever you are ready."

Tem's heart leaped in her chest. She remembered that basilisks could smell fear, and she didn't want Caspen to think she was afraid. And yet she hesitated. She'd never disrobed before anyone, certainly not a man. She was only ever naked at home, when she bathed or when she touched herself. And even then, she avoided looking at herself in a mirror. There was nothing natural about this to her—she didn't know how to show herself to someone else. Not even the dream could have prepared her for this.

At her hesitation, Caspen clasped his hands together.

"All journeys begin with a step, Tem."

She still didn't move. Her mother's voice was beating through her brain: *You will do as he says and try to learn something.*

But Tem wasn't accustomed to following orders. It went against every instinct in her body—it violated everything about who she was as a person. She couldn't just blindly obey him. She wasn't built that way. She never had been. So she said, "You first."

Caspen's eyebrows shot up, then darted immediately together. At his reaction, a sharp knife of anxiety stabbed Tem's chest.

Do not offend him, or else he may not allow you to come back.

Her heart dropped to her feet. What if she had just offended him? What if he hurt her? Or worse—what if he transformed into his true form, looked her straight in her eyes, and killed her? She would apologize. She would get on her knees and beg for forgiveness. She would disrobe and let him look as long as he liked.

Before she could do any of those things, Caspen said, "As you wish."

Now Tem was surprised. She had no idea whether anyone had requested this of him before. But there was no taking it back, and she didn't want to anyway.

Caspen stepped closer, stopping only when he was a few feet away. He was so much taller than her; she had to crane her neck to meet his eye.

He looked down at her calmly, as if this entire process was of no concern to him. And she supposed it wasn't. He'd seen dozens of girls before her and would see hundreds after. This was a duty for him—nothing more.

For Tem, it was everything.

Caspen removed his shirt slowly, grasping the bottom and pulling it up over his head in an impossibly smooth motion. Half of him was still clothed, yet Tem could barely handle what she was already seeing. His body was unreasonably fit, his torso corded with hard muscle. His trousers were slung low enough to reveal the sharp angles of his lower abs, which pointed downward like two arrows. Tem felt her entire face flush at the sight, accompanied by a wild urge to pull his trousers down herself. But Caspen's hands were already untying them, and before Tem could take another breath, they dropped to the ground.

Caspen's cock was nothing like the ones on the marble statues leading up to the church.

His was unfathomably long and straight as an arrow. He wasn't even hard yet, and Tem was already wondering how the hell it was going to fit inside her. She'd never taken anything that big. She wasn't even sure it was possible. It was the perfect extension of him—exactly as formidable and beautiful as he was. Tem stared at it in awe.

Suddenly she understood his reputation as the Serpent King. Everything she'd ever heard about Caspen made sense now that she was seeing this final part of him. The way the villagers spoke of him in hushed tones, the way his girls were always chosen by the prince—all of it justified by what was between his legs. Why should he submit to anyone when he was superior in this most fundamental way? Why cede his power when his was so much greater?

Tem was overwhelmed by the sight of him. She wanted to feel him inside her. She wondered if he wanted that too. Immediately, she banished the thought. She wasn't the first girl he'd had in his cave. And yet somehow, it felt like this was just for Tem.

Caspen let her look, watching her reaction with the slightest trace of warranted arrogance on his face. Eventually, he whispered, "Now you."

It was only fair.

Somehow, her nerves had abated now that he was naked. Seeing Caspen vulnerable made Tem feel brave, and she knew she was ready for what came next. With steady hands, she unlaced her dress and let it fall to the ground so she was standing in her underclothing.

Caspen's eyes didn't leave hers as he said, "And the rest."

Tem pulled off her underclothing.

The warm air of the cave caressed her skin, enveloping her in a breathless wave. It was impossible not to think about the fact that *she was naked*. But before she could dwell on it, Caspen circled her silently, looking her up and down. She looked at him too, observing the way he walked with undeniable control, his steps smooth against the roughness of the cave floor. She saw the way he observed her clinically, without emotion. Tem realized that while this was very new to her, this was absolutely nothing new for him. He had done this many times before. She was nothing but a number to him—he wasn't looking at anything he hadn't already seen.

Finally, Caspen stopped in front of her. He studied her eyes, her cheeks, her hair. Eventually his gaze slid down her neck to her collarbones, passing over her breasts, and landing on her stomach. He extended his hand, the tips of his fingers mere inches from her skin. But he didn't touch her. Instead, she felt a sudden warmth below her belly button, and the firelight dimmed.

"What are you doing?" she asked.

"I am checking to see if you are fertile," he said without making eye contact.

"And? Am I?"

Caspen's eyes flicked up to hers. "Patience is a virtue, Tem." He said it like a reprimand.

Tem sighed. "So I've been told."

His gaze returned to her stomach. Tem resisted the urge to tap her foot as she waited, *patiently*, for the examination to yield a result. She should have expected something like this. Sex and fertility were intertwined with the basilisk's influence. It was rumored that they drew power from it—that their ability to seduce humans was intrinsic to their nature. It was the reason they were tasked with training the prince's future wife: they were the only creatures who could be trusted to mold girls into women.

After what felt like an eternity, Caspen said, "You are fertile."

Tem didn't know how to feel about the announcement. Part of her wished she weren't—it would have meant she was out of the running for the prince. But if that were the case for Tem, she wouldn't achieve what she had come here to achieve. She would never be kissed, never be fucked. And that wouldn't do at all.

Caspen was speaking again.

"You will need to gain weight," he said. "The prince requested a fuller girl."

"I can't," Tem said without thinking.

Caspen's eyes narrowed. "And why not?"

She hung her head. "We…don't have much food at home. I have no way to eat more."

They had no shortage of eggs. But other food was scarce, and their social status as chicken farmers had long since distanced them from the kindness of their neighbors.

"Then you will eat while you are here," Caspen said. "I will feed you after our sessions, starting tomorrow."

Tem nodded, still staring at the ground.

"And do not cut your hair," he continued. "The prince likes it long."

Tem's hair currently fell just below her shoulders, although it was longer when it was wet, before her curls set in.

"Lift your chin," Caspen commanded.

She did so.

"Sit down." He gestured at the rock ledge behind her. "And spread your legs."

She did so.

The moment her knees parted, Caspen's jaw tightened. Up until now, his gaze had been detached, almost unfeeling. Now his eyes glowed brightly, lit with raw intensity. He kneeled suddenly in front of her, leaning forward and closing his eyes. True to his word, he still didn't touch her. But he breathed in deeply, and she saw his nostrils flare, accentuating the sharp angles of his face.

"Ylang-ylang," he said quietly, "and sandalwood." His eyes opened. "Who told you to do that?"

"My mother," Tem said, trying to focus on anything other than the fact that he was kneeling between her very naked legs. "She said it would give me courage."

Caspen stared at her for a long time. "And did it?" he whispered.

Tem gave a small shrug. "I'm not sure."

He was still kneeling, still holding eye contact. But now his gaze returned to the center of her, and he spoke another command: "Open yourself."

Tem's stomach clenched. "I don't understand," she whispered.

"Use your fingers," Caspen said slowly. "And let me see inside you."

He was mere inches away. Tem couldn't fathom revealing this part of her, but she knew she wanted to. So she took her fingers and spread herself open, showing him what she'd never shown anyone before. As soon as she did so, Caspen's pupils dilated wide within their golden irises, their expansion mimicking her own. He looked for a long time, so long it became difficult to hold herself open as she slowly became wet beneath his gaze. What was he doing down there? Memorizing her anatomy? Determining how to teach her? Either way, it was exhilarating to bare herself to him. She wanted his approval, and she wondered if he would give it.

Tem was not the only one affected by the process.

For the first time, she experienced what it was like to influence a man. Caspen's arousal was undeniable—he grew harder the longer he looked at her, and she felt a surge of pride at being the one who caused it, along with an intense curiosity she could barely suppress. She wanted to touch him—to feel the effect she had on his body. She wanted to do what Vera had bragged about doing—take him in her hands and stroke him until he finished. The thought turned her on so much that her fingers slipped into her wetness. The motion felt good, and without thinking, she did it again, right in front of Caspen's gaze.

She thought he might reprimand her, but he didn't. Instead, she heard a low hiss and realized it was coming from him. The hiss echoed throughout the cave, bouncing along the walls and surrounding them with its vibration. Tem wasn't sure whether she should be scared of the sound.

"Do you approve of me?" she asked.

The hiss stopped immediately. Caspen's eyes snapped to hers. "My approval is irrelevant," he said sharply. "It is the prince's approval you should seek."

Tem was suddenly self-conscious. She stifled her aching wave of desire, kicking herself for being so insolent. Caspen was a basilisk—she was an idiot for thinking she could have any effect on him.

She withdrew her hand, embarrassed at her presumption.

"I did not tell you to stop," Caspen said.

Tem stared at him. His pupils had grown wider; there was almost none of his golden irises to be found. It was like looking into the depths of darkness itself; there was only endless blackness. Tem knew, on an instinctual level, that they were entering uncharted territory.

Tentatively, her hand returned.

She went slowly at first, sliding two fingers in and out steadily, watching Caspen as he watched her. Then she went quicker, caressing the parts of her he would soon have access to, coaxing herself into something she couldn't stop. She showed him how she liked it—doing what she did when she was alone in her room, after her mother had gone to bed, when the world was dark and the cottage was quiet, when she closed her eyes and pretended someone was watching her. She wanted Caspen to see her truly, in the way she'd always wanted to be seen: as someone worthy of a man's touch.

Eventually, the hiss returned.

Caspen's gaze was unwavering. The fire reflected in the sheen of his skin, and Tem swore she saw the shadow of scales dappled over his chest.

She was already wet, but the sight of him made her wetter.

He was completely hard, his cock standing as erect as a soldier, his very nature defined by what was between his legs. She wanted him to give in. She wanted him to grab her, to thrust with impatient necessity, to collapse into her like a dying star.

But Tem knew that wouldn't happen tonight. Caspen had said as much, and Tem respected that. The student would not override the teacher. Still, that didn't mean they couldn't share in this together, that he couldn't show his commitment in another way, proving himself with an act of reciprocation. She hoped he might participate in her experience. And to her intense pleasure, he did.

Without a word, Caspen's hand went between his legs.

He gripped himself and started to rub, his shoulders tensing with each long stroke, showing Tem what she would soon do. She couldn't look away from his hand. It moved in a relentless rhythm, tightly at the base, then smoothly over the top, rubbing consistently in long, steady motions, his breath hitching with each stroke.

Caspen went slowly at first, then faster and faster. Up and down, just like Vera had said. Any trace of hesitation was gone from his eyes as his basic instincts took over, his desire dominating every barrier between them. He arched his head, exposing his throat. The hiss was low, thrumming around them, enveloping Tem in its insistent frequency.

Then Caspen stood, looking down at her, his strokes quickening with urgent devotion.

Tem knew she wasn't the first girl to be naked in this cave. She knew she wasn't special, that there was nothing she could offer Caspen that he hadn't seen before. Still, it felt as if this experience was unique to them, like he'd never looked at another girl this way, like she was the only one he would ever do this for. She wondered if it was true. She dearly hoped it was.

Suddenly, he stepped forward, and her breath caught in her throat.

For a moment, Tem thought he might break—that he might give in and mount her. Instead he leaned down, his other hand gripping the rock next to her head, his body positioned directly above her. His hand never stopped, and neither did hers. It was thrilling to see the way he touched himself. To know he was doing it because of her was beyond euphoric. She wished she could run her hands over him. She wanted to feel him against her palms, to understand who he truly was, to touch everything he was letting her see.

But he was impassable. The only way to connect with Caspen tonight was to do exactly what they were doing now. So Tem matched his pace, fingering herself to the same song, proving to him their rhythms were compatible, syncing her cadence with his.

With her other hand, she touched her breasts, squeezing and cupping them, making sure he knew what he could have if he wanted it. He was leaning so close she could feel the desperate gasp of his breath on her face. He stood between her legs, their bodies mere inches apart.

Tem wondered if he would think of her the next time he did this. Would he picture her, like she would surely picture him? Would he wish it were her hand instead of his, rubbing up and down, servicing him, encouraging what grew naturally? Or would he imagine her doing other things, like kneeling in front of him, taking him in her mouth, consuming him like she wanted him to consume her?

She wished she could taste him. She wondered if he would ever let her.

For now, his eyes traveled along her body, watching the way she moved, drinking in her naked skin like he needed her flesh to survive. Always, his eyes returned to what her hand was doing between her legs. Tem stared up at him, her back arched, exposing every part of her. She was completely defenseless, yet she felt irrefutably safe.

"Deeper," Caspen said, his voice rough.

Pride surged through her. He approved. He wanted more.

But Tem wanted more too.

Instead of going deeper, she withdrew her hand, gripping her thighs and pulling them all the way apart, opening herself just for him.

"Won't you do it?" she whispered.

He leaned down even farther, lowering his face so it was directly over hers. He was so close to touching her, his chest an inch away.

Tem could smell smoke on his skin.

"*You* will do it," he said, his voice a growl.

At his order, a chill went through her body. He was the one in charge—she shouldn't have questioned him. And yet Tem knew she held some power here. He wanted her to go deeper—he had said so himself. She would gladly give him what he wanted as long as it was appreciated.

"Stand up straight," Tem said. She wanted him to see it.

Caspen's eyebrows furrowed in surprise. She wondered if he'd ever been given an order before. For a moment, she thought he might reprimand her. Then he stood up straight, and Tem knew she had him. So she went deeper, using both hands, pushing herself to the brink, no longer trying to delay the inevitable, teasing herself the way she wished he would tease her. Caspen stared at her hands between her legs, seeing the way her fingers moved in and out—steady as the tides—watching as she rubbed her most sensitive area with small, perfect circles.

He saw exactly how wet she was. He knew it was all for him.

Tem was close to finishing. But she tried desperately to draw it out, going slowly, wishing they would experience it together. She wanted Caspen to finish at the same time, to share this with him so they would be bonded beyond the constraints of student and teacher. She wanted to know that he breathed for her like she breathed for him.

Caspen was close too.

She could tell by the way he kept changing his pace at alternating intervals, slowing down whenever he looked at her for too long. Each time he did it, he closed his eyes, and when he opened them, it was like he saw her for the first time all over again, his hand continuing as if it had never stopped. His breath came in short bursts, his pulse beating erratically in his throat. They were approaching the edge together, building toward their imminent conclusion.

Tem couldn't hold out any longer.

"Together?" she managed to say.

"No." Caspen shook his head, his voice a shadow of a breath. "You first."

Tem was so close, she couldn't protest. If that was what he wanted, she would gladly give it to him. So she looked up at him, feeling the swell of inevitability grow, unable to resist the wave that was about to crest. It was the easiest thing in the world to surrender to Caspen, to show herself at her most vulnerable, to lower her walls just for him. She imagined the way he would feel, the way he would taste, what it would be like if he pushed her hands aside and let himself have her. Just the thought was enough to take her there.

Finally, Tem finished.

A second later, Caspen finished too, releasing himself into his hand with a shuddering groan. He was breathing hard, just like she was. He bowed his head, the back of his neck glistening in the firelight. His shoulders shone with sweat, their sinew pulsing beneath his skin as he panted softly in the aftermath.

Tem couldn't catch her breath. She felt an undeniable surge of power knowing she made him finish without laying a hand on him. She didn't dare imagine what would happen when she could touch him.

Caspen raised his head to look at her.

Tem wished she could kiss him. Instead she held his gaze, trying to read his mind. What did he think of her? Was he pleased? Did this solidify their bond, or was she nothing but a stupid child to him, no different from the dozens of other girls who had come to his cave? Surely he wasn't thinking the same thing as her—that she had never felt a connection with anyone like this, that they had something special, something significant.

Tem wanted to speak, but it seemed wrong somehow, to put something so vast into words. Now that she knew what he could do in front of her, she needed to know what he could do inside her. She would die if she never got the chance to be with him fully.

Caspen straightened, rolling his shoulders.

Tem straightened too, staring wondrously at the substance in his palm. The sheen of it caught the flickering light of the fire, and she found herself standing up, reaching for it without thinking.

Caspen jerked his hand away sharply.

"Oh. I'm sorry—" Tem stuttered, immediately embarrassed. "I've just never…seen that before."

He tilted his head, looking at her with a thoughtful expression. "It is similar to yours." He held his hand back out slowly. "You may look if you wish."

She nodded gratefully, leaning forward.

His cum was something between a liquid and a solid, thick and shiny, a handful of liquified pearls.

"It's beautiful," she whispered.

"Then it is like you."

The words were a breath. She barely heard them. But he had said them, and Tem knew she would never forget the first time a man had called her beautiful.

Tem's throat tightened. Was it possible he wasn't as ambivalent as she thought? Was it possible he desired her the way she desired him? In the warm afterglow of what they had just shared, anything seemed possible. Tem wondered if he would have done the same thing with Vera. Had she bonded with her basilisk in a similar way? Or had she merely undressed and stood there, like Tem was originally meant to do?

They stared at each other for an eternity, the truth of the moment registering in both of them. Then Caspen cupped his hands together, holding his pearls in his palms. For some reason, Tem knew to remain silent as he closed his eyes, furrowing his brow and bowing his head. She felt a sudden rush of air, and the fire dimmed completely, going out in a single *whoosh*. A moment later, it flared back to life. In the light, Tem saw there was an object in Caspen's hands. He held it out to her.

"Take it," he said.

She looked down at his palms, which cradled something resembling a claw. It was smooth and curved, thick on one end and tapered to the size of a finger on the other. She took it in her hands, feeling the hardness of it. It might be made of stone.

"What is it?" she asked, lifting it into the light. It was warm to the touch and heavier than it looked. She studied the curve of it, fascinated by its smoothness.

"It does not have a name," Caspen said. "At least not one in your language."

"What is its purpose?"

"It will connect us while we are apart."

"How?"

Caspen stepped closer. "You will keep it inside you."

"Inside me?"

"Yes." His eyes traced back down her body, landing between her legs.

Tem understood. Her blush returned.

"It should fit perfectly," he said.

Tem looked up at him, and she was surprised to see his eagerness.

"Do not tell anyone you have it. And do not show it to anyone. It is for you and only you."

He stared at her with an intensity she didn't understand. She could only nod; his gaze was too strong. She looked down at the claw.

"What will it be like?" she whispered.

"Warm," he said. "It is the exact temperature of my human form."

Tem nodded.

"It will feel good," he continued. "I will make sure of it."

"How?"

"Like I said, it will connect us. I can make it…pulse."

"Pulse?"

He smiled, and she melted.

"When it pulses, you will know I am thinking of you."

Tem stared at the extraordinary thing. She turned it over in her hands, feeling its weight, noticing the way it shone, as if it were made of starlight. She couldn't believe it was formed from his very essence. Tem had never seen magic like that before.

"Try it." Caspen's voice broke her from her thoughts.

She looked up at him.

"Right now?"

"Yes."

This morning, Tem couldn't have imagined doing anything like this. But after what happened in the last hour, she felt a bravery she wasn't used to and knew she was capable of following his command. So she sat back down on the ledge, once again spreading her legs in front of Caspen.

She looked up at him, awaiting instruction.

"Take the larger end inside you," he said.

Tem did as she was told. She inserted the thicker end of the claw slowly, keeping her hand steady while she did it. She'd never taken anything this big inside her—it was hard and smooth, different from the way her fingers felt when she touched herself, and she found despite her wetness, it was difficult to insert it.

When she winced, Caspen spoke. "Do it slowly. It is not meant to hurt."

Tem nodded, taking a deep breath and sliding it up as far as she could. It was a curious sensation, and she found she liked it. Still, it was impossible to imagine Caspen's cock inside her when this was already a tight fit.

She stopped with the tapered tip still visible, curved up against the most sensitive part of her. She pressed her finger against it tentatively, experiencing the way it cradled her.

"Does it feel good?" Caspen asked quietly.

She looked up at him, and with a rush of epiphany, she saw he was hard again. Not all the way, like before, but he was partially raised, and Tem knew she had caused it.

"Yes," she whispered.

They stared at each other for a long time, Tem sitting and Caspen standing. It felt like a significant moment, and Tem knew not to break it. She wondered if he would touch himself again, but he didn't. He seemed to enjoy simply looking at her, and she enjoyed letting him.

The fire was burning low by the time Caspen finally murmured, "We are done for tonight. You may get dressed."

Tem felt brave once more and said, "So can you."

His mouth slid into a devious smile. "I appreciate your permission."

"I gladly give it."

Caspen's smile widened. Tem noticed that he watched her even as she put her clothes back on, his eyes tracing over her body until the last possible second. She watched him too, seeing the muscles roll in his shoulders as he pulled on his shirt, observing the defined veins on his arms as he tied his trousers. She sensed a restrained energy in his body, and she couldn't wait to feel it.

When they were both dressed, Caspen gestured gracefully.

"I will walk you out."

Tem nodded, following him toward the cave entrance. She could feel the claw inside her and was sure she would never get used to it. It took effort to walk normally.

It was a shock to enter the cold evening air after the warm embrace of the cave, and Tem shivered as they stepped outside. The grass was wet beneath her feet; it had rained while they were inside. At the start of the path, Caspen looked at her. His face was attentive, his eyes flashing in the dark.

"You will return tomorrow night. Do not be late."

Without another word, Caspen turned to leave.

"Wait," she cried despite herself.

He stopped, his back to her.

"Will you think of me?" Tem whispered.

Caspen didn't turn. She stared at his shoulders, broad and strong in the dark. His silence was absolute; she could hear nothing but the rustlings of the forest around them, overlaid by the pounding of her own heart. He stood there for so long she wondered if he had even heard her. Finally, he said, "I told you I would."

"I know. I just…" Tem paused, crossing her arms and taking a deep breath before finishing, "I wanted to hear it again."

Caspen still didn't turn.

Instead, an aching pulse shot suddenly between her legs. It passed through her so sharply that she gasped, doubling over in surprise, overwhelmed by the sheer intensity of it. She had to cry out; the sensation was too strong. She had never felt anything so good—it eclipsed every sensation she had ever given herself; it made her entire insides unfold in a spiral of petals, like she had become one with the moon and the stars.

Tem could barely keep her balance as the pulse intensified, forcing her to her knees. She curled into herself, her fists gripping the grass. She couldn't breathe; she couldn't think. She felt nothing but the most profound pleasure of her life. Tem knew in that moment without a shadow of a doubt that she was alive.

Then it was over.

By the time she looked up, Caspen was gone.

CHAPTER THREE

---◦•✳•◦---

THE NEXT MORNING AT BREAKFAST, HER MOTHER FIXED HER EGGS, AS USUAL. TEM sliced an apple on the side and set the honey pot on the table, the way she did every morning. Everything was as it had always been—everything was exactly the same. Except for Tem.

She was forever changed by her time in the cave. She'd lain in bed all night, wide awake, replaying everything that had happened. She remembered what she saw when Caspen dropped his trousers. She remembered what it felt like to touch herself, to see Caspen grow hard at the sight of her, to finish in front of him.

Tem tried to eat but could not. The moment she raised her spoon, the claw pulsed, and she gasped.

When it pulses, you will know I am thinking of you.

The thought was like dewy grass on a spring morning. She could imagine nothing better than knowing she was on Caspen's mind. She wished desperately for another pulse—she wanted him to think of her again—to think of her continually until they were reunited that evening.

But another pulse didn't come.

Tem's heart sank. Was that all she was worth to him? A single pulse—nothing more? What if it had been an accident, and he hadn't been thinking of her at all? Shame flushed her cheeks, and she turned back to her plate.

Breakfast passed in silence. Tem knew her mother was dying to ask about her time in the caves, but every time she opened her mouth, Tem shot her a glance that made it clear she didn't want to talk. She couldn't possibly tell her what had happened. She'd need to come up with a story that didn't involve her completely crossing every boundary the training was supposed to have in place.

In the meantime, it was Sunday, which meant the entire village went to church.

As Tem climbed the church steps, she looked at the stone statues of the gods—the ones whose anatomy was so staggeringly inferior to Caspen's. If these were the gods, then what did that make him?

They were late, and the church was already full. Tem followed her mother to the back row, sliding into the pew after her. When she sat on the hard wooden bench, the claw pressed against her insistently. She was immediately warm between her legs and wished she were alone. She had to sit delicately, her thighs tensed on the hard wooden bench, her hands gripping her knees.

"Something wrong, my dear?" her mother asked.

Tem shook her head. There were no words for the experience. "Nothing, Mother."

She looked around the church, trying to locate Gabriel as a way to distract herself. He was sitting at the end of their row, his arm around a boy who was decidedly not Peter. She couldn't help but smile.

The service began. They prayed to Kora, goddess of fertility. It was Kora's benevolence that influenced the training, that blessed the girls with fertility, that ensured the prince would bear a male heir. It was in Kora's name that Tem was to offer her body as an option for the prince. Kora was a mother to all, and it was said she visited new mothers the night before they gave birth to bless them with a safe delivery. Tem wasn't sure she believed it. There were plenty of women who died in childbirth. The queen herself, for instance. Everyone knew that the prince had grown up without a mother. Had Kora forgotten to visit her?

It was halfway through the service when the first pulse came.

Before Tem had a chance to catch her breath, a second one quickly followed. But this couldn't be happening right now. Not now, not next to her mother, not in *church*. Sitting still was impossible. Tem clutched the pew with both hands, squeezing her eyes shut as she tried to control her breathing.

Another pulse came, and Tem let out the tiniest whimper.

Do not make a sound.

Tem froze. The voice was Caspen's, and it had come from inside her mind. But how was that possible? Before she could wonder further, another pulse came, this one so strong that Tem had to grab the pew in front of her to keep from crying out. Her mother looked over with a frown.

"*Cramps*," Tem mouthed.

Her mother nodded.

It was the only thing she could think of to explain the way she was leaning forward, trying desperately to find a way to sit that didn't accentuate the pulses, which were coming in increasing frequency. There didn't seem to be any pattern to them. They varied in intensity and duration, sometimes quick and sharp, sometimes slow and lingering, each one leaving her more breathless than the last. They were so chaotic that Tem almost wondered if they were accidental. She couldn't believe the basilisk was thinking about her at all, much less thinking about her for this long. Tem looked around for something—*anything*—to distract her.

Her eyes landed on Vera.

She was at the end of a pew, leaning against Jonathan. Her shoulder looked like it was twitching, her arm jerking up and down in a steady rhythm. Whenever she sped up, Jonathan's head would roll back, and every time it did, Vera's shoulder would stop moving. Then it would resume a moment later with renewed vigor.

With a jolt, Tem realized what she was watching.

Tem looked around in bewilderment. Surely someone would see—surely someone would *notice*. But Vera and Jonathan were at the very end of a nearly empty pew, at an angle that hid Jonathan's lap. Anyone who glanced at them wouldn't know she was pleasuring him. Tem only knew because she knew Vera and also because she was so painfully turned on from the pulses that she felt as if she had suddenly acquired some inhuman ability to spot sexual activity from a mile away.

Whether out of sick fascination or latent jealousy, Tem couldn't look away. The pulses seemed to sense her arousal, somehow syncing to the motion of Vera's arm. They were purposeful now; Tem had no doubt that Caspen was thinking of her, and he must know she was thinking of him. The pulses were *building, building, building*. Even as the rest of the church started to sing a hymn, Tem couldn't join in. All she could do was stare at Vera's arm pumping up and down, imagining it was her arm instead, imagining it was Caspen's cock instead of Jonathan's.

Tem clamped her mouth shut as the final pulse came.

But it was impossible not to cry out. The hymn had reached a crescendo, and so had Tem, and just as the final note ended, Tem watched as Vera's head dipped beneath the pew, remaining in Jonathan's lap for a brief moment before rising again. She licked her lips in triumph.

The pulses lingered, drawing a residual moan out of Tem, which she didn't bother trying to silence. She was so wet, she could only hope it hadn't soaked through her dress.

"Someone wants you." Her mother's voice tore Tem from her trance.

"What?"

"I said, someone wants you." Her mother pointed to the end of their pew, where Gabriel was waving at her.

"Oh. Right."

The hymn was over. People were beginning to leave.

Tem stood with the rest of the crowd, filing toward the aisle, where Gabriel was waiting.

"Well?" he said when she reached him, hooking his arm into hers. "Are you a changed woman?"

Tem had no idea how to reply. She could feel her wetness dripping down her legs and felt a sudden kinship with Jonathan.

"Yes," she said honestly.

"Delightful." Gabriel squeezed her arm. "Tell me everything."

"Not while we're in church."

It was an empty protest. Nothing that had happened in the past hour had been appropriate for church.

"Oh, come on, Tem. Kora would be proud. She'd want you to give me all the juicy details."

Somehow, Tem believed him. Of all the deities, surely the goddess of fertility wouldn't object to anything related to sex. But still. Her mother was mere feet away, and Tem wasn't about to talk about this anywhere near her.

"I have a couple roosters to deliver. Meet me at the square in an hour?"

"With bells on." Gabriel gave her a mock salute before disappearing into the crowd.

Tem tried to act as normal as possible as she followed her mother home, but between the claw inside her and the wetness on her thighs, she was beginning to feel like a walking sin. The moment they were inside, Tem ran to the bathroom and immediately took a cold bath. As she washed her body with soap, she couldn't help but wonder what Caspen was doing right then. Had he climaxed, like she had? Was he still thinking of her? Did the claw only pulse when his thoughts were sexual, or would it pulse if she crossed his mind at all? What did basilisks do in their free time anyway? Tem tried to imagine Caspen at his version of church, sitting in a pew. Did basilisks worship Kora, like the humans did? Or did they have gods of their own?

Tem toweled off and dressed quickly, heading to the coop to gather the roosters.

Ever since it was discovered that the crow of a rooster could kill a basilisk, each household in the village was granted one rooster to be kept as a form of protection against the snakes in the event that they breached the mirrored wall. Despite their lifesaving properties, the roosters were not welcome gifts. A dead weasel was preferable for most people, especially since dead weasels didn't make any noise. Nobody wanted to wake up to incessant crowing at the crack of dawn, and for many families, the roosters ended up as dinner. Whenever that happened, Tem was tasked with replacing them.

By the time Tem had corralled the roosters and grabbed two dozen eggs for the bakery, nearly an hour had passed, and she had to rush to meet Gabriel at the square.

He was waiting under the clock tower, leaning jauntily against the bricks. He straightened when he saw her.

"Finally. Thought you'd forgotten about me."

"Never," Tem said as Gabriel took the basket from her arms. "You're unforgettable."

"Of course I am. Now give me details."

Tem told him everything that had happened in the caves, including how she had touched herself in front of Caspen, and he had done the same. The only thing she left out was the claw. Caspen had said not to tell anyone, and she had no desire to disobey him. Besides, it felt nice to have a secret, even if it was a small one. Tem's life had been so uneventful for so long that the prospect of keeping something from Gabriel was oddly thrilling. He'd had plenty of nights that she knew nothing about; now she had one of her own.

"Caspen sounds delicious."

"He's a basilisk, Gabriel. He's terrifying."

"Terrifyingly *delicious*."

If he hadn't been carrying her basket for her, she would've shoved him. "He's the Serpent King. His girls are always chosen. You don't understand the pressure I'm under."

"Tem. It's *good* that you're with the Serpent King. Imagine if you'd gotten a basilisk with no talent whatsoever."

"I wouldn't care."

"Oh yes, you would. I know you. You'd be whining about how you're with a boring old basilisk instead of one that knows what he's doing. Admit it. It's better this way."

Tem scowled. Gabriel was right, and they both knew it. Regardless of her mother's ambitions for her, Tem was participating in the training for her own selfish reasons, and those included getting as good at sex as possible just to prove to herself that she could do it. Like it or not, Caspen was the easiest route to that goal.

At the thought of sex, the claw pulsed.

Tem froze. They were in the middle of the road, in broad daylight. There was nowhere to hide if Caspen decided to send her anything else.

Gabriel stopped, looking back at her. "What's the matter with you?"

"Nothing," Tem said. "Cramps."

"Ah." Gabriel nodded knowingly. "Woman troubles."

"Something like that."

She stood still for just a moment longer, but to her relief, another pulse didn't come.

The rooster delivery was uneventful, and Tem was thankful Gabriel was there. People in the village liked him; they tolerated her. Gabriel had always protected Tem to the best of his abilities, but he was a year older than her and hadn't always been around when they were in school. He hadn't been able to stop the schoolyard bullies from chanting "chicken shit girl," but he had always been there to wipe her tears on the way home.

By the time they reached the bakery, Tem wished he could do that delivery as well. But she knew Gabriel's shift was about to start, and he kissed her on the cheek with a flourish before heading up the hill to the castle. Gabriel worked as a dishwasher in the castle kitchens, a job that gave him unending access to the stable boys. Which was just the way he liked it.

With a heavy sigh, Tem turned toward the bakery.

"*So*," Vera said shrilly. "How was it?"

Once again, Vera was leaning conspiratorially over the counter. Only this time, everything was different. This time, Tem was no longer the girl who had never seen a naked man. Between her experience in the cave and the presence of the claw inside her, the last twenty-four hours had been life-changing, plain and simple. But she couldn't say that out loud. Vera was such an insufferable blabbermouth that the entire village would know every detail by the time the sun had set. Tem settled on her usual strategy, which was to ask her something in return.

"How was it for you?"

"It was thrilling," Vera gushed, leaning forward. "My basilisk wants me. I can tell."

"What makes you think that?"

"The way he looked at me."

"Mine looked at me too," Tem said.

"Of course he did. That's what they're supposed to do."

Tem set her jaw. "He looked at me for a *long time*."

Vera sneered. "Well, so did mine. Forever, practically. And by the time he was done, I was wet. I'm sure he could sense it."

Tem had nothing to say to that.

"And that wasn't all," Vera continued.

Tem stiffened. Was she about to say that her basilisk had touched her? Kissed her? Done something beyond what Caspen had done with Tem? She braced herself, ready to hear confirmation that she had somehow messed things up already, that Vera was further along in the training after just a single night in the caves.

"He told me that I'm the prince's type. Apparently, he wants a curvy girl." Vera's eyes raked snidely over Tem. "A girl like *me*."

Tem felt her anger flare. "Caspen said that I—"

"*Caspen?*" Vera hissed, her face pinched with sudden jealousy. "He told you his *name*? Mine didn't tell me his. He didn't even *touch* me."

"Mine didn't touch me either," Tem admitted. But she left out the part where he'd undressed for her, as she had for him. She left out the part where they'd touched themselves in front of each other. And she certainly left out the part where he'd given her a piece of himself and that piece was inside her right now.

"Well, why would he?" Vera snapped.

Tem shrugged. The words hurt, but the hurt was alleviated by the pulse between her legs, and she wondered whether Caspen had felt her pain. She closed her eyes, focusing on the sensation. It was gentle at first, then more insistent. Tem couldn't help but smile; he was teasing her, the pulses lasting far longer than usual.

"And *what* exactly are you smiling at?" Vera interrupted her thoughts.

Tem's eyes flew open. "Nothing," she said, stifling her expression and brandishing the basket. "Take your eggs."

Vera huffed away, making a big show of retrieving Tem's payment before handing it over. "I guess I'll see you tonight," she said.

"You sure will," Tem replied.

She left the bakery with a spring in her step. For the first time in her life, an interaction at the bakery hadn't left her in tears. Not only that, she still had one more card to play with Vera: as soon as she found out that Tem was with the Serpent King, she'd be so jealous she might actually respect Tem enough to leave her alone.

The rest of the day passed in a blur of farm chores. Tem went through the motions mechanically, cleaning out the chicken coop on autopilot. She couldn't think of anything but tonight. How would the basilisk greet her? Would they talk about the pulses he had sent during church? Would they finally touch? Kiss? More?

The claw didn't pulse for the rest of the day, and Tem's heart was pounding by the time night fell and she joined the line of girls headed for the caves.

Her mother didn't escort her this time; she simply clasped her hands in hers, ran her fingers over Tem's freckles, and kissed her on the forehead before ushering her out the door.

When they reached the end of the trail, Tem was sick with anticipation. All she could think about was what might happen tonight. She could do nothing but put one foot in front of the other, and by the time she entered the cave, the pain in her chest was borderline unbearable.

There was Caspen, standing calmly in the center of the room. Tem's heart only beat faster as he closed the distance between them.

"Tem," he said quietly, and she remembered the deep smoothness of his voice. "How are you?"

"Oh," she said, clearing her throat. "I'm fine. How are you?"

He smiled, baring his teeth, but didn't answer. Instead, he nodded at the fireplace built straight into the stone wall. A thick mat had been laid out in front of it.

"Come," he said. "Let us begin."

Tem followed him to the mat.

Just like last time, he splayed his hands and said, "Whenever you are ready."

This time, Tem didn't demand that he undress first. Instead, she pulled her clothes off slowly, letting them drop to the ground in an easy pile. Caspen watched her, his mouth still tilted in a smile. He wasn't even touching her yet, but Tem could feel his power from here. Without a word, he undressed too, and once again, she let her eyes wander over his infuriatingly perfect body. Gabriel was right. Caspen was delicious.

Tem felt the same surge of power when she saw he was already on his way to being hard. It was incredible knowing he was hard because of her. It felt like the most intoxicating thing in the world to have this effect on him—to finally be perceived by someone other than her mother and Vera, someone who *mattered*.

"Lie on your back," Caspen said.

She did so.

"Open your legs."

She did so, and he knelt between them, pulling her thighs around his so he was centered above her. This wasn't the first time she'd been exposed in front of him, but it was the first time he'd touched her, and the second his skin met hers, Tem felt a *jolt* of energy so strong that her heartbeat would not be soothed.

The claw was still inside her, and Caspen caressed the tip of it with his finger. He wasn't touching her yet—just the claw—but he was so close that Tem could feel herself getting wet just from the thought.

"Did you enjoy what I sent you?" he asked quietly.

"Yes." She nodded, hoping he would send another pulse right now. But he didn't. Instead, he slid his finger along the curve of the claw and pulled it out in a single, smooth motion.

Tem gasped at the sudden emptiness.

Caspen set the claw aside. His hands returned to grip her thighs, pulling her even closer. Tem had never felt so vulnerable.

He paused.

Tem had absolutely no idea what to expect and briefly debated asking what they were about to do. Thankfully, Caspen spoke before she had the chance to.

"In order to understand a man's body, you must first understand yours," he said, his eyes tracing over her. "Do you know your own anatomy?"

Tem felt her inexperience rear its head once more. "I'm...not sure what you mean," she whispered.

Caspen extended his fingers, trailing them gently up her thighs. When he reached the center of her legs, he touched the most sensitive part of her, brushing against it with his fingertip. Tem had only touched that part herself, and now that Caspen was doing it, she feared she might go slightly insane.

"I mean," he continued, "do you know what this is called?"

"No," Tem managed to say, and it was the truth.

"A clitoris."

Tem had no idea it had a name. She knew it only as the part she teased just before she was about to finish—the part the tapered end of the claw pressed against, which throbbed with pleasure whenever Caspen sent a pulse.

"The prince may play with it," he said.

"Play with it?"

"Yes. Like this."

Caspen applied pressure with his finger, the veins in his arm flexing suddenly as he rubbed her clitoris *hard*. Tem cried out in surprise and pleasure. She could barely think, much less speak. Yet she felt the need to say, "Am I to be played with?"

Caspen withdrew his hand. The sudden absence of his fingers left her cold. He leaned in, and Tem flinched at the hardness in his eyes. "You are to do exactly what the prince wants. If he wants to play with you, you will let him. If he wants to do anything at all, you will let him."

His words were harsh, and Tem knew they were the truth. She was not the one with the power—she was here for the prince's pleasure, not the other way around.

"Right," she whispered. "Sorry."

Caspen's expression softened.

"You have nothing to be sorry for."

His fingers returned to her clitoris, and for a moment, all he did was touch her. Tem felt the familiar stirring of desire rear its head, and she wished she could sit up and touch him too. She wondered if Caspen wanted her to. He was clearly hard, but she had no idea whether that meant he was actually enjoying himself since he didn't stroke his cock like he did last time. He only touched her clitoris, and although it felt amazing, she desperately wanted more from him.

As soon as she thought it, he slipped two fingers all the way inside her.

Tem gasped. Caspen's eyes flicked to hers. If she didn't say something, she was going to moan, and that seemed inappropriate given Caspen's silence. So she said, "Does that have a name too?"

Tem's mother had always called it her "womanhood," which was decidedly vile. Vera called it her "flower," which was even worse.

If Caspen thought the question was weird, he didn't say so, instead answering calmly, "Pussy. Center. Vagina. Cunt. You can call it whatever you like."

The words were bizarre. Tem couldn't fathom calling it any of them. "What do you like to call it?"

The corner of his mouth twitched. "Pussy," he said simply.

Tem wondered what the prince liked to call it.

"Do you like that?" Caspen murmured, cutting off her thoughts.

"Yes," Tem said.

"Good." His fingers went deeper. "It is only the beginning of what you will experience."

Tem couldn't imagine anything more than this.

"It is my job to teach you what to expect," he continued.

She nodded, although she wasn't listening. What he was doing felt so good, she couldn't think straight; it was as if someone had poured honey into her brain, and all she could taste was sweetness. It felt as if every molecule in her body was on fire, like he was stirring the edges of her into a singular perfect shape. It was different from the pulses, which were cerebral—reverberating and lingering in her body like electrical surges. His fingers, on the other hand, were undeniably physical, forcing her to stay in the present and experience *exactly* what was happening.

Now that Caspen was touching her, Tem felt suddenly jealous that anyone else had shared this experience with him. She wanted to ground him in this moment—to remind him that it was *her* that he was touching, and nobody else.

"You're so…" Tem could barely get the words out. "…good at this."

Caspen let out a small laugh. "As I should be."

"Will it feel like this with the prince?"

Maybe she was imagining it, but she swore Caspen frowned. His words were clipped as he answered, "He has had anyone he wanted his entire life. So he is familiar with a woman's body."

Tem felt her stomach flip. Even though Caspen was teaching her—and *touching* her—she still felt like she would be clueless when she finally faced the prince. How could she possibly compete with girls like Vera, who had touched and been touched by men many times before? It was unfathomable. She couldn't hope to compare.

As these thoughts were thundering through her head, Caspen drew away.

"Sit up," he said.

Tem did so, her brown eyes on his golden ones. His skin was glowing in the firelight, as if the blaze originated from inside his body.

"Give me your hand," Caspen said.

Tem held out her hand, and he took it in his. He touched the tips of her fingers against the end of his cock.

"Do you know what this part is called?" he asked.

"No," she whispered, trying to keep her voice steady. He was so hard, she was having trouble concentrating.

"It is the head," he said. "See how it curves?" He brushed her fingers over the tip. "It is sensitive to a man."

Tem felt the smooth dome. It was shaped like a mushroom and just as soft. "Like a clitoris," she said.

Instead of answering, his grasp on her fingers loosened, which Tem took as tacit permission to explore.

Slowly, she trailed her fingers down the shaft of his cock, feeling every vein that ran along his intimidating length. She brushed her fingertips all the way from the base to the head, then back down again. She touched even lower, cupping his balls in her hand, filling her palm with them and squeezing gently. Once again, she was struck by the inaccuracy of the statues at church. If that depiction of manhood was to be believed, balls were three-quarters of the package.

Caspen watched her as she touched him, completely unfazed. He didn't seem to be in any sort of hurry, content to simply let her explore him at her own pace. She supposed that nothing surprised him at this point—he must've seen everything there was to see over the course of years of teaching.

Tem, on the other hand, was very fazed.

Caspen was the only man she had seen naked in person. And technically, he wasn't even a man. Even so, she felt quite sure that other men couldn't possibly be equipped the way Caspen was. She placed two fingers tentatively along his length. Two fingers were what she used to touch herself, and Caspen's cock was far longer and thicker than that. She literally couldn't imagine it inside her.

"It will fit," Caspen said quietly. Her eyes flicked up to his. "If that is what you are worried about."

"Oh," she said. "Well, that's…good."

He tilted his head. "You do not believe me."

"No, I—" She pulled her hand away in embarrassment. "It's just…"

Caspen leaned forward. "What is it, Tem?"

He was looking at her with genuine curiosity, which she found rather unnerving. It was overwhelming to have those intense golden eyes on her, and Tem felt her face flush under his gaze. "It seems like it'll hurt."

His expression softened. He leaned in even farther, and the temperature of the air rose between them. "I will make sure it does not. Your first time may be difficult, but you have nothing to fear."

Tem bristled at his assumption that it would be her first time. Even if he was right. "I'm not scared," she said sharply.

But she didn't know if that was true. All she could think about was how Vera had been having sex for *years*. How was it that Tem was so far behind? She squared her shoulders.

"Teach me how to touch you."

The words were not a question, and at them, Caspen's expression shifted from something like mild curiosity to...*pride*. But that couldn't be right. Before Tem had time to identify it properly, the basilisk took her hand in his, wrapping her fingers around his cock so they were holding it together. Then he guided her hand first up and then down, rubbing the shaft from base to tip just one single time, as if to show her how the motion would go. Then he squeezed their hands tighter and increased the pace, stroking in a steady, quick rhythm. Tem knew this was what Vera had done with Jonathan under the bridge and at church. But Tem couldn't imagine that Jonathan's cock looked anything like Caspen's.

"Breathe, Tem," Caspen said.

She hadn't realized she wasn't.

Tem had no idea how Caspen could concentrate enough to instruct her at a time like this, especially when he was the one being pleasured. Eventually, he removed his hand.

Tem didn't stop—she did exactly what she had seen him do to himself, rubbing in long, even strokes, speeding up when she sensed he wanted her to. It seemed like such a simple thing, yet it had an extraordinary impact. Tem was amazed to see the effect on Caspen—to hear his breath quicken, to see a fine sheen of sweat bead up over his chest. In every way possible, she was affecting him, and she loved every moment of it. She had never been able to do anything like this to a man before and, up until last week, had only imagined she ever would.

It was intoxicating to be this close to him—so close she could smell the smoke on his skin. But it wasn't like the smoke that curled from the pipes dangling from the mouths of drunk patrons at the Horseman. It smelled like the wildfires that sometimes burned the forest during summer—like the smoke that lingered on clothing after spending time around a campfire. It was deep and rich and layered, and Tem felt as if she were drowning in the smell.

Somewhere along the way, Caspen's hands found her hips, pulling her even closer. Their faces were an inch apart; Tem could see the soft curve of his lips. With a jolt, she realized they still hadn't kissed. The same hiss she had heard during her first night in the cave returned now. It filled the stone room, echoing around them in an endless loop, growing louder with every stroke.

"Faster, Tem."

Maybe Tem was imagining it, but it didn't sound like an instruction to her. It sounded like a plea, like he was begging her instead of telling her.

Tem went faster.

Caspen's jaw was clenched, his fingers digging deep into her skin. His breath hitched with each stroke, and she knew he was close to finishing. But how to get him there?

She remembered the church—the way Vera had dipped into Jonathan's lap. She remembered what Caspen had said about how the head was sensitive to a man.

So Tem leaned down.

Immediately, Caspen grabbed her by the chin, pulling her face up to his. His pupils were so wide, they eclipsed his irises, reducing them to thin rings of gold. The effect was mesmerizing; Tem couldn't have looked away even if she'd tried. It was as if his eyes had opened up a portal between them—as if they were pulling her in with a magnetic force she didn't have the power to resist. She withdrew her hand, suddenly terrified.

"Was that wrong?" she whispered.

"No," he said. "But you will learn one step at a time. Master this first."

She nodded, half expecting him to reprimand her. When he didn't, she wrapped her fingers tentatively around his cock again. His nostrils flared as she did it.

"Take me there with only your hand," he commanded.

He was still holding her chin.

She began to stroke him again. He'd lost none of his hardness during the pause. If anything, he was even harder. She felt how firm he was, how utterly unyielding. It was addicting to hold this part of him, to know that she had the power to make him finish. She moved her hand steadily, alternating between slowing down and speeding up, doing her best to tease him toward the edge. She pumped as quickly as she could for several seconds, then suddenly stopped, squeezing the base of his cock with no warning. His head arched back with a groan, and without thinking, Tem pressed her lips to his neck. His skin was unthinkably warm—far warmer than it should be. She thought he might push her away. Instead, his hand tightened under her chin, holding her in place with inhuman strength. His other hand darted around hers, directing her final strokes. One—two—and on the third, he finished, his cum pouring into her palm in a warm, smooth handful.

"*Kora*," he breathed. His lips were a centimeter from her ear.

She stared at the substance in her fingers. Just last night, she had stared at it on his. His very essence. Tem couldn't believe this was what had formed into the claw. She couldn't fathom what kind of magic could turn a liquid into a solid. It was unheard of, even by basilisk standards. She wondered what other magic they possessed.

Caspen finally unlocked his fingers from around her neck, placing his palm over hers. The fire dimmed, there was a cool pulse, and when he removed his hand, her palm was dry. They sat for a moment in silence, and Tem realized how intertwined they were. She was practically straddling him, their faces level, their chests mere inches apart. All it would take was a shift of her hips to ride him. Before she could act on her impulse, Caspen's hands wrapped around her waist. He lifted her off him, setting her gently back on the mat.

Tem wasn't sure what to expect next. So when Caspen reached for the claw, her heart jumped to her throat. And when he turned to her, this time she knew she wasn't imagining the ravenous anticipation in his eyes. He didn't say a word. Instead he wedged his hand slowly between her thighs, coaxing them open with his fingers.

Then he grasped her hip with one hand and slid the thicker end of the claw inside her with the other. Not all the way—just enough to make her gasp, and as soon as she did so, he pulled it right back out. Tem bit her lip. A fevered moment passed. Then he slid it in again slowly, working it in and out, over and over, while she knelt before him. It was equal parts ecstasy and torture. Tem wanted so much *more*. She wanted him to ram the claw inside her as far as it would go. She wanted him to toss it aside and ram *himself* inside her, faster and faster, until they both finished together. Instead she could only remain where she was, her breathing uneven and shallow, her hands gripping the mat as the claw filled her again and again.

Finally, it was too much. Tem felt her orgasm start to build, and she knew if he kept going, there would be no stopping it. She rocked her hips to match his rhythm, sliding herself forward to meet the claw, not caring how desperate she looked, not caring whether she was violating a boundary. She only cared about herself, and somehow, she knew that was all Caspen cared about too. His hand found its way to her neck again, pulling her face up to his, forcing her to stare into his mesmerizing eyes.

"It is time, Tem," he whispered. "Come for me."

"I'm—" she gasped.

Before she could complete the thought, she came for him.

Caspen's hand contracted around her neck as she climaxed, squeezing just hard enough that her vision blurred. Then, just as quickly, he released her. Her gaze fell to his hand between her legs, and she watched as he rubbed her clitoris—just once, the absolute briefest of touches—before pushing the claw the rest of the way inside her. Tem gasped at the sudden *fullness*, her hips jerking forward to take as much of it as possible.

Caspen's eyes met hers.

There was nothing to say, so neither of them spoke. But Tem felt an overwhelming understanding sweep over her like a tidal wave. In it, she felt Caspen's satisfaction as if it were her own. His approval was undeniable; he was looking at her like he wanted to devour her, like she was the single most beautiful thing he'd ever seen.

A moment later, the look was gone.

Tem watched as his pupils shrank, the blackness receding. It was only when his eyes were once again gold that Caspen finally said, "Shall we eat?"

CHAPTER FOUR

N THE RUSH OF THE LAST FEW MINUTES, TEM HAD NEARLY FORGOTTEN THAT THE basilisk had promised to feed her after their sessions. She nodded, still numb from everything that had just happened.

Caspen stood, pulling on his trousers. "Wait here. I shall return shortly."

He disappeared into the shadows, and Tem used the time to dress.

Some minutes later, Caspen returned holding a tray. He crossed to the mat, sitting beside her and setting the tray between them. The food was fancy—far fancier than anything Tem was used to at home. There were candied nuts and dried fruits, cheeses, thin cuts of meat, raisin bread, and small chocolates. This was luxury beyond the simple stews her mother made, and Tem was almost afraid to touch it.

"Is it sufficient?" Caspen asked. He was looking at her as if waiting for her approval.

"Oh—yes," Tem said quickly. "Thanks."

"Of course."

He was still looking at her.

"Won't you have some too?"

Caspen raised an eyebrow. "Would you prefer I did?"

"Yes. It's no fun to eat alone."

He chuckled quietly, and Tem savored the sound.

"As you wish." He gestured at the tray. "But please, you first."

Tem reached for the bread tentatively, aware of his eyes watching her. The basilisk waited until she took a bite before taking one himself, and for a minute, they ate in silence.

Finally, Caspen said, "You are afraid of me."

It wasn't a question. Tem looked up at him. She'd denied it when they first met, but now it seemed pointless to do so. "How can you tell?"

"I can sense it."

"But *how*?"

He looked at her, his mouth tilting up. "Your heartbeat." He leaned forward, brushing the tips of his fingers gently across her chest. "It is irregular. And you flinch when I touch you."

Tem blushed. "I don't mean to flinch."

Caspen shrugged. "It is a natural reaction. I am not offended."

Tem nodded, although she wasn't sure she believed him. Her mother's warning was still fresh in her mind. "I…like it when you touch me," she said quietly.

The basilisk smiled fully, baring his teeth in the flickering firelight. It was a feral smile—one of triumph and victory. "I know you do."

Tem wanted to ask if he liked it when *she* touched *him*. But she was far too nervous to do so. Instead, she said, "I suppose you can sense that too?"

He leaned back on the mat, tilting his head to look up at her. "It would take an imbecile not to sense that."

Tem felt herself blushing again. Was she so obvious? So predictable? "Do you find me boring?" she asked before she could help it.

To her surprise, Caspen let out another low chuckle. "Not in the least."

Her heart leaped. "But you must have met a thousand people in your lifetime."

"Far more than a thousand."

His words hung in the air, their meaning ambiguous. If he had met that many people in his lifetime and he didn't find her boring, that must mean she had made some sort of impression on him—potentially a positive one. Was he saying he found her *interesting*?

The thought was too much to bear. Rather than ask for clarification, she reached for a chocolate. Before she could touch it, the basilisk caught her arm. Tem froze as he raised her hand to the fire, turning it so that her freckles caught the light.

"Have you always had these?" he asked.

"Yes," she said. To Tem's horror, a darkness passed over his face. "Are they…I mean… is that bad?" she stammered.

Caspen blinked. "No," he said quickly, dropping her hand. "Just…" He hesitated for a long time, as if choosing his next word carefully. "Rare."

"Rare?"

"Eat," he insisted, ignoring her question. "We will not be meeting tomorrow."

Doubt shot through her. "Why not?"

"The prince wishes to see his potential future wives. You will go to the castle with the other students."

Students.

With a single word, Caspen had reestablished distance between them. It didn't matter that she had pressed her lips to his neck, that he had pulled her closer when she had done so. It didn't matter that he'd given her an orgasm and squeezed her throat when she came. He was her teacher and she was his student and he was training her for a role—nothing more.

Tem ate the rest of her food in silence.

When she was done, Caspen walked her to the head of the trail. Then he turned without a word and disappeared into the darkness.

———•◦◆◦•———

Tem was a mess of nerves the entire next day. Nothing she did alleviated the twist of anticipation she felt whenever she thought about going to the castle. Normally, she would seek out Gabriel for relief. But he was busy helping the kitchen staff prepare for the event tonight, so there was nothing left to do but help her mother around the farm and try not to think about how slowly time was passing. To make matters worse, she couldn't stop picturing what had happened last night in the cave. Every time she thought about Caspen's cock in her hand, she felt a deep ache between her legs that made her want to run to her bedroom and never see daylight again.

The afternoon passed in a daze of chores and errands, the hours sliding by in a meaningless blur. Caspen sent no pulses. Tem hardly heard her mother when she spoke; she barely registered the crowing of the roosters. It was only when she had to visit the bakery to drop off the daily allotment of eggs that Tem was forced to engage in a conversation that lasted more than two words. It was with Vera, and as always, it was unbearable.

"*So*, Tem, are you ready to meet the prince tonight? I have my dress picked out already, of course. Brand-new and made of the finest pink silk you've ever seen. What will you be wearing?"

"Oh," Tem said, wishing she could drown herself in the vat of chocolate behind Vera. "I hadn't thought about it. One of my mother's dresses, I guess."

"You're going to wear something *used* in front of the *prince*?" Vera scoffed. She was counting the eggs so slowly Tem felt as if time were flowing backward. "That's rather embarrassing, don't you agree?"

Tem did agree, but it didn't change the fact that she had no other dress to wear. "I'm in a hurry," she said instead, which only made Vera's sneer deepen.

"Where could you possibly have to be? Can't the chickens lay eggs without you?"

"Would you just hurry the fuck up?" Tem snapped.

Vera's mouth fell open. Tem was almost as surprised as she was. Throughout all the years of cruel teasing, Tem had never retaliated against Vera.

"There's no need to be *rude*," Vera said, her heart-shaped face scrunched in disapproval. "That kind of attitude won't get you anywhere with the prince."

"It got me somewhere with the Serpent King," Tem shot back.

If Vera was shocked before, she was livid now. Her eyebrows pulled together, and she leaned over the counter, narrowing her eyes at Tem.

"You're with the *Serpent King*? You're *joking*."

Tem leaned in too, holding eye contact. "I'm *not* joking. And as you know, his girls are always chosen. So I may not have a new dress, but I doubt I'll need one to catch the eye of the prince."

Tem snatched up her payment and left before Vera could say another word.

By the time it was finally evening, the thrill of defying Vera was long gone, and Tem was oscillating between tentative courage and absolute terror. The claw hadn't pulsed all day, and she had no idea what that meant. Surely, on today of all days, Caspen would think of her. But then she remembered how he'd called her his "student," and the wall of shame came crashing down once again. Of course he wasn't thinking of her. *She* was thinking of *him* because she was an overeager girl who somehow kept forgetting that her teacher was a deadly creature who could kill her with a single glance. How painfully predictable of her.

She was in the garden aggressively weeding the walkway when her mother approached.

"A package came for you."

Tem looked up in surprise. "What is it?"

Her mother shrugged. "I didn't open it."

"Who brought it by?"

"It was on the porch when I returned from the coop. I put it on your bed."

For some reason, this news sent Tem's heart into a canter. Before she had time to wonder who it was from, the claw pulsed. *Caspen*. It had to be.

Tem practically sprinted to her room, feeling lighter than she had in hours.

The package was wrapped in black paper and tied with gold ribbon. Tem touched the ribbon first, running the tip of her finger gently over its length. When she pulled on the end, the knot unraveled easily, the paper falling open to reveal a shimmering pile of fabric. Tem held it up and saw it was a dress. Unlike the linen dress she had planned to borrow from her mother, this one was made of silk, no doubt like the one Vera had bragged about earlier. It was deep emerald in color, and Tem knew Caspen had chosen it to complement her skin tone.

Tem was brutally torn by the gesture. If the dress was meant to make her prettier, did that mean the basilisk wanted the prince to find her attractive? And if he did, did last night mean nothing to him?

Something glinted on the bed, and Tem set the dress aside to see a gold necklace nestled in the paper. When she picked it up, she saw there was a small charm attached.

It was deeply polished and shiny, glinting in the candlelight. With a gasp, she realized it was a claw—a perfect miniature of the one inside her. She stared at it in awe. Tem had never owned anything gold before. It was an expensive metal—a metal that Tem and her mother could never afford, a luxury reserved only for the royals. Tem had only one piece of jewelry to her name, a dull silver ring she wore on holidays. The ring paled in comparison to the necklace.

Tem immediately put it on.

The chain was long; the charm fell directly between her breasts. She knew Caspen had made it so, and at the thought, a pulse immediately began to build. Here he was finally, after an unbearable day of silence. Tem barely had time to close the door to her room before she was on the bed, her hand between her legs. Her other hand was clasped over her mouth; she knew her mother was mere feet away and would surely hear her cry out. She tried to stay silent through the pulses, but it was utterly useless. Caspen was sending them so quickly, she could barely catch her breath. It was as if he wanted to overwhelm her, forcing her to feel his presence one last time before tonight.

Tem could hear her mother making dinner and knew she would leave soon to get vegetables from the garden. The moment she heard the door slam, Tem finished triumphantly, arching her back with a moan. She could feel Caspen's pleasure, and it matched her own. There was something desperate about their connection tonight, and she wondered if it was because of what would happen later that evening. She lay gasping on the bed, trying to catch her breath, the gold chain tangled around her neck.

She bathed before putting on the dress, finding that it fit perfectly. It hugged her in all the right places, turning her body into something it had never been before—something meant to entice a prince. She ran her fingers through her hair, trying to accentuate its length before realizing what she was doing and stopping immediately. *She* liked her curls. The prince had better like them too.

"Tem?" Her mother was knocking on her bedroom door. "It's time."

When Tem emerged into the kitchen, her mother's hands flew to her mouth in shock.

Her mother spoke before she could. "There's a carriage waiting for you outside. It will take you to the castle."

Tem nodded. She had no cloak that would match the luxury of the dress, so instead she went without, stepping into the chilly night and winding down the garden path to the awaiting black carriage. A footman helped her inside, and she sat on the soft velvet bench before looking up at the ceiling, where the royal insignia was etched in gold leaf. It depicted a snake dueling with a rooster. The snake was twisted in obvious pain, trampled beneath the spiny feet of the rooster. It was a clear homage to the war, specifically to the victors. Tem knew that the royals bore the snake on many of their personal items as a reminder of what they had overcome. Personally, she saw it as a taunt. She couldn't imagine how a basilisk would feel looking at it.

As the carriage climbed the long hill to the castle, Tem thought about the evening. She was looking forward to seeing Gabriel, since she knew he would be working. But that was the extent of her excitement. The night was sure to be a long, insufferable sequence of formalities. No doubt she would be put on display, paraded around to the royals so they could see their potential newest member.

Tem clasped her hands together tightly.

And then there was the prince. She wondered if she would meet him tonight or if he'd keep his distance from the contestants. Caspen had said he wished to "see" his potential future wives. That didn't mean he wanted to talk to them. If it were Tem choosing her future partner, she'd want ample opportunity to get to know them. But that would come later, she supposed. After all, the elimination process hadn't even begun. The first elimination would happen next week, after the prince had a chance to kiss each girl. That was the traditional timeline, and that was the way things had been done for centuries.

The carriage wound to a halt.

"We've arrived, miss," the footman said when he opened the door.

Tem took a deep breath, unclasped her hands, and climbed out of the carriage. They had parked right in front of the castle, and Tem stared up at the enormous double doors in awe. She had never been here before. She'd only looked up at the castle from down in the village, seeing it from the very bottom of the hill, where it resembled a fancy dollhouse. Now that she was seeing it in person, she realized just how large it was. It sprawled for what felt like miles, its walls made of stones that almost seemed to glitter. When Tem got closer, she saw that the grout holding the bricks together was full of crushed pieces of mirror. Of course the castle would have a last line of defense built right into its structure. As she reached the doors, they swung open.

The first thing Tem noticed was the gold.

It was everywhere: framing the oil paintings on the walls, brushed in intricate patterns on the wallpaper, interlaced in whorls of wood. It was even beneath her feet, flecked into the marble tile of the entryway. Tem had never seen such a blatant display of wealth.

"Name?" a voice asked her.

Tem turned to see a man in a black robe holding a ledger and looking at her expectantly. "Temperance Verus."

The man consulted the ledger before giving her a brief nod. "Right this way."

He ushered her through the entryway into a long hall lined with thick maroon carpet. Tem barely had time to blink before he pushed her through another door.

"Don't wander," he said before snapping it shut behind her.

Tem was immediately overwhelmed with noise.

She was standing at the edge of a giant ballroom filled with people, most of whom seemed to be well on their way to getting drunk. Tem spotted a few residents of the village, but mostly she was in the presence of royals. She remembered how Gabriel had mentioned that Henry would be ferrying people in from neighboring villages. She could tell which royals weren't from around here by the way they dressed. Some were wearing furs despite the fact that snow wouldn't arrive for several more weeks.

Tem set her sights on the tables at the far end of the ballroom, which were piled high with food. The selection resembled the food that Caspen had given her in the cave: fancy meats and cheeses arranged in delicate displays. Tem grabbed a handful of nuts and shoved them into her mouth as she scanned the crowd for Gabriel. To her dismay, he was nowhere to be found. Instead, her eyes fell on Vera, who was giggling in a corner with another girl. When they looked over at Tem, the giggling stopped immediately. Tem gave them a condescending wave, knowing full well that by now, Vera would have told everyone who would listen that Tem was being trained by the Serpent King. The wave was not returned.

The ballroom was lined with thick marble columns, elaborately decorated with carvings of Kora. Like everything else in the castle, they were accented with gold. Tem couldn't comprehend why such an excessive display of wealth was necessary. Everyone knew the royals were rich, but she had no idea the inside of the castle looked like *this*. She stared at the tables loaded with food. She thought of the many nights in her cottage when she and her mother had gone to bed hungry. It didn't seem fair. It didn't seem right.

Tem wished she could go find Gabriel, but the man at the door had told her not to wander. *And why shouldn't I wander?* she thought with sudden conviction. *This could be my castle someday.*

So Tem turned on her heel and made her way back through the crowd. She slipped into the hallway, sighing in relief at the sudden silence. The hallway stretched out for what seemed like forever in both directions. The walls were covered in dark oil paintings depicting long-dead members of the royal family. There were centuries of history here—centuries of heirs birthed solely because of the help of the basilisks.

Tem stopped in front of a particularly large painting of a battle scene. It reminded her of the insignia on the roof of the carriage. Dozens of snakes—*huge* snakes—were slithering over the ground, headed for a group of horse-bound riders. Some of the riders held roosters, some held mirrored shields. It was the final battle before the war was won; Tem could tell by the way the sky was painted deep bloodred. All the old songs spoke of the red sky on that final day. They said that Kora herself bled to make it that color.

Tem felt suddenly overwhelmed. There was a tight, twisting pain in her chest that had nothing to do with her nerves. She turned away from the painting, heading toward the first door she could find. By pure happenstance, it was a bathroom. The sink was gold, of course, and Tem splashed her face with water in an effort to cool down. She was just reaching for the towel when the door banged open.

A girl with a head of thick, icy-blond hair bound in. She was clutching a flute of champagne, her cheeks tinged with pink. One of the other contestants.

"Oh," the girl said when she saw Tem. "Sorry. I didn't know there was anyone in here."

"It's fine," Tem said quickly. "I was just leaving."

"No, no." The girl waved her off, sloshing her champagne in the process. "Don't leave on my account. I'm only here because I needed a break from the party. It's overwhelming, isn't it?"

"Yes," answered Tem honestly.

"I'm Lilly," the girl said, extending the hand that wasn't holding the champagne. "Well, technically Lilibet."

"I'm Tem. Well, technically Temperance."

"Temperance is a pretty name."

"So is Lilibet."

The girl rolled her eyes. "Hardly. It sounds like a toilet accessory."

"Does it?"

"*I* think so. But that's what nicknames are for." The girl tipped the rest of her champagne into her mouth before asking, "So what do you think of the prince?"

Tem shrugged. "I haven't met him yet."

"Hm. Well, when you do, tell him he lost a bet."

"Excuse me?"

"He bet me he wouldn't find any of the girls pretty." Her eyes flicked over Tem's dress. "But I have a feeling he won't be able to resist you."

Tem was becoming more confused by the moment. "I'm sorry. I thought you were—"

"In the running to marry my own brother? *That* would be the scandal of the century."

Tem's mouth fell open. She was talking to the prince's older sister. She should've known by the name Lilibet. Everyone had to memorize the royal family tree in school, but Tem hadn't thought about it in years.

Lilly laughed at the expression on Tem's face. "So? Aren't you going to ask me how to win his heart?"

Tem didn't know how to answer that. The only heart she really wanted to win was Caspen's.

At her silence, Lilly's face split into a grin.

"Ah, so you're *not* here to grovel at his feet. Interesting. Come to think of it, that might be exactly what wins you his heart. He always wants what he can't have."

A sudden cheer echoed outside the bathroom.

Lilly glanced at the door. "I'd better go. It was nice to meet you, Tem. And good luck! Not that you'll need it."

With that, the princess was gone.

Tem stared at the place where Lilly had stood, wondering what the hell had just happened. Another cheer broke out, but Tem had no desire to return to the party. Instead, she splashed some more water on her face, glanced at her reflection in the mirror, and slipped back into the hallway.

She wandered aimlessly through the castle halls, heading vaguely upward, taking a staircase whenever she encountered one. Eventually, she found herself in a room that looked like a study, with books on the walls and a heavy wooden desk at one end.

Tem took in the ornate rugs, the golden trim, the rich oil paintings. It was utterly different from her humble home, with its rough wooden floors and shuttered windows. She couldn't believe such wealth existed. She could understand why her mother admired such things when she had none of her own. For the first time, Tem felt compassion for what she'd interpreted as her mother's endless coveting. Maybe she had simply yearned for more, as Tem did.

Her eyes traced along the deep mahogany shelves, landing on an enormous, fanged skull that rested on a velvet pillow. As if in a trance, Tem reached for it. Just as her fingers were about to touch the bone, a jolt shot through the claw, up her spine and down her arm, forcing her to yank her hand back immediately. Caspen's voice thundered through her head, as strong and clear as if he were standing in the room with her:

Do not touch that.

"Why?" Tem whispered aloud to the empty room, cradling her hand against her chest. It still throbbed with his energy.

Because it does not belong to you.

His voice was so angry, she wanted to cry. Too late, Tem realized what she had been reaching for. Without warning, Caspen's mind overtook hers, and she saw a horrible montage of war: basilisks against humans, battles fought deep within the caves, the eventual near extinction of Caspen's entire family. Tem felt devastation and didn't know whether it was his or hers.

I'm so sorry, she thought, but Caspen was already gone. Her mind was empty, the claw suddenly cold. She stared at the skull numbly, wondering how humans could be so cruel. She couldn't get the images out of her head—so much blood, so much death. Both sides had suffered, but it was clear the basilisks had sustained far greater losses. It was just like the painting she had seen downstairs.

Tem was just about to try to call Caspen back when she heard "Looking for something?"

Tem whipped around.

A young man stood in the doorway, staring at her. He leaned against the doorframe, his angular face cocked to the side. His ice-blond hair was parted and slicked back, his sharp cheekbones catching the dim light of the candles. He wore a velvet suit of deep maroon, with a jeweled snake pinned to his lapel. There was a slim elegance to him that seemed vaguely familiar, and Tem realized he looked just like Lilly. They had the same thick hair, the same full lips.

So this was the prince.

CHAPTER FIVE

———••✳•••———

S HE'D NEVER SEEN THE PRINCE UP CLOSE—HE WAS ALWAYS WAVING FROM A BAL-
cony or sitting in a carriage in a parade. He was quite tall, his head nearly brushing
the doorway. Tem didn't have an answer to his question, so she said the only thing
she could think of.

"Is it real?"

The prince stepped into the room. "Is what real?"

Tem pointed at the skull. She wanted him to refute what Caspen had shown her.
She wanted him to tell her it was merely a trinket—nothing more than plaster and clay.

Instead, he said, "What do you think?"

During her silence, he approached, stopping when he was standing beside her.

"You're displeased," he said quietly.

"No, I—" Tem started, but she had no idea how to finish. "I'm…just surprised."

It was half the truth at least.

"I'd rather you didn't lie to me," the prince said. "Plenty of people do that already."

She looked up at him in surprise. His honesty was making her uneasy. She figured
the royals were well-mannered and careful with their words. She hadn't expected him
to speak so candidly.

Rather than reply, Tem simply looked at him, and he did the same.

His eyes lingered on the low cut of her dress, taking in the curves the clingy fabric
had given her. The open hunger on the prince's face was so different from anything
she'd ever known from a man. Caspen's desire for her was always masked—lurking just
under the surface, hidden beneath a restrained facade of indifference. The prince's face
hid nothing, and Tem felt an odd thrill at the thought. Before she could help herself,
she whispered, "You lost a bet."

He cocked his head. "I beg your pardon?"

Rather than explain herself, Tem turned back to the skull. "Seems like a morbid
thing to keep around, doesn't it?"

"It's a family heirloom," the prince explained. "My father considers it his most-
prized possession."

Tem felt a bristle of anger. "What kind of family keeps a skull as an heirloom?"

"Mine, I suppose."

Tem shook her head. It was despicable.

The prince seemed to read her mind because he said, "We're not all bad, you know."

She had a hard time believing that. The visions Caspen just sent her flashed through her mind again—pain and bloodshed and suffering. All at the hands of his family. Maybe the prince didn't fight in the war, but he was descended from people who did. And he clearly supported their actions.

Just when the silence became precarious, the prince extended his hand. On his wrist was a shiny gold cuff, etched with a snake that matched the one on his lapel.

"Thelonius. Although I prefer Leo."

Tem took his hand. It was warm and completely enveloped hers. "Temperance. Although I prefer Tem."

He held her hand a moment too long. "Temperance," he said the syllables slowly. "It certainly is a pleasure to meet you."

"Thanks," she said, because she didn't know what else to say. It wasn't exactly a pleasure to meet him.

A slight smile twisted his lips, as if he knew she was being evasive. "Are you enjoying the party?" he asked.

"It's...impressive."

"That wasn't a yes."

"Oh." Tem blinked, surprised again by his bluntness. "I just mean...I'm not used to these types of events. Parties, I mean. I...haven't been to many."

At her reply, he smiled fully, and Tem saw that his lateral incisors were sheathed in gold and tapered to points.

"I suppose it is a little stiff, as these things generally are."

Tem shrugged. "It's better than being at home."

"Is it?" He arched an eyebrow. "I can't imagine being in your position."

"What do you mean?"

"I mean I would be furious if I were you, paraded in here like a lamb to the slaughter."

Tem frowned. She may be speaking with the prince, but that didn't give him the right to insult her. "I am no lamb," she said quietly.

He raised an eyebrow. "No." His eyes went to her dress again. "You certainly aren't."

There was silence, and in it, Tem felt his heat. She understood suddenly that although he was a prince, she was the one who held the power here. She wondered what it would feel like to wield it.

Leo broke the silence. "Can I offer you a drink?"

Tem nodded, if only to get a break from his probing stare. Leo turned to the liquor shelf, tapping his fingers lightly along the selection of crystal tumblers before resting on one that contained amber liquid. His nails were perfectly manicured.

"Do you like whiskey?" he asked, his back still turned.

"I...don't know."

He looked over his shoulder at her. "You've never had it?"

"Once," she said. It was the truth: she and Gabriel had tried it at the Horseman after several rounds of beer. She genuinely couldn't remember if she'd liked it.

Leo grinned. "Whiskey it is then."

He selected two faceted glasses and poured an inch of liquid into each. When he handed Tem hers, their fingers brushed. His skin was warm. She stared down at the amber liquid. The harsh smell definitely rang a bell.

"Shall we do it together?" Leo asked.

She was surprised to hear herself answer "Sure."

"Very well. To Kora," Leo said, clinking his glass to hers.

"To Kora," Tem said back. Then she raised the glass to her mouth and took a delicate sip of the whiskey. It burned fiercely on the way down her throat, and she pursed her lips in surprise.

Leo downed the contents of his glass in one gulp. "Well?" he asked once she'd swallowed. "What do you think?"

"It tastes like fire," she said.

"That it does."

Tem was still trying not to cough. "How can you drink it so easily?"

Leo laughed, and the sound was like teacups clinking. "Lots and lots of practice."

The prince poured himself another glass and drank it slowly, as if he had all the time in the world to stand there with her. His behavior had the easy entitlement of privilege. Tem got the impression that nothing bothered him, and even if something did, he could make it go away with a snap of his slender fingers. He watched Tem with sharp intelligence, his eyes holding hers for longer than what she would consider socially acceptable. Vera had been wrong, she realized. His eyes weren't green. They were something closer to gray.

"So. How's it going so far?" Leo asked.

"How's what going so far?"

"You know, the training, or whatever it is they're calling it."

A blush rose on her cheeks. Was he really asking her about her sessions with Caspen? The process was hardly a secret—everyone in the village knew this was the proper way for a prince to choose a wife. But it was a sensitive subject for Tem. She was already embarrassed by her inexperience—she had no desire to discuss it with the very person she might be sleeping with in a matter of weeks.

"I don't believe that's any of your concern," she said quietly.

His mouth twitched. "On the contrary, I believe I'm the only person it concerns."

Her blush deepened, and she hated it. Tem didn't like the way the prince was making her feel. It was as if he enjoyed her discomfort, and she felt the power shifting back to him as he said, "Sex is best with someone who knows what they're doing. Wouldn't you agree?"

Tem didn't answer. She hadn't had sex yet, with someone who knew what they were doing or otherwise.

At her silence, Leo's smirk widened. "Then again, experiencing something for the first time can be…rewarding. If that's your situation."

Tem felt the whiskey burning in her stomach and, with it, her anger. She hated the way Leo was speaking to her. But even more, she hated the way Caspen had abandoned her. The claw was cold, his presence entirely absent from her mind. She was on her own. So she took a deep breath and said, "You don't know my situation."

Leo leaned in. "I'd like to."

He was far too close for comfort.

"Am I to take that as a compliment?" she asked.

"Certainly not. That dress looks beautiful on you. That's a compliment."

"I hardly consider it one."

Leo's mouth twisted in a condescending smile. "What could possibly be wrong with it?"

"You complimented the dress. Not me."

Tem didn't know where her courage came from. She shouldn't be talking like this, especially not to the prince. But she was angry—at Leo, at the situation she was in, and perhaps at herself for letting her insecurities impact her so greatly. Whatever she was feeling, it lit a fire in her that was stronger than any whiskey, and she was in no mood for banter.

Leo considered her answer. "Perhaps. But the implication is that the dress is only beautiful because you're the one wearing it."

"Implications aren't compliments."

Leo frowned. She doubted he was used to being defied.

He stepped closer. Despite downing two whiskeys in the span of a minute, he didn't seem affected by the alcohol at all. His eyes narrowed. "You already know you're beautiful, don't you?"

Tem had only been called beautiful once, by Caspen. And yet his word had made her believe it, so she answered honestly, "Yes."

"In that case, would you even care to hear it from me?"

Again, she spoke the truth: "No."

The cruel smile slipped from his face—definitely not used to being defied. "Then I won't burden you with it."

"How considerate of you."

A vein in his temple pulsed. It felt as if their entire conversation had been a battle of wits, and Tem wasn't sure who had won. *This* was the person she was supposed to give herself to? How could she be expected to compete for his affections when the way he was looking at her made her feel as if she'd been turned inside out?

"Shall we rejoin the party?" Leo said finally, his voice hard. "You're the guest of honor after all."

His timing couldn't have been better. Tem wanted nothing more than to get out of this room.

Leo gestured stiffly with his hand. Without another word, Tem followed him out, and he walked a step ahead of her all the way back to the ballroom. The moment they arrived, he left her. She watched his lanky frame navigate the crowd with understated authority, his whiskey glass still in his hand. People moved for him, and if they didn't, a casual wave of his long fingers cleared his path.

In the prince's absence, Tem knew a moment of peace. Then Vera appeared. Her eyes ran greedily down Tem's body, not unlike the way Leo had looked at her just minutes before. But instead of sexual attraction, there was nothing but pure jealousy in Vera's eyes.

"*That's* your mother's dress?"

Tem considered lying, but the truth was so much better. "No," she said. "Caspen gifted it to me."

Jealousy turned to utter loathing. "The *basilisk* gave you that?"

"The *Serpent King* gave me that."

Vera stood silently, gaping like a fish. It had taken twenty years, but finally, Tem understood how it felt to have the upper hand. She savored it.

Just then, Gabriel appeared at her elbow, holding a beer. "Piss off, Vera," he said cheerfully.

Vera's face contorted into a sneer. She and Gabriel had never gotten along—possibly because he was friends with Tem, possibly because he always somehow ended up kissing the boys Vera liked. Either way, they hated each other.

"There's no need to be *rude*," she hissed.

"I know there's no *need*. I'm rude because I want to be."

Vera didn't bother with a retort before flouncing haughtily away. Gabriel handed Tem his beer. She sipped it gratefully, using it to wash away the taste of the whiskey.

"Can't stay long," he said. "The kitchen is chaos tonight."

"Thanks for sneaking away."

"Of course." He tilted an eyebrow at her. "*So?* Have you met him yet?"

There was no need to ask who he was referring to.

"Just did."

"*And?*"

Tem sighed, avoiding his eyes. "I don't know, Gabriel. It was…strange. I couldn't really tell what he was thinking."

He was thinking he wanted to fuck you.

Tem nearly jumped out of her skin at Caspen's voice, which was so crystal clear, it sounded as if he were standing right next to her. He chose *now* to return to her mind? Tem tried to send a question back to him—to ask him if he was still angry about the skull—but it was like throwing water at a wall. There was a barrier between them that it seemed only he could bypass. Tem felt a slight twinge of annoyance.

Gabriel was speaking, but she hadn't heard it.

"What?" she asked.

"I said, he was probably thinking how diabolically good you look in that dress."

Even though it was just Gabriel, Tem blushed.

Before she could come up with an appropriate answer, the energy in the ballroom changed. When a moment ago there had been raucous chatter, now a sudden hush fell as movement broke out at the far end of the room.

"What's happening?" Tem whispered.

"The first elimination," Gabriel whispered back.

But that was impossible. It was far too soon—the first elimination wasn't supposed to happen for another week, after the prince had a chance to kiss each girl.

"Are you sure?"

"Everyone in the kitchen was talking about it. He'll be cutting two girls tonight."

"*Two?* Based on *what?* He hasn't gotten to know any of us yet."

"Looks, I suppose."

"And you're just telling me this *now?*"

"Vera distracted me! The girl is a terror. Anyway, I figured you knew already."

But Tem hadn't known. And she couldn't believe what she was hearing. There was supposed to be a proper order to the training process—one that shouldn't involve surprise eliminations. It wasn't fair. Then again, none of it was really fair. Lilly's words ran unbidden through her mind: *I have a feeling he won't be able to resist you.*

Tem glanced down at the dress Caspen had given her, remembering the way the prince had looked at it with hunger in his eyes. Would it be enough? Or had she insulted him by not accepting his compliment? He'd abandoned her the moment they'd returned to the ballroom—did that mean he wasn't interested in her? Their conversation in the study had been unconventional from start to finish and had ended on decidedly less-than-friendly terms. Tem had no idea where they stood.

Tem had gone her entire life without men liking her based on her looks. Why should the prince be any different? She'd probably be the first girl to go. But if she was eliminated tonight, her mother would never forgive her. Even worse, she'd never see Caspen again. She would have no excuse to go into the caves, no reason to see him. Without Caspen, Tem would probably die a virgin.

She couldn't be eliminated.

The crowd was moving, forming a semicircle around one end of the ballroom, where something was being assembled. Tem squinted to see what looked like podiums of various sizes, arranged in ascending order of height. She counted eleven of them. Tem frowned. If two girls were to be eliminated, there should be twelve podiums. Then she remembered the girl who had run off right before they entered the caves.

Tem glanced around for Vera. She was fluffing her hair and shooting meaningful glances at Leo, who was leaning against a column, looking bored by the proceedings.

"If the ladies could please form a line, we can begin."

The command came from a handsome middle-aged man in a uniform. His blond hair was flecked with gray. Tem recognized him as Lord Chamberlain, the most senior officer of the royal household and the king's brother. Tem had seen him around the village, attending to business on behalf of the king.

Gabriel gave her arm a squeeze. "Better get up there."

She shot him a terrified glance. "Kill me. Right now."

In response, he pressed a quick kiss to her cheek. Then he gave her a little push, and she had no choice but to join the line of girls walking through the crowd. By the time they reached the podiums, Tem's heart was beating out of control. Everyone was looking at them. And maybe it was simply her imagination, but it felt like everyone was looking at *her*. Hundreds of pairs of eyes raked over her dress, hundreds of stares pointed directly at her body. She'd never felt more like an animal in a cage than she did right now.

"That's it, right along here." Lord Chamberlain ushered them into an orderly line, turning them so they were standing in front of the podiums, facing the crowd. When they were all in position, he said, "Your Highness? It's time."

Leo emerged from the crowd, whiskey still in hand. His eyes trailed lazily over each girl, looking them up and down one after the other. Vera gave an odd shimmy when he passed by her, which was met with a bemused twitch of his lips. When his eyes landed on Tem, her heart caught in her throat. Leo stepped forward until he was right in front of her.

He leaned in.

But instead of sealing her fate, he tilted his head to the side, bringing his lips to the cheek of the girl standing right next to Tem. Tem was close enough to hear the words he whispered into the other girl's ear: "Sorry, darling."

The girl let out a strangled sob. Leo straightened, taking a casual sip of his whiskey as if none of this was of any concern to him. Then he turned to the girl to Tem's right, leaning in and saying the same two words to her.

Both girls were immediately ushered away, leaving a gaping space around Tem. It was only then that she realized her hands were shaking. It wasn't just the fact that the girls had been eliminated. It was the *way* Leo had done it—choosing the girls directly on either side of her, whispering in their ears specifically so she would hear, as if to show Tem that he *could've* eliminated her but *didn't*. Was this all a game to him? Didn't he care that he was in the process of choosing a wife? Leo was acting like none of this mattered to him at all. Tem couldn't understand his apathy.

Lord Chamberlain was speaking again.

"Congratulations, ladies. It is an honor to stand where you stand. As the final event tonight, His Highness will place you on the podiums. The lucky lady in first place will receive a private date with the prince."

Too late, Tem realized what was happening. It wasn't just a surprise elimination. The remaining girls were to be ranked, in front of everyone, based on how attractive Leo found them. The podiums were meant to display them in descending order of beauty.

It was insulting. There was no other word for it.

Tem wanted to run, just like that girl who ran from the caves. But she couldn't run. She was frozen in place as Leo pointed at girl after girl, assigning them to their podiums with a careless flick of his fingers until Tem and a girl with strawberry-blond hair were the only ones left standing. Only two podiums remained: the tallest and the shortest, best and worst, first and last.

Prettiest and ugliest.

Tem already knew what Leo was going to do. Still, it felt like a dagger twisting in her chest as he pointed at the blond and jerked his head at the tallest podium. Tem could practically feel Vera's sneer searing into the back of her skull from where she stood on the third podium. Leo didn't even bother to point at Tem. He simply knocked back the rest of his whiskey, holding her eye contact the entire time.

Tem didn't step onto the last podium. She couldn't. She could only stand in pure defiance, determined to wield the only power she had left. She looked Leo straight in the eye, refusing to look away even as the silence drew on. Everyone knew she was being trained by the Serpent King; everyone knew that meant she was supposed to be the best. To be ranked last was a complete and utter humiliation. Worse than that, it was a message. Leo wanted to punish her for rejecting him earlier. He wanted her to know, beyond a shadow of a doubt, that he was in control. Message received.

Lord Chamberlain broke the silence. "A round of applause for our winner!"

The crowd erupted into applause, and the blond girl waved as if she were already queen.

Tem could feel a stubborn swell of tears threatening to break free. But she refused to cry. Instead, she turned them into pure, simmering anger, which she channeled straight at Leo, whose shoulders were already slipping away through the crowd. Without thinking, Tem ran after him, shoving people aside and bursting into the hallway.

He was several yards away, about to ascend the stairs.

"Leo," she yelled. "*Stop.*"

He turned to face her, his expression moving quickly from surprise to smug satisfaction. "Something the matter, Temperance?"

She walked right up to him, stopping only when they were a foot apart. "You ranked me *last.*"

His mouth twisted into a cruel smile. "So I did."

"Care to tell me why?"

"I didn't think you'd notice."

"You might as well have called me ugly. Of course I noticed."

Leo leaned in. "You made it clear you don't want me to call you beautiful. Why shouldn't I call you ugly?"

"Because it's a lie."

Disbelief flashed across Leo's face. Tem seized the moment, stepping closer.

"And I'd prefer you didn't lie to me, Leo. Plenty of people do that already."

His own words hung between them. In the silence, Leo studied her face. He seemed to be working something out in his mind, and Tem decided to let him. She had nowhere to be—nothing was as important as this. She let him look as long as he liked, and when he finally opened his mouth to speak, his words had a bitter edge:

"I saw the way you looked at the skull, not to mention the way you look at me. You don't respect my family. You don't even want to be here."

His words echoed Caspen's: *You do not seem desperate to be here.* But Tem recognized them for what they really were. Leo was *asking* her whether she wanted to be here—whether she wanted *him.* It was a question that surprised her, given that the entire elimination process was based on his choice, not hers. It was assumed that the girls all wanted to be here. Her wants should be irrelevant to him.

But rather than give in—rather than answer him and reveal her hand—Tem decided to take her power back. So she leaned in, using her body in the same way Vera did with Jonathan, making sure Leo's full attention was on her before she turned his question back on him.

"Do *you* want me to be here?"

Their faces were inches apart. Suddenly, the castle disappeared, and they were the only two people in existence. Tem saw Leo's answer in his eyes—in the way his gaze traced hungrily down her neck to the golden claw that rested between her breasts. She saw his answer in the way his body angled itself to mirror hers, in the way his grip tightened on his whiskey glass, in the way his tongue brushed briefly over his lips as if it longed to taste hers. She saw his answer, but he said it anyway:

"Yes."

Tem leaned back, once again putting distance between them. "Then act like it."

CHAPTER SIX

TEM HAD NEVER BEEN SO TIRED IN HER ENTIRE LIFE.

The night at the castle hadn't turned out at all the way she'd expected. Between her interactions with Leo and the surprise elimination, Tem didn't know what to think of the entire process. Had she blown her chance with the prince? And if she had, did she even care? She didn't know the answers to those questions. All she knew was that tonight she would be back in the caves with Caspen.

She was desperate to see him. She wanted to make sure he wasn't angry with her over what happened with the skull. She wanted to ask him about the dress—whether it was meant as a symbol of his affection or whether it was meant to catch the eye of the prince. She wanted to see him naked, and she wanted him to see her. But she didn't know where they stood.

So when she walked into the cave to find him waiting there, she had absolutely no idea what to expect.

"Tem," he said quietly.

"Caspen," she said back.

He only said her name—nothing more. He didn't tell her to undress, like he had the last two times they had met. He didn't bring up the dress he had given her or the little gold necklace. He didn't ask how it had gone with the prince or congratulate her for making it through the first elimination. He just stood there, staring at her for a long moment before gesturing to the mat next to the fireplace. Tem crossed to it slowly, watching him as she did so. They sat at the same time, their bodies six inches apart.

Caspen still didn't speak. Instead, he raised his hand to her face, cupping her cheek in his palm and brushing his thumb over the curve of her bottom lip.

Tem knew, without a doubt, that she was about to have her first kiss.

For some reason, kissing seemed far more daunting than what they had already done. There was something simple about touching him and him touching her back. But a kiss required connection. It required them to move in tandem, to establish a rhythm with each other and an intimacy that she'd never experienced with another person before. To kiss someone was to *taste* them and to let them taste you. Tem couldn't imagine a greater responsibility.

Caspen's fingers laced into her hair, wrapping around the nape of her neck and pulling her closer. Without thinking, Tem pressed her palms against his chest, holding him back.

"Wait," Tem whispered. "Please."

Caspen raised an eyebrow. "Wait for what, Tem?"

"I don't know. I'm just not ready."

To her surprise, Caspen laughed softly. "Of course you are not ready. It is impossible to be ready for something you have never done before."

Tem swallowed. He wasn't making her feel any better. Caspen seemed to sense this, because he pulled her even closer, brushing his lips lightly along hers—not kissing her yet, only touching her skin with his. It felt like sparks exploding across her mouth.

"Just take what I give you," he breathed. "And when you are ready, give it back to me."

He waited until she nodded.

Then he kissed her.

When his lips pressed against hers, all Tem's fears disappeared. So *this* was what it was like to be kissed. It felt like she'd finally found something she'd been missing—like everything that had been off-kilter her entire life was balanced at last. Caspen's lips were soft and full, moving against hers more gently than she thought was possible. Tem let him guide her, following his lead as he slipped his tongue inside her mouth. Tem received it curiously, tracing it with hers, savoring the warm wetness before returning the favor.

They kissed for a long time. Tem didn't know how long. But somewhere along the way, her dress slipped from her shoulders. Then Caspen's shirt came off. They were both naked, intertwined on the mat, kissing like they had all the time in the world to do so. Caspen touched her gently, running his palms over her breasts, her hips, her thighs. He teased her nipples with his fingers, hardening them between his knuckles before cupping her entire breast and squeezing. She'd never been touched like that before. It felt so good, she never wanted it to stop.

Caspen's body was almost too warm for comfort. But she welcomed his skin against hers, wrapping her legs around his waist and pressing herself against him. The claw was still inside her, and Caspen had begun sending pulses, slow and lingering, their rhythm corresponding with the way they were kissing. Each one made her ache for him even more. Eventually he slid the claw out, replacing it with his fingers. She spread her legs so he could go deeper, arching her back to meet his touch, moving her body in tandem with his. She couldn't hold back her moans. There was no point in even trying. All she wanted was for him to never *ever* stop touching her.

Tem clasped her hand over his, holding it in place so she could slide herself up and down his fingers, grinding back and forth, back and forth, until she felt her orgasm building. Caspen's pupils dilated as he watched her pleasure herself, and she wondered if he enjoyed this even more than doing it himself.

With her other hand, she reached between his legs, pressing her palm against his cock—not even stroking it yet—just feeling how hard he was for her. She wrapped her fingers around it, pulling him even closer.

"Fuck me, Caspen," she breathed.

"Not tonight, Tem," he said against her lips.

Tem didn't understand. She wanted to have sex. She was *ready* to have sex. But for some reason, Caspen was withholding it from her. He defined the boundaries of their relationship—if it even *was* a relationship. But Tem knew it was. She knew they had crossed a line somewhere, probably the first night they met, when she'd asked him to undress and she'd touched herself in front of him. She was not just his student, and he was not just her teacher. They were more than that. They had to be.

"Please," she said as she tilted her hips, pulling his fingers deeper.

"Do not ask me again." His voice was strained—he was begging her.

"But I want you," she whispered.

Pain flitted across his face. She knew she hadn't imagined it.

"You will have me," he said. "Just not tonight."

He didn't say he wanted her too.

Tem pulled away. She felt suddenly exposed, like she'd revealed far too much of her heart to someone who didn't care to see it.

"Tem." He tried to pull her back, but she didn't let him.

She stared at the fire, watching the flickering flames, imagining they would consume her. She heard Caspen sigh.

"It is too early, Tem. We have barely begun our lessons."

Lessons. Student and teacher. Boundaries. Caspen's favorite defense.

"And how would you grade me so far?" she said sharply, looking him in the eye.

A long pause. "Do you truly want an answer?"

She clenched her jaw, biting back pain. "Yes."

He studied her face before replying. "You do not follow instructions. You are stubborn. And impatient. Those are not qualities the prince will appreciate."

Tem couldn't believe what he was saying. She glared at him. "Isn't that *your* fault? Maybe you should be a better teacher."

Caspen shook his head. "It is not possible to teach an unwilling student."

"Don't give me that shit again. I'm perfectly willing. I just made that crystal clear."

"You are perfectly willing to have sex but not to do any of the other things I mentioned."

"You want me to be *patient*? To follow *instructions*? You think that'll make the prince want me? Trust me, he only wants one thing. And you're not teaching me how to do it."

It seemed like the angrier Tem got, the calmer Caspen became. He was perfectly still, looking down at her with his arms bracketed on either side of her body, holding her in place beneath him. His cock was still hard.

"The prince will expect you to yield both your body and your mind. If you cannot give him both, there is no point in training you at all."

"Maybe I don't want to yield my mind. Why should I?"

Caspen didn't answer.

Tem propped herself up so their faces were an inch apart. "Why shouldn't *he* yield?" she insisted.

"Because he is the prince."

"So he can do whatever he wants?"

"The royals make their own rules."

"That's not fair."

"No. It is not."

Tem blinked. Had Caspen just agreed with her? It seemed like his reply had slipped out before he could stop it, like he hadn't meant to say it.

They stared at each other for a long moment. His next words were barely a whisper. "You are not meant to be tamed, Tem."

What was he saying? That he didn't think she had a chance with the prince? Tem bristled at the thought. If her own teacher didn't believe in her, then he was right: there was no point in training her at all. Or was he saying that he didn't *want* her to have a chance with the prince? That he wouldn't change her, even if he could?

"What's that supposed to mean?" She meant to say it harshly, but it came out as a whisper.

Now Caspen was the one to pull away. He sat up suddenly, and Tem felt a rush of cool air as his body heat left her. "We are done for the night."

Tem's mouth fell open in shock. "Excuse me?"

"You heard me. Get dressed."

"But—"

"Get *dressed*, Tem."

Tem flinched. He had never raised his voice at her before. His face was a cold mask of detachment, his aggressive tone in horrible contrast to the way he'd been treating

69

her all evening. There was nothing gentle about it. Tem was reminded suddenly that underneath the man, he was a monster.

Tem got dressed.

Caspen disappeared while she was pulling on her clothes, and when he reappeared, he had a tray of food. But instead of sitting and eating with her, he set the tray down on the mat and left without another word. The cave was glaringly empty without him, and Tem fought to hold back tears. How had the night ended so poorly when it had started so well? It was then that she realized he had taken the claw with him. She didn't bother eating. She just ran home.

The next time she came to the cave, it was clear they were back to square one.

For the next three nights, Tem sat on the mat, stroked Caspen's cock until he came, then ate her food alone. Caspen didn't give the claw back; he didn't talk to her. He didn't even look her in the eye. The meetings were so impersonal that Tem couldn't help but wonder if this was how they were for the other girls and their basilisks. Would this have been what happened if she hadn't asked him to undress the first night they met? Was this what it was like to have no connection to the person she was touching? She didn't know how long it would go on this way. All she knew was that she hated it.

Things were no better during the daytime. Tem spent every waking hour doing farmwork or running errands, anything to keep her mind off Caspen's unbearable indifference. Her visits to the bakery were nothing short of agony. Vera's cruelty knew no bounds; she'd taken Tem's low podium ranking as permission to return to her preferred method of torture, which was finding every opportunity to disparage the fact that Tem was a chicken farmer. Her taunts were rudimentary but effective. Tem weathered them in silence, delivering the eggs to the bakery and receiving her payment without saying a word. Vera clearly thought Tem was unworthy in every single way. Tem almost agreed with her.

Even her home was no longer a sanctuary. Her mother hovered nervously, watching Tem's every move as if she knew the training wasn't going well. Gabriel was no help either. He was sequestered away in the castle, working long hours in the kitchens to accommodate all the extra guests. Tem hated going to the Horseman alone, and even when she braved it, Vera was always there, ready with a fresh wave of taunts.

On the fourth night, Tem decided she'd had enough.

She went to the cave, like she always did. She sat on the mat, like she always did. But the moment Caspen went to untie his trousers, Tem spoke abruptly.

"I'm not doing that again."

Caspen blinked. She took advantage of his surprise, crossing her arms and continuing.

"You came in less than a minute last time. I'd say I've mastered that particular exercise, wouldn't you?"

It was meant to dig at him in more ways than one. Despite his obvious attempts to distance himself from her, there was no denying the hold she had on him. It was almost too easy getting him to come. All it took was for Tem to sit a little too close, to let her breath skim over his shoulder, and Caspen couldn't resist his climax. She savored the feeling, knowing it was her one advantage in their silent battle of wills. But she was done being silent.

Caspen's eyes narrowed. Finally, he looked at her. It felt like an eternity since she'd stared into his golden irises. She used the opportunity to lean in, forcing him to maintain eye contact.

"I'm. Not. Doing. That. Again."

There was a moment of silence, and in it, Tem could almost *see* the two sides of him fighting with each other: one side that wanted to keep her at arm's length and the other that couldn't resist her. Tem wanted him to give in. But the only way to win was to do the exact thing he thought she couldn't do: be patient. So she sat there silently and waited.

Finally, just like she knew he would, Caspen gave in.

"What would you like to do instead, Tem?"

Tem knew what he expected her to say. But she didn't want to have sex—at least not tonight. Instead, she said, "I want to talk."

Caspen blinked again. "About what?"

That was easy. "You."

Now he looked surprised. He tilted his head in that reptilian way of his, assessing her with uncanny intelligence. "In that case," he said slowly, "what do you wish to know?"

She would have to be careful with her first question. She didn't want to scare him off or make him regret talking to her. She would start small and build from there.

"Do you have any siblings?"

If he had looked surprised before, now he looked downright confused. It was a ridiculous question—she didn't even care about the answer. But it was meant to disarm him, and by the expression on his face, it had done just that.

"Yes," he said. "I do."

"How many?"

He shifted as if considering standing up and leaving. But he stayed where he was, his eyes still on hers as he answered, "Four."

"What are their names?"

Caspen hesitated. Tem thought he might not answer. And then: "Apollo, Agnes, Cypress, and Damon."

They were odd names. Tem used them as inspiration for her next question. "Do basilisks have last names, like humans do?"

"Yes. In a sense."

"In what sense?"

"We take the name of our quiver as our last name."

"Quiver?"

"It is like a clan."

"So what's your clan name?"

"Drakon."

Tem paused. "Caspenon Drakon," she said, trying the syllables out on her tongue. "That's your full name?"

"Yes."

"Sounds sort of silly, don't you think?"

Caspen let out a bark of laughter the likes of which Tem had never heard from him before. His normally fierce eyes crinkled around the corners, softening his entire face into something almost human. At his reaction, Tem laughed too. It was the first time they had done that together.

"It's *true*," she insisted. "It rhymes."

Caspen shook his head, still smiling. "That may be the case. But I would not suggest saying that to another basilisk, should you ever meet one. They will not take kindly to it."

"I didn't realize snakes were so easily offended."

Caspen's smile only widened. "I would not suggest calling us 'snakes' either. Not unless you have a death wish."

"Seems like a lot of rules to follow."

"Knowing you, you will not follow any of them."

There was a pause, and in it, Tem savored the way he was looking at her—like the barrier he'd erected the last three days was falling. She wanted nothing more than for it to stay down.

Caspen spoke next. "What is *your* last name?"

"Verus."

He lifted his chin, considering her. "Temperance Verus," he said quietly.

She loved the way her name sounded in his mouth. "That's me," she said just as quietly.

Eventually, Caspen relaxed.

He stretched out on the mat as they talked, one arm behind his head, the other resting on Tem's legs. It was a small gesture, yet Tem felt as if they were deeply connected by it, as if he were literally holding them together with his hand. He didn't pull her closer or do anything to deepen the moment. But it still felt intimate, and it was exactly what Tem had been craving from him for three long days. They talked for hours, about nothing and everything. Eventually, Tem lay down too.

They didn't kiss. Instead, Caspen undid the lacings of her dress one loop at a time, pulling it off her body until she was in nothing but her underclothing. Then he pulled that off too, and she was once more naked beneath him.

He still didn't kiss her. It seemed like all he wanted to do was to touch her. Caspen brushed his fingertips gently up her thighs, over her hip bone, and along the curve of her hip. He traced up the center of her stomach, resting his palm in the valley between her breasts. Tem wondered if he could feel her heart, which was beating so fast she could practically hear it. His hand was moving again, sliding up to wrap around her throat. Her pulse thrummed in her temple, pounding an incessant rhythm into her brain.

Without thinking, Tem's hand went to his neck. Caspen's eyes widened at the motion. Then they narrowed, and she heard his voice in her mind:

Squeeze, little viper.

Tem squeezed. She felt the cords of his throat contract beneath her palm, the hard line of his esophagus compressing between her fingers. What would happen if she kept squeezing? Would he let her? She was holding his life in her hand, just as he so often held hers. Tem recognized that this was a moment of trust between them—that she was meant to decide how it ended.

When she released him, he released her too.

They stared at each other for a long time. Caspen was the one to break eye contact, leaning forward and pressing his lips to her jaw. He trailed his kisses downward, gently biting her breast. Tem let out a tiny moan when he did it, and she felt him smile against her skin.

"So sensitive," Caspen whispered, his fingers brushing over her nipple, coaxing it into an obedient point. "I could make you come just from this."

Tem scoffed. "I doubt it."

Caspen's nostrils flared.

Then he lowered his head, taking her nipple into his mouth and sucking it between his teeth. Tem gasped. She'd never felt *anything* like that before. Her hand darted immediately to the back of his neck, her fingers lacing tightly into his hair. She needed something to hold on to—something to steady her against the sheer *ecstasy* he was making her feel.

Tem couldn't believe what Caspen was doing. He alternated between sucking her nipple and teasing it lightly, working it back and forth with his tongue. Every few minutes, he would stop, using his fingers to soften it before taking it in his mouth once more. He swirled his tongue in continuous, lazy circles, tracing the peak of her breast until Tem was completely wet between her legs. She could feel it dripping onto the mat. She'd never wanted to touch herself as badly as she wanted to right now. But if she did that, Caspen would win.

I will win regardless, his voice reverberated through her mind.

"No talking," Tem chastised him. She could barely get the words out.

Just when she was used to one motion, he did something different, sliding her nipple first through the ridges of his teeth before flicking it lightly with his tongue. He was teasing her, she realized, taking her to the edge and then back again, bringing her closer and closer each time. But Tem was stubborn. She wouldn't let him win this. She tried to think of something, anything, to distract her.

Chicken shit. Vera's insufferable giggle. Mother fussing around the cottage.

It was no use. There weren't enough distasteful things in the world to combat the euphoria that was spreading through Tem like fire.

Caspen's mouth completely covered her nipple. This time when he sucked it, he did it for so long and so tightly that she let out a helpless whimper, arching her back and grasping him desperately. As soon as she was sure she couldn't take another second, he pulled suddenly away.

Tem gasped in surprise.

It was that finally—the *absence* of sensation—that brought her straight to the edge. Her fingers tightened in his hair, trying to pull him closer, but his head didn't budge. Instead, Tem watched as Caspen's tongue closed the distance, gliding over her nipple just once, leaving it glistening in the firelight.

Then he blew on it.

Cool air caressed her gentler than a whisper, and Tem felt the last of her self-control finally break as her nipple immediately became so hard it ached. Her body had betrayed her. She could resist no longer.

Orgasm hit her like a tidal wave, crashing forth from the deepest eddies of her body and pulling her into an endless well of pleasure. She rode the wave gladly, basking in the sweet release, allowing herself to come undone just for him. Without hesitation, Caspen plunged his hand between her legs, and the moment he touched her clitoris, she cried out, bucking her hips to meet him. Caspen matched her energy, fingering her *hard*, his mouth returning to her nipple so he could play with both parts of her.

It was incredible. There was no other word for it. Tem could barely catch her breath; she felt as if she were seeing stars.

"*Caspen*," she gasped.

He raised his head so they were at eye level, his fingers slowing into a gentle caress. "You should not have doubted me."

She clung to him. It felt like her soul had been cracked open. "I hate that you have this much power over me."

To her surprise, he laughed.

"What's so funny?"

His grin only widened. "Of the two of us, I am not the one with the power, Tem."

Tem had no idea how to react to that. To believe that she had power over Caspen was to believe that she had influence over a centuries-old creature who could turn her to stone with a single glance. It wasn't a fantasy she could afford to indulge. Yet she knew their relationship had progressed far beyond the bounds of student and teacher. She shouldn't even be here—the other girls had surely long since gone home, and she was still in her basilisk's cave, naked, talking to him as if they were lovers. It was impossible. And yet she wouldn't want it any other way.

"Lucky for you, I'm a merciful ruler." She touched one of his shoulders and then the other, mimicking the motion for granting knighthood.

He grabbed her wrist, kissing the freckles on the palm of her hand. "Lucky me indeed."

They ate together that night and every night after. Caspen returned the claw to her and sent pulses constantly—in bed, in church, on the way to the bakery. On one particular day, they came so frequently that Tem had to pretend to be sick, waving her mother away and insisting that she needed to sleep it off. She spent the day naked in bed, soaked in sweat and her own wetness, wondering how the hell Caspen had enough time on his hands to think of her this often.

Tem suspected that his behavior had something to do with the upcoming elimination.

The letter arrived while Tem's mother was out running errands, so Tem was alone when she received the large white envelope stamped with the wax seal of the royals. Its contents were brief—a simple invitation requesting her presence at the castle the following night. Tem turned it over in her hands, marveling at the thick paper laced with gold leaf.

Then she began to worry.

CHAPTER SEVEN

---•◦✳◦•---

THE PRINCE WOULD BASE HIS DECISION ON A KISS.

Tem didn't know how or when the kiss would happen, but it was traditional for each girl to kiss the prince on the night of the first elimination. Then again, the first elimination had already occurred, so the process clearly wasn't following the conventional norms. What if she didn't get the chance to kiss him at all? What if Leo simply eliminated girl after girl without ever touching them?

Her worries followed her to the cave that night, the curved stone walls enveloping her in suffocating warmth. The only light was the fireplace, which glowed behind Caspen, illuminating his outline like a ghost.

The elimination hung over them like a shadow. They both knew what would happen tomorrow, but neither of them spoke of it. Instead, Caspen brought her straight to the mat, undressing her as he kissed her, pressing his mouth against hers as if he could claim it as his own. Tem accepted his tongue willingly, showing him without a question what she wanted.

Eventually, his lips moved to her neck. Then they moved even lower. Caspen kissed slowly down her stomach, pushing her legs apart as he did so. His hands went to her thighs, opening them and pulling them around his shoulders. A sudden wave of panic hit Tem as she realized what Caspen was about to do.

"*Stop*," she cried sharply.

He stopped, looking up at her in surprise.

Tem was overreacting—she could tell by the look of confusion on Caspen's face. She shouldn't be telling him to stop—it went against their roles. But they were past the point of student and teacher. Now they were lovers, and Tem wanted an equal say. She had never had a man's mouth between her legs before, and she knew she wasn't ready to experience the thing Vera had bragged so cruelly about.

Caspen's hands tightened on her thighs. "What is the matter, Tem?"

She shrugged, unwilling to put it into words.

Caspen sat up slowly, considering her. The firelight flickered on his face, and she saw he was genuinely concerned.

"It will not hurt," he said. "Quite the opposite."

"I know," she whispered. "But it's the first time for me."

He tilted his head. "Everything we have done together has been the first time for you. Why is this any different?"

Again, Tem couldn't put it into words. There was silence as she tried to formulate her thoughts, and Caspen waited patiently for her to do so. Finally, she murmured, "Yes to one thing isn't yes to the rest."

"That is true." He paused, tilting his head in the other direction, clearly trying to understand her outburst. She was still trying to understand it herself. "But have I not earned your trust?"

Tem considered the question. "You have."

"Then why not let me do this?"

Tem's chest felt like it was full of rocks.

Who would want a girl who tastes like chicken shit?

"I'm afraid," she finally admitted.

"Of what?"

She shrugged, refusing to say anything else. How could she explain it to him? He was a basilisk, the Serpent King—he wasn't afraid of anything. Sex meant next to nothing to Caspen. But it meant everything to Tem. He had no idea what it was like to be her—to be fragile and human and vulnerable. This wasn't something he could understand.

Caspen pushed her knees together gently, as if to undo what just happened. "We can wait until you are ready, if that is what you wish."

When she still didn't speak, he crawled so he was lying next to her.

They were silent for a while, and she knew Caspen was letting her determine what happened next. She wasn't ready to confide her true fears. Instead, she whispered, "Do you like doing it?"

Caspen's breath was on her cheek. "Why do you ask?"

"I'm just curious."

He looked at her for a long moment before answering. "Yes. I like doing it."

"Why?"

He shrugged, the muscles rolling in his shoulders. "Instinct, I suppose."

"But what do you like about it specifically?"

She could tell this was the first time anyone had ever asked him that. Surely, he found this line of questioning bizarre. But he indulged her anyway, saying, "It is a way to bestow pleasure on someone. It is a way to understand them and to taste them."

At his words, Tem realized she would not be able to avoid her fears. She would have to face them, no matter the consequences. So she asked the question that was gnawing at the edge of her throat. "What if you don't like the way I taste?"

To her surprise, Caspen smiled. "That is impossible."

"Why?"

"Because." He propped himself up on his elbow. "This part of you tastes like heaven." He brushed his lips up her neck, whispering the rest of his sentence right into her ear. "I have no doubt the rest of you tastes the same."

A shiver went down her spine.

When Caspen pulled away, they looked at each other in the firelight, and Tem realized she'd never felt so vulnerable in her life. This was scarier, somehow, than when she had disrobed in front of him for the first time. This was the culmination of everything she had ever dared to fantasize about—that a man would want to taste her—and she felt as if she were falling headfirst off a cliff into an roiling ocean of unknown.

Caspen seemed to sense her distress because he pulled her closer. "This should not be a concern, Tem. You have nothing to fear."

She nodded. But her doubt must have shown on her face, because Caspen sighed and said, "Shall I prove it?"

"Prove what?"

"That you taste good."

She frowned. "How?"

Caspen paused. Then he took Tem's hand and moved it slowly down her body until it was between her legs. He guided her first two fingers inside her gently, keeping eye contact the entire time. When Tem didn't protest, he pushed her fingers deeper, only stopping when she let out a soft moan. Then he pulled them back out, holding her hand between them. Her wetness glistened in the firelight.

He paused, and in that moment, every one of Tem's fears erupted inside her.

Then he smiled, and she knew what he was going to do. Still, it was an out-of-body experience to actually watch Caspen raise her hand, part his lips, and place her first two fingers gently in his mouth. She felt his tongue move between them, showing her exactly what he would do between her legs. When he was done, he kissed her fingertips. Then he smiled.

"As I said. Heaven."

Tem had never felt anything close to the way she felt right now. Caspen had always made her feel safe, but this time was different. This gesture was deeper—more nuanced and profound than all the other times he'd touched her.

Caspen was looking at her with such calm patience, she could have cried.

"How do you always know?" she whispered.

"Know what, Tem?"

"How to make me feel better."

He chuckled softly. "I never know. I just try something and hope for the best."

Now it was her turn to laugh. At her response, Caspen laughed too, and for a moment, Tem was perfectly happy.

He pulled her against his chest, and they lay there together, bodies intertwined.

"Is there anything else you wish to discuss?" he asked quietly.

She considered the question. When she first met Caspen, she never would have imagined they'd have a conversation like the one they were having now. She never thought she'd be telling him her fears and secrets—never thought he'd be asking her to tell him more.

There was really only one other thing she wanted, and it had been on her mind for a while now. But to actually say it seemed insurmountable, like climbing the tallest mountain with nothing but her bare feet to carry her. Yet she knew if she said nothing, she would regret it.

"I wish you would let me in."

He was silent for a moment before replying, "In what way?"

Tem considered how much she wanted to say. She wanted to ask about their mental connection, specifically why he could speak to her but she couldn't speak back to him. It was just another way their power was imbalanced, and she wondered if he could control it—if he was somehow blocking her from accessing him. Rather than say what she was thinking, she raised her finger, tapping it gently against his temple.

He caught her wrist with his hand, pressing her palm against his cheek. "I cannot control that, Tem."

"It seems like you can."

He shook his head. "It is beyond the boundaries of my power."

"Then why does it feel like there's a wall between us? Why does it feel like you're shutting me out?"

He shook his head again. "I do not know."

Tem was silent. She believed him because she knew he couldn't lie. But it felt like he was keeping something from her—like he knew more than he was revealing.

She decided to change the subject.

"There's an elimination tomorrow."

Caspen's eyes fell to her lips. "Yes. There is."

"Well?" she insisted. "Shouldn't you give me some advice or something?"

A muscle tensed in his jaw. "I have no advice to give."

"Seriously?"

She was pushing him, and they both knew it. She wanted him to validate their bond—to acknowledge the fact that there was something between them.

But Caspen only dipped his head, resting his lips on her throat as he said, "I do not wish to discuss this, Tem."

A twinge of anger twisted her gut. "You don't wish to discuss the exact thing you're training me to do?"

His teeth grazed her jaw. "No."

"Even if it means I'll be unprepared tomorrow?"

He lifted his head. "Even then."

From the look on his face, it was clear he was done with this conversation. But Tem wasn't. "You can't have it both ways, Caspen."

His eyes narrowed. "And which ways are those?"

"You can't prepare me for the prince without actually doing so."

"I have prepared you enough. You will only be required to kiss him tomorrow."

"And if I'm required to do more?"

"You will not be."

"You don't know that. There's already been an elimination. That wasn't supposed to happen either."

Caspen frowned, and Tem knew she had an opening.

"What if we're required to stay at the castle after tomorrow night?"

Traditionally, the final three girls were chosen at a formal ball, after which they moved into the castle for the last part of the elimination process. It was meant to increase their proximity to the prince, to ensure he had a chance to sleep with each girl.

"You will not be," Caspen said again. "It is too early."

Tem shrugged. "That's what you think. But the royals make their own rules. You told me that yourself."

Caspen's frown deepened. "I would have been informed if that were the case."

"Are you sure? Doesn't seem like the royals care about keeping you informed."

The skull in the study flashed through her mind, and she wondered if it flashed through Caspen's.

He sat up. "Enough, Tem."

She sat up too. But instead of retaliating with another dig, Tem placed her hand on his cheek, cupping the carved edge of his jaw in her palm. He was right; it was enough. Tem knew she was lashing out for reasons that had nothing to do with him. She was nervous for tomorrow; she was frustrated with herself; she was feeling desperate and unsteady and utterly out of control. She was consumed with *need*.

Tem wanted more. She'd wanted more since the very first night she'd come into this cave. But she couldn't rush Caspen. He was immovable—an ancient basilisk who wouldn't be swayed by her or anyone else. As much as she wanted more from him, she wouldn't get it until he was ready to give it. So for once, she stood down.

"I'm sorry," Tem said quietly.

Caspen's eyes met hers. He gave a small smile.

"You have nothing to be sorry for."

They spent the rest of the evening doing nothing more than kissing. Whenever Tem tried to take things further, Caspen stopped her. Every time her hand went below his waist, he pulled it back up. Every time her knees opened, he closed them. When he walked her to the head of the trail, his gold eyes lingered on hers before he kissed her gently on the forehead. Then he was gone.

A dress arrived for her, just like last time.

This one was deep maroon, with gold embroidery at the waist. It was low-cut; Leo would love it. Tem pulled it on slowly, wondering once again what it meant that Caspen was dressing her in something that would make her attractive to another man. She put the necklace on too, centering the gold claw on her chest. The other claw was inside her. Unlike last time, Caspen didn't send her any pulses. Instead, he was completely absent from her mind the entire afternoon, and even when the carriage arrived to take her to the castle, there was nothing but a gaping emptiness where his presence used to be.

The castle was just as she remembered it. Tem once again gave her name at the door before being ushered into the same ballroom as before, the impossibly high ceilings making her head spin. The crowd was rowdier than the last time she'd been here. It seemed that the royals had no shortage of alcohol. There were bottles of whiskey and tankards of mead lining the tables scattered throughout the room. Tem looked around for Gabriel but didn't see him anywhere. She did notice Lilly, who gave her a cheeky wave before disappearing into the crowd.

Leo was sitting at a table, his arm draped around the blond girl he'd ranked first during last week's elimination. She was practically in his lap, laughing at his every word. When Tem passed them, Leo arched an eyebrow and raised his whiskey in her direction. She ignored him.

Instead, she poured a whiskey of her own, downing the fiery liquid in a single gulp. It burned on the way down, just like it did the last time she'd had it. But it also steadied her nerves, and Tem basked in the brief moment of peace as the alcohol numbed her senses. That was when she heard it:

Help.

The word was barely audible at first—nothing more than a whisper in the corner of her mind. Tem froze at the sound, and for a single, panicked second, she thought it might be Caspen. But when the voice came again, she knew it wasn't his.

Help me. Please.

This voice was desperate and strained. It sounded weak—like whoever was speaking was on the brink of passing out. Tem closed her eyes to block out the party, concentrating with all her might. But the voice didn't come again. All that remained was a heavy rock of dread in her stomach. Whoever the voice belonged to was in pain. Tem's heart hurt for them, and she didn't even know them. The dread deepened.

She wanted to get out of the castle. There was something dark going on here— something *wrong*. It grated against her energy in a way she didn't understand, and all she wanted to do was leave.

Tem wove through the crowd, heading toward the enormous double doors at the end of the ballroom. She pushed past everyone in her way, clawing toward the green hedges of the garden. The freezing night air hit her the second she was outside, lifting goose bumps on her arms and chilling her straight to the bone. There was a birdbath just a few yards away. Tem clung to it, gripping it with both hands, staring down into the still water. It took several minutes before she had the strength to look up again, and when she did, she realized it wasn't just a hedge she had seen. It was a maze.

The walls of the maze stretched on in an endless structure of sculpted corners. Tem couldn't see past the first passageway, but she knew it must go on for miles. A hedge maze was exactly the kind of useless thing the royals would spend money on.

Behind her, footsteps approached. Leo's reflection appeared in the water.

"Perfect," Tem muttered in greeting.

"Good evening to you too," Leo said with an amused smile.

She heaved a huge sigh, turning to face him. "Good evening, Leo."

His smile widened.

"You've abandoned your date," Tem said tartly.

Leo shrugged. "She won't mind."

"I think she might."

"What I meant was *I* won't mind. She's not much of a conversationalist."

"Then why spend time with her?"

He smirked. "She's talented in other areas."

Tem scowled. It was standard for the girls to throw themselves at Leo during the elimination process. Most of them would try to have sex with him long before the final elimination. And Leo would surely let them. Of course he would brag about it. Tem wanted to slap him. Instead, she said, "If that's the case, why waste time talking to me?"

"I prefer your company. I want you here, remember?"

"Can't imagine why."

Leo ran his eyes over her greedily. "Can't you?"

He was far too close for comfort. Tem shifted away, gripping the sides of the birdbath until her skin turned white. Leo swirled his drink, which was nearly empty.

"You don't seem to enjoy these parties, Tem."

"Well spotted."

"We could go somewhere else if you prefer," he said.

"Where?"

"My room."

Tem rolled her eyes. "No, thank you."

"Shame," Leo sighed dramatically. "It's been a while since anyone's stayed overnight. Perhaps my seduction method needs tweaking."

"Seduction method?"

The words slipped out before she could stop them. Leo's eyes flicked to hers.

He seemed to sense he had an opening because he stepped closer, tilting his head so their faces were aligned. "Yes," he said quietly. "I have a method. Would you care to hear it?"

She wanted to say no. But she couldn't. "I'm sure you're going to tell me anyway."

"I take a girl up to my room," Leo continued as if she hadn't said anything. "I pour her champagne." He paused. "Then I draw a bath."

Tem wrinkled her nose. "Seriously?"

"Yes." Leo's mouth twitched. "Girls love baths."

Tem was getting a migraine from how often she was rolling her eyes.

At her reaction, Leo smiled, extending his hand to touch the bottom of her hair, twirling a wavy strand between his thin fingers. She should have pulled away. But she didn't.

"We take a bath," he continued. "We drink champagne." Leo looked her in the eye. "And then we have sex." He was still twirling her hair gently. For some reason, it gave her chills.

"And that works?" Tem whispered.

"Every time."

They stared at each other, just the two of them, standing at the edge of the maze.

"And you, Tem?" he asked softly. "Would it work on you?"

He was far too close. But for once, Tem wasn't pushing him away. There was something about Leo that was drawing her in. She couldn't put her finger on what it was, but it was concrete and strong, and she couldn't seem to resist him the way she usually did. But she couldn't let herself give in either.

So she said, "I'm not really a fan of baths."

Leo smiled. The muscles in his neck strained as he arched his head to look at the stars. "I'll never get a straight answer from you, will I?"

"Probably not. But isn't it more fun that way?"

"Yes," he said. "It certainly is." He looked down at her, the smile still on his face. "We could always skip the bath, you know."

Tem shrugged. "I'm not really a fan of champagne either."

He laughed outright at that. "In that case, I suppose I need a new method for you."

"Let me know when you find one."

The second she said it, victory flared in Leo's eyes. "I shall," he said quietly.

Tem rolled her eyes again, but it was too late. She'd let their banter go too far, and now Leo thought he had a chance. The worst part was he did. Tem didn't know what it would take—certainly not a bath and champagne—but given the right circumstances, she would go to his room.

"You know," Leo said, swirling the ice cube in his glass. "We're meant to kiss tonight."

Tem sighed. "I know."

"Any preference on where and when?"

"Are you saying I have a choice?"

"That's exactly what I'm saying."

Tem crossed her arms, looking incredulously up at him. "Do *you* have a preference?"

"Of course. But I'd rather hear yours."

Tem couldn't help but wonder what his preference was. She shrugged. "My preference doesn't matter."

"I beg to differ." He sounded sincere.

Tem eyed him warily. "I'd prefer we didn't kiss at all."

She could barely get the words out. But she had to see how he would react. To her surprise, he smiled down at her, flashing his gold incisors in the moonlight.

"And I'd prefer you didn't lie. But you knew that already."

They held eye contact for a long moment. Then Leo swirled his glass once again before dumping the ice cube into the birdbath with a soft splash. His smile widened as he turned away.

"The night is young, Tem. Find me when you're ready."

Then he was gone.

Tem stayed outside until it became unbearable to do so. When she couldn't take the cold any longer, she made a beeline for the closest table with food on it. She was just stuffing an unholy amount of cured bacon in her mouth when a familiar voice slid into her ear. "Don't eat too much, Tem. You might get *fat*."

It was Vera, of course, looking down her nose like she always did.

"The prince prefers a curvy girl," Tem said around a mouthful of bacon.

Vera scoffed. Then she groaned, rolling her shoulders.

"What's wrong with you?" Tem asked despite herself.

"Nothing, it's just…" Vera's mouth twisted. "My back is killing me."

"Why?"

She scoffed. "All this *sex*, of course. You'd think we could at least do it in bed, like civilized people. Anywhere would be better than the floor of a dirty old cave. But I guess that's all you can expect from a snake."

Tem's mouth fell open. Thankfully, at that exact moment, a girl in the crowd waved at Vera, and she disappeared.

Vera's basilisk is having sex with her.

The bacon turned in her stomach. Maybe it was just Vera getting another jab in. Maybe she wasn't *actually* having sex—she just wanted Tem to *think* she was. But Tem had to know for sure.

She spent the next hour tracking down each girl left in the competition, subtly steering the topic toward their time in the caves, the twist in her chest becoming tighter with each conversation. They were all having sex. Every single one of them. Which meant that Tem was the only girl whose basilisk wasn't fucking her. It felt like the surprise elimination all over again, like she was the ugliest girl in the room—like she was the girl that nobody wanted.

Tem's insecurities curled around her like vines, squeezing her stomach and compressing her lungs. How long had the other girls been having sex? Since the first night in the caves? But no—Vera had said that her basilisk didn't even touch her that night. So at least they were equal in that. But it didn't matter. They'd been unequal every day since, and Tem was once again the least experienced girl in the room. Suddenly she couldn't breathe. She needed to get away from all these people, and she needed to do it *now*.

Or maybe that wasn't what she needed at all. Maybe what she needed was one person in particular. The only person who she knew, without a shadow of a doubt, wanted to fuck her.

It took all of thirty seconds to locate Leo. He was leaning against a column, watching the party, his head cocked back against the stone in bored indifference. At the sight of him, Tem felt the familiar cinch of stubbornness, the refusal to give in. But why shouldn't she? Leo had made it clear he wanted to have sex with her. And he was obviously the only one. Why shouldn't she kiss him? The night was not so young anymore. And more importantly, she was ready.

People parted for Tem like she was made of fire. By the time she got to Leo, a small circle had already cleared. He looked down at her calmly as she marched right up to him, grabbed his face, and kissed him.

It wasn't right.

It wasn't Caspen.

But it was a kiss, and she needed it, and Leo kissed her back without hesitation, pulling her against him as if he'd been expecting this from her all along. And maybe he had.

Leo was a good kisser. Frustratingly so. The rest of the party disappeared as his fingers tangled in her hair, arching her head back to meet his lips. His tongue dove into her mouth with expert rhythm, sliding against hers and coaxing a tiny moan from the back of her throat. She prayed he didn't hear it. But from the way his grip tightened, she knew that he had.

Suddenly her back was against the column. Leo's hands were moving lower. The kiss was barely appropriate anymore, and Tem had a sudden vision of Jonathan and Vera groping each other at the Horseman.

Tem pulled away. Leo let her go, but just barely. He was holding her so tightly that their lips were still touching as he whispered, "That wasn't so bad, now was it?"

People were staring; Tem felt as if she were in a fishbowl.

"Your Highness?" Lord Chamberlain's voice floated past Tem's heartbeat, which was pounding in her ears.

"What is it?" Leo said without looking away from Tem.

"You have now kissed every girl. It is time."

"Very well."

Leo finally released her, taking a step back and adjusting his cuff links. Then, to Tem's utter surprise, he held out his hand. She took it cautiously, watching as he laced his fingers through hers. Their hands remained clasped together as they made their way toward the podiums, the entire ballroom watching them as they passed.

Leo didn't hesitate. He walked Tem straight up to the first podium, holding on to her until she was standing facing the crowd. In a final gesture, he pressed his lips to her fingers. Then he dropped her hand and pointed at the next girl.

Leo eliminated two contestants: the blond he'd ranked first the last time and a girl with choppy, brown bangs. Tem barely registered any of it. She simply stood on her podium—the *first* podium—and wondered how the hell she had gotten here. She was beginning to understand Leo's game. It was clear he was rewarding her for the kiss, that she'd used her body as currency to buy herself this position. Leo was straightforward in that way. He was a man of his word, as ridiculous as that felt to admit. At least with him, she understood the rules of his game.

When the elimination was over, Tem was immediately ushered back to the carriages along with the other remaining girls. She stared numbly out the window the entire way home, replaying what had happened.

"Miss? Did you hear me?"

They'd arrived at her cottage. The footman was talking to her.

"Sorry, what?"

"I said, someone will come for you tomorrow night. Be ready at eight."

It took Tem a moment to register his words. Then she realized what he was saying. Leo had ranked her first: that honor came with a reward.

Tem had a date with the prince.

CHAPTER EIGHT

---◦◦※◦◦---

'M SO PROUD OF YOU, MY DEAR."

It was the next morning. Tem was barely awake.

"I'm only the second girl he's taken on a date, Mother. Don't get your hopes up."

"That's a *good* thing. It means you have a chance to make a good impression before anyone else does."

Tem pushed her eggs around her plate. She had no idea if she even *wanted* to make a good impression on Leo. He hadn't exactly made a good impression on her.

"I'm missing a night of training for this," she grumbled.

"That doesn't matter, Tem. A date with the prince is far more important. Your training is meant to prepare you for him. There's no point in the training if you don't catch the prince's eye."

Tem sighed. She'd caught Leo's eye all right.

The events of last night were still a blur to her. She'd tossed and turned until dawn, replaying her kiss with Leo again and again until she'd memorized every moment of it. She remembered his tongue in her mouth and his hands on her waist. She remembered the way he'd gripped her like she was the very air he breathed. Kissing Leo was different from kissing Caspen—the prince was younger and looser and *free*, with none of the restrained power or deep, complicated seriousness that radiated off the basilisk. None of the depth of character either.

But at least the prince wanted to fuck her.

Tem still couldn't believe she was the only girl who hadn't had sex yet. It seemed like some sort of evil joke, like the universe was conspiring against her. She felt a deep, jagged anger toward Caspen for allowing this to happen. How could he withhold this from her? Especially when her very future depended on it? It was unspeakably cruel.

Regardless of how she felt about Caspen, for once in Tem's life, she was looking forward to visiting the bakery. She couldn't wait to see the look on Vera's face now that Tem had a date with the prince. But to her surprise, Vera wasn't there. Instead Geoff, Vera's father, was standing behind the counter.

"Where's Vera?" Tem asked. She was eager to rub her new development in her face and didn't like the idea of leaving without doing it.

"Sick," Geoff grunted.

"Oh." Tem frowned. "With what?"

Geoff shrugged and began counting the eggs.

Tem's frown deepened. It wasn't like Vera to miss work. The bakery was her stage; it was where she held court over the entire village, gossiping and passing judgment with little to no regard for consequences. She'd once worked during a snowstorm just because there was a chance the boy she liked might come in to order his favorite pastry. Vera was a force of nature, and Tem couldn't imagine a common cold taking her out.

"Well, do you know when she'll be back?" Tem insisted.

Geoff shook his head. "Soon."

He'd never been one for extended conversation.

"Fine," Tem sighed. She'd just have to brag tomorrow.

By the time she'd done her rounds with the roosters, it was midafternoon and Tem was starting to get nervous. She had no idea what a date with the prince would entail. Would they be alone? Chaperoned? Would they go somewhere or stay at the castle? She wished the training process had prepared her for dating. She wasn't good at talking to boys, much less a prince. Caspen should've given her conversation lessons. Add that to the list of things he was failing to teach her.

No dress arrived for her this time.

Tem didn't know what to think of it. Was Caspen withholding from her because he was angry she had secured a date with the prince? Tem was secretly pleased by the thought. She was not, however, pleased that she had nothing to wear. She was halfway through tearing her room apart in search of something suitable when her mother knocked on the door.

"Dear? A man is here for you."

Tem froze, a heap of underclothing in her arms. *A man?*

She poked her head into the kitchen to see the footman from the other night standing awkwardly in the doorway.

"Miss?" He brandished a package at her. "The prince requested you wear this."

Tem sighed.

Now she understood why there had been no dress from Caspen. Of course Leo wanted to pick something for her to wear, just another way to control her—to make sure she knew he was in charge. Tem loathed the thought.

She snatched the package from the footman before slamming her door and tossing it onto the bed. Half of her was dying to see what it was. The other half had no intention of wearing it.

You will wear it.

Tem jumped. It was Caspen's voice. He'd been absent all day, and he chose *now* to show up? Tem tried to send him a thought back but found that she couldn't. Her words pressed up against the same wall that had always stood between them. Instead she spoke them out loud.

"Says who?"

His reply came with humorless rigidity: *Says the prince.*

"And you? Do you want me to wear it?"

But he was gone.

Tem stared at the package. With a sigh, she ripped the paper perhaps more aggressively than necessary, and a dress tumbled into her hands. It was beautiful. There was no doubt about it. Tight and velvet and dangerously low-cut. But Tem hated it. It was sexy and revealing and clearly meant for Leo's pleasure alone. Caspen's dresses had complemented *her*, accentuating her beauty. Leo's dress had a decidedly different purpose: to reveal as much of her body as possible. Tem's ingrained stubbornness balked at the idea of wearing such a dress. All she could think about was how different it was from what Caspen would have chosen.

But it didn't matter what Caspen would have chosen. He didn't care about her. He refused to have sex with her. And he certainly wasn't going on a date with her tonight.

There was nothing for it.

By the time she'd pulled the dress on, it was time to go. Tem kissed her mother goodbye and bundled into the carriage, her stomach already twisting itself into a knot. She had no idea what to expect, and the long ride to the castle didn't help. All she could think about was Caspen. Why was there a one-way barrier between them? Why wouldn't he let her speak to him? Why did he insist on keeping his distance when all she wanted was to pull him closer? His apathy was infuriating, and she was almost thankful that the night's events would provide a welcome distraction from the anxieties eating away at her mind.

When the footman dropped her off at the castle entrance, Tem took a deep breath before knocking on the door.

To her surprise, Leo opened it.

The prince leaned casually against the doorframe, his head cocked to the side as his eyes raked over her body, taking in every detail of her dress.

"Stunning," he said. "As always."

Tem crossed her arms. "You picked it out."

He cocked his head in the opposite direction. "I thought it would suit you. Don't you like it?"

"I like making my own choices."

"Ah." His mouth quirked into a smile. "So I've offended you already."

"I'm not *offended*. Just annoyed."

Leo extended his hand. "Then allow me to make it up to you."

Tem glared at his hand. Then, after a very long moment, she took it. The prince intertwined his fingers with hers, pulling her inside the castle and into a room just off the foyer. It was large and warm, with a crackling fireplace on the far end. Oil paintings lined the walls, and the smell of pipe smoke clung to Tem's nostrils.

"What is this?" Tem whispered.

Leo dipped his mouth to her ear. "What do you mean?" he whispered back.

"I mean, I thought we were…going on a date."

"Is meeting my family in the parlor not sufficiently romantic for you?"

Tem took a moment to remember the royal family tree. There was Leo, of course, the only son of Maximus, the king. His mother had died giving birth to him. He had one sibling: his older sister, Lilibet, who was married to Edward Fitzwilliam, a duke of somewhere or another. They had two children, Aurora and Desmond. The king's brother, which made him Leo's uncle, was Lord Chamberlain, but Tem couldn't remember his name. He had no wife, which meant no children.

"Um," Tem said. She had no idea how to respond.

Leo chuckled at the look on her face. "Dating me isn't like dating some village boy, Tem. You're the future queen. That comes with formalities."

Before Tem could process his use of the present tense, the door opened.

"So it begins," Leo muttered.

"*Tem!*"

It was Lilly. She was wearing a yellow dress, and she looked beautiful as she bounded right up to them and pulled Tem into a tight hug. Then she smacked Leo on the shoulder.

"I was right, wasn't I? You like her."

He swatted her hand away. "That doesn't make you right about everything," he hissed.

"Just the important things."

Leo rolled his eyes. Then his expression sobered, and his voice dropped. "Is he in a good mood today?"

Lilly pursed her lips before dropping her voice too. "No."

Tem looked between the two of them. "Who are you talking about?"

"My father," they said at the same time.

As if they had spoken him into existence, a man appeared suddenly at Lilly's side. His cold eyes latched immediately on to Tem's before slipping briefly down her body. Not for the first time, she wished Leo had chosen a less-revealing dress. It hardly seemed appropriate to meet the king with this much cleavage.

Leo spoke before Tem could. "Father, this is Temperance."

The king's large hand engulfed hers, the golden bracelet on his wrist a twin to the one on Leo's.

"Temperance," he said slowly, and she had the distinct feeling he was looking straight into her soul. "The chicken farmer's daughter."

Chicken shit girl.

Maximus's eyes slid to Leo's. "You said she was beautiful."

His words hung in the air. They sounded like an accusation.

"She is," Leo said, his voice hard.

"If you insist."

Tem could feel tears rising and fought to suppress them. Beside her, Leo's entire body was tense. The silence grew slowly contentious as father and son stared at each other, neither of them willing to break it. Tem glanced between them, completely bewildered by the stalemate. There was clearly a deep history here, but Tem had no idea where it originated. Even Lilly was uncharacteristically silent, hovering nervously next to Tem and biting her lip.

Just when the moment became precarious, Maximus dropped Tem's hand.

Before she had a chance to process the interaction, someone else grabbed her. The next few minutes passed in a whirlwind as Tem met person after person, shaking hand after hand. She tried to memorize their names and ranks while keeping everyone's lineage straight, but eventually they blended together. It was like meeting an assortment of sunflowers—all equally beautiful, all with nothing of substance to offer. At some point, Leo was pulled away by Lord Chamberlain, and Tem found herself in a corner alone. She took the opportunity to survey the crowd.

Leo's family was extensive and tall and...*royal.* They carried themselves with unmistakable grace, so unlike the hunched weariness of the people in the village. Everyone in this room was a stranger to manual labor—their palms were smooth; their fingers dripped with gold. Tem touched the tiny golden claw around her neck. She still wasn't used to wearing something so valuable. She wondered what it had cost Caspen to acquire it. A voice suddenly shattered her thoughts.

"Temperance."

It was the king.

Tem shifted uncomfortably, distinctly aware of his disparaging gaze. "Your Majesty." She gave an awkward curtsy. It was difficult to move in the dress without exposing an unceremonious amount of thigh.

"Thelonius has taken a liking to you."

I wish he hadn't, Tem thought violently. Out loud, she said, "It appears that way."

"Are his feelings reciprocated?"

She fought the urge to make a face. "That's really none of your business," she muttered.

Maximus leaned in. He had the same gold incisors as Leo. "Who my son loves is invariably my business."

"Loves?"

"He can't take his eyes off you."

"Maybe he needs his eyes checked," Tem said tartly.

"Do not make light of this. Even now, he watches."

Tem scanned the parlor for Leo. He was leaning against the fireplace, whiskey in hand, staring at her with a slight smile on his lips. When their eyes met, he raised his glass in her direction.

Maximus's fingers wrapped around Tem's arm, digging painfully into her skin. "Everyone has their place, Temperance. Wouldn't you agree?"

"I don't know what you mean."

"I mean"—his fingers tightened—"there is a natural order to things. A hierarchy, if you will."

Tem scrunched her nose. She didn't like where this conversation was going.

"We must honor that hierarchy," the king continued. "Otherwise, things may become...unbalanced."

"Unbalanced?"

"Yes. Unbalanced."

He was still holding her arm.

"Take the basilisks, for example. They provide a service. Their place is beneath us."

Tem hated the way he was speaking to her—as if he were explaining a simple concept to a small child.

"Should the snakes ever question their place, the balance may falter. So tell me, Temperance: Do you know your place?"

Tem didn't answer. She was afraid if she did, she might say something rather rude.

"It is my son's duty to choose a suitable wife." Maximus's sharp eyes met hers. "Are you worthy of that privilege?"

Tem held his gaze. "Your son will be the judge of that."

"Apparently my son's judgment is questionable."

A thorn of resentment pricked Tem's side.

She didn't want Leo. Couldn't want him less. But Maximus was insulting her, saying she wasn't good enough for his weasel of a son. And why shouldn't she be? She was just as good as Vera—or any of the other girls—despite the fact that the world had told her otherwise. Tem tried to quell the anger inside her, but it wouldn't be stopped. She turned to face Maximus.

"If I wanted your son, I'd have him," she said coldly. Then she wrenched her arm from his grasp and walked straight toward Leo.

He raised his eyebrows. "Let me guess," he said as she approached. "My father told you you're not worthy of me."

"How'd you know?"

To Tem's surprise, a harsh darkness flashed across Leo's face. "That's his specialty, I'm afraid."

Tem frowned. There was no mistaking the change in his mood. Without thinking, Tem reached for Leo's arm. The moment she touched him, he relaxed, his expression sliding into one of practiced indifference. He downed the rest of his whiskey.

"Shall we?" he asked.

"Shall we what?"

"Get on with our date. Unless you'd prefer we stay here and mingle with my family all evening."

Tem would not prefer that.

At the expression on her face, Leo laughed. Then he crooked his elbow, clearly indicating he wanted Tem to take it. So she did. Without another word, Leo steered her from the parlor and out to the back patio, where a small, candlelit table was overlooking the maze. He pulled out one of the chairs, gesturing elegantly for her to sit.

"After you," he said.

Tem sat slowly, watching Leo the entire time. He seemed calm, but there was a glimmer of rage just beneath the surface that Tem had no idea how to address. She decided to break the tension. "This is…lovely." She waved her hand at the table.

"You're lovely," Leo said without missing a beat.

Tem scoffed. "Don't do that."

"Do what?"

"Compliment me. You're terrible at it."

"I can't be that bad. You're still here, aren't you?"

"I'm still here because I'm hungry. And it seems like there might be food."

Leo smiled. "There will most certainly be food."

"Great."

"Is that the key then?"

"To what?"

"To you. If I feed you, will I earn your favor?"

"I'm not a horse, Leo."

Leo let out a deep laugh. "Clearly not."

Tem rolled her eyes and promptly changed the subject. "You father seems…intense."

Leo's laugh turned bitter. "That's the kindest way I've ever heard him described."

"How would you describe him?"

True, unfiltered pain flashed across Leo's face. He leaned back in his chair, arching his neck to look at the stars. Tem let the silence sit, studying the tight angles of his jaw. Finally, he whispered, "Heartless."

He dropped the word with such aching bitterness that a chill shot down Tem's spine.

"Leo." She said his name softly, in a way she'd never said it before.

Leo met her eye, and for a moment, Tem saw his facade drop. She saw that the cocky prince was only a boy—a boy with a strained relationship with his father. She wondered what had happened between them and if he would ever tell her. Tem wanted to ask more.

But Leo gave a dismissive flick of his fingers and said, "I don't want to talk about my father." His face slid back into a smirk. It was clear the moment was over.

Tem sighed. "Then what do you want to talk about?"

"You, of course."

"What about me?"

"What do you like to do for fun?"

Tem blinked. She hadn't expected such a casual question from the prince. She didn't really have hobbies, at least not like normal people did. The farm took up most of her time, and when she wasn't helping her mother, she was at the Horseman with Gabriel. She decided to simply state the truth. "Drink."

Leo smiled. "Charming."

She shrugged. "You asked."

"So I did."

He was still looking at her, and she was still looking at him.

"What's your poison?" he continued.

"Whatever's cheapest. Yours?"

"Whatever's strongest."

"Charming."

"You asked."

A butler appeared out of nowhere to place a salad in front of Tem. He placed the same salad in front of Leo, filled their wineglasses, then vanished.

"We've established that you're not a horse," Leo continued as if there were no interruption. "But do you like spending time outside?"

Tem considered the question. They were outside right now, and she liked that fine. But she didn't inherently prefer it. "Not particularly."

Leo cocked his head. "Why not?"

"Time spent outside is usually time spent working on the farm."

"Ah," he said. "Of course. The farm."

For some reason, it seemed like her answer amused him.

"Something funny?" Tem prompted.

"Certainly not." He rearranged his expression until it resembled neutrality. "I just can't picture you on a farm."

His eyes went to her breasts. They'd been going there all night, but now they lingered.

"Surprising," Tem shot back, "considering you act like a pig."

Leo let out another deep laugh. The meaner she was to him, the more he seemed to enjoy himself. "I can't help it if I like what I see."

"You're only seeing it because you chose this dress."

"I thought you said you weren't offended."

"And I thought you said you'd make it up to me."

"So I did."

Leo waved down the butler and whispered something in his ear.

Tem ignored him, instead shoving a mouthful of salad in her mouth. It was a fancy thing, with feathery greens and a sweet dressing. Nothing like the hearty vegetables they grew on the farm. Even the silverware was gold. A single fork from this table would probably feed a family in the village for a month.

The butler reappeared, setting a small velvet box in front of Tem.

"What's this?" she asked.

"A way to make it up to you," Leo answered.

"I don't wear jewelry."

"You're wearing a necklace."

She touched the little gold claw, feeling its warmth. "This is…special."

Leo nodded at the box. "That could be special too."

Tem shook her head. "I don't want it."

"You don't know what it is."

"It's a bribe. And I don't take bribes."

Leo leaned forward. "Perhaps you would if it was the right bribe."

Tem crossed her arms. "You're not used to hearing the word *no*, are you?"

Leo leaned back. He smiled. "No."

They stared at each other, the small velvet box sitting between them. Tem wasn't going to open it. There was nothing he could say to make her do so. If she opened it, it sent the message that she could be swayed by trinkets and gold. If she opened it, he won. She didn't need Leo thinking she was shallow, and she certainly didn't need another necklace.

Leo sighed, raising his wineglass to his lips. "So difficult to please. What am I going to do with you, Tem?"

Tem returned her attention to her salad. "That's for you to figure out."

There were two more courses after the salad—a butternut soup with crusty bread and a tender roast. Tem devoured it all. Leo barely ate—he seemed content to drink his wine and watch her. No doubt he was used to the castle food anyway. The meal was a luxury for Tem. For Leo, it was just another dinner.

"Tell me something," Leo said presently. "Why are you here?"

It felt like an echo of what Caspen had said in the caves. *You do not seem desperate to be here.* Tem was getting a little tired of people questioning her decisions.

"You told me to be," she said shortly.

"You make it sound like you didn't have a choice."

"I didn't."

To Tem's surprise, Leo frowned. "You always have a choice, Tem."

She snorted at that.

"Do you really think I'd stop you from leaving?" he asked.

"No. But I want to stay."

The words were out before she could stop them. Tem didn't even know why she'd said them.

Leo's eyebrows shot upward at her admission. "Do you? You won't even accept my gift."

She put her fork down. "That doesn't mean I don't want to stay," she said quietly.

It didn't matter that she didn't want Leo's gift. If she left now, she'd be out of the competition. If she left now, she'd have to go home to her mother, to the farm, to Vera's cruel taunts. She was telling the truth: she wanted to stay. So she might as well make something of it.

Tem shifted in her seat, leaning forward so the dress offered an especially flattering view of her cleavage. Leo's jaw tightened at the sudden movement, and she took advantage of his surprise to say, "Do you know what else I want?"

Leo took far too long to answer. "What's that, Tem?"

"An apology."

He blinked. "For what?"

"For ranking me last during the first elimination."

His eyes slowly found their way back up to hers. "I thought we were past that."

"We aren't."

Leo sighed, running a hand through his hair. "I'm sorry I ranked you last."

Tem shook her head. "Say it like you mean it."

He flashed his gold teeth. "Is that an order?"

She held his gaze. "Yes."

The abject hunger in his eyes was undeniable. He trailed a single finger down the stem of his wineglass, taking his time before answering.

"Tem," he said quietly, "you were the most beautiful girl in the room that night. I never should have ranked you last. It was just another way to lie, and I'm sorry I did it."

For the second time tonight, Tem felt a chill. Leo seemed to sense her moment of weakness, because that infernal smile spread across his face once more.

"Do you accept my apology?"

"Yes," grumbled Tem.

"Good." He smirked.

Tem rolled her eyes. "*Don't* give me that look."

"And what look is that, Tem?"

"Like you've just won something."

Leo tapped his long fingers nonchalantly on the table, the smirk still twisting his lips. "Haven't I?"

"Can't you just behave yourself for once?"

"Life's no fun when you behave."

Tem had nothing to say to that. *The royals make their own rules.*

She was just about to drown herself in the rest of her wine when she heard it:

Help.

Tem froze. It was the voice—the same one she'd heard the last time she was at the castle. Her eyes slid to Leo, who was still watching her. Against her better judgment, she asked, "Did you hear that?"

He raised an inquisitive eyebrow. "Hear what?"

"Nothing."

It was no use. Of course he hadn't heard it—the voice was in her head, the same way Caspen's was. But if that was the case, did that mean the voice belonged to a basilisk? She wished suddenly that she could talk to Caspen. He would know the answer.

Please. Help me.

Tem stood abruptly.

Leo looked up in surprise, genuine concern flashing across his face. "Tem? Is every-thing all right?"

She shook her head, trying to clear it. "Just…too much wine."

Leo stood too, offering her his hand. "Shall we take a turn about the garden?"

Tem wrinkled her nose.

"A *turn?*"

Leo grabbed her hand. "Just follow me."

She allowed Leo to steer her down the patio stairs, noticing how he laced his fingers through hers so she couldn't drop his hand. They entered the garden together, but Tem stopped when they reached the edge of the maze.

Leo looked down at her. "Scared we'll get lost?"

"No," said Tem automatically. She didn't doubt Leo knew his way around the maze. She only doubted whether he'd let her out once he got her in there.

"Come on then." He gave her a condescending wink.

Tem let him pull her into the maze.

The world went instantly quiet. Even the birds—a sound she'd become accustomed to constantly hearing—were silent within the towering green walls. Leo took the lead, steering them through turn after turn. Tem wondered if he had the maze memorized. Eventually, he broke the silence.

"So, Tem," he said. "Do I have a chance with you?"

She looked up at him in shock. It was a bizarre question. The entire training process was designed so that *she* was the one vying for a chance with *him*. "I…don't know."

"Yes, you do."

"No," Tem insisted. "I don't."

It was the truth. Up until an hour ago, she'd thought there was nothing redeemable about Leo. But he'd revealed his true self when he'd talked about his father. There was a *person* under his insufferable exterior. And that person had a chance with her.

They were stopped on the path.

Leo leaned in, his eyes narrowing. "I don't believe you."

"Well, you should."

"Well, I *don't.* Your indifference is infuriating."

"I'm not indifferent."

"You certainly act like it."

"That's your interpretation."

He snorted. "You know you're the only girl who isn't throwing herself at my feet?

All the others had their hands down my trousers the first night they met me. But not you. How *should* I interpret that, Tem?"

She shrugged stiffly. "Interpret it however you like."

He leaned in even more. "What I would *like* is for you to tell me how you feel about me."

He was far too close to her. But despite his proximity, Tem found she didn't want to lean away. She liked the way he smelled. And she liked the way he was looking at her. Tem wasn't used to men looking at her that way—like they wanted her, like she was worth something. The feeling was like a drug.

Lilly's words ran through her mind: *He always wants what he can't have.*

Was that the reason Leo was pursuing her? Because she was the only girl whose hands hadn't been down his trousers? It wasn't a good enough reason for Tem. She needed him to want *her specifically*, and not just because he couldn't have her.

So she said, "I'm telling you the truth. I don't know how I feel about you yet."

"Yet?"

"I've known you for two weeks, Leo. And during those two weeks, we've only spent a few hours together. Do you really think that's enough time to form an accurate opinion?"

Finally, he leaned away, considering her. "Well, when you put it that way, perhaps not."

Tem rolled her eyes. "Exactly."

Neither of them spoke as they wound their way back through the maze. Eventually, the castle loomed into view. They were nearly on the patio when Leo spoke again.

"Aren't you curious to know how I feel about you?"

"I think I can guess."

"Can you?" Leo looked down at her. "Then by all means, Tem." He splayed his hands open. "Guess."

Tem looked up into his gray eyes, deciding how much she wanted to say. It was a delicate subject, and if she didn't tread carefully, she might offend him. Then again, nothing seemed to offend Leo. It was almost as if he enjoyed her insults. Tem wondered if she was the only person in his life who didn't completely cater to his every want and need. If that was the case, it put her in a position of power, and she savored it.

"I think I confuse you."

Leo raised an eyebrow. "How so?"

"I think you like me, but you don't know why. You want me, but you wish you didn't. You're used to getting what you want, but part of you likes that you can't get me."

His other eyebrow rose. "Can't I?"

"No," Tem said firmly. "Not until you've earned me."

His eyes flicked down her body, then back up again. "And you think you're worth earning?"

Tem held his gaze. "*You* think I'm worth earning."

"Hm," he said, the corner of his mouth turned up in amusement. For a moment, they simply stared at each other, and Tem wondered if this was how Leo acted with the other girls. It felt as if they were connecting on an unexpected level—one Tem could never have anticipated and one she didn't fully understand.

It was only when they reentered the castle that Tem realized the date was about to end. When they reached the foyer, Leo turned to face her.

"I'm not going to kiss you," he said.

Tem was too shocked to react properly. "Why not?"

He stepped closer. "Because if I kiss you, I'll try to take you upstairs. And you're not going to let me."

Tem opened her mouth, but he kept talking.

"And you were right. I'm not used to hearing the word *no*. And I don't want to hear it from you. Certainly not after I had to see you in this dress"—he brushed his fingertips along her waist so lightly she almost didn't notice until it was over—"all fucking evening."

"You chose it," she whispered.

"Apparently I'm partial to torture." There was a pause, and he stepped even closer. "I'm not going to kiss you. Instead, I'm going to picture everything I want to do to you *without* that dress on. And I'm going to pretend that someday you'll let me do it."

Her throat tightened. She couldn't breathe, couldn't think.

"You were wrong about one thing though," Leo continued, his voice eerily calm.

"What's that?" Tem managed to say.

He took her hand in his, turning it over and pressing his lips to the freckles on her palm. He murmured his next words against her skin. "I know exactly why I like you."

Then he disappeared into the parlor.

Tem stood alone, her heart thrumming in her chest. There were no words to describe what had just happened. It was as if an invisible thread now connected her to Leo, as if his vulnerability and candor had weakened her defenses against him. She couldn't have predicted a single second of this evening, and she had no idea how she felt about anything anymore.

Tem was just turning to leave when she heard a voice in the parlor. She froze, her hand on the door. The voice belonged to Maximus. He was speaking in a hushed tone—practically whispering. She paused, listening hard as he said, "You are enamored with her."

"How do you know? You've barely spent ten minutes with us."

"I know you, Thelonius. I have seen you like this before."

A pause. Then Leo said, "If you have seen me like this before, then you know what I'm going to do."

"You cannot choose her."

"And why not?" Leo countered, his voice considerably louder. "If I can't make my own choice, then what's the point of the elimination process?"

"She's a chicken farmer."

"*So?*"

"You are only doing this because you know it will anger me."

A pause.

"Maybe that's part of the fun," Leo said coldly.

Tem heard the clink of a glass and wondered if whiskey had been poured.

"I will not have you repeat the mistakes of your past," Maximus continued.

"Evelyn was *not* a mistake."

The king let out a dull laugh. "You were a fool then, and you are a fool now."

Another pause. When Leo spoke, his voice was laced with hate. "I let you control me once. I won't let you do it again."

"We have a reputation to uphold, Thelonius. This is not how things are *done*."

"Things are done the way we say they are. Isn't that what you're always telling me? *Laws are made to be broken*."

"I won't have my son wed to a chicken farmer."

"Then you won't have a son."

There were footsteps as one of them walked away.

Before she could be discovered, Tem walked away too.

CHAPTER NINE

—••✳••—

TEM HAD NO IDEA WHAT TO EXPECT THE NEXT NIGHT IN THE CAVE.
To be fair, she never knew what to expect from Caspen—whether he would be attentive or distant, caring or cold. Would he ask her about her date with the prince? Would she have to tell him about how they had dinner on the patio? How Leo hadn't kissed her? Or would Caspen pretend that the prince didn't exist, like he always did? The last time they were together, Caspen had tried to taste her. Whatever was in store for her tonight, Tem was quite sure she wasn't ready for him to do that.

And then there was the fact that they hadn't had sex.

Part of Tem wanted to yell at Caspen for holding out on her. She couldn't understand his behavior, and she didn't know how much longer she could survive without an explanation for it. The other part of her was terrified of pushing him away. Their connection was already perilous to begin with; the very last thing she wanted was to give him a reason to sever it.

Her worries followed her throughout the day—on the farm while she did chores, to the bakery where Vera was still infuriatingly absent, and all the way to the entrance of the cave. But the moment she saw Caspen standing next to the fireplace, they fell away. There was no trace of worry on his stony features, no sign that he had any troubles whatsoever. His eyes were focused on her and her alone, and she knew she wasn't imagining the heat in them.

"Come here, Tem."

She would've come whether he told her to or not.

When they were finally toe to toe, Caspen raised a single finger to her chin and tilted her face up to his. With that isolated motion, Tem allowed herself to forget the date with the prince. It was clear Caspen wasn't going to ask about it anyway. She forgot her anger, her frustration, her insecurity. She remembered that these precious hours in the cave were all they had, and she didn't want to waste them talking.

"What shall we do tonight?" Caspen murmured.

Tem couldn't believe he would ask her that. It undermined everything the training was supposed to be. It put *her* in charge. She wondered if it was his way of appeasing her—if he knew somehow that she needed to feel in control right now.

She took a moment to think about her answer. There were a hundred things she wished to do. But only one thing made sense to do tonight. Something that, if Tem did it, she might gain the courage to receive it in return.

"I want to taste you."

Primal hunger bloomed in Caspen's eyes. "As you wish," he said quietly, his finger slipping down the expanse of her throat. "On your knees."

Was worshipping one god really so different from worshipping another?

Tem knelt for Caspen the same way she knelt for Kora, looking up at him as he untied his trousers and slipped them down his hips.

He gave her no instructions. Instead, his fingers laced into her hair, grasping the back of her neck and pulling her forward. His other hand held his cock level with her mouth.

He paused.

In what felt like slow motion, Tem's lips parted.

Caspen let out a tortured moan as her wet tongue touched his velvet skin—soft and hard, water and stone. Tem saw his eyes roll back as he moved her head with his hand, coaxing himself farther and farther down her throat. Just as he'd taught her how to touch him, Caspen taught her this too. He directed her movements, guiding her back and forth, up and down. She was taking the very core of him inside her—tasting the part of him that exemplified his formidable power.

And yet Tem felt power too.

There could be no question of Caspen's pleasure—he was gripping her hair like his life depended on it, and with such an important part of him in her mouth, Tem wondered if maybe it did. He pulled her closer, deepening their union, sinking into her one glorious inch at a time.

Eventually, his grip on her loosened, and the message was simple: *Now you.*

Tem obeyed without hesitation, continuing the motion, feeling saliva build at the corners of her mouth as she took him down her throat, trying to consume as much of him as possible.

But there was only so much she could take.

She'd always known he was big; it was an undeniable truth. But to have him in her mouth meant feeling his length in a different way. It meant her lips straining to take him, her jaw being pried open beyond what she thought was physically possible. When he hit the back of her throat, she winced.

"Relax, Tem." His voice came from somewhere above her.

Tem tried to obey, but it was an impossible request. She couldn't take him—he was simply too big.

Suddenly, Caspen pulled away, leaving her empty.

Then, to Tem's complete shock, the basilisk knelt down in front of her. Her heart skipped several beats as his chest, then his shoulders, then finally his blazing eyes came into view.

"You must relax, Tem. It is the only way."

Even when he was kneeling, he was still taller than her. She shook her head, looking down at her hands.

"I don't think I can."

"Tem." He cupped her chin in his palm, pulling her gaze up to his. "You can do anything. Of that I am certain."

His eyes were completely black. They bore into her like bottomless pools, darker than the deepest corners of the cave—darker than death itself. Tem felt a part of herself cower at the sight. But another part liked what she saw. She recognized his darkness, and she felt a kinship with it.

Caspen shifted his weight back, lowering himself even farther for her. "Try it from here," he said. "If you need to rest, use your hand." He released her chin, letting her determine when she was ready to try again.

In the absence of his touch, Tem took a moment to simply breathe. Her mouth felt numb, and her palms were damp. *All* of her was damp.

"Tem," Caspen whispered. "Do you want to stop?"

She shook her head. "No."

He leaned in, and the temperature rose several degrees. "Are you sure?"

A fire flared within her. Of *course* she was sure. She'd been sure ever since she was thirteen and realized she wanted to kiss a boy. *Caspen* was the one slowing their progress. *Caspen* was the one holding her at arm's length. *Caspen* was the one who refused to have sex with her even when his duty demanded it.

She was sure. Even if he wasn't.

Without another word, she lowered her head. Except this time, she didn't try to take him all at once. This time, she let herself explore, lifting him with her hand and trailing kisses all the way down his shaft. She swirled her tongue where the base of his cock met the swell of his balls, immediately aware of the way his hand returned to her hair when she did it.

Now, with Caspen on her level, Tem could relax.

She took her time, pacing herself even though the last thing she wanted was to go slow. His cock was warm, every vein standing out beneath taut skin. Tem worked her way back up his shaft, taking only his head into her mouth and sucking on it gently. Caspen gave a sharp intake of breath, his fingers tightening in her hair. When she was sure she had his full attention, she took him as deep as she could over and over, losing herself in a motion that felt as steady as the tides. Vera had made it sound so clinical, like a transaction to be performed. But that wasn't true at all. Tem could never have anticipated there would be a rhythm, a harmony, a *flow* to it that was as natural as her own heartbeat.

With each dip of her head, Caspen's groans grew more desperate. Eventually, his body began to move beneath hers. Tem breathed through her nose as he took control, thrusting into her mouth with sudden urgency, tilting his hips up so that his cock slid smoothly in her throat.

Then out.

Then in again.

Tem closed her eyes, surrendering to him completely. She realized he was sending her pulses—taking care of her while she took care of him, ensuring she felt just as much pleasure as he did. She could barely stand the heat between her legs. Her wetness was dripping down her thighs, and if the task at hand didn't require so much focus, she would have tried to touch herself at the same time.

At some point during the experience, Caspen's presence entered her mind.

His consciousness curled around hers like a vise, gripping her at the base of her skull. The edges of her vision blurred, and she was suddenly lightheaded. A moment later, strength entered her, and she realized it came from Caspen. She felt his energy join with hers, her mind clearing immediately as he fortified their connection. Tem found she could go on, quicker than before, and she sensed Caspen's approval, feeling it in the back of her brain as if he were nodding inside her mind. It was an overwhelming sensation being intertwined with him like this. Tem knew she could do nothing but give in—there was no fighting his presence, and she didn't want to anyway. She only wanted to please him, and it was clear she was doing exactly that.

Caspen's breathing was ragged and strained; his thighs were slick with sweat. Tem knew from the way his moans had progressed that he was completely at her mercy. She was his weakness—the one thing he would never be able to fully resist. He *needed* what she was giving him.

His cock felt unbearably rigid; it was becoming impossible to take him all the way down her throat. He seemed different than earlier—*harder* somehow, as if there were metal beneath his skin rather than muscle. Tem remembered that he had told her to use her hand if she needed to rest. So she pulled away, releasing him from her mouth and grasping him with her hand instead. The moment she raised her head, Caspen's lips crashed down onto hers.

The kiss had none of the controlled grace she had become accustomed to.

Instead, it felt as if Caspen were trying to extract her soul from her body as he tore her dress off and yanked her forward, pulling her onto his lap so she was straddling him while she stroked him. He sent pulse after pulse—some of them so intense they bordered on pain. Every time Tem tried to catch her breath, he sent another, each one piercing her deeper than the last. It was overwhelming in the extreme. Just when she thought she couldn't go on, Caspen's hand joined hers, his long fingers tightening her grip around his cock, quickening her strokes to a lightning pace. They were moving in tandem now, kissing with feverish intensity, every inch of her body touching every inch of his. Tem was quite sure if he sent one more pulse, she would explode.

A split second later, her hand felt as if it were on fire.

The air tasted suddenly sharp, like metal. When Tem looked down, there was a dark red streak on Caspen's cock. At first, she didn't understand what she was seeing. It wasn't until she lifted her hand that she realized her palm was bleeding. Tem couldn't comprehend the sight. She looked questioningly up at Caspen, and her shock only increased. His eyes were shut, his jaw clenched tightly. There was smoke rising from his skin.

But it wasn't skin at all—it was scales, and they were interlocking and spreading across his chest at an alarmingly fast rate. The same scales were on his cock; they had rubbed her hand raw. Tem watched in horror as his body began to change before her eyes—his torso elongating, his shoulders expanding. Too late, Tem understood what was happening.

Caspen was transitioning into his true form.

A deafening hiss filled the cave as Caspen lurched backward, pushing Tem away.

"You need to leave," he growled. She barely understood the words—two razor-sharp fangs were warping his mouth. His tongue was splitting in two.

"No," she said.

Caspen's hands were fisted into the mat, his back arched at an unnatural angle. "I am not asking."

Before Tem had a chance to respond, his body jerked violently. It was as if someone had pulled him up by invisible strings before suddenly letting him drop. He fell back to the mat with an anguished roar, a sound so tortured that Tem wanted to cry.

He's fighting it, she realized with sudden clarity.

But even Caspen could not resist the will of nature. Smoke filled the cave as his body thrashed with otherworldly strength. Somewhere in the fog of her shock, Tem remembered that if he looked her in the eye while wearing his true form, she would die. His next command clapped like thunder in her mind.

LEAVE ME, TEM.

But she couldn't leave Caspen. It was the last thing she would ever do.

Despite every one of her instincts screaming otherwise, Tem moved closer. He was barely a man anymore. His once-smooth skin was now a shiny expanse of black scales. Sharp, ridged horns were puncturing his back, growing straight out of his spine. His angular head was pointed at the ground, and she knew it was his attempt to protect her. She pressed the palms of her hands to what remained of his shoulders. He was blazing hot—it took everything she had to keep touching him—but the second she made contact, he stilled.

"Caspen," she whispered. "Stay with me."

A great shudder passed through him. Tem felt his scales ripple beneath her fingers, and despite their searing heat, she didn't relinquish her grip.

I cannot.

"Yes," she insisted. "You can."

His consciousness was still joined with hers. She focused on their connection—tugging on the dark strands of his mind, pulling him even closer. He groaned, and another shudder tore through him.

Tem. You must go.

"I'm not going anywhere."

It is not safe. I will hurt you.

"You won't. I know you won't."

The hiss surrounding them grew louder. His body was still changing, his head slowly rising toward hers.

I cannot control it, Tem.

"You have to try."

I AM TRYING.

His rage was palpable. Tem was dripping with sweat; she couldn't hold on much longer. Smoke seeped from between his scales, stinging her eyes.

"Focus on something else," she begged. "Focus on me."

Caspen didn't reply. Perhaps he was beyond response. But Tem would not be dissuaded.

"Focus on me, Caspen."

She said it firmly, like an order.

Close your eyes, he ordered back.

"No. Stay with me."

Something was dripping onto the mat. Tem looked down to see blood seeping from Caspen's mouth. He was biting his own tongue.

"Caspen, please," she whispered.

The energy in the room shifted suddenly, as if a strong wind had blown through the smoke.

For the love of Kora, close your eyes.

"Caspen," she whispered again. "Please."

CLOSE YOUR FUCKING EYES, TEM.

Tem closed her eyes.

The moment she did so, Caspen wrenched himself away from her. He was retreating into his body, tearing himself apart just to keep himself together. Tem didn't need to see him to know what was happening. She could do nothing to help him. She could do nothing but pray. But even her prayers weren't enough.

She heard the ferocious growl that reverberated around the cave; she felt his mind violently extract itself from hers. The very air around her felt as if it had been set on fire. Tem knew, on an instinctual level, that he had transitioned—that she was now in the presence of a predator.

For some inexplicable reason, she was not afraid.

Instead, she felt the same peace she had felt the night before she came to the caves for the first time. She felt the same breath on her cheek—just one single breath, softer than a feather against her skin. She knew now what she had suspected then: it was Caspen in the dream—he had drawn her to him like a moth to a flame.

Her eyes were still closed. But she longed to open them—*needed* to open them. She wanted to see Caspen in his true form. She wanted to understand this final, most fundamental part of him. It didn't matter that it would surely kill her. Tem had never been afraid of dying anyway.

So she opened her eyes.

Thick, black smoke filled the cave. It choked her throat and forced tears down her cheeks. A dark mass came into view in front of her. Even when she squinted, she couldn't make out his full shape.

Tem.

His voice was in her mind, in her body. It was *everywhere*.

"Caspen," she said in return.

At his name, the claw pulsed, and Tem let out a desperate whimper.

It was so much stronger than usual—as if his true form allowed his power to operate at full force.

"Again," she pleaded.

Another pulse came, more intense than the first. Tem cried out as her clitoris throbbed with pain instead of pleasure.

Beautiful.

One word. But it was all she needed.

Tem's hand went between her legs, pressing on the claw, fortifying their connection. The smoke skimmed over her skin in whorls and eddies, brushing her hair from her shoulders and exposing her breasts. She arched her back, wanting him to see that she would do anything—*withstand anything*—for him. His next words filled the cave, penetrating every inch of the air:

I could eat you alive.

"I could let you."

Something was blossoming within her—something real.

Tem was seconds away from coming. She raised her hand, reaching for him. At first, there was only smoke. Then her fingers found purchase, brushing against the same scales she had felt earlier. She shifted forward, pressing her naked body against his.

Tem knew immediately that she had gone too far.

Caspen let out a roar of agony that nearly popped her eardrums. It echoed around the cave as Tem scrambled backward, shielding her head with her hands. She could see his outline shrinking into the smoke. He was transitioning again—returning to his human form. Scales became skin; spikes became muscle. Tem felt the temperature drop as he retreated even farther, curling away from her into the darkness.

"Caspen," Tem started. "I'm sorry—"

Before she could finish, the smoke cleared, and there was once more a man kneeling in front of her. Sweat ran in delicate rivulets down his chest, dripping along the hard lines of his torso. The firelight shone on his glistening body, making him appear as if he were glowing. His cock still had her blood on it.

"Caspen?" Tem whispered.

He looked at her, and she went cold at the fury in his eyes.

"What were you thinking?" he hissed.

"What do you mean?"

"I mean what were you *thinking*? I could have killed you."

"But you didn't."

"That fact is nothing short of a miracle. You should have done as you were told. You should have left."

"I couldn't leave you—"

"I cannot control myself when I am wearing my true form, Tem. You have no idea the danger you were in."

"You obviously can—" She reached for him, but he jerked away.

"You are a *foolish*, *reckless* girl. You do not follow instructions, and you do not use

110

your brain." Caspen stood, crossing to her dress and throwing it down in front of her. "Get dressed," he said. "And go."

He was shutting her out. She couldn't bear it. Not again.

"Caspen," she whispered. "Don't do this."

"I will only tell you one more time. *Leave.*"

"Caspen, please."

But he refused to look at her.

Tem blinked away tears. She pulled her dress on gingerly, trying not to use her right hand, which was still bleeding. She was almost at the entrance of the cave when she heard her name.

"Tem."

She turned. Caspen was behind her.

"Give me your hand," he said quietly.

Tem hesitated. Then she held out her hand, and he took it in his, unfolding her fingers so they were splayed open. Tem winced as he did so, and his eyes flicked up to hers before immediately returning to her palm. Her skin was red and raw, tiny drops of blood seeping to the surface between her freckles.

Caspen didn't say a word. He simply placed his palm over hers, and she felt a pulse transfer through his hand. Unlike the hot, lingering ones he sent her through the claw, this one was cool and soothing, and the fireplace dimmed for a brief moment before the pulse disappeared. When Caspen lifted his hand, her palm was smooth and healed.

"Thank you," Tem whispered. She curled her fingers tentatively, surprised to see there was no lingering pain.

Caspen didn't reply. He merely turned and disappeared into the shadows.

With no other option, Tem left.

It was the first time in a long time that Caspen hadn't walked her to the head of the trail, and she felt his absence deeply. Tem had no idea where they stood after tonight. She couldn't understand why everything had gone so wrong—it felt like things had progressed in a way they never had before. Clearly, they were connected on an unprecedented level. Tem had never heard of anyone else bonding with their basilisk like this. There were so many unfinished conversations between them—so many frayed threads that led nowhere. It was nothing short of torture. But each time they got closer, Caspen pushed her away.

By the time Tem got home, she was in the depths of despair.

Her mother was already in bed, and Tem had no desire to lie in the dark with nothing but her thoughts for company. Instead, she walked out to the garden, sitting on her favorite bench and looking up at the stars. She saw the Alpha Serpentis—the brightest star in the Serpens. It was supposed to shine brightest for the viewer when they needed it most, and tonight, Tem felt as if it were shining just for her.

She wondered if Caspen was looking up at these same stars. Or perhaps he had simply retreated beneath the mountain and removed her from his mind entirely. But Tem refused to believe that. It didn't seem possible that he wasn't thinking about what had happened tonight—that he wasn't thinking about *her*. Surely, their connection wasn't one-sided.

Tem decided it was time to find out.

She closed her eyes and concentrated, saying his name in her mind as forcefully as she could:

Caspen.

Silence.

But Tem was determined. She would not let things end like this—she needed to know that what they had was worth repairing. So she said his name again, this time crying it out in her mind: *Caspen!*

Silence.

When Tem opened her eyes, they were filled with tears. Perhaps she shouldn't have bothered; perhaps communication with Caspen was contingent on his consent, and she was wasting her time trying to speak to someone who didn't wish to speak to her.

It was utterly unfair.

She was sick and tired of choices being made for her. She was sick and tired of Caspen holding all the power. A wave of frustration swept through her, and she stood up, screaming his name to the stars as if she could shake them from the sky:

CASPEN!

Silence. And then:

There is no need to yell, Tem.

CHAPTER TEN

———•◦✳◦•———

T EM FROZE.

Caspen's voice was inside her head, as it always was, deep and luxurious and knowing. It shocked her so much that she sat back down on the bench, her mouth hanging open.

"I'm sorry," she whispered.

Speak to me using your mind, Tem.

"Oh," she said out loud, then clamped her mouth shut and thought it instead:

Oh.

She could feel his amusement, and with it, a weight came off her chest. Finally, the barrier between them was lowered. Finally, they were connected, just as they were always meant to be. Talking to Caspen was like sending her thoughts down a long, dark corridor and through an open door—one that, until now, had been locked tightly. It felt natural to be joined with him like this, and Tem couldn't believe it had taken so long for him to allow it.

So, Tem. Is there something you wish to say to me?

Now that they were having a conversation, Tem found herself suddenly afraid. She wasn't sure what she wanted to say, and she certainly wasn't sure how to say it. But Caspen was here, in her mind, and she didn't want to lose access to him. So she asked, *Did I do something wrong? Earlier, I mean.*

He was not beside her, but she could hear him sigh.

You did nothing wrong.

She felt relief at his words but wasn't sure if she believed them. *But I did do...something, didn't I? Or at least...I caused something.*

It felt like forever before he spoke again. When he finally did, his voice was but a whisper inside her head. *What happened was not your fault. It was mine.*

Tem summoned the courage for her next question. *But what exactly happened? I don't understand.*

For the first time, Tem sensed Caspen's hesitation. He was always so sure of himself; now his caution scared her. She worried he might not answer, or worse, cut off their connection altogether. Instead, his voice returned, still quiet, still subdued:

I lost control.

Tem processed his answer, wishing for so much more. She remembered the way he had pulled away from her when she'd pressed herself against him—his roar of agony that had nearly ripped her apart. She needed answers, even if he was unwilling to give them.

Did I hurt you?

Caspen's presence grew in her mind.

It is I who hurt you.

She shrugged, and she was sure he could see her.

You healed me.

His disapproval was obvious, probing at the back of her neck. It was a curious sensation, and although it wasn't necessarily pleasant, she savored it because it meant that he was still here. Tem needed to keep him with her.

She spoke before he could: *Will our lessons continue?*

The probing stopped abruptly. *Of course they will continue.*

An incredible lightness shot through her. *So you're not angry with me?*

His mood softened. *I am angry with myself.*

Tem could feel his sadness and, beneath it, deep regret. She wanted nothing more than to run back to the cave to comfort him.

Before she could act on it, Caspen said: *It is not your concern. Like I said, you did nothing wrong.*

She felt him start to fade and only wished to pull him back. *Please don't go.*

His presence paused. *I cannot stay, Tem. We should not be talking like this in the first place.*

But why?

Because it will only lead to pain.

She shook her head. *You have never caused me pain.* The wind caressed her cheek, and she swore he had sent it.

I did tonight.

He was fading again, pulling away. She had to keep him. *If this will only lead to pain, then why did you give me…a piece of you?*

Caspen's presence grew, as if his hands were on her shoulders. The claw was still inside her, and she felt it pulse. *I should not have done that either.*

His words crushed her. Of course he regretted it. Of course she was not worthy of the gesture. She swallowed her shame. *Shall I return it to you?*

Caspen flared in her mind. *I did not say I wanted it back. Only that I should not have given it to you. Do not assume I regret my actions. I am not someone who makes my decisions lightly.*

His words came in an avalanche, so quickly Tem could barely keep up. She blinked, trying to remain calm as she asked, *So you don't regret it?*

His answer was quiet. *No.*

Tem gripped the bench, as if by doing so she could grip him. *Will you think of me?*

His reply was barely a whisper, lost in the wind. *Constantly.*

Caspen relinquished his grip on her mind, and she felt his energy subside. Tem tried to hang on, but she knew this time he wouldn't stay. His presence faded, and she was all alone in the garden, once again staring at the stars. Where a moment ago she had been warm, now she shivered.

She tiptoed back through the house, passing her mother's door and hearing her reassuring snores. Tem's room was dark but warm, and she undressed slowly, pretending that Caspen was watching. The tip of the claw gleamed between her legs, its pearly sheen glowing in the darkness. It was the most beautiful thing in the world to her—certainly the most beautiful thing she had ever owned. Although she wondered if she did truly own it. Could one even own a part of someone else? Was any part of Caspen hers to own? Tem wasn't sure. All she knew was that he owned her completely, whether he wanted to or not. Tem touched the claw, pushing it deeper into the place Caspen had not yet been but she dearly wanted him to go.

The moment she did so, he returned to her mind.

His arousal matched her own; she could feel how much he wanted her, his heat traveling down the shared corridor of their connection. The tapered tip of the claw pressed against her clitoris, and when she imagined it was Caspen pressing her instead, she felt weak.

Tem climbed into bed, the sheets soft beneath her fingers. His voice came to her as she was pulling the covers over her shoulders:

Leave them.

Joy erupted in her chest at his command. She hadn't quite believed him when he said he would think of her; then again, she never quite did. Yet here he was, mere minutes later, keeping his word.

Tem left the covers by her feet, lying back on the pillows and shuddering in anticipation. A single pulse tingled between her legs, traveling up her body and peaking her nipples. The pulse quickened and, with it, her heartbeat. She tilted her knees open, brushing her fingers down her stomach, preparing to touch herself.

Be still.

Tem froze, her hand halfway down her body.

Watch.

Tem sat up curiously, staring between her legs. At first, nothing happened. She only felt a gentle vibration, which made her ache even more.

Then the claw began to move.

It slid in and out of her slowly, moving entirely on its own accord. Tem watched in mesmerized awe, transfixed by its steady momentum. She could not look away; it was a marvel to behold such magic and more amazing still to feel it. The claw seemed to glow as it penetrated her, never going all the way inside her—always stopping itself with the tapered end, which acted as a fingertip would, applying pressure against her clitoris with each penetration.

Kneel.

Tem did so, the curve of her ass resting on her heels, her thighs forming an open angle on the bed. She gripped the blankets tightly, focusing on her breathing as the claw went deeper, prompting her to move her hips in order to rub herself against the mattress. The combination of sensations felt so good she arched her back as a moan escaped her throat.

She was wet now, and it was soaking into her sheets. But Tem didn't care; she couldn't stop rubbing herself, and she knew Caspen wouldn't want her to anyway. She slid her hips back and forth, concentrating on the point of the claw, which was hard between her legs. If only Caspen were here. If only she could ride him the way she was riding her sheets. If only he could feel just how much she wanted to give herself to him. Tem needed him to know how turned on she was, how utterly obedient and pliable her body had become.

She pictured it with all her strength: her on top, him underneath, her palms splayed flat on his chest, his hands gripping her ass. She imagined how he would pull her against him with sharp thrusts, again and again, until they finished in unison.

As she pictured them together, she felt Caspen's hunger grow.

He sent her a vision back—the mirror of her own, but this time from his perspective. He was looking up at her as she rode him, her face flushed with heat, her breasts pushed together.

Was that what she looked like to him? Surely, he was embellishing the vision. Tem had never seen herself like that: beautiful, fierce, a sexual being—a *woman*. It was incredible to see what he saw, to view herself through the lens of his desire.

The claw moved in tandem with her, sliding in and out so she could pleasure herself on top of it. Caspen's presence in her mind only grew—she could feel him there as clearly as she felt herself.

Get on all fours.

The order was a growl. Tem obeyed immediately, feeling a rush of cold as the air met her wetness. But it lasted only a moment before the claw burned hotly and she cried out, twisting her fists into the sheets. She tried to remain still as Caspen sent it deeper and deeper inside her, but it was impossible not to react. The tip remained pressed against her clitoris, and the deeper he sent it, the more the pressure increased.

Beautiful.

The claw went deeper.

Perfect.

Even deeper.

Angel...fucking angel.

She could barely take another second.

Beautiful, perfect Tem. Fucking perfection.

It went on. Caspen whispered word after sweet word, pushing her closer and closer to orgasm. When she was just moments from finishing, the pressure suddenly disappeared.

Tem gasped in surprise, realizing he was teasing her, bringing her to the edge and then denying her a climax. Tem wanted to protest, but before she could, he sent the claw in again, his presence so strong she could have sworn he was behind her. For the second time in a row, he brought her to the brink but wouldn't let her finish. Instead, he said:

Take it out.

Tem could barely comply—it went against everything she wanted and needed. But she did so anyway, the smooth hardness slippery in her hands.

Lie on your back.

Tem did so.

Place it on your throat.

Tem set the curve of the claw so it encircled the front of her neck. It was so heavy she felt pressure on her airway. Caspen's growl of pleasure deepened.

Now finish.

It was the easiest thing in the world to slip her fingers between her legs, rub them against her clitoris, and finish. When she came, she could have sworn the claw tightened around her neck, and Tem thought she might choke. Before she could panic, the claw loosened, and a wave of euphoria swept through her. Tem's joy was nothing compared to his.

She felt Caspen's climax in conjunction with her own, his pleasure rushing in a relentless wave so unfathomably deep that she feared she might slip beneath it and never come up again. Tem had no idea this was what it felt like for him when he came. It was so much stronger than anything she had ever known—she couldn't believe he could survive such pleasure. It was impossible to tell where her climax ended and Caspen's began; perhaps they were one and the same. His pleasure was hers and vice versa. There was no end to their connection, no limits to what they could achieve together.

Tem lay there, naked, the claw still clamped around her neck. The afterglow of their orgasms was so strong, she barely heard Caspen when he asked: *Did you like that?*

His voice was a purr.

Yes. Did you?

When his answer took a moment to come, Tem panicked. When it finally did, he said, *Of course I did.*

Pride rushed through her. He was pleased. He approved.

What did you like the most?

Tem genuinely wanted to know the answer. Caspen was so mysterious; it seemed like she was always the vulnerable one. She wanted to know more about him, to learn how to please him and for him to trust her to do so.

I liked the way you did what you were told.

It was not the answer she wished for. Tem wanted him to like something about *her*—something that she specifically had provided.

He must have sensed her disappointment, because his presence coiled in her mind, settling at the base of her skull.

It is not my approval you should seek. You must save your heart for the prince. You know this, Tem.

Tem did know it. But that didn't make her seek his approval any less. Caspen himself had told her she was not meant to be tamed. Why should she tame her heart?

I just want to know what you like about me.

She could feel his amusement, and she didn't like it.

She hardened her tone, snapping, *Are you laughing at me?*

His amusement only increased. *Certainly not. I am merely wondering what made you this way.*

She frowned. *Made me what way?*

His answer was a single word: *Persistent.*

Tem was surprised. No one had ever called her persistent before. She supposed it was true; she was not one to give up. Even as a child, she'd learned that if she wanted something to happen for herself, it was up to her to achieve it.

I was just born like that, I suppose.

He laughed, and it sounded like church bells ringing. *Then if you must know, that is what I like about you.*

Tem couldn't help but smile. She lay there for a while longer until she became cold. She sat up slowly, and when Caspen didn't protest, she crawled up to the head of her bed. When Tem went to place the claw in her bedside drawer, she heard:

Stop.

She paused, her hand out.

I may want you again.

Anticipation rushed through Tem. Eagerly, she slipped the claw back inside her. It went easily; she was still wet. Then she pulled the blankets up and, despite her excitement, fell straight to sleep.

Caspen had her twice more that night.

The first time, Tem was awoken by a pulse shooting abruptly through her. It shattered her dreams, immediately setting her skin on fire. Caspen sent pulse after pulse in increasing intensity until she cried out, her legs crossed together tightly, her fingers pressing the claw even deeper. It was equal parts exhilarating and exhausting, and when it was over, Tem was covered in sweat and gasping for breath.

The second time was different.

The pulse was soft and tentative, reverberating through her so gently, she didn't even feel it at first. But it nudged her awake insistently, and as the wave built, Tem felt as if she were being unraveled from the inside out—as if Caspen were unfolding her in a field of sunlight. Her climax was long and lingering, buzzing gently along the edges of her body before fading into nothingness. When it was finally over, she heard his deep voice whisper, *Sleep, Tem.*

Tem slept.

She awoke to her mother's insistent knock on the door.

"Wake up, dear. There is someone here to see you."

Tem groaned, rubbing her eyes. There was only one person she wanted to see, and she was quite sure he wasn't in the kitchen. When she stumbled out of her bedroom, Gabriel's cheerful grin lit up the room.

"Morning, sunshine."

Tem glanced at her mother, who was standing pointedly in front of the drying rack.

"Hey." Tem sat next to him at the table. "What are you doing here?"

"Delivering this." He brandished a letter.

Tem recognized the royal stationery. "Why do you have that?"

Gabriel shrugged. "Peter was going to deliver it. I tagged along."

Tem smiled, pressing a kiss against his cheek. "I'm glad you did."

Everyone watched as she opened the letter. There were just three lines of thin black text, which she read out loud:

Temperance Verus,

The prince requests your presence at the castle this evening for a formal group dinner.

    Kindly be ready at 8:00 p.m.

"What's that?" Gabriel pointed at the back of the letter.

Tem turned the letter over. There, scrawled in messy red ink, were two additional words:

Torture me.

Leo's voice ran immediately through her mind: *Apparently I'm partial to torture.*

Apparently Tem was too.

Gabriel plucked the letter from her fingers. "Torture me?" he asked.

Tem sighed. "Leo," she said simply.

She wondered if the other girls had gotten a personalized addition to their letters. Somehow, she doubted it.

The last twenty-four hours had been such a blur that Tem hadn't had a chance to think about what she'd overheard in the foyer at the end of her date with the prince. But it all came back to her now. She remembered how Leo had argued with Maximus, how his father had chastised him for making the same mistakes of his past. Was Evelyn the mistake he was referring to? Tem knew nothing about her, but she knew Evelyn meant something to Leo. Could Evelyn be the cause of the rift between father and son?

Tem remembered something else from their conversation—something that made her blood run cold with resentment:

You are only doing this because you know it will anger me.

Maybe that's part of the fun.

If Leo was only pursuing Tem to make his father angry, then he had no respect for her as a person. That was unacceptable to Tem. She was not a strategy; she would not allow herself to be used to further the prince's agenda. It didn't matter that it gave her an advantage in the competition. It also reduced her to a prop in Leo's game. And Tem was far more than that. She was a catch, and she refused to be seen as anything but.

"So?" Gabriel was saying.

Tem blinked. "So what?"

"How are you going to torture him?"

"I'm sure I'll think of something."

"Tem," her mother scolded. "You should be trying to impress him."

"Torturing him *is* how I impress him, Mother. You wouldn't understand."

Her mother shook her head.

Gabriel, on the other hand, smiled wider. "You know, if he's into pain, you might consider—"

"*Out!*" her mother cried.

With one last rueful grin, Gabriel left.

Tem performed her chores on autopilot, thinking about the invitation. She wasn't surprised there would be a group dinner tonight. There were nine girls left, which meant that they were in the second stage of the elimination process. The events would become more intimate from this point forward, to ensure each girl had as much time as possible with the prince. Tem wasn't sure how she felt about having more time with Leo. Attending an event at the castle meant she wouldn't be able to go to the caves tonight. The thought disappointed her; she wanted nothing more than to see Caspen.

We will see each other tomorrow.

Tem nearly jumped out of her skin as she remembered that their minds were connected now. She'd spent so long trying to destroy the barrier between them that she wasn't used to it being down.

How long have you been there?

Not long.

Tem frowned. She didn't like that he'd listened to her thoughts without her consent.

I meant no harm, Tem. You are...hard to ignore.

Somehow, she knew it was a compliment. Before she could reply, he spoke again.

From now on, I will only come when you call.

His presence faded.

Tem wanted to call him back but didn't. It was hard enough that she had to see Leo tonight. It would be harder still if Caspen was listening to every word.

The package arrived at seven.

It was larger than the one Leo had sent her last time, and when Tem opened it, she realized why. Three dresses fell onto her bed. One was silver, which Tem immediately rejected. She didn't want anything clashing with the gold of her necklace. The next dress was a deep purple and so low-cut that Tem actually blushed. Typical Leo. The last one, inexplicably, was modest. It was black and form-fitting, with a high neck and long sleeves. Tem arranged the dresses on the bed so she could see all three at once.

Tem recognized that Leo was letting her choose for herself, that he'd heard her when she told him she liked making her own choices. Could it be possible that he wasn't the pig he portrayed himself to be? A glance at the neckline of the purple dress refuted that possibility. Yet his gesture wasn't lost on Tem.

She considered the dresses. Then she considered Leo's request.

Torture me.

It was one thing to show Leo everything he wanted. It was another thing entirely to show him nothing at all. Besides, who was she to deny the prince?

Tem smiled and reached for the black dress.

CHAPTER ELEVEN

———•◦✳◦•———

VERA WAS THE LAST GIRL TO ARRIVE AT THE CASTLE.
Tem watched as she flounced into the foyer with her nose turned up, snatching a glass of wine from the butler and downing half of it in one go. Her mouth was a bright circle of cherry-red lipstick, and she reeked of flowery perfume. The combination was an assault on the senses.

"Are you feeling better?" Tem asked as politely as she could manage.

Vera squinted at her suspiciously.

"Why do you care?"

"Your father said you were sick. I'm just making conversation."

Vera sighed. "If you *must* know, Jonathan ended things with me."

Tem almost laughed. It was just like Vera to be sad about Jonathan ending things while simultaneously competing for the prince's hand in marriage. Nothing was ever enough for Vera; she always had to have it all.

"Well…I'm…sorry to hear that."

"You should be."

"Excuse me?"

"You *should* be sorry. If I had been with the Serpent King, I'm sure I would've known how to keep him."

"Are you *serious*?"

Vera flipped her curls over her shoulder. The other half of the wine disappeared into her mouth as a butler ushered them into a dimly lit dining room along with the rest of the girls. A large circular table was arranged in the center of the room, surrounded by plush velvet chairs. Shiny gold name tags adorned each plate.

"You're *so* ungrateful, Tem," Vera hissed as the butler distributed more wine. "Of all people, *you* have the best teacher. Everyone knows that's the reason you got your date."

Tem had nothing to say to that. Little did Vera know that the Serpent King was hardly teaching her anything, and she'd only gotten her date because Leo wanted to make his father angry.

"The prince obviously likes you," Vera continued. "You're dressed like a nun and he still can't stop staring."

Tem glanced across the dining room to see that Leo was already there, leaning against the far wall. His eyes were on her thigh, which was exposed by the high slit in the dress. It was the only skin visible, yet somehow he'd managed to find it.

She shook her head. "He's only staring because he hates this dress."

"Whatever." Vera rolled her eyes. "Dresses don't matter tonight anyway."

"What do you mean?"

Vera suddenly had the same look on her face she got whenever she was about to drop a particularly scandalous piece of gossip. She leaned in, her red lips pinched with glee. "The Frisky Sixty is tonight."

Tem's stomach dropped. "How do you know?"

"My snake told me. Didn't yours?"

Tem was too shocked to reply.

The Frisky Sixty was a notorious part of the elimination process. Each girl would have sixty seconds with the prince, behind closed doors, with nobody else present. The villagers had dubbed it the "Frisky Sixty" because sixty seconds really wasn't enough time to do anything other than take your clothes off. And that was exactly what the girls were expected to do. The prince was choosing a wife after all. The Frisky Sixty gave him the opportunity to see what each girl had to offer. It was an antiquated, offensive, and abhorrent tradition. But it was also the simplest means to an end. What better way to guarantee that Leo would make an informed choice than to show him his options ahead of time?

Tem tried to dull the sharp prick of indignation that pierced her side. She couldn't believe Caspen hadn't informed her this was happening tonight. Then again, why would he? He hadn't prepared her for any other part of the competition either. She wanted to give him the benefit of the doubt—she wanted to believe that he hadn't known about this. But Vera's basilisk had known, and he had told her. Surely, the Serpent King would've been informed. Tem wasn't just unprepared; she was beginning to feel like Caspen was sabotaging her.

A gentle *clink clink clink* filled her ears. The butler was tapping a knife on a wineglass. The room hushed as he said, "Please be seated. Dinner is served."

Everyone obeyed, milling around the table and looking for their name tag. Tem had just found hers when Leo's nimble fingers swiped it out from under her.

"What are you—" Tem started to say, but he was already walking to the other side of the table and switching her name tag for the one next to his. He sauntered back to place the other name tag where Tem's had been a moment ago. It was Vera's.

"Trust me, you don't want to do that," Tem said.

"Trust me"—that familiar mischievous smile twisted his lips—"I do."

Tem could only imagine the conversation she would have at the bakery tomorrow. But she couldn't go against the prince.

With a sigh, Tem followed Leo to the other side of the table. He pulled her chair out for her, and she sat reluctantly, already bracing herself for what was to come. She chanced a glance at Vera, who was staring daggers at her.

Tem turned to Leo. "You've just made my life significantly more difficult."

He arched an eyebrow. "How so?"

"Vera will be furious."

Leo smiled widely. "Vera will get over it."

"I assure you, she won't."

He shrugged. "I want you next to me. Is that such a crime?"

Before Tem could answer, the butler served the first course, and dinner began.

The wine was flowing; Tem lost count of how many times her glass was refilled. By the time they were on the second course—a tender roast chicken—Tem was getting drunk. She wasn't the only one. Leo was drinking whiskey like it was water, and with every glass he downed, his movements became increasingly unpredictable, as if someone had loosened his joints. Tem couldn't imagine why he needed the liquid courage. The prince was the only person at this table who didn't have to be vulnerable tonight. All he had to do was watch.

The girls took turns flirting with Leo, alternating between fawning over him and giving each other scathing looks. It was pathetic to watch, and Tem found herself daydreaming. She was just about to replay her orgasm from last night in her mind when she heard it:

Help.

It was the voice again—the same one she'd heard before.

An idea occurred to her suddenly. If she could talk to Caspen, maybe she could talk to the voice. She reached out with her mind, opening another corridor and sending her thoughts along it:

Where are you?

The voice was barely audible. *I am here.*

Tem felt a surge of accomplishment. Now she was getting somewhere. *Tell me more. Are you in the castle?*

No answer.

Tem tried again. *How can I find you?*

Still no answer. The roast chicken was cleared away and replaced with a white layer cake. The butler refilled her wine. Between the conversations around the table and the buzz from the alcohol, it was difficult to concentrate. Tem closed her eyes, forcing herself to focus.

I want to help you. What can I do?

This time, the answer came quickly: *Do not trust the king.*

Tem's eyes flicked to Leo. He was listening to the girl on his right, who was alternating between chatting vigorously and biting her lip in a way she clearly thought was seductive.

Why shouldn't I trust him?

But the corridor had closed; the voice was gone.

It was then that she realized Leo was touching her.

His gaze hadn't wavered—he was still looking at the girl on his right. But his fingers had begun trailing their way along the slit in Tem's dress, skimming up the exposed skin of her thigh.

She slapped his hand away.

It was as if she'd done nothing at all; Leo didn't even blink. But a moment later, his hand returned to her leg, his long fingers gripping her knee with surprising authority.

He turned to her. "Would you do me a favor, Tem?"

His gray eyes were awfully close. For the first time, Tem realized they were flecked with green.

"Depends on the favor."

"Kiss me."

"You're drunk."

"And you're glorious. Kiss me."

"In *front of everyone?*"

He leaned in. "Unless you've changed your stance on baths and champagne."

"I haven't."

"Then kiss me. Right now."

It wasn't a request anymore. It was an order, and Tem had no idea what would happen if she didn't obey. Her eyes flicked to Vera, who was watching their interaction like a hawk. When she looked back at Leo, he gave her a devious smile.

"Unless you'd prefer I kiss someone else," he said quietly.

A pang of jealousy shot through Tem. She couldn't explain it, but she didn't want Leo kissing anyone else. Especially not Vera.

But she also couldn't give in. Not when he was acting like she owed him this.

Tem pushed his hand away again. "I'd *prefer* that this evening didn't run late. I have an early morning on the farm tomorrow."

Leo's eyes narrowed. "I see. Well, I certainly wouldn't want to keep you."

He snapped his fingers, and the butler appeared, leaning over his shoulder. "Is it time, Your Highness?"

"Yes."

"Very well. Who would you like to see first?"

Without breaking eye contact with Tem, Leo pointed at Vera.

The butler nodded. He rang a small bell, and the table fell silent.

"His Highness would like to begin the evening's events." The butler extended his hand to Vera. "Would you kindly follow me, miss?"

Pure triumph blossomed on Vera's face. She shot Tem a withering look before taking the butler's hand and allowing him to guide her to a door at the far end of the dining room.

The butler turned back to Leo. "Your Highness?"

Leo stood, whiskey still in hand. Without a backward glance, he followed Vera into the room. The butler closed the door behind them.

The rest of the girls erupted immediately into giggles and whispers. Tem could only imagine the snide victory Vera must be experiencing now that she was finally alone with Leo. She probably couldn't get her clothes off fast enough.

And what would Leo think of her? Would he like what he saw?

Tem's stomach roiled at the thought.

Sixty seconds passed far slower than Tem ever imagined it would. By the time Vera emerged, it felt as if an hour had gone by. The table hushed as she threw open the door, adjusting the neck of her dress with exaggerated emphasis. Her lipstick was smeared. She threw a pointed smirk at Tem before leaving the dining room.

The butler approached the table and extended his hand to another girl, who blushed deeply before taking it.

And on it went.

It was clear that Leo was the one deciding the order of the girls. It was the podiums all over again. Tem had no doubt she would be last. She was an afterthought—only worthy of seeing the prince after he'd had his fill of everyone else. Tem felt suddenly hyperaware of her body—of every curve and divot, of everything nobody but Caspen had ever seen. Was she really about to expose herself to someone who'd done nothing to earn it?

The minutes passed agonizingly slowly.

Girls emerged from the room in various states of undress. The fifth girl was still half-naked—she stumbled out with her dress off her shoulders, shooting Tem a rueful grin as the butler ushered her away.

The sixth girl went in.

What would happen if Tem refused to undress? If she simply stood there silently and waited for time to run out? Would Leo eliminate her on the spot?

And what would happen if she *did* undress?

Epiphany crashed into her like a wave.

Tem realized she had wasted far too long worrying about her body and not nearly enough time considering the very real implication of what would happen if she got naked in that room. If she was alone with the prince—if she took off her clothes in front of him—Leo would see every part of her. Every. Single. Part.

The claw was still inside her, its smooth point pressed against her clitoris. She had no way to take it out—the butler was standing five feet away. Even if she could remove it, where would she put it? On the table? The thought was impossible.

The sixth girl came out. The seventh girl went in.

Tem had only two minutes left before it was her turn. She closed her eyes, speaking into her mind.

Caspen.

A dull wave of panic threatened to overtake her as she held her breath, momentarily terrified that he wouldn't answer. Then: *Tem.*

She felt sick.

He must have sensed this, because he asked, *What is the matter, Tem?*

There was no other way to say it. *I'm about to spend sixty seconds with the prince. Alone.*

Maybe she was imagining it, but she swore she felt a wave of displeasure from Caspen's end of their connection. When he spoke, his voice was controlled.

Yes. And?

So he'd known the Frisky Sixty was tonight. And he'd chosen not to tell her. She made a mental note to yell at him for that later. For now, she had to make use of her limited time.

And it's customary for the girls to undress.

In the pointed silence that followed, Tem felt a ripple of anger. Caspen had been doing this for centuries—he was familiar with the entire training process and knew perfectly well what traditionally occurred during those sixty seconds. Why was he forcing her to explain it?

Are you going to undress?

Now Tem was floored. Given their history, the question was almost cruel. She narrowed her eyes.

I haven't decided yet. What do you think?

There was no mistaking the anger in his voice. *What I think is irrelevant. Your duty is to impress the prince.*

Don't you dare speak to me about duty.

I beg your pardon?

The door opened. The seventh girl came out. The eighth girl went in.

You have neglected your duty since the very first day we met. Everyone else was informed about tonight but me. Everyone else has had sex but me. You're doing me a disservice, and you know it.

Caspen bristled. *Are you questioning my methods?*

I thought that was obvious.

His anger only grew. *What is obvious is that you are impatient, insubordinate, and childish.*

Tem didn't have time to be hurt by his words. *Anyone would be impatient in my position.*

Is there a reason for this conversation? Or did you only call upon me to argue?

Tem's stomach twisted. He was going to make her say it. *If I undress, the prince will see what you gave me.*

A pause.

I can remove it, if that is what you wish.

Tem frowned. She couldn't read his tone. *If you remove it, would you...give me another?*

The pause was longer this time.

Tem could physically feel the seconds ticking by.

I would give you anything you asked for, Tem.

It was an evasive answer. She was beginning to expect those from Caspen.

There was no time to think it over properly. She had less than a minute before she would be face-to-face with Leo. She had no idea whether she would undress. All she knew was that Caspen hadn't prepared her for this. He had purposefully kept vital information from her. And now she—and she alone—would suffer the consequences of his actions.

Remove it.

Caspen's reply was made of ice. *As you wish.*

Tem winced as he slammed the barrier between them back down. A moment later, a bursting pulse shot through the claw. Rather than growing in strength, this one blazed brightly and then diminished, and by the time it was over, Tem felt achingly empty, as if nothing were ever there in the first place.

The eighth girl came out.

"Good luck," she said when she passed Tem. "He's in a mood."

Tem didn't have time to wonder what that meant. The butler was already beckoning her forward. Tem stood slowly, noticing every beat of her stammering heart. The butler opened the door for her, revealing a darkly carpeted room with books on the walls. A library.

Tem stepped inside. The butler closed the door.

Less than ten minutes had passed since she'd seen Leo, but it was clear he'd had several more whiskeys during that time. He was reclined in an armchair, his hair mussed, his shirt unbuttoned. His trousers were undone; Tem could see the white linen of his undergarments. A smear of red lipstick pulled the corner of his mouth into a gruesome shape, continuing in a blotchy streak down his neck. Vera's handiwork.

Despite herself, Tem felt a rush of heat at the sight of him. She'd never seen the parts of Leo that were exposed right now—the sharp angle of his clavicle, the dip of muscle just below his hip. His cock was hard, straining against the fabric of his trousers. Tem wondered dimly whether he'd had it out a moment ago.

Leo sat up straight when he saw her.

"Tem," he rasped.

She stood in absolute silence.

An elaborate metal hourglass rested on the desk. Its glass body was filled with gold flakes, all of which had settled to the bottom. No doubt it was perfectly measured to last sixty seconds. Leo's long fingers grasped the hourglass but didn't turn it yet. Tem spoke before she lost her nerve.

"If you expect me to take my clothes off—"

"I expect nothing of the sort," he interrupted her.

Tem scoffed.

Leo's mouth twisted in a smile. "Do you not believe me?"

"Why would I?"

Leo's eyes traveled over her body. Even when she was covered from neck to toe, it felt like he was looking straight through her. "What I expect and what I want are two different things, Tem."

"And what exactly do you expect?"

"I expect you to be difficult. Like you always are."

Tem crossed her arms. "And what do you want?"

Leo took a long swallow of whiskey. "Whatever you're willing to give me."

But Tem knew better. She knew the nature of men and the way they coveted. She knew Leo wanted what he couldn't have. How long until he took it?

"And what did *Vera* give you?"

He rubbed the back of his hand over his mouth, smearing the lipstick even more. "Nothing worth having."

"Oh, please."

"Sixty seconds with you is worth an hour with Vera," he said quietly.

Tem shrugged with an indifference she did not feel.

Leo stood unsteadily, grasping the table for balance.

Tem had never seen him drunk like this before, and she hated the sight. She jerked her head at the hourglass. "Are you going to turn that over?"

Leo tapped a single finger on the sculpted metal. "If I turn it over, will you take off that dress?"

Maybe it was her anger at Vera. Maybe it was the way Caspen had cut off their connection without consulting her. Or maybe it was the realization that she couldn't control even the smallest thing in her life right now. Either way, Tem had had enough.

"You can't just have whatever you want," she snapped.

Leo's face slid into a smile as he saw he had finally forced a reaction from her. "Maybe not," he said quietly. "But I can certainly imagine whatever I want." His eyes traveled slowly down her body as he stepped toward her. "Whenever I want it."

By the look on Leo's face, Tem knew exactly what he was imagining. She felt herself blushing and forced herself to suppress it. Why shouldn't he picture what he'd never have?

"Imagine all you want," she said. "I'm not taking off this dress."

The corner of his mouth twitched. "Yet," he whispered.

He was standing so close, Tem could count his eyelashes. He had a tiny scar on the bottom of his chin. She could smell his cologne, which was rich and musky, like cigars smoked outside during summer.

She expected him to try to kiss her, but he didn't. Instead he just stood there, far too close, watching her.

"You know," he said, his voice barely a murmur. "You can imagine whatever you want too."

She should punch him in the face. But Tem was finding it hard to think straight, finding it hard to remember why she was resisting him in the first place. "I don't want anything from you," she said.

Leo smiled, as if he knew it was not quite the truth. "So, *so* difficult."

"You like it."

Leo looked her straight in the eye. "I do. But that doesn't mean I'll tolerate it forever."

"Excuse me?"

"I have to eliminate two girls tonight, Tem. Why shouldn't I eliminate you?"

"Because you'd never see me again."

He shrugged. "Maybe that's not such a bad thing. I'm getting a little tired of my cock being permanently hard whenever you're around."

Tem's mouth fell open.

Leo chuckled softly. "Don't tell me that surprises you."

Tem didn't know what to say.

Leo placed one hand on the door behind her head. He leaned in, whispering his next words right into her ear. "The real question is whether you're wet whenever I'm around."

Tem's heart felt like it was about to leap from her chest.

Leo's lips were just brushing her skin, the sensation impossible to ignore. His teeth nipped her earlobe. "Are you wet, Tem?" he whispered.

Tem was.

She couldn't help it. She knew it was the last thing Leo deserved from her. But his mouth was near her neck. And he smelled good. And the way his body looked under his shirt was making her want things she had absolutely no business wanting. So she said, "You tell me."

At her words, Leo's entire demeanor changed. Where before he'd been pointedly detached, now his eyes narrowed with determined focus. Without a moment's hesitation, Leo slid his hand through the slit of her dress. She hadn't worn any underclothing—the tight fabric hadn't allowed for it. Leo's jaw clenched when he realized this.

"*Fuck*, Tem."

Tem's lungs seemed to contract as his hand dove between her legs to feel exactly how wet she was for him. She gasped as he slipped one, then two, then three fingers inside her. When he went for the fourth, Tem pushed his hand away.

Leo smirked. "That's all I get?"

"We only have sixty seconds."

His smirk deepened. "I never turned the hourglass."

He had a point there.

"Besides," he continued, "I'm in charge. If I want to keep you longer, I will."

"Could you get any more entitled?"

"Yes. I could. I could argue that I'm entitled to your cunt, whether you want to give it to me or not."

Tem raised her chin in defiance. "You're not entitled to any part of me."

Her response seemed to amuse Leo. "Always such a fucking tease, Tem."

Tem grit her teeth. "If I'm such a tease, why bother keeping me around?"

To her surprise, Leo laughed.

"If you think being a tease would turn me off, you don't know me at all."

He always wants what he can't have.

Tem looked up at Leo, who held her gaze calmly. It was unnerving how nothing seemed to faze him, especially considering how many whiskeys he'd had since the start of the evening. Tem felt as if she could say anything at all and he wouldn't even blink. She decided to test that theory.

"What if I never let you fuck me?"

He tilted his head, considering her. "Is that a threat?"

"It's a question. A simple one actually."

He laughed again. "*Actually*, it's not simple at all. The entire point of this process is for me to find a wife I want to fuck. If you're not willing to fuck me, then I don't see the point of keeping you here."

"Don't you?" Tem said. She felt nothing but power in that moment.

"No." Leo glanced lazily over at the hourglass. "I don't."

Now Tem was the one to move closer. She sidled up to him, draping her body against his in the same way she'd seen Vera do to Jonathan—in the same way any woman could do to a man. Despite Leo's best efforts to remain indifferent, she felt his breath hitch when her hips pressed against his cock. He made it so *easy*.

"I don't need to fuck you," she said softly, her lips grazing his throat. "I don't even need to take my clothes off. You want me so badly, you'd marry me just for the chance to see me naked. Am I wrong?"

Tem didn't know where her courage came from. She was risking everything on this—her place in the competition, her mother's reputation, *her* reputation. She was banking on Leo's predictability, assuming that what his sister had carelessly said about him in the bathroom was not only completely true but a surefire indicator of his future behavior. It was the biggest gamble she'd ever taken, and if she was wrong, it would cost her everything.

A vein was twitching in Leo's neck. Tem wanted to lick it.

Instead, she waited. When he finally spoke, his voice was a raw groan.

"You're never wrong, Tem." His eyes were hooded, the greed in them unmistakable. "I hate that about you."

His lips were on hers before her heart could take another beat.

Leo's hands grabbed her waist, nearly lifting her off the floor as his body curled down to intertwine with hers. She could taste every ounce of whiskey he'd consumed—along with something sweet, like honey.

They didn't bother going slow.

His tongue was in her mouth; her chest was pressed against his. Tem matched Leo's energy, giving him exactly what he was giving her, kissing him as hard as she wanted with no regard for consequences. It was liberating to be with him here—completely alone—where no one could see what they were doing. Tem felt irrefutably free, like she was flying over open water. She wondered if Leo felt the same.

When she ran her tongue over his gold teeth, she felt him smile.

"Do you like those?" he murmured against her lips.

"No," she murmured back.

"Liar."

Leo bit her bottom lip, pulling it toward him—not enough to cause her pain, just enough to make her want to bite him back. So she did.

The next thing Tem knew, her spine was slammed against the door. Leo's hands, which until now had been wrapped around her waist, were hiking her dress up to her hips. His cock was hard between her legs, the fabric of his trousers the only barrier between them. Tem imagined for a moment what it would be like to rip that last barrier away. She knew it was exactly what Leo wanted. But she also knew he had just seen Vera—and seven other girls—naked. He'd gotten enough of what he wanted tonight. Tem wasn't about to give him any more.

She gave him a sharp shove backward, breaking them apart.

"I'm still not taking my clothes off for you," she said.

Leo leaned in so his arms formed a cage around her head. "You assume I wouldn't fuck you with your clothes on."

Tem rolled her eyes. "*Don't push it.* You should be happy I let you kiss me."

He raised his hands in mock surrender. "I am." He lowered them slowly, and the smirk faded. "I am very happy."

There was a pause, and Tem wondered if she was happy too.

For a minute, they simply looked at each other. In the silence, Tem allowed herself to truly see Leo. He was breathing hard, just like she was. His hair was a mess of chaotic spikes, and his lipstick-smeared shirt was surely ruined. He looked perfectly, incandescently human. In that moment, despite herself, Tem felt her heart bend in his direction.

"You never turned the hourglass," she whispered.

Leo smiled. "You're right."

He crossed to the table and flipped the hourglass on its head. Tem watched as the sparkling gold flakes began to fall. When Leo returned to her, he kissed her again. It was a proper kiss this time—one that built slowly, warming Tem from the inside out. His tongue traced along hers as his arms pulled her closer with unprecedented tenderness. He held her as if she were something precious to him—something sacred.

In the sanctuary of his embrace, Tem forgot about the evening. She forgot about Vera, about Caspen, about the voice in the castle. There was only this kiss, right now, with Leo. When they finally pulled apart, the hourglass had long since run out.

"So," Tem whispered, her lips still an inch from his. "Will you keep me around?"

Leo smiled, his gold teeth flashing in the dim light. "For as long as you'll let me."

CHAPTER TWELVE

—••◦✳◦••—

TEM WENT STRAIGHT TO BED WITHOUT WASHING UP.
She told herself it was because she was tired, but she knew in her heart it was because she didn't want to wash Leo's scent off. His cologne lingered in her hair, on her dress, on her hands. It reminded her of the way his body had felt when it was pressed against hers—how he'd hiked up her dress and touched her. Tem pictured those long fingers of his, imagining what else they could do. She fell asleep thinking about Leo.

She woke up thinking about Caspen.

It was her first day without the claw, and Tem felt its absence the moment she opened her eyes. She touched her clitoris tentatively, missing the way it used to cradle her.

"Tem, dear?" Her mother knocked on her door. "Are you awake? They expect us at the square."

It was then that Tem remembered what day it was.

Every autumn, the village celebrated the anniversary of their victory in the war with a weeklong festival honoring the royals. It was a time of reverence and gratitude, culminating in an extravagant celebration in the town square. Tem and her mother always provided rooster feathers to symbolize the defeat of the basilisks. This year, the festival was even more important: it was rumored that a special ceremony would occur.

The Passing of the Crown was a long-standing tradition in the royal family. Whenever a prince was about to take a wife, the king would pass him his crown. It wasn't an official transfer of power—that would occur at the wedding. Rather, it was a way for the current king to acknowledge the future king's potential. The gesture represented a father's faith in his son's ability to rule. It was an extremely important event and a way for Maximus to give Leo his blessing.

Tem rolled onto her back, closing her eyes.

Do not trust the king.

She still had no idea where the voice had come from. But she knew it was somewhere in the castle, and Tem vowed that the next time she was there, she would find it.

Tem joined her mother in the chicken coop to gather feathers for the festival. When they arrived at the town square, it was packed with people. Tem immediately found Gabriel and joined him in hanging golden flags from the eaves of the shops surrounding the square.

The day passed in a series of menial tasks.

Tem alternated between thinking about Leo and thinking about Caspen. She wondered if either of them was thinking about her. Her attempts to contact Caspen had been fruitless; the wall between them remained firmly in place, and every time Tem tried to send a thought down the corridor in her mind, it was met with resistance. Eventually, she stopped trying.

"You're awfully quiet," Gabriel prompted. They were hanging flags outside the butcher shop.

"I'm thinking."

"About?"

Tem sighed. "Last night."

She told Gabriel everything that had happened at the castle, leaving out only her conversation with Caspen and the disembodied voice. He asked her to describe her sixty seconds with Leo in excruciating detail, giggling with unrestrained glee at everything that occurred behind the closed door.

"So?" he asked when she'd finished.

"So what?"

"*So* who's a better kisser? The snake or the prince? Come on, Tem. You can tell me."

"I am *not* answering that."

"I'll bet it's the prince," Gabriel continued as if she hadn't said anything. "He seems like he's got something to prove. Guys with something to prove are always better in bed. It's like they're grateful to be there or somethi—"

"If you say one more word, I'm telling Henry what you did with Peter."

Gabriel's eyes widened. "You wouldn't dare."

"I would."

Gabriel placed his hand over his heart in mock hurt. "Sex has changed you, Tem. You're not the woman I used to know."

"I haven't had sex yet."

Gabriel waved his fingers dismissively. "You've had a cock in your mouth, Tem. Some would consider that sex."

"*Henry. And. Peter,*" Tem hissed.

"Fine, *fine.*" Gabriel hung another flag, his lips pursed thoughtfully. "But this discussion isn't over."

Before Tem could protest again, Vera appeared. She shot a disapproving look at Gabriel before turning to Tem. "Did you enjoy the Frisky Sixty, Tem? I know *I* did."

Tem sighed. She was already in a foul mood, and Vera was only making it worse.

"Good for you," she said stiffly.

"The prince enjoyed it too."

"Good for him."

Vera wrinkled her nose, clearly wishing for more of a reaction. "He requested me first, after all. Obviously, he was eager to see me."

"Or eager to get it over with," Tem snapped back.

Gabriel let out a snort.

Vera glared at him. "And when did you take *your* turn, Tem? Rumor has it you went last."

Of course a rumor like that would spread. Vera was probably the one spreading it.

"I may have been last," Tem said through her teeth. "But I also stayed longer than sixty seconds."

Vera's face pinched.

"*What?*" she snapped.

Tem squared her shoulders. "The prince didn't even want to touch the hourglass. I had to remind him to turn it over."

Vera gaped like a fish, her eyes popping out of her heart-shaped face. It was the perfect retort; there was no way to disprove it since Vera had left before Tem went into the library. Even better given that it was actually true.

For once in her life, Vera took the hint and disappeared without another word.

"Feeling petty today, are we?" Gabriel said.

Tem threw him a look.

"What?" He grinned. "I like it when you're petty."

"*Please* shut up."

Gabriel pressed a kiss to her cheek before graciously shutting up.

Hours passed. They hung the rest of the flags. Eventually, Gabriel left to work dinner service at the castle.

Tem needed the alone time anyway.

She spent the afternoon helping the carpenters set up the stage for the Passing of the Crown. Tem wasn't particularly skilled at woodwork, but she was no stranger to manual labor, and she found that losing herself in the hammering helped to soothe her anxiety. By the time she was ready to head home, night was falling. Tem took the trail through the woods, winding slowly among the trees.

Suddenly, she heard a voice behind her:

"Hey!"

Tem turned around.

The voice belonged to Jonathan. He was flanked by another boy who Tem recognized from school. Christopher.

"Your name's Temperance, isn't it?" Jonathan asked, walking right up to her.

"Yes," she said. "But I go by Tem."

"Right. Tem."

Both boys were grinning at her, but they weren't friendly grins. They were predatory and unpredictable, and Tem felt a sudden urge to run.

"We heard you're with the Serpent King. Is that right?"

Tem cursed Vera and her big mouth.

"Yes," she began slowly. "But I—"

"So he's taught you quite a lot then, I'd assume?"

Tem shifted uncomfortably. It was getting dark, and the boys were blocking her path home. She wanted to leave, but she couldn't get around them.

"I'm…still learning," she mumbled.

"Is that right?" Jonathan's grin widened, and so did Christopher's. "We'd like to learn too. Right, Chris? Maybe you could teach us something."

He looked at Christopher, who nodded greedily, his eyes never leaving Tem's.

"I really need to get home," she said, her voice cracking.

"No. You really need to teach us something."

Jonathan stepped closer, and Tem stepped back. She was utterly defenseless. She wished suddenly that she had kept one of the hammers from earlier.

"Please," Tem begged. "I have to get home."

Jonathan grabbed her dress, twisting the fabric in his hand. "But we're not finished," he sneered. "We haven't even started."

Tem tried to yank herself away, but Christopher was suddenly behind her, pulling her arms back as Jonathan ripped the front of her dress open.

"*No,*" Tem cried. "Leave me alone."

"Why?" Jonathan asked. "I'm just helping you out. You should get used to being touched like this." He grabbed her breasts, *hard*, and she yelped in pain. "After all, this is what the prince will do."

Tears filled Tem's eyes as she heard Christopher laughing in her ear. Jonathan was hurting her; his cruel hands were far different from the way Caspen and Leo touched her, and she wished desperately that she were anywhere else but here.

Jonathan stepped back, untying his trousers.

"Why don't you show me what you've learned?" he sneered, dropping them to the ground. Tem stifled a wave of disgust as she realized he was already hard, his cock standing up to reveal his balls. He was less than half the size of Caspen, and for some reason, the thought gave her strength.

Tem knew what to do.

She stood suddenly still, no longer struggling as Jonathan stepped closer, stroking his cock with one hand.

"Come on then," he said with a grin. "Show me."

He was just close enough to make it work.

Without a second's hesitation, Tem flung her leg up as hard as she could, crushing the hard bone of her knee into the soft tissue of Jonathan's balls. He screamed, doubling over and falling to the ground. Christopher's grip on her loosened as he gasped in surprise, and Tem took the opportunity to wrench herself from his hands.

Without thinking, she leaped off the path, heading for the caves. She could think of nowhere else to go. In the other direction was only forest, and she knew she wouldn't make it all the way home before the boys caught her.

"Hey!" she heard Jonathan yell behind her "Come back, you little *slut!*"

But Tem was sprinting hard, her breath coming in short gasps as she flung herself through the door in the wall. The second she passed through it, Jonathan's taunts ceased. Tem didn't slow down, letting her feet carry her up the slope to the base of the mountain. She barreled straight for the farthest cave, scrambling through the entrance and scraping her palms on the rocks. It was completely dark inside—the fireplace wasn't lit, and the air was cold. What if he wasn't here? What if the boys followed her, and now she was cornered? What if—

"Tem?"

Caspen emerged from the shadows. He was wearing a loose linen shirt and trousers, his eyebrows raised in surprise. With a snap of his fingers, the fireplace flared to life.

"What are you doing here?"

"I…" Tem started but didn't know how to finish. Now that she was here, she realized just how foolish of a plan this was. Caspen owed her nothing. Why should he grant her refuge? She had shown up to his home completely unannounced, while they were on less-than-friendly terms. What if it made him angry?

Caspen stepped closer. "You should not be here," he said, confirming her worst fears.

Tem nodded desperately. "I know. I'm sorry. It's just…there were these boys, and they—they—"

But she stopped again, too ashamed to go on. Instead, she took a step back, ready to leave before she made things worse.

"Wait," Caspen said. His gaze fell to her torn dress, which she was holding together with her hands. He frowned. "What did they do?"

There was genuine concern in his voice. At his tone, she swallowed, trying to calm herself down.

"They...touched me."

Caspen went completely still. "The way I do?"

"Yes. Well, no, not really." Tem could feel herself blushing. But she couldn't seem to stop the words. "They were rough. I...didn't like it."

Caspen's eyes flicked back to her ripped dress. He stepped even closer. "What are their names?"

Tem clamped her lips. Something about the way he asked it made her certain she didn't want to answer.

"Tem." His voice was a low, controlled growl. "Answer me."

"Jonathan...and Christopher. They're a year older than me. Jonathan..." Tem dropped her voice in shame. "He was the one who touched me. Christopher only helped him."

Caspen was standing with his fists clenched at his sides.

When he didn't say anything, Tem mumbled, "I shouldn't have disturbed you. I should go—"

"No." Caspen shook his head. "You will stay."

Tentative relief shot through her.

"Take that off." Caspen nodded at her dress, which she was still holding together tightly.

Tem hesitated. She didn't want to be naked right now, especially after what had just happened. She hadn't come here for one of their lessons; she had come here for comfort. Perhaps she had been foolish to expect the basilisk to provide it. Perhaps he expected payment for his protection.

Before Tem could decide how to respond, Caspen pulled off his shirt. He held it out to her, and she took it cautiously.

"Thank you," she whispered.

He nodded, his eyes never leaving hers. He continued to watch as she let her dress drop to the ground. Before she could put on his shirt, Caspen stepped forward.

"You are hurt," he said. Tem followed his gaze to her breasts, where Jonathan's greedy fingers had left several grape-size bruises.

"I'm fine." She shook her head.

Caspen reached for her, and she jerked away sharply, pulling the shirt up to block him.

Caspen dropped his hands, his eyebrows knitting together. "I only mean to heal you, Tem. Nothing more."

"Oh," Tem said. "Sorry."

"You have nothing to be sorry for." He paused. "I will do it later if you prefer."

His voice was soft. Tem wasn't used to that tone from him. Their relationship had only recently become a reciprocal one, and she didn't know what to make of the way he was treating her tonight. But she knew one thing: Caspen would never touch her the way Jonathan had.

"You can do it now," Tem whispered.

She lowered the shirt slowly.

Caspen's eyes lingered on hers before returning to her chest. He stepped closer, cupping her gently, his hands warm against her breasts. The fire dimmed as a coolness spread from his skin to hers. When he was done, Caspen brushed his thumbs over her nipples, caressing them tenderly, as if his touch could undo Jonathan's. Tem closed her eyes, savoring the way it felt.

"You should only know pleasure," Caspen murmured, tracing the curve of her breasts before filling his palms with them. "Never pain."

"Tell that to Jonathan," Tem said without thinking. It was the first thing that popped into her mind, and she immediately regretted it.

Caspen's eyes narrowed. He looked her in the eye, and she saw all the anger in the world there. "I intend to."

Tem had never heard such fury in his voice before. "I…don't want anyone to get hurt," she whispered.

Caspen smiled coldly, dropping his hands. "We cannot always get what we want, Tem."

He turned away, and she was left there, shivering. She pulled his shirt on quickly. It smelled of smoke. When she was covered, Caspen beckoned to her.

"Come."

"Where are we going?" Tem asked.

"To my chambers."

"Oh," Tem said. She'd always figured Caspen spent his nights curled up in the cave, nestled among the stones while wearing his true form.

"Follow me." Caspen nodded at a passageway nearly invisible in the shadows. "And keep your eyes down."

The temperature rose significantly as they left the dim light of the cave. Caspen's shoulders were broad in the dark, and Tem stayed close behind him as they wound through a stone tunnel, passing doorway after doorway. Tem realized suddenly why

Caspen had told her to keep her eyes down. If a basilisk wearing its true form emerged and looked her in the eye, she would die.

There was no light in the tunnel, and Tem found herself tripping over the rough stone floor. At one point, she lost her balance, and Caspen's hand darted around her waist, preventing her from falling.

"Steady, Tem," he said quietly. He kept his arm around her until they reached a door identical to all the others. Caspen pushed it open. "After you," he said.

Tem entered slowly, her eyes struggling to adjust to the darkness. With a snap of his fingers, Caspen lit a torch, and suddenly she could see the room they had entered.

It was massive.

There was an enormous bed against the far wall, covered in deep maroon sheets and silk pillows. The mattress was set directly into the stone, with a small set of steps leading up to it. A full-length gilded mirror was propped in the corner, and Tem stared at her reflection as Caspen snapped his fingers once more, filling a fireplace with flickering light. It was warm here—just like the tunnel. The stone floor was smooth and adorned with rich rugs.

"Is it what you expected?" Caspen asked, his eyes on her.

"I'm...not sure," Tem answered honestly. She hadn't expected anything, really. "It's more...human...than I thought."

"That is because when I dwell here, I wear my human form."

"Where do you dwell when you wear your true form?"

The corner of his mouth twitched. "Elsewhere."

It was clear she wouldn't get a more specific answer from him. She wasn't sure she even wanted one. It was a deeply intimate thing to show someone where you slept. Tem was already grateful to be here, and she didn't want to give him any reason to kick her out.

"Thank you for having me," she said quietly. "I know it's an imposition."

Caspen crossed his arms, the muscles in his bare shoulders rotating under his skin. "You are not an imposition."

It was all he said, yet somehow it put her at ease. Caspen was looking at her calmly, and she knew he wouldn't lie about something like that. She wasn't even sure he *could* lie. Legend said that basilisks burst into flames if they spoke anything other than the truth.

"What is on your mind, Tem?"

She blinked, startled at the question. It was significant that he had asked. They both knew he could easily explore her thoughts himself. But he seemed to be treading carefully in light of what had just happened.

"I was wondering if the stories were true."

"Which stories?"

"The ones about basilisks."

"That depends," Caspen said, tilting his head. "There are many stories about us."

Tem nodded, trying to muster the courage to ask what was on her mind. "Do you really burst into flames when you tell a lie?"

To her surprise, Caspen threw his head back in laughter. Tem had never seen him laugh like that before, and she couldn't believe she had caused it.

"What's so funny?" she asked, suddenly self-conscious.

Caspen smiled. "Your question," he replied. "It is not what I expected. And to answer it, no, I would not burst into flames. But lying is…uncomfortable."

"Uncomfortable?"

"Yes. It requires effort, and our bodies reject it."

Tem nodded. So there was some truth to the legends after all.

Caspen's mouth tilted in an amused smile. "Is there anything else you wish to ask me?"

Tem considered the question. There were plenty of things she'd always wanted to ask him, but now that she had the opportunity to do so, she couldn't remember any of them. There was only one pressing matter she could think of.

"Why do you have a mirror?"

Caspen arched an eyebrow. "To check if I have anything in my teeth."

It took Tem a good long moment to realize he was making a joke. "Oh," she said. "Right."

She had no idea how to react to his humor. Caspen was watching her with such obvious amusement, she couldn't help but blush.

"You are wondering how I can look in a mirror without dying," he said before she could figure out how to recover.

"Well…yes."

"The same way I can look at you now without killing you. My gaze is not lethal when I wear my human form."

Tem frowned. "But that means you can…" She trailed off. She was going to say that if it was true he could look in mirrors when wearing his human form, it meant he could bypass the mirrored wall that surrounded the village.

"What is it that I can do, Tem?" he asked softly.

But there was no point in saying it. If the basilisks were going to invade the village, they would have done so long ago. The fact that they hadn't meant they knew the wall was useless and chose to remain outside it anyway. Tem couldn't imagine why.

So she shook her head. "Never mind."

Caspen watched her thoughtfully, as if he didn't quite believe her. "If you think of anything else, do not hesitate."

Tem never expected to get such an open invitation from him. She nodded, and he nodded too. Then he said, "Would you like a drink?"

She blinked in surprise. "What kind of drink?"

"Anything you wish."

Tem couldn't have named a single drink if she'd tried. The evening had already been so overwhelming, it felt as if her brain had been squeezed through a sieve.

"I'll have whatever you have," she said finally.

He nodded. "I shall return in a moment."

In his absence, Tem sat tentatively on the end of the bed.

She wondered whether anything like this had ever happened to the other girls. Had Vera seen her basilisk's chambers? Or was this a habit specific to Caspen—something the Serpent King did with everyone he taught? Up until now, her interactions with him had been strictly surface level. Even when they were connected with their minds, they didn't discuss anything of true significance. Now they were spending time together in a different way: talking and getting to know each other, as if they were dating.

Tem stifled the thought. They were *not* dating, and the basilisk was *not* her boyfriend. He was a fearsome creature—one who was her mentor and her teacher, training her for a role. He could not possibly care about an ordinary girl like her. Not to mention that their last conversation had consisted of Tem telling him to remove the claw so she could undress in front of Leo. Caspen was probably furious with her.

And yet.

He had healed her. He had taken her into his private chambers, and he had protected her. Those were not the actions of someone who didn't care. He could have sent her away when she showed up with her ripped dress. Instead, he chose to comfort her. Surely that meant something. Tem stared at the fireplace, losing herself in the flames. She knew what she hoped would happen tonight.

But would it?

Sometime later, Caspen returned with a bottle of dark liquid. Tem thought it might be wine, and when he poured her a glass, she knew from the smell that she was right. Caspen sat next to her on the bed before pouring himself a glass too, and they drank together in silence. The wine was sweet and made Tem feel even warmer than she already was. Sitting and drinking with Caspen reminded Tem of the meals they had shared, and another question occurred to her. She remembered he had encouraged her to ask.

So she said, "What do you eat when you wear your true form?"

Caspen was unperturbed by the query, answering easily, "Many different things. Fish if I feel like swimming. Small game if I feel like hunting. It depends on my desires."

She nodded, processing the information. For all their proximity to the basilisks, nobody seemed to know anything specific about them, and Tem found it fascinating to finally learn some of the things she had always wondered about. Now that she had started, she couldn't resist asking more.

"What does it feel like when you transition? Is it like putting on different clothes?"

Caspen smiled, leaning back on the bed and propping himself up to look at her. "It is more like taking *off* clothes. My true form is the most natural version of me. It is the way I am meant to exist, so it takes no effort at all to inhabit it."

"So it's not painful?"

"Not in the least." He shook his head. "It is ecstasy."

"Then why use your human form at all? Why not remain as a basilisk?"

"Because nobody tries to kill me when I am human."

"Oh," Tem said quietly, feeling immediately foolish for asking. She knew all about the war; she shouldn't have brought it up, especially when he was being so hospitable. "I'm sorry."

Caspen extended his hand, placing his palm on her thigh. "You have nothing to be sorry for."

It was the second time he'd said that tonight. His hand was heavy on her leg, and she tried to ignore how close his fingers were to everything she wanted him to touch.

Tem took a huge gulp of wine.

"May I ask *you* something?" Caspen said quietly.

"Of course." Tem nodded, surprised by the request. She couldn't imagine what the basilisk could possibly want to know about her.

His hand tightened on her thigh. "How did you get away from those boys?"

"Oh. Um…" Tem paused, embarrassed at having to recount the story. "Why do you ask?"

Caspen's jaw clenched. "Because I need to picture you getting away," he said, his voice low. "Otherwise, I only picture you getting hurt, and that I cannot bear."

At his words, a chill ran down Tem's spine. Once again, she was on the verge of convincing herself that he cared. Once again, she was indulging in a fantasy that would never come to fruition. But she indulged it anyway, answering his question as steadily as she could.

"I…hit Jonathan with my knee."

To her surprise, Caspen's face split into a sudden grin. "Did you really?"

"Yes," Tem said, thrown off by his reaction. "It was quite effective, actually."

"I do not doubt it," Caspen replied, still smiling.

Tem wasn't sure what to make of his mood. "Is that amusing to you?"

At her tone, Caspen's expression sobered somewhat. "Not inherently. I just know how much a knee can hurt." He tapped his finger gently on her kneecap.

Tem couldn't help but smile. He'd probably been kneed many times during his centuries of training girls for the prince. She was happy she hadn't contributed to that statistic.

They drank in silence again. Tem remembered something Caspen had said, and she knew she had to ask. "What are you going to do to them?"

Caspen's eyes flicked to hers. They both knew who she was referring to. "There is no need for you to know," he said quietly.

"I want to know."

Caspen sighed, finally withdrawing his hand from her leg. He set his wine on the floor before reclining on his back, his gaze pointed up to the ceiling. When he spoke, his voice was a whisper. "I am going to punish them."

"But how?"

He still didn't look at her. Tem set her glass on the floor and reclined too, positioning her body close enough to feel his heat.

"Tell me," she murmured. "Please."

Caspen sighed again. He closed his eyes as if to block out her request. "Tem," he said quietly. "Some things do not concern you."

Tem had nothing to say to that. If he didn't want to tell her, she couldn't force him to do so. Still, she worried what powers he might possess. What could a basilisk do to ordinary boys like Jonathan and Christopher? Caspen could infiltrate minds; he had access to magic she could only imagine. There was no limit to the damage he could cause.

"It was nothing serious," she said quietly. "They were just...playing around."

Caspen's temple tensed. "You are not to be played with."

A memory came back to Tem with striking force—the question she had asked Caspen the first time he'd touched her: *Am I to be played with?*

His answer had been different then.

"They're just boys," she whispered.

"Boys who hurt you. They will answer for that. Now let it be."

Tem pursed her lips. It was clear there was no arguing with him, and she wasn't sure she wanted to anyway. It was true the boys had hurt her, and part of her did want them to answer for it. But she worried Caspen would take it too far—that he would cause irreparable harm. Tem didn't want blood on her hands.

But clearly it was out of her control.

Tem laid her head on the mattress, studying the sharp angles of Caspen's face.

He turned to look at her, his expression softening. "I only wish to protect you," he said quietly.

"This isn't protection."

"Then what is it?"

"Retaliation."

"Would you have me do nothing?"

"I would have you be merciful."

Caspen snorted. "*Mercy* is for fools. I owe nobody my mercy."

"Not even me?"

A pause. They studied each other in the flickering firelight.

"I owe you many things, Tem. But mercy is not one of them."

Many things. What did he owe her?

Her heart slammed in her chest as he raised his fingers to her face, brushing gently along her cheek.

"Am I not allowed to protect you?" he murmured.

"You are," she murmured back. "I just didn't realize you wanted to."

Caspen held her gaze. "Protecting you is only the beginning of what I want to do."

CHAPTER THIRTEEN

—•◦✳◦•—

TEM COULDN'T BEGIN TO UNDERSTAND THE WAY CASPEN WAS LOOKING AT HER. IF she didn't know better, she'd allow herself to hope. But hope was painful, and there was no room for it in her heart. So she sat up.

Caspen sat up too, and for a moment, there was silence. When he spoke, his voice was a whisper.

"Do you know why I gave you a piece of myself?"

He was referring to the claw. Tem had always wondered why he'd done it, what exactly it had meant to him. "No," she said quietly. "Why?"

His fingers returned to her face, cupping her cheek with his palm. "You surprised me."

Tem's heart stopped at his words. It was the ultimate compliment considering how many people he had met in his unusually long life.

"How?"

The corner of his mouth twitched. "You asked me to undress."

"Oh. I can't believe I did that. I figured it would make you angry."

"On the contrary. It made me curious."

"Curious?"

"Yes." He was still holding her face. "It made me want to know you."

"But why?"

"*Because*, Tem." He pulled her closer. "You are worth knowing."

Tem shook her head. It was incomprehensible. There was no other word for it. To think she could offer anything of value to a basilisk was an impossibility. She didn't understand, and she feared she never would.

"We were strangers," she whispered. "How could you think that?"

Caspen traced his thumb under her chin, pulling her gaze up to his. "I find you extraordinary, Tem."

Tem couldn't fathom that.

At her expression, Caspen leaned in. "Is that so difficult to believe?"

Tem scoffed. "You're the extraordinary one."

Caspen tilted his head in the way he did when he was considering something. "What do you find extraordinary about me?"

"Everything," she answered immediately.

"Be specific."

Tem frowned. She had no idea why he would demand this of her. But it wasn't a hard question, and she easily answered, "Your knowledge. Your patience. I have neither."

"My knowledge I have gained over centuries. My patience likewise. Those things do not make me extraordinary, and you should not measure yourself against them."

Tem was surprised at his tone. He almost seemed angry. "I meant to compliment you."

"You complimented me at the expense of yourself."

She shrugged. "I don't know how to do it otherwise."

He shook his head. "*You* are the extraordinary one."

"No. I'm not. I'm utterly ordinary."

Caspen sighed. "That is patently untrue. But I do not expect you to believe me."

"You don't?"

"No," he said, the gold of his eyes flashing in the dim firelight. "You do not see yourself as I do."

He spoke calmly, as if his words were the ultimate truth. Yet Tem could not believe him. Years of cruel taunts ran through her mind—Vera's, the other schoolchildren's. Tem knew what other people thought of her; she knew how she felt in comparison to others. She hoped to one day see herself as Caspen did, but she doubted that day was today.

Still, she asked, "How do you see me?"

His eyes remained on hers for a long moment. "It would be easier to show you."

Before Tem had time to wonder what that meant, Caspen was pulling her to her feet. He positioned her so she was in front of the full-length mirror with him standing behind her. Gently, the motion so slow she barely noticed it was happening, he unlaced the linen shirt and slipped it from her shoulders. It fell to the ground. Then he brushed her hair back so she was completely uncovered.

Despite herself, Tem blushed. She rarely used the mirror at home, and when she did, she never looked at herself naked—certainly not for any prolonged amount of time. Her body had changed, she realized, since the last time she had really seen it. The awkward angles of her childhood were long gone. She had curves now, and rather impressive ones, thanks to the additional meals after her training sessions with Caspen. Her skin was tanned from hours spent outside on the farm, and her hair had lost its tight curls as it lengthened, framing her face with soft, graceful waves.

Caspen's hands were moving again, tracing lightly up her arms to the base of her neck. His fingers covered, then squeezed her throat before brushing over her breasts and continuing down to her waist. When he reached her hips, he wrapped his arms around her, pulling her tightly against his body. His chin rested on her head.

"Look at you," he whispered. "Perfection."

Tem stared at the two of them in the mirror. She supposed it was possible someone might consider her pretty. But it took only one look at Caspen to dispel the notion that *he* could believe anything of the sort. His muscles were perfectly toned; his arms flexed in rigid precision around her waist. His jawline stood out in sharp contrast to the soft lines of her face, and his hair was somehow perfectly styled. Tem felt an insistent jab of jealousy as she looked at him. She would never hold herself the way he did, with such easy elegance—she would never look that *effortless*. She felt herself retreating inward, to the place where she'd learned to hide from the bullies at school. Caspen's voice was suddenly in her mind.

Do not do that.

Do what?

Do not compare yourself to me. I already told you, I am nothing to aspire to.

It was so deeply false that Tem actually snorted. She tried to pull away, but Caspen only held her tighter.

I am not letting you go until you grasp this.

Then we're going to be standing here a long time.

Caspen's annoyance surged, then retreated. In its place came a gentle wave of understanding—a beam of pure empathy that seeped right into Tem's heart and warmed her to the core.

We will try something different.

Tem had no idea what to expect.

A moment later, a curious sensation overtook her. It felt as if Caspen were *pulling* her—drawing her consciousness away from her body and down the shared corridor between their minds. For a moment, everything went completely black. When light returned, Tem was still looking at herself in the mirror. But instead of looking straight ahead, she was looking down, and she realized with a jolt that this was *Caspen's* perspective. She was inside his eyes—inside his *mind*—and she was seeing herself literally from his viewpoint.

Tem started to panic. What if she couldn't return to her mind? What if she—

Relax, little viper.

Caspen's voice was so loud, Tem saw her reflection jump in the mirror. It came from all directions, as if she were standing in the middle of a tiny room and a hundred people were yelling his words at her. Tem tried to say something back but found that she couldn't. Her panic only increased and, with it, his amusement.

Untamable, as always.

As soon as he said it, Tem felt her panic disappear. She was calm because *he* was calm.

Now pay attention.

His focus and hers returned to the mirror.

It was like looking at herself through a kaleidoscope—the childish toys she had played with at the market after church—except instead of seeing a rainbow of fractured colors, she saw herself through all five senses. Suddenly she could smell her own scent—at least how she smelled to Caspen—which was warm and rich and something else she immediately recognized but couldn't name.

The sea, Caspen supplied softly. *You always smell like the sea.*

Tem had never been to the sea. But her mother kept a bottle of salt spray on her dresser, and ever since Tem could remember, she had stolen spritzes from it for herself, spraying it in her hair to texturize her curls and rubbing it on her wrists so she could smell it throughout the day. She'd always been drawn to that clear glass bottle, always loved the cool, salty spray that made her dream of places far away from her life on the chicken farm.

Tem's eyes—*Caspen's* eyes—traveled over her body once again. The sensation was completely unnerving, and if Caspen weren't holding her up, she was sure she would've fainted. But every time she came close to panicking again, Caspen calmed her down, soothing her with his mind as he showed her how it felt to look at her.

His gaze wasn't sexual exactly, although it was impossible to remove sex from a basilisk's mind entirely. It was more intimate than anything, and Tem watched in fascination as Caspen's eyes explored the curve of her hips, the dip of her collarbones, the soft crease where her thighs pressed together. She felt his craving for her—the ache of want that lurked just beneath the surface of his thoughts—and the herculean effort it took him to suppress it.

There was such unrestrained certainty in his desire—such unparalleled *ownership*—that Tem finally understood what Caspen had said earlier. Protecting her was his most basic instinct. It was at the forefront of his mind, even greater than his lust, which was stronger than anything she had ever felt. Caspen wanted—*needed*—her. There was nothing he wouldn't do for her, nothing he wouldn't sacrifice—including himself—if it would guarantee her safety. Tem couldn't believe Caspen was willing to be this vulnerable. It was like seeing straight into his heart. Everything he had said was true.

He found her extraordinary.

Again and again, his gaze fell to her neck, where her pulse was visibly beating. She made a mental note that he liked that area.

That should not come as a surprise.

She had forgotten he could hear her thoughts. At this proximity, he could probably control them.

Nobody could control you, Tem. But even if I could, I would not.

She watched as Caspen traced his fingers slowly across her waist. The sensation was completely foreign to Tem. She could feel every one of her own heartbeats pounding insistently beneath his fingertips, speeding up as he trailed his hand down her stomach. The temperature of her skin increased the lower his hand went, and when he slipped his fingers inside her, she gasped but not because she felt anything between her legs.

Instead, she felt what *he* felt, which was a tidal wave of hunger so deeply animalistic and desperate that she had no idea how he didn't unleash it immediately. He wanted her *so* badly—more, if it was even physically possible, than she wanted him. He wanted to taste her, he wanted to fuck her, he wanted to bury himself inside her. He wanted to hear the sounds she made when she came, and he wanted to hear them over and over and over again. He wanted to be the only one who understood her body, the only one who knew what turned her on, the only one to pleasure her.

Caspen wanted her on a primal level—one that went far beyond the limitations of his true form or her courtship with the prince. He wanted her in a way that was possessive, irreversible, and guaranteed to result in consequences if he didn't have her. He wanted her more than life itself because a life without her wasn't one he cared to live.

Finally, Tem understood the effect she had on Caspen—how irresistible she was to him. how far beyond the physical their connection truly went. She saw how they had been balancing on a treacherously thin knife's edge ever since the night they met, and Caspen was finally done fighting the inevitable. She was his sun. He revolved around her.

"Now do you believe me?" he whispered in her ear.

Tem was back in her own mind, standing in front of the mirror.

For once, the answer was yes. But rather than say it, Tem did what she knew Caspen wanted most; she turned around and pressed her lips to his.

They fell onto his bed together, their bodies intertwining on the silk sheets.

He had kissed her many times already, but this time was different. This time, Caspen gave Tem no commands. This time, they were equals, both deserving of pleasure from the other. He was no longer her teacher; she was no longer his student. They were just two lovers, experiencing each other the way lovers should.

Tem had seen inside Caspen's mind, so she knew everything he wanted to do with her. And yet he followed her lead, kissing her with tender devotion, only deepening the kiss when she pulled him closer, only slipping his fingers inside her when she spread her legs. His restraint only turned Tem on more. He was letting her take the lead, ceding his power—something he'd never done before.

He caressed her gently, his touch like a ripple in a still lake. Tem touched him too, pulling off his trousers and wrapping her fingers around his cock. Caspen let out a shudder as she did so, and at his reaction, Tem felt a sudden surge of confidence. She placed her palm flat on his chest, pushing him away from her.

Momentary concern flashed across Caspen's face. Tem smiled softly to reassure him. Then she tilted her knees, allowing her legs to fall all the way open.

She was ready now.

"*Tem*," Caspen breathed.

It was all he said, yet it was more than enough. For a moment, he did nothing but stare reverently at the center of her. Blackness overtook his eyes, driving away any trace of gold. The air around them grew even warmer as he bent forward, trailing his lips along the curve of her stomach. His fingers wrapped around her thighs, pulling them open even more. Caspen kissed the inner hollows of her legs—one and then the other.

He paused to look up at her, silently asking permission one last time. Tem nodded.

Then he lowered his head, and his mouth met the part of her she'd only ever dreamed a man would taste.

The second Caspen's tongue touched her, a swell of hunger passed through his mind and into Tem's, blurring the lines between them until she didn't know where his desire ended and hers began. Tem moaned as he swirled his tongue slowly around her clitoris, easing his entire mouth against her. They had barely begun, yet she already felt like she was seconds away from losing control. Despite herself, she was suddenly self-conscious.

Tem. Caspen said in her mind. *Let me do this for you.*

Tem closed her eyes.

He was so, *so* good at this. Tem shouldn't have been surprised; he'd had centuries of experience after all. But she wondered if his presence in her mind made him even better. It seemed like he was catering to her every thought. When she wished he would go deeper, he did. When she wished he would touch her a certain way, he did.

First his tongue was on her clitoris, then it was inside her, dipping into her wetness, tasting the heaven he'd wanted to taste for so long. There was no mistaking how much he liked it. She felt his adoration in every stroke, heard his devotion in the way his moans joined hers. He slid a finger inside her, and the temporary change in sensation made her weak. Tem knew he was widening her—coaxing her apart like the petals of a flower—preparing her for what was to come later.

She gasped as Caspen slipped another finger inside her, holding her open to give his tongue even greater access. It was exhilarating to have his head between her legs—to see him bow to her as if he were in prayer. Tem had no idea how she'd survived without such pleasure for so long, and if she never felt it again, she wouldn't survive that either.

His tongue was unstoppable, his fingers pushing deeper and deeper. It felt better than she'd ever imagined, and she'd imagined it a hundred times. Caspen was losing himself in her, gaining as much as he was giving, devouring her as if he had been starving until this moment.

He began pumping his fingers in a steady rhythm, sucking on her clitoris at the same time. The combination of sensations was so overwhelming Tem covered her mouth with her hand, afraid of the noises she might make.

Suddenly, he stopped.

Her eyes flew open as Caspen sat up. He leaned forward, pulling her hand away from her mouth.

Do not hide from me.

Tem understood that there was nothing she could do that would push him away. He only wanted *more* from her—more from her body, more from her mind, more from her heart.

Instead of leaning down again, Caspen placed his entire palm between her legs, splaying his fingers flat on her stomach and working the heel of his hand back and forth over her wetness. The strict, repetitive motion was nearly more than Tem could bear. Her clitoris was throbbing beneath his relentless touch, and suddenly she couldn't have stayed quiet if she'd tried.

Caspen watched her as he touched her, his eyes drinking in every inch of her body. Her hands went to her breasts, squeezing and cupping them in a mirror of their first interaction. Only now it was Caspen's hand between her legs instead of her own; now they were doing what they were always meant to do—becoming what they were always meant to become.

Demand flared in Caspen's eyes. He could only go so long without tasting her.

His head dipped again, and this time, Tem threaded her fingers into his hair, pulling him as close as she could. She let out a desperate whine; it still wasn't enough.

Caspen stilled his tongue.

Use me, Tem.

Tem understood his command. She tightened her grip, arching her hips to meet his mouth, grinding up against him again and again. He gripped her right back, making it easy for her to take exactly what she needed from him. Tem moaned shamelessly.

There was simply nothing in the universe that felt better than this. She knew what was building within her; she knew she was about to fall apart for him.

Just when her climax was imminent, Caspen pulled away.

Tem drew in a sharp breath. She was *so* close. But Caspen had always been this way; he never let her have it easily.

Her clitoris was swollen and tender. She let out a helpless whimper as Caspen trailed a single finger over it, the motion setting her entire body on fire. His voice surged into her mind.

Mine. Only mine.

Tem nodded eagerly. *Yours. Only yours.*

His hiss of approval reverberated around the room.

Caspen lowered his head again, and this time, he stayed there. Between his fingers and his tongue, Tem couldn't control herself anymore. Her moans became desperate as her back arched away from the sheets.

Caspen, she cried into her mind.

I need it, Tem, he said back. *Give it to me.*

All her walls were down, all her defenses destroyed. There was nothing Tem wanted more than to give Caspen what he wanted and get what she wanted in return.

So she let it build.

The insistent wave of pleasure grew, and Tem knew neither of them would stop it this time. Anticipation pricked up her spine; her body was tensing—coiling—preparing for release. She grasped the sheets as Caspen angled his fingers up, pulling a moan from her throat as he pressed against the very core of her. When he clamped her clitoris tightly between his teeth, she was done for.

Tem cried out as her body finally let go.

If it weren't for their connection in her mind, she might not have known Caspen was coming too. But she felt his pleasure lace undeniably into hers, taking her further than she could have ever gone alone. As they rode their waves together, Tem felt something seal itself between them—a bond that could never be broken. They belonged to each other now; there was no going back to the way things had been before they'd shared this essential, fundamental thing.

Tem was completely wet from her climax, but it was clear Caspen had no intention of stopping. He was licking away her wetness—*swallowing it*—savoring it like it was the best thing he had ever tasted. There could be no mistaking his enjoyment. Even if they hadn't been connected through their minds, she would have heard it in his groans—groans that only became more urgent the more he tasted her.

The air was getting undeniably warmer.

Tem knew they were in uncharted territory. It was impossible not to acknowledge the danger she was in—the danger they were *both* in. If Caspen lost control like he did last time, there was no guarantee he wouldn't hurt her. They were all alone in his chambers; if anything happened, she was completely unprotected. Tem knew they were taking a risk. But she also knew how precious she was to him.

Caspen's tongue was suddenly rough and coarse against her clitoris. Tem gasped at the sudden change in texture, her body jerking backward in surprise. Caspen only held her tighter, his hands clamping her hips in place, holding her down so he could lick her even deeper.

The dynamic between them was shifting.

His sole purpose was no longer only to pleasure her. Now Caspen was taking as much as he was giving—consuming her wetness like he needed it to survive. A deafening hiss filled the cave as he pushed his tongue even farther inside her. It went impossibly far—she ached as if she were being stretched. Tem moaned as he teased her clitoris and penetrated her center *at the same time*. Realization hit her like a bolt of lightning.

His tongue had split.

Tem recognized the extraordinary self-control Caspen must have been exhibiting in order to transition only this single part of him. Smoke rose from his shoulders, filling the air and skimming up Tem's body in soft, shadowy streams. Tendrils curved around the sides of her breasts before flowing up her arms and pinning her wrists to the mattress.

It didn't matter that he was a predator and she was his prey. Whatever happened next was inevitable. There was no stopping him, and she didn't want to anyway. Caspen had a need that begged to be fulfilled. A hunger only Tem could sate.

Her legs were open wide; every part of her was exposed. He feasted on her with reckless abandon, his head dipping over and over as he ravished her with his tongue. Tem was helpless, her hands pinned above her head by the warm tendrils of smoke. It didn't matter; she didn't want to move anyway. There was nothing she wouldn't let him do, no part of herself she wouldn't give to him if he wanted it. His hunger awoke a twin flame in her—one that yearned to be fed.

Tem could do nothing but surrender—to Caspen, to herself, to *pleasure*.

His tongue was on her clitoris. And inside her. And when his fingers penetrated her too, she nearly came right then and there. It was too much; she was going to explode.

"*Caspen!*" she cried.

He only buried himself deeper. She was thrashing against the smoky constraints, her hips bucking as he stimulated something in her she hadn't known she was capable of feeling. Everything culminated in a pinnacle, the splayed edges of her body colliding in a single perfect point. Tem's core contracted.

With a rush of euphoric release, she came.

Caspen's hiss of approval was deafening. There could be no doubt she was giving him exactly what he needed—that her orgasm was feeding the part of him that craved her.

Tem felt suddenly weak, as if she had just sprinted a long distance. Caspen licked her softly, and she knew he had returned his tongue once more to its human form. He pressed kisses down her inner leg, keeping his fingers inside her as he bit her thigh, pinching her skin between his teeth, surely leaving a bruise, giving her an undeniable reminder of their union.

Tem couldn't wait to look at that bruise tomorrow.

Finally, Caspen raised his head. They looked at each other in silent awe, as if neither of them could believe what had just happened. As if what they had shared was beyond comprehension.

He propped himself up and leaned in for a kiss. His tongue slid against hers, and she tasted herself on it.

See?

The rest of his question went unsaid, but Tem knew what he was asking. There was only one answer:

Yes.

He pulled away slowly.

Caspen laid his cock between her legs, his head nearly touching her belly button.

He placed his hand over the base of his shaft, pressing it against her wetness and sliding his cock slowly through the channel of his palm, mimicking the motion she knew he wanted to do inside her.

"Tem." His eyes raked up her body. "I need you. Now."

She raised her gaze to his.

"So have me."

CHAPTER FOURTEEN

⸺•◦✳◦•⸺

CASPEN WASTED NO TIME.

His hands grasped her hips, angling her body toward his.

The second his cock touched her, Tem's mind went blank. She could no longer think. All she could do was *feel*. She felt the heat of the air and the sweat on her skin. She felt Caspen's unrelenting gaze as he began to enter her, sliding only an inch of himself inside before sliding right back out. Even that was too much for Tem—she could barely take what he was giving her. He slid in again, going an inch farther this time.

Tem watched the point of their connection in utter awe. She couldn't believe how good they looked together—like her body was his sanctuary and he was finally coming home.

They both wanted this. They both needed this.

Caspen's breathing was ragged. He was concentrating hard; Tem saw once more the staggering strength it took for him to hold back. She knew he wanted nothing more than to ram himself inside her. But she also knew she couldn't handle that, and Caspen surely knew it too. It was his duty to take care of Tem—to set the pace and keep her safe. She trusted him to take that duty seriously.

They were halfway there.

"Kiss me," Tem whispered, desperate for more of him.

Caspen kissed her.

Tem spread her legs as much as she could, straining to take him—doing everything in her power to let him all the way in, to feel him as deeply as he wished to feel her.

At last, it was time.

Their minds were so entwined that Tem didn't know whether it was her voice or his that spoke just a single word as he sank all the way inside her.

Finally.

It was the completion of a circle that had begun the night she'd first dreamed of him. They were always meant to end up here. All roads led to this.

Slowly, with the utmost care, Caspen pulled out.

Then he pushed back in.

Tem gasped as he established a rhythm, teaching her this one final act, legitimizing their bond with each steady thrust. She received him willingly, drinking in every inch of him. She stared up into his eyes—eyes that were blacker than the bottom of the sea. Those eyes had seen centuries of life.

Now they were seeing her.

"Do I feel good?" Tem whispered.

It was the only thing she'd wanted to know since the moment she met him. From the way he gripped her, she knew his answer. But instead of saying it out loud, Caspen sent an overwhelming surge of affirmation into Tem's mind. He was penetrating her in more ways than one, his consciousness curled around hers like vines on a tree.

Tem. Tem. Tem.

Just her name. Over and over.

He said it as if he could never say it enough—as if he were grounding himself in this moment, right here, with her. Tem had never been adored like this before. Caspen's joy vibrated from his body to hers in an endless current. She couldn't believe she was the source of such rapture. He wanted nothing and no one but her.

All the times he'd been teaching her how to seduce the prince, he'd also been learning how to seduce her. He knew everything about her body; he knew how and where she liked to be touched and how long to do it for.

And she knew the same.

Weeks of lessons had made Tem fluent in the language Caspen taught her to speak. She knew if she arched her neck, his nostrils would flair as he inhaled her scent. She knew if she squeezed his throat, he'd squeeze hers in return.

Caspen. Caspen. Caspen.

She chanted his name back, showing him his joy was reciprocated—showing him they were unbreakable. Caspen kissed her as he fucked her, his tongue moving as if it were made to dance with hers. He had been holding out on her, she realized. He was so good at sex. Impossibly good. Centuries of training had turned him into some kind of intuitive *beast*—a beast that knew exactly how to fuck her.

He guided her into different positions, showing her all the ways they could be with each other. First, he sat back on his knees, lifting her hips so he could watch her take his cock. Then, he returned to her, pulling her legs over his shoulders so they were interlocked like puzzle pieces. It was intimate beyond belief; they were so close that Tem could see her reflection in his pupils. She moaned as he slid in and out of her, his cock unbelievably hard, his pace as steady as the tides.

Tem lost all track of time. There were no windows in Caspen's chambers, and it was impossible to tell whether hours or minutes were passing. Just when she thought she couldn't go on, Caspen sent her an insistent wave of his own desire, which was ten times the caliber of her own. She couldn't believe she was having this effect on him. She'd always known it was difficult for him to resist her, but now that she was in his mind, she saw exactly what it was like for him to be with her in this way.

Every sound she made sent him into a furor. He sought pleasure from *her* pleasure. He had waited so long for this, and now she was finally here, wrapped around his cock, his for the taking. He never wanted to let her go.

Eventually, Caspen slid his hands up her thighs, turning her onto her side. He was behind her now, nudging her legs open with his knee in order to give his fingers access to her clitoris. Tem gasped as he touched her and fucked her at the same time. It was everything she'd dreamed of and more. It was heaven, plain and simple.

They stayed that way for a long time—longer than Tem thought was possible. No doubt Caspen could tell how much she liked it. Her wetness was on his cock, on his fingers, on the sheets. She wasn't embarrassed; she knew it was exactly what he wanted. Every few minutes, he raised his fingers to his mouth to taste her before touching her again.

Just when she felt her orgasm begin to build, Caspen turned her around. They faced each other on the mattress, and for a moment, he merely stared at her. He didn't say a word—either out loud or in her mind. But Tem saw everything he was feeling as clearly as if he had told her himself. She saw how much this entire evening had meant to Caspen—how much pleasure it brought him to see her like this: vulnerable, naked, spread out in front of him. She was all his.

Caspen reached for her.

This time, it was quicker than before. Tem could barely breathe, but it didn't matter. She knew what was coming; she knew they were almost there.

Caspen's skin was scalding. The smoke had returned, threading into Tem's hair and skimming hotly up her back. She was wet with sweat, but it didn't matter; so was he.

There was only one thing left to ask.

Together?

Caspen's response was the perfect mirror of hers.

Together.

The threads of their consciousness joined into a single stream, rushing toward their inevitable conclusion. They had finished together before, but not like this—not while he was *inside* her. If Tem hadn't had those previous experiences with Caspen, she might've been scared of what was about to happen, of exposing herself in such a way in front of him. Instead, she felt only an overwhelming wave of bliss as he took what he needed from her and she took what she needed from him. It was a basic truth: she was made for Caspen, and Caspen was made for her.

Tem.

Even in orgasm, her name was his beacon.

Caspen.

Finally, they came.

He held her face to his, their mouths consuming each other's moans. It felt as if Tem were unleashing a lifetime of trying to fit into a box that was too small for her—two decades worth of trying and failing to find her place in a world that didn't care who she was and didn't expect her to be anything more. Her place was here. With Caspen.

Extraordinary.

Tem barely heard him. She felt only the most intense and searing pleasure she'd ever felt in her life as she fell apart, just for him.

In the aftermath, Tem knew peace.

One look at Caspen told her he knew the same. His face was relaxed, his expression the most carefree she had ever seen it. He was looking only at her; nothing else drew his focus. She was the most important thing in the world to him. As he was to her.

Tem ran her fingers through his hair. She'd always wanted to do that.

Caspen took her hand in his, turning it over and kissing the freckles on her palms before trailing his lips up her wrist. He kissed her inner elbow, her shoulder, her collarbone. He dipped his head to her breasts.

"Caspen," she whispered, pulling his face back up to hers.

"Tem."

"Do you do this with all the girls?"

To her surprise, he laughed. "No." He kissed her. "I do not."

She'd only half meant the question. But she was still glad to hear his answer.

Caspen looked her in the eye, becoming suddenly still. "Was it everything you hoped for?"

Now it was Tem's turn to laugh. She couldn't believe he was asking her that. "Yes," she said. "And more."

He nodded. "Next time you will come twice."

"Next time?"

"I plan on doing this many times with you, Tem. If you will allow it."

She laughed again. "I'll allow it."

He kissed her.

Tem felt his cock press against her. He was already on his way to being hard.

"*Seriously?*" she said.

The corner of Caspen's mouth twitched. "Such is the basilisk way."

They fucked again and again.

There wasn't a single moment Caspen wasn't inside her. Her body was a drug, and he was an addict getting his fix. Tem was no better—she couldn't get enough of him. They fucked so many times Tem became unbearably sore; she wasn't used to this much sex, and her entire body began to bear the consequences of Caspen's touch. Her back ached from arching it; her throat was raw from crying out; her lips became bruised from his bite. Despite her pain, she only wanted him more, and she had him again and again, even after it felt impossible to go on.

Finally, Tem was spent. Every thrust was agony; her entire body ached. She could no longer pretend she wasn't in pain, and she was afraid if they kept going, she might start to bleed.

"We should stop," Caspen whispered. His lips were against her ear, his cock still inside her. "I am hurting you."

Tem couldn't deny it. He was in her mind, and she knew he could feel her body's protests. He pulled out of her slowly, removing his length one inch at a time.

"Aren't you tired?" she asked when she was empty.

He chuckled. "No. Not in the least."

She pulled him back toward her. "Then I can try—"

"Tem." He clasped his hand around her wrist. "No."

"I don't want to disappoint you."

Caspen laughed again, pressing a kiss to her neck. "You could never."

"Don't lie."

He shook his head, his lips brushing along her jaw. "I cannot. Remember?"

She did remember, but she didn't believe it. Her insecurities ran far too deep for mere legend to soothe them. She knew he wanted more, and she hated her body for withholding it. Tem reached for him again, intending to pleasure him with her hand. He pushed her wrist down onto the mattress.

"*Tem*," he said sharply. "Stop."

Tem was on the verge of tears. "Just take the pain away," she insisted. "Then we can go on."

Caspen shook his head. "That cannot become a habit. It would be wrong to use you that way."

"Then how am I supposed to satisfy you?"

He smiled. "You have already satisfied me several times tonight, Tem. Surely, you noticed."

She knew he was purposefully keeping things light. But Tem wouldn't be persuaded. "I'm not enough for you," she whispered.

At her words, Caspen sighed. There was silence, and in it, they looked at each other, breathing in sync. "You are human, Tem," he said finally. "I do not expect anything beyond what a human can achieve."

"And if I wasn't human?"

Caspen frowned. "What do you mean?"

"Would a basilisk be able to match your stamina?"

He tilted his head. The motion was so distinctly reptilian that Tem only felt more justified in her question.

"It would depend on the basilisk," he said slowly. "We are not all identical. But yes. Sex in my true form is…"

He didn't finish his sentence. Tem found she didn't want him to. She didn't need to know all the ways she was inferior. She didn't need to hear confirmation that a female basilisk would be a far better match for him than she ever would. She already knew it.

At the look on her face, Caspen leaned in. "I chose *you* to be in my bed, Tem. Do you think I make my choices lightly?"

Tem knew he didn't. But she also knew he had chosen others in the past, and he'd all but confirmed he'd enjoyed them better.

"I think even you can make mistakes," she whispered.

Caspen sighed. "If my words do not comfort you, what will?"

Tem had no answer. She couldn't fathom that Caspen was satisfied with her, regardless of what he said. So instead of saying anything, she kissed him. Soon Tem felt the familiar stirrings within her that wanted more. She pulled Caspen's hand between her legs.

"Tem," he murmured against her lips. "I cannot keep saying no to you."

"Then don't," she murmured back, guiding him deeper. "Say yes."

"Tem," Caspen said again. But he didn't stop touching her.

He explored her gently, sliding his first two fingers in and out with slow, soft strokes. When he brushed over her clitoris, it was so tender that she winced. His fingers retreated immediately.

She tried to pull him back, but he placed his palm on her chest, right between her breasts. He pressed down, and Tem felt a coolness pulse through her. When he removed his palm, she was no longer warm. The heat between her legs remained, but she felt suddenly indifferent, as if she no longer wanted to have sex. The sudden change left her breathless.

"What did you just do?" she gasped.

"I took away your desire so you will not crave me anymore."

Tem stared up at him in horror. It was true; the fiery thirst that had consumed her a second ago was gone.

"Put it back," she said immediately.

"Tem," Caspen sighed in exasperation. "If I put it back, you will just keep wanting to—"

"I *said*, put it *back*."

He frowned. She had never used that tone with him before, and it was a surprise to them both. "I do not understand," he said slowly. "You told me to take away your pain—"

"That's different." Tem cut him off sharply. "Pain is a physical sensation. Desire is an emotion. Emotions are a part of who I am. You can't manipulate my feelings. It's an abuse of your power and a betrayal to me. It's worse than what Jonathan did." She grabbed his hand, holding it to her chest. "So put it back. Right now."

Tem saw many thoughts swirling behind Caspen's eyes. But finally she watched as comprehension, then regret rose slowly to the surface.

"I did not think of it that way," he said quietly. He pressed gently against her chest.

Tem felt the pulse again, and with it, her desire returned, as hot and desperate as before. But this time, she didn't act on it. Instead, she threw Caspen's hand off her and glared at him, waiting for him to speak.

Finally, he did. "Forgive me, Tem. I only meant to help."

"I know what you meant to do," she snapped. "And in doing so, you diminished me. You can't suppress my feelings when they're an inconvenience to you. I'll never trust you if you control me like that again."

He listened to her in silence.

"Promise me," Tem said, still looking him straight in the eye.

"I promise."

"Be specific." Now she was the one making demands.

Caspen took a deep breath, his chest rising steadily. "I promise never to alter your feelings again. You have my word."

They stared at each other.

"I'm so angry at you," Tem said finally.

To her surprise, the corner of Caspen's mouth twitched. "Yes. I can tell."

"It's not funny."

"Of course not." He arranged his expression into one of purposeful seriousness. "It is just that I have never seen you this angry before. You set your jaw." He touched her chin gently. "It makes you look strong."

"I'm strong whether I look it or not."

Caspen's finger traced down her neck. He smiled once again. "That I know."

They lay in silence for a long time, the only sound the soft crackling of the fire. Tem thought about what had just happened. Could Caspen control anyone's emotions or just hers? If his power was truly so limitless, it meant that the basilisks were even stronger than anyone knew. And considering they could bypass the mirrored wall, there was no telling what they could do.

But these were worries for another day.

For now, Tem was here, in Caspen's chambers. And she didn't want to waste time thinking about anything other than that.

Eventually, they found their way to each other again.

Tem traced his skin with her fingers, exploring the peaks and valleys of his torso. His body was so unfathomably *hard*. She could almost picture the scales right beneath the surface of his skin and wondered if she'd ever see them again.

When she touched his cock, he let out a soft hiss.

Tem ran a single finger gently down his shaft, starting at the base and following a vein all the way to the end. He was completely hard by the time she got to the head.

She shifted closer to him, pulling only the tip of his cock inside her. "Do you want me?" she whispered.

"Do not ask me that."

"Why not?"

"Because what I want and what you need are two very different things."

"I just need you."

"Tem." He shook his head. But he didn't push her away.

Instead, Caspen rolled onto his back, pulling her on top of him. Tem understood she was meant to take the lead—that he wanted her to do only what she could bear, since if he had his way, he would only fuck her harder. She rolled her hips slowly back and forth, straddling him with her palms splayed flat on his torso, sliding herself up and down his cock at a pace she could handle. She liked teasing him this way; it was satisfying to withhold something from Caspen, especially when she knew how badly he wanted her.

Tem rocked herself along his cock, tilting her body forward so that her clitoris was stimulated against the base of his shaft. She watched Caspen as he watched her, knowing how much he liked seeing her come. His eyes flicked greedily from her face to her neck to her breasts. His jaw was tense with restraint.

Her orgasm built quickly; she yelped as it slammed into her, leaning down to kiss him as she came.

When she did so, Caspen's hands slid suddenly down her body, grabbing her hips and yanking them against him so he could thrust into her from below. She tried to sit up, but he bit her lip, holding her to him as he thrust even faster. It was almost more than Tem could handle, but she shut her eyes and let him do it, feeling the raw desperation of his rigid body beneath hers, his teeth nearly tearing through her lip as he finished with a single violent thrust.

When his head fell back on the mattress, his eyes were wild—dark and bottomless, as if she were looking into the depths of a never-ending well. There was *so* much desire there, so much naked hunger and unrestrained strength, the depths of which were so unfathomable, Tem felt momentarily afraid. She remembered without a shadow of a doubt that although he wore his human form, he was a monster. She saw the darkness fade, his chest rising and falling as he steadied his breathing, slowly returning to himself.

What had she gotten herself into?

Tem touched her finger to her lip, and it came away bloody. At the sight, Caspen sat up.

"Tem," he said, rough traces of hunger still clinging to his voice like tar. "Forgive me."

It was the second time he'd said that tonight. Tem didn't know how to answer. Of course she forgave him. Part of her liked that she was so irresistible to him that he couldn't stop. But he had hurt her—there was no denying it.

Part of her liked that too.

"I'm fine," she said. The same thing she said after Jonathan.

Caspen raised his hand tentatively to her lips. When he touched them, the firelight dimmed, and she knew he had healed her. But the memory of his bite would likely never fade, and they both knew it.

"I...lost myself," Caspen said quietly. "It will never happen again."

Tem met his eye. "Yes, it will."

She didn't know how, but she knew it to be true. She was a human and he was a basilisk, and they were tempting fate every time they were together. It would happen again, and she would let it. There were no greater truths in the world.

"I am...not used to this yet," Caspen said, clearly choosing his words carefully.

"This?"

"You."

Tem nodded. She understood this was hard for him. There was nothing more painful than trying to suppress your true feelings. For a basilisk, those feelings were surely stronger than a human's. It must be agony to resist them.

"What can I do?" Tem whispered.

Caspen laughed softly, shaking his head. "Nothing. You can only make it worse."

She recoiled.

"Tem," he said, pulling her against him. "You know what I mean. The closer we get...the harder it is for me."

She nodded, tears forming in her eyes.

"Do not cry," he whispered. "I cannot bear to see it."

Tem shrugged, trying to hold it in.

"You have every effect on me," Caspen said quietly. "But I cannot give in. Otherwise…" He trailed off, his fingers whispering over her jaw.

She leaned into his touch, savoring the warmth of his skin on hers. Tem couldn't help it. She didn't care about the danger. She needed him. "Why does it happen?" she asked.

"Why does what happen?"

"The transition. Why does it happen every time we're…together?"

Caspen sighed, tilting his head up to the ceiling. "It is complicated, Tem."

"So explain it."

He sighed again and looked her in the eye. "Basilisks and humans are not meant to be together. We are your enemy. We are your predators. We are predisposed to destroy you—to take pleasure in your pain. When we are together, I walk a line between pleasing you and…hurting you. My human form craves the former. My true form craves the latter."

Tem processed his words slowly.

Just as she realized their meaning, Caspen spoke it out loud: "Some part of me enjoys hurting you."

His words were thick with shame, and Tem knew it had cost him dearly to say them. But she found it wasn't a surprise. She thought about how he'd bit her lip, drawing blood. How he'd thrust into her even after she'd tried to pull away. She remembered the untethered darkness in his eyes when he'd finished. His hunger.

Hunger for her.

Caspen had told her that her body should only know pleasure—never pain. But what if his pleasure could only come from her pain?

She reached for him again.

Caspen caught her wrist and gently rolled her off him. "Tem," he said. "Enough."

Tem wanted to protest. But she knew she had no more to give. Caspen knew it too; his mind was inside hers, and she couldn't hide her pain from him. She looked him in the eyes and saw there was no anger or impatience there. Perhaps it was easier to stop; perhaps he didn't trust himself around her anymore.

Tem nodded, accepting his final command.

Caspen pressed his lips to hers, and all they did was kiss. When Tem couldn't kiss any longer, they simply lay there, and Caspen brushed his fingertips up and down her body.

"Sleep, Tem," the basilisk murmured in her ear.

She did so.

When she woke, Caspen's arms were still around her.

Tem watched him as he slept, realizing it was the first time she'd ever seen him do that. He breathed impossibly slowly. Tem tried to hold her breath in between each rise and fall of his shoulders but found she couldn't make it a single time. There was something inherently peaceful about his expression—it was completely devoid of his usual intensity and seriousness. He looked younger, whatever that meant in the grand scheme of his long basilisk life. There was a tiny fleck of blood on his temple. No doubt from when he'd bit her lip.

Caspen's cock was pressed against her thighs, already hard.

Does that thing ever take a day off? she wondered.

It does not.

Tem nearly jumped out of her skin as Caspen opened his eyes. "You could warn a girl before doing that," she managed to say.

In reply, he kissed her.

"Caspen," she murmured as he worked his way down her neck. "We can't. I need to get home."

He rubbed his entire palm between her legs. "Do you?"

"The farm—I—"

But it was useless. She was already wet, and she couldn't pretend to give a shit about the chickens right now.

He slid the head of his cock inside her, then stopped, his eyes flicking to hers.

"Keep going," Tem said preemptively. She was so sore, she had no idea whether she could even take him. But she wanted to, and that would have to be enough.

Caspen considered her, his head tilted to the side. Whatever inner dilemma he was experiencing was clearly weighing on him. But Tem knew if she waited him out, he would give in. After a moment of watching her, Caspen's eyes flicked down her body. His pupils dilated. Then he rolled her so they were facing each other on the bed, her legs around his waist. His cock slid a little farther inside her before stopping.

Relax, Tem. Let me in.

But she couldn't relax. Nothing about this was *relaxing*. Tem felt feral and agitated, like she needed to be fucked *right now*, as quickly as possible, before Caspen gave up on her. But one glance at him told her he wasn't giving up anytime soon. He looked perfectly calm, his arms locked around her. He held her in place as he slid his cock in a half inch at a time. But even that was too much for Tem.

I can't relax.

Yes, you can. Open yourself up for me.

I'm too sore. And you're too big.

The issue is mental. You need to relax.

I can't.

Tem. I am not going to force myself inside you. You need to let me in. Show me you can take me.

She groaned. His gaze was infuriatingly steady.

Your pussy is soaking wet, Tem. Let me feel how wet you are.

Can't you just feel it from out there?

He pulled her closer. Another half inch went in. She squirmed, but his arms only tightened.

Take my cock, Tem. I know you can do it.

She liked it when he talked to her. It made her even wetter.

Say more things like that.

Caspen's hand grabbed her throat, forcing her head up so she had to look him in the eyes.

I know you want my cock, Tem. You woke up wanting it, and you want it even more now. I know exactly how wet you are for me. Your pussy is mine. So give it to me.

She closed her eyes, but he didn't stop talking.

Give me what is mine, Tem. I know you want to. I know you want my cock all the way inside you.

An inch went in.

Let me in so I can make you come. And as soon as you come, I will lick you clean, and then I will make you come again. Let me in, Tem.

Another inch.

Let.

Me.

In.

Her eyes flew open.

There you are.

They both moaned as the last few inches slid inside her, filling her completely. For a moment, neither of them moved, both of them drunk on the way the other felt. Then Caspen pulled all the way out and *slammed* back into her, rolling her onto her back at the same time so she was spread open beneath him. Tem yelped in equal parts pain and pleasure, her fingernails sinking into his shoulders as he thrust again and again, the steady *smack smack smack* of his cock syncing perfectly with her moans.

Her first orgasm came out of nowhere, rearing its head so suddenly that Tem gasped in surprise as much as pleasure. She arched her hips only to be met with the hard relentlessness of his cock. True to his word, the second she came, Caspen pulled out, dipping his mouth between her legs and licking her until he had swallowed every last drop of her wetness. Then he yanked her hips against his and slid once more inside her. She was becoming one with him, their bodies conforming to each other like waves against sand.

"More," she begged.

Caspen drew away, and for a moment, she was afraid he was displeased.

Then his hands grabbed her, lifting her and turning her so she was on her knees facing the mattress. Tem cried out as his cock entered her again. Caspen groaned, and she knew he was beyond the point of stopping. He thrust harder and harder, his hips slapping against her ass so quickly she could barely stand it. But she didn't dare ask him to go slow—she knew he couldn't have if he tried. Just when she was about to finish, Caspen leaned down, grabbed the base of her neck, and yanked her upright so her back was pressed against his chest.

The sudden change in position left her breathless.

"Caspen," she gasped. "I was close."

"I know you were." His grip moved to her throat, turning her head to his. He spread her legs with his knees, his other hand working her clitoris rhythmically between his fingers. "I want to see your face when you come."

"You see my face every time."

"And it is not enough."

He was still thrusting into her—never giving her a break, never stopping. His fingers tightened around her neck. She could barely breathe.

Let go, Tem.

Her eyes squeezed shut as she surrendered to his grip, allowing him to push her straight into oblivion. As the pendulum of her release began to swing, Caspen's hiss filled his chambers. His thrusts only quickened as his climax joined hers, and Tem felt their combined wetness begin to drip down her thighs. They shattered together.

Eventually, his thrusts slowed, then stilled.

Caspen shifted his weight backward as he pulled out of her. His hand went between her legs, gathering their cum and holding it in his palm. Tem's breath caught in her throat as she realized what he was doing. He placed his other palm over his hand, and just like last time, the fire dimmed completely before suddenly flaring back to life. Another claw was in his hand.

This time, it was made of two luminous substances instead of one.

Tem looked at it in wonder. It was the most beautiful thing she had ever seen. Two shimmering swirls combined to make a single claw. The best parts of them, joined together in one object. When Caspen held it out to her, she shook her head.

"I want you to do it."

His mouth twitched.

Then he pulled her onto his lap so she was straddling him. Slowly, keeping his eyes on her the entire time, he slid the thicker end of the claw inside her. She stayed steady, holding on to his shoulders as he worked it all the way in. When it was fully inserted, Caspen wrapped his arms around her, burying his head against her neck and breathing in her scent.

"Stay with me today," he murmured into her hair.

Tem smiled against his skin. "I can't. I have to get back to the farm. The festival begins tonight."

At her words, Caspen stiffened.

Too late, Tem realized what she had said. The festival was a way to commemorate the basilisks' defeat. It was not a topic she should have brought up around him. "I'm sorry," she said quickly. "I didn't think—"

Stop.

He said the word in her mind, and Tem immediately stopped.

I do not hold you responsible for the sins of your ancestors.

Tem wasn't sure how to respond. Caspen may not hold her responsible, but it was impossible to extricate her from the past. She was only here because the basilisks were meant to train the prince's future wife. Their relationship was a *product* of the sins of her ancestors.

"The festival is stupid anyway," she murmured.

Caspen pressed a kiss to her collarbone. "That it is."

He accompanied her to the head of the trail, as always. When he kissed her goodbye, his hands slid over her body one last time, as if he wanted to memorize it.

Then he was gone.

Tem walked the rest of the way home in a daze. She was so sore that she had to move exceedingly slowly, and by the time she reached her cottage, the sun was directly above her.

"Out *again*, Tem?" her mother said as soon as she walked in. "I told you that boy is bad news."

It took Tem a good long moment to realize she was referring to Gabriel. "I'm sorry, Mother."

There was no point in explaining where she'd really been. If her mother thought she was out drinking with Gabriel, that was indisputably better than the truth.

"You look a mess. Wash up, then I want you in the garden."

Tem barely had the energy to nod.

She washed up. Then she spent a long, brutal afternoon in the garden. The late-autumn sun beat down on her in a relentless haze, and if it weren't for the pulses Caspen sent her using the claw, she doubted she would've made it through the day. All she could think about was having sex with him. If she could've run back to the cave to fuck him all over again, she would've.

Patience, Tem.

He was amused. She was restless.

Night finally fell, and it was time for the festival.

Tem and her mother made their way toward the village, where everyone was gathered in the square, as expected. But instead of the raucous sounds of the festival, there was only silence, broken by the occasional hushed whisper.

Tem frowned, turning to her mother. "Why is everyone so quiet?"

Her mother shrugged.

Tem spotted Vera's pink ribbon near the front of the crowd and pushed her way toward it.

"What's going on?" Tem asked when she reached her.

But Vera only shook her head. One hand was clamped tightly over her mouth, and the other was pointing straight ahead.

Finally, Tem saw what everyone was looking at.

There, in the middle of the square, were two stone statues. They were hunched on the cobblestones, cowering with their hands above their heads, as if in an attempt to protect themselves. Flayed ribbons of dried blood spattered the ground around them.

Tem's stomach turned to ice as she immediately recognized their faces.

Jonathan and Christopher.

CHAPTER FIFTEEN

⸺•◦✳◦•⸺

T HE MURMURS OF THE CROWD WERE GROWING LOUDER NOW, ONE QUESTION, repeated over and over: *How did this happen?*

Only Tem knew the truth.

"We were meant to meet up tonight," Vera whispered. "I think he wanted to get back together."

It was just like Vera to find a way to make such a horrific moment about her. But Tem had far more pressing things to worry about.

I only wish to protect you, Caspen had said.

Now it was Tem who wished to protect Caspen. The villagers would not forgive such an act of violence against one of their own. The royals wouldn't either. The consequences of Caspen's actions would reverberate far beyond simply settling a score in Tem's honor. It was a violation of the truce struck centuries ago, and it would not go unpunished.

Caspen had been inside her mind all day. When did he have time to do this? Tem replayed the day hour by hour, thinking about their connection. There hadn't been a moment when he wasn't with her. The only time they hadn't been communicating was when they were asleep last night in his chambers.

Tem paused. *She'd* been asleep.

There was no way to know whether Caspen had stayed with her the entire night. She'd been so exhausted from the sex that she hadn't woken up once. He could have easily slipped out under the cover of darkness to kill Jonathan and Christopher before returning to her. Tem thought about the fleck of blood on his temple. She'd assumed it was hers.

"What do you think will happen tonight?" Vera's whisper broke Tem from her thoughts.

The first night of the festival was always a wild one; the villagers usually drank mead and danced in the town square until dawn. But there would be no dancing tonight. People were already retreating to their homes and locking the doors behind them.

Tem shook her head. "I don't know."

All she knew was that she needed to talk to Caspen. She reached for their connection, feeling for the door that joined the corridor between their minds.

But it was shut.

Tem shouldn't have been surprised. Surely Caspen was deep beneath the mountain, surrounded by his own kind. She wondered if the other basilisks knew what he'd done. Or worse, if they'd sanctioned it.

"Tem." Her mother was suddenly beside her. "We're going home."

Before Tem could protest, her mother was already steering her away.

They walked in silence. Her mother stared purposefully ahead, her hands clasped at her sides. She didn't seem afraid. Rather, it was as if she was preparing herself for something imminent, something she'd expected for a long time.

"Mother?" Tem asked quietly.

"Yes?"

"Is there any way to bring them back?"

Her mother shook her head.

"No, my dear. They are petrified. It is permanent."

"But if there was some magic—some way to reverse—"

"You cannot reverse death, Tem. Their souls have gone to Kora."

Neither of them said a word the rest of the way home.

Tem planned to sneak out to see Caspen when her mother went to bed. But her mother sat awake in the kitchen until well past midnight, and Tem ran out of excuses to sit up with her. Eventually, she had no choice but to retreat to her bedroom and stare at the ceiling. Hours passed. Her mother never went to bed. By the time Tem finally drifted off, the roosters were starting to crow. She awoke in the same position she'd fallen asleep in.

Her mother was still in the kitchen when she emerged. Before either of them could speak, there was a knock at the door. A footman handed Tem a letter.

Temperance Verus,

Tonight's event will proceed as planned.
Kindly be ready at 8:00 p.m.

Tem turned it over, surprised at the twist of disappointment she felt when she saw that there was no additional note scrawled in red ink this time.

Then she remembered what tonight's event was.

Seven girls were left: they were halfway through the elimination process. At this point in the competition, it was tradition to host the girls and their teachers at the castle to give the prince an opportunity to fine-tune their training. It meant that Tem was about to be judged on her progress.

It also meant that Caspen was going to meet Leo.

Tem's stomach performed an uncomfortable flip at the thought. She couldn't imagine a stranger duo: the formidable basilisk and the human prince. Both powerful in their own right. But they couldn't be more different from each other.

Tem didn't bother trying to check in with Caspen through their connection. He hadn't answered her all night, and she doubted he would start now. Instead, she helped her mother with the farm work, feeling more miserable by the hour.

Jonathan and Christopher were dead because of Tem.

There was no way around it—no way to spin the situation to make it anyone's fault but her own. She should have tried harder to dissuade Caspen. She should have tried *at all*. But Tem knew in her gut that Caspen would not have been dissuaded. He was possessive, uncompromising, and he considered her to be *his*. There was nothing she could have done to prevent this.

Two packages arrived for her this time.

Neither package contained a note, but Tem knew immediately when she unwrapped them who had sent which dress. Caspen's was green; Leo's was red. Caspen's had a drape to it that would lie beautifully on her waist. Leo's had a slit up the side—a clear nod to the dress she'd worn for the Frisky Sixty. She knew which one she wanted to wear.

And yet she hesitated.

Both Caspen and Leo would be attending the event at the castle. Both would see immediately whose dress she had chosen. Tem felt a sudden stab of annoyance. Why had they both sent her something to wear? Why were they forcing her to choose? It wasn't fair.

She stared down at the dresses, willing one of them to disappear. When neither did, she decided to take matters into her own hands.

"Mother?"

Her mother looked up from the stove.

"Yes, dear?"

"Do you have a dress I can wear for tonight?"

Her mother frowned.

"I thought…" Her eyes flicked to Tem's bedroom, where the dresses were still laid out on the bed.

"Those don't fit," she said bluntly. It was half-true. They didn't fit Tem's needs.

Her mother pursed her lips before nodding. "Let me see," she said.

Tem followed her into the main bedroom, her eyes going immediately to the bottle of salt spray on her dresser. She touched the clear glass, remembering how Caspen had said she smelled like the sea. Her mother rustled through her closet, pulling out two dresses and holding them up. One was brown; that wouldn't do at all. Tem's eyes immediately went to the other.

It was white, and it was linen, and it was wildly inappropriate for a formal event at the castle. But it was good enough for her mother, so it was good enough for Tem.

"That one," she said.

Her mother handed her the dress.

Tem kept the claw inside her and the gold chain around her neck. By the time the carriage arrived to take her to the castle, she still hadn't heard from Caspen. It was difficult not to resent his absence.

"Miss?" The carriage door opened, and a footman extended his hand. "We've arrived."

Tem allowed herself to be steered into the castle.

The ballroom was just as it always was: sparkling with gold and filled with people. Tem scanned the crowd for Caspen, but he wasn't there yet. Before she had time to wonder when he would arrive, she felt a hand on her arm. It was Gabriel.

"Going for a casual look tonight, are we?" He kissed her cheek. "I like it."

"You're probably the only one."

"Please, Tem. If the prince doesn't want you in linen, he doesn't deserve you in silk."

Tem grinned. He was right.

"Do you know when the basilisks will be here?" she asked.

Gabriel shrugged. "Any minute now."

Tem scanned the room again, this time looking for Leo. She spotted him immediately, leaning against a marble column like he always was. Maximus was by his side, saying something in his ear. They both looked worried. Tem could imagine why.

No doubt the violation of the truce weighed heavily on the royals' minds. It was no coincidence that the basilisks were coming to the castle tonight. Surely the royals intended to control the situation—to assert their dominance in a public setting.

Help.

Tem froze.

The events of the last few days had been so overwhelming that she hadn't thought about the voice even once. But now that Tem was once more in the castle, everything came back to her in an arresting wave. She had promised herself that the next time she was here, she would find the voice. Tem turned to Gabriel, ready to excuse herself.

Before she could say a word, he nudged her and whispered, "Showtime."

The basilisks had arrived.

The entire ballroom fell silent as the seven teachers entered. Their effortless grace was mesmerizing: they could have been gliding on ice.

"So," Gabriel whispered. "Which one's yours?"

All the basilisks were objectively beautiful. But Caspen was on another level.

He stood half a foot taller than the others, his gold eyes appraising his surroundings with barely masked disdain. Wherever he moved, the crowd parted for him like water.

Tem simply pointed.

"*That's* Caspen?" Gabriel hissed.

"Yes."

"You little liar."

"Excuse me?"

"You little *liar*, Tem. You failed to mention that he was a perfect specimen of a man."

"He's not a man."

"Trust me, Tem. *That's* a man."

Tem rolled her eyes. "Would you please behave? This is hard enough without you gawking at him like he's some kind of deity."

"Have you *seen* him? He *is* some kind of deity."

"For Kora's sake."

"I've never seen a more beautiful man."

Tem sighed. Neither had she.

"I can't believe you get to have *sex* with him."

Tem sighed again. Neither could she.

The tinny sound of clinking glass cut through her thought.

"Attention, everyone." Maximus was walking to the center of the room, his voice just as deep as Tem remembered it. Leo remained by the column, a glass of whiskey dangling from his fingers. When he met Tem's eye, he winked.

Gabriel followed her gaze. "Did the prince just *wink* at you?"

Tem shoved him. "He did not."

"You should wink back."

"I'd rather die."

Gabriel squinted. "He's got quite the jawline, hasn't he?"

"No," Tem hissed through gritted teeth. "He doesn't."

"Oh, please, Tem. I know jawlines, and *that's* a jawline."

Gabriel waggled his fingers coquettishly at Leo, who raised a bewildered eyebrow.

Tem smacked his hand down. "*Fine*, he has a nice jawline."

"Probably has other nice bits too."

Tem had nothing to say to that. The king was still speaking.

"It is with great honor and privilege that we welcome our guests here tonight. My son and I are most grateful for their services."

Maximus's wording wasn't accidental. Tem suddenly remembered their conversation in the parlor: *They provide a service. Their place is beneath us.*

The king was minimizing the basilisks, reducing them to their roles as teachers. His speech was a warning, a way to remind them that the royals held the power. But did they? The mirrored wall was useless. The villagers lived once more in fear of the monsters beneath the mountain. If there was peace to be had, it was no longer guaranteed. If it ever was.

Tem watched a muscle in Caspen's jaw twitch as Maximus continued.

"The elimination process is a time-honored tradition. It ensures that my son"—the king's eyes flicked briefly over to Leo—"makes the right choice. And perhaps more importantly, it ensures that the balance of our kingdom remains intact."

Should the snakes ever question their place, the balance may falter.

"If you would raise your glasses"—Maximus raised his, along with everyone else in the room—"I'd like to make a toast."

Gabriel took Tem's hand and raised it ironically, as if it were a glass.

Maximus paused before speaking, and his eyes ultimately settled on Tem's as he said, "To making the right choice."

Everyone but Leo downed their drink.

Gabriel pressed his lips to Tem's fingers before dropping her hand. "Well, I'm off. See you in a bit?"

"Sure," Tem said. "See you."

Gabriel disappeared.

Before she was ready for him, Caspen was in front of her.

"Tem," he said, his voice an eager murmur.

It had only been a day since they'd parted, but it felt like a lifetime to Tem. She wondered whether it felt the same for him or if she'd slipped from his mind as easily as a snuffed-out candle.

"Caspen," she said back, his name barely making it past the lump in her throat. "How are you?"

It seemed like a stupid thing to ask. But she had no idea what else to say to him, especially considering their circumstances.

"I am well. And yourself?"

She could only nod. It felt like something was compressing her lungs, making it impossible to breathe.

"Can I get you a drink?" he asked quietly.

"Yes, please," she managed.

He disappeared, reappearing a moment later with a delicate flute of champagne. He held it out to her.

"I hate champagne."

Caspen smiled, and her heart skipped a beat. "Forgive me," he said. "I did not know."

"Well. Now you do."

His smile widened. "What would you prefer to drink, Tem?"

"Whiskey."

She didn't know why she'd said it. But for some reason, in that moment, she'd thought of Leo.

Caspen disappeared again, and when he reappeared, he handed her a whiskey.

"Thank you."

"My pleasure."

He stepped closer. "You are not wearing the dress I sent."

Not a question. Simply a statement.

"The prince sent me one too."

Caspen tilted his head.

She couldn't read his expression.

"I see," he said quietly. "And you could not choose."

Another statement. "I *could*," Tem clarified. "But I didn't want to."

"I see," he said again, his eyes traveling over her body, taking in the humble white linen.

In the silence, Tem felt her heart hammer in her chest. She needed to ask Caspen about Jonathan and Christopher—needed to hear the confession straight from his lips. But there was one issue that was more pressing.

"I've been hearing a voice," she said before she could stop herself.

Caspen's eyes snapped back to hers. He frowned. "A voice?"

"Yes. In the castle. Well, in my head. But it's coming from the castle."

Tem figured this announcement would be met with confusion or at least incredulity. Instead, Caspen looked over his shoulder as if to ensure no one else was listening.

He stepped closer. "We cannot discuss this here."

His response bewildered her. She'd expected him to ask some clarifying questions—or *any* questions at all. His lack of surprise could only mean one thing.

"Can you hear it too?"

He pursed his lips but didn't reply.

Now Tem was the one to step closer. "If you can hear it, then you know it's asking for help."

"I said I will not discuss this here."

It was all too much. She was so tired of Caspen withholding information from her.

"*Excuse me?* There has to be something we can—"

But Caspen cut her off. "*I will not discuss this here.*"

Tem stepped back, her eyes stinging with tears. Despite his harsh command, Caspen didn't look angry. On the contrary, he seemed almost sad. When he spoke again, his voice was soft.

"Tell me, Tem. What is your opinion of the prince?"

Tem could feel her palms start to sweat. Why was Caspen asking her this? Was he jealous? Or was he simply checking in on his student?

"He's..." She paused, her eyes searching the crowd for Leo. He was slipping through a doorway at the far end of the ballroom, flanked by a girl on one side and a basilisk on the other. One of the seven private meetings he would be conducting tonight.

Tem shook her head, attempting to focus.

"He's a royal. They're all the same."

Caspen leaned in. "Does he favor you?"

A direct question. One she couldn't avoid. She answered it honestly. "Yes. I think so."

Caspen's eyes narrowed.

A sharp throb shot through the claw. It was so intense that Tem gasped, her hand shooting between her legs in an attempt to alleviate the pain. Unlike the gentle, aching pulses Caspen usually sent her, this one was so jarring, she knew it was not meant for pleasure.

Tem looked up at him in shock. "That *hurt.*"

Regret flashed over Caspen's face. He opened his mouth, but before he could speak, Tem was already turning away.

Caspen grabbed her arm. "Where are you going?"

"To take it out," Tem snapped.

"*No,*" he cried. She had never heard him so desperate. "Tem, I—"

"How dare you?" she hissed. "How *dare* you use it to cause me pain? I put it in because I trust you."

Caspen's face was a dark mask of remorse. "I did not mean to hurt you."

"You never do."

"I reacted, and—"

"*You're* the one who trained me for him."

Caspen stared down at her. His eyes went hard. "I am well aware of that, Tem."

"Then what do you want from me?"

His hand slid slowly down her arm until his fingers were just brushing hers. Tem was distinctly aware of the way they were standing together, sequestered alone at the edge of the ballroom. The claw pulsed softly.

"Everything."

Tem shook her head. "Don't say that."

"Why not?"

"Because you don't mean it."

"Of course I—"

"If you wanted me, you would let me in. But you don't. You never have. You keep secrets from me. You never give me a straight answer. You *silence* me."

"You cannot be silenced, Tem. That much is very clear."

"Did you kill Jonathan and Christopher?"

Caspen lifted his chin, looking down at her. "Of course I did."

"I told you I didn't want anyone to get hurt."

"And I told you some things do not concern you."

"Loss of human life concerns me."

"Their lives were hardly a *loss*."

The pulse quickened. They were arguing, but he was turning her on. "Stop that," she demanded.

"Why?"

"It isn't fair," she insisted. "I have no way to retaliate."

"You speak as if we are at war."

"It feels as if we are."

The pulses stopped. She hated how much she missed them.

Caspen leaned in, his eyes holding hers. "It is not my wish to wound you, Tem."

"Then what is your wish?"

The crowd seemed to disappear around them.

"To prepare you."

"For what?"

The pulse returned, gently this time, throbbing rhythmically against her underclothing. She closed her eyes, savoring the sensation.

They were still closed when she heard Caspen whisper, "For what comes."

When Tem opened her eyes, they were no longer alone.

Another basilisk stood beside Caspen. This one had black hair that brushed his shoulders and cheekbones so sharp they reflected the light. He was several inches shorter than Caspen, with the same rigid posture. He appraised Tem with clear contempt.

"So, Caspenon," he said, still looking at Tem. "This is your student."

Something about the way he said "student" made it clear he meant it as an insult.

"Her name is Temperance," Caspen said, his voice purposefully even. Tem recognized his tone; it was the one he used when he was attempting to restrain his anger.

"*Temperance*," the basilisk said slowly, tilting his head to get a better view of her. "Interesting."

"And you are?" Tem asked before she could help herself.

The basilisk blinked, as if surprised she was addressing him directly. "I am Rowe Seneca."

"Interesting."

Rowe is dangerous. Do not anger him.

Tem nearly jumped as Caspen's voice returned to her mind.

Why not?

But he was already gone again.

Rowe's gaze fell to the golden claw around her neck. A cross between disbelief and rage flashed over his face. He looked at Caspen.

"Tell me that is not what I think it is."

Caspen tensed. "That is none of your concern."

Rowe stepped closer, and Caspen's hand darted to Tem's waist. Rowe's eyes followed the movement with disgust. "You are a disgrace to your quiver," he snarled.

Caspen's grip only tightened. "And you are a burden on yours."

Rowe let out a bitter laugh. "Better a burden than a traitor."

The ballroom seemed to shrink as Caspen leaned forward, his face mere inches from Rowe's. "Remember your place. Or I shall remind you of it."

Rowe stared up at him in defiance, but Tem didn't miss the unmistakable flash of fear in his eyes. An endless moment passed as the two basilisks glared at each other. Tem didn't dare break the silence. It was clear there was history here, but she had no idea what it could be. She remembered what Caspen had told her about basilisks: how their quivers were like their clans. Rowe was from another quiver—perhaps one that had tension with Caspen's. She couldn't begin to imagine the political climate of the basilisks. Surely, it was even more complicated than the royals.

They were still standing in silence when Vera appeared.

"Run out of dresses, Tem?" she chirped.

Her voice snapped the basilisks from their stalemate. Rowe turned to Vera. "I told you to wait for me until the prince called us in."

Tem raised her eyebrows. Rowe was Vera's basilisk.

Vera's eyes went jealously to Caspen's hand, which was still on Tem's waist. She touched Rowe's arm in an imitation of the gesture.

"I know, but I—"

He brushed her off. "Leave us," he barked.

Vera's face pinched. It was a dismissal and not a kind one. For a moment, it seemed like she might protest. But one glance at Rowe's face seemed to change her mind. With a final dissatisfied huff, she flounced away.

Rowe turned back to Caspen, continuing as if Vera were never there. "I should rip that from her neck." He pointed at Tem's necklace.

Caspen immediately angled himself so that he was between her and Rowe, his body acting as a shield. "Only if you wish to lose your hand."

"The way you protect her..." Rowe's nostrils flared. "*Disgusting.*"

"Say one more word," Caspen hissed, and Tem felt a chill rush down her spine. "And you will join your father."

Horror flared in Rowe's eyes, followed by pure, unfiltered loathing.

Then he turned and was gone.

Tem looked up at Caspen. He was staring after Rowe, his jaw locked. She had so many questions, but she was sure he wouldn't answer any of them. Before she could decide where to begin, a butler appeared beside her.

"His Highness will see you now."

There was no time to decompress after what just happened. The butler was already ushering them through the crowd, toward the doorway at the end of the ballroom. Tem felt a sudden prick of fear. Not only was Caspen about to be face-to-face with Leo, but he was already angry. There was no telling what he might do if provoked. Leo wasn't exactly a peacemaker; he was even more prone to disruption than Tem was. The butler opened the door.

There stood Leo.

CHAPTER SIXTEEN

T HE PRINCE HELD A GLASS OF WHISKEY, WHICH HE SWIRLED CASUALLY. HIS EYES
flicked briefly over Tem's dress before landing on Caspen. For a moment, nothing
happened.

Then Leo stepped forward.

He moved slowly, stopping only when he was in front of the basilisk. They were dead
even in height, but Caspen's build made him seem taller. Tem would have paid good
money to know what each of them was thinking. But Caspen's mind was still closed off
to her, and she'd never been able to access Leo's. She merely watched helplessly as the
two men in her life stared at each other. Leo broke the silence.

"Thank you."

Caspen blinked. "For?"

Leo looked down at Tem. "For her."

Caspen stiffened. His hands were slowly forming into fists.

"She's really something, isn't she?" Leo said nonchalantly.

Tem wondered if he had any idea the danger he was in.

"Yes," Caspen said through his teeth. "She is."

"Of course." Leo shot a grin at Tem. "She's also rather difficult."

Caspen didn't acknowledge that. His voice was monotone as he asked, "Are you
satisfied with her performance?"

There was a pause, and Tem's stomach squirmed as she remembered the point of
this meeting was to *grade* her.

Leo laughed. "Define performance."

Caspen's gaze slid to Tem before snapping immediately back to Leo. "You have not
yet slept together?" His words lingered in the room like smoke.

Leo took a sip of his whiskey. "You sound surprised. Don't you two
communicate?"

A pulse went through the claw. If only the prince knew *how* they communicated.

"I assume *you've* slept together," Leo continued without missing a beat. "Care to tell
me what I have to look forward to?"

Tem's mouth fell open. Leo had always been cavalier about sex, but hearing him discuss it so flippantly was still a shock.

Caspen bristled. Tem's palms began to sweat again.

"She will satisfy you," he said stiffly. "And if she does not, it is my failure. Not hers."

Tem processed his words. She'd never thought about the training in that way. She hadn't considered that she was a reflection of Caspen and if the prince didn't choose her, it was just as much his fault as hers.

"Hm." Leo swirled his whiskey. "You assume you know what will satisfy me."

Caspen rolled his shoulders.

Tem said a silent prayer to Kora for Leo's life.

"I assume nothing beyond what I know of human men."

Leo frowned, and for the first time since the conversation began, his tone hardened. "And what do you know of human men?"

Another pause. Caspen's eyes locked onto Leo's, and Tem felt a tangible shift in the energy of the room as he said, "That they are easily satisfied."

There was no mistaking the challenge in Caspen's voice. He'd essentially called Leo simple. Predictable. He was belittling him, implying that Leo—and all humans—had no depth. Tem knew it was not an insult the prince would tolerate.

Leo's fingers tightened on his whiskey. He bared his gold, tapered teeth.

"You forget your place, snake."

Caspen went immediately still.

It was a mirror of the conversation she had just witnessed between Caspen and Rowe, only this time, Leo was the one putting Caspen in his place. Tem was reminded suddenly that although Caspen was an important part of her life, he was meaningless to Leo. To the prince, Caspen was nothing more than a tool—a means to an end—a cog in a tradition that was hundreds of years old. Leo believed the same thing his father believed: the basilisks were beneath him.

How wrong he was.

"Enough," snapped Tem.

They both looked at her, eyebrows raised.

"I'm not *livestock*." She barreled on before either of them had a chance to interrupt. "You can't just talk about me like I'm not here."

It was deathly quiet. Tem could hear her pulse pounding in her skull. She turned to Leo.

"I'm your future wife. And I deserve to be treated as such."

Leo's eyebrows hiked up even farther. Tem held his gaze. It seemed safer than looking at Caspen, who was palpably radiating anger. The prince seemed to be considering something—considering *her*. For all the times Leo had looked at her before, Tem wondered if this was the moment when he truly saw her as a *person*, not as a commodity. It was the bare minimum of what she deserved.

"You're right," Leo said finally.

Caspen said nothing.

This time, Tem let the silence sit. She wanted them to think about what she'd said—to truly comprehend her place in this process. It was unacceptable to her that they thought this was about them. *Tem* was the one with a choice to make. *Tem* was the one who held the power. If she chose to walk out of this room, neither the basilisk nor the prince could do anything to stop her. They both wanted her. They should start acting like it.

Leo reached for her hand.

A sudden wave of rage surged inside Tem's mind. But it wasn't hers; it was Caspen's. For once, Tem didn't let him in. She slammed the door shut between them, doing everything she could to keep him out. She took Leo's hand, focusing on the way it felt—warm and strong, his long fingers intertwining with hers as he asked, "What do you need from me, Tem?"

He said it quietly, as if they were the only two people in the room. Tem considered the question. There was only one thing she needed from Leo—the same thing she needed from herself.

"Patience."

The corner of his mouth twitched. "Not my specialty, I'm afraid."

The rage was growing stronger. It took everything she had to suppress it.

Just when resistance became impossible, Leo turned to Caspen. "Leave us."

Tem expected him to protest. Or perhaps explode. Instead he gave a curt nod, and a moment later, he was gone. As soon as the door snapped shut, Caspen's rage retreated from her mind. Tem blinked, shaking her head to clear it. Leo was still holding her hand.

"Tem." His grip tightened. "What's wrong?"

"Nothing. But I should…check on him."

Leo frowned. "Why?"

"Because…"

She could come up with nothing to say. There was no logical reason why she would need to check on her teacher, and they both knew it. But the fact remained that she had to see Caspen. So she said the only thing she could think of. "I'll be right back, Leo. I promise."

Leo was still frowning. It was a long, weighted moment before he responded. "Of course. Take your time."

Tem didn't give him a chance to change his mind. She extracted her fingers from his, pushing through the door and back into the ballroom. Caspen's tall frame was at the edge of the crowd. She ran for him, not caring who was in her way.

"Caspen!"

He turned, his expression unreadable.

"*She will satisfy you?*" Tem hissed when she reached him, disguising her hurt with anger. "How could you say that about me?"

Caspen let out a humorless laugh. "I did my duty, Tem. Nothing more."

He turned away, but Tem grabbed his arm. "Your *duty?* Is that all I am to you?"

Caspen whirled around, closing the distance between them in half a second. "You know very well what you are to me, Tem. But my hands are tied."

She glared up at him. "Actually, it's *my* hands that are tied."

Caspen's eyes narrowed. "Are they? You are his *future wife*, are you not? Such an esteemed position is hardly a burden."

Tem stepped back as if she had been slapped. "I said that to defend myself," she whispered. "And it's just a fact. You know it is."

"The only *fact* is that he wants you. Even more so now that he senses a challenge from me."

"Senses a—"

"And if he thinks he can take what is mine." Caspen cut her off, leaning even closer. "He is wrong."

This time when he turned to leave, Tem let him.

The sounds of the ballroom became a dull roar as she closed her eyes. Caspen hadn't said Leo's name—not once. Perhaps it was a way to degrade him—to undermine the hierarchy the royals insisted on enforcing. Jonathan's and Christopher's statues flashed suddenly through Tem's mind. She would not allow that to happen to Leo. Not ever.

Tem opened her eyes.

There was Gabriel, laughing with a butler. There was Vera, pining after Rowe. Nobody in the crowded ballroom knew what Tem had just endured—what Caspen had done and was capable of doing. It was becoming too much for Tem to bear. She could not continue to carry such secrets alone.

Somehow, she found her way back to Leo. He looked up as she entered the room.

"What was that about?" he asked. He had a funny expression on his face, as if he were trying to figure something out.

"Nothing," Tem said automatically. It wasn't her best, but she had nothing left to give.

Leo stepped closer. "I'd rather you didn't lie to me, Tem. Remember?"

Tem sighed. Of course she remembered. But she also couldn't tell Leo the truth. So she said, "I'm just tired. It's been a long day."

She knew he didn't believe her.

"Is he always like that?" Leo asked.

"Like what?"

"A bit of a brute."

"Caspen is not a brute."

The words came out sharper than she'd intended. Leo raised an eyebrow at her tone.

"Have I offended you?"

"You insulted someone I care about."

Too late, Tem realized it was utterly the wrong thing to say. The look of pure disgust on Leo's face was exactly the one Rowe had given Caspen earlier.

"You *care* about him?"

Tem tried to recover, reaching for his arm. "I just don't think he's a brute. He prepared me for you after all. Don't you think we owe him our gratitude?"

Leo jerked out of her grasp. His voice was flat when he spoke again. "Preparing you for me is his duty. I owe him nothing. And neither do you."

"Leo…" she started, but he shook his head, and she fell silent.

He stepped closer. His gray eyes were shards of ice. "Is this why you won't fuck me? Because of *him*?"

Tem's mouth opened, then closed.

In the silence, he studied her.

She didn't dare speak. Leo was smart; he would not be fooled by words. Tem had no choice but to let him come to his own conclusion. When the prince finally spoke, his voice was a quiet murmur of realization.

"He means something to you."

Tears began to form. Tem was being pulled in a direction she had no control over—being forced to reveal something she had never intended to reveal. Everything was coming to a head *right now*, and there was nothing she could do to stop it.

There was no point in lying. Leo would see right through it if she did.

So Tem whispered, "Yes."

True hurt and disbelief flashed across Leo's face. "How much?" he asked.

"How much what?"

He leaned in so she couldn't look anywhere but at him. "How much *exactly* does he mean to you?"

Tem couldn't believe this was happening.

"He…" she started but had no idea how to put it into words. How much *did* Caspen mean to her? A lot. But she couldn't say that to Leo.

Before she could come up with an answer, he was already asking a far worse question. "Do you love him?"

She needed to lie. That was all there was to it; she needed to conceal the truth, just this once. But Tem couldn't do it. The more she tried, the tighter her chest became. It was like trying to speak through a suctioned tube. She could barely get the word through her teeth: "No."

Leo's entire body was rigid. Tem wanted to reach for him but didn't. There was nothing to say—no way to fix this. She knew without a shadow of a doubt that she'd just set something in motion that couldn't be undone. For a moment, Tem was afraid Leo might scream at her.

But then, inexplicably, he softened. His shoulders slumped as his eyes dropped to the floor. It was a long moment before he spoke, and when he did, his voice was hoarse. "Am I to share you?"

Tem couldn't believe the agony in his voice. She had forgotten that underneath Leo's bravado, he had a heart just like hers. A heart that was capable of want—of *love*. Leo's ego shielded him from vulnerability; it was easy to forget how sensitive he was. But in moments like these, Tem understood him better than she understood herself. She knew what it meant to yearn.

"That's…up to you, I suppose," she said quietly.

The prince looked at her with such devastation she wanted to cry. "No, Tem. That's up to you."

Tem reached for him again, but he stepped away.

"Go to him," he said.

"What?"

"You love *Caspen*,." His voice was sharper than a knife. "So go to him."

Tem flinched. "Leo, please—"

"Just. Go."

Then he turned and was gone.

Alone at last, she let the tears fall.

There was no point in lingering. Tem ran from the castle, trying not to think about what would happen if Leo eliminated her tonight. First and foremost, her mother would never forgive her. The farm had only become more of a burden since Tem was away so often training for the prince. Her mother had taken side work to make ends meet— watching small children for the women in the village, tending to the neighbor's cats when they were away from home. It was a lifestyle that wasn't sustainable. Tem's courtship with the prince was their only lifeline: the only thing that would save them. And now that was probably gone.

Go to him.

Leo's words raced through her head over and over as she made for the carriages. Part of her wanted to obey—to go to Caspen and lose herself in his arms. Another part of her remembered the wave of rage Caspen had felt when Leo took her hand. What if that rage became directed at her? He'd already used the claw to hurt her tonight. There was no guarantee he wouldn't do it again. But if she went home, she would have to face her mother, and Tem couldn't stand the thought of telling her what had just happened.

"Where to, miss?" the footman asked as she climbed into the carriage.

"The forest."

Tem spent the entirety of the ride with her head in her hands. Despite her distress, no tears came. Instead, she felt only an endless wave of adrenaline that set her teeth on edge. She was done waiting for answers from Caspen. It wasn't fair that he withheld information from her the way he did; it wasn't fair that she was constantly in the dark. Tem needed to know where she stood with him. She needed to know that in a single night, she hadn't lost everything that ever mattered to her.

When the carriage arrived at the edge of the forest, the footman helped her out with an incredulous look.

"Wouldn't you rather I take you home, miss?"

"No," Tem said simply.

She walked quickly into the trees, keeping her eyes on the ground. The last time she'd been on this path, Jonathan and Christopher had assaulted her. Now they were harmless stone statues, frozen in the middle of the square. How things had changed.

The cave was dark, the fireplace cold.

Tem didn't bother waiting for a welcoming committee. She dipped immediately into the shadows, traversing the passageway using nothing but her memory. When she reached the door to Caspen's chambers, she paused. There was no telling what kind of mood he'd be in. Did he even want to see her? Both Caspen and Leo had discovered that the other meant something to her tonight. It seemed too cruel a punishment for her to lose them both because of it.

Without another second's hesitation, Tem opened the door.

The fireplace was lit, but the room was empty.

Tem sat on the edge of Caspen's bed and wondered suddenly if this had been a terrible mistake. What was she thinking, coming to his chambers without an invitation? What if he didn't want to see her—or worse, what if he had sought refuge with someone else? Her stomach turned at the thought. She could hardly expect loyalty from Caspen when she herself was entangled with the prince.

The fire began to burn low.

What if he never showed? Tem had no idea where Caspen might be or if he even knew she was here. He could be somewhere deep in the forest, hunting in his true form. He might not return for hours. Tem stood, resolved to go back home. That was when she heard it.

"Temperance."

Her full name.

Tem looked over to see Rowe in the doorway. He must have just returned from the castle. She was immediately aware of how vulnerable she was—alone under the mountain with a basilisk that wasn't Caspen. The situation was far outside her control.

"I came to see Caspen," she managed to say. "Is he here?"

"He is close by," Rowe replied smoothly, tilting his head as if listening to something. "And getting closer."

Tem's heart picked up the pace. If Caspen was close, she was almost safe.

Rowe stepped into the room, and Tem instinctually stepped back. The basilisk chuckled at her retreat. "Are you afraid, Temperance?"

Tem said nothing. Rowe smiled, and her blood ran cold.

"Answer me," he commanded.

"Yes," she whispered. "I'm afraid."

His smile widened. "As you should be."

Tem raised her chin. It was the only thing she could do to defy him.

Rowe crossed slowly to the fireplace, keeping his eyes on Tem the entire time. He moved the way Caspen did, with the same unattainable grace.

"I must confess," he said musingly, as if this were a casual conversation and not a deeply dangerous scenario, "I cannot understand Caspenon's infatuation with you. You are not much to look at."

Tem couldn't muster the energy to be insulted. She knew there was no winning with Rowe.

"Of course," he continued, "Caspenon has always been...*sentimental*."

Tem reached desperately for Caspen with her mind, but the door between them was still shut tight. "He knows what he wants," she said stiffly.

"That much is clear," Rowe sneered. "Yet I doubt he knows the price he will pay if he gets it."

"I don't understand," said Tem despite herself.

"No." His eyes flicked down her neck to the little golden claw. "You would not."

Tem fought to control the conversation. "If anything happens to me, Caspen will seek revenge."

Rowe laughed darkly. "Do not speak on things you do not understand. Revenge is already mine to seek."

For a moment, the only sound was the crackling of the fire.

Rowe glanced over his shoulder at the doorway as if he'd heard something. Then a sly smile pulled at his lips as he said, "But perhaps not tonight." When his gaze returned to her, he looked her up and down one last time. "Until we meet again, Temperance."

As if he were never there to begin with, Rowe disappeared.

Tem let out a long breath. The hairs on the back of her neck were standing straight up, and she couldn't shake the feeling that she'd just dodged certain death. All the tears that had refused to come earlier now threatened to engulf her. Rowe was dangerous. There was no doubt about it. And clearly he had a personal problem with Caspen—one he was willing to use Tem to exacerbate. *Revenge is already mine to seek.* What did that mean? What had Caspen done?

Before she could dissect it further, she heard her name again. "Tem?"

This time, it was Caspen standing in the doorway. He crossed to her immediately, stopping just short of touching her. "What are you doing?"

"I had to talk to you."

"You should not have come here alone."

"I know."

"It is dangerous for you. I cannot protect you if—" He cut off, his eyes traveling over her with sudden concern. His nostrils flared. "Rowe. I can smell him. Was he here?"

Tem shook her head. If one more thing went wrong tonight, she was going to scream. "Caspen," she said. "I don't want to talk about Rowe."

Caspen pursed his lips. It was obvious he wanted to say something else, but Tem was grateful when he refrained. The weight of the evening hung between them as they studied each other.

Tem chose her question carefully. "How do we move forward?"

Caspen sighed. "That...depends."

"On?"

"Tem," he sighed again. "I do not wish to discuss this now."

But Tem was fed up. She was done letting Caspen decide what they could and could not discuss. He wouldn't talk about the voice in the castle, he wouldn't talk about the status of their relationship, he wouldn't talk about anything of value. It was enough. She refused to live in a state of limbo any longer.

"How do we move forward?" she insisted, her voice sharp.

Caspen's eyes narrowed. She had never used that tone with him before. "I cannot predict the future, Tem," he said, his voice equally sharp.

"I'm not asking you to. I'm just asking what you want."

"You know very well what I want."

"But I *don't*," she cried. "You never confide in me. You never tell me how you feel. You expect me to read your mind, then you get angry when I can't do it. *You're* the one who won't let *me* in. Not the other way around." Tem was on the verge of tears. She waited a moment before finishing quietly, "You never talk about the future. I…don't know what I am to you."

Caspen was looking at her with unrestrained disbelief. She didn't know if he was shocked by her words or the way she had said them. Either way, it was a long time before he spoke, and when he did, his voice was barely a whisper.

"*You* are my future. It is as simple as that."

Now the tears fell.

Because it was not simple. Not at all. Even though it was everything she'd ever wanted to hear from Caspen, Tem had no idea how they were supposed to be together. She didn't fit in with his people, nor he with hers. A future with Caspen was of no benefit to her mother or the farm. Things had never felt more impossible.

"Why didn't you tell me sooner?"

He shrugged, the motion stilted. "It makes this complicated."

"Was this not already complicated?"

Caspen shook his head. "It is more so now. You cannot comprehend the difficulty I am in."

"Then tell me."

He shook his head again. She'd pushed him too far; he was closing himself off from her. But Tem would not allow that anymore. If they had a future together, she deserved to have a say in it.

"Caspen." She touched his arm, stepping closer. "Tell me."

For a long time, Caspen stood motionless. Then he traced his fingertips along her shoulder and down the gold chain until he was touching the little claw between her breasts.

"This is not just a necklace," he said softly.

"Then what is it?"

Caspen paused, his fingers stroking the charm. "It is…a gesture of intent."

Tem frowned. "Intent to what?"

His eyes found hers.

"To marry you."

CHAPTER SEVENTEEN

—••◦✳◦••—

A RE YOU SAYING WE'RE *ENGAGED*?"

The room grew suddenly warmer. Tem could hardly breathe.

"No," Caspen said quickly. "You would need to accept the proposal in order for us to be engaged."

"Oh," said Tem, still reeling from this revelation.

Now Rowe's extreme reaction to the necklace made sense. Surely a basilisk and human pairing was uncommon or even frowned upon.

"Well…" she said slowly, "I accept."

To Tem's surprise, Caspen's face darkened. "You cannot accept."

"Excuse me?"

"What I mean to say is *you* cannot accept. My quiver, should they approve the match, would accept on your behalf."

Tem absorbed this information. It was utterly bizarre; she'd never heard of someone being unable to accept their own proposal. It begged an obvious question: "Will they approve the match?"

"I very much doubt it."

"*Excuse me?*" she said again.

"Tem." He took her hands in his. "It is not personal. Basilisks and humans rarely mate. What we have is unusual, and my quiver will be wary of it."

Tem was still trying to process the fact that Caspen had proposed to her. She thought back to when he'd given her the necklace; it was the morning after he'd touched her for the very first time. He'd made her come, and she'd done the same for him. Afterward, they'd shared their first meal together. Tem remembered how electrifying their connection had been that night, how exhilarating and *significant* it had felt to bring each other to orgasm. That night had meant a lot to her. Only now did she realize it had meant even more to Caspen.

There was one last thing Tem needed to know.

"How long have you loved me?"

Caspen held her gaze as he whispered, "Far longer than you have loved me."

Tem wondered just how long that was.

Was it the moment she'd touched herself in front of him? Or earlier, when she'd first taken off her clothes in the cave? Or earlier still, when he'd visited her in her dreams? Had he known then that he loved her? Had she known too?

Caspen had always been an anomaly to her, a creature far beyond anything Tem could encapsulate with mere words. It shouldn't surprise her that things had progressed for him in a way she never could have predicted. There was no point in trying to comprehend a basilisk. And yet Tem was not afraid of his declaration. She was not afraid of *him*. She never had been. Caspen had always treated her as his equal, despite the inequity between them. He was the only one who built her up—who told her constantly that she was enough.

As they looked at each other, something blossomed in Tem's heart. There was a sincerity to his gesture that she appreciated more than he would ever know. To be told she was someone's future wasn't something Tem had ever expected to hear. She thought girls like Vera were the only ones who could catch the eye of a man—that every other girl in the world was worthy of affection but her. Caspen had shown her that wasn't true. He'd opened her up—in more ways than one—and she would be forever changed because of it.

Caspen wore an expression of obvious caution, no doubt waiting to see how she would react to what he'd just told her. There was no reason to make him wait any longer.

Tem stood on her tiptoes and kissed him.

Caspen met her lips with his, pulling her into his arms with monstrous strength. The kiss was everything she needed and more. It was confirmation that the risks they were taking were worth it—that they would always choose each other despite everything standing in their way.

The kiss deepened. Tem grabbed at every part of him, pulling him against her, wishing she could *consume* him. Everything about him made her feral, like an untamed animal that had just been let out of its cage. She focused on nothing but Caspen, pushing away everything that happened tonight, pouring herself into this moment until she was blind with desire. Her hands slid down his trousers to feel his cock. As soon as she touched him, he pulled away.

"Tem," he said, his voice strained. "We should not."

"Why not?"

Caspen brushed his fingers gently over her bottom lip. "It is too easy for me to lose control around you."

Tem remembered how he'd bitten her last time. How he drew blood. "You love me," she said.

"I do."

She leaned into his touch. His eyes were turning black. "So control it."

His thumb pulled at her lip, opening it. "I cannot," he whispered.

Her hand returned to his trousers, but he stopped her before she could pull them down.

"Tem," he said firmly. "I do not trust myself."

"*I* trust you."

Caspen only shook his head. "I have done nothing to earn it."

"But you love me," she said again.

"My love for you is my burden to bear."

At his words, she pulled abruptly away. "I'm a burden to you?"

"No," he said. "Of course not. That is not what I mean."

"Then what do you mean?"

He tilted his head to the ceiling as if asking Kora for answers. "I mean that I never should have let this happen."

She yanked herself from his grasp. "Then why *did* you let it happen?"

"Because I am *weak.*" Caspen practically yelled it.

Tem stepped back in shock.

He stepped closer. "I am *weak* when it comes to you, Tem. I cannot control my actions. I cannot follow logic or reason. All I think about is you. I wonder what you are doing and who you are doing it with. I obsess over every moment you are with the human prince, and I want to rip his head from his shoulders every time he touches you. It is not rational. It is not acceptable. But it is my reality, and there is nothing I can do about it."

Tem felt suddenly faint. "Is loving me really so horrible?" she whispered.

"Of course not."

"Are you saying I make you weak?"

He shook his head. "No."

"Then what *are* you saying? Are you angry with me?"

"*No.*"

"Is that the only word you know? Because—"

"*Tem.*" He placed his hands on her shoulders, looking her in the eye. "I am not angry with you. I am angry with myself. I should have known better. I am the one who gave in to temptation. *That* is what I mean when I say I am weak."

"Temptation? Is that what I am?"

His grip tightened on her shoulders. "Temptation, salvation, heaven, hell—you are everything, Tem. You are my undoing. You are beyond comprehension. There are no sufficient words to describe you, either in my language or yours." His hands moved to her face, cupping her jaw. "My compass points to you. I could not change direction even if I wanted to."

Tem stared into his eyes, losing herself in those bottomless black pools.

Her compass pointed to him too. It always had. They were drawn together by something bigger than themselves—something neither of them could control or reverse. Tem knew the future would not be easy for them. But she also knew there was nobody else she wanted a future with. It was the easiest thing in the world to lean in and kiss him again.

Caspen's lips were soft, his body hard.

Even beneath his mask of restraint, Tem could feel how much he wanted her. His skin was just as hot as the flames in the fireplace, singeing her wherever she touched him. Rather than try to undress him again, Tem undressed herself, pulling off the white linen and letting it fall to the ground. Caspen's eyes slid over her naked body, drinking in every inch of her skin.

Beautiful.

Suddenly, the barrier between them was down. His voice returned to her mind and, with it, his entire presence. Tem welcomed him easily, opening up her consciousness to accommodate his, savoring the way his mind intertwined with hers. Caspen's hands went to her waist, tracing her curves with just his fingertips. Then he dug into the soft flesh of her hips, lifting her and setting her on the bed.

This time when Tem pulled down his trousers, he didn't stop her. As soon as his cock was exposed, she leaned forward to taste him. Caspen held her back, remaining standing at the edge of the bed.

Turn around.

Tem turned around. A moment later, his hands were on her shoulders, pulling her down so she was flat on her back, her neck arched over the edge of the mattress. Caspen brushed a single finger along her throat, coaxing her head back even farther. From this angle, he looked like a monument. For him, the view was even better. Tem wondered if he liked her this way—her whole body laid out before him, every inch of her exposed for him to see. Caspen cradled her head in his hands.

Hold still for me.

Tem relaxed into his grip as his thumbs framed the center of her throat. Slowly, patiently, he slid his cock into her mouth. She closed her eyes as he went deeper, letting him hold her in place, content to do nothing but feel how he filled her.

In and out, in and out, steady as a heartbeat.

The claw began to pulse, and immediately, Tem was aroused. Her nipples peaked, and she touched them tentatively.

Yes, Tem.

She remembered that Caspen was watching her—that she had his undivided attention—that he was looking down at everything she was doing. The thought was electrifying.

Tem squeezed her breasts. Perhaps it was her imagination, but she swore Caspen became even harder. His cock was like marble in her throat, a formidable column in limitless motion. The pulses were relentless; her back arched as her clitoris throbbed with need.

Take it out.

Tem felt for the tip of the claw, hooking her finger around it and pulling it out.

Touch yourself.

Caspen's commands were sharp and desperate. He *needed* this.

Tem had to concentrate in order to obey. It required all her focus to keep her throat relaxed for him while using her hands on herself. But after a moment, it became second nature. There was nothing easier than bringing herself pleasure, and there was nothing better than doing it in front of Caspen. The room grew warmer as she slipped her fingers deep between her legs. Caspen groaned, his cock pushing even farther into her mouth. His hands left her neck and found her breasts, teasing her nipples and flicking them with his fingers.

She moaned around his cock. It was nearly agony to be stimulated in so many places at once. Being with Caspen was always like this—always new, always overwhelming, almost too much for her to handle. But Tem liked it that way. She liked how Caspen pushed her to her limits, because she knew she did the same to him. Their relationship had never been one-sided; he was just as addicted as she was.

Suddenly, Caspen's fingers joined hers. The angle of his cock changed as he leaned down over her, cupping her hands with his and pushing them both deeper. Tem relinquished control, letting him guide her, letting him pump their fingers in and out together. But soon, even that wasn't enough. Caspen's hands gripped her thighs, pulling them all the way apart. He leaned down even farther, and she lifted her hips to meet him. His tongue found the very center of her, and Tem slipped away into paradise.

There was nowhere to hide, no way to resist. Tem could only surrender to the suffocating *closeness*, threading her fingers into Caspen's hair and holding his head between her legs so he was just as anchored as she was. His cock was all the way down her throat. His torso was flat against hers, his body pressing her into the bed. They were perfectly aligned—an endless circle of completion with no beginning and no end. They were one body. There was no difference between her needs and his. She used him just as he used her, both of them experiencing pleasure in a never-ending loop. Caspen's teeth teased her clitoris as his tongue sank into her wetness. His groans vibrated against her chest, his ascension imminent.

Tem could tell Caspen was close. Yet she had to know: *Do I have you?*

His fingers contracted on her thighs. *You have me.*

A split second later, Caspen came.

For the first time, Tem tasted him—*all* of him. His cum was warm and soft and *smooth*, flowing down her throat like melted gold. She swallowed it all, eager to possess everything he was willing to give her. His cock was still in her mouth when her own orgasm arrived. Caspen groaned again, and Tem knew he was swallowing her too. She shuddered as he licked her, savoring her wetness with deep, sensual strokes. Then he stood upright, pulling his cock slowly out of her mouth. When he finally released her, Tem sat up, turning to look at him.

His eyes were black, his chest slick with sweat. Tem was sweating too, she realized, and her neck ached from holding such an unnatural angle for so long. But she didn't mind. She liked feeling the effects of sex on her body—liked the way Caspen left his mark on her.

He was already reaching for her, pulling her into a kiss.

They kissed slowly, discovering the way they tasted together. Tem sucked gently on his lower lip. He did the same. Their mouths became gorgeously intertwined, and Tem could feel his tongue splitting in two as smoke rose from his shoulders. She kissed him deeper, pressing her body fully against his torso as his hands tangled in her hair. There was only one thing she wanted, and she spoke it into his mind:

More.

But Caspen pulled away.

"I already told you, Tem. We should not."

His eyes were shut—she knew he was too scared to look at her. Smoke was curling around his body in probing tendrils, and the air felt as if it were on fire.

Tem placed a reassuring hand on his chest. "Please, Caspen. Try."

He didn't move.

She dropped her voice to a whisper. "Try for me."

He was still for another long moment. A low, steady hiss filled the room. Then he opened his eyes. "I cannot guarantee your safety."

She nodded. "I know."

Tem knew he would yield. He wanted her too badly to resist. Still, it felt like time slowed to a crawl as Caspen cupped her face in his hands and looked her directly in the eye. His thoughts came to her in a devout whisper: *Kora herself could not sway me as you do.*

Tem smiled. *Fuck me, Caspen. Now.*

He smiled too, and she saw the beginnings of his fangs.

They fell back onto the mattress as Caspen centered himself between her legs. His lips were once more on hers, the head of his cock just beginning to enter her.

And how shall I fuck you?

Slowly.

Caspen slid inside her with unhurried, leisurely grace. Tem moaned at his poignant pace. It felt so unbelievably good, she barely heard him as he lowered his lips to her ear and said, "Tell me what you like."

He'd never asked her that before. Their lessons in the cave had always been about him and, by extension, the prince. Anything Caspen knew about her sexual preferences had been learned through their experiences together. She couldn't believe he was asking her, point blank, what she liked in bed.

"I like it when you can't resist me."

He kissed her jaw. "What else?"

"I like it when you turn me on in public." She was referring to the claw.

"What else?" He murmured it against her skin, burying himself in her in every way possible.

"I like it when you make me come."

Caspen brought his lips once more to her ear. "That is not difficult to do."

He was still fucking her slowly, as if he had all the time in the world to do so. Tem had no idea it could feel like this—that it wasn't always wild and fast and desperate. It was one thing to feel desired, another entirely to feel cherished. Caspen demonstrated his love with every slow thrust, matching his movements to her breathing until she was practically in a trance. He kissed her neck, arching it back so she was vulnerable—yet secure—in his arms.

Tem had never been this wet before. Now she understood what it meant to truly take him, to receive his cock the way it was meant to be received—all the way to the base, thrust after merciless deep thrust. Heat rose on her cheeks, her whole body covered in a fine sheen of sweat. She felt flushed, as if she had a fever.

"Tell me what you like," she managed to whisper.

Caspen smiled. "I like it when you say my name."

Tem crossed her legs around him, pulling him even deeper. "What else?"

"I like it when you cannot catch your breath."

She couldn't catch it right now. "What else?"

"I like the sounds you make when I fuck you quickly."

Despite what Caspen said, he didn't fuck her quickly. He kept doing what *she* liked while telling her what *he* liked. It was exactly what Tem wanted from him, and it only turned her on even more.

Caspen's hand went between her legs. He massaged her clitoris gently, syncing the motion with his thrusts so that every time he went all the way inside her, his fingers applied even more pressure. It was almost beyond what Tem could handle.

"I *know* you like that," Caspen said quietly.

Tem couldn't even nod. He was guiding her toward her climax—getting her ready for release. His eyes were black pools, watching her in complete rapture. She wanted to come for him, to show him how devoted she was to their union—to show him that she was *his*.

Just when she was moments away, Caspen retreated, rolling onto his back. "Ride me," he ordered.

Tem obeyed, straddling him and sinking down onto his cock with a shameless moan. She jerked her hips quickly, chasing the euphoria she knew was imminent. They were surrounded by smoke: Caspen was alternating between shutting his eyes and staring at her neck, and she knew he was fighting to stay in control. Tem would not make it easy for him.

Her orgasm was building, building, *building* inside her—growing with ferocious determination, threatening to drown her in its insistency. She was seconds away again, and this time, she would let nothing stop her. Tem dug her fingernails into Caspen's skin, anchoring herself in the moment. It was heaven to ride him like this, to take ownership over her own pleasure and get herself where she needed to go.

Tem cried out as she soared into ecstasy.

The moment she finished, a change came over Caspen, and she knew he was done holding back. He grabbed her breasts so hard that she yelped. The second she did so, he released her, skimming his palms down the curve of her waist and squeezing her ass with both hands.

"I can't keep up with you," she gasped.

At her words, Caspen sat up straight, wrapping his arms around her and pulling her tightly against him. For a moment, they were both perfectly still, their lips centimeters apart, their bodies intrinsically intertwined. Tem could feel Caspen's heart beating steadily in his chest, so much slower than her own, which was galloping like a wild horse. She felt knowledge in his heartbeat—a deep, vast *knowing* that had been around far longer than she was alive and would exist far past her death. She wondered how long that heart had been beating.

Then Caspen arched his hips, penetrating her rhythmically from below. He held her gaze, watching her calmly as her breath hitched with every thrust.

"Please, Caspen," she breathed.

Tem didn't even know what she was begging for.

His grip tightened, holding her in place as he thrust into her again and again. She was on top but he was in control, setting the pace like he always did. Tem shut her eyes and moaned, surrendering to him because it felt too good not too, surrendering to him because she had no other choice.

"Tell me," she gasped. "Tell me how you feel about me." She needed to hear him say it. Now, while they were joined together.

Caspen didn't hesitate. "I am undone by you," he said. "I crave your scent, your skin, your voice. I think about you all the time, to the point of destruction. You are unbearably overwhelming. I cannot resist you no matter how hard I try."

To hear Caspen describe her in the exact way she felt about him was unfathomable. Tem wanted to hear more.

Before she could ask for it, Caspen was already speaking, his words accentuated with every thrust. "I am afraid of how much you mean to me. You occupy every inch of my mind. If anyone ever hurts you, I will rip them apart. No one compares to you. No basilisk or human has ever captivated me the way you do. I want to fuck you all the time. I want to come inside you."

His pace was increasing. Tem couldn't breathe.

"You."

Thrust.

"Are."

Thrust.

"Perfect."

This time when she came, he spoke a command into her mind:

Open your mouth.

Tem did so without question.

Caspen's hand wrapped around her throat, arching her neck back so he could position his face directly over hers. He opened his mouth but didn't kiss her. Instead, he made a guttural sound—something between a hiss and a growl, something completely and undeniably inhuman. Tem felt him come at the exact same time as a black liquid emerged from his mouth.

Tem's eyes stayed wide open as the substance dripped down the back of her throat.

It tasted like smoke.

When the last of the liquid had slid from his mouth to hers, Caspen finally kissed her. He was soaked with sweat, and so was Tem. Their combined wetness was spreading all over their legs, but neither of them bothered to clean it up. There was no point; Tem liked being covered in him. The vibrations of their union ebbed away slowly, and it wasn't until the air began to cool that Tem finally asked, "What was that?"

The gold was returning to Caspen's eyes. He hooked a single finger through the chain around her neck, pulling her closer.

"My venom."

"Your *venom?*"

"Yes."

"But won't that *kill* me?"

Caspen scoffed. "Of course not."

Tem sat up straight, hardening her voice. "Don't you *dare* make me feel stupid for asking that. Everyone knows basilisk venom is lethal."

Caspen's expression softened. "My venom is only lethal if I bite you. It is harmless on its own."

"*What?*"

This was complete news to Tem. All her life, she'd been raised to think that basilisk venom was deadly.

"Venom is fatal when administered straight from the fang," Caspen continued.

"So I'm not going to die?"

He pressed his lips to her neck. "Not from what I just did."

Tem felt a sudden swoop of anticipation. What *had* he just done? She'd never heard of a basilisk giving its venom to a human, even if it wasn't lethal. He'd told her to open her mouth, and she had obeyed. No part of her had hesitated to follow his order because she trusted him. It was that simple. But was she foolish for doing so?

She pushed him away. "You should have asked me first."

Caspen frowned.

Tem continued before he could. "You can't just decide what to do to me. I deserve an equal say."

"I cannot consult you on every single decision I make, Tem."

"You can when your decisions concern my body."

He didn't respond.

"I would have said yes, Caspen," Tem whispered. "To anything you asked. I always say yes to you. So just ask next time."

He looked at her finally. "Very well," he said quietly. "I will ask next time."

Tem nodded. Then, "But what…exactly did you do?"

"I already told you. I gave you my venom."

"I know *what* you did. But why did you do it?"

Caspen's eyes met hers. "You are not safe in my world, Tem. Every time you come here, it is a risk."

Tem knew her excursions under the mountain were dangerous. But she also knew they were worth it. "*You* keep me safe," she said.

He shook his head. "I am not always here. You were alone with Rowe tonight."

"He didn't do anything."

"Only because I was nearby. Next time, he will not hesitate."

"To do what?"

"To crest you."

Tem frowned. Crest her? It wasn't a term she'd heard before. "What does that mean?"

Instead of answering, Caspen lifted her off his lap and set her next to him on the bed. Anticipation slipped down her spine as he said, "The crest is a way for a basilisk to gain power."

Tem mulled this over. Basilisks drew their power from sex. Was he worried Rowe was going to have sex with her?

"Caspen." She laid her palm on his shoulder, leaning in. "Nothing happened between us. I promise."

He shook his head. "The crest is not sex."

"Then how does it work?"

"Limited contact is required for the crest. Rowe would only need to touch you"—as if to demonstrate, Caspen wrapped his hand around her throat before finishing quietly— "in order to crest you. When you are crested, you are forced to orgasm. It is a violent, nonconsensual act. My venom will protect you from this."

"But why would Rowe want to give me an orgasm?"

"Think of it as taking, not as giving."

"I don't understand," Tem said.

"The crest is a way to extract power from a human. When you climax, the basilisk who crested you becomes stronger. Rowe wishes to draw power from you."

"Can't he crest anybody? Why me?"

"He can." Anger crept into Caspen's voice. "But I took something dear to him. He wishes to do the same to me."

"What did you take?"

Caspen didn't answer.

Revenge is already mine to seek.

Tem used the pause to sort through her thoughts. She was struck again by how little she knew of Caspen's world and how out of step she was in it. There were untold dangers around every corner here—dangers she couldn't anticipate because she didn't know they existed in the first place. It was a problem that was beginning to feel insurmountable. She understood that she was at a disadvantage—that Caspen often had to act in her best interests, without her knowledge. But she didn't always like the way he did it. And it wasn't the first time; the stone statues of Jonathan and Christopher flashed through her mind. Yet another decision Caspen had made to protect her. Tem still considered herself responsible for their deaths. She probably always would.

Tem needed to know more. But Caspen clearly didn't enjoy this line of questioning. This conversation was a minefield, and it was becoming increasingly impossible to navigate it.

She counted thirty long seconds before asking, "Why have you never crested me?"

"Because it is a violation."

"I want you to do it."

Caspen shifted so they were facing each other. "No, Tem."

"Why? Does your venom prevent it?"

"My venom prevents anyone else from cresting you. Technically, I still could. But I would never do so, Tem. You do not deserve that."

"Are you saying it'll hurt?"

"Not at all. But it is still a form of abuse."

Tem had already made up her mind. Experiencing an orgasm from Caspen in such a way would surely be incredible. She needed to know how it felt. "Do it," she said again.

But Caspen was shaking his head. "There is more to it, Tem. The crest forms a bond between human and basilisk. One that cannot be broken."

"Aren't we already bonded?"

"Not in this way. If I crested you, you would be compelled to do what I say, always. It would remove your agency."

Tem frowned. She didn't like the sound of that.

Caspen drove his point home. "I could give you any order, and you would have to obey. If I told you to stab yourself with a knife, you would do so without hesitation."

"You would never tell me to do that."

"Of course not. But the bond extends beyond verbal suggestion. If I were starving and there was no food, you would cut off your arm to feed me, whether I ordered you to or not."

Tem made a face. "Ew."

A smile twitched Caspen's lips. "Precisely. Ew."

They were silent for a moment.

"Can you crest other basilisks?" she asked.

"It is forbidden for a basilisk to crest another basilisk. It is only meant for—"

"Humans," Tem finished the thought. Of course it was.

"Yes." Caspen studied her face in the flickering firelight. "Humans can withstand the crest because you are meant to give us power. Basilisks are not meant to dominate each other. It is an abomination of nature to crest our own kind."

"But it's possible, right?"

"Yes," he said again, quietly this time. "It is possible."

Something about his tone made Tem ask, "Have you ever done it?"

His jaw locked. Tem tried to ignore the sharp stab of jealousy that shot through her at the thought of him using the crest on someone else.

"Caspen," she whispered, fearing his response. "Is there a basilisk who is bound to you?"

To her surprise, he said, "No."

Tem thought he might elaborate, but he didn't. There was only one thing left to ask. "What happens to a basilisk when they're crested?"

Caspen took an eternity to answer.

"They die."

CHAPTER EIGHTEEN

⸺••✳••⸺

T EM WANTED TO KNOW MORE. *NEEDED* TO KNOW MORE.

But she feared she had already asked too much—probed too deep into Caspen's past after an already stressful evening—and he was on the brink of shutting down because of it.

She pressed her lips to his cheek.

"We don't have to talk about it right now," she murmured. Her wording was purposeful; Tem wanted, without a doubt, to talk about it at some point. But it would do no good to push Caspen any further. They had both been through enough tonight.

Tem shifted closer to him, wrapping her arms around his neck. He relaxed against her, and for a moment, neither of them spoke. Then Caspen murmured, "You should go home, Tem."

Her stomach flipped. She pulled away. "Are you upset? I didn't meant to—"

"I am not upset." At the look on her face, he softened his tone. "I promise I am not upset, Tem. But it is true that you should go home."

Tem frowned. They were engaged, or nearly so. She had hoped they would stay together at least until the morning. "But why?"

"The quivers have called a council meeting. I must attend."

Tem had already asked too many questions tonight. But Caspen seemed far more willing to discuss this topic, so she asked another.

"What's the meeting about?"

"Me."

"Oh."

Tem touched his shoulder. "Are you sure I should leave? I could wait for you."

He shook his head. "I do not want you here alone."

Tem had no rebuttal for that. After what happened with Rowe earlier, she could hardly argue she'd be safe. "What will happen at the meeting?" she asked.

Caspen cupped her hip with his hand. Despite telling her she should leave, he didn't seem eager to get rid of her. "My recent…exploits…will be discussed."

Tem thought of the golden claw around her neck. Surely, the quivers would have plenty to say about the fact that Caspen had proposed to a human. And there were also the murders of Jonathan and Christopher to contend with.

Tem shifted even closer. "Will you get in trouble?" she whispered.

Caspen's lips skimmed her shoulder. "Perhaps."

Tem climbed back onto his lap, touching just the tip of her finger to the head of his cock, which was already hard. "What will happen to you?"

"That is up to the king to decide."

Tem paused. "I thought you were the Serpent King."

To her surprise, Caspen chuckled softly. "Only humans call me that. It has no bearing on my actual title."

This was news to Tem. Everyone referred to Caspen as the Serpent King. He was a legend—the entire village had talked about him since before Tem was born. There wasn't a single girl eligible for the training who didn't know his reputation.

"In that case." She angled her hips, lowering herself onto his cock. "What is your actual title?"

Caspen waited until she was fully seated before answering. "I am the son of the king."

Tem was a little too distracted by the way he felt inside her to fully absorb this information. But as she slowly began to slide herself up and down his cock, she managed to focus enough to say, "So…you're a prince?"

Caspen was equally distracted. His fingers were wrapped tightly around her thighs, guiding her movements. Eventually, he answered, "Yes. I am a prince."

Tem let that revelation sink in for a moment. It was absurd. She was involved with not one but *two* princes. *At the same time.* It was nothing she could have ever predicted for herself.

But she would marvel at that later. Right now, there was only one prince she wanted.

Caspen let her set the pace, kissing softly up her neck as she rode him. Tem used his shoulders to steady herself, gripping his warm skin while establishing a rhythm. She loved having sex like this: slowly, intimately. Caspen liked it too. He gazed at her with unfiltered adoration, pulling her closer every chance he could. His hands touched every part of her, brushing up her hips to caress her breasts, holding his palms flat so she could press her nipples against them each time she arched her back. He understood her implicitly, without being asked. He knew she wanted to gain experience—to learn what her body liked—to use him to do it. There was no ego when it came to her pleasure. Both of them wanted her to enjoy it.

Tem was getting close. Her clitoris was tender; her nipples were hard. She was thrusting quickly now, riding him desperately, eager to come. Caspen's fingers wound around the back of her neck. His other hand gripped her ass, yanking her hips against his in rapid succession.

That was all it took for her.

"*Caspen,*" she cried.

That was all it took for him.

Their climaxes fused together, rushing forward in a ferocious wave that threatened to drown them both. Tem would never get used to this: the raw exchange of energy that only sex could draw forth. They clung to each other, gasping, as the tide of their union flowed between them. Their faces were an inch apart. Tem brushed the tip of her tongue over his bottom lip, tasting the shadow of his venom. She bit him lightly, pulling his lip into her mouth.

Harder, Tem.

She clamped down, drawing blood. Caspen let out a rough grunt but didn't pull away. It felt natural to Tem—she wanted to taste every part of him. She already had his venom inside her. Why not his blood too?

Tem gently sucked his lip. When she drew away, she watched in fascination as the wound healed itself, just as Caspen had done for her.

He smiled. "Did you like that?"

She nodded.

"Good."

"Did you?"

"Yes."

"But I hurt you."

His smile only widened. "You can do anything you like to me, Tem. Trust I will enjoy it."

There was no mistaking the desire in Caspen's eyes. Tem watched it slowly fade as his pupils shrank and his eyes became golden once more. He pressed a light kiss to her shoulder.

"I will walk you out," he said.

Tem wanted to protest. She wanted to stay here with him forever. But she also knew that he had more pressing things to do—things that might affect their future. She supposed she had better let him do them.

Tem slid the claw back in. Caspen walked her out.

When they arrived at the head of the trail, Caspen pulled her into his arms and held her. They stood there, clasped together, his body the only thing keeping her warm.

"Will you tell me how the meeting goes?" she murmured against his chest.

"Yes," he murmured back. "But it will run quite long. Probably until morning."

"Wake me up."

"No." He shook his head. "You need sleep."

Tem didn't bother protesting. He was right; she needed sleep. It had been a harrowing twenty-four hours, and her adrenaline was running low. The thought of her cozy cottage bed was exceedingly appealing, and the thought of falling asleep even more so.

Caspen must have sensed this, because he kissed her on her forehead and said, "Go, Tem."

Tem went.

On the walk home, she realized she had no idea whether she was still in the competition—she'd left the castle before Leo had announced the final five girls. Now her heart performed a nervous swoop as she considered what the future might hold. She was one step away from being engaged to Caspen. But what if the council punished him? Or worse, punished her? Tem knew nothing of the ways of basilisks. If there were ramifications for an engagement such as theirs, she had no hope of predicting what they might be.

And then there was Leo.

What must he think of Tem? A student in love with her teacher. She would have to leave the competition if things progressed with Caspen. Her exit would undermine the entire elimination process. It was unheard of.

Or was it?

A conversation came back to her suddenly, striking her with the force of lightning:

"Has anyone ever left?" she asked.

"Once," Caspen said. "But she was not my student."

Why had that former student left? Tem wished she knew. She wished for a lot of things—for the council to approve her engagement, for Leo to forgive her, for her mother to live a life of leisure. But these were not wishes that would be granted tonight. For tonight, all Tem could do was go home and sleep. So she did.

The roosters crowed her awake.

Tem savored a few moments alone in the kitchen as she watched her mother tend to the garden. The festival would surely resume tonight. The Passing of the Crown was in a few days, and the proper buildup would need to commence. Tonight's event was a significant one: the prince would kiss each of his remaining prospects in front of the entire village, during which the villagers would vote for their favorite girl. The voting was simple: whoever the crowd cheered for loudest was the winner.

On its surface, it seemed like a way to include the villagers in the elimination process. Whoever the prince picked would eventually be their queen after all. The subjects of the kingdom deserved to have a say in who ruled them. In reality, it had little to no bearing on who the prince actually chose. It was all for show—nothing more than a way to appease the crowd and make them feel as if they had a voice. For Tem, the *chicken shit girl*, it was just another public humiliation. That was if Leo hadn't already eliminated her.

Tem would never forget the way he'd looked at her last night—like she'd torn his heart straight from his chest. She hadn't known she was capable of making a man look at her like that. Now she held two men in the palms of her hands. Tem looked down at the sprinkle of freckles scattered across her skin. She thought about how she'd threaded those very same fingers through Caspen's hair as he'd buried his head between her legs last night.

The claw pulsed.

Tem reached for Caspen with her mind, but the corridor between them was shut. Before she could worry about this, she heard "How did it go, my dear?"

Her mother stood in the doorway. Tem had no idea how to answer her. The last thing she wanted was to shatter the illusion that they had hope for a better future. But she couldn't tell her mother where she stood with Leo—not when Tem herself barely knew.

"It went…better than expected."

Considering she'd expected the meeting between Caspen and Leo to result in bloodshed, it was the best thing she could think to say.

"That's wonderful."

Tem didn't reply.

The claw pulsed again, harder this time. It was so strong, she could feel her wetness beginning to drip down her legs. Tem excused herself hurriedly, desperate to be alone. The bathroom was closest, and by the time she reached it, the sensation was nearly unbearable.

Tem barely managed to shut the door before crossing to the only window, fully prepared to climb out and run back to the caves. All she could think about was getting to Caspen. She needed to taste him, to let him taste her. She wanted nothing more than to be in his chambers, alone, so they could touch each other without anyone watching. Tem bit her lip, ready to cry out—ready to finish. Suddenly, the pulses ceased.

Her mouth fell open in shock.

To be brought to the edge, to come so close to the brink, only to be denied, was nothing short of torture. She waited, her hands on the windowsill, desperate for just one more pulse.

But it didn't come.

Instead, Caspen whispered a single word into her mind:

Stay.

Tem stood there, frozen, staring out the open window. A breeze swept into the bathroom, snapping her from her stupor.

Caspen wanted her to stay. He had denied her, then rejected her. Was there a worse feeling in the world? They were supposed to be engaged; he was supposed to be getting the council's approval *right now.*

Tem held back tears as she closed the window, pulling the curtains shut. She didn't know what to do with herself. Half of her wanted to cry. The other half felt downright ravenous, as if she could rip apart raw meat with her teeth. She hated how much control Caspen had, even when he was nowhere near her. Just when she was about to return to the kitchen, another word came, sending her heart into a gallop:

Undress.

And just like that, he had ensnared her again.

She could not defy him. She didn't even want to.

Tem had no idea if Caspen could see her. But she pretended he could, undressing slowly, the way she did the first night they met. She undid the buttons of her nightdress one by one, pulling it from her shoulders and letting it drop to the floor. She slipped out of her underclothing, letting that fall too. When she was fully naked, she waited for another command, knowing it was only a matter of time before it came. Finally, it did:

Draw a bath.

She crossed to the bathtub, turning on the water and adding scented oils. She'd never been partial to baths. But this was one she knew she would enjoy.

Tem sat in the tub as it filled, watching as the bubbles rose up her legs. The pulse began again, coaxing her back into its familiar warmth. She leaned against the white porcelain, arching her neck. Goose bumps dotted her skin, and her nipples became so hard that they hurt. She placed her palms over them tentatively, cupping her breasts in her hands.

Squeeze.

She did it, and it was heaven.

Again.

This time, she moaned, the sound disappearing beneath the tumble of the running water. Her whole body felt as if it were made of glass, as if she might shatter at the slightest provocation.

Do you like doing that for me?

Yes.

What else would you do for me, Tem? Show me.

Tem dipped her hands into the bath, wetting them with oil and water. Then she touched her breasts again, rubbing them gently, picturing Caspen in front of her, imagining he was watching her every move. The oil was slick and smelled of roses. She softened her nipples, then hardened them again, feeling Caspen's desire grow to match her own.

She wished he would come to her. She wished he was here to see her like this, to place his hands over hers and squeeze as hard as he liked.

Take it out.

She hesitated.

Do it, Tem. Right now.

Tem didn't want to remove the claw; she liked the way it filled her. But she didn't want to disobey him either, so she hooked her finger along its curve and pulled it from between her legs. Even taking it out felt good, and she sighed at the emptiness.

Lick it.

Tem didn't hesitate. She touched the claw to her lips, starting from the thinner end and running her tongue slowly along its curve. As she did it, she tasted herself, and somehow, she also tasted Caspen. It was only once she reached the end of the claw that she realized it had grown in her hand. Where before it could have fit in one palm, now she needed both hands to hold it. She stared, enraptured, as it changed shape into something she recognized: something long and hard and formidable. It was the most important part of Caspen—the part he trusted her to hold—and Tem was honored to hold it.

She took the end in her mouth, swirling her tongue around its wide tip, doing what she knew he liked. Then she took it all the way down her throat, slipping it in and out in a steady rhythm.

Faster.

Tem obeyed, propping her elbows on the side of the bathtub so she could take him as deep as possible. She did this until she sensed, rather than heard, when Caspen was close to finishing. A raw ache ran through her, and she recognized it as the twin to hers. Tem knew she had mere seconds before he came, so without hesitation, she pulled his length out of her mouth and slid it once more between her legs. She winced as she did so; the smooth stone was unforgiving—so much harder than his actual cock.

As soon as it was inside her, pleasure exploded in her mind. The swell was so undeniably strong that Tem cried out, throwing her head back in utter surrender, allowing his surge of gratification to obliterate every thought in her brain besides the one in his:

Mine.

Tem was still riding out her orgasm when their connection closed.

She lay back in the bathtub, panting, her body flushed with pleasure. She remained there until the bath water was cold, sitting in silence as the claw returned to its normal shape, pressing insistently against her clitoris. Tem rinsed herself before dressing and rejoining her mother in the kitchen.

The rest of the day passed in a slog of menial farm chores.

After the lightness of her orgasm, Tem found she was dreading the festival with every fiber of her being. She couldn't decide which was worse: getting eliminated from the competition and having to tell her mother she'd failed or staying in the competition and kissing Leo in front of the entire village. There were no good options here. It seemed like there never were.

By the time they were traipsing toward the village, Tem was sick with anticipation.

Night had fallen; the only light was the warm glow of the town square in the distance, which was lit up like a chandelier. By the time they reached the festival, the celebrations were well and truly underway. Colorful candles were strung from one side of the square to the other, giving the cobblestones a magical quality. The space was packed with vendors selling food, trinkets, and ribbons like the ones Vera always wore in her hair. The statues of Jonathan and Christopher had been removed—the only thing in the center of the square was the large wooden stage. Tem scanned the crowd for the one person she knew would settle her nerves.

As expected, Gabriel was by the mead.

"Gabriel," she said when she reached him. "Am I out?"

Gabriel threw his arm around her. He'd clearly started early. "Don't know, dearest. The prince didn't eliminate anyone."

"*What?* Why?"

He shrugged. "Nobody knows. Didn't even meet with half the basilisks. He had an argument with the king, then made everyone leave."

"He fought with his father?"

"He did indeed."

A chill rushed through Tem. It was because of her. It had to be. There was no other possible explanation as to why Leo hadn't proceeded with the elimination.

"Well, what *happened?*"

Gabriel was drinking his mead with the same arm that was around Tem's shoulders. She kept having to dodge his glass every time it went to his mouth.

"You sure ask a lot of questions."

"*Gabriel.*" She grabbed his arm, pulling him so they were face-to-face. "Focus. What did Leo say to Maximus?"

"You know," he said lightly, tapping the tip of her nose with his fingertip. "You're rather bossy tonight."

Tem sighed.

Gabriel pressed his lips to her cheek before answering. "I didn't hear what was said. I was in the kitchen. But I'm sure Vera knows."

Tem's eyes found Vera, who was standing on the edge of the square looking decidedly less superior than usual. Was she one of the girls whose basilisk never met with the prince? Tem remembered the jealousy on Vera's face when she saw Caspen touch her waist. Perhaps she was angry that her evening with Rowe had been cut short.

"I'd rather not talk to Vera," Tem muttered.

"You and me both."

Tem rolled her eyes, grabbing Gabriel's glass of mead and downing the rest of it in one gulp.

He gasped in mock surprise. "Thief."

"Oh, shut up. The next one's on me."

Gabriel laughed. "How very generous of you."

Everyone drank for free during the festival. The alcohol was provided by the royals, and it was notoriously strong. Tem and Gabriel spent the next hour flitting around the square, drinking far more than they should. For Tem, it was a way to distract herself from what might happen later. For Gabriel, it was just another weeknight.

They were on what felt like their tenth glass of mead when Caspen's presence loomed suddenly into her mind.

Tem.

Tem immediately spilled her drink onto the ground.

"Oy," Gabriel yelped as he leaped backward. "Careful!"

"Sorry," Tem muttered. To Caspen, she said: *How was the council meeting?*

A long pause.

Eventful.

It was a typical Caspen answer. Just enough to appease her—not enough to actually tell her what had happened.

Are you in trouble?

Another pause. *No.*

She had to trust he wasn't lying. Still, it seemed impossible that there would be no consequences for his actions. Tem decided to push the matter: *Will your quiver accept our engagement?*

This time, the pause lasted so long, Tem thought he might have closed the door between their minds. A flare of irritation snapped through her.

Caspen? Will they accept?

His voice came back to her. *On one condition.*

Which is?

His hesitation was palpable. She sent an insistent wave of impatience at him, making it clear she would not wait any longer.

Tell me.

Not now.

Why not now?

We will discuss it the next time you are here.

Tonight?

No. You will come to me tomorrow.

But we—

I have matters to attend to tonight, Tem.

But—

Caspen severed their connection.

A hot coil of anger curled inside Tem. She *hated* it when he did that. It made her feel helpless in a relationship where there was already a significant imbalance of power.

"Tem." Gabriel's arm was around her again, jolting her abruptly back to the present.

"What?"

"Mr. Jawline has arrived."

All the mead in the world couldn't prepare Tem for the sight of Leo. He was flanked by his father and Lord Chamberlain, his long legs closing the distance to the stage. Lilly followed close behind, and Tem wondered what she thought of all this. It must be strange to watch her brother go through a public courtship process. Then again, nothing the royals did was particularly normal.

"He looks sad," Gabriel whispered, pulling Tem from her thoughts.

Tem studied Leo's face. His mouth was a tight line, his eyes on the ground as he walked. A wave of tenderness flowed suddenly through her. The last thing she wanted was to see Leo sad. To think he might be sad because of her was unbearable.

Gabriel nudged her. "Guess you'll just have to cheer him up."

To Tem's surprise, she found that she wanted to. Before she could reply, Leo clapped his hands, and the crowd fell silent.

"Would the seven beautiful ladies I've had the pleasure of courting please do me the honor of joining me onstage?"

Tem watched as Vera nearly sprinted through the crowd. With a heavy eye roll, she handed Gabriel her mead and followed suit, falling into line behind the other girls. When they reached the stage, Lilly extended her hand to each girl, helping them up the steps. When her hand touched Tem's, she winked.

Tem didn't have a chance to wink back.

Leo's eyes were already on her as she ascended the steps, and Tem couldn't help but wonder what he was thinking. Was he angry? Or simply sad, as Gabriel had said?

The crowd was getting loud again; it seemed they couldn't stay calm for more than a few minutes at a time. Unlimited mead tended to have that effect. Their cheers only grew as the girls lined up in a row and Leo extended his hand to Vera, who was first in line. She took it eagerly, following him to the front of the stage. The crowd roared as they faced each other. Realization dawned.

Leo was going to use each kiss to decide who to eliminate.

It was even worse than the podiums. Was Tem about to be eliminated in front of the entire village? She couldn't imagine anything more embarrassing. Perhaps she should have expected this. The royals were heartless after all.

A sharp knife of jealousy twisted Tem's stomach as Leo placed his hands on Vera's waist. She remembered the prince's words from last night, whispered through a haze of hurt:

Am I to share you?

She was not the only one being shared. Leo had his own advantage in their silent battle of wills; he was not fully in her grasp, and she was an idiot to think he ever had been. Tem didn't care that they were in public; she wanted nothing more than to run forward and rip Leo's hands off Vera. Instead, she watched as he leaned in and kissed her straight on the lips.

The cheer of the crowd was deafening.

It was no surprise: Vera was the village favorite. Adored by every man, envied by every woman. Tem could never hope to compete with such undeniable allure. The kiss was short—but passionate—and when they finally broke apart, the cheer lasted for so long that Leo had to hold up his hands in protest, waving the crowd down to a reasonable level before reaching for the next in line. Leo kissed girl after girl. The crowd roared on.

The knife twisted deeper with every kiss.

By the time Leo got to the second-to-last girl, he didn't even bother looking at her. Instead, his eyes bore straight into Tem's as he leaned in. She held his gaze as they kissed, determined not to look away—determined not to let him faze her. It didn't matter that everyone was watching. It didn't matter that the crowd was cheering for the girl who was currently in Leo's arms. Tem didn't like watching him kiss anyone else. And she certainly didn't like the way he was flaunting it in front of her. It was especially unfair given the lengths she'd taken to keep her connection with Caspen a secret. Tem had never used that to make Leo jealous. Maybe she should have.

By the time Leo was headed her way, Tem was angry.

Only one thing would make her feel better. One thing would make Leo remember who they were to each other. Tem was glad Caspen was no longer in her mind. He didn't need to see the way she grabbed Leo's shoulders and yanked him closer. He didn't need to hear the moan that escaped her throat as she pressed her lips hungrily to his. Immediately, she could feel his cock growing hard. Tem wanted to touch it.

Instead, she kissed Leo with everything she had, allowing herself to give in to temptation, allowing herself to feel something for the human prince. After all, wasn't that what Leo wanted? For Tem to want him? Maybe she didn't want him in the same way she wanted Caspen; maybe her connection with Leo wasn't ethereal and otherworldly and *magical* the way it was with the basilisk. But it was real. It always had been. There was no denying that Tem was drawn to Leo just as he was drawn to her—that they needed each other in a way that couldn't be defined.

Leo wasn't perfect. And Tem liked that.

His body folded against hers, his fingers lacing deep into her curls. The slightest hint of whiskey lingered on his tongue. Tem drank it in—drank *him* in.

Leo kissed her for far longer than he kissed the other girls. There would be no mistaking his preference for her now, if there was ever a question to begin with. When Tem finally drew away, Leo barely let her go. His slate-gray eyes were inches from hers, and she saw nothing but victory in them. She knew the prince loved a challenge—that he viewed Caspen as a competitor, an *opponent,* and Tem as the prize to be won. She knew she'd given him exactly what he wanted. But perhaps, for once, it was what she wanted too.

"We kissed for too long," she whispered.

"Impossible," he breathed. "I'd kiss you forever if I could."

It was then that Tem noticed the crowd was silent.

There were no cheers for her like there were for Vera—no frenetic roar of approval. The villagers had one vote to cast, and it was not for Tem. There were only two people clapping for her: Gabriel and her mother. She couldn't pretend to be surprised.

Leo didn't acknowledge the silence. He simply guided Tem back to her place in line, pressing a kiss to her wrist before dropping her hand and turning to the girl beside her.

Leo leaned in, his angular face tilting to the side as he said, "Sorry, darling."

The girl stepped back in horror.

Tem flashed suddenly to her first night at the castle, when Leo had eliminated the girls in the exact same way. Everyone watched in silence as he walked farther down the line, stopping in front of a girl with red hair who immediately started crying. She fled the stage before he even had a chance to speak. Leo stood still for a moment, staring at the empty spot before him. Then he turned once more to the crowd.

"Thank you for your vote." He glanced at Vera, who preened insufferably at the end of the line. "Rest assured your voice has been heard."

The crowd cheered again. Several mead glasses met their deaths on the cobblestones. Without another word, Leo descended the stage to join his father, whose face was a mask of rage. Tem could only imagine what Maximus was thinking. To watch his son favor the town pariah was surely cause for fury. The king would not take kindly to Leo's insolence. It would strain their already fragile relationship and put Tem straight in Maximus's crosshairs—somewhere she had no desire to be. But these were worries for another time.

For now, mercifully, the show was over.

Tem filed off the stage with the other girls before finding her way back to Gabriel. He handed her a glass, which she immediately downed.

"I'd give it an eight," Gabriel said.

"Excuse me?"

"Your form," he said. "Eight out of ten."

"My *form?*"

"Bit too much tongue for me, but I suppose the prince might be into that. Next time, stand on your tiptoes. Otherwise, he's a touch too tall for you."

Tem let out an incredulous laugh as she realized he was rating her *kissing.* She knew it was just a way to distract her from her poor showing with the crowd. Gabriel always knew how to make everything better. Tem never had a lot in life. But she'd always had him.

They spent the rest of the evening standing at the edge of the crowd, playing a drinking game where they took a sip whenever Vera fluttered her eyelashes at someone. Eventually, Tem's mother appeared by her side.

"It is getting late, my dear."

"Of course, Mother. See you at home."

Her mother shook her head. "I am staying in the village tonight."

"Oh."

Tem had forgotten that her mother was tending to the butcher's young daughter while her parents were out of town. The crowd's silence loomed once again in Tem's mind. How had it felt for her mother to witness Tem's public disgrace? A slick thread of guilt tightened her throat. It was an old wound, split open again.

On a whim, Tem embraced her mother. They rarely touched in such a way. Tem could count on one hand the times they'd held each other for longer than a brief moment. If her mother was surprised, she didn't show it. She simply tucked her head against Tem's shoulder and squeezed her back.

When they drew apart, Tem said, "See you tomorrow, Mother."

Her mother gave her a small smile. Then she left.

"In that case." Gabriel wiggled his eyebrows at her. "Horseman?"

Tem sighed. They hardly needed to drink more. But her mother wouldn't be home, and she couldn't go see Caspen. What else was she supposed to do with her evening?

"Horseman."

They stumbled to the bar together. When they reached it, people were already trickling in from the festival. Gabriel pressed a kiss to her cheek. "First round's on me."

Tem didn't protest.

She slid into their favorite booth, ignoring what felt like everyone's eyes on her. No doubt people would be talking about tonight's events for a long time.

Her thoughts returned to the conversation with Caspen and the one condition under which his quiver would accept their engagement. What kind of condition could it possibly be? And what "matters" did he have to attend to in the meantime? A wave of annoyance swept through Tem. She wasn't over the fact that he'd cut off their connection with no warning. It was unacceptable that he chose to exercise his power in such a one-sided way. They couldn't have a proper relationship if he didn't communicate with her. Tem was always in the dark, always the last to know. It had to stop.

Gabriel slid into the booth and handed her a beer. "Here you are, dearest."

"Thanks." She managed a smile. They clinked their glasses and took a sip together.

"You know." Gabriel leaned closer. "Old Steve is looking pretty good tonight."

"Not another word."

"I'm just saying. If it doesn't work out with the prince, you can marry him. I bet *he* likes a bit of tongue."

"Can't I just marry you?"

"Please, Tem. I'm swimming in stable boys."

Tem sighed.

"Although," he said musingly. "You might try fucking in a carriage sometime. *Roomy.*"

Tem rolled her eyes. Then she looked at Gabriel. He was drunk, and so was she, and for some reason, all she wanted was to tell him everything that was happening in her life. She wanted to tell him about the claw, about her bond with Caspen, about Jonathan and Christopher. The secrets were beginning to eat her alive.

"Gabriel," she said slowly. "What if I told you I was responsible for something bad?"

He took a long swallow of beer. His glass was half-empty already. "I'd be intrigued."

"What if it was really, *really* bad?"

Gabriel shrugged. "I'd be very, *very* intrigued."

Tem took a gulp of beer. Was she really about to do this?

Before she could decide, Gabriel held up his hand. "Tem," he said in a pseudo-serious tone. "If you're going to tell me something important, I need hard liquor."

She had to smile at that. Quite frankly, she needed hard liquor in order to tell him. "Fine."

Tem stood and made her way to the bar, where Old Steve was leering at her. Before Tem could rummage in her pocket for coins, she heard:

"It's on me."

Tem's blood ran cold. She'd recognize that voice anywhere.

Leo.

CHAPTER NINETEEN

EO'S LANKY FRAME WAS LEANING CASUALLY AGAINST THE BAR, HIS EYEBROWS arched in preemptive amusement.

"*What are you doing here?*" Tem hissed.

"Buying you a drink. I thought that was obvious."

"You can't be here."

"Yet here I am."

"Leo." She grabbed his arm and yanked him toward the door. "Get out."

"You know I love it when you order me around." His hands wrapped firmly around her waist, pulling her back. "But I'm afraid I'll have to disobey." Leo corralled Tem easily, pressing her body against the bar with his.

She tried to elbow him, but it was no use. He had her pinned.

"You look beautiful, by the way."

"*By the way?* Is my beauty an afterthought?"

Leo's cheeks cracked into a smile. "So difficult to please."

Tem was still trying to wrestle herself away from him. "You've always been terrible at compliments."

"If you say so."

"How did you know where to find me anyway?" she snapped.

"It's a small village, Tem. I asked the first person I saw."

"Remind me to kill them."

"And be an accomplice to murder? Unlikely."

She glared up at him, but he only smiled wider. "You're gorgeous when you're angry," he purred.

"I'm gorgeous all the time. Now tell me what you're doing here."

A pause. Leo's smile faltered. "I'm afraid my father and I had a…disagreement."

"What kind of disagreement?"

"I'd rather not say."

"I'd rather you did."

"Your friend is waiting, Tem. Shouldn't you introduce me?"

"Shouldn't you go somewhere else?"

"I chose to come here."

"But *why?*"

Another pause. Then: "I wanted to see you."

Tem sighed. Leo always wanted to see her. But did she want to see him? It wasn't exactly convenient timing; she was about to confide in Gabriel. That would now have to wait. There was no doubt that her kiss with Leo had awakened something in Tem— something she was willing to explore. And from the way the prince was holding her, she knew he wouldn't leave no matter what she said.

"*Kora.*" She relented finally. "But you're paying for *every* round, not just the next one."

Leo grinned. "Naturally."

Tem rolled her eyes and, with one final shove, disentangled herself from his arms. "Whiskey," she said simply. Then she left him at the bar and huffed into the booth next to Gabriel.

"Is that who I think it is?" Gabriel asked.

"Yes," snapped Tem.

"What the *hell* is he doing here?"

"He had a fight with his father."

"Daddy issues," Gabriel said knowingly. "Sexy."

"Just shut up and enjoy your free drinks."

Gabriel was still smiling when Leo returned to the table and handed them each a whiskey.

"Thanks…Your Highness."

Leo laughed. "Please. Call me Leo."

"Call me Gabriel."

"I certainly shall."

"What's with the hardware?" Gabriel pointed at Leo's mouth, where his gold teeth glinted in the dim light of the bar.

Tem elbowed Gabriel. But Leo only smiled wider, showing the full extent of the metal.

"They're traditional," Leo answered. "The men in my family get them when we turn twenty, among other gifts."

"Not the women?"

He shrugged. "The women get gold in other forms. Jewelry, usually."

"Must be nice to be able to afford gold."

"*Gabriel,*" Tem said.

Leo touched her leg, halting her protest. "It is nice," he said carefully. "But I don't pretend to have earned it."

"Hm." Gabriel glanced at Tem. "I like him."

"That makes one of us."

Leo grinned at her. "Your opinion of me is more favorable than you let on."

Tem rolled her eyes. "And how do you know that?"

"I'm here, aren't I? You let me stay."

"You were a damsel in distress. I had to."

"You *chose* to, and I am very grateful."

Tem rolled her eyes again. His hand was still on her thigh. "Don't get used to it," she whispered.

He smiled again, flashing those gold teeth. "I certainly won't."

Gabriel leaned forward. "*My* opinion is *very* favorable, if it helps."

Tem kicked him under the table. "It doesn't."

Leo shot him a wink. "It *does*, thank you."

Tem kicked him too.

By the time the Horseman was shutting down, Leo had paid for four more rounds, and Tem was having trouble seeing straight. Gabriel was no better off. He kept throwing his arms around Tem and Leo, declaring that he would be the best man at their wedding.

"We'd be honored," Leo said every time.

"That would require a wedding," Tem said every time too.

Leo only laughed.

They left the bar together, all linking arms. Gabriel extracted himself with some difficulty before saluting them with a flourish.

"It's been a pleasure, gentlemen."

"I'm a lady," Tem said.

"Barely."

She smacked his chest.

Leo held her back. "That's our best man you're accosting."

"*That would require a wedding*," Tem insisted.

In response, Leo pressed his lips to her cheek.

"Get a *room*," Gabriel crooned, wiggling his fingers at them before disappearing into the darkness.

"I intend to," Leo said against her ear.

Before Tem could smack him too, another voice cut through the air:

"*Thelonius.*"

They both turned.

There, mounted on a horse whose shiny white coat was completely at odds with the dismal grime of the street, was Maximus.

Leo immediately threw his arm in front of Tem, pushing her behind him as the king dismounted. He strode toward them with fury in his eyes, his gaze flicking first to Tem, then back to Leo.

"Running away is for children," Maximus said. "I expected more from you."

Leo lifted his chin in defiance.

"You remind me of my youth every day. It shouldn't surprise you when I act my age."

"Enough. You will return with me now."

"I don't think so."

Maximus looked once again at Tem. "Is this what drew you away? The chicken girl?"

Tem opened her mouth, but Leo was already defending her.

"Her name is Temperance. You might want to learn it, considering she's going to be my wife."

"I will take away your title before I let you choose her."

"And crown Lilly king? That's rather progressive of you. I didn't realize you'd changed your stance on women in leadership. Mother would be so proud."

"Enough."

But Leo wasn't done. "I will make my own choice, Father. There's nothing you can—"

"*Enough*," the king spat out. "You will return with me now."

Leo went completely rigid, his fingers twisting tightly in the fabric of Tem's dress, still holding her behind him. His next words were so quiet—so *deadly*—that Tem felt a chill go down her spine as he said, "I will return when I fucking well feel like it."

Something dangerous glimmered in Maximus's eyes. He stepped forward—just a single step—to say, "Ignorant boy. You will face consequences for this."

Leo stood his ground. "Then I will face them with my wife."

Father and son stared at each other.

After an endless moment, Maximus turned, mounted his horse, and was gone.

They stood alone in the street, Leo's gaze locked on his father's retreating form. Tem placed her palm tentatively between his shoulder blades, feeling the tension in his body.

On a whim, she said, "Take me somewhere, Leo."

He turned slowly to face her. "Where shall I take you, Tem?"

"I don't know. Impress me."

Leo tilted his head, considering her request. "Very well."

He held out his hand. Tem took it.

They wound through the streets together, heading toward the church. When they reached it, they didn't walk up the steps, like Tem figured they would. Instead, Leo took her around the back, where a sprawling graveyard stretched to the top of a sloping hill. She nudged his shoulder.

"Are you planning to kill me?"

A small smile. "Not tonight, Tem."

They walked slowly among the graves. For once, Tem was content to let Leo lead. He seemed to know where he was going, although she couldn't imagine who would be buried here. His mother, the queen, was the only person in his immediate family who was dead. Surely, the royals had their own crypts deep beneath the castle. There would be no reason to bury the queen among the villagers.

Eventually, they stopped. But not at a grave.

Instead they had ascended the hill overlooking the graveyard, where a bench sat beneath a drooping willow tree. Leo's gaze was trained on the trunk. Tem squinted to see what he was looking at. Two letters were carved into the whorled wood:

E + L.

Something tugged at Tem's heart.

"E and L?" Tem whispered, although she already knew.

Leo stared at the tree, his eyes unfocused. "Evelyn and Leo," he whispered back.

Evelyn was not a mistake.

"Who was she?"

"She was…important to me."

Tem squeezed his hand.

"What happened to her?"

Leo's jaw tightened. He turned to face Tem. "A prince is allowed to bed whoever he likes before the training. It's encouraged, actually—the more the better. But relationships are forbidden. I'm supposed to save commitment for my wife. So when I met Evelyn, I figured she would just be another girl in my bed. But she wasn't. She was…" He paused, and Tem could see the pain in his eyes. "…everything."

A long moment passed before he spoke again.

"We used to meet there"—he gestured at the bench—"to talk for hours. I'd never talked to anyone like that before. In the castle, everyone talks *at* me. Evelyn talked *to* me. And she listened. I think that's why I fell in love with her. Then my father found out."

The tug on Tem's heart intensified. "What did he do?" she asked despite herself.

"He didn't approve. He never does. Evelyn came from a family of fishermen. Her parents were dead; her aunt had raised her. She was a year older than me, so she wasn't eligible for the training. He told me I had to end it."

"And did you?"

"No," Leo said simply. "I didn't."

Tem turned that information over in her mind. Leo had courted a girl—a girl his father didn't approve of, a girl just like Tem. She understood now why Maximus was so against their relationship, why he insisted on keeping them apart. This was a pattern for Leo. It begged the obvious question:

"So…what happened?"

Leo sighed. "We made plans to run away."

That shocked Tem. "You were going to leave your family for her?"

"*Evelyn* was my family."

Tem felt a chill go down her spine. She looked up at Leo. His eyes held nothing but hurt. "You loved her," Tem whispered.

"Yes," he whispered back, his voice nearly breaking. "I certainly did."

Leo spoke with such finality that a small part of her soul was wounded by his words.

Tem tried to imagine Leo in love, Leo happy, Leo with Evelyn. The same knife of jealousy that had pierced her earlier twisted again in her now. *You don't care about him*, she reminded herself. *This is all for show.* Yet even as she thought it, Tem knew it wasn't true. She cared now, whether she wanted to or not.

Leo dropped her hand. He continued quietly, "The morning we were meant to leave, she didn't show up. Eventually, I figured she had changed her mind, and I left."

Tem stared at the carving on the tree. Just those two letters—nothing else. She knew if she waited, Leo would elaborate.

Still, the silence stretched on for minutes before he finally said, "I had my servants ask around about her. But she was gone."

"Where did she go?"

He shook his head. "I don't know." Leo paused, and his next words were a broken whisper. "I…still come here most mornings. Just in case."

He fell silent, and this time, Tem let the silence sit, wondering if she'd ever seen Evelyn at school. She'd never been particularly concerned with anyone in the grade above her; Tem's schooldays had been spent simply trying to survive. Perhaps Gabriel had known her. The village was small; it was entirely possible. But if Evelyn had gone away, there was no telling where she could be now.

Tem took a moment to consider what this part of Leo's past meant for their future. If he was still in love with Evelyn, his heart was closed off—not just to Tem but to anyone. The elimination process was pointless if he wasn't ready to fall in love again.

She thought about how Leo had been drawn to her from the very beginning—how he seemed to revel in the way their courtship got under his father's skin. What was the point in telling Tem about Evelyn if all it did was show her that Leo wasn't available, that he was using her? Was Tem just a placeholder—somewhere for the prince to store his pain while he worked through his grief? Did she even have a right to be angry if that were indeed the case?

"Why did you bring me here?" she asked softly.

Leo sighed. "Because you asked me to impress you. And the only thing that seems to impress you is honesty. So I'm trying to be truthful about my past." He paused, meeting her eye. "If it was a mistake, I pray you'll forgive me. But I want you to know who I am."

"It wasn't a mistake." Tem didn't think twice before the words left her mouth. She meant them.

Leo nodded. "I'm glad."

Tem stared up at him, every bone in her body wishing things were different. She wished they had more time to get to know each other—that perhaps she might reveal herself to him in the same way he had just revealed himself to her. Leo was being honest and open—something Caspen couldn't seem to accomplish.

Before she could decide how to move forward, Leo said, "You don't trust me, do you, Tem?"

She could only tell him the truth. "Not really."

Leo nodded, as if her answer didn't surprise him. "What can I do to change that?" he asked quietly.

Tem sighed. "I don't know, Leo. I'm not sure anything you do would change that."

There was another silence, and in it, Leo reached for her, touching the tips of his fingers to her waist. "I'd like to try."

The place where he touched her was warm. "Then tell me the truth," she whispered.

"About what?"

"Your intentions."

Leo tilted his head. "What do you mean?"

Tem gestured at the carving on the tree. "Are you only pursuing me because you know it will anger your father? Or do you really want me?"

Leo didn't answer at first. When he did, his voice was soft. "Both."

She knew it was the truth. "I don't like being used, Leo," Tem said quietly.

She expected him to reply right away.

Instead, he stepped closer, raising his other hand to cup her face gently in his palm. His gaze dropped to her mouth, and she thought he might kiss her. But he brushed the tip of his thumb over her bottom lip, so gently she barely felt it, so slowly an eternity passed by the time his finger trailed from one side to the other.

When it was over, Leo whispered, "Did you like that?" He was barely an inch away.

"Yes," Tem whispered back.

Leo smiled. "That's a start."

"Leo…"

But she couldn't finish. She couldn't possibly tell him that she still didn't trust him—not now, not when they were standing by the bench where he had sat with the first girl he ever loved, not when he had finally chosen to be vulnerable with her. Not when Tem was keeping so many secrets herself. So instead, she took his hand in hers, intertwining her fingers with his.

They stood together, hands clasped, the graveyard silent around them.

Tem didn't know how long they stayed there. It was bitterly cold by the time they left, and Leo took off his cloak, moving to place it over her shoulders.

Tem waved him away.

"But you're shivering," Leo said quietly.

"Then I'll shiver."

Hurt flashed across Leo's face.

"Very well."

With a jolt, Tem realized the gesture was genuine. She was so used to Leo's actions as moves on a chessboard; she almost couldn't tell when he was being real.

"Wait." She put her hand on his arm.

Leo paused, still holding his cloak. His eyes searched hers, deep apprehension in them.

"You can give it to me."

A shadow of Leo's smile returned, and he stepped closer.

Tem stayed perfectly still as he draped his cloak over her shoulders. He brushed his fingers along the nape of her neck, gently lifting her hair so her curls fell loosely down her back.

He looked so content as he did it—so undeniably fulfilled—that despite the warmth of his cloak, Tem got full-body chills.

Leo looked her in the eye. "I understand you don't need me to take care of you," he said quietly. "But it is my pleasure to do so."

Tem nodded, her throat suddenly tight.

She knew Leo liked to take care of her. She remembered how he'd paid for her drinks at the Horseman, how he always made sure she had enough to eat. Such gestures were how he built trust between them. But it only worked when Tem let him do it, and nothing could be more difficult.

Tem pulled his cloak tighter around her shoulders as they walked back toward the church. Did Leo wish he were giving Evelyn his cloak instead of Tem? And did Tem wish it were Caspen giving her his cloak instead of Leo? She didn't know anymore.

When they were once again standing on the main street, Leo looked at her. "What next?"

Tem looked back at him.

She knew he didn't want to go home. And normally, neither would Tem. But her mother was tending to the butcher's daughter, and Tem found she didn't want to be alone.

So she took the lead, guiding them wordlessly through the cobblestone streets, steadily approaching the edge of the village. Leo's shiny black shoes were out of place here; Tem found herself blushing as they reached her tiny cottage. If Leo thought her accommodations were depressing, he didn't say so. Instead, he followed Tem as she pushed through the garden gate, asking only:

"Are your parents not home?"

"I've never met my father," Tem said. "And my mother is tending to a child in the village."

Leo didn't respond.

As soon as they were inside, Tem pulled Leo's cloak off his shoulders and hung it on the coatrack before pointing at the kitchen table. "Sit."

Leo's lips twitched, but he didn't smile. "If you insist."

Tem knew her mother kept a stash of alcohol in the kitchen for the rare occasion when she needed a drink after a particularly long day on the farm. She searched for it while Leo sat, eventually locating the bottle in the cupboard behind the flour.

She held it up.

"Only if you'll join me," Leo said in reply.

Tem found two glasses and poured them full. She handed one to Leo.

"To Kora," she said.

"To Kora."

They clinked glasses, drinking together just as they had the first night they met. Leo downed his glass in one gulp. Tem refilled it immediately.

"Are you trying to get me drunk?" he asked, his teasing tone a shadow of what it usually was.

"You're already drunk."

"That I am."

Tem looked at him. His jaw was set, his body still tense. She didn't know how to comfort him, but she found that she wanted to.

"Your father is wrong, you know," she said quietly.

Leo looked at her. "No, he isn't."

"You don't even know what I was going to say."

"You were going to say that my father is wrong, that I'm not a child—that I'm capable of making my own decisions and that he should trust me to live my life the way I want to live it. But it's not true. I am being utterly selfish in choosing you. There will be consequences for my actions. And if I know my father, they will not be pleasant."

Tem took another sip of her drink. "I was *going* to say that you're not ignorant. You're one of the smartest people I know."

Leo raised an eyebrow. "Careful, Tem. Too many compliments and I may develop an ego."

Tem rolled her eyes. "Please. We both know it's far too late for *that*."

Finally, Leo smiled.

They drank in silence for a while, and eventually, Tem said, "Has he always been like that?"

"My father? Yes, always. Why do you ask?"

Tem shrugged. "He's so angry. I'm just surprised that you turned out…" She trailed off, unsure how to phrase it.

Leo was still looking at her.

"How did I turn out, Tem?" he asked softly.

"Like you," she answered.

There was nothing specific in her answer. She hadn't said anything, really. And yet it felt like she'd given him a compliment, and for some reason, she hoped he took it as one. Perhaps he did, because he asked, "Have I managed to impress you?"

Tem thought about how Leo behaved tonight. He'd treated Gabriel—someone far beneath his status—with kindness. He'd responded to her constant digs with nothing but humor. *He's always done that*, she realized. All he'd ever wanted was to earn her favor, even though it was Tem who was supposed to be earning his. Leo's vulnerability revealed a different side of him—a side Tem liked. So she whispered, "Yes."

"I'm certainly glad to hear it."

Tem found she was glad to say it.

The moment deepened. She was suddenly aware that they were alone, in her cottage, with nothing to prevent what happened next. Leo smiled fully, flashing his gold incisors. His gaze remained trained on hers as he said, "You're difficult to please, you know."

"So I've been told."

Leo raised an eyebrow at her. Some of his usual attitude returned.

"Good thing I've always liked a challenge."

Tem rolled her eyes.

"*Don't* get ahead of yourself. If you're expecting to fuck me tonight, you can forget it."

He laughed softly. "I wouldn't dream of expecting that."

She shot him a look, but he only smiled wider.

"What I expect and what I want are two different things, Tem."

The words were familiar; he'd said them during the Frisky Sixty, when she'd refused to undress for him. How simple life had been back then.

"You're not sleeping in my bed either," Tem said bluntly.

Leo smirked. "A bed isn't required for what I want to do."

She glared at him. "You can spend the night in the kitchen. The chairs are hard as rocks."

His smile widened. "Delightful. I look forward to it."

Tem didn't have anything to say to that, so she said nothing. It was obvious Leo was enjoying himself. To Tem's utter surprise, she was enjoying herself too. She wasn't exactly…having *fun*—too many emotional things had occurred tonight for that to be the case. But there was something satisfying about her back-and-forth with Leo: their banter felt natural, like she was competing against a worthy opponent. But she didn't know what Leo wanted. And she doubted Leo did either. The wound with Evelyn was clearly still fresh. Yet here he was, in her kitchen, and Tem knew she didn't want him to leave.

Tem downed the rest of her drink, and Leo downed the rest of his.

"We've established that I'm not going to fuck you," he said. "But are you going to let me kiss you?"

Tem crossed her arms. "Will you stop that?"

He frowned. "Stop what?"

"Flirting with me." She expected Leo to have an immediate comeback, but instead, he tilted his head.

"Does it really bother you?" he asked quietly.

Tem's answer came against her will. "No."

Leo shifted closer. The walls of the kitchen seemed to shrink. "Then why would you want me to stop?"

"Because when you flirt with me, I flirt back."

"That's the idea."

"And when I flirt back, I feel like I'm betraying…myself."

She wanted to say Caspen. But somehow, she couldn't bear the thought of speaking his name in front of Leo. The prince was still watching her, his head cocked to the side. Tem sat silently, staring at her whiskey glass. When Leo spoke again, his voice was sincere, his teasing tone completely gone.

"I didn't know it made you feel that way. I certainly don't mean to assault you in your own home."

He paused. Tem wanted to say something, but she couldn't seem to breathe.

At her silence, Leo continued, "I'm grateful for your hospitality, so I will refrain from flirting with you tonight. But know this, Tem." He leaned in, and she smelled his cologne. "Flirting with you is a pleasure. And a compulsion. One that, if I'm being truly honest, I doubt I can stop."

Tem stared at her whiskey, unable to look him in the eye. Her throat was tight.

"Tem," Leo said softly. "I understand, more than anyone, how you feel."

"Don't—"

"And I *understand*," he said, cutting her off, leaning even closer, "that your loyalty lies elsewhere. Contrary to what you may think, it is not my intention to make that more difficult for you. I know what it is to have an occupied heart. But I cannot help how I feel. And you've made it very clear that I am not entitled to any part of you—that your heart as well as your body are to be earned. I ask only for the chance to do so."

Now Tem was sure she was blushing.

"You may think he is right for you," Leo whispered. "But perhaps I am right too. And should you choose to kiss me tonight, he never has to know."

Leo was *so good* with his words. Always saying the exact thing that would give her pause. It was an infuriating talent and one that was serving him extremely well right now.

His breath feathered her cheek as he finished quietly, "So are you going to let me kiss you?"

Tem closed her eyes.

She couldn't deny that she was drawn to Leo. But she also couldn't deny the look she'd seen in his eyes when he told her about Evelyn. He loved her—*still* loved her—the type of love that didn't fade easily, if it ever did. Tem didn't want to kiss someone who loved someone else. He was not the same man who had walked into the Horseman. This man had a past. A past that could have a profound effect on their future.

Tem opened her eyes. "Not tonight."

To her surprise, Leo smiled.

"Is something funny?"

"No," he said simply.

They stared at each other in the darkness. Despite the autumn evening, the kitchen was warm, and Tem felt agitated. Why was it that immediately after she'd turned down a kiss from the prince, suddenly it was all she wanted to do? She had to break the moment.

"I'm going to sleep."

Leo ran a single finger around the rim of his glass. "Very well. Good night, Tem."

There was a pause, and Tem almost didn't want to leave. But she was exhausted.

She needed time to process what had just happened between them, and she didn't trust herself to make any more decisions tonight.

Tem was just pulling her bedroom door shut when suddenly she was met with resistance. With a jolt, she realized Leo was holding the door from the other side. She let go of the handle slowly, watching as he pulled it open, leaving a six-inch gap between them. For a moment, Tem thought he might step through. But he didn't. Instead, he said quietly, "In case you change your mind."

Then he turned away.

In case she changed her mind?

Could Leo tell somehow that Tem had been on the verge of changing her mind already? He seemed to be inside her head nearly as often as Caspen was. At the thought of Caspen, Tem crossed to her bedside dresser. With a glance back at the open door to make sure Leo couldn't see her, she stripped down to her underclothing, reached between her legs, and removed the claw. She didn't know why she did it. Something was guiding her tonight that she couldn't explain; something was drawing her to Leo in a way she'd never been drawn before. Tem studied the smooth curve, stroking it with her thumb.

A moment later, her hand was empty.

She stared at her palm in shock. The claw was gone—disappeared as if it were never there in the first place. It had happened only once before—at Tem's request, before the Frisky Sixty. Did Caspen know what she was thinking about doing with Leo? She felt for him with her mind, but the door between them was firmly shut. Tem flexed her fingers in disbelief. There was no point in dwelling on it any longer.

Instead, Tem climbed into bed and fell asleep immediately. But she awoke just hours later, and no matter what she did, sleep wouldn't return. She tossed and turned violently, trying not to stare at the open door.

But she couldn't ignore it.

She thought about how she had taken Leo in tonight. He was right; it was her choice. And she had made it readily, without outside influence, simply because she'd wanted to. She thought about Caspen, whose voice was painfully absent from her mind. He was always the one drawing the line between them. It was always Caspen who decided when and how their relationship would progress. Now Tem was the one drawing the line with Leo—keeping distance between them, policing his behavior and holding him at arm's length.

Now the person setting boundaries was her.

And why exactly was she so against the human prince? What was it about Leo that Tem found so abhorrent? Was there really anything wrong with him, or was it just that Maximus was his father—something over which he had no control, something he himself had expressed disgust over? Should a son suffer for the sins of his father? Maximus judged Tem constantly, with no justification or remorse. Was she really going to do the same to Leo?

Leo had never lied to her. He'd defended her in front of his father—more than once—at great personal cost. She'd never taken his constant advances seriously, but now Tem wondered whether that was just because she'd gotten so used to the polar opposite from Caspen. Was she only interested in affection when it was being withheld from her? Leo had proven time and time again that he wanted her, even when she didn't believe him. Leo, whose opinion of her was informed by her actions, yet her opinion of him was formed by her own prejudice. Leo, whose only sin was his lineage. Leo, who despite the fact that girls were throwing themselves at him left and right had only pursued Tem. Why should she deprive herself of what she knew they both wanted? Leo was right. Caspen never had to know.

Tem got out of bed.

She crossed to the door, which was still cracked open. As if in a dream, she walked through it. Leo was still at the table, fast asleep, his head tilted back against the wall. His sharp cheekbones were softer in the dark, his thick blond hair mussed in the back. She stared at his exposed neck, his prominent Adam's apple. He was completely defenseless. For some reason, seeing him like that confirmed Tem's decision.

She touched his shoulder.

At the contact, Leo's eyes flew open. He looked up at her calmly, as if he knew what she was about to say.

Tem said it anyway. "I changed my mind."

CHAPTER TWENTY

THERE WAS ABSOLUTE SILENCE AS THEY STARED AT EACH OTHER.

For some reason, Tem felt perfectly at ease. From the look on Leo's face, he did too. His mouth turned up at the corner as he stood slowly, his eyes never leaving hers.

Leo whispered, "What are we about to do, Tem?"

Her mind was already blank, her arms wrapping around him. "Whatever we want," she whispered back.

Then she kissed him.

It wasn't their first kiss, yet somehow it was new. Somehow, this time, it felt as if they were on equal footing—like Tem's cottage was far away from everything that had been weighing on them, like they both knew they were safe with the other here. They kissed slowly, neither of them in a rush, neither of them giving in to necessity just yet.

Tem tugged on Leo's shirt. "Take this off," she said.

He laughed softly. "If you insist."

She watched as he took it off. Leo's torso was angular and lean, so different from the brutal muscles on Caspen. There was a tiny scar under his chin, and she touched it tentatively.

"What's that from?" she asked.

"Carriage accident."

Tem giggled.

"Is that funny?" he murmured.

His hands were moving too, skimming down the curves of her hips.

"Only rich people have scars from carriage accidents."

"I am a rich person, Tem."

"Don't remind me. It's one of your more abysmal qualities."

Leo laughed.

Then he dipped down, grabbed the backs of her thighs, and picked her up. Tem completed the motion, wrapping her legs around his waist as he carried her to the bedroom. When they fell onto her bed, Tem understood exactly how much Leo wanted her. His hands were all over her body—greedy and insistent—yanking her underclothing off with unapologetic urgency. Tem lost herself in his grip, savoring the way he wanted her—*needed* her—and the way she wanted him in return. The moment they were both naked, they gasped together as skin met skin for the first time. Tem's hand slid between Leo's legs just as his hand slid between hers, and she let out a yelp as he pinched her clitoris.

"*Leo.*"

She saw his smirk even in the dark.

"Tem." His voice was a barely restrained growl. "Don't expect me to be gentle when you've made me wait this long."

Tem decided not to make him wait any longer. She wrapped her fingers around his cock—the second cock she'd ever felt—and began to stroke.

Leo sucked a tight breath between his teeth.

"*Fuck,* Tem."

Tem smiled.

Leo's cock was the perfect extension of him—long and proud and *regal,* yet another embodiment of his unchecked ego. Tem understood why he conducted himself the way he did, why he felt the need to answer to no one, why he moved through the world with such careless arrogance. She felt an undeniable surge of power with her fingers wrapped around his shaft. It was a privilege Tem couldn't have comprehended before this very moment and one she didn't intend on wasting.

"Do you like that?" she whispered.

In response, Leo slipped his fingers inside her.

Nobody had ever touched her that way but Caspen. But her body knew what to do, and Tem knew to let it. Caspen's words came suddenly back to her:

He has had anyone he wanted his entire life. So he is familiar with a woman's body.

Leo was familiar indeed. He knew exactly how to touch her. He knew how to play with her clitoris; he knew how to stroke that channel inside her that made her *burn* with need. Tem couldn't pretend she hadn't imagined this. She couldn't pretend she hadn't looked at his nimble, beautiful fingers and imagined how they would feel caressing the most sensitive part of her. All her imagining couldn't have prepared her for how it felt in real life. He was breathtakingly intuitive—changing his rhythm based on the sounds she made, applying pressure exactly where and when she wanted it. He was *listening* to her, and she wasn't even talking.

They moved in tandem, her hand between his legs and his hand between hers. Their breathing was synced, their cadences aligned. It was so easy to touch him. Caspen had taught her what to do after all. Tem knew how to tease a man, how to make Leo *groan*, and how to make him like it. He touched her too, coaxing something from her that she couldn't resist, forcing her to acknowledge that he could perhaps be right for her.

They were moving quickly now, every inch of Leo pressing against every inch of her, the friction of their skin sending Tem straight into a desperate frenzy. She felt like an animal in heat.

Her lips were on his neck.

"Leo," she whispered. He was holding her together and pulling her apart.

"Ask for it, Tem," he ordered.

"Now," she whimpered in his ear. "Please, Leo. Right now."

Leo obeyed immediately. Without another word, he grabbed her hips and centered himself, looking down at her for a single, silent moment. Tem looked back, spreading her legs, holding herself open just for him. She noticed the way his pulse beat in his temple—his expression a wild cross between fierce desire and deep satisfaction, reveling in his victory, even now. He angled his hips, and she did too.

The moment his cock touched her, Tem's mind erupted in agony.

It was as if someone were splitting her head in two with a blunt axe. The sensation was so strong that she screamed, lurching away from Leo and curling herself into a ball.

"Tem? What is it? *Tem!*"

But Tem couldn't answer. There were no words to describe the torture overtaking her mind. She felt nothing but torment, heard nothing but a single, anguished cry, repeated over and over into eternity, never-ending, as bottomless as the ocean. It was indescribable pain, and she didn't even know whether it was hers.

"Tem." Leo touched her shoulder. The pain worsened.

"Caspen." It was all she could manage to say. "He's here."

"Where?" Leo asked, bewildered.

Tem pointed at her head. The pain was growing, shutting everything else out.

"He's in your *mind?*"

But Tem couldn't reply. The pain was too excruciating for her to form a single thought. Her head was a maelstrom of grief, anger, and bitter jealousy, each emotion so strong, she felt as if she were being run through with a knife.

"Tem, look at me. *Tem!*"

Leo was calling her. He was calling her, and she couldn't answer.

Her head was filled with a montage of her time with Caspen. She saw the moment they met in the cave, when she asked him to undress. There was their first kiss, from his perspective, as he wove his fingers into her hair and pulled her against his lips. She saw the time he almost transitioned. She saw him heal her after Jonathan. She watched as they fucked in his chambers for the first time, wild and desperate, two people who could finally be together without restraint. *How long have you loved me?* she'd whispered just last night. *Far longer than you have loved me*, he'd whispered back. Tem couldn't take any more. She could barely breathe. But she drew on every ounce of strength she had left to send a single word down the fractured corridor of their minds:

Stop.

As suddenly as the pain had come, it was gone. The pressure on her head finally released as their connection broke, shattering into a thousand shards of glass. Tem gasped in equal parts shock and relief, the sudden absence of agony nearly agony in itself.

"Tem? *Tem.*"

Leo was still saying her name. She had no idea how much time had passed—no idea what she had screamed while Caspen was in her head. She looked up into his terrified eyes.

"Leo," she whispered.

"I'm here." He held her face in his palms. "What can I do?"

But Tem couldn't speak. Instead, she began to cry.

Leo pulled her tightly into his arms as her shoulders shook. She sobbed against his skin, not bothering to hold back her tears, not bothering to pretend she didn't feel every ounce of despair that Caspen felt. She was so tired of him shutting her out, of only letting her in when it was convenient for him—of making her feel like she was under his control. Tem wanted to think for herself, *act* for herself. How could she have a say in her future when she couldn't even accept her own proposal? Nothing was simple with Caspen; nothing was straightforward. It never had been. She resented him for driving her into Leo's arms, and she hated how much solace she had found in them.

Eventually, her sobs ceased.

They lay quietly, Tem's head resting on Leo's bare chest, his arms wrapped around her, their legs intertwined. Leo drew gentle shapes on her skin, his fingers brushing up and down her arm in slow, comforting strokes. Every few minutes, he kissed her on the top of her head.

"I'm sorry, Leo," Tem whispered eventually. Her voice was hoarse.

His fingers stopped. "For what?"

"That we didn't…that I couldn't…"

He shook his head, his fingers resuming their journey. "I don't mind, Tem," he said quietly. "I'll take what I can get."

His words gutted her. They hurt even more coming from Leo, who somehow always had to take what he could get when it came to Tem. He received what attention she could spare; he took what affection she would give him. Leo never got all of her, and he never complained. He took what he could get, even when it was never enough. It was yet another reminder to Tem that giving half of herself to two people wasn't sustainable. Something would have to break. She hoped it wouldn't be her.

"It may happen again," she said.

Leo shrugged. "If it does, we will deal with it."

Tem noticed his use of the word *we*, as if they were in this together. Maybe they were.

Another minute passed before Leo asked, "How can he be in your mind?"

She heard the hesitant curiosity in his voice and remembered that up until tonight, Leo didn't know about her mental tie to the basilisk.

"I don't know exactly," she answered truthfully.

"But he…can speak to you?"

"Yes."

"And what did he say?"

"Which time?"

Leo's fingers stopped again. Tem realized too late that he'd assumed Caspen had infiltrated her mind for the first time a moment ago.

"He has spoken to you multiple times," Leo said.

It wasn't a question. There was no point in denying it.

"Yes."

"You…maintain a connection with him?"

His shock was obvious. Tem fought to deescalate the situation. "*He* maintains a connection with me."

It was the truth. Or at least part of it. It was true that Tem savored their bond, but Caspen was the one who controlled it.

Leo's grip was tightening around her.

"And what *exactly* is the nature of your connection?"

Tem had no idea what to say. No answer would satisfy Leo: no explanation would make this situation acceptable to him. How could she possibly tell him the extent of her mental bond with Caspen? How could she tell him that they had *sex* through that connection, that Caspen would turn her on and she would do the same, that they had brought each other to orgasm more times than she could count? It was incomprehensible, even to Tem.

"He speaks to me…and I…answer."

"I see," said Leo quietly. "He speaks. And you answer."

His voice was steady. But Tem knew they were in very dangerous, *very* uncharted territory.

She held her breath as he said, "How often does this occur?"

"It's…not consistent. I can't predict it."

"And what did he say to you tonight?"

Another question she wished he hadn't asked. She couldn't tell Leo how Caspen felt—how their entire relationship had flashed before her eyes in an avalanche of aching torment.

"He didn't *say* anything, really. He just…" Tem broke off, trying to put the experience into words. "He's jealous," she finished simply.

"Well," Leo murmured, and to her surprise, his tone softened. "We can hardly blame him for that."

Tem wanted to say something else. To apologize again. But she knew it wouldn't make a difference. Instead, she tilted her head and kissed Leo on the lips. He kissed her back, and for a moment, Tem felt peace. They didn't try to have sex again. They simply kissed slowly, their bodies intertwining under the covers. Tem was still terrified Caspen might return, and she knew Leo must have been too.

They kissed until Tem was too tired to kiss anymore. When they stopped, Leo simply held her, cradling her body against his. She fell asleep with her head tucked underneath his chin.

When Tem awoke, her legs were tangled in Leo's. He was still asleep, his arms wrapped securely around her. When she tried to lift her head, she immediately regretted it; she had a headache so severe that she doubted it was just from the alcohol. It had to be an aftereffect of Caspen's infiltration.

At her movement, Leo's eyes opened.

Without a word, he leaned in and pressed his lips to hers. Their bodies merged even closer, their skin still warm from sleep. Eventually, Leo slipped his hand between her legs. What he was doing felt so good, it took everything Tem had to whisper, "We can't, Leo. My mother."

"Is tending to a child in the village."

"Will be returning any moment."

"We'll make it quick."

"I don't want it to be quick."

Leo laughed softly at that. "Good to know."

He was still touching her. "Leo," she said gently. "Stop."

He stopped.

They stared at each other in the dim morning light. Even though Tem had just denied him, Leo looked irrefutably happy.

"What are you smiling at?" she asked.

His smile widened. "I'm glad you changed your mind."

"Even though…"

She couldn't say the words. The night had been an utter disaster, all things considered. Caspen's presence hung between them like an unspoken curse, and Tem doubted very much that Leo's experience with any of the other girls in the competition had gone at all the way this one had.

Leo shrugged. "A small price to pay for your company."

But Tem would not be convinced. "I can't control it, Leo."

He looked her right in the eye. "I understand, Tem."

It was all he said. But it was enough for now.

They dressed in silence, stealing glances at each other before leaving the cottage. When they reached the garden gate, Tem turned to face him.

"Well," she said. "I'll see you soon."

"That you shall."

There was so much more she wanted to say. But the words wouldn't come.

Tem turned away.

"Wait." Leo grabbed her hand. "Would you do something for me?"

She looked back at him. "What?"

His hand tightened in hers.

"Hold on to it."

"Hold on to what?"

"Whatever it was that made you change your mind last night. Just…try to hold on to it. Please?"

They stared at each other, and in that moment, Tem realized how much last night had truly meant to Leo—how deeply and desperately he wanted to be with her, how badly he hoped what little progress they'd made wasn't ruined by her lingering connection with Caspen. Tem wanted to reassure him, but she didn't want to lie. So she simply nodded instead.

"I'll try."

Leo nodded too. Then he dropped her hand, turned, and disappeared down the street.

Tem stood as if in a trance. It had been one of the most formative nights of her life. Not only was her relationship with Caspen hanging in the balance, but suddenly, Leo had stepped up in a way she'd never thought possible. *I know what it is to have an occupied heart*, Leo had said. It was horrible was what it was. Tem did not want to feel this way for two people—did not want to split herself in two.

Her mother appeared on the garden path.

"My dear," she said. "How are you?"

What a question.

There was no way to answer it. In response, Tem merely shrugged. They returned to the kitchen together, and her mother held up the half-empty liquor bottle.

"Really, Tem?"

"It wasn't just me," Tem said quickly.

"That *infernal* boy," her mother muttered, and Tem knew she would assume it had been Gabriel. There was no point in correcting her.

Tem tried to busy herself with farm work, but the chickens provided no distraction whatsoever. She could think only of the way Leo's hands had felt on her body—of how he'd been able to ignite something in her that she once thought only Caspen could ignite. Tem had no choice but to comprehend the most fundamental thing that now rang true: her heart was in two places, and things would not be easy for her.

Leo.

And Caspen.

She loved them both.

It shouldn't have come as a shock to her—too many things had brought her gradually to this conclusion to make it any sort of a surprise. Still, she marveled at how she could feel such a draw to them both, how she could *want* two people in the same way—a way that was guttural and raw and real.

She was engaged to Caspen. Or nearly so. And one day—depending on factors well outside her control—she might be engaged to Leo too. Tem could imagine it now: walking down the aisle in a white dress, pledging herself to the human prince for the rest of their lives. It wouldn't be difficult. It was merely an extension of everything she'd felt for him up until this point, a way to solidify their connection into something real—something tangible.

And yet.

Caspen was in her veins. He was in her blood, in her mind, in her soul. He was the breath in her lungs; he was her tether to life. Caspen was everything.

So why did he make her feel so empty?

Tem performed her morning chores dutifully before taking the usual basket of eggs to the bakery. By the time she got there, she was dreading what came next.

There was Vera, dressed in pink.

"*So*, Tem?" she sneered, her heart-shaped face positively glowing with anticipation. Clearly, she was no longer grieving Jonathan. "Who do you think the prince will take to the castle?"

Tem remembered the way the crowd had roared for Vera and the way they had stood in silence for her. She knew Vera had savored every moment of Tem's humiliation.

"I don't know," she said stiffly. "Whoever he wants, I suppose."

"Yes, but"—Vera leaned forward, and Tem nearly choked on her perfume—"who do *you* think he wants?"

Considering the way Leo had touched her last night, Tem had a fairly good idea who he wanted. But she couldn't tell that to Vera.

"I'm sure he'll consider what's best for the kingdom," she said carefully. "Not just what's best for him."

Vera's smile widened. "And who do *you* think is best for the kingdom?" she sneered.

Tem stared resolutely at the eggs.

Not even a second passed before Vera barreled onward. "His father spoke to me, you know."

Tem's eyes snapped up to hers. "What?"

"The *king*"—Vera savored the word as if it were chocolate—"told me that *I* was his first choice."

"That *choice*," Tem said with equal emphasis, "is for the prince to make. Not the king."

"Perhaps." Vera shrugged. "But surely the prince will take his father's opinion into account."

Maximus's words came back to Tem suddenly: *I will take away your title before I let you choose her.* Tem hadn't considered he might truly be serious. It would be a scandal of the utmost caliber if Maximus were to interfere with the elimination process. It would undermine the facade of control he fought so hard to preserve.

Vera was still talking: "After all, a father knows what's best for his children." Her eyes narrowed, and her mouth twisted cruelly. "Not that you would understand, Tem."

Her words were a white-hot knife in Tem's gut. It was a low blow, even for Vera.

But Tem understood that Vera was angry. She had seen how Leo had kissed her, and despite the crowd's—and apparently the king's—approval, Vera felt threatened.

The thought was oddly empowering.

"I'll take these now," Vera said cheerfully, snatching the eggs from Tem's hands. She flounced off in a wave of perfume, leaving Tem to stew over what had just happened. When she returned with payment, Tem took it and left without another word. Their conversation played over and over in her mind on the way home.

What if Vera was right? What if Maximus had a say in who Leo chose? If that were true, Tem had no chance with the prince at all—a prospect she had no idea how to process. No matter what happened during the competition, Tem had always assumed Leo would be the one to make his own choice. But what if this decision—the most important one of his life—was made by his father? It didn't seem remotely fair.

Tem worried for the rest of the day until finally, the night came.

By the time she reached the base of the mountain, her skin was covered in a cold sweat. Tem was just as nervous as the very first time she'd gone to the caves, if not more so. It felt as if her entire body were on edge—like every cell was pricked with bated anticipation.

When she reached Caspen's cave, she paused.

Beyond the all-encompassing darkness was her future—her *husband* if his quiver allowed it. That was no small thing to Tem. There was no part of this that she took lightly, no part of this that didn't sway her to her very core. She touched her fingertips to the cold, rough stone, wondering what awaited within it. Would Caspen be angry with her for letting Leo stay the night? He had seen them together—naked and inter-twined—in her bed. Would they talk about the pain Caspen had inflicted on her—the torture he had wrought in her mind? There was only one way to find out.

Tem stepped into the darkness.

Caspen was waiting for her, as he always was. He stood silently in the middle of the cave, and even now, his beauty took her breath away. The basilisk didn't say a word. Instead, he turned, and Tem followed him in silence to his chambers. It wasn't until they were facing each other before the fire that Caspen finally spoke.

"I am sorry, Tem."

Tem blinked. She hadn't been expecting that. "For what?"

Caspen let out a long breath. He stepped forward so they were mere inches apart. "First and foremost, for hurting you last night. I am aware of your perception of our power dynamic, and I do not wish to reinforce that."

Tem turned his words over in her mind. She noticed how he'd specified her *percep-tion* of their power dynamic, as if her perception wasn't correct. But it was. Caspen held the power. He always had. Before she could press the issue, he continued.

"I also wish to apologize for any confusion regarding my intentions."

"Your...intentions?"

"I thought I had made my feelings for you clear. Apparently, I had not."

"Oh," Tem said, because she had no idea what else to say.

Despite what he'd just said, Caspen didn't actually proceed to make his feelings for her clear. He was always talking like this, saying things in a vague way, avoiding straight-forward declarations. No doubt a habit honed from centuries of finding ways not to lie.

Tem would wait no longer. "What *are* your feelings for me?"

Caspen sighed as if this was very difficult for him. "I love you."

His words should have been a soothing balm. Instead, they were a cage—a trap that Tem would not fall for once again.

"I know you do," she said firmly. "And it does not help me."

She meant it. Nothing about Caspen's feelings helped her. His love for her did not remedy her family's reputation, his love for her did not solve her infatuation with Leo, his love for her did not ensure her future. Caspen's love for her fixed exactly nothing, and Tem was utterly tired of that fact. She wanted to yell at him.

Instead, she said, "Things cannot go on as they have been."

"I agree," Caspen said quietly.

He raised his hand, brushing a single finger along her jaw. Despite herself, Tem leaned into his touch. Already, she could feel herself softening toward him. That was all it ever took with Caspen—a single touch, and she was his again.

But she would not be so easily seduced this time.

Too much had happened in the last twenty-four hours; too much had *changed*. Tem was no longer the girl she used to be. There was no coming back from what had occurred between her and Leo, no undoing what had already been done. She was done taking no for an answer, done playing by the rules of Caspen's game.

Tem looked straight at him. "I almost fucked Leo last night," she said bluntly.

Caspen's eyes narrowed. "I am well aware of that, Tem."

"So?" Tem insisted. "Are you going to do something about it?"

Caspen's gaze bore into hers. He let out a dry laugh. "No."

She stared up at his infuriatingly perfect face. "*No?*"

"If you think the human prince matters to me, then you are sorely mistaken."

The human prince.

It was clear now.

Tem saw finally how Caspen viewed Leo: not as competition but as nothing but a nuisance. Leo didn't even rank in the grand scale of Caspen's worries. What could a human prince do in the face of a basilisk one?

Perhaps the human prince did not sway Caspen. But he swayed Tem.

There was no denying it, no erasing their connection. Leo gave her something that Caspen could never provide: security. Leo wanted her. It was plain and it was simple, and it was far easier than anything that might come from courting a basilisk. Why shouldn't Tem go with the surefire option? Why shouldn't Tem go where she was wanted?

"He may not matter to you," she said quietly. "But he matters to me."

At her words, Caspen stiffened. "I see."

For a moment, neither of them spoke. For some reason, Tem felt a flare of anger. Of course Leo meant something to her. Her relationship with Caspen was so nebulous—so fraught with strife—that he should not begrudge her this slight chance at happiness.

"Tem," Caspen said quietly. "I do not blame you if you wish to seek solace elsewhere."

He was clearly hurt. But his words only made her angrier.

"I don't *want* to seek solace elsewhere," she snapped. "I want to seek solace with *you*."

He shook his head. "Perhaps I cannot provide it."

"*Bullshit*." Tem stepped forward, grabbing the chain around her neck. "Does this mean nothing to you?" She brandished the claw. "Is this a *lie?*"

"Tem," Caspen said quietly. "You do not understand what it will take for us to be together."

"Because you won't tell me."

Caspen looked up at the ceiling. "Because I would not have you do it."

Here it was: the mysterious condition that his quiver required of her in order to accept their engagement. Tem couldn't wait any longer to hear it. She grabbed Caspen by the neck, forcing him to look her in the eye. "Why not?"

"It is unthinkable. And you would never consent to it. And even if you did consent to it, my quiver's approval is not guaranteed."

"What is it?"

"It is not worth discussing, Tem."

"You mean *I* am not worth discussing."

Caspen put his hand over hers, holding her against him. "That is *not* what I mean."

"It shouldn't matter what other people think."

"It does not matter. *You* are the only thing that matters to me."

Tem looked straight at him. "It doesn't feel that way."

Regret darkened Caspen's eyes. "Then I have failed you."

She didn't reply, because there was nothing to say. His words were not enough anymore. Tem knew how Caspen felt one day and not the next. He was the one thing she truly couldn't handle: inconsistent.

The fire crackled, and Tem resisted the urge to throw herself into it.

Caspen's gaze fell to her lips. "I am merely trying to protect you," he whispered. "Basilisks do not respect humans. You are considered the enemy. By being with you, I betray my own kind."

"But you said that it happens, that there are pairings of humans and basilisks."

Caspen sighed. "Yes. There are."

"Then how did they come to be?"

"Through great difficulty and sacrifice. Mostly on the side of the human."

"What do you mean?"

Caspen was silent for a long time. Tem knew she only had to wait him out. She would not be dissuaded this time. She would find out exactly what it would take to be with him so she could make an informed decision about her future.

"There is a ritual," Caspen said eventually.

"What kind of ritual?"

"One that would legitimize our engagement. But only if you can withstand it."

"*Withstand* it?"

"Yes."

"You make it sound like an attack."

"It may as well be one."

"What is it?"

But he hesitated. It was clear this was difficult for him.

"Caspen," Tem insisted. "Tell me."

"I already told you it is not worth discussing."

"Yet clearly I wish to discuss it."

"Yet clearly I do not."

"But *why?*" Tem tried to pull her hand away, but Caspen tightened his grip.

"It would disrespect you," he said.

"You're being awfully vague."

But Caspen only shook his head. At his reaction, Tem tried to pull away again. This time, he grabbed her wrists and held her still.

"Tem," he said, his voice low, his face centimeters from hers. "I am ashamed that my people allow this."

"Allow *what?*"

When he didn't answer, she pushed him away, crossing her arms and staring into the fire. This was beyond infuriating. Her heart was pounding; her shoulders were tense. All she wanted was to run from this room. But more than that, she wanted Caspen to be transparent with her. And she knew it would only happen if she stayed. So Tem stood there stubbornly, waiting him out.

Eventually, Caspen spoke. "Basilisks are sexual creatures," he said slowly.

"Yes." Tem nodded. "Obviously."

"The ritual is ancient," he continued. "It is the one way humans can prove themselves to us, in the one language we understand."

She turned to face him. "But what does it entail?"

His next words were barely a murmur. "Our culture revolves around our king." Again, he paused, and the fire crackled.

"*So?*" Tem insisted.

"So," Caspen said, and she knew they were coming to the crux of the issue. "In order to earn my quiver's favor, you would need to prove yourself to him."

"And how would I prove myself to him?"

Caspen closed his eyes, as if he couldn't bear to look at her. "The same way you proved yourself to me."

His words sank in slowly, then all at once.

Finally, Tem understood: "I would have to have sex with your *father?*"

CHAPTER TWENTY-ONE

❖

F
OR A SINGLE, STATIC MOMENT, TIME STOOD STILL.

Then Tem cried, "That's *barbaric*."

Caspen opened his eyes. There was nothing but remorse in them. "It is tradition, Tem. You will find they are often one and the same."

"I can't believe you expect me to—"

"*I do not expect you to do anything*." Caspen grabbed her shoulders, shocking her into silence. He sighed, hanging his head and pressing his forehead gently to hers. "Put it out of your mind. It will not come to pass. I will never request it of you."

To Tem's surprise, she felt a flare of anger. "Why not?" She stood taller. "Do you think I'm incapable?"

Caspen sighed again. "Tem. Do not do that."

"Do what?"

"Do not bait me into saying something you will hold against me. It is not that I think you are incapable. It is that I would never subject you to something that should not be expected of anyone. It is not a tradition I wish to be a part of."

"Then why did you propose to me in the first place?"

Caspen's grip on her tightened. "I proposed to you because a life without you is not a life I care to live."

His words stopped her short. A life without Caspen wasn't a life she cared to live either. But it didn't make what he'd done any better.

Now it was Tem's turn to close her eyes. She was still aware of Caspen before her, of the burning fire beside them. But she took a moment to delve deep within herself, to listen only to her own mind. Tem couldn't believe Caspen had kept this from her. And yet she understood why he'd done so. She was quite sure she wouldn't have been able to absorb this information even a week ago. But things were different now. *She* was different now.

Tem opened her eyes. "If it's the only way I would be accepted, why wouldn't you beg me to do it?"

A slight frown wrinkled Caspen's brow. "Because it is an insult, Tem."

"It's also tradition."

"*Fuck* tradition."

To her surprise, there was true anger in his eyes. Caspen was sometimes firm, often strict, but he rarely used profanity with such emphasis. Tem recalled their conversation about his strained relationship with his father—a relationship that surely wouldn't improve if Tem were to have sex with him. It occurred to her that she was not the only one who would be affected by the ritual; Caspen would suffer in his own way.

"It is meant to test you," Caspen continued. "Basilisks value sex above all else. It is how we measure our capability, how we determine who succeeds, who ascends, who rules. It is both a revered and deeply primal act—one that, the more it is done and the better you are at it, the higher your position in our society. The king holds the highest male ranking. He earned that position through sex."

"*Earned?*"

"Yes, Tem. Such is the basilisk way."

Tem was in shock. At the look on her face, Caspen sighed.

"If the king approves of you, everyone will. Or at least they should. The idea is that if you are worthy of the king, then you are worthy of any basilisk."

So it was an initiation. Tem could understand that on a basic level—she could understand *theoretically* how the basilisks would want a human to prove themselves worthy.

"But he is your *father*," she whispered.

Caspen sighed again. "Yes. I am well aware of that. But this has always been the way things are done. I would not be the first son to experience this situation with my father."

Tem shook her head. There were no words.

She thought about Leo's relationship with his father. She could only imagine that Caspen, also a prince, had similar problems—problems that couldn't be fixed with a single conversation, problems the depth of which Tem couldn't possibly fathom.

There was no way she could do this, no way she could mount a father the same way she mounted his son. Tem had always known how the basilisks valued sex. But this was so far beyond the scope of sanity that she was having a hard time processing it.

She looked up at Caspen.

"What happens if I don't do it? Can we still be together?"

"We can. But…"

He faltered. Tem waited him out.

"My people will not accept you," Caspen said finally. "They will consider you an accessory—a plaything—a—" He paused, searching for the right word. When he finally found it, he finished quietly, "They will look upon you as my pet, Tem."

Rage shot through her. Tem was nobody's pet. "Is that the future you want for us?" she said sharply. "As owner and pet?"

"No." He shook his head. "Of course not."

"Then how do you suggest we proceed?"

In the pause that followed, Tem watched as a thousand emotions passed through Caspen's eyes—regret, desire, and concern foremost among them. All he wanted was for her to be safe—for her to fit smoothly into his life without the struggles that inevitably came with their relationship. But it was not destined to be so. Now Tem knew the truth—that she would never be accepted, that she would never be able to stand beside him as his equal in the eyes of his people unless she did this single unfathomable thing.

Caspen didn't reply. Instead, he kissed her.

In his kiss, she felt everything he couldn't say. She remembered the parts of her that had been stifled and miserable until the moment she'd met Caspen in the cave. Her life was empty before Caspen. He'd shown her that she was capable, that she *mattered*. It was a revelation Tem now believed wholeheartedly, and she was no longer willing to settle for less than she deserved. Even if that meant having no one at all.

Caspen's lips were gentle on hers. He didn't pull her closer or try to undress her. Tem knew he was purposefully holding back, and she was grateful for his restraint. The only advance he made was internal; she felt him tentatively brush along the edge of their connection, as if he were knocking on the door to her mind.

Tem didn't let him in yet.

She allowed the kiss to deepen first, letting Caspen slip his hands into her hair, letting him pull her body against his. His desire was obvious, and so was hers. But Tem was taking her time now. The only thing she wanted was to enjoy this kiss.

It wasn't hard to do so.

Caspen's hands cradled her face, holding it to his. His tongue caressed hers softly, coaxing a moan from her throat. He brushed his lips briefly to her cheek before returning to her mouth, paying her such care and attention that she felt like the only girl in the world.

Eventually, she opened her mind.

Neither of them said anything at first. Instead, Caspen's presence curled around hers, holding her the same way his hands did: tenderly, as if she were something exceedingly precious to him. It was only when Tem let the last of her guard down that he whispered, *I love you, Tem.*

Tem loved him too. Their connection was undeniable; it rippled through every inch of Tem's body, vibrating from her head to her fingertips. She could feel her resistance slipping with every stroke of his tongue, her desire to be with him rapidly eroding her desire to be angry at him. Caspen was in her mind, and she knew he could sense this. Still, he didn't take things further. Instead, he pulled away. They stared at each other for a long moment, the only sound the snap of the fireplace.

Caspen spoke first. "Will you take a walk with me?"

"Where?"

"I must show you something."

He waited until she nodded before taking her hand in his.

They entered the passageway together, and Tem immediately trained her eyes on the ground.

"Where are we going?"

"Patience, Tem."

"I can't take any more surprises, Caspen."

He didn't reply.

They wound deeper and deeper beneath the mountain, passing doorway after doorway. It was impossible to know how time functioned here, nothing to tell her whether the sun or the moon was above them.

Caspen?

He squeezed her hand. *Tem?*

Is this where you spend your time?

Sometimes. I also venture outside to hunt. But yes, beneath the mountain is where I dwell.

Tem's eyes began to adjust to the stark darkness. *How much farther?*

It is not far. I promise.

True to his word, they stopped a few minutes later.

They were standing at the entrance of an enormous room. Great stone arches curved above their heads into endless blackness above. Tem tried to look up at the ceiling, but even when she squinted, she couldn't see it.

"Where are we?"

Instead of answering, Caspen guided her forward.

Tem shivered as they walked along the cold stone floor. Unlike Caspen's chambers, which were warmed by his fireplace and his own body heat, this place was cold; she felt the undeniable pull of death here. Tem curled herself against Caspen.

"Almost there, Tem."

She followed his lead, foraying even deeper into the darkness. Finally, they reached what appeared to be the center of the room. Caspen stopped, and Tem stopped too.

Before them stood a great stone monolith.

It disappeared up into the ether, far beyond what was visible to her human eyes. Even when Tem craned her neck, she couldn't see the top.

"What is this?" she whispered.

Caspen's hand tightened in hers. "It is a memorial."

Tem could just make out etchings on the stone—etchings that looked like names. She squinted, attempting to read the carved words. "Who are they?"

Caspen didn't respond, and Tem didn't ask him to. She stepped closer, peering at the names on the great stone slab, all recorded with complete precision.

With a jolt, Tem recognized a single word: *Drakon*.

"Your quiver..." she said, stepping even closer.

"Yes."

Another word jumped out at her: *Seneca*.

Rowe's quiver.

"What happened to them?"

"They went missing."

Tem frowned. "When?"

"After the war."

"*After* the war?"

"Yes."

Tem processed this information. It didn't make sense. The war was over; the royals had defeated the basilisks and brokered the truce, and there had been no battles since. She couldn't imagine why basilisks would go missing.

"Where have they gone?"

As soon as she asked it, she found she already knew the answer.

Help me.

The voice she'd heard—the disembodied plea that plagued her every time she went to the castle—it had to be a basilisk. Caspen's answer confirmed what she already knew.

"The castle."

Tem felt a chill go down her spine.

"The royals would have you believe that all has been quiet since the war," Caspen continued, his voice low and urgent. "But that is not the case. My people have gone missing for centuries."

"But *why*?" Tem stuttered. "Why would the royals keep basilisks in the castle?"

"To use us."

"For what?"

Now Caspen hesitated. He turned to her, his jaw tense. "Tem," he said quietly. "I must ask you something. And you must answer with complete honesty."

Tem blinked. He was so deeply serious—so obviously concerned—that she had no idea how to react to his tone. She said the only thing she could think to say: "Ask me."

Still, Caspen hesitated. He touched her waist, drawing his fingertips slowly down her body. "Are you loyal to him?"

Tem understood he was asking about the human prince. There was no doubt that Leo held a piece of her heart. But so did Caspen. He always would.

"I am loyal to you."

Not a yes or a no. Simply a statement of fact. It was the best Tem could give him, and Caspen seemed resigned to her answer. His hand gripped her tightly, his fingers digging into her hips as he said, "The royals use basilisks for bloodletting."

Tem frowned. "Bloodletting?"

"It is a process where our blood is alchemized into gold. This"—Caspen touched the golden claw around her neck—"is a piece of me."

Comprehension hit Tem like a tidal wave. The necklace was not just a gesture—no mere trinket to symbolize his intentions. Caspen had *bled* for her.

"They hunt us, Tem," he continued, his words rushed and tight. "They take us to the castle, and they bleed us until we have nothing left to give." He gestured at the memorial. "Hundreds have died there."

Tem reeled from this revelation. It was difficult to comprehend such cruelty. Everything made sense now—how the royals had accumulated so much gold, how they used their wealth to wield power over anyone who tried to cross them, how Maximus kept the basilisks in their place. She thought of Leo's teeth, of his tapered incisors sheathed in gold: a symbol of wealth, of power, of dominance. Their fanglike shape was nothing but an imitation and a mockery of the basilisk from whose blood they were made. Tem fought a wave of nausea as she remembered how her tongue had touched those teeth just last night. Something even worse occurred to her.

Did Leo know about this horrible practice?

Would he sanction it the same way his father had? Leo hated the basilisks. It was a hatred formed by years of prejudice—a hatred that ran irreversibly deep. Tem remembered Leo's gold cuff: the same one that encircled Maximus's wrist.

Like father, like son.

"Is there a way to help them?" Tem whispered. "To get them out?"

"Yes," Caspen said slowly, his golden eyes searching hers. "But it will be…difficult."

Tem was sure of that. There was no way to rescue the basilisks in the castle without alerting the royals of their departure. Surely any plan to get them out would involve bloodshed. Tem didn't want to imagine which side would suffer more.

"Tem," Caspen murmured, breaking her from her thoughts. "The time will come when you will have to choose."

Tem didn't want to believe it. She *refused* to believe it.

And yet somewhere in the depths of her soul, she knew Caspen was right. She knew, without a doubt, that she would be forced to pick a side—that eventually, her heart would inevitably break.

"I don't want to choose," she whispered.

Caspen smiled sadly. "I know."

The room seemed to grow colder.

Tem's fingers touched the little golden claw around her neck. She thought about how it was made from Caspen's body—from his blood. There were no words for what he had done.

Her eyes found his. "Caspen," she whispered.

He pressed a single finger to her lips. "Tem," he murmured. "It was worth it. For you, I would give anything." His hands moved to either side of her face. "I love you."

He'd said it just minutes ago. But this time it was a plea, a question to which only Tem had the answer. He was asking if she was on his side, if her feelings for Leo were nonnegotiable, if she would choose the basilisks over the humans.

Tem didn't have the answers to any of those questions.

Caspen looked at her, and for the first time, she saw how difficult their situation was for him. It wasn't unlike the way Leo had looked at her just this morning. Both men wanted Tem for themselves. But there was a factor that neither of them could predict: her. She did not want to pick a side; she did not want to choose. There had to be another way.

They stood at the memorial for a long time. Eventually, Tem began to shiver again, and they walked back through the passageways together. When they reached Caspen's chambers, Tem reclined on his bed. Caspen followed, wrapping his arms around her before releasing a weary sigh against her shoulder. Tem knew he had not asked for any of this.

Neither had she.

Caspen's fingers skimmed gently up her back. "Please, Tem," he whispered. "Tell me I have not lost you."

It was impossible to miss the desperation in his voice. But it didn't matter really how Caspen felt. The only thing that mattered was what Tem was willing to do—how far she was willing to go for him.

"You haven't lost me," she whispered.

Caspen pressed a soft kiss to her neck. Then to her cheek. Then to her lips.

Tem kissed him back, forgetting everything that had happened in the last twenty-four hours. She forgot how Leo had showed up at the Horseman, how he had come to her cottage, how he had touched her while she touched him back. She only knew this moment, right here, with Caspen.

They moved slowly at first, remembering the way the other felt. Tem undressed herself, enjoying the way Caspen watched her as she did so. He was still holding back—still waiting for permission to take things further. Tem was ready to give it.

Caspen.

Tem.

Touch me.

Caspen trailed his fingers slowly down her body, brushing them along the dip of her waist before pulling her beneath him. Tem tipped her knees open, and Caspen's eyes immediately turned black.

So beautiful, Tem.

You always say that.

Because it is true.

Craving bloomed within her as Caspen slid two fingers deep into her center, all the way to his knuckles. Then he paused. They both stayed perfectly still, each of them watching the other. Caspen's gaze traced over her body with boundless veneration.

Tem would never get tired of being looked at that way.

His fingers moved steadily in and out of her, warming her with each stroke. His other hand wrapped around her neck, arching her head back so he could bend down and kiss her throat. It felt so right to be connected to him like this, to move together as if they were never apart to begin with. Caspen understood her in a way no one else ever could; her body was an instrument only he could play.

Caspen waited until Tem was dripping with wetness before removing his fingers. His hand went to his cock, but he didn't enter her. Instead, he said, *May I?*

Tem found it significant that he had asked. She knew it was a gesture, a way to seek her forgiveness. He was asking permission to fuck her, begging for the privilege of being inside her. It made Tem feel powerful, and she liked that feeling.

Yes.

Even with her consent, Caspen still went slowly. He positioned himself between her legs, wrapping them around his torso one after the other. His eyes met hers as he finally entered her, sliding only an inch of his cock in before pulling back out. Tem moaned as he did it again, going just an inch farther this time, holding himself back from everything she knew he dearly wanted to do.

More, Caspen.

He gave her more.

Tem gasped with relief as he filled her completely, and Caspen did the same. He was her home, and she was his. Their union was sacred. It was the truth.

Tem pushed Caspen so she could climb on top of him.

She wanted him to see every inch of her—to show him everything he needed permission to have. Caspen's eyes were black with desire, any trace of gold completely gone. His skin was hot; it was nearly unbearable. Beads of sweat rolled between Tem's breasts, pooling on Caspen's torso. She dug her fingers possessively into his skin, claiming him for herself.

Touch me, Caspen.

He touched her.

He ran his palms over her ass, her hips, her breasts. He brushed his fingertips over her nipples, coaxing them into eager peaks. Tem leaned into all of it, pleasuring herself exactly the way she wanted, taking her climax into her own hands. For once in her life, Tem was in control. She couldn't contain her moans. It felt *so good* to ride him—to slide up and down his cock, to fill herself to the brim.

Caspen simply watched her, letting her do whatever she wanted, touching her when and where she told him to. She wasn't worried about him; his climax was inevitable in the same way the sun rose in the east and set in the west. She was concerned only with herself, chasing nothing but her own pleasure, knowing that no matter what she did, his cock would remain rigid beneath her.

Sit up.

Caspen sat up. There was sweat on his temple. She licked it.

From this angle, her clitoris was stimulated nearly to the point of torment, and she flicked her hips as quickly as she could to reinforce the sensation. Caspen held on to her as if his life depended on it. And maybe it did. Maybe, given what they were up against, all they really had was each other. Maybe this was the only thing that mattered—this fleeting minute, this cosmic moment of connection that could be taken away at any second. Tem only wanted him more—only wanted him deeper. If she could slice herself open and wrap herself around him, she would. And she knew Caspen would do the same.

Smoke rose from his shoulders. It curled around her neck.

More.

Caspen shook his head. *Do not tempt me.*

Tem pressed herself against him. *More, Caspen.*

He could not resist her. She knew it as well as he did.

His eyes were black, his skin scalding to the touch. The smoke tightened as a low hiss filled the room. Caspen was close. She could feel it in every thrust; she could sense it in every breath. His shoulders were tense beneath her hands. Even Caspen could not resist the draw of pleasure. The moment her climax began, so did his.

Tem.

Her lips were on his neck.

Tem. Tem. Tem.

They moved to the rhythm of her name, falling over the edge together.

TEM.

Without thinking, she bit him.

Instead of pulling away, Caspen only pulled her closer. *I am yours, Tem.*

She sucked on his neck, pulling the warm fabric of his skin between her teeth until she felt it break—until she tasted the stunning metallic of Caspen's blood. Hot wetness poured into her mouth in a willing wave as she took what he'd already given her. Tem wanted to mark him, to inflict a shadow of the pain he'd inflicted on her. Caspen's fingers gripped her head, holding her against him. He gave himself to her the same way she gave herself to him—the same way any lover would relinquish their power to the other. When Tem released him, she arched her head back in triumph. Caspen kissed her throat.

Little viper.

Afterward, they lay together, her head on his chest. Tem ran her fingers over his neck. The wound had already healed.

"Will I see you tomorrow?" she murmured against his skin, memorizing the way he tasted.

He sighed gently, pulling her closer. "I am afraid not. I have matters to attend to."

Again with the mysterious matters. Tem didn't bother asking about them. She didn't even want to know what they were at this point. "What about the next day?"

"It is the Passing of the Crown."

"So?"

"So," he sighed again. "You will be expected at the ceremony."

There were five girls left in the competition. The next elimination would occur at the ball, after which the final three would stay in the castle until the prince chose his wife. Tem had never imagined she would make it this far.

Tem tried to kiss him. It seemed better than talking.

To her surprise, Caspen didn't take the bait. He held her back, looking straight into her eyes as he said, "Tem. I know the human prince loves you."

Now it was Tem's turn to sigh. "He doesn't know what he wants."

That was also true. Leo was still in love with Evelyn. As a result, he was unpredictable—ruled by emotions and prone to dangerous spontaneity. He was entirely human and always would be.

"He wants *you*."

Tem sighed again. "What would you have me do?"

Caspen pulled her even closer. "I would have you remember who you belong to."

"I could never forget," Tem whispered. She wanted to have sex again. But there were still questions to be answered, things that gnawed at her soul with incomparable insistence. "You never told me who you crested."

Caspen went suddenly still. His dark eyes locked on to hers. "That was deliberate."

"I know. But you need to tell me."

"Why?"

"Because you are done keeping secrets from me. And your past matters."

Caspen observed her with the same deep intelligence she'd come to expect from him. It was so easy to get lost in his eyes, to forget what she was asking in the first place.

"It should not matter," he said.

"But it does." Tem placed her hand gently on his chest. "Caspen," she whispered. "Tell me."

Their bodies were draped together. There was no space between them—no room to hide.

Eventually, Caspen spoke. "The Drakons have had difficulties with the Senecas for centuries, long before the war with the humans."

Tem remained silent, syncing her breathing to his.

"Both quivers have fought for power. At times, it has become violent." Caspen paused. "My father," he said slowly, "values power above all else. He is willing to sacrifice anything for it."

Tem thought about how Caspen's father was the true Serpent King. She could only imagine what it took to gain and keep such a title.

"Are you?" she asked.

Caspen's eyes flicked to hers. "Am I what?"

"Willing to sacrifice anything for power?"

Caspen pulled her closer, as if he were afraid she might slip away. "Not anything."

For some reason, Tem grew cold. "Caspen," she whispered. "Tell me what happened."

"It is not complicated," he said quietly. "My father wanted the throne. Another basilisk was in the way. My father asked me to crest them, and I did so."

"Who?"

His lips drew into a tight line. "Rowe's father."

Tem remembered the conversation in the ballroom with perfect clarity:

Say one more word, and you will join your father.

She recalled the way Rowe had looked at Caspen with complete hatred—the way he had called him a traitor. Caspen had killed his own kind. He had crested another basilisk and made enemies in the process. Tem couldn't understand why a father would ask such a thing of his son.

"Why did you do it?"

Caspen sighed. "There is no limit to what I would do for those I love."

Tem couldn't help but notice the parallels of their situations. When faced with an impossible choice, Caspen had chosen the harder path—the path with consequences. Now, when faced with the prospect of the ritual, Tem felt a similar pull. She pressed her lips gently to his.

There was no limit to what she would do for those she loved either.

CHAPTER TWENTY-TWO

ORNING ARRIVED BEFORE TEM WAS READY.

Caspen accompanied her to the head of the trail, as always. He kissed her goodbye, as always. Only this time, it felt different. This time, she knew what it would take to be a part of his world, and the knowledge sat in her core like a stone. When Caspen pressed his lips to hers, it felt like an apology.

Tem walked home alone.

Her mother was weeding the garden, and Tem joined her wordlessly. She pulled weed after weed, pouring all her bottled-up energy into the task at hand.

Inevitably, her thoughts turned to the ritual.

It was vile. Plain and simple. Yet Tem understood it. Sex was currency to the basilisks. It made sense that the only way to join their ranks was through seduction—that the only way to earn their approval was to perform the act of sex itself. But not even Tem could deny that sleeping with Caspen's father was at best unusual and at worst horrifying. What kind of society would allow for such a thing?

Such was the basilisk way.

Tem sighed, yanking out another weed. If she did the ritual, she could be with Caspen fully, the way they were meant to be together. But if she did not, she would never be properly accepted into his world. She was at an impasse, and she had no idea what to do.

"My dear?"

Tem jolted back to the present, where her mother was looking at her expectantly. "What?"

"You seem quiet. Are you well?"

Tem stared at the weed in her hand. Against her will, she began to cry.

Her mother immediately dropped her rake and embraced her. "Whatever is the matter, Tem?"

Tem only cried harder. She had no words for her situation, no way to express just how helpless she really felt. It was, simply put, impossible.

Her mother held her until her sobs quieted. Tem marveled at the contact; it was the second time in two days they had hugged like this. She wondered suddenly if the elimination process brought other mothers and daughters closer together. It was a shared experience after all. Her mother had gone into the caves just as Tem had—she had taken the same emotional and physical journey. For the first time, Tem considered confiding in her mother. She had been in love once. And love, if nothing else, was universal.

"Mother?" Tem asked against her shoulder.

"Yes, dear?"

"Why did you leave Father?"

Her mother stiffened.

"Please," Tem whispered. "I need to know."

A long moment passed. To Tem's surprise, her mother didn't pull away. Instead, she tucked her head against Tem's so they were more comfortably intertwined, and Tem wondered if it was easier for her mother to speak on this topic when she wasn't looking directly at her daughter.

"I left him because we could not be together."

"Why not?"

"His family would not allow it."

Tem considered this. Was it possible that this was where her mother's pain began? Had her father's family looked down on her, and she'd lost the love of her life because of it?

"I'm sorry, Mother."

Now her mother pulled away. "Why, my dear?"

Tem shrugged. They held hands. "Things have never been easy for you."

Her mother shook her head. "I only wish for things to be easy for *you*." She paused, then smiled. "The prince favors you, my dear. He kissed you longer than anyone else. I think you have a real chance with him."

Guilt twisted Tem's stomach. She had just learned what it would take to be with Caspen, and she was seriously considering doing it. Things had escalated far beyond the scope of the competition; Leo's favor was no longer the only thing at stake, and ultimately it didn't matter whether she had a chance with him. If she chose Caspen, she would forsake Leo.

Her mother turned Tem's hands over in hers, tracing the freckles on her palms.

"You hold the stars in your hands," she whispered. "Just like your father."

She'd said it a thousand times before. But this time, she said it sadly, as if it were not a good thing.

"Mother," Tem said quietly. "How do you know if someone loves you?"

Her mother met her eye. "When they would sacrifice their happiness for yours."

Tem processed her words, wondering whether Caspen or Leo would sacrifice their happiness for hers. More importantly, would she sacrifice her happiness for theirs? Caspen was already asking her to choose a side. It was only a matter of time before Leo did too. But why should Tem be the one to make such a sacrifice? Why shouldn't *they* be forced to choose *her*?

Her mother spoke again. "We should finish our work."

"Of course."

They spent the rest of the day in amiable silence, and Tem used the time to think about their conversation. It was a wonder her mother had told her anything at all. But Tem was glad to learn what little detail she'd divulged, and every time she looked at her hands, she thought about her father. Did he miss her mother? Did he miss Tem? Clearly, he hadn't been willing to sacrifice *his* happiness for theirs. Perhaps all men were built that way. Perhaps it was women who bore the burden of sacrifice.

At last, it was evening.

Tem collapsed onto her bed, forgoing dinner. She briefly considered inserting the claw before remembering that it was gone. Instead, she trailed her fingers between her legs, touching herself the way she had her entire life, doing what she'd done long before she met Caspen. There was something special about doing it this way, with no one else to direct her. Her eyes closed as she moaned softly, her fingers slipping into her wetness. She thought of Caspen—of the way he'd penetrated her just last night. She thought of Leo—of the way he'd pinched her clitoris until she'd cried out.

Then she thought of them both.

Was it really so wrong to picture them all together? Perhaps her mind was her last true sanctuary, the only place where she would never pick a side. She didn't want to choose, and here she didn't have to. It wasn't something she'd ever fantasized about before: the three of them intertwining like silken strands of a braid. But once she began, she found she couldn't stop.

Tem imagined herself kissing Caspen. Then Leo. Then both.

She lost herself in a vision of lips and hands and *need*, picturing the ways they could move with one another. It seemed a natural thing to her: to give herself to the men who loved her. Why shouldn't they seek pleasure together? Why shouldn't she be worshipped by the two people who wanted nothing more than to claim her as their own? She wanted to sit on one cock, then the other. She wanted to taste them both.

Her fingers worked desperately against her clitoris, rubbing until she couldn't hold back any longer. She saw Leo before her, Caspen behind her. Their movements coalesced in a heated blur until blond became black, gray became gold. They were all one—all the same.

Tem cried Kora's name when she came.

As she drifted off to sleep, she imagined the princes on either side of her, cradling her body between theirs.

The next day dawned cold and joyless.

Tem completed her farm chores on autopilot, forcing herself to stay busy until dusk. When the sun was finally setting, she joined her mother on the path to the village.

The town square was packed with restless people, and Tem scanned the crowd for Gabriel, but he was nowhere to be found. She wandered the square alone, taking in the elaborate decorations. There was gold leaf everywhere—plastered on the shutters of the cottages facing the square, lining the wooden stage, even flecked across the cobblestones. Tem shuddered at the sight.

The Passing of the Crown always occurred at this point in the competition, when the prince was nearly ready to choose a wife. It was a way for the current king to express faith in his son's choice—to show that the next generation was ready to rule. If the Passing of the Crown went well, the villagers could expect the king to cede power to the prince on his wedding day.

Someone pressed a glass of mead into Tem's hands. She sipped it slowly, losing herself in the bustle of the square. It wasn't until a hush fell over the crowd that she looked up to see Leo ascending the stage.

He walked straight to the edge, facing the villagers. Behind him stood Lilly, radiant in a green cloak that made her blond hair even brighter. Next to her was Maximus, whose face was drawn in tight apprehension. Tem could only imagine what he was thinking.

"Thank you all for being here tonight," Leo said, his voice carrying over the square. "You honor me with your presence."

To Tem's surprise, this announcement was not met with applause. Instead, a murmur swept through the crowd—one tinged unmistakably with disapproval. Before Tem could worry about this, Maximus stepped forward too.

"As you all know, the Passing of the Crown is a momentous occasion," the king began. "It is a tradition that has gone on for centuries and will go on for many more."

His speech was long, and Tem found her mind wandering. She thought about Caspen and how the basilisk traditions were so very different from the human ones. If only all it took for her to be accepted by his people was a simple ceremony like the one she was about to watch.

Then again, were the two traditions really so different?

The Passing of the Crown was also a test of a father and son's relationship. There was no law that said Maximus *had* to pass the crown. Tem had never heard of a king withholding his blessing from his son, but surely in the long history of the kingdom, it had happened. She couldn't imagine anything worse for the royals. Tensions were already running high now that the truce was broken; it would not be wise to present anything other than a united front, especially when the villagers were growing restless. There was a palpable shift in their energy tonight—an underlying ripple of tension that hung in the air like fog. Tem didn't like the feeling, and for some reason, she feared it.

Her thoughts snapped back to the present as Maximus clapped his hands together sharply. Tem watched as Lord Chamberlain stepped forward and placed a golden crown on the king's head. Tem knew this was meant to symbolize the current state of power. Maximus turned to Leo, who knelt at the front of the stage. The crowd fell silent as Maximus raised his hands, touching just his fingertips to the crown.

He hesitated.

Tem remembered how Maximus had criticized Leo for acting childish, how he didn't trust his instincts. She thought about how he'd spoken to Vera personally to tell her she was his favorite. Leo's affiliation with Tem would no doubt give the king pause. But if Maximus didn't pass the crown, he risked undermining the facade the royals fought so hard to keep intact—the illusion that everything was perfect, that there were no cracks in the foundation. As much as Maximus might want to teach Leo a lesson by not passing the crown, the ramifications of such an act would reverberate far beyond tonight's events. It would damage the royals' reputation and sow seeds of doubt about their ability to rule. It would upset the balance.

An eternity passed.

Then, with the same steady control she'd come to expect from the king, Maximus lifted the crown from his own head and set it slowly on Leo's. For a moment, there was silence.

A voice screamed from the crowd, "*Justice for Jonathan!*"

Everyone turned collectively toward the source of the cry. Jonathan's older brother, Jeremy, was standing on a wooden crate with his fist in the air. Tem felt a chill go down her spine at the sight.

"Justice for Jonathan!" he yelled again.

"And for Christopher!" another voice cried.

Tem heard several sounds of approval. The villagers agreed.

She looked back at Leo, who was slowly standing. His eyes held a coolness Tem knew well.

"Such a loss is devastating," Leo said, his voice firm and clear. "It is unacceptable, and my family mourns with yours. You have my word that the snakes will not go unpunished."

"How?" Jeremy said. "How are you going to punish them?"

Now Leo glanced at his father. Maximus lifted his chin, the motion so subtle it was nearly imperceptible. It was a test, and one Tem dearly hoped the prince would pass. The king was telling his son to take the reins. If Leo was worthy of the crown, he would one day need to navigate situations just like these.

Leo cleared his throat before continuing. "I understand and share your need for justice. But these matters require lengthy discussion. We will not make any rash decisions."

"*Fuck* your discussions. My brother is dead. We should drive the snakes from their caves!"

The crowd roared. A flicker of fear curled in Tem's stomach. The villagers were agitated; there was no calming them. The chant began slowly. Tem barely heard it at first, but it built to an unstoppable rhythm, and there was no mistaking the words that grew into a frenzied roar.

"Kill the snakes! Kill the snakes!"

A frown creased Leo's forehead. He turned once more to his father, who glared at him before stepping forward with undeniable authority. Tem flinched at the look on his face.

"My people," Maximus cried, raising his hands in solidarity. "I feel your pain."

But the crowd would not be appeased. They wanted blood.

"Kill the snakes! Kill the snakes!"

Even Maximus could not control this. He raised his hands higher, as if to fend off the chants.

"We will ensure that the snakes pay for their sins," he yelled over the cries of his people. "They will suffer the consequences of their actions."

But it was not enough. The villagers only grew louder.

Tem understood that they were angry—that a most fundamental part of their livelihood had been offended. The truce was supposed to protect them; it was supposed to guarantee their safety. If they could not trust the truce, they could trust nothing. The villagers lived under the protection of the royals, and when that protection failed, what did they need the royals for? It was not a good position for Leo. It was perilous.

Tem was jostled around as the cries of the crowd grew louder. Her eyes met Leo's, and she saw a sudden flash of concern in them—concern not for himself, she realized, but for her. He stepped toward the edge of the stage—toward her. Tem quickly shook her head. If he entered the crowd, he would surely be swarmed. She gave him a look that said: *I'm fine.*

Leo didn't seem convinced.

For the first time, Tem feared for the human prince. His jaw was tight, his fists clenched at his sides. He was not immune to danger just because he was the son of the king. It only made him more prone to it. Tem knew she hadn't imagined the precarious moment of delay when Maximus passed the crown. And now this.

Before she could do anything else, Leo's eyes widened in fear.

A man was climbing onstage.

The villager lunged immediately in the prince's direction, his arms outstretched, his mouth an angry slash. Leo raised his hands in defense, but it was Maximus who stepped forward to block the blow.

Tem gasped as another man joined the first.

She could do nothing but watch as the two men advanced on the prince and the king, their hands curled into fists. It was unprecedented; she'd never seen such a blatant display of insurgence. Another figure launched themselves onstage, and this one she recognized: Gabriel. He shoved the first man away from Leo before turning to the second. Members of the royal staff were now running forward as more villagers swarmed the stage. The crowd screamed, and Tem covered her ears against the sound.

A hand grabbed her arm. It was her mother.

"Come, my dear. It is not safe."

She was right; it wasn't safe. The crowd was in a furor, yelling and chanting and throwing things at the royals. Glasses shattered on the cobblestones as people tore down the great golden banners draped across the square. It was madness.

Tem watched as Maximus grabbed Leo by the shoulders and yanked him back toward Lilly, who was standing with her hands over her mouth. Tem's mother was pulling her in a similar fashion, directing her to the edge of the crowd. The last thing Tem saw was the golden crown on Leo's blond head as his father ushered him off the back of the stage.

Tem and her mother hurried along the path home, not stopping for anything. Their little cottage seemed extra quiet after the chaos of the town square, and her mother immediately crossed to the sink and began washing the dishes. Tem knew it was a way to soothe her nerves, and she stood beside her in solidarity, drying dish after dish.

Neither of them spoke.

Tem used the silence to reach for Caspen with her mind. He answered immediately: *What is it, Tem?*

I just came from the Passing of the Crown. The villagers are angry. They speak of revolt. Silence.

Tem continued: *You violated the truce. They won't forgive it.*

She felt Caspen bristle.

I am not the only one with unforgiven sins.

Tem shook her head. *More people will get hurt if you don't make things right.*

Caspen let out a humorless laugh. *We do not concern ourselves with their kind.*

You mean my *kind.*

A pause. Caspen's reply was merciless. *I told you there would come a time when you would have to choose.*

And if I can't?

Again, silence. Their connection was still open, but Caspen wasn't speaking. Tem waited him out, resisting the urge to break the standoff. She would not allow him to avoid this conversation; she would not give in.

Finally, Caspen responded. *Then you may find that your choice is made for you.*

Now Tem bristled. *And who will make my choice? You?*

I will never control you, Tem.

For the first time, Tem wondered if that was true.

Do you really want war, Caspen?

It does not matter what I want. War has already begun.

Not a yes or a no. Another half-truth. Another lie.

Tem thought of the tension between the quivers—of the way Caspen's father had come to power. The villagers may be angry now, but the basilisks had been angry for centuries. Peace teetered on a knife's edge.

Suddenly, a knock came at the door. She set down the towel and opened it.

There stood Leo.

Tem immediately cut off her connection with Caspen. Whatever came next, she was certain he didn't need to hear it.

"Leo," she breathed, deeply aware of her mother watching them. "What are you doing here?"

"I had to see you." He was still wearing the crown.

"Well, that's…" Unexpected was what it was. But there was no point in saying that. Instead, she said, "Why?"

Leo leaned slightly closer, and Tem's heart broke into a gallop as she saw a small cut on his cheek. A single drop of blood seeped onto his skin. "I wanted to make sure you were safe. The crowd…"

Leo didn't finish his sentence. He didn't have to. The crowd's behavior went beyond mere rowdiness; it bordered on rebellion. Tem understood why he wouldn't want to voice such a thought, especially in front of her. She was touched by his presence; it showed he cared.

"I'm fine," she said. "I was more worried about you."

Something close to joy flitted across Leo's face. Then he shrugged. "My father put me in a carriage. I had it come here."

There was a pause, and she realized how close they were standing. It was entirely improper; her mother was *right there*. Yet Leo's eyes traveled over her body, and she wondered if he was thinking about the last time he'd been here. Tem remembered the way they'd touched each other on her bed, how his cock had been hard against her palm.

"Tem," he said quietly, and she snapped back to the present. "The ball is soon."

"I know."

He shifted closer. "Will you be there?"

It was an odd question. Tem was one of the final five girls; her attendance was required. She wondered if this was the real reason he'd come—if he needed reassurance that he still had her favor.

"Why would you ask me that?"

Leo raised his hand to touch the bottom of her hair, tracing a strand with his fingertips. He pulled gently on the loose curl before releasing it. "Because I never know what to expect with you."

"Well. You can expect me to be there."

He nodded. "And what else can I expect?"

"What do you mean?"

"I mean." He tilted his head toward her, and she smelled his cologne. "Will he be there too?"

Tem noticed how Leo didn't say Caspen's name, as if saying his name would invite him in.

"The basilisks don't attend the ball," she said stiffly.

"That's not what I meant."

Tem knew what he meant. He was asking if Caspen was in her mind—if she would bring him, even subconsciously, with her. Tem didn't know how to answer him.

"He might be," she said honestly.

Leo's jaw twitched. "Very well."

There was a long moment of silence in which Tem could hear her mother pretending to bustle around the kitchen. It didn't matter that they weren't alone. All that mattered was letting Leo know he still had a chance. So she stood on her tiptoes and pressed her lips to his.

Tem knew she didn't imagine the sound of surprise her mother made. But she ignored it—and everything else—concentrating only on showing Leo how much he meant to her. He kissed her back without hesitation, his hands shooting forward to yank her against him. His urgency only made her want him more. She clung to him shamelessly, holding his body as tightly as she could against hers. Tem had no idea how long the kiss lasted, but the prince was the one to pull away.

She looked up into his gray eyes, wondering what he was thinking. Tem was so used to her mental connection with Caspen that she wished she could connect in the same way with Leo. But unlike Caspen, Leo never hesitated to be vulnerable with her.

So she simply asked, "What are you thinking about?"

To her relief, he smiled. "I am thinking about how I wish your mother wasn't home."

Tem blushed. She hoped dearly that her mother hadn't heard that. Leo touched his fingertips to her cheek, as if to wipe away the color. In return, Tem did the same, wiping away the single drop of blood.

"And you, Tem?" he whispered. "What are you thinking about?"

Tem was thinking about all the things that were on the verge of going terribly wrong. But there was no point in voicing any of them. When it came down to it, there was really only one thing she was thinking about: "You."

He smiled, baring his golden fangs. "Finally an answer I like."

At the sight of his teeth, she grit hers.

The context of their circumstances couldn't be ignored. Tem would never forget the secret she now knew about the royals, how deep their cruelty truly ran. She had to believe that Leo didn't know what was in his mouth—that princes were indoctrinated into this horrifying tradition only once they were crowned king.

Tem needed a way to bring the two sides together: a way to protect Leo and everyone she loved. If Tem had a foothold in basilisk society—if she had some influence in Caspen's world—she could enact change. Or at the very least warn Leo of what was to come.

Tem waited until the prince was safely in his carriage and on the way back to the castle before opening the door to Caspen's mind. She spoke just a single sentence before severing their connection:

I will do the ritual.

CHAPTER TWENTY-THREE

•••✳••••

ER MOTHER RETIRED TO HER BEDROOM, AND TEM DID THE SAME.
The visual of Leo being swarmed onstage ran repeatedly through her mind, and she knew she would never forget the stab of fear she'd felt at the sight. But there was no use in fixating on it tonight. All she could do for now was try to sleep and prepare herself for what was to come.

So Tem slept.

The next morning brought little relief. Tem awoke to the crowing of the roosters, as she always did. She hated the sound, as she always had. Her chores were completed without complaint, and she took only enough breaks to eat her meals. Her mother didn't ask about the prince's visit—it seemed their shared moment of intimacy had passed. Tem wondered whether there was a similar distance between Leo and Maximus today. Would father and son discuss what had happened at the Passing of the Crown? Had Leo noticed the king's hesitation before setting the golden crown on his head? Tem dearly hoped he hadn't. It was a difficult thing to face the rejection of a parent. She wouldn't wish it on anyone.

Before Tem knew it, evening had arrived.

She walked slowly through the woods, noticing the way the birds were barely chirping. Autumn was rapidly turning to winter; soon the mountain where the basilisks dwelled would be covered in snow. The temperature rose the moment she entered the cave.

Caspen was already waiting for her.

Without a word, he tilted his head, and she knew to follow him. When they reached his chambers, Caspen turned to face her. His expression was a mixture of caution and reverence. It was no surprise to Tem that the first words out of his mouth were "May I ask what prompted your decision?"

Tem didn't reply. She found it quite telling that Caspen didn't try to talk her *out* of her decision. Only further confirmation of what she already knew: he secretly wished for her to do it.

She said the same thing she'd said to Leo: "I changed my mind."

Caspen looked like he wanted to ask another question, but he didn't. Instead, he said, "Thank you, Tem."

He was grateful to her for agreeing to the ritual—for deciding to put her body on the line for him. But Tem wasn't ready to be benevolent just yet. "When will it happen?" she asked.

Caspen splayed his broad, graceful hands. "Whenever you choose."

Tem looked up at him. "I want to do it before I move into the castle."

She said it confidently, as if it were a guarantee. Caspen knew as well as she did that according to tradition, the ball was when the prince would choose the final three girls. Of course, Leo might not choose her. But considering the way he'd so clearly feared for her well-being last night, the way he'd shown up at her doorstep just to make sure she was unharmed, Tem knew in her soul that he would.

Caspen interrupted her thoughts. "In that case," he said slowly, "I will make the arrangements for tomorrow night."

Tomorrow night. Twenty-four hours from now.

Tem swallowed her fear, remembering why she was really doing this—remembering what was at stake if she failed.

"I need to know more," she said.

Caspen tilted his head. "More?"

"About the ritual," Tem insisted. "I need to know everything."

"Very well," Caspen said. "What do you wish to know?"

Her first question came easily. "Where will it take place?"

"There is an auditorium specifically for its purpose."

The fear threatened to return. "So it's public?"

"Yes."

Tem couldn't help but blush. Imagining that many people—that many *basilisks*— watching her have sex was enough to make her weak. "How many basilisks will be there?"

"Everyone in my quiver will attend."

"But is it…more than a hundred? Two hundred?"

"I do not know the exact number. But yes. Hundreds."

Tem closed her eyes.

Hundreds.

When she opened her eyes, Caspen was watching her.

"And what of your father?"

"What of him?"

"You need to teach me how to—"

Caspen held up his hand. "Do *not* speak of it."

"I need to know what he—"

"I do not wish to *discuss*—"

"Well, I *do*."

They stared at each other. The topic was uncomfortable for them both. But Tem was right. If the future of the kingdom hinged on her excelling at the ritual, she needed to know exactly what to expect. Caspen knew his father better than anyone; he was the only one who could prepare her for this.

"It's just another lesson," Tem whispered. "That's all."

Caspen shook his head.

She touched his arm gently. "You taught me everything else. So teach me this."

Caspen turned to the fire, staring at it for so long that it actually began to dim. Finally, he spoke. "You will be on top," he said, still not looking at her, "to signify you have come to the ritual willingly."

"The whole time?" Tem asked, her voice small.

"Yes. He will not kiss you or touch you more than necessary."

Tem looked up at him. "I know I made you promise never to alter my feelings," she said. "But will you make me calm during it?"

Caspen shook his head. "I cannot interfere. My father will hold it against you."

Tem nodded.

"But I will make you calm before and after," he said. "You have my word."

She nodded. "Will you be watching?"

"Yes."

The thought repulsed her. "I'd really prefer you didn't."

Caspen's jaw clenched. "Trust me, I would prefer that too. But I must, Tem. I have to make sure his hands do not stray. If they do, I will kill him."

"Are his hands known to stray?"

By the look on his face, Tem could guess the answer.

"I'd rather you didn't kill your own father because of me."

"It would be because of him."

"Still."

The entire conversation was absurd. Tem couldn't believe they were talking about this—that she was really going to have sex with Caspen's father in a public auditorium. Nothing about this was normal.

"What else?" she asked.

"He values confidence. He will sense if you are afraid or if you doubt yourself."

"I'm not afraid."

The barest of smiles touched Caspen's lips. "You never are."

They both stared at the fire.

"Is that it?" Tem asked.

Caspen sighed. "There is more. You will have sex with me as well as my father."

Tem stared up at him.

"At the *same time?*"

"No," Caspen said quickly. "One after the other. My father has seniority, so you will be with him first. Ideally, you will bring him to climax. If not, then the ritual is already over. If you succeed, you will have sex with me next. It is imperative that both my father and I finish quickly. If it draws on, he is less likely to give his blessing. In both cases, we will come outside you."

Tem frowned. "Why?"

"To present proof to my quiver. That way, there can be no question of your achievement."

Tem processed this information. She had no idea there would be so many rules. "Is that all?" she whispered.

"Nearly. If you succeed in both cases, you are worthy of my father's blessing. Should he decide to give it, you and I would go to a designated suite."

"A suite? What happens there?"

Caspen sighed.

"Well?"

"We would be expected to…celebrate the king's decision."

"Celebrate how?"

The pause lingered.

"Oh, for Kora's *sake*," Tem cried. "Just tell me, Caspen. Tell me *all of it*, right this second, or I'm walking home."

Caspen didn't protest. He simply said in a monotone, "We would celebrate by having sex. Continuously."

"*Continuously?*"

"Yes. The closest comparison I can make is to what humans call a honeymoon. It is customary for the new couple to sleep together until midnight. If we do not, my father could revoke his blessing."

"He could revoke it at any time?"

"Yes."

"But how would he know if we didn't have sex until midnight?"

Caspen answered in the same quiet tone. "The suite is public, just like the ritual. Everyone will be watching us."

It was incomprehensible—the whole thing. There was nothing in Tem's mind except pure, unfiltered disbelief, and it threatened to consume her in an unstoppable wave. She felt the sudden need to sit down.

"Is that all?" she breathed.

"Yes. That is all."

Tem had never been so happy to hear it.

She closed her eyes. A moment later, Caspen embraced her, and she let him. Tem leaned against his chest, trying not to think about what would happen tomorrow. But there was no avoiding it. Everything culminated here.

"Tem." Caspen's voice was a strained whisper. "Please. Tell me what you are thinking."

She opened her eyes. "I'm thinking I had no idea what I was getting into when I told you to undress the first night we met."

His arms tightened around her. "Yes. Of that I am quite sure."

There was nothing else to say. Tem was numb.

Caspen held her for a long time, and eventually, they climbed onto his bed, pulling off their clothes as they went. They didn't have sex. Instead, they stared at each other in the dimly flickering firelight as Caspen traced his fingertips up and down Tem's body. She knew he was using the motion to calm himself just as much as her.

It seemed as if they were on the verge of something significant—something that would alter their relationship forever. Tem had no idea how the ritual would affect them—whether it would change their dynamic for better or for worse. Caspen was a basilisk, so he respected his people's customs. But he was also a man, and a possessive one at that. Tem couldn't imagine that sleeping with his father would improve things between them.

They drifted off together, Caspen's hand still on her waist.

She was awoken by her name:

Tem.

Caspen's voice was clear as day, ringing through her mind like a bell. Tem sat up straight, her heart pounding like she'd just run a mile.

"What is it?" she asked.

He didn't answer. His eyes were closed, his body motionless except for the gentle rise and fall of his chest. Tem leaned down, squinting her eyes at him. A slow smile pulled her cheeks as she realized he was asleep.

Caspen must be dreaming about her.

As soon as she thought it, she knew it was true. His mind must be interacting with hers—the barrier lowered, the corridor between them wide open.

Tem.

There it was again.

Tem shifted so she was facing him. She closed her eyes, concentrating as hard as she could.

Caspen.

No response. The corridor between their minds felt clogged, as if it were filled with smoke. Tem wondered if it was because Caspen was unconscious. She waited for him to call to her again, and when he didn't, she felt sudden disappointment.

Her name was only worth saying twice? That wouldn't do at all.

Tem touched his temple, concentrating on their connection. She pushed through the smoke, feeling her way down the corridor and toward the door to his mind. Just outside it, she stopped.

Was this a violation?

Tem didn't want to infiltrate Caspen's mind without his permission. But he had never told her not to do so. And he had pulled her into his mind once before, when they'd stood in front of the mirror together. Besides, did they not belong to each other? What secrets could he possibly have that weren't hers to know?

Tem entered Caspen's mind.

It was completely dark; there was nothing to *see.* Rather she *felt* sensations all around her, curling against her own mind like vines on a tree. First and foremost was sexual desire—it surrounded her with such intensity that Tem felt immediately turned on. She searched for something else—*anything* else—to focus on, finding that there was only one other clear presence in Caspen's mind: worry. A thick thread of anxiety loomed in the background of his consciousness, casting a pall on everything around it.

What was he so worried about?

Tem tried to see the emotion but found that she could not. Instead, she could only *feel* it, concern and apprehension lacing into her as surely as if they were her own emotions. When she probed further, she realized the worry was surrounding *her.* Not the version of her that was currently inside Caspen's mind but the version of Tem he thought about when she wasn't around. He was worried about her. Although that wasn't quite right; it was more that he was worried *for* her. Perhaps because of the ritual. But Tem had a feeling it had nothing to do with tomorrow's events. It was a broader worry—a deep echo of uneasiness that bordered on fear. Fear for her.

Tem.

Caspen was awake. His voice boomed around her in the same way it had when they'd stood in front of the mirror together. She felt his consciousness join hers, and suddenly she was not the only one active in his mind. When he opened his eyes, Tem saw what he saw, which was her own body kneeling on the bed beside him. She was struck once more by the way he perceived her, as if she were the most beautiful thing he had ever seen. His gaze traveled over her hungrily, taking in the curve of her hips and the way her hair curled gently around her shoulders.

Tem was in two places at once—his mind and her body—and she found that she had control in both. She smiled, and a bright surge of joy shot through Caspen's mind. He reached for her, threading his fingers into her hair and pulling her face down to his. When their lips touched, Tem felt what he felt when he kissed her: pure, aching desire. She kissed him back, savoring the hunger that flooded his mind as he pulled her even closer. Caspen's hands went to her body, his palms flat against her skin to feel as much of her as possible. Every time she moaned, a wave of lust overtook him. It was a wonder he didn't tear her apart.

The kiss deepened.

Caspen rolled on top of her, nestling himself in the cradle of her hips. Tem spread her legs to accommodate him, and as soon as she did so, the worry vanished from his mind. His only focus was her; he only wanted *more*. Still, he didn't initiate sex. He followed her lead, letting Tem set the pace, letting her determine when and how things progressed. Tem felt firsthand the restraint it took for him to go slowly. She saw how his gaze lingered on certain parts of her body—her neck, her collarbones, her lips—how he concentrated on a single thought every time he came close to losing control: *Keep her safe.*

He thought it over and over relentlessly whenever Tem's naked body became too much for him to resist.

Keep her safe. Keep her safe. Keep her safe.

It was extraordinary to experience him this way. He was utterly enamored with Tem—nothing mattered to him except for her experience. His pleasure came from her pleasure. Anything she did turned him on; the mere thought of her was enough to harden his cock.

He palmed her breasts, and she watched as her cheeks flushed.

Caspen groaned at the sight.

See what you do to me?

He was addressing her now, within his own mind. Tem still didn't know how to answer him when they were joined like this. So she used her body to communicate, pulling him closer and kissing him on the lips. Heat flared all around her.

Perfect, perfect girl.

Tem only kissed him harder.

Caspen slipped a finger inside her, then another. Tem felt her own wetness—how soft and inviting her center was to him. He touched her gently, dipping ever deeper, adjusting his technique based on the sounds she made. He knew her body intimately, knew exactly what to do to make her moan. He bit her earlobe, she yelped, and he bit it again.

Something was brewing in the back of his mind now: something dangerous. Tem recognized it as the part of him that wanted to transition—the part that wanted to shed his human form and rip into her with no regard for consequences.

Keep her safe.

The words were quiet—strained. It was becoming more difficult to follow them.

Tem realized she had some power here—she could help him resist his instincts. She placed her palms on his torso, pushing him away and creating distance between them. Caspen let her do this. Then she took the hand that wasn't inside her and brushed the tip of her tongue over his fingertips. She was distracting him—forcing him to focus on something that wasn't sex. The monster inside him settled, content to watch her as she sucked gently on his first two fingers. Caspen leaned forward, pushing them deeper into her mouth, all the way to the back of her throat. Tem closed her eyes, letting him penetrate her this way, letting him feel how far she could take him.

Look at you.

For once, Tem could do so. She watched herself through Caspen's eyes, seeing every-thing he saw—seeing everything he loved. She felt how warm and wet her mouth was—how proud he was that she willingly took any part of him inside her. There was ownership in his gaze but not control. He didn't want to dominate her; he only wanted her all to himself. It was no different really from the way she felt about him. Tem wanted Caspen to belong to her and her alone.

I already told you, Tem. You have me.

Caspen withdrew his fingers from her mouth and pressed his lips there instead. His cock was completely hard, and Tem wrapped her palm around it, beginning to pull him inside her. Caspen followed willingly, and the moment he was all the way in, she finally understood what it was like for him to fuck her.

It was pleasure like she'd never known. It was so much *bigger* for him, so much *more.* Basilisks experienced sex on a spiritual level—one that humans couldn't hope to comprehend. It was as if he wasn't complete until he was inside her, as if only a fraction of himself existed without Tem. She felt the way he listened to her body, adjusting his movements based on cues as subtle as her heartbeat. Even her skin told a story. Caspen's fingertips sensed every bead of sweat, every goose bump, every tiny variation in tem-perature. He knew she was about to orgasm before she did; he could hear the difference in the cadence of her breath. Of all the things Caspen had taught her, Tem never thought she'd be learning how to have sex with *herself.* It was extraordinary.

Caspen propped himself up on his elbows so he could watch her face with every thrust. Tem stared back at him, her expression open and trusting and at ease. She was happy and fulfilled in his arms; she was at peace. Nothing brought him more pride than seeing her that way. There was no greater honor than being inside her.

The monster was rapidly returning. Smoke seeped off Caspen in black swirls. When they skimmed Tem's body, they were an extension of him—touching her like his hands would, feeling her just the same as he did with his fingers. The hiss that filled the air was deafening from within his mind. Tem almost wanted to cover her ears. But the imminence of orgasm was far more pressing. As it built in her, it built in Caspen, and Tem could feel how unstoppable the force of a basilisk's climax truly was. He would not transition; he would keep her safe. But he also wouldn't hold back a single ounce of the pleasure that threatened to shatter the confines of his human form.

At the very last moment, Caspen pushed her from his mind.

It wasn't because he no longer wanted her there. Rather, it was so she could experience the orgasm he'd worked so hard to give her. Tem returned to her own mind just as her climax hit, and she gasped as the first moments of pleasure reverberated through her body. She looked up at Caspen, who was looking down at her.

Her eyes slammed shut as she came.

Caspen's hands gripped her hips, his fingers digging deep into her skin. He held her against him as he thrust into her, again and again, so quickly Tem could barely breathe. He was coming too—just as intensely, just as *desperately* as she was.

When they were finally finished, they lay together, his head resting on her chest. Tem ran her fingers through his dark hair, marveling at what had just happened.

Eventually, Caspen asked, *Why did you come into my mind?*

You said my name in your sleep.

She felt him smile against her skin. *I see. And?*

And what?

He raised his head to look her in the eye.

Did you find what you were looking for?

Tem thought about what she'd sensed in his mind: the dark cloud of fear that surrounded his thoughts of her. She wanted to ask about it. But she also wanted to savor this moment with him. So she said, *Yes.*

Good. You are welcome anytime.

They fell asleep together.

When Tem awoke, her first thought was of the ritual. She couldn't believe it was happening tonight—that in a few short hours, she would be doing unthinkable things in order to prove herself to Caspen's quiver. She wanted to stay here with Caspen until it was time. But her mother needed her on the farm, and there was no possibility of lingering.

Caspen walked her to the head of the trail. Instead of kissing her, he placed his hands on her shoulders.

"It will begin at dusk," he said. "Come when you can."

Tem nodded. She was trying to remain calm, but her stomach wasn't cooperating.

"Do I need to…bring anything?" She didn't know what else to ask.

Caspen shook his head. "No. But do not exert yourself today. You will need your strength."

Tem nodded again. Before she could begin to worry, Caspen kissed her. They kissed slowly, and by the time they drew apart, Tem was wet again.

"I wish I could stay with you," she whispered against his lips.

"Soon," he whispered back.

Tem dawdled through her farm work, trying not to think about tonight. Her mother was gone, running an errand in the village, so at least she didn't have to visit Vera. But on a day like today, Tem would have welcomed the distraction. Her chores were done early; there was nothing to do but worry. When her mother returned, they spent the afternoon together in the kitchen, mending their winter cloaks. Hours passed in silence, and Tem's mind spun.

Her thoughts wandered to her very first night in the caves—how the girl in front of her had run screaming back down the path. Tem wondered where that girl was now and whether she regretted fleeing from her fate. She remembered what her mother had said to her that night after she'd spread oil on her thighs: *They will give you courage.*

Tem could use that courage now.

"Mother?" she asked.

Her mother looked up from her sewing. "Yes, dear?"

"Do you still have the ylang-ylang and sandalwood?"

Her mother frowned. "Yes. Why do you ask?"

Tem hesitated. They were well into the training process; there was no reason why Tem would need the same thing she'd needed on her first night in the caves. Yet she felt much the same as she had that night: like everything she'd ever known was about to change.

"I…need courage tonight."

It was all she could say without revealing anything else. Her mother's frown deepened, but she didn't ask any more questions. Instead she set her sewing aside and retrieved the amber glass vials, motioning to Tem to lift her skirt. She spread the oil gently on each thigh, and Tem felt immediately calmed by the contact. It reminded her why she was doing this: for the people she loved.

"Thank you," she whispered when her mother was done.

In response, her mother kissed her on the cheek.

The walk was cold and windy.

Tem hunched her shoulders against the autumn chill, hurrying her way to the base of the mountain. Caspen was already waiting for her in the warm darkness of the cave, and he took her hand in greeting, brushing his lips against her wrist. Tem followed him to his chambers, and they sat on the edge of his bed. Instead of initiating sex like they normally would, they stared at each other in anticipatory silence. Caspen squeezed her hand in his.

"You do not have to do this."

Tem rolled her eyes. "*Don't* say that to me."

"Tem." Caspen pulled her closer, forcing her to look him in the eye. "I will say it until the very last moment, so you know you have a choice."

But Tem just shook her head. Because she didn't have a choice—not really. She was on a mission now, one that Caspen couldn't possibly understand. It wasn't just about him. Or her. Or even Leo. This was about the future of the kingdom, and Tem would not falter now.

"I've made my choice," she said.

Caspen gave her a small smile. "So stubborn," he whispered.

"You should know that by now."

The small smile grew. "That I should."

They lay in bed for a while longer, watching the fire and talking about anything other than what was about to happen. Finally, it was time to go. When Tem began to stand, Caspen stopped her. He tugged at the bottom of her dress.

"There is no need for this," he said.

Realization dawned.

"I'm supposed to go…*naked?*"

"Yes."

"But *why?*"

"Basilisks have different rules than humans do."

"I don't understand."

"We are sexual creatures."

"I know that already."

"What I mean to say is that we are…open."

"What do you mean by 'open'?"

"Out there"—Caspen nodded his head at the doorway, beyond which Tem knew lay the winding passages—"if a basilisk chooses to wear their human form, they will not burden it with clothing."

Tem frowned. "You're saying they're...naked...all the time?"

Caspen's mouth twitched. "That is exactly what I am saying."

"So everyone just...*sees* everyone else?"

"Yes."

"But *why?*"

"Because it does not matter to them, Tem. *You* do not matter to them. To a basilisk, the human form is inferior to our true one. The human obsession with privacy is not one the basilisk shares or understands. They do not respect your body."

Tem bristled. "Does my body not deserve respect?"

"Of course." He pressed his lips to her shoulder. "Of *course* it does. But there is no need for clothing when you will be removing it anyway."

Tem had no argument for that, so she pulled off her dress.

They walked together through the winding tunnels, deeper beneath the mountain than Tem had ever gone before. It was completely dark except for the occasional torch, and Tem had to rely on Caspen for guidance. He held her waist, directing her every time they came to a fork in the passageway. Eventually, they stopped in front of an ancient pair of wooden doors. Caspen pushed them open.

The auditorium wasn't at all what Tem expected.

It was lined with torches and circular in shape, with rows of stone benches that sloped gently down toward an enormous stone statue. Tem craned her neck to look up at it. When she realized what she was looking at, her heart stopped. She turned to Caspen.

"You said the ritual was in an auditorium."

"It is."

She pointed at the statue. "Then explain *that.*"

Caspen looked up, following her gaze. "That..." He trailed off, and Tem finished for him.

"That's *Kora.*"

"Yes. It is."

Tem stared up at the statue numbly. It was the largest depiction of Kora she had ever seen, carved from a stone that looked like marble, with delicate threads of gold laced throughout it. The goddess was in a seated position, cross-legged, her elaborately braided hair nearly touching the arched ceiling.

"Where—" Tem started, but the question died on her tongue. There was only one obvious place the ritual could occur. Kora's hands were resting palm up in her lap, splayed open to form a perfect level surface, right in the center of her legs. An altar.

"Her hands," Caspen said, even though Tem already knew.

"And you expect me to—"

"I do not *expect* you to do anything."

"You know that's not what I mean. This is…"

But there were no words.

Caspen walked her all the way down to the altar, his arm still around her waist. They stood in front of the statue, looking up at Kora's peaceful face.

"She's beautiful," Tem said, almost despite herself.

"Like you."

Just then, the double doors opened, and people began to file in.

Caspen pulled her closer. "I love you," he murmured in her ear. "You do not have to do this."

"Please stop saying that."

Caspen didn't reply. He only held her tighter as the auditorium filled. Tem had expected a crowd full of snakes, but all the basilisks wore their human forms.

It is so that no one accidentally kills you.

Tem supposed that made sense. Still, it was unnerving to see so many naked people at once—it wasn't something Tem was used to. And they were so *beautiful*. The women all had soft curves, and the men were all tall, imposing presences. It was hard not to feel woefully inferior when she was surrounded by so many stunning bodies.

Tem looked up at Caspen. His eyes were narrowed; she had never seen him so tense. She had no idea what to do when he was like this. Usually he was the calm one; it was always Tem who was spiraling about something. Now he was holding on to her like she was the last person alive, his fingers twisting into her skin so tightly that she winced. He couldn't continue like this. The last thing she needed was for him to snap at his father when his energy was so unpredictable.

"Caspen," she said softly, pressing her lips to his chest, then his collarbone, then his jaw. "Calm me down."

He leaned into her touch, relaxing his grip ever so slightly. "As you wish."

A soothing wave flowed from his mind to hers, slowing her scattered heart rate. Somewhere along the way, their lips touched. They kissed slowly, and Tem knew everyone would be watching.

"I love you," Caspen whispered when Tem finally pulled away. "You do not have to do this."

The problem was she loved him too. And in order to be with him, she had to do this.

A sudden hush fell over the crowd. Tem followed their gaze to the double doors, where a tall figure was standing.

The Serpent King had arrived.

CHAPTER TWENTY-FOUR

—•◦※◦•—

TEM HAD THOUGHT THAT CASPEN WAS FORMIDABLE.

All the hard lines on him were even harder on his father. They had the same proud posture, the same rigid musculature in their torsos. But where Caspen's face had an ethereal quality to it, his father's beauty was intimidating and harsh. His eyes were fully black, with none of the gold of Caspen's. They roamed over the auditorium, taking in first the crowd, then his son, then finally Tem. She flinched as his gaze met hers. Beside her, Caspen's entire body went rigid. He was holding her so tightly she could barely breathe, yet she wished he would hold her even tighter. He whispered in her ear:

"He will not harm you. He knows I will never forgive him if he does."

Tem could only nod.

"If at any point you change your mind and you wish to stop, you need only look at me, and I will put an end to this."

"And how will you put an end to it?"

His answer was a single word: "Quickly."

"I'd *really* rather you didn't kill your own father because of me."

The king began to walk toward them. Something flared within Tem—a familiar sensation, something she'd felt many times before with Caspen. Perhaps it was the king's resemblance to his son that made her feel warm. Or perhaps it was something independent of Caspen entirely. The king was naked, just like everyone else, and Tem couldn't help but flush at the sight of his cock. It was the same perfect shape as Caspen's, only slightly thicker at the base. He was already hard, which was no surprise.

At this point, Tem was no stranger to rigid cocks.

The basilisks knelt as the king made his way through the crowd. Time slowed with every step he took, and by the time he was right in front of them, it had stopped altogether.

For an endless moment, father and son stared at each other. Tem could only imagine what they were thinking. Then the king held out his hand. With a jolt, Tem realized she was meant to take it. Caspen's lips dipped to her ear.

"You do not have to do this."

Tem didn't reply.

Instead, she took the king's hand. It was enormous; his palm swallowed her fingers as he led her up the steps of the statue. A hiss rippled through the crowd as they ascended, and Tem resisted the urge to cover her ears against the deafening noise. When they were standing right in front of Kora's hands, the king turned to face her.

The soothing wave of calm slowly dissipated. But Tem didn't look at Caspen. Instead, she looked at the king, seeing everything she was about to touch. She knew she shouldn't be turned on. She *shouldn't* be.

But she was.

Tem couldn't help it. The warmth she'd felt when the king first walked in had only increased the longer he was naked in front of her. She would understand if it was merely a physical sensation—she was looking at a beautiful body after all. But Tem felt an odd, magnetic pull toward him that she couldn't explain. The king was tilting his head just as Caspen always did, considering her in that familiar, reptilian way. His expression was inscrutable. But Tem recognized a spark of heat in his eyes, identical to the fire that burned perpetually within Caspen's. Something else stirred within her: a familiar stubbornness that was welded into her bones. She *wanted* to do this. And she wanted to do it well.

"What is your name?"

The king's voice was rough, like gravel. Tem heard echoes of Caspen's voice in it— they shared the same deep cadence and cavernous tone.

"Temperance."

The parallels to her first night in the cave were undeniable. She'd stood before Caspen in the same way and introduced herself just as she was doing now.

"Temperance," the king said slowly, testing it out. His black eyes bore into hers, and Tem had the distinct impression he was looking straight into her mind.

She squared her shoulders, tilting her chin upward. "And yours?"

The king's eyebrows rose a quarter of an inch. Then he said smoothly, "I am Bastian."

Now that they knew each other's names, Tem felt oddly calm. The king was no longer some nebulous, unknown force. Bastian was just a man like any other, and Tem was a woman who had been trained to seduce him.

"Do you understand your purpose here?" Bastian asked.

Purpose. Somehow, the question felt bigger than the ritual.

Did Tem understand her purpose?

"Yes."

The king didn't ask anything else. It would seem the time for talking had passed.

Without another word, he turned and climbed into Kora's hands, reclining on his back so that her palms cradled his shoulders. It was clear Bastian wasn't going to initiate anything; it was up to Tem to begin the ritual. And that was just fine with her. It gave her control in a situation that felt entirely out of her command, and she used the brief moment alone to close her eyes, preparing herself for what was about to happen.

Her mind was blank, Caspen's presence noticeably absent. She missed him, but she didn't wish he were with her. The next few minutes were not about him. They were about Tem, and they were about Bastian, and they were about showing everyone in this room what she was capable of. For some reason, she was perfectly calm. Some part of her *liked* this—the thrill of a challenge. She'd never felt particularly capable her entire life in the village—never excelled at much of anything. But she would excel at this.

Tem opened her eyes.

It was time.

She stepped forward, pressing her hands against the warm, smooth stone. Then she climbed onto Kora's palms, placing her knees on either side of Bastian. The second she opened her legs, the king's nostrils flared, and she knew he must smell the sandalwood and ylang-ylang on her thighs. Tem didn't ride him yet—didn't even touch him. She merely looked down at him, noticing all the things about his body that reminded her of Caspen's. His skin held the same smooth, flawless luster. His jaw was the same angular shape. The two men were undeniable predators—Bastian was eyeing her like he wanted to devour her right then and there. It was a look she'd grown used to getting from Caspen, and it was a look she'd always liked.

Tem also noticed the ways in which they differed.

Bastian's hair was streaked silver at his temples. He had a scar on his shoulder in the shape of a jagged lightning bolt. Perhaps an old battle wound. Whereas Caspen's chest was bare, Bastian's was covered in dark hair that tapered in a trail toward his cock. Tem wanted to run her fingers through it. Instead, she slowly leaned down, extended her hand, and cupped his balls in her palm. She had no idea if this was allowed, but she wanted to feel this part of him—the vulnerable part—to remind the king that she was in charge. Caspen was right: Tem was stubborn. And she was ready to begin.

Bastian didn't protest. He simply watched her, his cunning eyes narrowed in focus. Tem wondered what he was thinking, whether he had already formed an impression of her. Did he believe she could bring him to climax? Or was he merely waiting for her to fail? It didn't matter what he believed. *Tem* knew she could do this.

Her hand moved from his balls to his cock, her fingers wrapping around the impossibly thick base. She didn't bother stroking it. Instead, she centered herself above

Bastian, lowering herself until his cock was almost touching her. Her eyes flicked once more to his. The king looked up at her as if to say: *Do it. I dare you.*

Tem was not afraid.

She slid herself slowly down the first few inches of his cock. She already knew what to expect; Caspen had taught her how to take a cock like this inside her. The feeling of expanding—of *stretching*—was one she knew well. Still, it was difficult to get all the way to the bottom, and despite her efforts, she couldn't make all of him fit. But it didn't matter. As soon as Bastian was inside her, Tem's trepidation fell away, and her instincts took over.

She moved her hips slowly, testing his cock, learning how it felt to ride him. The heat she had seen in the king's eyes was unmistakable. Tem knew what it looked like when a man was aroused, and it was exactly how Bastian was looking at her now. She used it to her advantage, building into a steady pace, establishing a rhythm. She knew she had to make him finish quickly, but she also knew the power of the buildup. Caspen's words played in her head: *He values confidence.* So Tem looked down at the king with haughty assurance, as if *he* were lucky to be here with *her.* She pretended Bastian was the one who needed her approval, not the other way around, and fucked him exactly the way she thought he should be fucked.

She dug her fingernails into his torso, using the hard planes of his abs to steady herself as she slid up and down, working herself back and forth the same way Caspen taught her. Tem pictured Caspen's hands on her hips, guiding her, training her to understand a man's body. She leaned forward even more, pushing her breasts together, daring the king to look at them. But he didn't. He held her gaze with practiced detachment, the only sign that he was enjoying himself the endless black pools of his pupils, which were trained on her in uninterrupted rapture.

Up until now, Tem had been avoiding the base of his cock. Bastian was bigger than his son, and it was only when she let herself take him fully that her body began to protest. The moment he filled her completely, Tem couldn't help but wince.

As soon as she did so, Bastian grunted.

Caspen's words came to her suddenly:

We are predisposed to destroy you—to take pleasure in your pain. When we are together, I walk a line between pleasing you and...hurting you. My human form craves the former. My true form craves the latter.

Bastian was no different from Caspen in this way—he also craved her pain. If she wanted to make him finish—and finish fast—it would cost her something to do so.

Tem rolled her hips quickly, riding through the pain, concentrating instead on the effect she was having on Bastian. His jaw was locked, and with each shallow breath he took, his body only tensed more. She slammed herself down on his cock, harder and harder, allowing yelp after yelp to escape her lips. Pain merged with pleasure. They were one and the same.

Suddenly, Bastian was fucking her back, moving his hips to meet hers. She had no idea if that was standard, but if the goal was to make him finish, it had to be a good thing. Tem glanced at his hands, which thankfully weren't straying. But there could be no doubt that the king was participating in the ritual, which meant that Caspen was watching his father fuck her. Tem tried not to think about that. Instead, she let herself go, arching her back and moaning whenever the base of his cock put pressure on her clitoris.

The king was close. She could see the muscles in his neck straining with each thrust. He was half sitting up now, his eyes boring into hers, delicate tendrils of smoke seeping from his skin. It was the point when he should climax—Tem knew it from her sessions with Caspen, and she knew it instinctively as a woman. Yet the king was not finishing. Before Tem could begin to panic, she felt a sudden presence overtake her mind. For a moment, she thought it might be Caspen. Then she realized it was Bastian.

Up until now, Caspen was the only basilisk who had ever entered her mind. His voice was as familiar as her own. But his father had a different presence—older, *ancient,* vaster than the sea. He spoke just two words before retreating:

You first.

It was the same thing Caspen had said to her their first night together in the caves. Like father, like son. But this wasn't supposed to be part of the ritual; Caspen hadn't said anything about *her* finishing—only his father and himself. What if this was the only way that Bastian would finish? What if his approval was contingent on her climax?

Whatever the case may be, Tem wanted to finish. And not just because he'd told her to. It would be a lie to say she wasn't turned on by the ritual. She imagined the king was Caspen, and in a way, he *was* Caspen. The two men weren't really so different. Both were intimidating. Both were powerful. Tem was attracted to that power: she always had been. She focused on the way his cock felt inside her, allowing herself to feel real pleasure, just for a moment. The moment she felt it, she *pushed* it in Bastian's direction as hard as she could—as if she could reverse his infiltration into her mind and infiltrate his instead. Bastian's nostrils flared, his eyes narrowing to slits. In that moment, she knew she had him.

With a single, final thrust, Tem came.

The second it happened, the king grabbed her waist, lifting her off his cock with undeniable finality. Tem gasped at the sudden emptiness, watching in stunned shock as the king finished on her thighs. She stared at his cum on her skin—blending with the ylang-yang and sandalwood oils—just as thick and shimmery as Caspen's. It occurred to her distantly that Caspen only existed because of that exact substance.

Bastian set her on Kora's stone fingers before stepping down from the altar. He slid his hand over Tem's thighs and raised his palm high above his head. Tem realized he was showing his cum to the audience, offering irrefutable proof that she had succeeded. A deafening hiss rose from the crowd, and Tem felt immediately as if she might faint. Before she could fall, a pair of hands grabbed her, their grip familiar and strong. The second Caspen's skin touched hers, peace spread through her. It reverberated down her spine in a soothing wave, and she knew he was keeping his promise to make her calm. He lifted her off the altar, pulling her tightly against his chest.

His lips were on her ear. "You were *perfect*, Tem."

"Perfect?"

"Utterly."

She leaned against his shoulder.

Bastian lowered his hand, and the hiss quieted. He turned to Caspen, and although he said nothing aloud, Tem knew they were speaking to each other using their minds.

Without warning, her calm faltered.

Caspen was supposed to be controlling her emotions; she shouldn't be able to feel the anxiety that suddenly erupted in her chest as her heartbeat quickened into a frantic canter. Tem couldn't tell whether the feelings were hers or Caspen's. Anxiety turned to fear—the same fear she'd felt when she'd visited Caspen's mind just last night. Without warning, Tem heard a single sentence of their exchange:

I will not allow it.

The words were spoken by Caspen, and when he said them, Bastian's brow furrowed. Tem froze in place as a flash of anger passed over the king's face. His reply was swift: *You will do as I say.*

Just as uncertainty began to twist her stomach, the king turned to her. He held out his hand, and the moment he did so, the wave of calm returned.

Tem looked at Caspen. He nodded. As if on autopilot, she raised her hand and placed her palm gently on the king's, directly over his cum. His fingers wrapped around hers, lifting her arm high into the air. The second he did so, the hiss of the crowd returned.

Caspen's face split into a proud smile. Not a word had been spoken, but she understood that she had done the impossible.

Tem had earned the king's blessing.

Bastian dropped her hand before retreating into the audience. The hissing grew louder—it was all Tem could hear, reverberating through her like a tidal wave. She looked at Caspen, and when his eyes met hers, she saw a wild mix of concern, desire, and fierce pride. She knew he was worried for her, but she also knew how meaningful this moment was for him—for *them.*

"It is our turn now," he said, his voice low. "Can you go on?"

She nodded again. The ritual had barely begun; the king's blessing was only half the battle. Tem knew she was ultimately seeking the approval of Caspen's quiver and that they would make their decision based on everything that would happen *after* she slept with the king.

"You are in charge, Tem. I will follow your lead. What do you wish for me to do?"

Tem had only one answer:

"Just kiss me."

Caspen kissed her, and the moment he did so, Tem felt herself unwind. There was no ritual, no audience, no king. There was only Caspen, who she trusted unequivocally with her body and with her heart. They kissed as if they were the only two people in the room, and they may as well have been. His hands dipped to the backs of her thighs, lifting her onto the edge of the altar. He remained standing as his cock slid inside her.

Tem.

Caspen.

He felt so good. He felt so right. He felt like home.

Tem knew she could make Caspen finish—she'd done it a hundred times before. But this time, they needed to be quick. So she sent him vision after vision of her touching herself—alone in her room, where he had never been, sometimes using the claw, sometimes using her fingers, showing him what she did when they were apart. She replayed her moments of climax again and again, knowing they would overwhelm him—knowing they would push him straight to the brink.

It pushed her there too.

"Caspen," she moaned. Just his name—nothing more.

Caspen pulled out of her immediately, his shoulders hunching forward as he finished into his palm with an urgent groan. Before Tem had time to breathe, he slapped his hand hard against her hip, sliding it all the way down her thigh and leaving a wet, slick streak for everyone to see.

There was no mistaking the approval of the audience. Their collective hiss had become deafening. Tem finally tore her gaze away from Caspen and looked out into the crowd.

Her mouth fell open in shock. "Caspen," she gasped. "What's happening?"

Caspen followed her gaze.

The basilisks were all having sex.

Some with each other, some with themselves. In pairs, in groups, in sweaty, roiling piles of limbs. Men with women, men with men, women with women. There was no order to it whatsoever—Tem had never seen anything like it. It was already enough of a shock to see hundreds of naked people at once, but to watch them all fuck each other was far beyond anything Tem could comprehend. She watched as three women tore into each other with an intensity that bordered on violence. One man was on his knees as another man thrust his cock into his mouth. Another man kissed one woman while a different woman sat on his cock. It was complete and utter chaos. The hiss reverberated off them in a continuous wave, throbbing with their collective movements. It seemed to be growing somehow into something that wasn't just a sound. Tem felt the pressure of the air begin to change. She recognized the smell of smoke.

"Caspen?" Tem whispered, her voice small.

Caspen grabbed her face. To her surprise, his eyes were dark with fear.

"You need to leave," he said. "Right now."

"What? No, I'm not leaving you."

He was trying to pull away from her. She wrapped her legs around him tightly, holding him closer. He was already hard again.

"Tem, please," he said desperately. "You need to leave."

"Tell me what's going on."

"They are about to transition."

"All of them?"

"There is no time to explain. You must close your eyes. And do not open them until I tell you."

"What? Why—"

"When they come, they will transition. *I* will transition."

"I don't understand."

"I cannot stop it, Tem. I am one with them. Just close your eyes."

"What do you mean you're one with—"

"Close your eyes, Tem!"

It was an order. Tem closed her eyes.

The hiss grew to an unspeakable volume, filling her from the inside out, drilling into her skull with such intensity she could barely stand it. Her legs were still wrapped around Caspen, but a moment later, they were being pushed apart. Whereas one moment ago, she had been pressed against his warm, damp skin, now she felt hard scales scraping against her thighs. He was embodying his true form—right now—right in front of her. But she couldn't see him. She could only feel the shape of his body change from distinctly human to distinctly…not. His natural temperature was already higher than hers, but now it felt like she was touching a tin roof in the peak of summer. Tem's skin began to burn. She lurched backward, curling into herself, trying not to touch any part of him. All she heard was the earsplitting hiss of the crowd, ripping her eardrums to shreds.

Tem had no idea how long it lasted. The hiss reached a thundering crescendo, and she knew they must be climaxing. She covered her ears, shutting out the screeches, shutting out everything that made the hair on the back of her neck stand up in anticipatory fear.

Eventually, the hissing stopped.

"Tem."

Her name.

"You can open your eyes now, Tem."

She didn't move.

"Open your eyes for me."

Tem opened her eyes.

At first, she saw nothing but smoke.

Then she saw Caspen—the human version—looking down at her. Tem raised her head. She was curled up on the altar, cradled in Kora's hands. The room was emptying; all the basilisks were once again wearing their human forms. Bastian was nowhere to be found.

She sat up straight, placing her hands on Caspen's chest. His skin was hot.

"Are you hurt?" she asked him.

He let out a dull laugh. "You are the one I am worried about."

"I'm fine."

His gaze fell to her thighs, where fresh pink burns were forming. He pressed his palms to her skin, healing the burns with a cooling pulse.

"I am sorry," he whispered.

"I'm fine," she said again.

He just shook his head.

"What now?" she asked. "Do we still…"

"Yes." Caspen nodded. "The ritual must continue. That is, if you…"

"I can do it."

Caspen pursed his lips. But instead of protesting, he gathered her gently in his arms, lifting her off the altar and setting her on the ground. His fingers touched her waist as he led them through the tunnels, and Tem knew they were headed to the suite where they would have sex until midnight. Tem wanted to ask a hundred questions, but she also wanted to preserve her energy. So she spoke to Caspen using her mind:

I still don't understand what happened. Why did they all transition?

The ritual collectively turned them on. When that happens, it has a hive effect. We all become one, and if one of us comes, we all do.

Tem processed this. It was a terrifying concept.

But why *did it happen?*

Because of you.

Tem couldn't believe what he was saying.

That's…good, isn't it?

Yes. But it is also dangerous, especially for you. If you had opened your eyes—

But I didn't. I'm fine, Caspen.

He pressed a kiss to her temple before changing the subject. *Are you ready for what comes next?*

Tem knew what came next would not be easy for her. She thought of all the nights she'd spent with Caspen up until now—how he'd always accommodated her when she needed a break from having sex. He wouldn't be able to do that this time. They were meant to have sex repeatedly, without stopping, until the ritual was complete. She didn't know if her body would be able to withstand it.

I think so.

It was the best she could give him. His grip tightened on her waist.

I will keep you safe, Tem.

She knew he would try. But she also knew what she had just seen: Caspen was bound to his quiver—bound to his true form. He would not be able to suppress his instincts forever.

Tem wanted to ask Caspen about the moment between him and his father—about the fear that had seeped from his mind into hers. But this didn't seem like the time to broach the subject.

Besides, they had arrived at the suite.

A large room opened up before them with the same stone walls as the rest of the caves. There was no ceiling; Tem could see the night sky. Caspen followed her gaze.

It is how we will know when to stop. When the stars show that it is midnight, the ritual is over.

In the center of the room was a large, low bed. There were no blankets or pillows—only a fitted, black silk sheet.

The bed was completely exposed; there was no barrier around it whatsoever. But unlike the altar, which had been the focal point for the audience, this was like a fishbowl, where anyone could walk by them at any time. Basilisks were already roaming around the suite, some of them leaning against the walls, some of them seated in groups on the floor.

Are they going to watch the whole time?

They will come and go as they please.

Some of the basilisks were mere feet away from the bed. *They're so close.*

Caspen pulled her face to his. *Just look at me, Tem.* He brushed his thumbs over her cheeks. *Look only at me.*

She nodded. If she looked only at him, she could pretend they were in his chambers, like they had been so many times before. He was still inside her mind, keeping her calm as they approached the bed together. Tem climbed onto it first, falling onto her back and looking up at Caspen, his face framed by stars. He leaned down, pressing his lips first to her stomach before kissing a path up her body. The second he touched her, she felt safe.

I love you.

His words caressed her mind like a whisper. She sighed beneath him, spreading her legs and letting him in like she always did. Tem was sore already. But she was also wet, and she took his cock easily. Caspen slid in and out with unhurried thrusts.

I love you too.

They moved together slowly, ignoring everything around them, focusing only on each other. Tem noticed that Caspen kept her beneath him, as if he were shielding her.

When she tried to get on top, he held her down.

Caspen, what are you doing?

I am trying to preserve your privacy.

Well, cut it out.

She felt him smile against her cheek. *You are human, Tem. I know you are not used to being watched like this.*

I don't need you to protect me, Caspen.

I only meant to help.

This is going to be a very long night if we only fuck in one position.

He smiled again, and this time, he allowed her to roll so she was on top. A hiss echoed throughout the suite, and Tem felt a sudden stab of anxiety as she remembered what had just happened in the auditorium.

Will they transition again?

Tem didn't like the idea of being trapped in such a small room with this many basilisks wearing their true forms.

It is unlikely. The hive orgasm is extremely rare. Two in one day would be unheard of.

How rare?

The last one was before my lifetime.

That was a surprise to her, especially considering how sexual the basilisks were. She figured they were having hive orgasms frequently.

Caspen sat up, pressing his lips to hers. *Do not be afraid.*

Tem pushed him back down. *I'm not afraid.*

She splayed her hands flat on his chest so she could center herself as she rode him. The hissing was steady but didn't grow louder, and Tem allowed herself to relax. They were here for her after all. Why shouldn't they see what she could do?

Her first orgasm built gradually. Tem didn't mind taking her time when she knew there would be many more to come. She paced herself deliberately, savoring the way Caspen felt inside her. His eyes were black with lust, and Tem wondered fleetingly whether watching her fuck Bastian had triggered his possessive side, turning him on even more. Nothing would surprise her at this point; it had done something similar to Tem.

Just when she was close, Caspen grabbed her waist, lifting her and turning her so she was riding his cock facing the opposite direction. Tem gasped at the sudden change. A moment later, his hands went to her hair, pulling it back over her shoulders and exposing her breasts. Tem understood he wanted to display her, to show her off to the basilisks surrounding the bed. She watched them as they watched her, enjoying the way their eyes traced over her body.

One of the basilisks stepped forward. He extended his hand, reaching for her face. *Caspen? What's happening?*

He wants to touch you.

Should I let him?

That is up to you. Say the word, and I will tell him not to.

Her answer came easily: *No. Let him.*

Tem watched the basilisk as he brushed his fingers gently along her jaw. When he stepped back, another took his place. Basilisk after basilisk approached her, touching her briefly—never lingering—almost as if they wanted nothing more than to confirm that she was real. They touched her face, her hair, her lips. The men were strong and assured, the women soft and tender. Occasionally, a hand would dip to her breasts, but every time that happened, Caspen let out a low growl, and the basilisk would retreat.

Tem was close to finishing. The mere thought of doing so in front of all these people only made her want to more. She wanted to show them how good she was at this, how well Caspen had taught her.

The basilisks were still touching her, one after the other. With a jolt, Tem recognized the next basilisk in line.

Rowe.

CHAPTER TWENTY-FIVE

••✳••

N A SPLIT SECOND, CASPEN WAS UPRIGHT. HIS CHEST HIT TEM'S SHOULDERS AS HIS arms wrapped around her waist, halting her motions and pulling her tightly against him.

He should not be here. The ritual is only meant for my quiver.

The crowd parted for Rowe as he approached the bed, his eyes never leaving Tem's. The suite was silent; any hissing had stopped completely. Behind her, Tem could feel Caspen's temperature rising. She prayed he wouldn't transition while he was still inside her.

Rowe stopped at the foot of the bed. He raised his hand slowly.

Caspen's grip became even tighter. The room was so quiet Tem could hear her own heartbeat galloping frantically against her ribs. Rowe's eyes flicked to Caspen's. They stared at each other for a long moment, and Tem knew they must be speaking with their minds.

Rowe's gaze slid to her.

Tem stayed perfectly still as he brushed a single fingertip under the bottom of her chin, tilting her head toward his. When her neck was fully arched, he paused.

"She takes you so well," Rowe whispered.

Caspen wrapped his fingers around her throat, yanking her away from his grasp. "Do not touch what is mine."

A smile twisted Rowe's lips. It was a cold smile, utterly devoid of anything but malice. He looked Tem straight in the eye and said, "I hope he breaks you."

Before Tem could think of a response, Rowe stepped back, disappearing into the shadows.

Tem looked to Caspen for guidance as the crowd's collective hiss returned. He was staring after Rowe, his jaw clenched. Tem touched his face gently, pulling his gaze to her.

"Caspen," she whispered. "Look only at me."

At her words, he relaxed. His grip on her throat loosened; the tension left his chest. He lifted her once more, turning her again so she was facing him. Tem moved her hips purposefully, knowing they wouldn't be interrupted this time. The wave inside her began to build as Caspen's fingers went to her clitoris, applying pressure where she needed it the most.

Caspen, she cried into his mind, *I'm—*

Before she could finish her thought, she came.

Caspen came too, releasing himself inside her as he pulled her hips quickly against his. She felt his wetness join hers, spreading over their thighs and dripping onto the sheet. There was ownership in his grip. The way he held her told everyone that she was *his,* that she belonged to *him.* Tem gave herself over to it, letting him pound into her as hard as he wanted, letting him mark her in any way he liked.

They fucked again. And again.

Every time Caspen came, he became hard mere moments later. There were times when he didn't even bother pulling out. They had sex for hours, and eventually the bed became soaked with their cum. At one point, two basilisks stepped forward, and Caspen fucked Tem standing up while they changed the fitted silk sheet.

The crowd ebbed and flowed. Basilisks came and went, watching for just a few seconds or for hours at a time. Some of them touched themselves, and some of them simply stared. It was overstimulating to the point of distraction. Sometimes Tem found herself watching them as they watched her, staring at the endless parade of beautiful, naked bodies.

Only one person stayed the entire time.

Bastian stood off to the side, nowhere near the bed. He never touched himself, although he was clearly erect. He merely stood there silently, focused on Tem. Whenever she caught herself staring at him, she forced her gaze back to Caspen, losing herself in his eyes, which were getting blacker with every orgasm.

He was starting to transition.

There was no mistaking the scales that had begun to harden his skin. They spread slowly but surely down his chest in a dappled wave, multiplying by the hour. There was no way to stop it—no way to reverse it. They were here finally, at the point Caspen had always feared. Caspen was becoming more aggressive—his hands squeezed her breasts, her neck, her ass. His fingers tangled in her hair, holding her mouth directly on his as he claimed her.

The stars inched along the sky above them but not nearly fast enough. After a particularly rough climax, Caspen cradled Tem's face in his palms.

You will bleed if we keep going as we have been.

So heal me.

No. I will not hurt you just because I can heal you.

I don't care, Caspen.

I do.

Tem knew Caspen was worried for her. But beneath that worry was the insatiable desire she had come to recognize in him. She knew that at some point—*soon*—he wouldn't be able to stop even if he tried. Tem remembered what she had seen when she'd infiltrated his mind. He was addicted to her; everything she did turned him on, and even when she was in pain, it only turned him on more, the basilisk instinct overtaking the part of him that wanted to keep her safe.

She could see how difficult it was for him to hold back—how he couldn't look at her for too long, especially when she was on top, how close he was to losing control with every single thrust. It was only a matter of time before he gave in and ravaged her the way he really wanted to.

Just hurt me, Caspen.

No.

There's no other way.

I will find another way.

And what way is that exactly?

I will be gentle.

But he couldn't be gentle. Every time their eyes met, she could practically feel his hunger. The scales on his shoulders were spreading; his skin was scorching to the touch. She could taste smoke on his tongue. He was transitioning before her, his body slipping into its true form against his will. Nobody—not even Caspen, with his unparalleled self-control—could change his fundamental nature. Tem was prepared to argue again. But before she could, Bastian stepped forward.

Tem froze as father and son stared at each other once more.

Her heart leaped in anticipation. Was there a problem? Had they done something wrong? Was the ritual over? Tem glanced up at the sky. It was not yet midnight. She looked at Caspen, but his face revealed nothing. After a moment, Bastian stepped back again, crossing his arms and leaning once more against the wall.

What did he say?

Caspen's eyes met hers. *We have one hour left.*

Dread pooled in Tem's stomach. An hour.

It was far too long. She knew her body; she couldn't go another hour like this.

I will try to be gentle, Tem. But I…

Caspen didn't finish his sentence. Tem finished it for him: *But you can't.*

He was still thrusting slowly, still trying to resist. He buried his head in her shoulder; he couldn't even look at her anymore. She could feel his heartbeat—normally so slow and steady—beating erratically against her chest.

He was fighting. But he was losing.

Caspen's body refused to behave; the monster inside him was dying to get out. Tem pressed her palms against his shoulders. His skin was white-hot.

Just hurt me, Caspen.

No.

Even if you're gentle, I'm not going to make it.

He shook his head. But they both knew she was right.

Hurt me, Caspen. Then heal me. It's the only way.

I cannot.

You don't have a choice.

I will not.

But it was not a matter of will. *I trust you, Caspen.*

It was true. There was no one she trusted more.

The crowd of basilisks had grown. Tem wasn't surprised; this was the grand finale after all. This final hour would determine whether everything had been worth it— whether *Tem* was worth it.

Caspen rolled on top of her. Tem knew it was his way of protecting her from himself. This way, her body was covered—she was no longer on display, and Caspen could control the pace. Tem heard just a singular thought in his mind, desperate and deliberate: *Keep her safe.*

He clung to it like a life raft, syncing his thrusts to its rhythm, chanting it again and again and again. It was a temporary solution; nothing could prevent what was coming. Caspen was pressing her into the mattress; his skin was burning her alive. Despite being soaking wet, Tem felt as if she were straining to take his cock—as if he were growing inside her. He no longer felt the way he always felt. He felt harder. Tem remembered the first time she'd stroked him in the cave, how her hand had bled.

Keep her safe. Keep her safe. Keep her safe.

Even his presence in her mind was shifting, changing from something that felt human to something completely foreign to Tem—something animalistic and feral. It gnawed at the edges of her brain, clouding her vision and consuming her consciousness with its insatiable hunger, crushing her—*smothering* her.

Caspen's cock was hard and unyielding and *ridged*, changing into something that was far too big for Tem's body. It was stretching her—forcing her legs open beyond the point of comfort, far beyond what Tem's hips could accommodate naturally. Blood joined her wetness.

The fine line between pain and pleasure blurred until it was nonexistent, both sensations twining together in her body and her mind in an indistinguishable thread.

Keep her safe.

But Tem was fading. It had been too long a day; she had been through too much. Hours of sex had left her exhausted, and she was becoming a mere shell of herself.

Keep. Her. Safe.

Her body strained to take him, but it was impossible. Caspen was ripping her apart—breaking her, just like Rowe hoped. Every time he pulled away, each ridge of his cock shredded her on its way out before he pushed back in again. Her blood was everywhere. Tem shut her eyes against the wave of panic gripping her like a vise.

Then, with a horrible *crack*, Tem felt her pelvis break.

Pain slammed into her so sharply that she screamed.

At the sound of her scream, Caspen came with a feral roar—one that shattered her eardrums and cracked the stone walls of the suite. He released such a powerful wave of energy that the basilisks surrounding them knelt in unison, bowing their heads immediately to the floor.

The last thing Tem saw before she blacked out was Bastian walking toward them once more.

•••••

Caspen's presence returned slowly to her mind, trickling into her skull like water. She barely heard the first time he whispered her name:

Tem.

It was only when he spoke again that his voice became clearer:

Please, Tem. Come back to me.

Tem opened her eyes.

She looked up at Caspen's dark, concerned face. The only thing she knew was pain. "Just take it away," she begged, the words barely a whisper. "Caspen. Please."

No sooner were the words out of her mouth than Tem felt the pain subside, and she gasped in relief. It ebbed steadily away as her body stitched itself back together. Nothing had ever felt so good in her entire life. Relief washed over her as the pain in her pelvis retreated and her hip bones realigned.

Tem tried to sit up, but Caspen immediately held her down.

"Lie still," he said, his voice tight with fear.

Tem allowed her head to fall back on the mattress. They were still in the suite, still surrounded by basilisks. A glimmer of starlight touched her face.

It was midnight.

Caspen gathered her in his arms, lifting her. Nobody stopped them.

Caspen carried her like that through the tunnels, all the way back to his chambers. When he laid her gently on his bed, she saw blood on his legs, and she knew it was hers.

"I'm sorry," she said, her voice hoarse.

He shook his head. "When will you learn that you have nothing to be sorry for? *I* am sorry."

Tem could only nod.

Caspen disappeared for a moment before returning with a clean linen. He pulled her legs open gently and began wiping the blood from her thighs. Tem watched him as he did it, and despite her exhaustion, she was struck by his tenderness. The linen was warm and soft. He cleaned every part of her, and when he was done, he ran the towel over his own legs, removing the last traces of the ritual.

Then he looked down at her. "Can I get you anything, Tem?"

"No."

"Are you sure?"

"I just want you."

The corner of his mouth twitched. He climbed into bed beside her, pulling her into his arms. "You have me."

In response, she kissed him, and for a while, that was all they did. But eventually, Tem wrapped her legs around him. She traced her fingers gently down his cock, coaxing it between her thighs.

"Tem," Caspen murmured. "It is over. You should sleep."

But she shook her head. "Please."

Caspen sighed. "I cannot say no to you, Tem."

"Then don't."

They had sex once more. Just the two of them, alone, with nobody watching. They fucked slowly, with no agenda or deadline. Several times, they stopped just to kiss before starting up again. Caspen brushed his lips softly over every inch of Tem's skin, pressing kisses to her neck, her wrists, her collarbones. He kissed each of her fingertips one by one, then he kissed the freckles on the palms of her hands. He had already healed her injuries, but it felt as if he was healing her all over again, the cooling pulse of his magic blooming wherever his skin touched hers.

Tem didn't think she could climax again. Yet somehow, with Caspen thrusting slowly between her legs, she felt herself building toward it once more.

"Caspen," she whispered.

"Tem," he whispered back.

She came. A moment later, so did Caspen. She fell asleep while he was still inside her.

Tem awoke in a fog.

Her mind was tired, her body more so. It was as if she had been trampled by a carriage. The moment she opened her eyes, she saw Caspen was already awake, watching her.

"Tem." His voice was low and hopeful. "How do you feel?"

Tem groaned in response. She was sore everywhere—her back ached; her hips hurt. For a moment, she didn't know where she was.

Then she remembered.

The events of the previous night rushed over her in a relentless wave, threatening to overwhelm her. She remembered the auditorium, the altar, the king's body beneath hers. She remembered every single time Caspen had entered her in the public suite and how by the end of it, she was nearly split in half.

"Tem." His voice came back to her, its urgency increased. "Please answer me. Are you in any pain?"

She could only nod.

At her response, Caspen sat up. He placed his palm flat on her stomach and closed his eyes. There was a cool pulse, and suddenly the aches disappeared. Tem felt immediately better physically, but she knew he could do nothing for the emotional exhaustion that clouded her brain like smoke.

"Caspen," she whispered. "Was I enough?"

He opened his eyes, looking at her with boundless reverence. "You were more than enough. You were extraordinary."

Her lungs felt as if someone were squeezing them. "But when we came back here…"

She trailed off. Caspen had carried her back to his chambers after the ritual was over. The memory of the journey was blurry, but Tem knew she hadn't imagined the blond female basilisk who'd sneered at her in the darkness of the tunnel, and she certainly hadn't imagined what the woman had said to Caspen:

"A mate who must be carried to bed like a child, bleeding and broken. Is this who the prince deems worthy?"

Caspen had snapped immediately back, "The *king* deems her worthy. An honor you cannot claim."

The exchange lasted mere seconds. But the words were seared on Tem's heart, and she knew she would never forget them.

Caspen's eyes held hers. "That was nothing, Tem."

"It was the truth," she said quietly.

"It was *nothing*. Jealous words from a jealous soul."

"Who is she?"

Now Caspen looked away.

She grabbed his chin, pulling his face back to hers as she said, "You don't get to keep secrets from me."

He met her eyes. The unsaid portion of her sentence hung in the air between them: *Not after what I just did for you.* Caspen knew it was the truth just as much as Tem did.

He let out a long breath before saying, "Her name is Adelaide. She belongs to the Seneca quiver. We have…history."

Tem knew as well as anyone what "history" meant. It meant they had slept together and that Adelaide had satisfied him more than Tem ever could.

"Did you love her?" Tem whispered.

"No."

She looked him in the eye, and she knew he was telling the truth. But that didn't make it hurt any less. "Then why is she so angry?"

"Our values do not align."

"How so?"

Caspen sighed. "Must we discuss this, Tem? You have just been through—"

"Yes. We must."

He sighed again, looking down at her in exasperation. "Adelaide does not believe basilisks should mate with humans. As a whole, the Senecas do not support it. She has… reservations…about our union."

"She hates me."

Caspen rolled his shoulders. "She does not know you well enough to hate you. But yes, she…is not fond of you."

"She is fond of *you.*"

"No. I promise you, Tem. It was not like that between us."

"Like what?"

"Like how it is with you and me. It was never real."

"But it was physical."

For what felt like the hundredth time, Caspen sighed. "Yes, Tem. It was physical. But it did not matter. *She* did not matter. If you choose to be upset over everyone I have ever slept with, there will be no end to your jealousy."

Tem recoiled. At her reaction, regret flashed across Caspen's face.

"I do not say that to hurt you. It is merely the truth." He paused, and his thumb brushed over her hip bone. "You know who I am."

Yes. Tem knew who he was. He was a prince: the future king and the most desired prospect under the mountain.

"She's a better match," Tem whispered.

"No. She is not."

"She's a basilisk."

"That does not make her a better match."

"But—"

"*Tem.*" His hand squeezed her hip. "Would you mate with a man simply because he is human?"

"We don't call it mating."

Caspen let out an exasperated breath. "I am making a comparison. Just because she is a basilisk does not mean we are compatible."

They both fell silent. His words made logical sense. But there was no logic in her emotions, and it was impossible for Tem not to feel insecure.

"What can I say to make you believe me?" Caspen whispered.

Now Tem sighed. There was nothing he could say, and they both knew it.

"Tem," he continued. "*You* have the king's blessing."

She gave him a look.

"And you have mine." He pressed his lips to her shoulder. "I am in awe of you."

Tem allowed a small sliver of pride to slip through her. She knew her body would bear the consequences of last night for a long time. But it had been worth it.

"Will your quiver accept me?"

Caspen kissed her skin again. "If they know what is good for them."

"When will they make their decision?"

"They have likely already made it. I will speak with my father today."

"But what happens if—"

"Tem," he said gently, pulling her closer. "Enough. There is nothing more you can do."

She fell silent, content simply to breathe for a while. It felt good to lie there, to do nothing but feel Caspen's arms around her.

His lips were right by her ear, and he murmured, "Can I do anything for you?"

Tem considered the request. Caspen had never asked that of her before, and she was not quite sure how to answer. Instead of speaking, she pressed her palm flat against his chest, trailing her fingers slowly down his torso.

Caspen grasped her hand, stopping her before she could go any lower. "Anything but that, Tem."

Shame shot through her. "Do you not want me?" she whispered.

"Of course I want you." He intertwined his fingers with hers. "I am merely following tradition."

"Not more tradition," Tem groaned.

Caspen chuckled softly. "This one is quite tame. We are not to sleep together the day after the ritual."

"Oh."

For once, a reasonable tradition. "In that case, I should get back to the farm."

Tem tried to sit up, but Caspen's arms tightened around her. "Be still," he said. "You need to rest."

"I'm fine," she insisted.

His mouth twitched. "You are stubborn."

They lay in silence for a moment longer.

But Tem could not remain here forever. It was true she had to return to the farm; otherwise, her mother would worry. Beyond that, there was still something else to contend with.

The ball.

Tem found it odd that Caspen hadn't brought up the event or the fact that she may very well be moving into the castle by the end of the week. Surely, that would have some impact on their engagement. Surely, he *cared*.

"Caspen," she said slowly, her breath against his cheek.

"Tem."

"What will happen to us?"

"When?"

Tem shot him a look. She was sure he knew what she meant but had avoided the truth on purpose. Tem clarified anyway. "When the prince chooses who will move into the castle."

"He will choose you."

The question he answered was not the question she had asked. Tem felt a twinge of annoyance at his evasion. "How can you be sure?"

Caspen smiled sadly. "Because you are perfect."

"If I am perfect, it's because you made me that way."

Caspen cupped her chin gently in his hand, looking her in the eye as he said, "You were already perfect."

They were beautiful words. But Tem would not be seduced by them.

"Answer the question. What will happen to us?"

Caspen sat up. Tem sat up too, her hand on the great slope of his shoulder, their lips inches apart. When she studied his face, she couldn't help but compare it to Bastian's. She could see how Caspen would eventually age—where his cheekbones would sharpen and his hair would tint with silver.

"I do not know what will happen," he said finally. "My quiver must accept you first. If they do, we can discuss what comes next."

"I want to discuss it now."

Caspen stood, crossing to the fireplace. Tem remained on the bed, watching him as he stared into the flames. The muscles in his back rolled as he crossed his arms.

He turned to face her. "When the prince chooses you, you will move into the castle with the final two girls."

"*What?*"

Tem had expected him to fight for her—to insist that she drop out of the competition.

His eyes held hers as he continued. "You will go to the castle, and you will stay there until the prince decides to marry you."

"But *why?*"

He turned back to the fire.

Tem stood, crossing to him. "Why did you make me go through the ritual if you have no intention of being with me?"

"I have every intention of being with you, Tem. But my world is dangerous."

"That's always been the case."

"Tem." His voice dropped. "*I* am dangerous."

The ritual had been traumatic for Tem. But it occurred to her suddenly that it might have been just as traumatic for Caspen. He was the one who had to look at her shattered body and know he was the one who broke her.

She touched his arm. "I'm fine, Caspen."

He placed his hand over hers. "A healed wound still bears a scar."

Tem understood what he was saying—that although he had healed her body, the memory of the ritual would surely haunt both of them for a long time. But it was over; they had done it. There was no going back. There was only the future, and Tem needed to know how they would spend it.

"Are we never to be together?"

Caspen's grip tightened. "There are circumstances surrounding our union that you cannot comprehend."

"So explain them."

"Tem," he sighed. "I do not—"

"Wish to discuss this?" she cut him off, pushing him away. "I never want to hear that from you again. You will discuss anything I request of you, and you will do it right now."

Caspen sighed.

He knew just as well as Tem that the time for shielding her had passed. She was in this now, and she deserved to know everything. There would be no more secrets between them. Tem needed the truth, and she wouldn't settle for anything less ever again.

"I have earned the right to honesty, Caspen."

His eyes met hers. "That you have."

It was still a long moment before he spoke. But finally, he said, "Things are…difficult at the moment between the quivers."

"Difficult how?"

"There are whispers of a coup."

"Against the king?"

Caspen nodded. "Yes. And by extension, myself."

"You?"

"I am the one who crested Rowe's father. I paved the way for my own father to be king."

"If you know there's going to be a coup, why don't you do something about it?"

"We *are* doing something about it. There is a council meeting tonight. My father will try to make peace."

"How?"

"The coup is not the only circumstance at play. The quivers have always had their troubles, but we are nonetheless united against a common enemy."

He didn't have to specify who that enemy was. Tem already knew.

Caspen continued. "My father has a plan to overthrow the royals. He hopes by doing so, it will quell the rebellion within our own ranks. If the Drakons are the ones to defeat the humans, the Senecas will fall in line."

Tem felt a dull stab of fear and realized it was for Leo. There was already friction between the basilisks and the humans. If Bastian planned on fueling that friction into fire, the human prince would be the obvious target.

"And what *exactly* is your father's plan?"

"The answer to that is…complicated."

"Why?"

"Because it involves you."

Tem blinked. "*Me?*"

"Yes."

"But how?"

Caspen reached for her waist. It was not a gentle grip; he held her as if he was afraid she might run away. He stared into her eyes for a long moment before asking softly, "Have you ever wondered why you cannot lie, Tem?"

She blinked. "Excuse me?"

"Even when the situation demands it—even when your life depends on it—you always tell the truth. Am I wrong?"

Tem scoffed. "Of course I don't like lying. Nobody does."

"It is not that you do not *like* to lie. You cannot."

Tem thought about all the times she had lied and how difficult it had been for her. How her throat had tightened, how she could barely get the words out. She thought about when Leo had asked her if she loved Caspen. How her answer had physically pained her.

Caspen pulled her closer. "Lying is nearly impossible for a basilisk. It costs us something to do so."

She stared up at Caspen, who was looking down at her as if he were bracing for impact. "Why are you saying this to me?" she whispered.

"Twenty years ago, a girl left the training process. She was pregnant by her basilisk."

Tem already knew where this was going. She knew it in her bones. Yet she whispered, "No."

"Yes," Caspen insisted. "*Yes*, Tem."

Tem wanted to block her ears—wanted to do anything but hear the next thing that came out of Caspen's mouth.

"Your mother is the one who left."

CHAPTER TWENTY-SIX

T HAT'S IMPOSSIBLE."

Even as Tem said it, she recalled the conversation she'd had with her mother mere days ago:

"Why did you leave Father?"

"I left him because we could not be together."

"Why not?"

"His family would not allow it."

Tem had assumed that meant her father's family had looked down on their occupation. But now she wondered if it meant that her mother had faced the same obstacles Tem had—the same ritual. Perhaps her basilisk hadn't been as supportive as Caspen was. Perhaps he had cast her out. Or perhaps his quiver hadn't even given her mother a chance to prove herself the way the Drakons had. Her mother had gone on to be a chicken farmer, to surround herself with roosters, the one thing that would protect her from snakes. She'd done everything she could to ensure she would never get hurt again.

Tem stared straight ahead at Caspen's chest. "Are you saying you know my father?" she whispered.

A weighted pause. "Yes."

Rage coiled within her. "Where is he? Is he *here?*"

Caspen shook his head. "No, Tem. He…went missing."

Tem's heart nearly stopped. She remembered the memorial—the etched names of the basilisks kept deep beneath the castle, the prisoners who were forced to give their blood so the royals could maintain their riches. She remembered the voice she'd heard in the castle, the one crying for help.

Her father.

"But I'm human, Caspen. Look at me." Tem gestured at herself. "I'm *human*."

"You only appear that way, Tem."

She gestured at him.

"*You* appear that way too."

"My human form is simply an illusion. It does not mean I am part human."

Tem burrowed her face in her hands. It was all too much. She couldn't imagine herself as anything other than human.

Or could she?

Tem had always felt out of place, like she was wearing the wrong clothes. She'd always hated the farm, always loathed the sound of the roosters. It grated against her on a molecular level—on an *instinctual* level. She'd always wanted something else from her life—something *more*. But she'd never expected this.

She looked up at Caspen, and her resolve hardened. "You knew."

Caspen shook his head. "I only suspected."

"At first, maybe. But eventually, you knew. And you didn't tell me."

"I am telling you now."

"That's not good enough."

Tem stepped back. She couldn't bear to look at him. She was so sick of his evasions, his half-truths, his twisted efforts to keep her in the dark. Tem was always the last to know. Even this most important, fundamental thing about herself—she'd had no idea. She was the last to be kissed, the last to be fucked. *Do you know your own anatomy?* Caspen had asked her once. Not at all, it would seem.

"How long have you known, Caspen?"

He didn't answer.

"How. Long."

The pause went on forever. Finally, Caspen reached for her hands, turning them over so her freckles caught the firelight.

"This is a distinct feature," he whispered. "Even among basilisks. It was no coincidence that you, a human, had such a rare thing. Your father has the same ones. That is when I suspected you were a hybreed."

Hybreed. Half human, half basilisk.

Tem had heard the stories just like everyone else—that such a creature existed. But they were stories, nothing more. Hybreeds were not supposed to be real. They were not supposed to be *her*.

"When I spoke to you using my mind, that is when I knew for sure," Caspen finished quietly. "Only basilisks can communicate with one another that way."

Tem stared down at her freckled palms. There was a pattern to them, she realized suddenly. All these years, and she'd never noticed that she had exactly twelve freckles on each palm, evenly split, with three freckles beneath each finger except her thumbs.

Tem shook her head. She pulled her hands from his grasp.

"Why didn't you tell me sooner?"

"Because I did not want to frighten you."

"Right," she spat. "Because we both know I am so easily frightened."

"Tem—" He reached for her again, but she smacked his hands away.

"Don't."

There was silence as they stared at each other, and Tem felt anger—true, unstoppable rage—begin to flow through her. Her chest was tight; it was becoming difficult to breathe. She fought to stay calm, asking her next question with her fists clenched.

"Why would you make me do the ritual if I'm not even human?"

"I did not make you—"

"*You know what I mean.*"

Caspen's face was drawn. It pained him to see her like this. But Tem didn't care.

"Only humans are subjected to the ritual. Nobody would suspect you were anything else."

To her surprise, his response satisfied her. What better way to convince everyone she was a human than to put her through a ritual that only humans were subjected to? But she still didn't understand why he'd done it.

"Why would you want everyone to think I'm human?"

"To protect you, Tem."

"From what?"

"*Everything.*" He threw his arms wide. "My father. My world. My quiver. If they find out you are a hybreed, they will—"

But he cut himself off. Now it was Caspen's turn to take a moment to compose himself. Tem waited impatiently for him to continue. When he did, his voice was low.

"I was a fool, Tem." He stepped closer. "I thought I could protect you, but I have made things incomparably worse."

Tem frowned. "How?"

"My father accessed your mind during the ritual. He knows what you are."

Tem remembered how Bastian had told her to finish first. She thought of the moment afterward, between father and son—how Caspen had said, *I will not allow it.*

"Caspen," she said with conviction. "What does your father want with me?"

Caspen closed his eyes. For once, Tem didn't rush him. Somehow she knew that they had arrived finally at the last piece of the puzzle. She was about to get the truth.

When he opened his eyes, Tem saw unmistakable fear in them. It matched the fear she'd seen in his mind—the dark cloud of worry surrounding his thoughts of her.

"He wants you to crest the royal family."

Tem's mouth fell open.

"Usually, contact is required for the crest," Caspen continued quickly, his voice low and strained. "But your power is unique. Hybreeds can crest many people at once without touching them at all. You simply need an opportunity where all the royals will be gathered together."

Tem felt lightheaded. "The wedding," she whispered.

Her wedding.

Caspen nodded. "Once you crest them, they will lose their free will. They will be vulnerable. My people would immediately take over."

Tem narrowed her eyes. "Was this your plan all along?" she asked. "For the prince to pick me so I could crest his entire family?"

"Of course not. I never wanted this for you."

"How do I know you're telling the truth?"

"I cannot lie, Tem."

"Yes, you can. You twist the truth all the time. How do I know you aren't doing it now?"

"What do you wish for me to say? You are precious to me, Tem." His voice almost broke. "I do not want anything to happen to you. My father is the last person I would want to find out what you are. He is the cruelest man I know."

"And yet you were willing to kill for him."

Caspen went perfectly still. "That was a long time ago. And it is my deepest regret. You know this."

But Tem only shook her head, struggling to grasp her new reality—a reality in which she couldn't trust Caspen.

"I don't know anything anymore."

They stared at each other in the flickering firelight, the only sound the crackle of the flames. Something had broken between them—something vital. Tem didn't know where they stood after this. She didn't know how to navigate a world where Caspen lied to her.

"This plan has been in place for centuries, Tem," Caspen said quietly. "My father knew that eventually the training would result in a pregnancy. Even if it took years, he was willing to wait for it."

Cold, slick doubt coated her throat.

"Is this why your father gave me his blessing? So I could perform the crest?"

To her surprise, Caspen shook his head. "No. The ritual is sacred—it is sanctioned by Kora. He cannot wield his blessing as a weapon in our war."

Tem didn't know what to believe anymore.

Caspen seemed to sense this because he continued. "It was not in his best interest to approve of you, Tem. The closer you are to me, the harder it is for him to manipulate you. He honored the outcome of the ritual. You earned his blessing, I promise you."

His words didn't make Tem feel any better. She didn't know if she believed him or if she even cared. Perhaps it didn't matter whether she'd truly earned the king's blessing or not. All that mattered was what she'd just learned—that Bastian had plans for her, that she was meant to help the basilisks regain power.

"Do you want me to crest the royals?" she whispered.

"*No,*" Caspen said sharply. "I do not."

"Why not?" Tem said accusingly. "Don't you want your people to take over?"

He paused. "I do wish for that." The second pause lingered a moment too long. "But it is dangerous for you to crest so many people at once."

"I thought you said the crest was a way to gain power."

"It is. But you have no experience wielding such power. There is no telling how it would affect you."

Anger, betrayal, and anguish rippled through her. She was done talking about this. "I'm going home."

"Tem," he said carefully. "We should—"

"I'm going *home*, Caspen."

Tem couldn't stand to be in his chambers another moment. She brushed past him without another word, ignoring the way he called her name after her, closing the barrier between their minds as she sprinted down the dark passageway. The cold morning air snapped in Tem's lungs as she emerged from the cave and ran through the woods, not stopping until she reached her front door.

"*Mother,*" she cried as she barged into the kitchen.

Her mother looked up from her sewing in surprise.

"What is it, dear?"

"Why didn't you tell me the truth?"

For a moment, her mother was perfectly still. Then she set down her needle and interlaced her fingers in her lap, looking calmly up at Tem. From the look on her face, it was clear she knew the moment of reckoning had come.

"I did not want you to feel different from anyone else," her mother conceded.

Tem scoffed. "It is *far* too late for that, Mother."

Her mother didn't want her to feel different from anyone else; Caspen didn't want to frighten her. These were mere excuses, nothing more.

"It would have been dangerous if you knew," her mother continued just as calmly, as if she'd been rehearsing her response for years. "The villagers would not have been kind."

"They were not kind anyway," Tem cried.

"Please, my dear. Try to understand."

But Tem only shook her head. She held out her hands accusingly, brandishing her freckled palms. "I *deserved* to know."

Her mother didn't respond.

Tem paced back and forth in the kitchen, trying to control her anger. It was unforgivable that she had been treated with such disrespect. This was her identity—her very *being*. To have so many people know her most intimate secret while not knowing it herself was nothing short of a violation. If she could not trust her own mother, who could she turn to?

She stopped pacing. "I am going to Gabriel's."

Her mother's eyebrows shot upward. "You cannot tell that boy, Tem. Nobody can know."

"Gabriel is trustworthy," Tem said sharply, although she didn't know whether *anyone* was trustworthy anymore. "And he is my friend."

"Tem—you—"

But Tem was already out the door. Contrary to what she'd just said, she was not going to Gabriel's. It was early; he was probably still asleep. Instead, she would go to the place where she knew she would find the one person who was unequivocally on her side.

I…still come here most mornings. Just in case.

The church wasn't far. By the time she reached it, the sun was rising in earnest, and Tem feared she would be too late. But when she started on the path through the graveyard, she saw a lone figure sitting on the bench on the hill.

Leo looked up in surprise as she approached.

"Tem?" His brows furrowed in concern as he stood. "What are you doing here?"

It was then that Tem realized she had no plan whatsoever. She couldn't tell Leo she was a hybreed. She couldn't tell him about the ritual, about the Serpent King's plan for the royal wedding, about the basilisks who were being tortured for their blood deep beneath the castle. There wasn't a single thing she could say to him other than the truth.

"I wanted to see you."

A curious expression came over Leo's face. When he didn't reply, Tem became suddenly aware that she had barged in on the prince's private moment, that the only reason he was here was because he was hoping *a different girl* would show up.

Tem took a step backward. "I'm sorry," she said quickly. "I shouldn't have—"

"Yes." He grabbed her hand. "You should have."

Tem stared at his hand, his long fingers interlacing with her freckled ones. "Spend the day with me," Leo said.

Tem let out an incredulous laugh. "Don't you have duties to attend to?"

"My duties can wait."

She was still standing two steps away, their hands clasped between them. "Leo…"

He stepped closer, pulling her against him.

She closed her eyes, breathing in the scent of his cologne. For the first time in a long time, she felt peace. Tentatively, she rested her head against his chest.

"Tem," Leo whispered. "What's wrong?"

Tem had no idea how to answer that. She was exhausted—she'd been up all night, and her body, as well as her mind, was utterly spent.

"I don't know, Leo," she said quietly. "I…" But she couldn't go on.

Leo tightened his hold. "Did that brute break your heart or something?" he murmured against her hair. He sounded sad somehow, although Tem couldn't imagine why.

"Nearly," she murmured back.

Leo pulled away, taking both her hands once more in his. "Spend the day with me," he said again. "Come to the castle. No one will bother us."

Tem shook her head. "I can't."

Leo pulled her closer. "You can't? Or you won't?"

Tem knew what he was really asking. Her spot in the final three was all but guaranteed. If she spent the day with Leo, it wouldn't be because of the competition. It would be because she wanted to. Tem felt the familiar stubbornness inside her—the refusal to give in.

Then Leo said, "It's your choice, Tem."

Her choice. Something Caspen and her mother refused to give her.

Tem looked up at Leo, who was looking down at her. She studied the narrow angles of his face, the sharp gray eyes that were constantly calculating his next move, even now.

She stood on her tiptoes and kissed him.

Leo's body conformed to hers as naturally as moss on a tree. His agile fingers slipped into her hair, tangling in her curls. He was warm and strong and *hard*, and Tem found she only wanted more.

"Is that a yes?" he whispered when they pulled apart.

"Yes," she said quietly. "As long as you don't draw a bath."

Leo's mouth twitched, but his expression remained serious, as if he knew this was a difficult decision for her. But there was victory beneath his restraint, and his grip on her tightened as he pulled her along the path and into a carriage waiting at the edge of the graveyard.

Neither of them spoke on the ride.

Tem leaned against Leo, letting her body rest for the first time in far too long. When they arrived at the castle, the prince guided her down a hallway lined with elegant sconces. They passed an enormous painting at the base of a staircase, and Tem stopped to stare at it.

There was Leo, looking deeply serious, sitting on a velvet armchair. Maximus was behind him, his hand on Leo's shoulder, matching gold cuffs glinting on their wrists.

"Father and son," Leo said quietly.

The familiar pinch in Tem's stomach returned.

Leo's arm tightened around her, pulling her along. She let him move her, following him up the stairs and down a long, carpeted hallway to a door at the very end.

He pushed it open.

Leo's room was enormous, as expected. There was a four-poster bed on one end and a fireplace on the other, the walls in between lined with overstuffed bookshelves.

"Would you like something to eat?" he asked. "I usually take breakfast around now."

It was then that Tem realized she was starving. "Yes."

"And to drink?"

"Anything but champagne."

Leo smiled as he pulled a tasseled rope on the wall. A moment later, there was a knock on the door, and a servant appeared. His eyes swiveled to Tem's before latching back on to Leo. They exchanged a few words before Leo shut the door.

"I'm afraid everyone will know you are here," he said with an amused smile. "That was one of our more talkative servants."

Tem shrugged. It didn't matter who knew she was here. All that mattered was that she was away from her life in the village.

Despite her desire to be here, now that she was actually in Leo's room, Tem found herself in a state of mild panic. What if he expected her to sleep with him? Surely, the prince assumed her presence meant she was ready and willing to jump into his bed. But Tem had no desire to have sex right now. The ritual had drained all her energy, and the last thing she wanted was another cock between her legs.

Leo seemed to sense this, because he said, "I don't expect anything from you, Tem."

She shot him a look. "But you want something."

He held her gaze. "All I want is your company."

When she didn't reply, he touched her waist gently.

"I understand that you are seeking refuge. I have no desire to take advantage of you when you came here for shelter."

Tem stared at the floor. She wasn't even sure she deserved his shelter at this point.

Leo finished quietly, "I'm a man of my word, Tem. Whether you believe me to be or not."

Tem didn't know what she believed. Then she shivered. Leo's room was freezing.

He saw this and immediately said, "I shall make a fire."

Tem took the opportunity to look around his room, peering curiously at the bookshelf. It was crammed full of books in varying languages, so many that the shelves were bending beneath their weight.

Tem turned to his bed, which was meticulously made. She very much doubted Leo was the one who made it. His bed frame was intricately carved wood, and on the closest bedside table were stacks of books topped by white candles. The candles had burned so low that the wax was dripping down over the spines of the books, pooling in hard circles on the wood.

"Do you like to read?" Leo's voice came from behind her.

Tem turned to see him leaning against the fireplace, watching her. "Not really," she said. "I mean, I would if I had time. Or books. But no, not really."

He nodded at the chairs in front of the fireplace. "Shall we sit?"

Leo waited until Tem sat before sitting himself. There was a moment of silence while they stared at the fire.

"Do you have a favorite?" Tem asked eventually.

Leo arched an eyebrow. "A favorite book?"

Tem nodded.

"I'm not sure," he paused. "It changes day to day."

"So what's your favorite today?"

Another pause. Then: "*The Raven and the Swan.*"

Tem knew that one. Everyone did; it was an old fable about a raven that wanted to become a swan. But no matter what the raven did—including swimming in the swan's pond and eating the swan's food—it remained a raven. It couldn't change its true nature.

"Why?"

Leo shifted in his chair, crossing one long leg over the other. "The raven wants more from its life."

"And you relate to that?"

His mouth twitched. "Somewhat."

Tem rolled her eyes. "Your life seems pretty good to me, Leo."

"That's because you're looking at it from the outside, Tem." He said it softly, his eyes on the fire.

"You have everything," she said and shrugged. "What else could you possibly want?"

He didn't reply for a long time. When he did, Tem barely heard the word:

"Agency."

"You *have* agency."

"It may seem that way to you. But my hands are tied in every way that matters. I can't choose what I do, where I go, who I date. Everything is decided for me."

"You have a roof over your head. You have food and books and a fireplace in your bedroom, for Kora's sake. And by the way, you *are* choosing who you date. Right now, actually. Are you really telling me you're unhappy?"

Leo looked at her, his eyes hooded. "Yes. I'm afraid I am."

Tem stared at him, trying to understand.

She, of all people, knew what it was like to truly have no agency. Her path had been decided for her the moment she was born in the same year as the prince, the daughter of a single mother with nothing but chicken shit to go home to. Leo had no idea what it was like to have everything decided for him. He was the son of a king, with more power than he knew how to wield, straining against a self-imposed cage.

"Do you not believe me?" Leo asked.

Tem sighed. "If you say you're unhappy, I believe you. But you have more power than you think you do."

"And how shall I wield that power?"

"I don't know, Leo. Do something—anything. Think about someone other than yourself."

"I think about you."

She ignored the compliment, leaning in. "Think about your family. Think about what they've done."

Leo frowned. "And what has my family done?"

Tem shouldn't have said that. Before she could figure out how to answer, there was another knock on the door.

Leo's eyes lingered on hers for just a moment before he said, "Come in."

Tem stared at the fire as the same servant from before set a tray of food down and left without a word. Neither of them touched the food.

Leo leaned in. "What has my family done, Tem?"

He said it like a plea. His voice was curious—apprehensive, even. As if he were afraid to hear the answer. Tem decided in that moment that he didn't know about the bloodletting. He *couldn't*. Leo would never condone such cruelty.

But she also couldn't imagine telling him.

What exactly would she even say? That there were imprisoned basilisks—including her own father—beneath their feet? That everything Leo owned was paid for in blood? Tem thought about the portrait of Leo and Maximus, both wearing matching gold cuffs.

Like father, like son.

Even if he had no knowledge of the bloodletting, Tem had no idea whether she could trust Leo. If the last twenty-four hours were any indication, she couldn't trust anyone. She knew Leo was angry at Maximus for how he'd treated Evelyn and for how he was already beginning to treat Tem. But was he angry enough to condemn his father's crimes? There were so many secrets, so many things Leo didn't know, and none of them would be easy for him to hear. She didn't want to keep things from him the same way so many things had been kept from her.

All journeys begin with a step.

But it was too soon. Leo may be angry with his father, but Tem very much doubted he was ready to discover the atrocities happening within his own home. Not when he had been raised his entire life to believe that basilisks were the enemy.

The truth would have to wait another day.

"You said it yourself." Tem shrugged in what she hoped was a nonchalant manner. "Your family controls you. You could stand up to your father if that's really what you wanted."

Leo tilted his head, appraising her.

She wondered if he could tell she'd wanted to say something else.

"And how would you suggest I stand up to him?"

"By making your own choices."

Her suggestion hung in the air. She didn't elaborate, and Leo didn't ask her to. He was still staring at her when Caspen entered her mind: *Tem. My quiver has made their decision.*

PART TWO

CHAPTER TWENTY-SEVEN

---•◦✳◦•---

T EM LET THE SILENCE SIT, FORCING CASPEN TO SPEAK AGAIN:

I know you are angry with me. But you should know that the Drakons have given you their blessing.

The news had no impact on Tem. She deserved his quiver's blessing after everything she'd gone through. She expected nothing less.

Caspen continued. *And I know you are with the prince.*

Now Tem spoke. *It's none of your business who I'm with.*

A testy pause. *I am not criticizing you. It is your right to spend time with whomever you choose.*

His words were taut.

Is that all? I'm about to eat breakfast.

Caspen's presence loomed larger, and she knew he wanted to keep her with him.

There is something else. I must attend the council meeting tonight.

You told me that already.

I wish for you to attend with me.

That was a surprise to Tem.

Why?

We are now officially engaged. That means you are the future queen. Your presence is expected.

He was the second person to call Tem the future queen. The first was Leo.

Is it safe for me to attend?

Caspen paused. And then: *I will ensure that it is.*

Tem heard the resolve in his voice. It brought her little comfort.

Tem? Caspen said when the silence dragged on. *Will you attend?*

Tem sighed. *I'll decide later.*

Another long pause. *Of course. I await your decision.*

Tem severed their connection without remorse.

"Tem?"

She blinked. Leo was staring at her.

"What?" she asked.

"Where did you go?"

"What do you mean?"

"I mean, you…went somewhere just now. Were you talking to him?"

Tem was surprised he could tell. There was no point in hiding it. "Yes."

Leo's brow furrowed. "What did he say?"

Tem hesitated. Was she really going to talk to Leo about her mind connection with Caspen? The day could hardly get any stranger. "He wants to see me tonight."

Leo's lips formed an unhappy line. "Do you want to see him?"

"I haven't decided yet."

"Does he know you're here?"

"Yes."

"I imagine that would make him angry."

It is your right to spend time with whomever you choose.

"Yes. It does."

"Is that why you came?"

Tem blinked. "What?"

Leo shifted, leaning toward her. "Did you come here just so you could make him angry?"

She considered the question. There wasn't one singular reason why she'd come here. A combination of things had collided into a single perfect circumstance that resulted in her having breakfast in Leo's bedroom.

"Partly. But I also came because I wanted to."

Leo's eyes held hers.

She had no idea whether he believed her. When he didn't reply, Tem whispered, "Should I leave?"

He shook his head. "I'd rather you didn't."

"Even after what I just told you?"

To her surprise, he smiled. "Especially after what you just told me."

Tem's stomach turned over. There was so much more she had to tell him. They hadn't even touched the tip of the iceberg. Leo didn't know she was a hybreed, that she was capable of cresting, that there was a mutiny being planned as they spoke. He didn't know anything that mattered.

When Leo saw the expression on her face, he sighed and said, "One thing at a time, please, Tem."

Tem pursed her lips. He was right. One thing at a time.

"You've made it clear you won't have a bath," Leo continued. "Or champagne. So tell me, Tem, is there something else you'd care to do?"

She thought for a moment. "Will you read to me?"

Leo arched an eyebrow. "What shall I read?"

"*The Raven and the Swan.*"

Leo tilted his head, studying her. Then he said, "Very well."

He stood, crossing to the bookshelf. On his way back to her, he lifted a blanket from the end of his bed and draped it over her shoulders. Tem was moved by the unexpected gesture. It reminded her of when he'd given her his cloak in the graveyard. The blanket was warm, the fire even warmer. Leo read calmly, and Tem found herself drifting off to the sound of his voice.

When she woke, she was still in the chair, wrapped in the blanket. Tem glanced over to see Leo fast asleep, his long legs still crossed, the book still open in his hands. The fire was almost out, and afternoon sunshine was peeking through the bedroom window.

"Leo," Tem whispered.

He didn't wake.

"Leo," she whispered again, reaching over and tugging on his sleeve.

His eyes opened and he sat up, looking around at her. "What's the matter?" he asked.

"Nothing," Tem said. "It's afternoon. You fell asleep."

Leo stretched, uncrossing his legs. "On the contrary, *you* fell asleep. I didn't think it polite to wake you."

Tem gave him a look.

He smiled, then it faded. "In truth, you seemed like you needed it." He paused, and his voice dropped. "I've...never seen you so peaceful."

Tem stared at him. He was being sincere. "Oh," she said. "Well. Thanks, I guess."

"My pleasure."

There was a moment of silence as they stared at each other. Then Leo's mouth twitched. "*Speaking* of pleasure," he said, snapping the book shut and setting it on the armrest. "We could—"

"No," Tem said firmly. "We couldn't. You're about to ruin a perfectly nice moment."

"Hm," he said, still smiling. "I rather think it would *enhance* the moment. But if you insist—"

"I do insist," she said, standing up. "Can you just take me home, please?"

"Very well, Tem." He stood too, shaking his head in amusement. "I shall take you home."

Tem followed him out into the hallway and down the stairs. To her intense relief, they didn't run into Maximus on their way out.

When the carriage arrived at Tem's cottage, she turned to Leo. "Thank you," she said.

He arched an eyebrow. "For what?"

"For being my refuge."

He took her hand in his, pressing his lips to her knuckles. "It was an honor."

Tem rolled her eyes.

His grip tightened. "I mean it. I know my time with you is somewhat…borrowed. But any moment with you—no matter how brief—is glorious."

Guilt twisted Tem's gut. Leo may be understanding now, but his patience was bound to run out. The prince was accustomed to getting what he wanted, and he wanted her. He would not tolerate her connection with Caspen forever. And if he were to learn exactly how deep that connection truly went, she doubted he would ever forgive her.

"Leo…"

He cut her off with a kiss.

Tem didn't bother resisting. They melted into each other, kissing without a single care, safe in the knowledge that nobody could see them within the four walls of the carriage. Leo's tongue was relentless, and so was Tem's. It felt as if they were making up for lost time, their bodies doing what their minds truly craved. Tem's hand went to his lap, palming his cock, feeling how hard he was through his trousers. Leo groaned, cupping his hand over hers and *squeezing* until she groaned too.

Tem pulled away. "Unbutton your trousers," she ordered.

Leo gave her a cunning smile. "I thought you weren't interested in pleasure."

"Well, now I am. Unbutton them."

"No. Not until you say it."

"Say what?"

"That you want me."

Tem scoffed. She began to stand, but Leo yanked her right back down.

"Say it, Tem." His lips were an inch from hers. "Say you want me, and my cock is yours."

They stared at each other. The air in the carriage was warm and already smelled like sex.

Tem thought about Caspen and how angry she was at him. She thought about how he'd lied to her—*betrayed* her. Why should Tem be loyal when Caspen was anything but? She was half basilisk after all. There was a part of her—a *significant* part—that craved Leo in the same way Caspen craved her. Why should she deprive herself of him?

It was a good thing Leo wasn't asking her to lie. "I want you," she whispered.

The smirk returned. "Good girl. Now unbutton them yourself."

Tem didn't hesitate. Her fingers flew along the seam of Leo's trousers, undoing the buttons before reaching down his undergarments and grabbing his cock. Leo inhaled sharply when she did it, and a second later, she had him fully exposed. He was completely erect—his cock just as long and pretentious as she remembered it. Tem dipped her head immediately. Leo gasped in surprise as she took him all the way down her throat.

"Tem," he breathed.

Pride curled within her. She lifted her head before lowering it again, creating a steady rhythm.

"You're so fucking good at this."

Tem barely heard him. She was concentrating on how hard he was in her mouth, how significant it felt to suck on the part of Leo that made him *him,* how badly she wanted to take him even deeper.

Leo's hand went to the back of her head, his hips moving to meet her. His fingers twisted in her hair, holding Tem in place as he thrust lazily up and down. He was taking his time, and Tem didn't mind.

She let out a tiny moan when his cock hit the back of her throat.

"*Fuck,* Tem."

The thrusts became quicker. It was amazing to see the effect she had on him—to see how impossible it was for Leo to control himself around her. Tem felt such power in that moment, such undeniable control, and she wanted nothing more than to keep it.

On his next thrust, she sat up, releasing his cock from her mouth and using her hand instead. Leo grabbed her chin, turning her head to his.

"Sit on my cock, Tem."

Tem let out a soft giggle. "No."

"Tem, I swear to Kora—"

But Tem wasn't listening. She lowered her head again, taking him once more down her throat. Leo's hand returned to her hair, twisting it around his knuckles so he could hold it away from her face.

"Need to fuck you—need to fuck you so badly—need you—"

Each phrase was punctuated by the rise and fall of her head as she slid her mouth up and down again and again. Tem wasn't used to this much verbal accompaniment. Caspen spoke occasionally, but it was usually to issue a command or impart selective praise. Leo was constantly vocal, and Tem found she enjoyed it. It was satisfying for her to hear in real time how he felt about her.

"Let me fuck you, Tem, *please.*"

The hand that wasn't holding her hair was roaming along the lacings of her dress, beginning to pull it off her.

But Tem was not going to fuck Leo today.

Not here, not in a carriage, not twenty yards from her cottage. Not when her body still bore the effects of the ritual. She wanted to fuck the prince in a bed—*his* bed—and she wanted to do it right. For now, she merely wanted to show him that she cared—that she was grateful for his hospitality and that his obsession with her would be worth it.

She sat up straight. "You can't fuck me, Leo."

"I assure you," he said as his hands—both of them now—worked to unlace her dress. "I can."

"No." She grabbed his wrists, pinning them against the back of the carriage. "You can't."

They stared at each other, both breathing hard. Leo's hair was disheveled, his cheeks tinged with pink. Tem was sure she looked similarly windswept.

"And why not?" Leo asked.

"Because I said so."

"That's hardly a reason."

"It is, actually. And it's the only reason you're getting."

"Tem." He arched his head back in exasperation. "Knowing you has been the single most torturous experience of my life."

Tem pressed her lips to his exposed neck, murmuring her next words against his skin. "You're the one who asked me to torture you, remember?"

"I'm rather regretting that now."

"How about a compromise?"

"What sort of compromise?"

"I'll take this off"—she released his wrists and pointed at her dress—"and I'll finish what I started"—she pointed at his cock, which was still hard—"but you can't touch me."

Leo let out a bark of laughter. "*Hardly* a compromise. That's simply more torture."

Tem shrugged. "Or I can go inside and you can finish by yourself. Your choice."

Leo's mouth twisted. "Wicked, *wicked* girl."

Coming from him, she knew it was a compliment.

"Do we have a deal?" Tem insisted.

Leo rubbed his hand over his face. "Yes, *fuck*."

"Good."

Before he could change his mind, she left her spot beside him on the bench and knelt on the floor of the carriage. Leo's temperament changed as soon as she was on her knees. Hunger flared in his eyes—pure, animalistic craving the likes of which she'd never seen on him before. His cock, which was already hard, became noticeably harder. Leo leaned forward, his elbows on his thighs, watching Tem with possessive focus as she slowly pulled her dress up over her head.

The moment she was naked, something crackled into existence. Tem felt the energy in the carriage shift—as if a bridge had opened between them. Leo's gaze traveled slowly over her body, and Tem let it. His eyes traced down her neck, lingering on her breasts before following the curve of her waist. Then finally, they landed on the center of her. He licked his lips.

Why not give him one more gift?

Tem slipped her fingers gently between her legs.

For once, Leo had nothing to say. He simply watched in reverent silence as Tem played with her clitoris, rubbing it with her first two fingers. Then she took those fingers and pushed them deeper, touching herself slowly, letting Leo see exactly what he wasn't allowed to do. She didn't bring herself to orgasm. Instead, she raised her fingers and brushed them over the head of his cock, coating it with her wetness.

"Remember our deal," she whispered.

Leo clasped his hands slowly behind his head before leaning back and looking down at her through hooded eyes.

"I will not survive you," he said, his voice a guttural whisper.

"Do you even want to?"

He didn't answer.

Leo watched as Tem turned her head, parted her lips, and touched them to the base of his shaft. At the same time, she palmed his balls, cupping them firmly and pressing her thumb into the nook where they met his cock. Tem worked her tongue slowly up the shaft, licking him from base to tip. When she reached the head, she sucked on it for at least ten full seconds, and by the time she was ready to move on, Leo's moans filled the carriage.

Tem used her hand to give him three strokes in rapid succession. Then she lowered her head once more, this time angling herself so he could see every inch of his cock disappear down her throat and reappear again. It felt so good to give him this—to show him the wait had been worth it.

Eventually, Leo began to break.

He extended his hand slowly, touching only the taut skin of her cheek while her mouth was around his cock. Tem swatted him away, and he retreated. But a moment later, he did it again, caressing her jaw with only his pinkie finger.

She straightened. "Leo," she warned. "I will leave."

He groaned, throwing his head back in agony. "*Tem*," he rasped. "You're *killing* me here."

"I know."

Tem went to dip her head again but paused instead. Why not kill him a little more?

Moving slowly so Leo was sure to see every second of it, Tem brought her hands to her chest, lifting her breasts so his cock was cradled between them.

Leo gripped the carriage seat with his fists, and she knew it took him everything he had not to touch her. His fingers tore into the cushioned fabric as she held her breasts in place and slid them up and down his cock, watching him as he watched her, seeing the way he could barely keep his hands at his sides. Just when she knew she was pushing him to his limit, she held still, tilting her chin up and tacitly signaling him to take over.

Leo shifted his hips, tentatively at first, as if to see what would happen. When Tem remained in place, he jerked them quickly upward, sliding his cock through her cleavage at a rapid pace. His head fell back—he couldn't even watch her anymore. The next time his hips rose, Tem freed her breasts, seamlessly replacing them with her mouth.

She took him deeper this time, knowing in her gut that the prince was close. She matched the pace he had set a moment ago, dipping her head again and again, working his cock until it was slick with her saliva. Tem's moans joined Leo's. She wanted him to hear how much she liked doing this—how satisfying it was for her to satisfy him. Tem knew he was mere seconds away.

Leo cried out, "Fuck, Tem—fuck—*fuck*—"

His hand returned suddenly to her hair, and for a moment, she thought he was breaking their deal. Instead, Leo pulled her sharply off his cock, his other hand shooting forward so he could finish into his palm. They both stared at his cum. Without thinking, Tem leaned down.

She knew Leo had a perfect view of her as she extended her tongue and licked the glistening substance from his palm with slow, soft strokes.

"Tem," he whispered as he watched. "Fuck."

She sat upright and smiled. "Is that your favorite word?"

"When it comes to you, it is."

"I want you to finish in my mouth next time."

"So there will be a next time?"

Tem rolled her eyes.

Then she pulled on her dress. Instead of kissing the prince goodbye, she simply exited the carriage, leaving Leo with his cock still out. The footman whistled at her as she walked down the garden path, but Tem ignored him; she was far too happy to be embarrassed.

The late-afternoon air contrasted starkly with the heat they'd generated in the carriage, and Tem paused at her front door, her fingers on the handle. Was it even worth going inside? She was in no mood to return to the conversation from that morning. Tem had nothing new to say, and she doubted her mother did either.

Seconds ticked by.

Her only other option was to go to the caves to attend the council meeting. But she wasn't sure she wanted to do that either. Caspen had lied to her. He'd concealed his knowledge of a deeply important, *vital* part of Tem's identity that would affect every aspect of her future. That wasn't something she could easily forgive. Yet now that she knew she was a hybreed, she wanted nothing more than to explore that side of her. Tem had always known there was no future for her in the village. Perhaps her future was in the caves.

But what kind of future would it be? One that began in violence—with the crest? It was unfathomable to Tem that Bastian would expect her to do something so pivotal. The magnitude of her role in his plan was not lost on her. He thought of Tem as nothing more than a pawn: a game piece in his reckless play for power. But Tem was so much more than that. She would not be manipulated; she would not be used. Whether she performed the crest or not, it would be on her own terms, not Bastian's. Nobody would choose Tem's future but her.

She dropped the door handle. It was time for her first council meeting.

Caspen wasn't waiting for her in the cave this time, and she wondered whether that was because he hadn't expected her to come. Either way, Tem traversed the passageway alone. When she reached his chambers, she paused.

Would Caspen be angry that she had cut off their connection so abruptly earlier? Would he know she had pleasured Leo in the carriage? In Tem's eyes, Caspen did not have a right to be angry about that. Not when he'd kept her in the dark for so long. Why shouldn't she have secrets of her own? Tem opened the door.

Caspen was by the fire, and when he saw her, obvious relief flashed over his face.

"Tem," he said quietly. "You came."

"Yes," she said as she closed the door. "I did."

Tem joined him by the fire. Caspen was naked, and without a word, Tem undressed too. She was no longer shocked by his customs and had no desire to rail against them. They were her customs now. Caspen's eyes went instantly to her body, and a moment later, he was hard.

He touched his finger to her bottom lip. "I can smell him on you, Tem."

She didn't reply. It should have occurred to her that there was no way to keep her dalliance with Leo a secret. Caspen was too intuitive—too much of a predator—not to sense where his prey had been.

"Are you angry?" she whispered.

He pulled her bottom lip with his thumb, opening her mouth. "You are mine, Tem," he said simply. "Whether you give your body to another does not change that."

Tem thought about how basilisks were so very different from humans and how she carried both traits within her. Adelaide's beautiful face and blond hair flashed through her mind.

"Are you...giving your body to another?"

His mouth twitched. "There is no one else I want. My body and my heart belong to you."

That was all it took to soften her.

It was just so *easy* with Caspen—so *right*. Tem felt their connection even when her mind was closed off to him, even when she was so angry she couldn't think straight. He was her other half. He was *hers*.

Caspen's hands cradled her face before brushing down her neck. He cupped her breasts—not unlike the way Tem had just cupped them for Leo—holding them in both palms.

His thumbs teased her nipples, hardening them.

Don't we have a council meeting to get to?

The basilisk smiled. *That we do.*

He released her breasts, instead taking her hand in his. They wound through the tunnels together, and already Tem was beginning to feel nervous.

Is there anything I need to know before we get there?

Caspen's hand tightened in hers. *The purpose of this meeting is to guarantee that the Drakons remain in power. My father hopes to unite the quivers against the royals, and he thinks if the Senecas know we have a hybreed, they will fall in line.*

Tem looked up at him. *Does he know that I haven't agreed to his plan?*

Caspen clenched his jaw. *Yes. He knows.*

Then why would he want me at this meeting?

Because we are newly engaged.

I don't understand.

You and I have a significant connection. Your presence contributes to my power. It may work in our favor.

Tem took a moment to process this. She'd never thought about how she might contribute to Caspen's power—how their relationship would benefit him politically. Before she could ask anything further, Caspen stopped in front of a large wooden doorway.

It is time.

Tem turned to him. She opened her mouth to say something—anything—but before she could, Caspen pressed his lips to hers. He was not gentle; she could feel his anticipation. Even now, his power was growing. The same energy Tem sensed on him whenever he was about to transition was present now, thrumming between them. Caspen's tongue found hers, and she wondered if he could taste Leo's cum.

I can.

Despite this admission, he didn't stop kissing her. His hands grabbed her ass; his cock pressed against her. Tem felt desperately warm and was suddenly grateful she wasn't wearing any clothes. By the time Caspen pulled away, wetness was dripping down her leg. He traced his finger up her thigh, trailing it through her center before raising it to his lips. He licked his fingers slowly, and Tem couldn't help but think of how similar it was to what she had just done for Leo.

Caspen smiled, as if he knew it too.

They entered the council meeting together.

CHAPTER TWENTY-EIGHT

——•◦✳◦•——

The ceilings were high, just like the auditorium where the ritual took place.

The floor was stone, as were the walls, and there was an enormous, white marble table in the center of the room. It was long and oval, surrounded by twelve marble chairs. Ten basilisks sat along the table—the Senecas on one side and the Drakons on the other. They all wore their human forms, and they were all naked.

At the head of the table sat Bastian.

It was jarring to see him for the first time since the ritual. Tem had a sudden memory of how he'd felt inside her—how she'd strained to take him. Her cheeks flushed at the thought.

What of your mother? Tem asked, desperate for a distraction. *Where is the queen?*

My mother is dead.

Caspen said it so simply—as if he were reporting the weather. Tem couldn't believe they'd never talked about it, that he'd never mentioned this deeply significant fact. What were the chances that the two princes in her life were motherless?

Caspen took the seat at the other end of the table, directly opposite his father. There was no additional chair for Tem. Instead, Caspen pulled her between his legs, his knees on either side of hers. She was grateful for the contact; his proximity made her feel less nervous, and she leaned back against his chest.

When everyone had settled, Bastian cleared his throat.

"We shall begin by congratulating my son on his engagement."

Rowe made a scoffing sound.

The king turned his black eyes to him. "Do you have something you wish to say, Rowe?"

Rowe only sneered.

"Speak," Caspen growled. "Or lose your tongue."

Rowe's response was cold. "Let us not waste time with pleasantries, shall we? We all know why we are here."

"Rowe is correct," Bastian continued as if the interruption was of no consequence to him. "There have been...tensions as of late." His eyes slid first to Caspen, then to Rowe. "Today we hope to ease those tensions."

The Drakons and the Senecas glared at each other from opposite sides of the table. Tem couldn't imagine a world where the tension in this room was eased.

Caspen pressed a kiss to her temple. *Be patient. We have barely begun.*

Bastian steepled his fingers.

"I understand that many of you are no longer content beneath Drakon rule. But we must honor the circumstances that granted us power. Otherwise, we forsake Kora, and we forsake ourselves."

There was a testy silence in which everyone looked at Caspen. Every basilisk in this room knew exactly which circumstances had granted the Drakons power.

"And why should the Drakons keep their power?" said Rowe, his jaw tight. "What have they done to earn it?"

Tem thought Caspen might say something in his defense. Instead, his hand went between her legs. A low hiss filled the room the moment he touched her. All the basilisks were staring at them—staring at *Tem.* It was then that she understood her role in this meeting. Caspen had said her presence contributed to his power. He was exercising that power now, drawing on their connection to bend the council to his will.

Tem couldn't complain. What he was doing felt like heaven, and she allowed herself to lean into him, savoring the way he touched her. Caspen shifted his grip, pulling her legs open to display her. His fingers dipped slowly in and out, spreading her wetness until she was dripping onto the marble chair.

The hissing intensified.

Rowe's eyes were fixated on Tem, who held his gaze. She could see the direct effect her bond with Caspen was having on him—his eyes were black, his hands clamped tightly on the edge of the table. He looked like a man who didn't want to yield but had no other choice.

Pride surged through Tem.

What now? she asked.

Caspen was unreadable, his hard features like slate in the warm darkness. His lips brushed her neck.

Now we begin.

Bastian was looking at his son with something akin to pride, and Tem knew his plan was working. If Caspen hadn't been turning her on right now, she'd feel indignant about being used. But his fingers were lulling her into a trance she had no desire to break, and she barely heard Bastian as he said, "I propose we put the royals in their place."

A disbelieving murmur swept across the table. Surely, there had been talk of rebellion before, of reclaiming what the basilisks deemed to be rightfully theirs. But now that the king was the one sanctioning it, the proposition held legitimate weight.

"And how shall we put them in their place?" Rowe asked.

Bastian's answer was simple. "We crest them."

Tem heard several incredulous sounds.

"The royals will attempt to resist us," another basilisk said. "We cannot hope to crest them all."

Bastian pointed at Tem. "She can."

"And what is so special about *her*?" Rowe snapped.

Bastian laced his fingers together. "She is a hybreed."

Instant chaos.

Several basilisks cried out in disbelief, while others smacked the stone table in protest.

Rowe's voice carried over it all. "If the Drakons knew of the existence of a hybreed and they hid it, *that is treason.*"

"I did not know," Bastian insisted, his hands raised. "Not until the ritual."

"*He* knew." Rowe pointed at Caspen. "He *had* to have known. He has been fucking her for *weeks.*"

"My son's business is his own," Bastian said. "I take no responsibility for his actions."

Tem found that ironic.

"This is absurd," a female basilisk on the Seneca side insisted. "You play us for fools."

Bastian shook his head. "I am merely championing our liberation."

"And let me guess," the woman continued. "As the liberators of our people, the Drakons would remain in power."

Bastian leaned back in his chair. "One would assume the Senecas will yield to those of us who are bold enough to defeat the royals."

It was a classic basilisk answer—evasive and ineffective. The council would not be swayed.

"Prove it," Rowe snarled. "Prove she is a hybreed."

Tem didn't wait for anyone's permission. She was already feeling for the corridor to Rowe's mind, gently opening the mental door that led to his consciousness. The moment she made contact, Rowe whipped his head around to stare at her, his mouth slack with shock.

Tem whispered two words softly into his mind: *Hello, Rowe.*

Rowe recoiled in disgust, slamming a barrier between them so fast that she flinched. "Impossible," he growled.

Behind her, Tem felt Caspen's amusement. *What did you say to him?*

I just said hello.

Caspen's amusement only increased. His fingers were still inside her, and his cock had been hard for a while now. Tem could feel it against her back and wanted nothing more than to turn around and mount him.

Not yet, Tem.

Tem squirmed in his arms. She was turned on to the point of distraction; she wanted to have sex *right now*. But Caspen held her in place as Bastian said, "I assure you, it is not impossible. And neither is our freedom."

"*Your* freedom," Rowe insisted. "Meaning the Drakons."

"Our freedom is also yours. We have a hybreed." Bastian spread his fingers wide. "And we plan to use her. She is a resource for us all."

"*If* the prince chooses her," Rowe spat. "And *if* she even agrees to be used."

"He will choose her," Caspen snapped. "My students are always chosen."

Rowe turned to him, his eyes narrowing.

Tem remembered that Caspen had a reputation to uphold—a legacy to defend.

"And she will not be *used*," Caspen continued, his voice dangerously low. "She is not your tool of destruction. She is my future queen. I decide what happens to her."

"Actually," Tem said quietly, "*I* decide what happens to me."

Everyone at the table turned to look at her.

Bastian cleared his throat. Caspen's grip on her tightened protectively.

"Of course," the king said evenly. "You have a say in this, Temperance. Is there something you wish to add?"

There were plenty of things Tem wished to add. But only one thing came to mind right now.

"Why should I do this for you? Why should I enslave innocent people?"

Bastian leaned forward. "The royals are hardly innocent."

His words reminded her of the ones Caspen had said—how he didn't consider human lives a loss. Tem thought of Lilly's young children, who had no fault in the war against the basilisks. Were they to answer for the sins of their ancestors?

"Perhaps the king is not innocent. But the rest of the royals would be collateral damage."

"There will be far more damage if you do not perform the crest."

Tem frowned. "What do you mean?"

Bastian shrugged with practiced ease. "The crest is an elegant solution to our problem. It involves no loss of life, no bloodshed. My people can regain power peacefully. If you refuse, we will be forced to carry out a…less elegant solution."

"You mean war."

"Yes," Bastian said simply. "Is that what you want?"

War was the last thing Tem wanted. But she didn't want to crest anyone either. "I want peace."

"I understand your position," Bastian said. "But the situation is bigger than yourself."

He spoke carefully, and Tem knew he was trying to control her. If she refused to perform the crest—if she denied the king in front of his council—the Drakons would lose the upper hand.

Tem didn't want to put Caspen at a disadvantage. But she wasn't willing to sacrifice Leo's family for him either.

"Give me a reason," Tem said.

Bastian raised an eyebrow. "A reason?"

"Tell me how the crest will benefit me."

The king considered her for a long moment, and the basilisks on both sides of the table shifted uneasily. Tem knew that everyone in this room wanted the royals gone. They wanted it more than they wanted power for themselves. And Tem was the catalyst.

When Bastian spoke, his voice filled the room. "The crest will free your father."

It was the one thing he could have said to give her pause.

Tem's father was the perfect example of the royals' cruelty—of their *greed*. She may be able to justify some things Leo's family had done, but never that. Never the blood-letting. It was unforgivable and unconscionable and evil. But did the royals deserve to be crested for it? Did they deserve to lose their free will? It didn't seem right.

But Tem refused to sanction open war.

She pictured Jonathan and Christopher, petrified in the town square. There would be more deaths—*countless* deaths—unless Tem put a stop to it herself. The future of the entire kingdom was at stake. Gabriel, her mother, every human who played no part in the basilisk war yet would be caught up in it anyway. If the crest would save innocent lives, it was worth it.

Tem, Caspen said softly in her mind, and she knew he'd heard her thoughts. *You should think this through.*

Tem ignored him. She'd thought it through enough. It was time to act.

"Fine," she said. "I will crest the royals."

We should discuss—

"On one condition."

Bastian splayed his hands open. "Please. Enlighten us."

Even Caspen fell silent as the room awaited her condition.

Tem cleared her throat before saying, "The human prince will not be harmed."

There was immediate uproar. The basilisks cried out in unanimous fury, with Rowe's voice ringing the loudest.

"It would appear that the plaything has fallen in love with her playmate," he jeered.

There were sounds of agreement, and Tem tried to ignore the unmistakable wave of disapproval coming from Caspen's mind. She didn't care if he didn't like it. She wasn't done yet.

Tem raised her voice. "And neither will his sister nor her children."

The uproar increased. It wasn't until Bastian pounded his fist on the table so hard it cracked the marble that everyone finally quieted down.

"That is more than one condition, Temperance," he said darkly.

"Those are my terms."

"This is not a negotiation."

"Isn't it? I'm a hybreed. You need what I can provide."

"Be careful how you speak to your king."

But Tem was done being reprimanded. "Be careful how you speak to *me*," she snapped.

The entire council went quiet. Behind her, Caspen drew in a careful breath, and for a moment, his fingers stilled. Tem paused, ready for him to say something in her mind. But he didn't. He seemed to be waiting to see what she would do.

So she said, "I suggest you consider my conditions. If you find them unfavorable, you're welcome to wait centuries for another hybreed to show up. I hate to imagine what additional damage the royals could cause during that time."

There was a long, tense silence.

Bastian was regarding her with something close to hatred. Tem knew she had crossed a line, pushed the boundaries of what was acceptable or even safe. But she was no stranger to kings looking at her with open animosity. Maximus had prepared her for this.

"Very well," Bastian said finally, his gaze leaving Tem's and traveling around the room. "You heard her. The hybreed is willing to aid in our cause."

The table was silent.

Bastian continued. "It is time to regain our rightful place in this kingdom. It is time to free our brothers and sisters. It is time to fight for those who cannot fight for themselves. And it is time to remember our common enemy."

Rowe stood. "That enemy is *in the room with us*," he screamed.

Caspen let out a sharp hiss. Unlike the aroused, sensual hiss he made during sex, this hiss was harsh and clearly meant as a reprimand.

Rowe hissed right back, and at the sound, Caspen stood too, pushing Tem to the side so he was leaning over the table at Rowe.

"Watch yourself," he said, his voice a spear in the dark.

"Look at you." Rowe's eyes were hardened steel as they traced over Caspen's erection. "Turned on by a blunt."

Caspen went immediately still. His black eyes narrowed to slits. "If you value your life, you will not say that word again."

Rowe smirked. "Is it not true? You chose a mate who is part human—a mate who is *weak*. And now you want us to—"

Caspen moved so fast that Tem didn't even have time to blink before his hand was wrapped around Rowe's throat. "*There is nothing weak about my mate.*"

Several basilisks leaped forward in an attempt to pull Rowe and Caspen apart. The enormous marble table scraped against the floor as bodies crashed into each other in a disorderly tangle. Tem knew Caspen was powerful right now, so when he finally released Rowe, it was because he *chose* to, not because the hands gripping his shoulders had any real impact.

Caspen yanked Tem back into his lap, his breath ragged in her ear. When everyone was finally reseated, ugly purple marks were forming on Rowe's throat where Caspen had choked him. Another second and Rowe would have been dead.

The council was absolutely quiet. What felt like a full minute ticked by before Bastian said, "Let us put it to a vote. All those in favor of cresting the royals?"

Eight hands went in the air. Rowe sat defiantly still. Caspen, Bastian, and Tem didn't vote.

"The majority has it."

Is it over? Tem asked.

Nearly.

The king continued, "All those in favor of the conditions our hybreed has imposed?"

No hands went in the air.

A flicker of anger crossed Bastian's face. His eyes went to his son's, and Tem felt Caspen nod.

It is time, Tem.

For what?

In reply, Caspen's hands wrapped around her waist, pulling her onto his cock. He thrust into her quickly, holding her just above his lap so he was in complete control. Tem had been wet for so long that she needed no foreplay; the entire evening had already been foreplay, and she was more than ready to take him.

She came so fast that she gasped.

Caspen finished a moment later, letting out a low groan as he lifted her off his cock, showing the council proof of their union.

The entire thing couldn't have lasted more than thirty seconds. But the change in the room was undeniable, just like when Caspen had fingered her earlier. Only this time, he'd garnered far more power from their connection. Tem felt it in the air—a palpable energy that radiated off his body in shimmering waves, drawing everyone in, drawing *her* in.

Bastian asked the same question again. "All those in favor of the conditions our hybreed has imposed?"

Every hand went up.

"Then it is done."

Now it is over.

To Tem's utter surprise, the king bowed his head at her. Then he stood, turned, and left the room. The rest of the basilisks stood too, and Tem watched as they formed a single-file line in front of her. She glanced around at Caspen.

What are they doing?

They are acknowledging my authority.

By staring at me?

You are the source of my authority. Our connection is what swayed them today.

There was an electric moment of silence. Then the first basilisk knelt before her. Caspen's hand shot forward, palm out, stopping the basilisk from coming any closer.

What's happening now? Tem asked.

They wish to honor you.

Honor me how?

There is a tradition in which each member of the council kisses you.

Are you serious?

It is similar to the human tradition of kissing the ring.

Tem almost laughed at that. It wasn't similar *at all*. But she supposed she understood it in concept.

They want to kiss me while you watch? Tem asked incredulously.

Yes. But, Tem...the kiss would not be on the mouth.

Then where would it be?

Caspen didn't say a word. Instead, his fingers went once more between her legs.

"Are you *serious?*" Tem said out loud.

Caspen's hand immediately retreated. *It is meant as a sign of respect. You do not have to accept.*

But will it help you if I do?

Yes. It will.

Then I accept.

Caspen hesitated only a moment before positioning her between his legs, their knees aligned in parallel V's. He pulled her thighs open, offering her to the basilisk kneeling in front of them.

The basilisk leaned in.

Time seemed to slow as he pressed a soft, reverent kiss to her clitoris. Then he looked Tem in the eye, nodded respectfully, and stood. The second basilisk stepped forward, kneeled, and did the same. Each member of the council followed suit, one after the other, men and women alike. As the line went on, Tem became wetter and wetter. Finally, the line ended, and only one basilisk remained.

Tem's heart pounded as Rowe knelt in front of her.

He dipped his head, holding her gaze. It was only when he was an inch away that he finally closed his eyes and lowered his head to her center. Rowe did what the others did not. The basilisks before him had merely pressed their lips against her, touching her for only a fraction of a moment. But Rowe's tongue dipped inside her—curiously, as if he wanted to taste her—and Tem couldn't hide the way her breath hitched with pleasure. As soon as it happened, Rowe drew away in disgust.

"She liked that," Caspen said. "Do it again."

Surprise, then embarrassment, then eager anticipation surged through Tem. She *had* liked that: the tiny flick of Rowe's tongue, the subtle pressure of his teeth. The rest of the council hadn't done anything to distinguish themselves. Only Rowe's kiss had given her a glimpse of true pleasure, and Caspen was in her mind, so he knew it too.

For a long moment, Rowe didn't move. Then slowly, he lowered his mouth. He brushed his tongue against her, one soft flick like before, and she nearly came apart right then.

"Again," Caspen commanded.

This time, Rowe dipped his head and kissed her—right *there*—right where Caspen kissed her nearly every night. He swirled his tongue expertly over her clitoris, drawing a desperate gasp from Tem that she couldn't control. She closed her eyes and surrendered to the sensation. It felt so *good*. Rowe's mouth was a wicked devil, pushing Tem to the brink of a cliff she never asked to climb. He gripped her thighs, pulling her against him, making it so she didn't have a moment to breathe beneath his relentless tongue.

Caspen's cock was hard against the base of her spine.

Rowe kept going. He licked her, sucked her, stroked her until she was whimpering beneath his lips, her legs spread open without a single thought besides the undeniable need to feel as much of this as she possibly could.

There was no council; there was no meeting. There was only Tem's pleasure and what she was willing to surrender to get it.

"Make her finish," Caspen growled.

He was in her mind, his power growing with every flick of Rowe's tongue, the deep hum of magic crackling louder with each minute Tem inched closer to coming. Tem couldn't believe this was happening. But she wasn't about to stop it—not when it felt this good and *especially* not when everything in her wanted Rowe to continue.

She was mere seconds from finishing when Caspen's hand darted suddenly around her, grabbing the back of Rowe's neck and holding his head down, ensuring he stayed between her legs as she climaxed. The last thing she saw was Caspen's fingers interlaced in Rowe's thick black hair before her eyes slammed shut and she cried out, shuddering in release.

Only when the last wave of Tem's orgasm had passed did Caspen relinquish Rowe from his grip with a dismissive shove.

"Stand," he barked.

Rowe stood.

With a jolt, Tem realized he was hard, his cock standing just as surely as he did.

"Look at you," Caspen said, his voice sharper than a knife's edge. "Turned on by a blunt."

Tem still didn't know what that word meant. But she knew she had never seen Caspen so angry, and despite the warm afterglow seeping through her, she felt suddenly afraid.

"Finish," Caspen commanded Rowe, his voice lethally quiet. "We both know you want to."

There was such danger in his tone that Tem found herself holding her breath. When Rowe didn't respond, Caspen straightened.

"Finish," he growled. "*Now.*"

Rowe did not want to yield. The strain from resisting Caspen's order was evident on his face. His body was rigid, his muscles tensed to the point of exertion.

But Caspen was the future king. He had won the favor of the council, and his power was the strongest it had ever been. Even now, Tem could feel it vibrating off him, clouding her vision with stars.

Finally, as if compelled by an otherworldly force—and perhaps that was what Caspen's power was—Rowe's hand went slowly to his cock. He wrapped his fingers around the base and began to pump. He finished pathetically fast; it took three strokes before his head arched back with a tortured grunt. He palmed most of his cum, but Tem saw a single drop fleck onto his foot.

She stared at it as Caspen said, "Refer to her by anything other than her name again and you will no longer have a cock to stroke. Do I make myself clear?"

Rowe nodded, his eyes still glazed over with orgasm, his chest covered in sweat.

"Say it," Caspen ordered. "Say her name."

Rowe blinked, his eyes focusing on Tem. "Temperance."

There was no mistaking the hot thread of hate in his voice.

"Good. Now get out."

Rowe didn't need telling twice.

The moment he was gone, Tem looked back at Caspen.

"You made him angry," she whispered.

"*He* made *me* angry."

Caspen's tone was so forceful that Tem swallowed the rest of her thought, which was that Rowe was not a good enemy to have right now, especially when they needed his support. Humiliating him in front of the council could bring nothing but trouble. But before she could worry about it, Caspen spoke again. "Everyone out," he said, his eyes never leaving hers.

Tem didn't even hear the rest of the council leave.

She only felt Caspen's hands on her waist as he lifted her, turned her in midair, and pulled her straight down onto his cock.

She gasped at the sudden *fullness*, her hips moving of their own accord, her body craving him just as surely as he craved her. Tem grasped his shoulders, using them to steady her as she took exactly what she needed from him. When their lips met, Caspen groaned, and Tem knew he liked her best when she was just like this: naked on his lap. He squeezed her ass, then her throat.

Tem didn't stop riding him. She needed what came next—needed to feel that ultimate release. Smoke was rising from Caspen's torso, but she no longer feared it. Something in her called to it. Something in her wanted *more*. Sex with Caspen felt different now that they were engaged, now that she knew who she really was.

Come for me, Tem. I need to see you come.

Tem was already coming. She threw her head back as her orgasm hit her, blossoming in her center and spreading up her spine. An overwhelming wave of approval washed over her, and she knew it was Caspen's. He loved seeing her this way—messy and sexy and free—coming for him exactly when he told her to. And Tem loved being this way for him.

Now she understood how she could share her body with another but only belong to him. How they were fated—beyond comprehension, beyond logic, beyond reason—their very matter intertwined in an impenetrable thread. They would not be broken. Ever.

Between the orgasm Rowe had given her and the one she'd just had, Tem felt as if she were made of sunlight.

Caspen pulled her off his cock and set her on the edge of the table, his face between her thighs. For a singular moment, he simply looked up at her, and Tem was reminded immediately of the first time they met, when she'd touched herself in the warm darkness of the cave, and he'd touched himself in return. She'd been so naive then.

Caspen lowered his mouth.

It was one thing for Rowe to taste her. It was quite another for *Caspen* to slip his tongue inside her, to show her without a shadow of a doubt that she was *his*, that they *belonged* to each other. His tongue traced slow circles around her clitoris, just enough to make her arch her back but not enough to make her come again. When his fingers entered her, she moaned, grabbing the back of his head and holding him against her. He licked her willingly, deliciously, the way every girl wanted to be licked—like she was the ultimate prize and the man between her legs was so lucky to have won her. He licked away all her wetness from the orgasm she'd just had, and by the time he was finished, she was wet again from what he was doing now. The marble table was hard beneath her ass. But it didn't matter. What he was doing felt so good that Tem could have stayed here all night. Just when she was moments away again, he stood, slid his cock inside her, and thrust until they finished together.

Tem rested there, her legs wrapped around him, their chests pressed together, their hearts beating in unison.

That was some council meeting.

Caspen laughed, the sound vibrating against her. *They are not usually so eventful.*

I should hope not.

He kissed her cheek. "You must be tired," he whispered. "We should sleep."

Tem nodded.

Caspen lifted her off the table before setting her on the cold stone floor. He took her hand, and they wound through the passageways together. When they reached his room, they collapsed onto his bed, folded in each other's arms. The last thing Tem heard before she fell asleep was Caspen's voice in her mind:

Thank you.

CHAPTER TWENTY-NINE

---✦·•---

W HAT DID ROWE CALL ME?"

Caspen opened his eyes. "I see we are already asking questions," he said, stretching his arms before pulling her against him. Tem had been awake for a while, watching him sleep. But now she needed answers.

"Caspen," she insisted. "Tell me."

"Rowe called you a blunt," he said, his voice still rough with sleep. "It is an insult used to describe humans."

"But I'm not human. I'm a hybreed."

"You are *part* human. That is already too much for Rowe."

"But why 'blunt'? What does it mean?"

"It refers to your teeth. Humans do not have fangs like we do. They will always be… blunt, so to speak."

Tem absorbed this information slowly. She thought about Leo's gold teeth and how they were shaved into points. Fangs, for all intents and purposes. But false ones.

"Do you think I'm weak?" Tem whispered.

The rage on Caspen's face was unmistakable. He cupped her jaw, looking her straight in the eye as he said, "You are perfect, Tem. I will not allow you to think otherwise."

She appreciated the sentiment. She just didn't believe it.

Caspen pulled her closer, pressing his lips to her neck. "Rowe is a fool if he thinks you are weak."

"He's just a fool in general," Tem muttered. She felt Caspen smile.

"That he is."

They were silent for a moment. Then Tem said, "I meant what I said."

Caspen raised his eyebrows questioningly.

She clarified. "I'll only do the crest if Leo's safety is guaranteed."

"I understand, Tem."

"Will your father keep his word?"

"Yes."

"How do you know?"

"Because he needs you to perform the crest. If he goes back on his word, he knows you will not deliver."

"And afterward? How do I trust that he won't go back on his word then?"

Caspen looked her once more in the eye. "You have my word as well, Tem. No harm will come to the human prince. Or to his sister."

Deep appreciation swept through her. Now Tem felt better. But the feeling lasted only a moment before another trickle of doubt set in. "What will happen to the rest of the royals?"

Caspen sighed. "I do not know."

"Yes, you do. Tell me."

He sat up, and Tem sat up too. "I do not know for certain. After you crest them, they will be bound to you."

"And then?"

"I do not know," he said again.

Tem stared numbly at his shoulder. It would be worth it. Whatever the cost, it would be worth it to avoid war.

"Caspen," she whispered. "What if I can't crest them?"

He took her face once more in his hands. "You can."

"I thought you didn't want me to do it."

He sighed. "I do not want you to do it if you are not ready. But if this is the path you have chosen, I will help you prepare."

"Prepare?"

"I will teach you how to harness your basilisk side. Once you do that, you will be able to perform the crest."

"Do you mean you'll help me…transition?"

He held her gaze steadily. "Yes."

"How?"

Caspen shrugged. "It is like you said. I have taught you everything else. Why not this?"

Tem smiled at that. But it quickly faded. "I'm…scared," she whispered.

His expression softened. "We do not have to do anything today. You can take your time."

But they were running out of time. The ball was mere days away; the wedding would be shortly after. If Tem didn't do this now—if she couldn't master this new part of her—Leo's safety wasn't guaranteed.

Something else gnawed at Tem's heart—a fear she didn't want to name. She looked up at Caspen, staring deep into his golden eyes.

"Caspen," she said slowly. "You said our connection is what made the council acknowledge your authority."

"It is."

"So you can…draw power from our connection? From me?"

He nodded. "I can."

"Even if I'm not near you?"

Another nod. "Yes."

Tem looked straight at him. "So when you send me pulses—when you turn me on—it makes you more powerful."

"It does." He said it calmly.

Tem frowned.

All those times he'd brought her to climax using the claw, he was drawing power from her. He was *using* her. She thought about the time in the bathtub—how it had occurred while he was meeting with the council, seeking approval for their engagement.

Caspen tucked a strand of hair behind her ear. "Why are you asking me this, Tem?"

"You're using me to gain power."

He didn't respond.

Tem tilted her head. "Am I wrong?"

Still no response.

She hardened her tone. "What if I didn't give you power? Would you still be with me?"

Caspen touched her chin, pulling her face to his. "Of course."

She gave him a look.

"Tem," he said as he leaned in. "Of *course* I would. It is true that you are a source of power for me. But that is not why I am with you. Do not forget that you are a hybreed. Everything I can do, you can do as well."

Tem absorbed the meaning of his words.

Caspen spoke before she could. "I am a source of power for you too, Tem."

It was an interesting thought. She wanted to know more, but another fear was seeping into her heart—one she didn't want to face. Her next question was a whisper. "What if I never transition? Will you still love me?"

Caspen pressed a kiss to her forehead. "I fell in love with you when I thought you were human. Please do not insult me by assuming I would not love you otherwise."

Tem hadn't thought of it that way. At first, she'd been angry with Caspen for concealing the fact that she was a hybreed. But now she considered his choice from a different perspective. If he'd never told her, she may never have found out, and they would have continued on as they had been: her as a human, him as a basilisk.

They might have lived like that for the rest of their time together. Caspen had never pushed her to do anything she wasn't ready to do—never needed her to be anything other than human.

His next words confirmed it. "I will always love you, Tem," he whispered. "In any form."

There was nothing more to say after that. Tem knew in her heart that Caspen's interest in her was not transactional, that their connection went far deeper than a mere exchange of power. He would have abandoned her long ago if that were the case. There was no guarantee she would be able to transition—no guarantee she would ever reach her full potential. He'd loved her before he saw her freckles. He would always love her.

Caspen kissed her again, and she kissed him back.

Eventually, he drew away.

"It is nearly morning," he said quietly. "Your mother will be waiting."

It seemed wrong to leave without having sex. But Tem was still exhausted; her body had been through far too much in the past few days, and she suspected Caspen knew this. He walked her to the head of the trail, kissing her deeply before letting her go.

The morning was a cold one; winter was beginning to set in. The last days of the autumn season were upon them, and soon the village would be covered in snow. Tem had always hated the snow. It was far too cold and made her feel miserable. Now she wondered whether that was a distinctly basilisk trait. Snakes coveted warmth—they were drawn to it in their deep, dark caves. There was so much she didn't know about herself—so much she had yet to discover.

Tem went about her farm chores in silence. She noticed the crow of every rooster, marveling at how they physically pained her. It was worse somehow now that she knew the truth. It was as if the glass had shattered on her life and she would never put the pieces back together again.

When she entered the cottage, her mother was waiting for her.

"My dear," she said quietly.

Tem sighed. There was still no closure between them—no resolution. "Mother."

A pause. And then: "I should have told you sooner."

Tem blinked. She hadn't expected to hear that at all.

Her mother stepped closer, taking Tem's hands in hers. "It was wrong of me to conceal something so important from you. I pray you'll forgive me."

Tem opened her mouth, then closed it again. Was she really going to blame her mother for keeping this secret when she was now keeping secrets of her own? Her mother had no idea what Tem had been up to under the mountain. She didn't know that her daughter was engaged to a basilisk—that Tem was practically following in her footsteps. So she said, "Of course I forgive you."

Relief flooded her mother's face. She squeezed Tem's hands, then dropped them. "I know you must have many questions. And I will answer them, but later. For now, I was planning on going to the bakery."

Tem knew it was her way of making peace, of sparing her from a needlessly cruel encounter with Vera.

"Thank you, Mother."

Her mother smiled. Then she left.

Tem spent the rest of the day in bed, alternating between worrying and sleeping. By the time it was midafternoon, she was already aching to see Caspen again. She was eager to begin her lessons—eager to transition. Now that she knew there was an entire part of her that lay undiscovered, she needed to explore it.

Tem couldn't wait until evening.

She left her mother a note and walked quickly to the caves, her shoulders hunched against the wind. When she arrived, she went straight to the passageway, confidently navigating the twists and turns she'd memorized long ago. Tem was almost to Caspen's chambers when something stopped her dead in her tracks.

Someone stood in the middle of the passageway.

She could barely see them in the near blackness, but her spine broke out in chills when they spoke.

"Temperance."

It was Rowe.

Tem didn't respond. She couldn't have if she'd tried.

Rowe stepped closer. "You know," he said casually, as if they were old friends. "You should not wander the mountain alone. It is not safe for humans."

"I'm not human." Tem hated how small her words sounded.

Rowe stepped even closer. "No?" His voice immediately lost its congenial tone. "Then what are you? A half-breed. An abomination of nature who thinks she is our salvation."

"I don't think that," Tem whispered.

"Stupid girl. You know *nothing* of the ways of my people."

"I know Caspen regrets what he did."

Rowe froze. It was a wild gamble to bring up Rowe's father. But Tem needed to distract him—to find a way out of this. She barreled onward before he could stop her.

"He didn't want to perform the crest."

Rowe's response was cold. "Yet he did so anyway."

"He only did so because he felt he had no other choice."

"*Yet he chose to do it,*" Rowe hissed. He stepped closer once more, and his breath was on her face as he said, "What he did was a sin. He will pay for it in blood."

Tem tried to control her heartbeat but found it was impossible. Rowe was standing far too close; every instinct in her body was telling her to run.

"Wouldn't you do anything for your family?" she asked desperately. "For your quiver?"

"His quiver has no right to the throne," Rowe snarled, his voice sharper than crushed glass. "And neither do you."

Cold fear bit through Tem.

Rowe was angry. At Caspen *and* at Tem. Before she could turn around, Rowe grabbed her arm, his grip painfully tight. His other hand went to her throat, his fingers tightening around her windpipe. But instead of choking her, Rowe's eyes bore into hers, his pupils dilating wide. For a single, terrifying moment, Tem thought he might kiss her.

Instead, Rowe's face twisted into a frown. "Unbelievable," he whispered. "He claimed you."

Tem had no idea what that meant. But she knew she had to get away. Rowe was clearly unhinged, and there was no telling what he might do next. With one final yank, Tem wrenched herself from his grasp as forcefully as she could. To her surprise, he let her go, his face still frozen in shock. Every instinct screamed at Tem to run.

Instead, she raised her chin and said, "If you ever touch me again, Caspen will kill you."

She didn't even know whether the words were true. If Caspen killed Rowe, there would be an immediate war between the quivers. Tem didn't want that to happen— especially not because of her. But Caspen was the only card she had left to play. He was powerful, and right now, she needed to remind Rowe of that.

Rowe didn't answer. Tem ran.

She sprinted the rest of the way to Caspen's chambers, frantically counting the turns one after another, somehow making it to the familiar wooden door.

Caspen looked up in surprise as she entered. "Tem? You are early."

She immediately burst into tears.

"*Tem.*" Caspen crossed to her, taking her face in his hands and pulling it up to his. "What is the matter?"

She shook her head, trying to control her sobs.

"Talk to me, Tem." Caspen's gaze fell to her throat.

She wondered if he could see where Rowe had grabbed her.

"Tem, please," he whispered. "What happened?"

She didn't answer, still catching her breath.

"You look just as you did after those boys hurt you. I cannot bear to see you this way."

At the mention of Jonathan and Christopher, Tem remembered the stone statues in the square. She imagined what Caspen might do to Rowe. "It's nothing like that." She shook her head again. "Really."

But Caspen's mouth formed a hard line. "Tell me what happened."

His voice was quiet. There was no point trying to hide from him. Even if she could lie convincingly, he would never believe her. She looked up into his concerned eyes.

"I ran into Rowe," she said finally. "He...was angry."

Caspen immediately stiffened. "About what?"

"The council meeting."

A muscle twitched in his jaw. "What did he say?"

Tem tried to look away, but Caspen held her face near his.

"He said I had no right to the throne." There was a pause, and Tem considered leaving out the rest. But something in Caspen's expression told her he wouldn't stop until he had the full story. So she finished quietly. "And then he said you claimed me."

Caspen straightened. "Did he touch you when he said that?"

"He grabbed my throat."

Shock passed quickly over Caspen's face. Then unfathomable anger took over. He dropped his hands. "Wait here," he commanded.

"Where are you going?"

"I will explain when I return."

Tem pulled him back. "You will explain *now*."

"Tem, stop. I must—"

"*Caspen.*"

At her cry, he went still. She threw her arms around his neck, holding him against her.

"I need to feel safe," she said quietly. "Please don't leave me."

His face was an inch from hers. She stared into his golden eyes, seeing nothing but rage in them.

"I must kill him, Tem."

A chill went down Tem's spine. It was exactly what she'd threatened Rowe with, but now that it was actually an option, she knew without a doubt she didn't want it to happen.

"It was *nothing*, Caspen. Truly."

But Caspen was already turning to leave again. "This cannot go unpunished."

She pulled him back. "There's nothing to punish."

He let out a dry laugh. "You are wrong."

"He only grabbed me."

"He tried to crest you."

That made Tem stop short. She frowned. "How do you know?"

Caspen's eyes went once again to her neck. "The crest is most effective when done by the throat."

Tem pictured the terrifying moment when Rowe had grabbed her and looked her in the eye. "But I didn't feel anything," she said slowly.

"That is because I claimed you for myself. My venom protected you from his crest."

Tem remembered how she had swallowed the smoky black liquid. "Are you sure?" she whispered.

"Yes," Caspen said, his body still angled toward the door. "Only the king could bypass that protection. He is the only basilisk with enough power to crest anyone he wants."

"What would have happened if Rowe had crested me?"

"I would have killed him," Caspen snapped. "Like I wish to do now."

"That's not what I mean."

He sighed, finally turning back to her. "Then what do you mean, Tem?"

"I mean…what would have happened to us?"

If possible, Caspen looked even angrier than he already did. "I do not know for sure. You are a hybreed, so you are both basilisk and human. The crest could have enslaved you. Or it could have killed you. If it had enslaved you, our bond as we know it would be broken. You would belong to him."

"I can't imagine that."

"Neither can I."

Tem tried to picture herself with Rowe instead of Caspen. The thought made her want to vomit. "But how could he think he'd get away with cresting me? He couldn't hide it, could he?"

"He would not hide it. That is the point. Everyone would know he crested you. He would fuck you in front of me, and there would be nothing I could do about it."

It was an awful thought. Tem couldn't imagine being bound to someone like Rowe—someone who hated her, someone who didn't care if she lived or died. Someone who would use her to torture Caspen.

"I wouldn't let him."

"You would not have a choice, Tem. The crest would bind you. Your only desire would be to please him."

"That's horrible."

"It is. To crest another's mate is unspeakably cruel. There is no way to reverse it. It is an unforgivable act of war. Rowe knows this."

"So…what happens next?" Tem asked softly. "You can't kill him. You know that."

Caspen sighed. "I know. But I must retaliate."

"Can't you just…I don't know…teach him a lesson somehow?"

The corner of Caspen's mouth twitched. It wasn't a happy smile. "That is exactly what I will do."

A sliver of dread pierced Tem's stomach, and she regretted her suggestion. But surely, whatever Caspen chose to do to Rowe would be better than killing him, wouldn't it? As long as there were no more deaths on her hands, Tem could justify the outcome.

She stepped closer to him. "Just…don't do anything tonight. Please. I don't want to be alone."

Caspen's hands found her waist. "I will not leave you alone."

"Ever?" Tem murmured against his lips.

"Ever," Caspen murmured back.

They kissed slowly, sensually, savoring the way the other tasted. Caspen unlaced her dress, and it fell to the floor. He whispered a question into her mind as his tongue moved against hers. *Do you want to try to transition?*

A lot had already happened tonight, and Tem was tired. But the allure of transitioning was why she'd come here in the first place. And if the incident with Rowe had taught her anything, it was that she needed to protect herself. Transitioning was the best way to do it.

Yes.

Caspen pulled away. *Come with me.*

He took her hand in his, and they entered the passageway.

Where are we going?

Down.

It was all he said. Tem didn't ask for more information, content to simply walk by his side as they descended deeper and deeper beneath the mountain. At one point, they crossed through a large circular room with a fountain in the middle. There were benches scattered throughout the space.

"What happens here?" Tem asked.

"It is a gathering place," Caspen said. "Think of it as a courtyard."

They continued walking ever downward, and Tem swore an hour passed before Caspen finally stopped them in front of a pair of double doors. He turned to her.

"I want you to try to relax."

Tem rolled her eyes. Caspen always wanted that.

"Tem." He placed his hands on her shoulders. "You need to be calm. And you need to believe you can do this."

She stared up at him. It was clear that *Caspen* believed she could do this, whether Tem believed it herself or not. That would have to be enough for now.

Tem nodded.

Caspen nodded too, then pushed open the double doors.

An enormous cavern unfolded before them. They were standing at its very edge, on a slope that led gradually down to a deep, wide lake. Glistening water went on for what seemed like forever—Tem couldn't see the end of it. The cavern was lit by torches, their warm light flickering off the surface of the lake. Stalactites hung from the ceiling in great jagged drips.

"This is…" Tem whispered. But there were no words. It was beyond beauty; Tem had never been somewhere so clearly steeped in *magic*. She could feel it in her bones—much the same way she'd been able to feel Caspen's power during the council meeting. There was a deep, ancient energy here, and Tem felt herself drawn to it.

Caspen guided her down the slope, right to the edge of the water.

"What is this place?" Tem asked.

"It is the center of the mountain."

"Why did you bring me here?"

Caspen stepped into the water, and Tem followed. "It is sacred," he said as they waded out until they were waist deep. "We believe that Kora herself bathed here."

Tem could believe that too. The lake was ethereal; she could see how a goddess would feel at home here.

"It may be easier for you to transition somewhere that is connected to nature."

"Why not outside?"

"There are people outside. If you transition and you cannot control yourself, they would be in danger. I do not want you to worry about hurting anyone your first time."

Tem felt a rush of gratitude toward him. He had clearly thought this through.

Caspen took her hands in his, turning to face her.

We will do this together.

He said it with a confidence Tem did not share.

A moment later, she felt him pull her into his mind in the same way he had done before. Tem made a concerted effort not to panic at the thought of leaving her physical body unprotected while he transitioned.

I will keep you safe.

Tem would have nodded, but there was no point. Even Caspen's conviction could not soothe her. She was too anxious—too frightened—to be at ease even in the shelter of his mind.

Relax, Tem.

Tem tried to relax.

She focused instead on the way Caspen felt, noticing how he was calm and steady despite what was at stake. It was a trait she'd always desired for herself. Tem felt too much, all the time.

You can use that, Tem.

Use what?

Your emotions.

How?

Transitioning is about becoming the truest version of yourself. You are emotional. Embrace that.

I thought you wanted me to be calm.

Perhaps what I want is irrelevant here.

Tem considered this. She was a hybreed. That meant she was just as much a human as she was a basilisk. It also meant that she would never be exactly like Caspen. There would always be a part of her that would not be tamed.

Now pay attention.

Tem knew that tone well. Her teacher had returned.

A subtle vibration was forming in Caspen's mind. It buzzed along the perimeter, building gradually into a low hiss. Tem felt it all around her; it dug into her brain like a hundred tiny talons, scratching at the essence of her being.

This is how I begin.

Tem realized what Caspen was doing: he was showing her how *he* transitioned in the hopes that she would be able to do so too.

The hiss grew until it surrounded Tem on all sides, building into a singular gleam of power. There was a great *swell*, and Tem felt a sudden wave of motion sickness. Caspen was breaking—*shedding*—unfolding himself from the inside out. It was like being in the middle of a volcano while it erupted.

Along with the mental sensation, Tem experienced what Caspen felt physically. It was exactly as he'd said: transitioning was like taking off clothes. Layer after layer of restriction fell away, revealing the feral beast beneath.

Join me, Tem.

The hiss grew. Tem was unbearably hot, as if she had a hundred fevers at once.

Something called to her—something that felt like Caspen but wasn't him, something primal and wild and free. Tem wanted to answer.

But she couldn't.

When she tried to access the deepest parts of her, she was met with resistance. There were shackles holding her down—chains of doubt and fear that would not budge no matter how hard she yanked at them.

You can do it, Tem.

I can't.

You are the only one standing in your way.

Tem was painfully aware of that.

Her consciousness pricked as Caspen passed the point of no return. Part of her ached to join him. An equal part recoiled in terror.

Trust your instincts, Tem. You can do it.

Tem felt as if she were splitting in two. *I'm telling you I can't.*

Thick, black smoke filled the cavern. Caspen was growing, his human form long gone. *Join me.*

They barely sounded like words anymore. Caspen's voice was just a hiss, thundering through her mind and rattling her teeth in her skull.

Tem tried again to break free—to fling away the anchors that weighed her down, to cast aside twenty years of pain and insecurity and self-doubt. Caspen's mind surrounded hers, pulling her toward him, forcing her in two different directions.

You can do it.

But Tem had had enough.

"I CAN'T!" she screamed. Her voice echoed endlessly around the cavern, cruelly repeating her own failure back to her.

A moment later, Tem was back in her own mind. She saw Caspen's outline shrink behind the smoke, and she knew he was returning to his human form. The sweltering temperature dropped to a tolerable degree, and before she could even blink, a man stood before her once more.

Caspen's hands went to her waist, holding her gently. "We will try again tomorrow, Tem. Do not despair."

Tem didn't even have the energy to nod.

Instead, she collapsed against him, tears stinging her eyes. The frustration and disappointment were too much for her. She had never felt so defeated.

Caspen held her as she sobbed, waiting until she was calm before carrying her out of the lake and through the passageway, murmuring soothing words the entire way back. By the time they reached his chambers, Tem was fast asleep in his arms.

When she woke, the first thing she felt was shame.

Tem couldn't imagine how things could have gone any worse. She was completely hopeless. It was one thing to feel out of place as a human, but to know she couldn't transition either was a blow she hadn't expected.

You cannot transition yet. *That does not mean you will never do so.* Caspen was awake, watching her.

I'm hopeless, Caspen.

Caspen touched a single finger to the bottom of her chin, raising her head to his. *I never want to hear you say that again.*

Tem was on the verge of tears. Caspen pressed his lips to hers.

Rest today, Tem. We will try again tonight.

By the time Tem got home, she had cried twice more and received a pounding headache in return. The farm work did nothing to soothe her, and despite cleaning the chicken coops with unhinged aggression, Tem's mood only worsened.

It wasn't fair that Caspen could transition so easily. There had to be some trick to it, something Tem was missing. And what if she never figured it out? What if she never accessed this part of her—the part that was capable of performing the crest? There was too much at stake for that to be the case. She *had* to master this. For Leo's sake and her own. She could not shoulder the burden of war.

Her mother mercifully made the trip to the bakery again. If this was their new normal, Tem certainly wasn't going to question it. She savored the time alone in their little cottage, taking the opportunity to smell the sea salt spray on her mother's dresser. It had been a long time since she'd used it, and she spritzed a tiny amount in her hair now, pressing her curls to her nose and sniffing deeply. For some reason, it made her feel connected to Caspen, and she wished the claw was inside her.

Just then, there was a knock on the door.

Tem bounded into the kitchen, half expecting to see Leo on her porch. Instead, it was a footman, who handed her a letter before disappearing. Tem opened it in a rush to read:

Temperance Verus,

The prince requests your presence at the castle for a formal ball in two days' time. The dress code is evening wear.

There was a note on the back, written in tangled red ink:

Next time, I get to torture you.

CHAPTER THIRTY

———••◆✳◆••———

TEM COULDN'T HELP BUT SMILE. THE MEMORY OF WHAT SHE'D DONE WITH LEO IN the carriage came back to her in a fevered wave, bringing a rush of heat to her cheeks. Then, just as quickly, her face fell.

Two days.

That meant Tem had only two nights left with Caspen. Two nights to learn how to transition. She crumpled the letter in her hand. She was done holding herself back.

Tem ate a quick dinner with her mother before setting off once more for the caves. This time, Caspen was waiting for her, and she knew it was to prevent another incident like the one that had happened with Rowe.

They didn't bother going to his chambers. Instead, they traversed the passageways that led beneath the mountain, crossing through the empty courtyard before continuing on to the cavern. When they reached the lake, they waded out into the water just as they had the night before. Caspen turned to her.

We will try something new this time. He leaned in, drawing her into a kiss.

This isn't new. She felt him smile against her lips.

We will transition while we are together.

You mean while we're having sex?

Yes.

And how is that going to help?

Caspen dipped his hands behind her thighs, lifting her and wrapping her legs around his waist. *I will talk you through it.*

Tem wasn't really listening anymore. His cock was rubbing against her, and she could feel her mind going blissfully blank. Maybe Caspen had a point. Sex was natural to her—sex with him even more so. Nothing made her feel more peaceful and alive than being with Caspen.

Are you ready?

Tem nodded.

They both moaned softly as he entered her.

Her arms wrapped around his neck as he thrust slowly upward, their motions creating ripples in the lake. Tem angled her hips to meet his, letting him all the way in. Caspen pressed kisses to her skin, distracting her from what she knew was to come. Eventually, she lost herself in his arms, thinking only of how good he felt inside her.

Every time she became anxious, Caspen would soothe her with his body and his mind. At no point did he let her panic; at no point did he allow her to spiral. Whenever a wave of fear threatened to overtake her, he quelled it.

Focus on me, Tem.

It was not hard to do so.

Their bodies were pressed together—two beings becoming one. Caspen pulled her closer with every thrust, bringing her to the brink of orgasm. Every time his hips met hers, her clitoris throbbed.

I want it, Caspen.

I know you do. He was thrusting faster, his eyes turning black.

I want it.

So take it.

He was growing in the same way he had during the ritual, his cock becoming bigger and harder and ridged. Only this time, Tem wanted to take it—was *going* to take it. She clawed at the edges of her mind, feeling for the same vibration of power she felt in Caspen's.

You can do it, Tem. Join me. Be with me.

There was pain interlaced with the pleasure now, coursing through her in shards of fractured lightning.

I know you can do it.

Caspen believed in her. Caspen knew she could do it.

Let go for me, Tem.

There was nothing she wanted more.

Let go.

Tem let go.

Everything in her plunged at once. The lake disappeared. There was no water, no cavern, no Caspen. Tem was no longer *there*, no longer *solid*. Instead, she was soaring toward something that she recognized—something familiar yet new. Something *real*.

Caspen was still inside her, but the place where she took him was changing—turning into something that could accommodate the most powerful version of him. She heard a hiss and realized it was her own.

Look at me, Tem.

Tem's eyes flew open.

For the first time, she saw Caspen in his true form. He was beautiful—far more beautiful than he was as a human, more beautiful surely than the gods. His body was covered in sleek black scales, shinier than the facets of a diamond, reflecting and refracting light in a kaleidoscopic waterfall. She stared into his eyes—eyes she no longer feared, eyes that had seen the worst parts of her and always loved her anyway.

Pleasure radiated through her. Caspen was inside her body and inside her mind, stimulating both at the same time, penetrating Tem without limits. Smoke surrounded them, caressing every part of her, intertwining them even more than they already were. She was hyperaware of the sensations within her own body, the way she was suddenly in tune with the blood in her veins, able to feel the way her muscles rippled and tensed.

Tem was unstoppable. Her power finally matched his.

She understood now how Caspen was so intuitive—how he knew exactly how to pleasure her. The same ability had been granted to Tem: she could hear his heartbeat, feel the subtle changes in the way his blood rushed through his body.

Caspen sent a surge of power right to where they were joined.

Oh. Tem closed her eyes in sheer bliss. *Do that again.*

Smoke enveloped her, and she arched her entire body back so she was looking up at the stalactites hanging far above them. He sent another, and Tem nearly blacked out.

Again.

Another.

Again.

And another.

Caspen wrapped his body around hers, surrounding her completely, making it so she felt nothing but him. He sent pulse after pulse—far more powerful than anything he'd ever sent her using the claw—until blackness began to overtake her. Just when she was sure she wouldn't survive another, Caspen sent one last pulse.

Pleasure like she'd never known slammed into her.

Tem roared in release—in *salvation*—as climax took her. No human words could describe such exquisite bliss. Every cell in her body was hot and open, willingly receiving wave after wave of glorious sensation as Caspen pushed her far beyond the limit of what she'd ever thought she was capable of taking.

It was paradise.

Nothing Tem had felt up until now could ever compare to this. She felt so *alive*, so *whole*, so filled with *purpose*. Tem wanted to give it back—to make Caspen feel everything she was feeling. She reached for her own power and sent *him* a pulse, wielding the wave of pleasure her climax had given her, using it to pleasure him in return.

Caspen let out a rabid sound—one of brutal joy. Tem sent another pulse, desperate to hear him make that sound again. No sooner had she released the pulse than he sent one in return, ripping the breath straight from her chest.

It was sensory overload in the extreme.

Tem had never experienced such rapid give and take, never been such a participant in someone else's experience. Everything she did to Caspen, he did right back to her. Each pulse she sent him was returned tenfold until she could feel her body vibrating with unrestrained power.

They were still connected, still intrinsically fused together. Tem never wanted it to end. She knew Caspen was right here with her, that they were on this journey together, that they would anchor each other no matter what came.

She couldn't tell one orgasm from another. They were endless, building into one great orchestra that unfurled her from the inside out. Caspen's voice bloomed suddenly in her mind:

I want all of you, Tem. Give yourself to me.

How?

Let me all the way in.

Caspen was so deep inside her she didn't know how to let him any further in. He surrounded her already. There was nothing more to give him.

Open your mind.

Tem had thought her mind was already open. But a moment later, she felt Caspen brush up against a barrier—one that shielded the deepest, purest piece of her: her soul.

To open it would require ultimate trust, ultimate surrender. It would mean showing him everything—the part of Tem she kept only to herself, the part that made her *her*. Tem couldn't imagine letting Caspen see that. But there was no one she'd rather show it to.

She began to lower the barrier.

Caspen growled in approval. Tem sensed the animal in him—the beast that craved her even when she was a beast too. His hunger for her ran so deep that a sudden loop of fear enlaced her. Caspen immediately suppressed it, his grip on her growing with each moment they were joined like this.

Let me in, Tem.

Tem closed her eyes and let Caspen all the way in. She felt him take the reins, pouring himself into her, filling her mind until they were no longer two beings but one. Tem had never experienced anything like this before. Their minds were combined: she was equal parts Caspen and herself. She saw his soul too, its flame a mirror to hers. He stroked her from the inside out until she was whimpering beneath his grasp.

Are you going to come for me?

She wanted to.

Yes.

Come for me, Tem.

This time when she came, Caspen came too.

They spun out into the ether together, their bodies taking from each other until neither of them had anything left to give. They were one and the same; they belonged to each other.

Caspen's mind tugged once again at hers, but this time in the opposite direction, this time in a reversal of what they had just done—toward the weight and heaviness of humanity.

Return with me.

It was easy to return to herself. The sensation was like falling backward—as simple as slackening her grip on the great thrum of power that joined her to Caspen, trusting that the ground would catch her when she landed.

And it did.

They were back in the lake, back in the cavern, back together. Tem opened her eyes to see Caspen's gold ones staring back at her. She smiled.

"I did it."

He smiled back. "Of course you did. You can do anything, Tem."

"I want to do it again."

Caspen laughed, the sound echoing around the sloping stone walls. *As you wish.*

They did it again. And again.

At some point, words were beyond them. They were simply moving, breathing, *existing* together—conforming to each other with nothing but their basest instincts and rawest desires. Tem herself ceased to exist. Instead, she was one with Caspen, one with Kora, one with her people.

Caspen was right—it did get easier. Tem transitioned back and forth three times, each time quicker than the last and the final time without using Caspen's mental connection to guide her. They had sex each time, for longer and longer, until finally neither of them could go on. For once, her stamina matched his.

Afterward, they lay panting on the shore of the lake, both of them returning slowly to their human forms. Beads of water trickled in rivulets down Caspen's torso, and Tem watched as scales became skin once more. She reached out her hand, placing her palm against his chest. He placed his hand over hers, holding them together.

It is heaven to be with you like this, Tem.

She shifted closer, pressing a kiss to the curve of his shoulder. Then she climbed on top of him, straddling his hips and looking into his eyes.

They didn't have sex again—Tem couldn't have if she'd tried. She simply ran her hands gently over his body, feeling the warmth of his skin against hers. Caspen let her do this, looking up at her in return, his palms resting gently on her hips. There was peace in this moment.

There was truth.

By the time they headed back to Caspen's chambers, Tem was so exhausted she could barely stand upright. They walked slowly, their hands clasped together, stopping only to kiss languidly in the darkness.

Eventually, they passed through the courtyard, only this time, it wasn't empty. Several basilisks wearing their human forms were gathered in a throng, speaking in hushed tones.

With a jolt, Tem recognized one of them.

Rowe stood on the other side of the fountain, talking to another basilisk.

Tem instinctively stepped closer to Caspen, squeezing his hand for comfort. He looked down at her.

"What is it, Tem?"

She opened her mouth to tell him. But at that exact moment, they passed the fountain, and Rowe's entire body came into view. Tem's warning died on her tongue.

Rowe's cock was gone.

It was not a clean cut. A warped mound of scar tissue protruded between his legs as if it had been ripped off instead of severed. Tem wondered suddenly if that was exactly what Caspen had done. The sheer force it would take to do such a thing made her feel sick. Surely, Rowe had used his power to heal himself. But the nature of the injury was so violent that Tem couldn't imagine the pain he'd endured before his skin knit itself back together again. The amount of blood he'd lost would have been nearly fatal. His balls were gone too—there was nothing left where everything had once been. Tem tried not to stare. But she couldn't look away.

Tem knew Caspen was angry with Rowe for trying to crest her. But it took seeing Rowe's mangled body to truly understand the scope of his fury. Rowe had tried to take what was his. In return, Caspen had taken the part of Rowe that basilisks valued the most—the part of him that directly contributed to his status in society. A basilisk without a cock was incomprehensible. It meant he couldn't participate in sex—the only thing that mattered to his people—in the same way everyone else could.

It meant he had nothing left to lose.

Caspen's words ran through her mind: *To crest someone else's mate is unspeakably cruel.* Tem wondered if this wasn't somehow crueler. Caspen had done the one thing Rowe would never recover from—something just as permanent and painful as losing your mate. It would be better to be dead. Surely, this was also an unforgivable act of war.

Tem was having trouble breathing.

"How could you—" she started but couldn't get the rest out.

Caspen simply kept walking, his head pointed straight forward. "I did what was necessary, Tem."

Tem looked up at him and saw nothing but rage. Not for the first time, she was struck by his power. It radiated off him in waves.

"You made him angry," she whispered. It was the same thing she'd said to him after he'd forced Rowe to finish after the council meeting. Except now, Rowe would never finish again. And it was all because of Tem.

"I know."

Caspen said it in a way that made it clear he was well aware of the severity of his actions.

They didn't speak the rest of the way back to his chambers. When they climbed into his bed, Tem was so exhausted from the night's events that she fell asleep the moment her head hit the pillow.

When she woke, she felt the full effects of what they'd done at the lake.

Her human form was aching. It felt as if she had been stretched too thin, like her skin was no longer the right size. There was a sporadic pain between her legs that wouldn't go away, and her limbs were suddenly heavy. Even her balance was off; it was as if she were a stranger in her own body. Just when she felt the urge to panic, warm, steady hands touched her.

Good morning, my love. Caspen was awake.

Good morning.

Tem turned to him, running her fingers through his hair and studying his face. It was fascinating to see the similarities between Caspen's human form and his true form. His hair was the exact same color as his scales; the angle of his eyebrows perfectly mimicked the triangular shape of his basilisk face. It was like she was finally able to see every part of him—to understand him on his most authentic level.

She gazed at him for a long time.

Caspen didn't try to kiss her. He merely let her look, exercising his seemingly endless patience as she traced her fingertips gently along his temple, then his cheek, then his jaw.

"Beautiful," Tem said.

Caspen smiled. "That is what I say about you."

"Well. It goes both ways."

He smiled wider. "How do you feel?"

Tem shifted, letting out a groan. "Sore."

Caspen nodded. "That is normal. Your body is not used to changing in such a way. We will practice again tonight."

At the mention of tonight, Tem remembered what was happening tomorrow.

"Caspen," she said quietly. "The ball."

His eyes held hers. "When is it?"

"Tomorrow night."

"I see."

There was a pause as Leo's presence loomed between them. Tem nestled closer to Caspen and asked, *Will we still see each other after I move into the castle?*

Caspen answered immediately. *Yes.*

But how?

We will find a way.

Tem didn't say anything else because there was nothing else to say. Even if she could find a way to visit Caspen while she was living in the castle, she still had no idea what would happen if all went to plan and Leo chose her as his wife. What would happen after the wedding—after she'd crested his family? Leo wouldn't want anything to do with her. And what of her engagement to Caspen? Surely, they were to be married at some point. But Tem had no concept of basilisk weddings—whether they were anything like what humans did, with a ceremony and rings. The little gold claw around her neck was the only token of their engagement, and it had been made from Caspen's blood. Tem couldn't imagine what kind of wedding would center around such an act. But these were questions for another time.

For now, she wanted every last second she could have with Caspen.

Caspen.

Yes, Tem?

Kiss me.

Caspen brushed his lips against hers, and Tem's worries fell away. Her body was too sore for sex. But she wanted it anyway, and Caspen had never been able to resist her. When he slipped inside her, she bit her lip in pain. Caspen paused.

We do not have to do this, Tem.

I want to.

I understand. But we do not have to.

Tem only pulled him closer. He thrust slowly, gently, making eye contact the entire time to ensure she was fully present. Eventually, he turned her onto her side, entering her from behind so their bodies were cupped together—two crescent moons in identical orbit. Tem closed her eyes, losing herself in the way his cock felt, allowing him to fully take charge. She was so wet, he slid in easily, her body accommodating every inch of his length.

It was different from the sex they had in their true forms. But Tem needed to fuck like this too, as a human, so she could feel connected to the part of her that felt like *her*.

Soon, she was close.

Caspen rolled her so she was on her stomach, his thrusts speeding up as he buried himself in her over and over again until they fell into orgasm together. Tem gasped as the euphoric rush hit her, clenching her muscles around Caspen's cock as he groaned against the back of her neck. Afterward, they remained clasped together, his arms still wrapped around her. He pulled out, and his fingers found her clitoris, caressing it gently. He slid his fingers inside her, and it wasn't until Tem felt pressure between her legs that she realized what he was actually doing. Another claw was forming deep in her center, molding itself perfectly to the inside of her body. Tem gasped as it pressed against her clitoris, curving into its final shape and coaxing her straight into another climax.

Caspen's other hand went to her throat, arching her head back so he could kiss her as she came.

"Caspen," she breathed against his lips.

"Tem," he breathed back.

He released her. The claw was solid inside her. Tem welcomed its weight.

Thank you.

Of course, Tem.

They kissed again. Finally, Tem broke away. *I have to get back to the farm.*

He buried his face in her hair, and she knew he was smelling her scent. *I want you to stay.*

You know I can't.

He only held her tighter. *Please, Tem. Stay.*

His request surprised her. There was a hint of desperation in his voice—of deep-seated longing. It was almost as if the closer they became, the more he was scared of losing her. Tem wanted to reassure him. But their relationship was not the only thing at stake. Tem had other people she loved now—other people to protect. Caspen could protect himself.

No.

He released her with a sigh.

They walked together through the passageway, and when they reached the head of the trail, Caspen pulled her against him again. He kissed up her neck, biting at her earlobe.

"Caspen," she yelped. "You have to let me go."

He only held her tighter.

Tem went still, allowing him to hold her. This was a different version of Caspen than the one she was used to. This version was not aloof, not secretive or harsh. This Caspen openly yearned. This Caspen needed her.

Something had changed between them at the lake, when their minds had combined. It felt as if he'd left a piece of himself with her, and Tem realized it was possible that he had. And perhaps she'd left a piece of herself in return. She had no idea what magic had occurred in that cavern under the mountain, no clue how deep their connection now went.

"Caspen," she whispered. "Let me go."

He let her go.

Tem returned to her cottage a changed woman.

The farm no longer looked like home. Perhaps it never had been. Whether Tem's future lay in the castle with Leo or in the caves with Caspen, she knew for sure it was no longer between these wooden walls.

Her mother was away, delivering the eggs. Tem spent the day doing chores, watching the hours tick slowly by. Caspen sent her pulses—too many to count. Tem savored them. She'd missed carrying the claw inside her, and now that she had it again, it was as if part of her had slid back into place. She experimented with sending pulses back, practicing the same thing she'd done in the cavern with intermittent success. It turned out Tem wasn't quite used to her power just yet. At one point, she sent a pulse so strong that Caspen roared in pain, shouting a word in a language she'd never heard.

Sorry.

His pain subsided, replaced by wary amusement. *It is no matter, Tem. You do not know your own strength.*

I didn't mean to hurt you.

I am not hurt. That was merely…a surprise.

Tem smiled. She sent him several more surprises that day.

By the time her mother returned, Tem had no desire to remain in the cottage. The pulses through the claw had given her energy; it was her first taste of what it felt like to draw power from Caspen, and she was aching to expend it. But instead of going to the caves, she wanted to savor what could be her last night in the village—to be young and impulsive one last time.

Without a second thought, she pulled on her cloak and set off for the Horseman. It was early; she figured she'd be the only one there. To her delight, she was wrong.

"Temperance." Gabriel threw his arms wide as soon as she pushed open the door.

He was seated in their favorite booth, several empty beer glasses in front of him. "It's been too long."

Tem slid in beside him. "Shouldn't you be at the castle helping prepare for the ball?"

"I'm injured," he said and brandished his thumb, which was wrapped in an astonishing number of bandages. "They sent me home."

Tem took a sip of his beer. "How'd that happen?"

"Had a little disagreement with a steak knife."

"Who knew cutlery could be so disagreeable."

"My thoughts exactly."

"Gabriel," Tem said slowly. "Thank you."

He cocked his head. "For?"

"For..." Tem paused, remembering the way Gabriel had protected Leo at the Passing of the Crown, how he'd shoved away the villager who'd launched himself at the prince. Tem knew he'd done it for her because he understood, even after only seeing them together briefly, how much Leo meant to her.

"Everything," she finished quietly.

Gabriel pressed his lips to her cheek. "Anything for you, dearest," he said just as quietly. He threw his arm around her, pulling her against him. "But enough about me. How's my future princess?"

The last time Tem was here, she'd been about to tell Gabriel what Caspen had done to Jonathan and Christopher. Then Leo had shown up, and the evening had gone in a completely different direction. So much had happened since then; there was so much more to tell.

"The future princess is tired."

Gabriel laughed at that. "I'd be tired too if I was fucking two people at once."

"You *are* fucking two people at once."

"Oh, that's right," he said, tapping his good finger against the beer glass. "I am, aren't I?"

Tem rolled her eyes. "Besides, I'm only fucking one person," she said resolutely.

Gabriel raised an inquisitive eyebrow.

"Is that so?"

"Yes."

"Come on, Tem. You mean to tell me you haven't taken a dive in the princely waters yet?"

She shook her head.

"*Really?* You know the ball is tomorrow night, right?"

"I know."

"Well then, you'd better hop on it if you want a chance at the crown. And by *it*"—he smacked her knee—"I mean *him*."

Tem closed her eyes in exasperation.

"Anyway, rumor has it that the king might interfere."

Tem's eyes flew back open. "Interfere with what?"

"The competition."

Gabriel was standing, ready to order more beer.

"Wait." Tem grabbed him, pulling him back down. "Interfere how?"

Gabriel sighed, as if this line of questioning was a great burden standing in the way of his acquisition of alcohol.

"If he doesn't like who Leo picks, he won't allow the wedding."

Dread pierced Tem's stomach. She remembered how Maximus had told Vera she was his favorite. "But how do you know that?"

"Henry said he heard the king and Lord Chamberlain talking."

"Well, what did they say *specifically*?"

"*Patience*, Temperance," Gabriel tutted. "I'm a little bit drunk, you know."

"I know," Tem sighed. She waited for Gabriel to continue.

"The king said, 'if he chooses her, I will choose another.'"

Tem didn't need to ask him who the king was referring to. If Leo chose her, Maximus wouldn't allow them to get married. But Gabriel had no idea what was at stake here. Tem *needed* to marry Leo in order to prevent war. Tem *had* to win the competition. There was no other option.

Tem no longer had an appetite for beer. "I have to go," she said. "Caspen is expecting me."

"On his cock."

Tem gave Gabriel a good shove for that.

She slipped from the booth and walked quickly through the village streets. She'd planned on staying at the Horseman for far longer, perhaps having a drink or two. But after this news, she only wanted to see Caspen—only wanted to find solace in his arms.

He was waiting for her in the cave.

Tem felt immediately drawn to him, as if the basilisk side of her awoke the moment he was near. She wondered if Caspen felt the same, because he drew her into a kiss so urgent she could barely catch her breath.

Are you ready to transition again?

Tem kissed him back. Transitioning again meant sex, and she was always ready for that.

Yes.

The kiss lasted a moment longer before Caspen took her hand in his and pulled her into the darkness of the passageway.

They had barely gone ten feet when it happened.

Tem felt nothing at first, only a slight *whoosh* of air as someone appeared before them. It was so dark she couldn't even tell who it was. Beside her, Caspen tensed.

Then her mind exploded in pain.

CHAPTER THIRTY-ONE

—··◦◦✳◦◦··—

T EM HAD NEVER EXPERIENCED A MENTAL ATTACK LIKE THIS BEFORE. IT CAME AT
her from all sides, piercing every part of her brain and shredding her mind with
brutal insistence. Beside her, she heard Caspen cry out, and she knew he was
experiencing a similar assault.

Fools. Both of you.

The voice belonged to Rowe.

He was shrouded in smoke. Tem saw only a bright flash of something sharp before
Caspen let out a strangled grunt of pain, his hands clasping his neck. Deep crimson
blood seeped between his fingers.

"*Caspen!*" she cried.

Rowe's presence surged into Tem's mind, crushing her with excruciating force. She
tried to slam the door shut between them—to cut off the corridor that allowed him
access to her. But Rowe was far too strong. He'd had centuries more practice wielding
the gifts granted to basilisks. Tem fell to her knees, surrendering to the assault.

Caspen's voice came to her then, tight with agony. *Transition, Tem. Do it now.*

But Tem couldn't. She was too new and in too much pain. Rowe's mental attack
was crippling her, cutting off her ability to access the power Caspen had only recently
taught her to wield.

It hurts, Caspen.

I know, Tem.

Panic clenched her chest. Caspen's voice was faint, as if he were far away. Rowe's
attack had caught him off guard, and now they were both vulnerable. Tem reached for
him, trying to pull him closer.

A hand grabbed her. But it wasn't Caspen's.

*Stupid girl. Filthy blunt. Did you think there would be no consequences for your
actions?*

Tem couldn't answer. There was no point in doing so anyway. Rowe's grip on her
tightened, his fingers twisting the skin around her wrist.

You little slut.

It was the same thing Jonathan had called her—the time-honored insult men threw at women they could not control.

Tem's back hit the hard stone floor as Rowe cast her violently aside. A moment later, Caspen's body crashed to the ground next to her. She turned her head to look at him, her heart nearly stopping at what she saw. Blood poured from the wound on his neck, dripping down his chest in horrible streaks. He wasn't healing himself. Perhaps he couldn't.

She'd never seen Caspen like this before—broken and in pain. Tem had watched many animals die on the farm. She knew what it looked like when someone was past the point of no return.

"Caspen," she whispered with what was left of her voice. "Crest me."

No.

The word was thunder in her mind.

Yes, she insisted. *It's the only way.*

I would rather die.

Well. I'd rather you didn't.

Rowe was coming closer.

If I crest you, everything will change between us.

Nothing will change between us. I'll still love you, and you'll still love me.

His blood was seeping onto the stone floor. *Our relationship as it is now will be forfeit.*

Only if you decide it is.

You will be bound to me. You will—

I know what will happen. I remember everything you said. But you need power, and I can give it to you. It's the only way.

Caspen's eyes fluttered shut. *I will not take your agency from you, Tem.*

Even if I'm asking you to?

It will corrupt your very nature. You are not meant to be tamed.

I'm a hybreed. I'll be fine.

You do not know that. It could kill you.

Rowe had reached them. His face stretched in a maniacal grin as he leaned forward, extending his hands. Time had run out, and they both knew it. Perhaps the crest would kill her. Perhaps it would enslave her. But if Caspen did nothing, Rowe would kill them both.

Caspen's voice was barely a whisper in her mind. *I never wanted this for you.*

Tem sent her next thought with everything she had left. *I've only ever wanted you.*

Slowly, Caspen opened his eyes. He raised his hand, wrapping his bloody fingers around Tem's throat. *You should only know pleasure.*

She finished the line. *Never pain.*

He closed his eyes.

For a moment, nothing happened. Then something inside Tem erupted, slamming into her from all directions with more force than she could comprehend.

She couldn't take it. She needed more.

She wanted it to stop. She would die if it did.

It was pain. It was pleasure.

It was *everything*.

There was no beginning and no end. The sensation bloomed from deep within her core to the tips of her fingers in a relentless *snap* of utter clarity. It was like being submerged in a perfectly warm bath—like floating in the world's stillest lake. Nothing could penetrate the warm numbness that enveloped her entire body. She had no problems, no worries. There was nothing and no one that could cause her harm. There was only utter and complete ecstasy.

Caspen's eyes flew open.

They were blacker than the night itself, endless pits of darkness that bore into Tem like knives. The wound on his neck was rapidly healing, stitching itself together as if it were never there to begin with. A deadly smile twisted Caspen's lips. As if in a trance, he stood to face Rowe, who opened his mouth but never got the chance to speak.

Instead, Caspen flicked his fingers—the gesture so casual Tem almost didn't catch it—and Rowe's back arched as if someone had snapped his spine in half. Tem wondered if that was exactly what had happened. Rowe fell to the floor, his face contorting as he screamed.

It was horrific. But Tem felt only bliss.

Caspen stepped forward and knelt over Rowe's mangled body. His fingers still dripped blood as he grabbed Rowe's neck and began to squeeze. Smoke rose from Caspen's shoulders, curling up the curved walls of the passageway.

Through the haze of Tem's rapture, her brain was trying to tell her something. She attempted to listen, pushing aside the waves of delirium the crest had given her, trying desperately to part the waters of her mind. Finally, a thought formed.

She tried to stand but couldn't. Instead, she crawled to Caspen, touching his shoulder and immediately recoiling. His skin was white-hot. It scalded her so sharply that the pain cut through the effects of the crest, delivering her firmly back to reality. She tried to reach for him with her mind.

Caspen.

He didn't answer. His mind was closed off to her, surrounded by impenetrable walls of flame. She spoke aloud instead.

"Caspen."

A muscle flexed in his jaw. He didn't look at her.

"Stop," she said, the word barely audible.

Rowe's fingernails were clawing at the back of Caspen's hands, drawing more blood.

"Caspen," she said again, louder this time. "Please stop."

He looked at her, and she flinched at the intensity of his gaze. "Why should I?" he growled. His voice was barely human.

"If you kill him, the Senecas will go to war with the Drakons. Your family, Caspen."

Rowe was choking. Caspen's grip tightened. "He deserves to die."

Tem pulled on Caspen's arms with all her might, ignoring the unbearable heat of his skin. It was like pulling on molten stone.

"Do your siblings deserve to die too?" She racked her memory for the names he'd told her so long ago. "Apollo, Agnes, Cypress, Damon? What about them?"

Caspen closed his eyes. Rowe's were wide open, staring up at Tem with paramount hatred.

"You said there was nothing you wouldn't do for your family," she continued. "So do this."

"Do not use my words against me."

"You're the one who said them." Her breath was a helpless rush. Smoke was filling her lungs. "Please, Caspen. Have mercy."

It was the second time she'd asked him for that. He hadn't granted it the first time.

"Do not *force* me to be something I am not, Tem!"

The words were a roar. He said them with such vitriol—such *loathing*—that Tem knew there was no going back from this. It was one thing for Tem to ask him to spare a human life. It was quite another to beg for Rowe's—Caspen's enemy, someone who had done nothing but try to hurt them both.

Rowe was no longer struggling. Time was running out.

"He isn't worth it," she cried.

Caspen let out a noise that made it clear he didn't agree. But Tem couldn't let Caspen kill Rowe. It would mean war. It would mean a target on Caspen's back and, by extension, a target on Leo's. And it would all be because of her. She couldn't have any more deaths on her hands.

Not even Rowe's.

"Be merciful," Tem whispered. "Please. For me."

For a moment, Caspen didn't relinquish his grip.

Then came a deadly whisper: "There is nothing I would not do for you, Tem."

Finally, he released Rowe, who let out a sputtering cough as he grasped at his own throat. Caspen sneered down at him in disgust before looking straight at Tem.

"This is the only time you will get mercy from me. Do you understand?"

Tem nodded because she couldn't do anything else. She understood that she had asked too much—that she had forced Caspen to go against his instincts, that he had compromised himself for her.

"I understand."

Caspen looked at her for a long moment before his expression softened. He touched her throat again—gently this time—and concern returned to his face. It was like watching the sun slowly set.

"Are you in any pain?" he asked.

Tem tried to answer him but found that she couldn't. She felt lightheaded, as if she might faint.

A moment later, she did.

<hr />

"Will she live?"

Caspen's words came to her through a fog. Tem was somewhere warm, a soft pillow beneath her head. Caspen's chambers. She was conscious, but she couldn't seem to move.

"She is breathing. Beyond that, I do not know."

The second voice belonged to Adelaide. Some vague part of Tem was distantly jealous.

"What can be done?" Caspen whispered.

"Nothing," Adelaide said just as quietly. "We must wait."

Caspen's voice turned suddenly sharp. "If you are lying to me, if this is some pathetic, jealous ploy to take her place, I will—"

"I would never stoop so low," Adelaide snapped, and Caspen fell silent. A second passed. She continued quietly, "I do not wish to prolong your pain, Caspenon. This clearly wounds you. If I had a solution, I would readily give it."

Tem opened her eyes.

Caspen was the first thing she saw. He was sitting on the edge of the bed, his brow furrowed in worry. Rowe's blood, as well as his own, was drying on his body. Adelaide was leaning against the wall, watching them with her arms crossed. She was naked, and Tem tried not to look at her infuriatingly perfect breasts.

"Tem." Caspen leaned forward, and Tem flinched. He retreated, concern flashing across his face. "How do you feel?"

What a question. Unanswerable, really. Tem asked a question of her own. "What's she doing here?"

Adelaide snorted. "I should be the least of your concerns."

Tem sat up. "I decide my concerns."

"Tem." Caspen leaned forward again, and this time, she let him. "Adelaide is here because the last known hybreed belonged to the Seneca quiver. She has some knowledge of your condition."

Tem looked at Adelaide, who was looking at her. "You…have met someone like me before?"

Adelaide shook her head. "No. But my family has."

A thousand questions came to Tem's lips—too many to ask. She started with "Did it work?"

Adelaide blinked. "Did what work?"

"The crest. I mean, am I…"

Tem looked to Caspen for guidance.

"Are you bound to me?" he finished.

Tem nodded.

"I do not know." Caspen cast a glance at Adelaide. "Is she?"

Adelaide shrugged. "How should I know? Give her an order and find out."

Caspen's eyebrows shot up, then knit together.

"Yes," Tem said, sitting up fully. "Good idea. Give me an order, Caspen."

Caspen glanced between the two women, who were both staring at him expectantly. "What sort of order shall I give you?"

"Anything. But make it something I wouldn't want to do."

Caspen's mouth twitched.

Tem rolled her eyes. "And don't you *dare* be cruel about it. I swear to Kora if you—"

"Stop talking, Tem."

For half a heartbeat, there was silence. Then Tem said easily, "Rude."

Adelaide clapped her hands together. "Good. Now if you will excuse me, I must—"

"Wait," Tem said. "What else do you know about hybreeds?"

Adelaide hesitated. Her eyes flicked to Caspen, who nodded.

"Humans with basilisk blood are rare," she said slowly. "Extremely so. Your existence is…an anomaly."

"What does that mean?"

"The two halves of you are paradoxical," Adelaide explained. "Your basilisk side is a predator, while your human side is prey."

Tem frowned. "I don't understand. Are you saying my body is trying to kill itself?"

Adelaide shook her head. "The opposite. You carry the balance of nature within you. It is an extremely powerful thing."

Tem was reeling from this information. She had to know more. "How powerful?"

Adelaide paused, tilting her head in the same way Caspen did when he was considering something. There was a moment of silence as her eyes traveled over Tem.

"I do not know the extent of it," she said finally.

Another pause. The only sound was the crackling of the fire.

Adelaide broke the silence. "I do know this: the two of you need to be careful. What happened with Rowe cannot happen again."

Tem blinked. "Why not?"

Adelaide nodded at Caspen. "Unlike my engagement to Caspenon, yours is bound by blood. You must keep each other safe. If anything happens to either of you, it could be centuries before we see another hybreed."

Tem's lungs contracted so tightly she could barely breathe. Nothing Adelaide had just said made any sense to her. She focused on the one thing she unequivocally understood. "*Your* engagement?"

Adelaide raised an elegant eyebrow. She glanced at Caspen, whose entire body had gone rigid.

"You had not told her we were once engaged," Adelaide said.

It was a statement, not a question.

"No," whispered Caspen. "I had not."

Adelaide glanced at Tem before bowing her head. "Then it would seem you two have much to discuss. I shall take my leave."

Tem didn't stop her this time. The moment the door closed, she turned to Caspen, who was already opening his mouth. Tem beat him to it. "You said it didn't mean anything—"

"That was the truth. It—"

"You said it was only physical—"

"It *was* only physical. I never—"

"*You were fucking engaged to her.*"

At her tone, Caspen pursed his lips, falling silent.

"You lied to me," Tem whispered.

"No." Caspen shook his head sharply. "You asked if it meant anything, and it did not. It is true that we were engaged. But it was not my doing. I did not propose to her"—he leaned in to touch the golden claw around Tem's neck—"as I did to you. There is no blood bond between Adelaide and me. Our families arranged it. It was purely political."

Tem still didn't know what a blood bond was. But that would have to wait. "*Political?*" she scoffed.

"Yes." He shifted closer. "It was a strategy to bring the Drakon and Seneca quivers together, nothing more. I was the one who broke it off."

"And when exactly did you break it off?"

Now Caspen fell silent.

"*When*, Caspen?" Tem asked again, firmly this time.

He sighed. "The first night of the training."

A wave of horror passed over Tem. "Before or after we met?"

From the look on his face, she knew the answer. He said it anyway. "After."

Tem's stomach turned. "Are you telling me you were *engaged* when I undressed in front of you?"

His voice was tight with pain. "Yes."

Tem felt as if the wind had been knocked out of her. That was the night she'd touched herself—the night she'd slipped the claw between her legs.

"But, Tem"—Caspen spoke quickly, clearly trying to get the words out—"the moment I met you, I knew I had to end it. I have loved you from the beginning. You know this."

Tem stared stiffly at the fire. She couldn't bear to look at him for another second.

At her silence, Caspen said, "Adelaide never meant anything to me, Tem. She will confirm it, if you wish."

Tem snorted. The *last* thing she wanted was for Adelaide to confirm anything about her engagement—or lack thereof—with Caspen.

When she didn't reply, Caspen began again. "Tem, I—"

But Tem held up her palm, and he fell silent. Hot, burning betrayal twisted her insides into a painful knot. It was similar to the way she'd felt when he'd told her she was a hybreed. Tem tried to control her heartbeat, but it was no use.

"I want to go home," she said, standing abruptly.

"You cannot leave." Caspen stood too, following her to the doorway. "You must transition—"

Tem whirled around to face him. "You think I want to have *sex* with you after what you just told me?"

Caspen tried to touch her shoulders, but she shook him off.

"We do not have to have sex," he said. "But you must practice, Tem. You need to—"

"I need to what? *What*, Caspen? Transition so I can become more like you? A *liar?*"

His jaw tightened. "Tem, please."

"No. I don't want to hear it. I'm going home."

"At least let me walk you out. Rowe could still be—"

"I don't need you to walk me out, Caspen. I don't need *anything from you*."

And with that, Tem ran from his chambers.

The passageway was empty; Rowe was long gone. Caspen's blood was drying in a pool, and Tem leaped over it on her way out. She broke into a sprint as soon as she was on the trail, not stopping until she was all the way home.

Her mother was already in bed; the cottage was silent.

Tem went immediately to her room. She tore the claw from between her legs and shoved it into her dresser drawer, not wanting to receive a single pulse from Caspen tonight. She severed their mental connection, making sure there was no way he could access her mind, even while she slept. Then Tem crawled into bed and cried herself to sleep.

The next morning was blustery.

Tem didn't mind; her mood matched the weather. When her mother knocked on her bedroom door to call her to breakfast, she simply pretended to be asleep. Tem wanted no part of the world today. She wanted no part of any of it—of Caspen's world, of Leo's, of her own. There was nowhere to go, nowhere to hide, nowhere that would shelter her from the reality of her situation.

Tem rolled over, staring at the ceiling. Her eyes traced the familiar knots in the wooden beams above her bed, and she wondered if it was the last time she'd be seeing them. She could recall a hundred nights crying herself to sleep in this very bed—a thousand where she'd been too tired to even do that. Her entire childhood had been spent struggling to fit in, struggling to feel *right*. Now that she knew the truth, somehow she felt little peace. Now there were two worlds she didn't belong to.

And what of the blood bond? Adelaide had said what happened with Rowe couldn't happen again—that they needed to keep each other safe. What did she mean by that? Caspen would have the answer. But Tem had no desire to speak with him. She wasn't interested in hearing any more lies.

Finally, Tem rose. Her mother was in the kitchen.

"I saw the invitation." She pointed at the letter on the table. "Are you ready for tonight?"

Tem sighed. Nothing could possibly prepare her for the ball. "I don't know," she said.

Sympathy creased her mother's forehead. "My dear." She crossed to Tem, placing a hand on her cheek. "You have made it this far. What's a little further?"

Tem sat numbly, staring at Leo's note.

It was true. She had made it this far.

Tem ate her breakfast in silence before retreating to the yard to do her chores. The day passed slowly. Tem spoke to Caspen only once, snapping a single sentence at him before slamming their connection shut again.

Don't bother sending me a dress.

She knew Leo would send one. And sure enough, when she returned from the chicken coop, a package was on the porch. Tem unwrapped it in the privacy of her bedroom, laying the dress out on her bed so she could see its full length.

It was far more formal than the other dresses Leo had sent her, and Tem knew this was a direct reflection of the type of event she'd be attending tonight. Unlike the tight, revealing dresses she'd worn previously, this one was closer to a gown. It was sky blue and made of soft, expensive silk. There was a matching shawl made of delicate, sheer fabric with golden stars woven into it. It was surely handmade; Tem had never seen something crafted with such meticulous care.

She took a bath, cleaning every inch of her body and washing her hair. She waited until her mother was busy making dinner before slipping into her room and spraying salt water on her curls. Then she pulled on the dress and the shawl. At the last minute, Tem slipped the claw between her legs. Even though she was angry with Caspen, the thought of leaving it in her bedroom when she might never return was too much for her to handle. The moment she inserted it, a gentle, tentative pulse nudged against her. Despite herself, Tem bit her lip. It felt *so* good. And she knew Caspen knew it too.

The pulse built slowly, and Tem grasped the edge of her bedside table. She understood the message: Caspen might not have sent her a dress, but he didn't need to. He had *this* connection with her, this profound bond that nothing—not even an argument like the one they'd had last night—could break. Tem let out a soft moan as the pulses grew stronger.

Then they stopped.

Her eyes flew open. He was testing the waters, reminding her what he could do, enticing her to return the favor. Tem was sorely tempted to open their mental connection and send him a pulse back.

But she would not give in. Not yet.

From then on, there was nothing left to do but wait. The carriage arrived on time, and when the footman knocked on their door, her mother pulled her into a tight hug.

"I am so proud of you, my dear," her mother said, pressing a kiss to her cheek.

"Thank you, Mother," Tem said back.

In the safety of her embrace, she remembered everything that was at stake, every reason why she was doing this. It wasn't about Caspen or Leo. It was about her family— the one person who had sheltered her and raised her and made sure she had a soft place to fall. There was nothing Tem wouldn't do for her mother.

By the time the carriage arrived at the castle, Tem was resolved to her fate.

She entered the foyer with her chin held high, ready for whatever the evening would bring. The ballroom was breathtakingly decorated. Flowers hung in great bunches from the ceiling; gorgeous crystal glassware was stacked in sparkling towers around the room. To her disappointment, Gabriel was nowhere to be found. Instead, Lilly appeared suddenly at her side, pushing a glass of champagne into her hands.

"Long time no see, Tem. Are you ready for tonight?"

Tem stared down at the champagne, half contemplating drinking it. "As ready as I'll ever be."

"My brother has been talking about you all week. It's a bit pathetic actually."

The information made Tem feel warm. She wanted to see Leo. Badly. "Is he here?" she asked.

"Should be," Lilly chirped, taking a sip of her champagne. "Probably discussing important, kingly things with our father."

At the mention of Maximus, Tem's stomach twisted into a knot. She wanted to ask Lilly if the king would contest Leo's choice, if he would stand in the way of a wedding. But she didn't want to get Gabriel in trouble. And she didn't want to assume Leo would choose her. So instead she said, "I'm going to find him."

"Suit yourself." Lilly gave her a little wave before flitting away.

Tem traded her champagne for a whiskey before making a lap of the ballroom. The royals were out in full force tonight; everywhere she turned, she saw necks, ears, and fingers dripping in gold. The sight made her feel sick. Tem leaned against the closest column, trying to catch her breath. She lowered the barrier in her mind but didn't reach for Caspen. Instead, she searched for another connection—one she knew was close by. When she found it, she said, *Can you hear me?*

The words disappeared into the void. Seconds passed. Tem tried again. *Do you know who I am?*

A long pause. Tem stared at her whiskey, her heart pounding against her ribs. Then her father's voice replied, *Yes.*

Hope rushed through Tem. *I'm going to get you out. I'm going to fix this.*

Her announcement went unacknowledged. Instead, she heard the same words she'd heard once before: *Do not trust the king.*

Tem frowned. Something occurred to her for the first time, and she couldn't believe she hadn't thought to ask it sooner. *Which king?*

But the connection was closed.

Tem downed the rest of her whiskey in an attempt to calm down. Truth be told, she didn't trust either king. Before she could think on it further, she felt another pulse.

This time, against her better judgment, she let Caspen in.

And just what do you think you're doing? she asked.

Missing you.

Tem rolled her eyes. *You're not forgiven.*

Another pulse. *I know.*

Are you going to apologize?

If that is what you wish.

Tem crossed her legs, trying not to gasp as he sent a pulse so strong her clitoris throbbed. *You never fight fair.*

I see no reason to.

Tem couldn't reply. She was too focused on resisting the orgasm that desperately wanted to break free. Caspen was relentless, sending her pulse after pulse until she was so turned on, she almost didn't feel the hand on her waist.

"Tem."

It was Leo. The pulses suddenly ceased.

She turned to face him.

"*Kora,*" he breathed, his wide eyes taking in the silk dress and golden shawl. "You look…" He seemed to be at a loss for words, finishing quietly with "Celestial."

"You're getting better at compliments," Tem said.

His face broke into a grin. "I'm certainly glad to hear it."

Tem smiled too, and for a moment, her worries disappeared. She looked up at Leo, taking in his velvet suit and the jeweled snake pinned to his cloak.

"Are you enjoying the ball?" Leo asked.

"No," Tem answered honestly. She'd been enjoying other things, but certainly not the ball.

His smile widened. "I thought as much. Shall we venture elsewhere then?"

"I'm not going to your room," Tem said curtly.

"Who said anything about my room?"

Tem rolled her eyes. If Leo had his way, they'd never *leave* his room.

He raised his arm, offering her the crook of his elbow. "I was thinking we could take a stroll, if it pleases you."

"Your father won't like that."

"Good."

In reply, Tem laced her fingers around his arm as he guided her through the ballroom, out to the patio, and toward the maze. Her wetness dripped down her thighs, evidence of the orgasm she'd barely resisted.

The moment they entered the great green walls, Tem felt calm for the first time that evening. The din of the ball died down as they wound deeper into the maze, the air becoming so cold that Tem shivered. Leo immediately set his cloak on her shoulders. This time she didn't protest, instead savoring the way it enveloped her in his scent. As they wound through the maze, the weight of the evening hung over her.

"Leo," Tem said as steadily as she could. "Am I in the final three?"

He glanced down. "Do you want to be?"

A direct question. Before she could answer it, they came upon a dead end.

The world went silent as they both stood still. A statue of a robed figure loomed over them, and Tem could just make out the name etched into the plaque at its base: *King Maximus III.*

Leo's father.

Tem turned to face the prince. He was looking down at her calmly, with the same practiced composure she'd come to expect from him. When she still didn't answer, Leo leaned in. His lips brushed hers as he whispered, "I'm asking you to give me your heart, Tem. I deserve to know whether it's even yours to give."

Tem couldn't handle the way he was looking at her. It was not unlike the way Caspen looked at her—as if she were something exceedingly precious. Something worth having.

"I can't promise you my heart," she whispered. "But I can promise it will always be mine to give."

Leo pulled away a fraction of an inch.

Tem knew it wasn't what he wanted to hear. But it would have to be enough for now. "Leo." She raised her hand, cradling his narrow face in her palm. "You told me not to lie to you."

He gave her a sad smile. "So I did."

There was nothing else to say. Tem kissed him.

From the way Leo kissed her back, she knew he'd been waiting all night to do so. His hands went immediately to her body, roaming beneath the cloak as he pressed her back against the statue. His fingers grabbed her hair, arching her neck so he could kiss up her throat.

When his lips found hers again, Tem was done pretending she didn't want him.

Leo was warm. And he tasted like honey. And his tongue was sheer heaven against hers, even though it wasn't Caspen's. The prince lifted her onto the base of the statue, pulling her legs around him. She was surrounded by hardness—Leo's body in front of her and the cold stone behind her.

It wasn't until he slipped his hand up her dress that Tem remembered what he'd find between her legs.

CHAPTER THIRTY-TWO

—•◦✳◦•—

T HERE WAS NO TIME TO PUSH HIM AWAY.

Tem froze as Leo's fingers found her center, brushing against the tip of the claw. His eyebrows furrowed in confusion.

"What…" Leo started but didn't finish. He pressed on the claw, pushing it against her clitoris.

Despite herself, a tiny moan escaped the back of Tem's throat.

Leo pulled away. "What the *fuck* is that, Tem?"

"It's…"

But there was no good way to explain it. And even if there were, Tem could tell by the look on Leo's face that although he might not know exactly what the claw was for, he knew it had something to do with Caspen. His next words confirmed it.

"It's from him, isn't it?"

Tem nodded because there was nothing else to do.

"What is its purpose?"

Tem shook her head.

"What is its purpose, Tem?"

"Leo, please—"

But Leo was already sliding his fingers inside her. He hooked them around the curve of the claw before yanking it out roughly and holding it up between them. For a moment, they both stared at Tem's wetness glistening in the moonlight. An unfathomable anger passed over Leo's face. He turned, throwing the claw as hard as he could down the dark passage of the maze.

"*No!*" Tem cried.

But he was already turning back to her, his fingers filling the space where the claw had just been, driving into her so quickly that her head arched back with a gasp.

Leo's other hand went to her throat, his eyes narrowing as he yanked her face to his. "He may have made you wet, but I will make you come."

Tem couldn't have protested if she wanted to. Leo's fingers were already sliding in and out with expert precision, persuading her body to relinquish control. A moment later, he was on his knees, and for the second time, Tem knew what it was to have a prince kneel before her.

Tem moaned as Leo's mouth met her wetness, the words he'd written on the invitation running wildly through her mind: *Next time, I get to torture you.*

If this was torture, Tem was happy to die from it.

Leo knew *exactly* what to do. He licked her with confident, targeted strokes, his tongue diving deep into her center before rolling against her clitoris. Tem gripped his hair with both hands, holding him against her so everything he did was amplified tenfold, so she didn't miss a single second of this ravishment.

He was consuming her, *devouring* her, gorging himself on her until she couldn't form a single thought.

"Leo," she moaned over and over again. "*Leo.*"

She understood he was reprimanding her—forcing her to remember how good he could make her feel. This was the dynamic between them, their endless battle. Now it was Leo's turn to hold the power, and it was Tem's turn to yield.

His fingers joined his tongue, and for a moment, Tem saw stars.

Leo was unrelenting, even as her grip tightened in his hair—even as she whimpered his name helplessly. Caspen had already been turning her on for hours; Tem was beyond close. But it wasn't until Leo sucked her clitoris suddenly between his teeth that her hips bucked and she came with a yelp, finally releasing the pent-up heat that had been building in her all day long.

The second she cried out, Leo stood. He yanked her dress down without a word and stalked back into the maze.

"Leo, *wait.*" Tem leaped from the statue, barely catching her breath as she ran after him. "This is a *maze.* You can't just leave me—"

Leo whirled around, his eyes flashing in the darkness. "I can do whatever I damn well please, Tem. That's what you do after all."

"That's not fair."

"Isn't it?"

"You know I can't control him, Leo. He—"

"You can control what you *put in your own body, Tem.*"

He turned again, and Tem had to run to keep up with him. "It doesn't matter what I put in my body. He's in my mind. He'll always be there."

Leo shook his head. "This cannot go on."

They had come to it at last: the moment when Leo's patience ran out.

"What do you suggest I do?"

"I suggest you shut him out."

"I *can't.*"

"Can't you? Or do you just not want to?"

Tem stopped, suddenly hurt. Leo knew very well how difficult this was for her, how much she hated the position she was in. If she could make it easier for herself—and for him—she would. But her bond with Caspen wasn't something she could just shut off. Nor did she want to. It was far more complicated than anything Leo could comprehend, and there was no possible way to explain it to him.

"You said you didn't mind," she whispered. "You said you would take what you could get."

Leo stopped too, his hands clenched into fists at his sides. "I know what I said, Tem," he growled, turning to face her. "But I want more. I want *all* of you. Anything less than everything isn't enough anymore."

"Why?" Tem asked, betrayal pinching her chest. "What changed?"

He shook his head. "That's the fucking problem, Tem. Nothing's changed."

She stared at him in disbelief, tears in her eyes.

Leo leaned in, and she craned her neck to look up at him. "I want all of you," he said deliberately. "Or I don't want you at all."

They stared at each other, both breathing hard. Then Leo turned once more, and Tem stayed two steps behind him all the way back through the maze.

When they reached the castle, Leo whirled around one last time. "And to answer your question," he snapped. "Yes. You're in the final three. Whether you want to be or not."

He swept away, leaving Tem alone on the edge of the ballroom. Leo's message was clear: he was punishing her for her connection with Caspen. He knew it was difficult for her to love them both—even more difficult when Leo presented himself as a viable option. It would be cruel to eliminate her, crueler still to keep her in the competition. He would force Tem to choose, to tear herself in two.

Torture indeed.

Tem found the closest glass of whiskey and threw it down her throat. She wished she could simply leave. But to go where? She couldn't go back to the caves. She couldn't go back to the farm. There was no place for Tem—no shelter from the storm. Her only option was to take another whiskey and slip into the crowd, losing herself among the guests until eventually she was drunk. At one point, Gabriel found her, pressing a quick kiss to her cheek before disappearing back into the kitchen with a wave of his bandaged hand. She barely noticed him. Instead, Tem watched as several footmen assembled the podiums, placing them at the end of the ballroom. There were only three. Tem remembered when there were eleven.

A sharp *clink clink clink* rang out, and Tem turned to see Maximus tapping a knife on a wineglass.

"Thank you all for being here tonight," he began, his shrewd gray eyes appraising the crowd. "My family is grateful for your support."

Beside him, Leo scowled.

"Would the five remaining ladies kindly step forward?"

Tem took one last gulp of whiskey before following the other girls to the podiums. They stood in a single-file line, the way they always did, facing the prince. Maximus was still talking.

"The time has come for my son to make an important decision. The three young ladies he chooses tonight will reside in the castle for the remainder of the elimination process. When he is ready, my son will choose a wife."

Beside Tem, Vera puffed out her chest.

Maximus continued. "The next time we gather, it will be for a wedding."

Dread darkened Tem's vision. The whiskey wasn't helping anymore.

Leo stepped forward, and the elimination began.

Instead of approaching the girls like he had in the past, Leo had them come to him. He extended his hand to the girl on Tem's right, and the crowd cheered as she walked forward, took his hand, and stepped onto the second podium. Tem didn't know the girl's name, and she didn't care to. She only knew the name of the girl Leo would pick next:

Vera.

Maximus's mouth twitched into a smile as Vera took Leo's hand and mounted the first podium. The crowd cheered even louder.

Tem stood between the last two girls, wondering if they already knew they were out. She straightened her shoulders. Leo didn't even extend his hand to her. He merely looked Tem in the eye before jerking his head at the third podium, directing her like a dog learning a trick.

Last again.

Tem didn't need to look at Maximus to feel the fury radiating off him as she walked forward to claim her podium. She stood there proudly, just as she always had, refusing to let anyone here make her feel like she was worth any less than the girls who stood beside her.

Vera was positively beaming; Tem could feel her condescending smile even from here.

Leo looked only at Tem.

There was such jealousy in his eyes. Such anger. The time for allowances had clearly passed; the prince was done giving Tem a break simply because he wanted her.

The time will come when you will have to choose.

Leo's future would be easier if he chose Vera. She was the village favorite and his father's favorite too. If Tem wanted him to choose her—and if she wanted to save his life—she had to give him a reason to do so.

Someone touched Tem's hand—a servant helping her down from the podium. Tem followed the other two girls out of the ballroom and up a flight of stairs. They were headed to Leo's floor. Tem recognized the towering portrait of father and son as she ascended the stairs. When they reached the landing, the servant directed each of the girls to their rooms. Tem's room was at the very end of the hallway, farthest from Leo's.

"Can I get you anything, miss?"

Tem blinked. She wanted many things: for Caspen to apologize, for Leo to understand her circumstances. But she couldn't have either of those. So she said, "Whiskey."

The servant nodded and disappeared.

Tem stood alone, staring at the bed in front of her.

It had all happened so fast. One moment, she'd been attending a ball, and now she was sequestered in the castle, doomed to wait until someone else decided her future for her.

She couldn't stand it. She needed to talk to Leo.

Tem opened her door and stepped out into the hallway, ready to find him. To her surprise, he was already there, leaning against the doorframe of the room right next to hers.

He wasn't alone.

Vera was giggling, pushing her breasts together as Leo twirled a lock of her hair around his fingertips, the same way he twirled Tem's. His eyes slid to hers. For an endless moment, they looked at each other. Then Leo cocked a single, cruel eyebrow. His hand found Vera's waist, pulling her down the hallway toward his bedroom. The last thing Tem saw before the door closed were Leo's fingers unlacing the back of her dress.

Tem was no stranger to lonely nights, but this was one of the worst.

The claw was gone, lost in the maze. Caspen was utterly absent from her mind, the emptiness so glaring and foreign she could barely stand it. Tem didn't dare reach for him. She didn't know what she would even say. He knew she was in the castle; he knew the prince had chosen her.

And then there was Leo.

Tem would never forget the look on his face as he pulled Vera into his bedroom. She kept picturing his long fingers unlacing Vera's dress—fingers that were inside Tem just an hour ago. No doubt they were already having sex in Leo's four-poster bed. Vera would do anything he asked, endlessly eager to please the prince. The thought made Tem want to cry, and she climbed into her bed, pulling the unfamiliar blankets tightly around her. Her room was cold, but she didn't make a fire. She simply stared at the ceiling, thinking about how just this morning, she'd stared at the ceiling of her childhood bedroom—the ceiling she'd wished so many times never to see again. Now there was nothing she wanted to see more. Eventually, her whiskey arrived, and Tem drank it in one gulp.

When she fell asleep, her dreams were filled with ice.

⋅•◆◆◆•⋅

The whiskey had not been kind to her.

Tem woke with a groan, massaging her temples in an attempt to alleviate her pounding headache. Her first thought was of Leo. She pictured him waking up next to Vera, their naked bodies intertwined, their lips touching.

The visual was enough to bring the whiskey right back up.

When Tem was done in the bathroom, she crossed to the closet, opening it to find a row of dresses in her size. She pulled on the closest one before placing her hand on her bedroom door and pausing. What to do next? Tem could think of only one thing, and it was undoubtedly dangerous. But she was here, in the castle, and she would use the situation to her advantage even if it meant taking a risk.

She knew about this part of the competition from school: the girls were given free rein of the castle and expected to spend time with the prince if he requested it. He would bed them as he saw fit. There were no rules regarding the speed or timing of the final eliminations: sometimes the girls were in the castle for days, sometimes for months. Leo was in charge now, and he would choose his wife when he was ready.

Tem stood at the door, still hesitating.

She had no desire to open this door if it meant seeing Vera emerging from Leo's room, her hair messy from sex, her eyes glazed over after a night of lovemaking.

Yet she had to open it.

The hallway was mercifully empty; perhaps Leo wasn't even awake yet. Tem descended the stairs to the ground level, her bare feet brushing against the gold-flaked tiles in the foyer. She stood there for a moment, listening to the sounds of the castle. A distant bout of laughter came from the kitchen, and Tem knew the staff was preparing breakfast. She took a moment to close her eyes, focusing her energy on a single word:

Caspen.

He answered immediately. *Tem.*

I want to see my father.

She said nothing of the elimination process, mentioned no part of what had happened last night in the maze. Caspen sensed her evasion but didn't address it. Instead, he replied, *That is not a good idea.*

Why not?

Someone may see you.

Tem was having trouble hearing him; it was as if they were talking through a wall. *It's early. No one is around.*

It is not safe.

I'm not asking permission, Caspen.

He bristled. Some small part of her enjoyed his distress. *Then what are you asking, Tem?*

Do you know where he's being kept?

No. I do not.

Haven't you asked him? Or any of the basilisks who were imprisoned here?

Bloodletting weakens basilisks. They cannot use their minds as we can.

Tem thought about how her conversations with her father were always brief—a few words at most—before his voice faded. *Fine. I'll ask him myself.*

She sensed his disapproval.

You need to be careful, Tem.

I will be.

You should—

But his voice cut off abruptly.

Caspen? Are you there?

No response.

Tem shook her head as if to clear it. She would worry about their connection later. Caspen wasn't the basilisk she needed to talk to anyway.

Tem concentrated again, feeling for another presence nearby. When she found it, she wasted no time. *Where are you?*

She stood in silence, awaiting an answer. His response was barely a whisper.

Below.

Tem pursed her lips as that connection faded too. It was their shortest conversation yet, and it wasn't much to go on. But it wasn't a stretch to guess what "below" meant. Surely, there would be dungeons in the castle, places where the royals kept traitors during the war. And where they kept basilisks *after* the war.

Tem slipped through the castle, searching for the first stairway that headed down. When she found it, she took it quickly, walking on the pads of her feet so she didn't make a sound. She was already rehearsing a story in her mind in case anyone found her: she would say she was looking for the kitchen, that she was hungry after a night of drinking at the ball. It was only half a lie; her stomach growled as she descended the endless staircase.

Eventually, the temperature began to drop.

Tem passed doorway after doorway, ignoring them all. The dungeons would be deep beneath the castle, lower than anything else, far away from anywhere a servant might stumble upon them accidentally. She walked for what felt like forever. But then, she came upon a metal door.

Tem knew immediately from the smell of the air that she had arrived.

Death and decay clung to her nostrils as she groped through the darkness for the door handle. It wasn't even locked. There wasn't a guard in sight—not a single person watching over the entrance to a long row of dark, hopeless cells. At first, Tem was shocked by the lack of security. But the moment she saw what was in the first cell, she understood why there were no guards down here. There was no need for security when the prisoners were this weak.

A female basilisk wearing her human form was shackled to the stone floor. There was nothing else in the cell, not even a cot. A complicated tangle of metal wires was fused to the basilisk's fingers, trailing up into a hole in the ceiling. Tem had no idea what their function was, only that they must be part of the bloodletting process. Even now, she could see the color of the wires change from silver to gold, pulsing intermittently as the basilisk's face twisted in pain. Tem's heart broke at the sight of someone—someone like *her*—being treated like this. It was abhorrent.

All the cells were filled.

Tem couldn't explain it, but she knew which cell contained her father. It was as if she were drawn to him by the invisible connection that had brought him into her mind in the first place. Tem followed their connection down the row of cells until she reached the very last one, stopping in front of it and squinting into the darkness.

There he was at last.

Even slumped against the rough stone wall, Tem could see her father's beauty. His shoulders were broad, his eyes burnished gold. But unlike the gleaming, molten brightness of Caspen's irises, her father's eyes were dull—almost closer in color to copper—and Tem wondered if it was an effect of the bloodletting. He was tall, just like all basilisks, but stooped beneath the weight of years of torture.

Her heart called out, *Father.*

It was strange to say that word to him. Tem had no memory of this man; by the time she was born, he was already gone. But now she studied his face, and despite the dim lighting, she saw their resemblance. He had hair just like hers; it was lank now, but

Tem recognized the same curls that also framed her face. His hands were resting palm up in his lap, silver wires fused to his fingers. Even in the darkness, Tem could count twenty-four freckles on his hands. Twelve on each side.

Her father opened his eyes. They stared at each other.

What is your name, child?

Tem's heart performed a mournful swoop. He didn't even know her name. *Temperance.*

She couldn't be sure, but she swore he smiled.

What is your name? Her mother had never told her.

Kronos.

"Kronos," she whispered it aloud, imagining a world in which she'd grown up saying it.

Her father tilted his head. *You should not be here, Temperance.*

She stepped closer. *I had to see you.*

It is not safe.

It was Caspen all over again. Tem shook her head, hooking her fingers through the bars of the cell. *I'm going to get you out. You just need to hold on until the wedding.*

Her father closed his eyes. *It is too late for me.*

Tem could see how weak he was—how perilous of a toll the bloodletting had taken on him. *Wait, please. I need to know—which king can't I trust?*

He took a long time to answer. But finally: *Ours.*

Bastian. *But why?*

Her father took a deep breath, and the shackles bolting him to the floor clinked softly. *He values power above all else.*

Most kings do.

Kronos shook his head, the motion clearly paining him. *Power corrupts.*

It was all he said. Tem thought about what Bastian had already done to gain his power, what he had asked Caspen to do. Power did corrupt. It was crookedly tempting and cruel. It turned men into monsters, or perhaps monsters into men. Which was worse? Tem didn't know anymore.

Kronos spoke again. *You have lingered too long. Go.*

Tem's grip tightened on the bars. *I don't want to leave you.*

Go, child. And do not return.

Tem knew he was right. She'd been down here far too long already. Leo could be awake by now. If he noticed her absence, it would only anger him further.

She dropped her hands reluctantly, taking one last look at her father. *I'll come back for you. I promise. Just hold on. Please.*

He didn't reply.

There was nothing else to say. Tem retraced her steps out of the dungeon until she reached the stairs that led back up to the castle. She ascended them as quickly as she could, and by the time she got to the main floor, her calves were screaming in protest. She was just crossing through the foyer when the parlor door opened and the last person she wanted to see emerged.

"Temperance," Maximus said slowly, his calculating eyes flicking to her bare feet. "What brings you out of bed at such an early hour?"

The question was casual. The implication was not.

Tem sensed immediately that Maximus knew she'd been searching for things he didn't want her to find.

When she didn't answer, the king stepped closer. "Does my son know you're sneaking around his home?"

Tem threw a question right back at him. "Does your son know what goes on in his home?"

Maximus paused, his eyes narrowing. "I do not know of what you speak."

A lie. There was only one secret she could be referring to—one horrible, abominable thing the royals kept to themselves.

Tem stepped closer too, looking defiantly up at him as she asked again, "Does Leo know?"

Maximus stared down at her. She could almost see the gears turning in his brain, deciding how to react. When he spoke, it was through gritted teeth. "He will learn when he becomes king."

At last, Tem had confirmation that Leo was innocent. She crossed her arms. "And how do you think he'll react?"

"He will understand he must do what is necessary to protect the balance of our kingdom."

"*Torture* is necessary?"

"I already told you, Temperance," Maximus said as if she were a child. "The basilisks provide a service. Their place is beneath us."

Tem hadn't realized when he'd said those words to her all those weeks ago that he'd meant them literally.

"You would do well to remember your place," he continued. "Or you may find it is decided for you."

You may find that your choice is made for you.

Tem raised her chin. "I decide my place. And as of now, it is right here. In this castle. With your son."

Maximus's nostrils flared. He leaned in, and Tem smelled cigars on his skin. "You will never have him."

She looked straight at him as she said, "He told me he intends to marry me."

The lie came easily, and as soon as she said it, rage flitted across Maximus's face. "That will not happen as long as I am alive."

"You can't stop us."

"Can't I?" Maximus leaned in too. "Do you think you are the first unworthy girl my son has fallen for? The first *whore*? Thelonius has a type. And you, Temperance, are exactly his."

Tem would not be wounded by petty insults. "Leo deserves to choose his own future."

"My son has proven himself incapable of that task."

It was then that Tem realized their conversation ran far deeper than just her courtship with the prince. Maximus was referring to Leo's pattern of behavior, how his son consistently chose love over duty. It was one of Leo's finer qualities. To Maximus, there could be nothing worse.

"There's nothing you can do," Tem snapped. "He has already decided."

Maximus laughed cruelly. "I have corrected my son's mistakes before. I will not hesitate to do so again."

Tem froze.

The king was admitting that he had played a part in the demise of Leo's relationship with Evelyn. Perhaps he had paid her to leave the village.

Perhaps worse.

"I am not Evelyn," Tem said quietly. "I will not be so easy to get rid of."

Maximus frowned, and Tem realized he hadn't known that she knew about Leo's first love.

Tem seized the advantage, driving her point home. "You tried to control him once. If you try to do it again, I will turn him against you."

Maximus's nostrils flared. "You would not *dare*."

"I *would*," Tem snapped. "And I would relish it."

She stepped even closer, and Maximus's eyes widened as she finished.

"When Leo chooses me, you will honor his choice. If you do not, I will tell him you were the one who destroyed his future with Evelyn. And you will lose him forever."

Maximus squared his shoulders. "My son would understand."

"Would he?" Tem arched her eyebrow petulantly. "Your son already considers you cruel. Somehow I doubt this would help his impression."

Maximus opened his mouth to retaliate. But another voice spoke before he could.

"Tem?"

Tem turned around to see Leo on the staircase. Concern for her clouded his face.

He stepped closer. "What's going on?"

"Temperance was just leaving," Maximus said coolly. "She got lost on her way to the kitchen."

Leo's eyes remained locked on Tem's. She arranged her face into a neutral expression.

"Yes," she said with a nonchalant shrug. "I was hungry."

The tiniest smile twitched Leo's mouth. "You always are," he said quietly.

The smile disappeared a moment later. They were still at odds, still in a battle of wills. Not even a shared common enemy in Maximus could bring her and Leo together right now.

The prince turned back up the stairs. Without a backward glance at Maximus, Tem ran after him. She'd just told the king that the prince intended to marry her. The last thing she needed was for him to see that they were barely speaking.

When they reached the landing, Leo stopped. "What did my father want?"

Tem pursed her lips. "He would prefer that I not wander the castle."

Leo shot her a look. "That preference hardly warrants a personal conversation. What did he really say to you?"

Tem avoided his eyes. She wanted to tell him what his father had done to Evelyn. But it wasn't time. Leo was still so angry with her. He wasn't ready, and neither was she.

Tem attempted to distill their conversation into something Leo could digest. "He thinks I'm not good enough for you."

Leo's expression softened almost imperceptibly. "Well," he murmured. "He is wrong." A moment passed. His expression hardened again. "Has he spoken to you today?"

Tem knew he was referring to Caspen. She decided to be honest. "Yes."

Leo nodded, his jaw tightening. She expected him to walk away, but he stayed where he was.

"What did he say?"

Tem hesitated. She certainly couldn't tell Leo about Kronos. Instead, she said, "We're in a fight."

Leo raised his eyebrows. "Is that so?"

"Yes."

"What sort of fight?"

Tem didn't answer.

"Well," Leo said slowly. "I hope you two can resolve it."

"You do?"

To her surprise, Leo let out a dull laugh. "Yes. I do."

"Why? I would think you'd want us to fight."

Leo scoffed, as if the answer was obvious. "A race won by default is no true victory, Tem."

"I'm a person, Leo. Not a prize."

He stepped closer, and she sensed his energy. "I know you're a person. A person who is capable of making choices. I want you to choose me because you want me, Tem. Not because you're in a fight with him."

With that, he walked away.

CHAPTER THIRTY-THREE

◦•✳•◦

T EM UNDERSTOOD HER PUNISHMENT WOULD CONTINUE—THAT LEO WOULD FAVOR the other two girls over her, possibly indefinitely, until she came to him herself. More torture. Lucky her.

She sequestered herself in her room for the rest of the day. A servant brought her meals, and she ate without tasting them. At some point, she felt Caspen's presence leaning on her mind once more.

Out of pure desolation, she let him in, speaking before he could. *I'm still angry with you.*

Then come be angry in my arms. I must see you.

I'm at the castle, Caspen. I can't just leave.

Find a way.

Why don't you come here if it's so easy? It wasn't a real suggestion. They both knew he couldn't come here.

Be reasonable, Tem.

Tem rolled her eyes. Then she sighed. The truth was she wanted to see Caspen. It didn't matter that she was angry with him. She missed him dearly; it felt as if a part of her were incomplete.

If I come, it will have to be at night.

*Then I will await you with—*His sentence cut off.

Tem frowned. *Caspen? Are you there?*

*Tem. I—*But he cut off again.

Their connection was spotty; she could barely hear him. It was as if someone was opening and shutting the door between their minds. Tem couldn't understand why this was happening. Their connection had always been crystal clear no matter how far apart they were from each other. All the more reason to see him.

By the time night fell, Tem had made up her mind.

As soon as the servant cleared away her dinner tray, she flung open her bedroom window, hoisting herself over the balcony and climbing down the trellis until her feet were firmly on the ground. She looked up at Leo's window, wondering who he would be sleeping with tonight.

It didn't matter. It wasn't Tem.

She took the backstreets through the village, winding around shadowy corners so that nobody would see her. The last thing she needed was someone spotting the prince's future wife on the streets after dark. When she reached the forest, Tem allowed herself to relax. The cave was just as she'd left it—dark and deep, its entrance beckoning to her like an open mouth.

There he was.

It had only been a short time since she'd seen Caspen but also an eternity. He was just as gorgeous as he always was—if not more so—and Tem wondered what chance she possibly stood against such beauty.

"Tem."

"Caspen."

He stepped forward, gathering her in his arms. As soon as his skin touched hers, Tem felt her resolve fade. He smelled good, and he felt even better. Her body had missed him, even if her brain was furious with him. By the time they got to his chambers, Caspen's hands were already sliding her dress from her shoulders, and Tem didn't tell him to stop.

Caspen threw her on the bed the second she was naked, pulling her legs open and sliding his cock deep inside her. His thrusts were relentless; she could barely catch her breath.

Tem rolled so that she was on top, forcing him to look at her. "Caspen," she whispered. It was neither a prayer nor an admonition.

"What do you want, Tem? Name it."

In answer, Tem pushed Caspen down, his broad shoulders hitting the mattress as he stared up at her. She moved her hips lazily, as if she had nowhere to be but here. "Tell me you love me," she whispered as she rode him.

"I love you."

"Tell me I'm everything you've ever wanted."

"You are everything I have ever wanted."

"Tell me I fulfill you."

"You fulfill me." He cupped her ass with both hands, pulling her all the way down his cock. "*Kora*, do you fulfill me."

She fucked him slowly, savoring every word. The affirmations were nearly better than the sex. Hearing how he felt about her turned her on beyond anything he could possibly do with his body.

"This is it for me, Tem," Caspen moaned. "*You are it for me.*"

"I'm going to come," she whispered.

"You had better."

Tem's orgasm built slowly, corresponding directly with the self-assured movements of her hips. She was pleasuring herself—*giving* to herself—making sure Caspen knew she was not to be taken for granted. The moment she reached her summit, Caspen grabbed her hips, angling himself so he could thrust into her from below.

His hips jerked once, twice, and on the third time, he pulled out suddenly, slapping his cock up against her stomach, finishing on her skin.

Without missing a beat, Tem grabbed his shaft, gripping him tightly and coaxing every last drop of cum from the tip. Just when she was sure he was done, she leaned down, cupping her mouth over his sensitive head, sucking *hard*—just once—before looking at him.

He was a mess for her. His eyes were black, his expression utterly devoted.

"Tem," he whispered. "Do that again."

She smiled. "Say please."

He didn't even hesitate. "Please."

Who was she to deny him?

She lowered her head, tracing her tongue along the tip of his cock. Already, she could feel him becoming hard again. Such was the basilisk way.

"All of it, Tem. Put me in your mouth. I know you can do it."

His words were a broken gasp. She savored his desire. It was incredible to hear him *need* her so much. It was always *her* needing him. Now their roles were reversed, and Tem found she liked it.

"Beg," she whispered. "Beg me, Caspen."

"A king does not beg."

"He does for his queen."

He groaned, and his hand went to the back of her neck. "Suck my cock, Tem. *Please*. I beg of you."

Tem traced the tip of him with her tongue. Still teasing him—still refusing to yield. "What would you forsake for me?" she whispered.

"Everything."

She nipped her teeth over the smooth curve of his head, cupping his balls in her palm. She squeezed. "Your title?"

"Yes."

Another squeeze. "Your father?"

"*Yes.*"

She allowed herself to look at him. His eyes were shut tight, the muscles in his jaw clenched to the point of exertion.

"Do you mean that?" she whispered.

His eyes flew open. "You know I cannot lie."

It was enough for her.

Tem took his cock in her mouth, pulling his full length down her throat. From the way he groaned, she knew he was watching her do everything he'd begged her to do. It was exhilarating to have him like this—defenseless, completely at her mercy. Caspen was a powerful creature. And he belonged to her.

"*Tem*," he moaned, his fingers twisting in her hair.

When he came, she swallowed every last drop of him. She released his cock, positioning herself above his body so they were face-to-face. "What am I to you?" she whispered.

Caspen lifted his lips to hers, whispering a single word into her mouth. "Everything."

They lay together afterward, content to do nothing but touch each other.

Tem knew eventually she would have to return to the castle. But that meant returning to Leo, and she wasn't ready to do that yet. Besides, she hadn't come here just for sex.

"I saw my father," she said quietly.

Caspen was gently fingering her. He paused before murmuring, "How was he?"

"Barely alive."

His fingers went deeper. "I told you not to go."

"You can't tell me what to do."

His mouth twitched. "That I know." He was still touching her. But the time for sex had passed. There was business to attend to now.

"Caspen." Tem pushed his hand away. "Adelaide said our engagement was bound by blood. What does that mean?"

Caspen's eyes went to the golden claw around her neck. He touched it. "It means that when I gave you this, my blood bound our lives together," he said. "It is an ancient magic, and it is irreversible."

Tem absorbed this information in shock. "So if I die…"

Caspen finished quietly, "I die."

She was floored by his admission, shocked by the lengths to which he would go in order to be with her and her alone. Tem should be angry that he'd done this—and so many other things—without asking. But for once, she couldn't seem to muster any rage. The risk of the blood bond was *far* greater for Caspen than it was for her. There was little chance he would die, from natural causes or otherwise. Tem, on the other hand, was a hybreed. She was a weapon; she would always have a target on her back. She had not yet mastered her basilisk side; she was vulnerable.

"Tem," Caspen said. "Are you angry?"

She shook her head. "No. But…it seems like such a risk."

He nodded. "It is a risk. Many basilisks choose not to bind their engagements in blood for that very reason."

"But you chose to bind ours."

"Yes," he said quietly. "I did."

"Why?"

Caspen looked at her for a long moment. His answer was simple. "Because I need you."

It was a familiar sentiment. Tem had seen it in his mind the very first time he'd let her in, and it was one that she shared. Still, the gesture was staggering. It was not lost on Tem that Caspen had given her the little golden claw shortly after they'd met. He'd bound himself to her—using his blood—long before they knew anything about each other. His love had been that strong—that *sure*. Tem couldn't conceptualize such clarity. It was flattering, to say the least. But it was also a problem. If anything happened to either of them, the other would be affected. The other would *die*. Adelaide was right. They had to be careful.

"Caspen," she said. "I need you to do me a favor."

He brushed a curl off her shoulder. "Anything."

"I want to talk to Adelaide."

Caspen frowned. "Tem," he said quietly. "I told you I—"

"It's not about the engagement."

He tilted his head. "Then might I ask why you wish to speak with her?"

"You can ask," Tem said firmly. "But I won't answer."

"So stubborn," he murmured, brushing his thumb over her bottom lip.

Tem didn't reply. She wasn't ready to name the gnawing seed of doubt that hung heavy in her heart. Not yet. Not until she had proof.

"Very well," Caspen said finally, and she heard the worry in his voice. "Will you be able to return tomorrow night?" He asked it as if he were actually asking something else—as if he wanted to know how things were going with her and Leo.

Tem didn't know what to tell him. She settled on "I'll try."

It was the truth at least.

Caspen nodded before pulling her into a deep kiss. Tem kissed him back with everything she had, trying to soak up some final remnant of joy before she returned to the castle. When the kiss ended, they simply lay there peacefully, seeking solace in each other's embrace.

Eventually, it was time to go back.

Caspen held Tem's hand until the very last moment, only letting her go when they reached the head of the trail. When his fingers fell from hers, she felt cold.

The walk back was lonely. By the time she reached the castle, dawn was imminent.

It had been a good deal easier to climb down the trellis than it was to climb back up. But somehow Tem made it back into her bedroom, pulling the window shut just as the sun began to rise.

She slept all day. There was nothing else to do.

When she woke, it was dusk. Tem tried to reach for her bond with Caspen, but she could barely sense it. She had to talk to Adelaide, and soon. She was about to climb out her window again when there was a knock at the door.

It was Leo.

She answered it, and there was a heavy pause in which they stared at each other. Then Leo said, "Tem."

"Leo," she offered in return.

"My father is throwing a dinner party tonight, and I must attend."

"How nice for you."

"I'd like you to come as my date."

That wasn't what Tem had expected at all. "But *why*?"

Leo ignored her surprise, answering smoothly, "Because I am in the mood to anger my father. Do we not share that interest?" He had a point there.

"I…" Tem started but stopped. She needed to see Adelaide. It was imperative that she confirm her suspicion. But she couldn't tell Leo that.

Before she could decide how to answer, the prince continued. "I will have a dress brought up for you. Meet me in the foyer in twenty minutes."

He swept away without another word.

Tem stood with her mouth hanging open, shocked at this turn of events. Was Leo manipulating her? Was this just another ploy to sway her heart in his direction? Tem was never sure with him. Regardless, she was starving. And she was *certainly* in the mood to anger Maximus.

So when the dress arrived, she pulled it on.

It was far too tight and low-cut to be appropriate for dinner. But Tem wore it anyway, willing to appease Leo if only for tonight. The golden claw still rested between her breasts, framed by the significant cleavage afforded her by the dress.

Leo was waiting in the foyer. He watched her walk down the stairs with his hands clasped behind his back, as if to prevent himself from touching her. Tem stopped on the bottom step so they were eye to eye.

"This dress is ridiculous," she said.

His mouth twitched. "That's the idea."

"You're depraved."

"I'm taking that as a compliment."

"That's your prerogative."

Leo extended his hand, palm up, and Tem took it. He guided her down the hallway into the same room where the girls had waited for the Frisky Sixty to occur. A circular table was set with gold cutlery and crystal glassware. They were the last to arrive. Leo pulled Tem's chair out, and she took it gingerly, trying to sit in a way that wouldn't accentuate her neckline. Leo's arm rested on the back of her chair. Maximus sat directly opposite Tem, his slate-gray eyes searing into hers.

"Your father is staring at me," Tem whispered.

At her words, Leo's eyes flicked to her dress. "He has good reason to."

"I highly doubt he's as influenced by this dress as you are."

"I should hope not."

Maximus was still staring at her. It was becoming rather uncomfortable.

Leo murmured in her ear, "I apologize in advance for anything you might be subjected to tonight."

"And what might I be subjected to?"

Leo paused, then said simply, "Unpleasantness."

From the way Maximus was looking at her like she was a bug on the bottom of his shoe, Tem could guess what kind of unpleasantness might be imminent. Then again, it couldn't be anything worse than what she'd already been subjected to her entire life. Maximus may be cruel, but he had nothing on Vera.

The only other person Tem recognized was Lilly, who was sitting next to her father, watching the proceedings with a sympathetic expression. The other chairs were filled with people Tem didn't recognize. She assumed they were Leo's extended family, here for the wedding.

"Aren't you going to introduce your guest to the table, Thelonius?" Maximus said coldly.

Leo smiled. "Certainly." He stood, grabbing Tem's hand and pulling her upright with him. "Please welcome my date, Temperance Verus."

To Tem's horror, everyone at the table looked right at her.

Before she could figure out whether they expected her to say something, Leo was already speaking. "She's one of the lovely women in the running for my hand in marriage. As you can see, she's already got a head start." He raised his arm so everyone could see their hands clasped together.

A murmur of laughter rippled across the table. With a single line, Leo had not only explained Tem's presence at the dinner but legitimized it. Where just moments ago, she'd been the recipient of discerning stares, now everyone was smiling at her. *He's good at that*, Tem realized. Disarming people was a talent of Leo's. He did it easily, with nothing but his words. She made a mental note to remember that about him.

As they sat back down, Maximus said, "How are you finding the castle, Temperance?"

"Oh," Tem said, surprised he was addressing her directly. "It's…something."

"It must be quite different from what you're used to in the village."

Tem was smart enough to spot an insult when she saw one. She refused to take the bait. "It's certainly eventful around here."

Maximus's eyes narrowed. He wasn't pleased that she refused to play his game. "And what does your father do, Temperance?"

The question made her blood run cold. Was Maximus aware that Tem was a hybreed? Or was he simply making dinner-party conversation? Surely, he couldn't know that one of the basilisks deep beneath their feet was her father. Or could he?

"My *mother* runs a chicken farm," Tem said pointedly.

There was a weighted silence as everyone at the table glanced at Maximus, who was glaring at Tem like he wanted to throw his wine at her.

"Chickens," he sneered. "How charming."

Before she could defend herself, someone else did it for her.

"Don't speak to her like that," Leo snapped.

It was the first time Tem had ever heard Leo raise his voice, and a chill went down her spine at the sound. He was staring at Maximus with pure, vivid loathing, his hands clenched into fists under the table. His reaction was so disproportionate to Maximus's comment that Tem knew there was no way this was only about her.

Tem reached for him.

She touched Leo's hand under the table, uncurling his fingers gently from a fist. Then she pulled his hand into her lap, holding it with both of hers. Leo didn't look at her while she did it. But when Tem squeezed his hand, he squeezed hers back, and his voice was steady again when he said, "Forgive me, Father. Too much wine."

Nervous laughter spread across the table, and a moment later, the chatter resumed. But Maximus didn't move, staring at his son with utter contempt in his eyes.

"Leo," Tem said, pulling his attention to her.

He turned, and the second their eyes met, his expression softened. He leaned in. "What can I do for you, Tem?"

"I'm starving," she said, her tone purposefully light.

Leo smiled, if a little stiffly.

"Then we had better feed you."

No sooner had he said the words than a butler appeared and began serving them from a golden tray.

The food was exquisite: tender roast beef, crispy potatoes, and herby green salad. It reminded Tem of the food she'd eaten on her very first date with Leo, where they'd sat on the patio before walking through the maze. It was strange to sit here with him now, in the same room she'd sat in before the Frisky Sixty. They had come a long way together, she and Leo. And the journey had not been all bad.

The next hour was spent making pleasantries and exchanging small talk. Tem learned that the other guests were indeed Leo's extended family, in town for the wedding. The thought made her nervous, but she didn't show it. Instead, she laughed and smiled and charmed herself into their good graces, pretending she was playing a part. And maybe she was.

The woman next to Tem was on her fourth glass of red wine. "I've never seen one before, you know," she purred, swirling her glass.

"Seen what before?" Tem asked.

"A snake."

"Oh," Tem said. Then she frowned. "They look just like humans."

"*Attractive* humans, I've heard. What's it like to fuck one?"

Tem's eyebrows flew upward. She glanced at Leo, who was mercifully engaged in conversation with the man on his left. She cleared her throat. "It's…life-changing," Tem said honestly.

"Oh, I'm sure it is," the woman crooned, leaning even closer. "Maybe I'll get lucky at the wedding."

Tem blinked. "Will the basilisks be attending?"

"They should be. At least that's what my sister says. Did I tell you about the time she—"

But Tem was no longer listening. If the basilisks were attending the wedding, that meant they would seize power the moment she performed the crest. It meant there would be no time to ensure a smooth transition from one king to the next, no time to ensure things happened in an orderly fashion. The change would be immediate. Lawless. And possibly dangerous.

When the main course was cleared, a butler served dessert.

A white ceramic dish containing a chocolate soufflé was set in front of Tem. It was covered in powdered sugar. She touched it with her fork, disturbing its pristine surface.

Leo watched as she took the first bite. "And?" he said.

"Pretty good."

"I suppose that's better than pretty bad."

"Marginally."

Leo laughed, and at the sound, Tem chose to do something she shouldn't. She leaned closer, lowering her voice so only Leo could hear. "Do you really want to make your father angry?"

He arched an eyebrow. "Always."

At his reply, she whispered, "Feed me."

For a moment, Leo did nothing. Then the familiar smirk returned to his face. He took the fork, scooped up a bite of the soufflé, and held it out to her. Tem leaned even closer, taking the bite slowly, keeping her eyes on Leo's while she did it.

Maximus watched the entire time, his expression irate.

When Tem finished the bite, she pressed her lips to Leo's cheek, leaving a smudge of powdered sugar on his skin. She smiled at him, and he smiled back.

"And you thought I was depraved," he whispered.

She wiped the sugar gently from his cheek. "Takes one to know one."

Dinner was followed by cocktails in the parlor, where, thankfully, Maximus left them alone. It was only when the fire was dying down and the guests were starting to leave that Maximus shot Tem a pointed glance, which she returned.

Leo's arm encircled her waist as they ascended the stairs together, and when they reached the landing, he stopped in his tracks. Tem thought he might say something or perhaps make a move on her. Instead, he closed his eyes, leaning his head back so it was resting against the wall.

He let out a deep sigh.

Tem stared at him, unsure what to do. It felt like a moment that should be private, and despite herself, she felt bad for Leo. Tem wondered suddenly if he decompressed like this after every dinner party. Growing up with a father like Maximus couldn't have been easy on him.

She touched his chest.

Leo's eyes opened. He placed his hand over hers, holding them together. They stared at each other for a long moment. Then Leo raised his other hand, brushing the tips of his fingers underneath Tem's chin. Perhaps she'd had too much wine. Perhaps she was simply overwhelmed by the events of the last few days. But for some reason, his touch felt so good that Tem couldn't help but close her eyes as he traced his fingertips along her jaw. She tilted her head so his palm could cup her cheek.

"Come to my room," he whispered.

She shook her head.

"Why not, Tem?"

"Because you're just going to try to have sex with me." Even though her eyes were closed, she knew Leo was smiling.

"I wouldn't dream of it."

She opened her eyes. He *was* smiling. "Promise?"

Leo smiled wider. "Having sex with you requires your consent, Tem. And you essentially just revoked that. There would be no point in trying. But if you insist, then yes. I promise."

Together, they entered his room.

CHAPTER THIRTY-FOUR

———••✦••———

TEM STOOD BY THE BAR CART AS LEO SHUT THE DOOR BEHIND THEM. EVERYTHING was the same as she remembered it: immaculately made bed, packed bookshelves, crackling fire.

"Would you care for a drink?" Leo asked.

"Please."

He poured them both whiskeys before sitting in one of the armchairs facing the fire. On a whim, Tem set her whiskey on the end table, crossed to Leo, and curled up beside him. He moved to accommodate her, pulling her against his chest with a deep, satisfied sigh. They stared at the fire for a long time, neither of them saying a word.

Tem breathed in his scent, savoring the cologne that lingered on his neck. He smelled so *good*. She savored other things too. Like the way his arms were wrapped securely around her. And the way a single lock of blond hair lay over his forehead. He was handsome, she realized. Or maybe she'd always known he was but had pretended he wasn't. Tem tried to imagine what it would be like to wake up next to him every morning for the rest of her life. Before she could picture it, Leo looked at her.

"Tem," he murmured.

Tem didn't think. She just pressed her lips to his.

They kissed slowly, their bodies folding together in the armchair. Tem expected Leo's hands to stray, but they didn't. Instead, she was the one pulling him closer. She was the one running her palms under his shirt, touching his ribs one by one, feeling the angled lines of his torso. She remembered what Caspen had told her:

You are mine, Tem. Whether you give your body to another does not change that.

Tem pressed her lips to Leo's neck. She wanted to taste him.

"Tem." The prince pulled away, but just barely. "Stop."

"Why?"

"Because you made me promise not to try to have sex with you."

"I don't see you trying. You just told me to stop."

"You make it rather difficult to keep that promise."

He pulled back in earnest this time, his eyes gleaming in the light of the dying fire.

His voice dropped to a whisper. "You can't imagine everything I want to do to you right now."

"Yes, I can." She traced her fingertips down the center of his chest. "But you're a man of your word, remember?"

"It is becoming impossible to remain one."

Tem giggled. She couldn't help it. It was fun to tease him, to force him to resist her, especially when she knew how badly he wanted to do the opposite. She liked playing these games with Leo. It had always been that way between them—a battle of wills, a test of who held the power. Tem was holding it now, and she didn't plan on relinquishing it.

"Tell me what you want to do to me," Tem whispered.

"Everything."

"Be specific."

Leo *moaned*, the sound vibrating deep in his chest. "I want to rip this off you"—his fist twisted the strap of her dress—"and throw it in the fucking fire. I want you to tell me what you like, and I want you to say my name while I do it."

"More, Leo. Be specific."

His hand went to her throat, pulling her head to his. "I want you spread open in front of me. I want to bury myself in your cunt until you can't fucking breathe."

"More."

"I want you all to myself. I don't want to share. I want my name to be the only thing on your lips, and I want my cum dripping out of you."

"*More.*"

His final words were a tortured whisper. "I want to do everything you'll let me do."

Tem sat up.

Leo's eyes widened. Then, just as quickly, they narrowed in hungry anticipation as Tem straddled him so they were facing each other in the armchair. She grasped the bottom of the dress and pulled it up over her head.

"*Tem,*" Leo said at the sight of her naked body.

Tem's finger darted forward to touch his lips. "Don't worry," she whispered. "You kept your promise."

"If you tell me I can't touch you this time—"

"Touch me, Leo."

Leo didn't hesitate.

He grabbed her with both hands, pulling her onto his lap so she was pressed against the hard length of his cock, which was barely contained by his trousers. He groaned while he did it, and Tem moved her hips to meet him, rubbing against his shaft to make him even harder. She took his hand and placed it on her thigh.

Leo's eyes fluttered shut. For a moment, he didn't seem to breathe. Then his eyes flew open, and he took over, sliding his hand between her legs and slipping his fingers inside her.

Tem gasped as he slid them in, then out, then back in again, driving them deeper every time.

"You're *dripping*, Tem," he whispered. "Is that all for me?"

Tem nodded.

"Say it," he commanded.

"It's all for you."

"Again."

She placed her hand over his, angling her hips so his fingers went all the way inside her. "It's all for you, Leo. Just for you."

Tem took control, sliding herself up and down. Leo watched her, enraptured, as if he had never seen anything like her before. His other hand wandered, touching her hips and her waist and her breasts. She let him do this, conforming her body to his touch, showing him how well they could move together.

At some point, Leo removed his fingers, and Tem watched as he raised them to his lips, licking her wetness from them slowly.

"So fucking sweet," he murmured.

Hot, possessive pride swept through Tem. "Just for you," she said again.

She dipped her own hand between her legs, and when she removed it, Leo licked it too, sliding his tongue into the groove between her fingers, closing his eyes as he did it. He looked radiantly happy, like he was savoring his last meal on earth.

As soon as he was done, he kissed her.

She tasted herself on his lips, just as she had so many times on Caspen's. Only this time, she also tasted the traces of honey that accompanied Leo's kiss, and the taste made her so ravenous that she filled her hand with his cock. He was harder than stone, straining against the confines of his trousers. But Tem didn't release him. Instead, she turned around, situating herself so her ass was in his lap, her knees on either side of him.

Leo gave a sharp intake of breath at the change in position. A moment later, he twisted his hand around the ends of her hair, yanking her head back so her spine was arched against his chest. His other hand slid up her waist to her breasts, squeezing one and then the other, running the hard peaks of her nipples through his fingers until she was whimpering beneath his touch.

Tem arched her back even more, pressing her breasts into his palm.

"So needy," he whispered. "What are we going to do with you?"

Tem plunged her hand between her legs to grab his cock.

Leo grunted at the contact, his fist tightening in her hair. "So *fucking* needy."

His hand left her breasts, and Tem gasped at the sudden absence. Then his palm hit her ass with a hard *smack*, and she moaned as he bucked his hips below her. He spanked her again. And again.

She was so wet, it was soaking into his trousers.

"You're going to turn around," he said, his lips on her ear. "And you're going to come."

Tem couldn't obey quickly enough.

By the time she turned around, Leo had spread his entire hand open beneath her, and she lowered herself onto his palm without a moment's hesitation. Tem rubbed herself back and forth with quick, contained movements, going steadily faster until her wetness was dripping down his wrist. Her skin felt as if it were on fire—like one single touch might ignite her into a blaze.

"That's it, Tem," Leo said, his eyes locked on hers. "Show me."

Her breath came in short, desperate gasps.

"Show me how pretty you are when you come."

Tem wanted nothing more.

She wanted Leo to see what he did to her—the effect he had even when she was pretending she didn't want him, that some part of her belonged to him, even if that part wasn't hers to give away.

At the last second, Leo slipped his fingers inside her, touching her *right* where she needed it, forcing her body to collect what it was owed.

She drove herself against him as she came, thrusting her hips with shameless urgency, drinking in every last second of pleasure he had to offer her. Tem knew he liked to see her like this—open and exposed, helplessly reliant on him for her climax. It confirmed what both of them knew but only one of them denied: she needed him.

Afterward, they kissed slowly, Tem still naked, Leo still clothed. Tem made no move to undress him. She'd done exactly what she wanted to do tonight, and she didn't intend on doing anything else.

"What will it take to get you on my cock?" Leo whispered. He was still touching her, playing lazily with her clitoris, his hand covered in her wetness.

Tem smiled. "Your undying devotion."

"You already have it."

She laughed. "There are two other girls you can fuck, Leo."

"I only fuck them because I can't fuck you."

Tem took his hands and placed them on her breasts. He thumbed her nipples as she said, "Then maybe you should eliminate them."

He raised an eyebrow. "Is that what it would take?"

She shrugged as if this was of no concern to her. "Maybe."

Leo arched his head back in exasperation. His hands remained on her breasts. "Tease," he said simply.

"Masochist," she said back.

He pinched both her nipples. Tem bit her lip.

She held his gaze as he caressed her breasts, brushing his long, slender fingers first up her cleavage then down it, continuing until his palms were on her hips. He seemed content to simply touch her, spreading his hands wide so he could feel as much of her skin as possible. Tem watched as he dipped his fingers once more into her center. But instead of pushing into her, he raised his hand and spread her wetness onto her already hard nipple, massaging it into her skin until she was aching with need. He leaned forward and opened his mouth.

"*Leo*," Tem moaned when his tongue met her breast.

Her fingers threaded into his hair as he sucked her nipple between his teeth. Then he flicked her clitoris, and she cried out. Everything in Tem wanted to pull him closer; everything in her wanted *more*. But she would not be getting more tonight.

"Leo." She pulled away. "I have to go."

His grip on her only tightened. "Where?"

"To sleep."

"No."

"Yes." Tem smiled.

He kissed her. His hands started to wander again.

Tem swatted them away. "*Behave*, Leo."

Leo let out a groan of displeasure. He touched her for as long as he could, up until the very last second, when Tem finally raised herself off his lap. Even then, he still touched her, stroking her exposed center as she bent over to retrieve her dress. When she stood, he leaned back to look up at her. She looked down at him, sprawled in the armchair, his hair disheveled, his eyes gleaming. He looked luminous.

"I want you to stay," he whispered.

Tem leaned over him, pressing a soft kiss to his throat. "I know you do."

"Please, Tem." He reached for her, but she straightened.

She shook her head. "You have to *earn* overnight privileges, Leo."

"Is that so?"

"Yes."

"Then I suppose I'd better endeavor to do so."

"I suppose you had." With that, Tem crossed to the door and left him.

The moment Tem was back in her room, she bolted for the window.

She had no idea how long she'd been with Leo. Too long. It was late—or perhaps early—and she needed to get to the caves and back before anyone discovered she was gone. What if Leo came to her room in the morning? What if he came to her room *right now*?

It didn't matter. Tem had to talk to Adelaide.

Her journey to the caves was a blur. The air held that certain electricity that came right before it rained, and Tem sprinted in an attempt to outrun it. She hurtled through the village, into the forest, and through the wall, bursting into the cave to find it empty. Tem groped her way down the passageway, not stopping until she reached Caspen's chambers.

He was already there, standing by the fire with Adelaide.

"Tem," he said immediately. His nostrils flared, and she remembered how he'd known she'd been with Leo after the carriage ride, how he could smell him on her. Surely, he would smell him this time. But she couldn't worry about that now.

"Caspen," she said. "I need to speak with Adelaide alone."

Caspen hesitated. Tem knew he was already in the dark, already worried something was happening beyond his control. She didn't have the capacity to comfort him.

"Of course," he said quietly. "Take as long as you need."

He pressed a long, tender kiss to Tem's cheek before sweeping from the room. Tem waited until the door was closed before turning to Adelaide.

"What is it, Temperance?"

Tem arranged her thoughts before speaking. "I…can't talk to Caspen anymore."

Adelaide raised an eyebrow.

"With my mind, I mean. Our connection is…broken. It's weak. I can barely hear him." Tem paused, gathering the courage to continue. "And I can lie. For the first time in my life. Easily—the way normal people can."

Adelaide crossed her perfectly toned arms. "Why are you telling me this, Temperance?"

Tem met her eye. "Because you know about hybreeds. And I need you to tell me what's wrong with me."

"I cannot be sure." Adelaide shrugged elegantly. "I am by no means an expert."

"Well then, *guess*."

She sighed. "When did it begin?"

"Right after Caspen crested me."

Adelaide's golden eyes searched Tem's. "I have never heard of anything like this before. I doubt anyone has. But it is possible that…" She paused, and it felt as if every cell in Tem's body were tilting forward. "The basilisk side of you is…dying."

"*What?* But the crest didn't work. I'm not bonded to Caspen."

"It did not work on the *human* side of you. You are made up of two things, Temperance. Perhaps the crest could only choose one or the other. It chose the basilisk."

"You say that as if it has a mind of its own."

"It may very well have one. Caspen had only crested a basilisk before you. So when he did it again, the crest was drawn to what it knew. The part of you that is human was spared from its effects. The part of you that is basilisk was not."

"So…what's going to happen to me?"

"I do not know."

"But if you—"

"If I had to *guess*," Adelaide said, "I would say that you are…wounded, so to speak."

Tem's heart fell.

This explained everything: her inability to speak to Caspen as easily as she once did, her newfound ability to lie. She was losing the best part of her—the part she'd only just gotten to know.

Adelaide was watching her in sympathetic silence.

"What happens if the basilisk side of me dies completely?" Tem whispered.

Adelaide sighed, answering gently. "The same thing that happens when anything dies. It ceases to exist."

"But then I'll be…" Tem couldn't say the words.

Adelaide said them for her. "You will be fully human."

The reality of this revelation sank in slowly. If Tem became fully human, she would lose the ability to crest. If that happened, Leo's life was in danger. Bastian had said that the crest was an elegant solution—that the alternative was all-out war. If she couldn't perform the crest, there would be bloodshed.

"How can I heal it?"

Adelaide pursed her lips. "I do not know that it can be healed. But if it were possible, it would require a significant amount of power."

Tem's mind was racing. Surely, cresting the royals would garner her a significant amount of power. But only if she could do it before the basilisk side of her died completely. She lifted her chin.

"How long do I have?"

Adelaide sighed. "I do not know that either. Caspen crested you days ago. That means the basilisk side of you has been dying for just as long. If the deterioration of your connection is as bad as you say, I would guess you have a week. Maybe less."

A week. Maybe less. Tem fought to ignore the panic threatening to overtake her. "You can't tell Caspen."

Adelaide opened her mouth to protest.

"You *can't,*" Tem insisted. "He'll never forgive himself if he finds out this is his fault. Promise me."

But the basilisk shook her beautiful head. "It will not matter what I promise. He will find out when he can no longer speak to you with his mind. Most likely he has already begun to feel the effects. It is inevitable, Temperance."

Tem held back tears.

"Listen to me," Adelaide said urgently. "That is the least of your worries. You must remember that you are bound to Caspen by blood."

Tem closed her eyes as she realized what Adelaide was about to say. Nothing could prepare her for hearing it.

"His life is linked to yours." Adelaide leaned closer. "If a part of you dies, specifically the basilisk part..."

Tem finished for her. "Caspen will die too."

CHAPTER THIRTY-FIVE

＊

ADELAIDE DIDN'T LINGER. THERE WAS NOTHING ELSE TO SAY ANYWAY. SHE LEFT Tem by the fire, and a moment later, Caspen returned, worry evident on his face. "Tem," he murmured, his arms already around her. "Talk to me. Please."

Tem closed her eyes. What could she tell him? That a part of her was dying? That he was dying too? There was no way to say it. And besides, Adelaide was right. He would find out eventually.

When Tem didn't answer, Caspen spoke again. "Tem," he said quietly. "I know I have not been…what you need of late. But I cannot bear it when you shut me out."

Realization hit her.

Caspen thought *Tem* was the reason their connection had been weak the past few days. He thought she was angry about his engagement to Adelaide, that she was pushing him away on purpose, to punish him. It couldn't be further from the truth.

Tem looked up at him, losing herself in the golden pools of his eyes.

She thought of all the decisions Caspen had made for her—decisions that involved her body. He'd proposed without telling her; he'd given her his venom; he'd bound their lives together by blood. He'd done those things to protect her. She understood that now, more than she ever had before.

They had been through so much together, *survived* so much together. The training, their engagement, the ritual—even Rowe. Caspen was her anchor. She would not allow anything to happen to him. She would do what was necessary to save him—to save herself.

Now it was Tem's turn to protect him.

Her path was clear. She would marry Leo. She would crest the royals. She would heal the basilisk side of her before Caspen found out that he was dying. It was time for him to trust her as she had once trusted him. Tem was the one keeping secrets now. And she would not apologize for it.

"I do not mean to shut you out," she whispered against his chest.

Caspen's fingers brushed gently through her hair. His want was evident; she could feel the hardness of his body, the way he drew her in. His lips were on her neck. Tem let him kiss her for one moment—just a single infinite moment—before pulling away.

"Caspen," she whispered. "I have to get back."

His grip only tightened. "Tem," he said, his voice low. "You need to transition."

He was right. She needed practice. But she couldn't linger here. "I can't stay, Caspen," she said again, softly this time.

His grip still didn't loosen. "We must prepare you, Tem."

But there was no time to prepare. Not now—not when it was nearly morning. If Leo discovered she'd gone to see Caspen, there would be no wedding at which to perform the crest anyway.

"I'll come again as soon as I can," she said. "I promise."

Caspen wasn't pleased. She could sense it in the way he kissed her at the head of the trail, holding her too tightly. He missed her. And she missed him. But there were bigger things than just their relationship to consider. Caspen's life now hung in the balance.

It had rained while she was in the caves, and Tem fought to keep up her pace on the muddy trail. By the time she was back at the castle, the sun was about to rise. The trellis was slippery; she nearly fell twice. But she managed to haul herself into her bedroom in one piece, running her fingers through her tangled curls and shaking the water from her hair.

There was a sudden knock on her door.

Tem froze. There was no time to take a bath, no time to clean herself off. All she could do was kick her muddy shoes under the bed, tear her dress from her body, and throw a robe over her shoulders before opening the door.

Leo stood before her. "Tem," he said breathlessly. "Good, you're awake. I came to tell you that I—" He cut off as he took in her wet hair. He frowned, and Tem's heart slammed in her chest.

"I took a bath," she said preemptively.

But the frown on Leo's face remained in place. He stood perfectly still as his gaze went behind her, where her dress was crumpled on the floor. His eyes traveled from the dress to the muddy footprints that led from the windowsill.

"Where were you?" he asked slowly.

Tem didn't answer. Something about the way he asked it filled her with dread.

Leo stepped closer. "Were you with him?"

Tem tried to change the subject. "What were you going to tell me?"

His eyes finally met hers. They narrowed. "I was going to tell you that I just eliminated Cassandra, and I was on my way to do the same to Vera. But perhaps I acted too soon."

"Leo—"

"Perhaps," he raised his voice, overpowering hers, "I have been living in a fantasy wherein you possess the same caliber of affection for me that I feel for you."

"I—"

"*Perhaps.*" He was nearly yelling now. "I have been a fool. So I shall ask you only once more, Temperance." He leaned in, and she flinched. "And I would prefer it if you didn't lie to me. Where the *fuck* were you?"

"Leo," she said, reaching for him. "Please try to understand. There's so much you don't know—"

"I know *you*," he said coldly, yanking his arm from her grasp. "And I know you are ruled by your heart instead of your mind."

"I'm not—"

But Leo would not be stopped. "I know everything we did last night you learned from *him*."

"You can't hold my training against me," Tem said desperately. "Every girl was taught the same way."

"The other girls didn't *fall in love with their teachers*."

Tears pricked Tem's eyes. "You know better than anyone that you can't help who you love."

His face went white. "How dare you say that to me? You cannot compare your infatuation with a snake to what I had with Evelyn."

"I'm not comparing. I'm just—"

"You have brought me nothing but pain since the day we met. I never should have let myself fall for you."

Tem recoiled. "Are you saying you regret choosing me?" she whispered.

Leo's face was the picture of fury. "I'm saying you are not at all what I expected, Tem."

Tem stood her ground. "You're not exactly what I expected either, Leo."

"Please. You've always gotten the better end of this deal. You get to be queen. Isn't that every little girl's dream?"

"Not mine."

"Well, it should be. And what do I get? A wife who loves someone else. Lucky me." His voice was bitter.

"I'm not your wife yet," she said quietly but firmly. "And if we can't get through this, I never will be."

Leo let out a dull, humorless laugh. "There's nothing to *get through*, Tem. *You* need to get over *him*."

"I can't."

"*Why?*" He stepped closer. "What is it about that filthy snake that has you so entranced? What lies has he spun to seduce you?"

But Tem couldn't answer him. She couldn't explain her bond with Caspen—couldn't tell Leo what she really was. Or could she?

What if, when faced with the truth, Leo chose a different path than his father had? If Leo knew that Tem was a hybreed, he would be forced to view the basilisks differently— not as the enemy but as a part of her.

Before she could follow that train of thought, Leo spoke again.

"All the other girls let me up their skirts on the first date. Vera can't get enough of my cock. She's begged me to fuck her more times than I can count. But not you. *Never you.*"

Tem knew his patience had run out, knew she had withheld herself for too long. Still, his next words sent a chill down her spine.

"End things with him, Tem. Or I'm marrying Vera."

He was gone before she could even blink.

Tem didn't know what to do with herself. She couldn't end things with Caspen. It wasn't an option. But she couldn't get eliminated either. She had to marry Leo. *Needed* to marry Leo.

One question remained.

Why *had* she waited so long to sleep with him?

She was attracted to Leo. She had feelings for him. Yet she couldn't pull the trigger— couldn't let him all the way in. To sleep with him would be to lie to him. If Leo knew who she really was, if he knew she was a hybreed, he wouldn't want her anymore. He would be repulsed by her; Tem was sure of it.

Or was she?

Tem never gave Leo the benefit of the doubt. She always assumed the worst of him, even when he'd only given her reason to assume the opposite. Did she truly have so little faith in him? Perhaps of the two of them, Tem was the unworthy one. Perhaps it had always been that way.

Leo would never get the chance to truly know her unless she gave him one. He loved only a version of her—the version she'd allowed him to see. It was time to show him all of her.

Leo deserved the truth.

But first she had to find him. He wasn't in his room, and he wasn't in Vera's. Tem searched the entire floor, throwing open door after door until she'd searched every room. All empty. She took the stairs two at a time, hesitating only a moment before poking her head into the parlor, bracing herself to potentially see Maximus. He wasn't there. Neither was Leo.

Tem stood in the foyer, breathing hard. Where could he be?

Then she remembered it was morning. There was somewhere Leo liked to go in the mornings—somewhere she'd found him before.

Tem waved down the nearest servant. "I need a carriage," she said.

The servant frowned. "You're not supposed to leave, miss."

"It's important."

The servant shook his head. "The girls are meant to stay in the castle."

"Is this a *prison?*"

"I am simply following orders, miss."

"Fine." Tem pushed past him, heading for the kitchen.

It took no time at all to locate Gabriel. He was washing dishes, laughing with the other kitchen staff as they prepared the morning meal.

"Gabriel," she cried.

He turned, his eyebrows rising in surprise. "Tem? What are you doing down here?"

"I need a favor."

He twirled a soapy spoon dramatically. "Anything for you, dearest."

"Can you get me a carriage?"

He winked. "You're lucky I know a stable boy."

Gabriel disappeared, returning a few minutes later with Henry. Or maybe it was Peter. Tem was finding it hard to focus on anything but getting to Leo as quickly as possible. She barely felt the kiss Gabriel pressed to her cheek before she followed Henry—or Peter—out to the stables. They secured a carriage, taking extra care to avoid discovery by the gardeners, who were performing their duties on the grounds.

Tem sat with her hands clasped in her lap as the carriage took her into the village. The journey was rough, the streets still wet from the rain the night before. By the time they arrived at the graveyard, Tem's stomach felt like it was eating itself. She had never been so nervous about anything in her life—not even for her first night in the caves. Back then, she hadn't known what she was getting into. Back then, her biggest worry was having her first kiss. Now she understood the gravity of what she was about to do, and she simply had to do it anyway.

Leo was there, sitting on the bench beneath the willow tree, just like she hoped he'd be.

He looked up as she approached. Only this time, he didn't seem pleased to see her. "Tem," he said as he stood. "Unless you've come to tell me that you—"

"I can't end things with him," she said.

Leo snorted. He turned to leave.

"But you deserve to know why." Tem grabbed his arm, and Leo paused, looking back at her with clear contempt in his eyes.

"You love him," he snapped. "That's why."

"I do love him." Tem stepped closer. "But that's not the reason I can't end things. At least…not the only reason."

Leo turned to face her. He didn't say anything. But she could sense his curiosity, and now that Tem had his attention, her heart beat even faster.

She knew what came next would determine not only their future but the future of the entire kingdom. The fates of everyone she loved depended on how Leo would react to what she was about to tell him.

So she asked, "Do you trust me?"

He blinked. "I do."

"I'm not asking if you like me. Or if you want to fuck me. I'm asking if you *trust* me."

A shadow of a smile lightened his face. "Just because I like you and want to fuck you doesn't mean I don't trust you, Tem."

"Leo. This is important."

He sighed, running a hand through his thick blond hair. "Very well. I trust you."

She looked into his eyes, seeing his sincerity. He trusted her. She could feel it.

"Then you should know the truth." But Tem paused. It felt as if the sky were falling down.

Leo was staring at her, his expression unreadable. He leaned in. "The truth about what, Tem?"

Me.

But she couldn't say it. She just couldn't. Instead, she borrowed Caspen's line: "It would be easier to show you."

There was a hairline pause. Then Leo dipped his head. "Lead the way," he said simply.

Neither of them spoke the entire way back to the castle. Tem couldn't help but think about the last time they were in a carriage together—how Leo had called her wicked, how she'd licked his cum right out of his palm. She wondered if he was thinking about it too.

When they arrived at the castle, they paused in the foyer.

"Is your father occupied?" she asked.

Leo shrugged. "Why?"

"I don't want him to see us."

The prince nodded slowly. "He usually meets with his advisors in the mornings," Leo said. "He will not disturb us."

Tem nodded. Something else occurred to her. "You can't tell him I'm showing you this."

Now Leo hesitated. The curiosity she'd sensed earlier reared its head again. She knew he understood that she was asking him to choose between her and his own father.

Leo made his choice:

"I will not tell him. You have my word."

It was enough for Tem.

They navigated the halls of the castle together, winding down staircase after staircase until Tem was once more standing before the door to the dungeon. She paused, turning to Leo. This was an unprecedented moment for them. A moment of truth.

At her hesitation, Leo asked, "Shall I do the honors?" He raised his slender fingers to the door handle.

Tem could only nod.

Leo waited just a moment longer before turning the handle and stepping through the door. Tem followed, her throat tightening as the cloying smell of decay invaded her nostrils. The cells were just as she remembered them, row after row disappearing into the darkness.

Leo took a few steps forward, then stopped. His head turned to the side, and Tem watched as his gray eyes fell on the occupant of the first cell.

"Tem…" he whispered. "What is this?"

In reply, Tem took his hand, guiding him closer to the cell.

Leo stiffened as they approached the bars. He stared at the basilisk slumped against the cell wall, taking in the tangle of golden wires fused to her fingertips.

"What's happening to it?"

It.

The basilisk was clearly a woman, yet Leo referred to her as an object.

Tem tried not to take this as a bad sign. "Basilisk blood has magical properties," Tem began, realizing she had no idea how to explain the bloodletting.

Leo stared at the wires. Tem had never seen him stand so still. "What kind of properties?"

Tem took a deep breath. "It can be alchemized into gold."

"Gold," he murmured.

"Yes," said Tem. "Gold."

For a moment, Leo simply stood there. Then he turned to face her, and Tem raised her hand.

"These," she whispered, brushing her finger over his lips, right where his incisors were. Her fingers fell to the golden cuff on his wrist. "This."

Leo shook his head. "No," he said.

"Yes."

His gaze returned to the cell. "This is *barbaric.*"

The same thing she'd said about the ritual. "Says the son of the man who allows it."

Leo opened his mouth, then closed it. Disbelief flashed across his face, followed quickly by deep shame. He looked utterly devastated; Tem might as well have plunged a knife into his chest. Yet underneath his pain, she saw reluctant comprehension dawning in his eyes. He might find it hard to believe what was happening in the dungeon, but it certainly wasn't hard to believe that his father would allow it.

"I am not my father, Tem," Leo whispered.

She wanted to comfort him. Instead, she forged onward. "Then prove it. Put a stop to this."

"How?"

"Do what you've always wanted to do. Wield your power."

Leo closed his eyes as if he could block out her words.

Tem stepped closer, clenching his hand even tighter in hers. "If you want things to change, you have to be the one to change them, Leo."

His eyes were still closed.

Tem barreled onward. "Is *this* what you want your legacy to be? Greed? *Torture?*"

Leo opened his eyes. "Of course not," he whispered.

"Do you think it's right?"

He was silent.

She couldn't tell whether she was getting through to him—whether he was coming over to her side.

"Tem…" Leo said slowly. "This is…"

"Wrong," she insisted. "It's *wrong*, Leo."

He took a deep breath. "But they're…*snakes*, Tem. They aren't… We don't consider them to be…"

"People?"

He pursed his lips.

Tem knew it would be nearly impossible to unravel twenty years of prejudice in one fell swoop. There was only one thing she could do that might fully convince Leo of the atrocities that were happening here: one single thing that might sway him.

"What if it were me in that cell?"

Leo frowned. "It wouldn't be."

"If your father had his way, it would."

"I don't understand."

Rather than respond, Tem led him down the long row of cells, her heart growing heavier with each step. When they reached the very end, Tem steeled herself for what was to come.

Her father was in the same position as before: slumped over, gaunt and weak.

But even in the darkness, Tem could see he had worsened. His eyes were closed, his breathing ragged. More wires had been fused to his fingers; his hands looked like they were bleeding gold. Tem didn't bother trying to speak to him using her mind. Even if she were still able to do it, she very much doubted he would answer.

Tem turned to Leo. There was simply no other way to say it.

"Meet my father."

Leo blinked.

"His name is Kronos."

At the sound of his name, Kronos opened his eyes, and Leo took a step backward.

Tem retained her grip on his hand, forcing him to remain next to her. "My mother went through the same training I did. She fell in love, just like I did."

Leo shook his head slowly, his eyes locked on Kronos. Tem filled the silence, trying to give him as much information as possible before he inevitably bolted.

"The royals have been capturing basilisks ever since the war. This is what they do to them. It's called bloodletting"—she pointed at the wires—"and it's the reason your family is so wealthy."

Leo gripped her hand to the point of pain.

Kronos closed his eyes.

"It's cruel, Leo. It's inhumane."

Her choice of words was not an accident. She desperately needed to humanize her father, to show Leo that his life mattered—and by extension, Tem's life too.

"It's been happening for centuries. And it will continue to happen until someone breaks the cycle. That person should be you."

Leo's jaw was clenched. He didn't look at her.

"I cannot break it off with Caspen. We have a bond that goes beyond love. We are…connected. I'm bound to him, Leo," she finished softly. "I will always be bound to him."

Leo pulled his hand from hers.

Tem fell silent.

All the parts of her were finally unfolded before him—all the secrets she'd kept for so long. He'd asked her not to lie to him, and she had. She'd lied *so much*. But she'd lied to protect him. She'd lied because she cared. Was it really such a sin to lie to protect the ones you love?

Leo turned to her. "You're one of…*them*?"

"Yes," Tem whispered. "I am."

His expression was unreadable. There was no telling which direction he was leaning in, which path he would choose.

Tem had only one card left to play—one last secret that could tip him in her direction. "Your father sabotaged your relationship with Evelyn."

Deep pain passed over Leo's face. "How do you know that?" he whispered.

"He admitted it to me."

At the flash of shock in Leo's eyes, Tem almost reached for him.

Instead, she drove her point home. "He said if you choose me, he will do it again."

Leo went still.

Tem could do nothing but wait to see where the cards fell. Leo would either reject her or choose to protect her. She was relying on nothing but instinct to hope he made the right choice. Perhaps his love for her was not enough.

Perhaps it was.

"Leo," she whispered. "Please say something."

Leo didn't say anything. He simply took her face in his hands and kissed her.

The moment his lips touched hers, something bloomed within Tem—a combination of safety and tenderness and *love*—something she didn't know she could feel for two people at once.

When the kiss ended, Leo didn't pull away. Instead, he looked Tem deep in the eyes and said, "I never really had you, did I?"

Tem stared back at him, noticing the traces of green in his irises. She thought of Evelyn. "I never really had you either."

A sad smile twisted his lips. "We both know you did."

There was a pause, and Tem didn't know how to fill it.

Leo's next words were a whisper. "I've been in love with you ever since I saw you in that green dress, Tem."

The dress Caspen had given her.

Tem thought back to that night—how they had agreed not to lie to each other, how she'd forced Leo to admit that he wanted her. How far they had come.

Before she could reply, Leo dropped his hands, a shadow of his former self returning as he asked, "What can be done?"

At his words, Tem felt immense relief. If Leo was asking that, it meant he wanted to help. It meant he was on their side.

"We need to try to make peace," Tem said. "We must change the future of your kingdom."

"How?"

Tem didn't know the answer to that question. But she knew who would. "I'm…not the person to ask."

"Then who is?"

Now she avoided his eyes.

Leo sighed. "Ah. Of course. Him."

Tem didn't reply.

They stood in silence, and she prayed she hadn't just made a grave mistake. Then Leo said, "Can you…arrange a meeting?"

He spoke slowly, his tone cautious and controlled. Tem knew this was the last thing he wanted to do, and it would be the last thing Caspen wanted to do too. But with Leo on their side, the future between the royals and the basilisks could be different from the one Bastian had planned. There was hope. And as long as there was hope, they had a chance.

"Yes," Tem said. "I can."

Neither of them spoke on the way back from the dungeon.

When they reached the top of the stairs, the prince turned to his room.

"Leo, wait," Tem said.

He paused, his hand on the door. An eternity passed. "Tem?" he prompted.

Her heart slammed in her throat. It took all her courage to say, "Can I stay?"

Leo's eyebrows rose an almost imperceptible amount.

He'd asked her to stay so many times. But now Tem was the one asking—*begging*—to stay. She wasn't just asking about the competition. She was asking whether she could stay in his heart—in the place he'd saved for her since the moment he saw her in that green dress.

Leo didn't answer.

Instead, he opened his bedroom door, swinging it wide to reveal his four-poster bed.

Tem could sense Leo's anticipation; she could feel the way his body was drawn to hers. She was drawn to him too. There was no denying it, no pretending that what they had wasn't real. This game of theirs had gone on long enough. Tem had revealed her cards, and Leo had too. There was no reason to resist anymore. She was done fighting the inevitable.

His lips were on hers before the door slammed shut.

There was perfect, complete rhythm to their movement; both of them touched the other as if they had always known this was the way it was supposed to be, as if they were destined to do this since the moment they met. She pulled off her dress.

"Tem," Leo said. "Get in my bed."

CHAPTER THIRTY-SIX

———⋆———

TEM GOT IN HIS BED. SHE LAY ON HER BACK.

"Fuck," Leo breathed.

Tem decided to take her time. She brushed her hands slowly down her body, caressing her breasts before letting her fingers dip between her legs. Leo undressed as he watched, unbuttoning his shirt and pulling down his trousers. When he was finally naked before her, Tem whispered, "Touch me, Leo."

He stepped forward. His fingers found her wetness, and she moaned in deep fulfillment.

"*Fuck*," he breathed. "You're so wet, Tem."

Her hand joined his, pulling him even deeper. "Just for you," Tem whispered. She knew he needed to hear it. And she wanted to give him what he needed.

Leo bent down to kiss her inner thigh. "How could you keep this cunt from me for so long?"

"You had to earn it."

"And now that I have?"

"It's yours."

Leo pulled away.

Tem looked up at him as he looked down at her, both of them comprehending the significance of the moment. "Leo," she whispered.

He smiled. "I know, Tem."

Then he lowered his head.

He licked her, his tongue softer than silk, pressing against the most sensitive part of her as if he knew exactly what it would do to her—as if he knew exactly how much it would make her *need* him.

"Leo, please," she whispered.

"Please what, Tem?" he murmured against her clitoris.

"Fuck me."

"Not yet."

Now Leo was the one resisting her, taking his time now that he finally had her in his bed. His hands gripped her thighs, holding them apart. Tem arched her hips, meeting his mouth as his tongue delved even deeper.

It was nothing like when he'd tasted her in the maze. That time had been aggressive and militant—almost like a punishment. This time was slow and sensual and intimate, and Tem felt connected to Leo in a way she never had before. He was cherishing her, adoring her with his tongue, kissing the center of her like it was the most precious thing he'd ever tasted.

"*Leo*," she cried as his fingers joined his tongue.

His response was wordless, yet Tem understood what he was telling her with every stroke; she heard his message in every moment that he lost himself inside her. He loved her.

Tem was approaching the edge. It was inevitable; she couldn't resist if she tried.

She threaded her fingers into his hair, holding his head between her legs. She felt no shame. This was everything they were always meant to do; this was the way they were meant to be.

"Fuck," Tem moaned. Leo's favorite word.

It was the easiest thing in the world to come against his tongue.

Leo swallowed every last drop of her. There was no limit to his allegiance, no threshold he wasn't willing to cross. Tem arched her hips, rewarding him for his devotion, letting him know without a shadow of a doubt that he had earned access to any part of her he craved.

When Leo raised his head, he smiled. "Do you want my cock, Tem?"

She nodded.

"Say it." His fingers slid in and out of her, teasing her beyond what she could take. "Say you want my cock."

Tem would obey. Just this once. "I want your cock, Leo."

"When?"

"Now."

"Where?"

Her fingers joined his. "Here."

Leo kissed her thigh again, forcing her to wait for him, forcing her to be patient.

But patience had never been her strong suit.

"Leo," Tem insisted. "Now."

He chuckled softly. "So fucking needy."

That wouldn't do at all.

Tem moved her hands to her breasts, squeezing them while he watched.

"Tem." His voice was a broken murmur.

"Fuck me," she whispered. "Right now."

Leo stared at her, enraptured.

She arched her back. "*Now*, Leo."

That was all it took.

The moment Leo centered himself between her thighs, Tem's mind ceased to function. There was no logic or reasoning. There was only *want* and *need*.

Tem moaned as Leo's cock touched her center. He paused, his eyes flicking to hers, silently seeking permission one last time.

She grabbed the back of his neck, angled her hips, and pulled him all the way in.

Tem had handled his cock before, so she knew it was big. But it was something else entirely to feel Leo *enter* her—to take him the same way she'd taken Caspen. It was incredible to watch Leo's face as he slid inside her. If his expression was any indication, he felt what Tem felt: pure bliss.

He kissed her neck. Then her lips. "Tem," he whispered against them.

"Leo," she whispered back.

They moved in perfect unison. Tem touched every part of his body, digging her fingernails into his back as his thrusts deepened. His cock roused something within her—something that had patiently waited until now to emerge. She wanted more of him. She wanted him to stake his claim on her. She wanted to stake her claim on *him*.

"Faster, Leo," Tem whispered.

She felt him smile against her neck. "I'm afraid I can't do that, Tem."

"Why not?"

"If I go any faster, we won't be doing this for very long."

She smiled, pride shooting through her as she understood the effect she had on him.

Tem arched her hips so his thrusts went deeper.

Leo's fingers tightened in her hair. "*Fuck*," he groaned. He pushed her down firmly, pressing her hips against the mattress so he was once more in control. "We do this my way, Tem."

"Is that so?"

"Yes." His fingers wrapped around her neck. "It is."

She looked up at him. "What if I don't want to do it your way?"

"You can have anything you want next time, Tem. But not this time."

Before she could respond, Leo drew away.

He gripped her hips with his hands, pulling them up so he could watch her beneath him. He stared at the place of their union with covetous rapture, honoring their connection with every thrust. Tem's fists twisted into the sheets as he fucked her, letting him see everything he'd only dreamed of seeing. Just as Tem could feel herself building toward her climax, Leo paused. His fingers flexed on her hips as he tightened his grip, holding her in place as he pulled his cock out until only the head was inside her.

He thrust in an inch. Then back out.

Then another inch.

Then back out.

It was befitting of Leo; it was *torture*.

He was teasing her, bringing her to the brink of where she needed to go without actually letting her get there. The prince was in control; the prince decided what happened next. Tem couldn't blame him. It was only fair.

"Do you want to come, Tem?" Leo thrust a little farther, letting her have just half of his cock.

Tem nodded desperately.

"Use your words," he ordered.

"I want to come."

"Beg for it."

"Let me come."

"Again."

She understood why he needed to hear it, why he needed her to ask for him over and over. After so many weeks of acting ambivalent toward Leo, he needed to hear that Tem craved him as much as he craved her. Tem, of all people, could understand how it felt to be unwanted and how good it felt when the opposite was finally true. She would let him take anything he wanted from her; she would let him have exactly what he'd coveted for so long.

Tem begged for it again and again, calling his name until she couldn't tell where she ended and he began. She vocalized everything she loved about him, telling him exactly how he made her feel. With every word she said, Leo's cock went in a little farther. Finally, he was all the way inside her.

Tem asked for it one last time.

"Let me come, Leo. Please. I want to come."

Leo pressed his fingers to her clitoris, and it was this finally that took Tem over the edge. "So fucking pretty," he whispered.

Tem barely heard him.

She was flying—*soaring*—plummeting into the abyss with absolutely nothing to stop her. Leo was still touching her, still pushing her where he'd always wanted to take her. It was as simple as breathing to give this to Leo, to fall apart just for him, to see the complete and total victory in his eyes as she came.

Her body was laid out before him. She had nothing more to hide.

Leo reached for her, sliding his fingers behind her neck and pulling her upright. To be this close to him after what he'd just made her feel was nothing short of paradise.

"I want to come together," she whispered.

Leo kissed her neck, then her jaw, then her lips. "We will."

Tem didn't argue. He was lifting his hips, thrusting into her from below. In one smooth motion, he reclined onto his back, pulling her on top of him. She immediately began to ride him.

"Be still," Leo said.

Tem didn't want to be still. It went against everything her body was telling her to do. "Why?"

"I want to look at you."

Tem whimpered, straining her hips against his command.

Leo's hands shot forward, gripping her waist and holding her down. "Be *still*," he ordered.

Tem was still.

Leo leaned back, appraising her. The future king. "You look so good on my cock, Tem," he whispered.

Tem wanted to move—to slide her hips forward to show him how good she looked *riding* his cock. But he had told her to be still, so she was. She watched him as he watched her, his eyes traveling over her body with haughty satisfaction.

"Who knew that the only time you took orders was in bed?"

Tem rolled her eyes. "Don't get used to it."

"I certainly won't."

He was still holding her in place, still looking at her like she was his greatest prize.

Tem looked at him too, noticing all the things she'd never let herself notice before. His body was sculpted beneath hers, the rigid length of his cock placed perfectly in her center. She wanted to ride him *so badly*. But they would do this his way first. Then they could do it hers.

Leo brushed his fingertips up her thigh, raising goose bumps on her skin. "I've imagined this so many times," he said, his voice a husky whisper.

Tem took his hand in hers, raising it to her breasts. She guided just the tips of his fingers over her nipples, one after the other. "Did you imagine this?"

Leo's expression was one of unrestrained hunger.

Tem guided his hand even higher, biting down on his thumb. She sucked it gently, holding eye contact the entire time.

"*Kora*," he breathed. His other hand was on her hip. His fingernails dug into her skin, coaxing her forward.

The time to be still had passed.

Tem rode him slowly, splaying her hands flat on his torso. Both his hands went to her breasts, giving them a hard squeeze before gripping her hips once more.

"So *fucking wet* for me."

It was true. She was dripping for him.

It made riding his cock easier, made it so that she could slide up and down without restraint, ignoring everything but the way he felt inside her. Leo let her ride him, and Tem *knew* he'd imagined this. It only turned her on more to think of him that way—to picture him touching himself in the quiet darkness of his room, perhaps in front of the fire, coming into his palm at the thought of her on his cock. It was part of the reason she liked Leo so much. He was obsessed with her.

Tem felt her orgasm building long before it arrived. She worked toward it slowly, taking her time, bringing herself there while the prince watched. Leo touched her the entire time. He ran his hands over her ass, her hips, her waist. He filled his palms with her breasts.

"You were made for me," he rasped.

Tem leaned forward so he could see even more of her. The angle was nearly unbearable. His cock penetrated her so deeply that she gasped.

"Take it, Tem."

Tem did as she was told.

She took it over and over until she knew she couldn't take it anymore. When she reached that point, she let herself go, surrendering to all the pleasure Leo provided her. Her climax was visceral and *raw*, beginning between her legs and spreading throughout her entire body, unraveling her to her very core.

Leo held out, waiting until Tem's orgasm had completely run its course before having his own. It was incredible to watch him come. Tem noticed everything: the way his hands tightened on her hips, the way his veins popped beneath his skin, the way he tilted his chin as if to get a better view of her. It was clear that *Tem* had made him come—not the sex but Tem herself. She was all he wanted—all he needed.

She was his muse.

"Leo," she whispered as he poured himself into her.

He sat up, wrapping his arms around her and pulling her tightly against his chest. "I know, Tem," he murmured as he rubbed her back. "I know." His fingers stroked her spine, and his lips pressed against her shoulder.

Tem drew in a shuddering breath. Leo's heart was beating frantically in his chest, even faster than hers. He'd wanted this for far longer than Tem had. Leo was the one who yearned for her; Leo was the one who wanted a future that may never happen.

Tem lifted herself up. She touched the head of his cock before trailing her fingers up his torso, spreading a thin trail of his own cum over his skin, marking him with irrefutable evidence of their congress. Then she licked her fingers.

Leo watched her in amazement. "You're so gorgeous, Tem," he whispered, his lips drifting to her neck. "So fucking stunning."

She grasped a handful of his hair. "So are you."

Leo let out a soft laugh, pulling her down onto the bed. "Is that right?"

"Yes. Boys can be pretty too, Leo."

They lay together for a long time, doing nothing but touching each other. Tem explored the soft blond hair that trailed down to Leo's cock, the smooth dips between his ribs, the prominent Adam's apple on his neck.

Leo explored her too, touching her thighs, her hair, her sensitive nipples.

They kissed while they touched, and eventually, Tem's hand found his cock. He wasn't immediately hard again like Caspen always was, but Tem didn't mind. Perhaps it was beautiful, in a way, that there were limits with Leo. Each time with him was precious—each time *meant* something. She was content simply to stroke him with her fingers, listening to the sounds he made while she did it. It wasn't until later, when he began fingering her, that he became hard once more.

"Leo," she whispered as he rolled on top of her. "You said I could have anything I wanted."

"So I did," he whispered back. "How do you want me?"

Tem pulled him closer. "Just like this," she whispered. "Right here."

Leo smiled. "Then so you shall have me." He slid inside her.

Somehow it felt even better than the first time. They both moaned in unison, their breaths becoming one. Leo cradled her head in his hand, holding her securely as he sank into her again and again.

"So soft, Tem," he whispered. "So wet."

Tem took him deeper and deeper, all the way to the very center of her, validating their connection in the best way she knew how. She wanted to seal them together indefinitely. She wanted Leo's heart imprinted on hers. She wanted to give him her heart in return.

"I'm close, Leo."

He slowed his pace. "Not yet, Tem."

"Why not?"

"You said you wanted to come together."

Tem wanted nothing more.

She let Leo set the pace, savoring the way his tongue tasted in her mouth, tracing it with hers. She remembered their first kiss—how he'd told her to find him when she was ready. It was always that way with Leo. He always waited for her—always made sure she got what she wanted, even when she didn't know she wanted it. He listened to her. He cared.

Leo's face was right in front of hers. When he looked into her eyes, Tem understood that this moment meant everything to him. He'd chased her for so long, never truly earning her favor until it was too late. She wanted to give this to him now, to be together before everything inevitably fell apart around them.

Tem relaxed beneath his thrusts, knowing they would find their way together. She felt the hardness of his body, how perfectly it moved within hers. Their song had taken a long time to write, but now it was all Tem wanted to hear. Leo wasn't perfect, and neither was she. Tem didn't know what their future held, didn't even know if she would survive the week. But she knew she wanted to try. For him.

"Tem," Leo murmured, his lips dropping to her neck. His thrusts were quickening. "I'm going to fuck you harder now." The words were strained; he was clearly holding back.

Tem nodded eagerly, showing him she wanted that too. "Fuck me harder, Leo."

Her hands left his head and wrapped around the bedpost, holding on tight as he drove into her. This was it: the moment for them both. Tem had been waiting for this ever since they'd met in the study and they'd drank whiskey together for the first time. This had been building between them since then.

Tem closed her eyes. She knew Leo was watching her—knew he wanted to see every moment of this. But Tem wanted to *feel* it instead. She wanted to understand how her body took his, how perfectly they would conclude their union. This could be goodbye after all. Tem didn't want to forget a moment of it.

Leo called her name.

Tem answered with his.

They came together.

Tem opened her eyes to see Leo above her, content and fulfilled, his thrusts slowing as their waves began to ebb. Tem brushed her hands up his torso, pulling his face down to hers. She kissed him, and he kissed her back, and for a very long time, that was all they did. When they pulled apart, Leo smiled, flashing his teeth. Tem touched the gold ones.

Leo's expression sobered. Already, reality was setting in. Already, it was time to think about the future.

"Tem," he whispered. "I didn't know. If I had…"

Tem placed a single finger over his lips. She knew he hadn't known. But Tem was not so naive to think he would have charted a new path if he had. Not without knowing her—not without falling in love with someone who contained the very thing he'd been trained to hate.

Her response was the same thing Caspen once told her. "I don't hold you responsible for the sins of your ancestors."

Leo nodded, although she couldn't tell if he believed her. But there was nothing she could say to comfort him. This sliver of happiness was temporary for them. The moment they left Leo's room, they would have to face what came next.

But that moment did not have to be now. They lay together, their breathing in sync, and Leo's fingers brushed over the little claw necklace. Tem hadn't bothered to take it off.

"Tem," he whispered. "How did you find out about…who you are?"

She noticed how he said *who* rather than *what*.

It was progress.

"Caspen told me I was a hybreed."

"A hybreed?"

"Half human, half basilisk."

"How did he know?"

Tem raised her hands, showing Leo the freckles on her palms. "These," she said as he looked at them. "My father has the same ones. He passed them on to me."

Leo pressed his lips to the freckles.

"And he could talk to me using his mind," she said. "That capability is only between basilisks."

They were silent for a long time. Tem simply breathed Leo in, smelling the way his cologne mixed with his skin, feeling the way his body felt against hers. She brushed her fingers up his chest, to his shoulders, then around the back of his neck. She paused.

There was a ridge there—a firm line of scar tissue. When Tem touched it, Leo flinched.

He pulled away. Tem pulled him back.

"Leo," she said. "Turn around."

He shook his head. "No."

Tem sat up, and so did he.

"Leo," she said again. "Now."

To her surprise, after a pause, Leo obliged.

He turned slowly, kneeling on the bed so his back was to her. The moment the firelight hit his skin, Tem reached for him.

There were *four* ridges, she saw now, each about three inches long, two on either side of his spine. She couldn't believe she hadn't noticed them before.

"What happened to you?" Tem whispered.

"Carriage accident," he said quietly.

Of course it was a lie. He'd said that about the scar under his chin, but that one was jagged and irregular, befitting an accidental injury. The scars on his back were purposeful, almost surgical, and they looked like they had been administered fairly recently.

"Leo," she said. "Tell me."

"It's nothing, Tem."

She brushed her fingertips over the scars, and he shuddered. "It doesn't look like nothing." Without thinking, she leaned forward, pressing her lips to each scar. She turned her head, resting her cheek on the back of his neck and wrapping her arms around his torso. They sat like that for a long time, until finally, Leo spoke.

"They're traditional," he answered. "My father has them too. His father gave them to him, and so on."

Four raised scars, perfectly identical. She thought of the statue in the maze: *King Maximus III.* Leo would be the fourth king in his line.

Father and son.

"But *why*?"

Leo's shoulders rose, then fell. "Why does my family do any of the idiotic things we do? It's like any other ceremony. The Passing of the Crown, the Cutting—it's all the same. Yet another opportunity to mark the progression of power. My family has always been this way."

The Cutting. More tradition.

Tem thought of that time at the Horseman—how Gabriel had asked about Leo's golden teeth. Leo had answered: *The men in my family get them when we turn twenty, among other gifts.*

Some gifts.

She thought then of the freckles on her hands—a gift from her own father, but not one that had made her bleed. Leo bore the marks of his family in the same way she did, but his were administered with a blade. She imagined Leo doing this to his own son someday, cutting into his skin and leaving a scar. She couldn't picture it.

Tem relinquished her grip on his back, crawling around so she was facing him.

"Are you going to do it to your child?" she whispered.

Leo twirled one of her curls around his finger. "I would prefer that my son not hate me, Tem."

It took her a good long moment to understand what he was saying. "You…hate your father?"

"Trust me." He smiled sadly. "The feeling is mutual."

He said it so bluntly that Tem felt a sudden rush of sympathy for Leo. She couldn't imagine what it was like for him to grow up in this castle with a father who hated him. Maximus's contempt for her was scathing. No doubt it was tenfold for his own son.

A healed wound still bears a scar.

She took his face in her hands and looked him straight in the eye. "Maximus was wrong for doing this to you."

Leo shrugged. "It's all he knows."

"That doesn't make it right."

The prince had no rebuttal for that. Instead, he kissed her, and she let him.

When they pulled apart, Leo whispered, "I know you won't end things with Caspen."

Tem nestled herself more securely into his arms. "How do you know that?"

Leo gave her a sad smile. "He's your Evelyn."

Tem did not reply, because she realized it was true.

"I don't want to talk about Caspen," she whispered.

His hand brushed slowly down the curve of her waist before slipping between her legs. "Then we won't talk," he murmured as he slid his fingers inside her.

He touched her slowly, kissing her while he did it. Tem spread her legs for him, letting him go deeper, letting him touch everything he had earned the right to touch.

Eventually, she asked for all of him, and he gave it to her.

By the time they had finished with each other, night was falling. The sky outside Leo's window was rapidly turning black, and Tem knew they couldn't stay here forever.

"If you want to meet with him," she said, her lips still on his, "we should go tonight."

Leo sighed. He propped himself up on his hands, looking down at her. For a moment, Tem wondered if he would go back on his word—if everything that had just happened wouldn't be enough.

Then Leo nodded. "Very well."

CHAPTER THIRTY-SEVEN

———•••✳••———

T EM KNEW CASPEN WOULD NEVER AGREE TO MEET WITH LEO. THEIR LAST MEET-
ing had gone so poorly, she wasn't at all optimistic about how things would go if
he saw the prince again. But even if Tem wanted to ask Caspen for a meeting, she
wouldn't be able to anyway—their mental connection was so weak, she couldn't even
feel for the doorway into his mind anymore.

They would simply have to show up and hope for the best.

Tem could feel the minutes slipping by as they dressed. She was still fighting a
timeline, still praying she would be able to fix what she'd broken before it was too late.

When they were finally ready, Tem took Leo's hand.

They walked to the stables together, and this time, Tem knew nobody would stop
them from leaving. The staff catered to Leo's presence immediately, bowing their heads
and preparing a carriage for them.

The ride was silent. Leo simply held her hand in his, stroking the pad of his thumb
gently over her skin. Occasionally, he would raise her fingers to his lips and kiss them.
Tem leaned her head against his shoulder, trying not to think of what was to come. She
didn't have a plan beyond getting the two princes to speak reasonably to each other
about the future of their people. Surely, two grown men could accomplish such a thing
for the greater good.

Surely, this wouldn't be an utter disaster.

The carriage dropped them off at the edge of the forest. They walked together into
the woods and onto the trail that led to the caves. When they passed through the wall,
Leo raised an eyebrow but didn't comment. Tem didn't feel like explaining how the
basilisks were only vulnerable to mirrors when they wore their true forms. It wasn't
anything the prince needed to know right now. Finally, they reached the base of the
mountain.

"Leo," Tem said quietly, stopping when they reached the entrance of Caspen's cave.
"Can I ask you a favor?"

He stopped too, looking at her in the darkness. Before she could speak, he said, "You
would prefer that he didn't know we slept together."

Tem pursed her lips. "Yes."

"I will not reveal it."

She gave him a dubious look.

He stepped closer. "I want you all to myself. Why would I tell him?"

"Because it would hurt him."

Leo shook his head. "It would also hurt you. And I have no interest in doing that."

"This is already hurting me, Leo."

The words just slipped out. Tem didn't even know if she meant them. But agony flashed across Leo's face, and he whispered, "I don't want to hurt you."

Tem sighed. "It's not you exactly. It's…"

He finished for her. "Us."

She sighed again, looking up at him. "Yes."

"Tem, I…" Leo started but didn't finish. He looked deeply unhappy, and Tem didn't know how to fix it. They both knew what she'd said couldn't be unsaid. But Tem needed him to hear it—needed him to know how painful it was for her to be caught between two parts of herself. It was slowly tearing her in half.

Leo looked at her sadly.

"I know you have always doubted my intentions," he said. "And I don't blame you, considering my past. But know this: I will never do anything to hurt you."

He leaned in.

"Know this also: I want you. And I know that's not what you want to hear. And I know you don't want me back—at least not enough to justify betraying whatever connection you have with him. But I cannot live without you. Even if it means I only have some part of you, that is far preferable to no part of you at all."

"Vera is the better match," Tem whispered. "You should just choose her."

"I'd rather have half of you than all of Vera. Even if it means sharing you for the rest of my life."

Tem stared at him. Had Leo just…*proposed?* Before she could process this, he spoke again.

"I know you belong to him, Tem. And I know I want you anyway."

"Leo…" she whispered, but she had no idea what to say.

What was the appropriate response here? What could be said to such a vulnerable admission? Leo had always been candid with her about his feelings, always crystal clear with his declarations of favor. But this one was different. This one was permanent.

"Can we just…get through tonight?" she asked. "For now?"

A resigned smile twisted Leo's lips. "Of course we can, Tem."

She knew they were limited by time and circumstance. She knew he wanted more. But it was beyond her control. "Thank you," Tem whispered.

Leo bowed his head. Then she dropped his hand, and they entered the cave.

Tem watched Leo as his eyes adjusted to the darkness and took in the fireplace and the mat in front of it. It was strange seeing him here in this place where Tem had taken so many first steps, where Caspen had taught her everything she'd always wanted to know. Tem no longer recognized the girl who had come to this cave all those weeks ago. That girl was gone.

Tem turned to Leo. "I should talk to him first," she said.

He nodded. "Very well."

"Just…wait here."

Leo nodded again. He seemed determined, like no matter what happened, he was resolved to his fate. Tem admired his bravery. It was no small feat to come face-to-face with a basilisk. To Leo, he was coming face-to-face with his enemy—the creature his family had villainized his entire life. It couldn't be easy for him to unravel that prejudice in real time.

She pressed a quick kiss to his cheek before dipping into the passageway. Her quiet knock on Caspen's door was answered immediately.

"Tem," Caspen said, and even now, her heart flipped at the sound of him saying her name. "What is it?"

She knew he hadn't been expecting her. The last time they'd communicated had been when she'd spoken to Adelaide. Tem still didn't know whether Adelaide had told him the contents of that conversation. She had no idea if he knew that the basilisk side of her was slowly dying—that his own fate was in question.

Tem looked up at him. He didn't look well. There were shadows under his eyes that had never been there before. Was he simply not sleeping? Or was this a symptom of the joined effect of the crest? She wanted to reach for him but didn't. Instead, she said, "I…need you to talk to someone."

Caspen raised an eyebrow. "Who?"

There was nothing for it. "Leo."

At the sound of his name, Caspen stiffened. His nostrils flared, and Tem knew he could smell the human prince on her. "Why?"

"I told him you would be willing to see him."

"You *brought* him? Have you lost your *mind*, Tem? He cannot be here."

"Well, he is. And he wants to speak with you."

If Caspen was shocked before, he was floored now. "*Why?*" he hissed.

"He wants to discuss the future of the kingdom. He wants to end the bloodletting."

Caspen's eyes were dark with fury. "There is nothing to discuss. There will be no peace as long as the royals are in power. You have seen what they are capable of."

"Leo isn't like the rest of the royals."

"He is *exactly* like the rest of the royals. He considers himself better than the basilisks."

She shook her head. "No. He doesn't. Not anymore."

"Of *course* he does, Tem. He is no different from his father. He will never show us mercy. He would have us all killed."

"Leo is not his father."

Caspen stepped closer. Tem resisted stepping back. "You are a fool if you believe that."

Anger coiled within her. "You don't know him, Caspen."

Caspen shook his head, leaning in. The shadows under his eyes hadn't been her imagination. He was gaunt, his features drawn as if he hadn't eaten in a long while. Tem hated seeing him like this. She had to fix it.

"You do not know him either, Tem. You cannot trust anything he says."

"I trusted you, didn't I?"

Caspen's eyes narrowed. "What does that mean?"

"I had no reason to trust you, but I did. Now look at us."

Caspen bristled. "Are you comparing me to him? Because I consider that an insult."

"I'm not comparing you. I'm just saying that—"

"You are saying that because you trusted me, I should trust him. But one has nothing to do with the other."

"That's not fair. You can't judge him without knowing him."

"I can do whatever I wish, Tem."

She knew he was angry. But she was angry too.

Critical analysis came second nature to Caspen, but for Leo, questioning his circumstances was a learned behavior—one he couldn't possibly master in the short time since Tem had told him who she was. She was willing to give him allowances that Caspen wasn't. She understood that he was still growing into the person she knew he could be—the person she knew he wanted to be. There was nothing black-and-white about Leo; he was not good or bad, cowardly or brave. He was many things at once. And Tem loved him for it.

She crossed her arms, standing her ground. "You're better than that, Caspen."

He laughed bitterly. "Am I? Why should I hold myself to a higher standard when you consider me equal to the human prince?"

"I never said you were equal."

"You may as well have." Caspen stepped closer, and Tem flinched. "Imagine what he would do if he knew what you really are."

She gritted her teeth. He wasn't going to like what came next. "He already knows."

Caspen went completely still. His eyes searched hers, and there was nothing but betrayal in them. Tem knew she'd violated his trust—knew she'd chosen to tell Leo she was a hybreed without consulting him first. But it was her secret to share. Caspen didn't have to like it.

"You *told* him? Do you have any idea how dangerous that is?"

"He deserves to know."

"What else did you tell him? Does he know about the crest?"

Tem hesitated. Leo didn't know about the crest, about how there was a plan for Maximus and the rest of the royals.

"No," she said, keeping her voice steady. "And he doesn't need to know."

"And why should he not know? It concerns his family, does it not?"

"His family will be spared," Tem insisted.

"Not all of them. Only himself and his sister. You made that very clear."

His voice was dangerously quiet. A flicker of doubt passed through Tem. Leo hated Maximus. He'd said so himself. But did he hate him enough to condemn him to the crest?

"Shall I tell him?" Caspen taunted, his eyes flashing like flint in the darkness. "Or would you like to do the honor of informing him of what will happen to his father?"

The doubt intensified. The last thing Tem wanted was for Caspen to tell Leo about the crest. If he reacted badly, if for some reason his hatred for Maximus didn't run as deeply as she thought, things between them could fall apart.

"You can't do that," Tem said.

"And why not?" Caspen asked.

Tem didn't like his tone. He was threatening her.

"Because it could ruin everything, and you know it."

"Everything? Or your relationship with him?"

"Nothing could ruin my relationship with him."

Caspen's eyes widened, then narrowed. Tem knew he understood what she was saying: that her connection with Leo had been solidified through sex. That it was permanent.

"I did not realize," he whispered, his voice deadly, "that you could be so easily seduced."

Rowe's words came back to her suddenly: *The plaything has fallen in love with her playmate.*

It wasn't a foreign thing to see Caspen so jealous, but it was to see him so petty. Tem wondered if it was an effect of the crest—if his usual stoicism was weakening along with the rest of him. He had always been steady. But no longer.

"I have to marry him, Caspen. That's always been the plan."

Little did Caspen know that his own life depended on that plan. He scoffed.

Tem continued. "Leo is on our side. I promise you."

Caspen arched his face to the ceiling, the cords of his neck standing out beneath his skin.

"*Kora*. You always do what you want, Tem. You never *think*."

This was going nowhere. Tem had to get them back on track. "Just talk to him. Please. Do it for me."

Tem knew perfectly well that it was the last thing Caspen wanted to do. But he also owed her this for all the things he'd kept from her. He couldn't be angry that she'd done something without asking him, and he knew it as well as she did.

After a seemingly endless pause, he said, "There is nothing I would not do for you."

Without another word, Tem turned.

Caspen followed at a distance, staying two steps behind her. Just before they reached the cave, Tem saw that his hands were balled into fists.

"Caspen."

He looked down at her.

She touched his arm gently. "Please," Tem whispered.

For a long moment, he didn't react. Then he uncurled his fingers, letting his hands hang loose at his sides. They entered the cave.

Leo was leaning against the wall but straightened when he saw them. He immediately glanced at Tem before looking at Caspen.

A long moment passed, and Tem held her breath. Leo said nothing. He seemed resolved to let Caspen take the lead. It wasn't until Caspen dipped his head in Leo's direction in the barest form of acknowledgment that Tem finally let out her breath. It was good enough for her.

Tem stepped between them, spreading her hands in what she hoped was a neutral gesture.

"Both of you have been told that the other is the enemy," she said quietly. "But that is a lie."

The two princes stared at each other, neither of them speaking.

"I'm living proof that you can coexist," Tem continued. "If you want peace, you need to break the cycle."

Caspen tilted his head, and Tem thought he might say something. Instead, Leo was the first to speak.

"I understand you may have…reservations about me," Leo said, addressing Caspen directly. "But I can assure you we are on the same side."

Caspen let out a dry, incredulous noise.

"Tem has informed me of my father's actions," Leo went on as if Caspen hadn't made a sound. "They are appalling, and they should not go unpunished. I'd like to help with that if I can."

Caspen still hadn't spoken, and Tem was starting to wonder if he was ever going to.

Leo continued doggedly. "You may not trust me, but Tem does. And I know you value her opinion."

Caspen blinked.

Then he looked at Tem.

They held eye contact for a long moment, and Tem felt the gaping void where their connection used to be. Caspen finally broke his silence.

"The only opinion I value is my own," he growled.

The two men stared at each other. Caspen's hands were slowly balling back into fists, and Tem rushed to break the moment before things got worse.

"You both want the same thing," Tem said. "Can we at least agree on that?"

They looked at her.

She realized she had inadvertently spoken too much of the truth and scrambled to move things along. "When Leo becomes king, he will cease the bloodletting immediately."

Caspen looked back at Leo. "Your *father* might mind."

"He won't be king anymore. He won't have a say."

Caspen's jaw tightened. "The bloodletting is the reason you have so much gold. If you cease it, you forsake your wealth."

Leo licked his lips, and Tem wondered if he was thinking about the golden fangs in his mouth. "Wealth obtained in such a way is of no value to me. There are far greater treasures than gold."

Tem didn't miss the way his eyes flicked to hers. Caspen stepped toward Leo, who immediately stiffened. For a single terrifying moment, Tem thought he might tell him about the crest. But then Caspen said, "Why?"

Leo blinked. "Why what?"

Caspen stepped even closer. To Leo's credit, he didn't step back. "Why are you willing to go against your own father?"

Despite how close Caspen was standing, Leo looked over at Tem for a long moment before answering. "I know how it feels to lose something you love," he said. His eyes slid back to Caspen's, and he finished quietly. "My father loves power above all else. I'd like to see him lose it."

Caspen didn't know Leo's story, didn't know he was referring to Evelyn. But Tem knew Leo's motivations better than anyone. The bloodletting wasn't just a misdeed that needed to be corrected—it was a way for Leo to heal from his past.

Caspen raised his eyebrows, and Tem swore she saw a modicum of respect pass over his face. Then he stifled it.

"No royal is so altruistic. What do you expect in return?"

"He doesn't want anything," Tem said.

"But I do," Leo said quietly. He turned to Tem, and her heart stopped. "I do want something in return."

A beat of silence passed.

Now Tem understood. Leo was willing to do this, but only on one condition: Her.

Caspen let out a dry snicker.

Leo held up his hand. "I do not expect you to stop seeing each other. I am not so naive to think that your bond could be ignored. Love demands to be felt."

There was a pause, and Tem's heart nearly broke. Leo was always doing this, saying deeply impactful things in a matter-of-fact manner. He was skilled with his words, even now.

He continued. "I understand that basilisks live very long lives. You will have nearly an eternity together." His gaze moved to Tem, and his next words were a whisper. "I just...want you while I can have you."

It was, as Bastian might say, an elegant solution.

Why shouldn't they share her? Tem was in love with them both. She was equal parts human and basilisk. Tem already knew that Caspen didn't consider the human prince to be his equal. As such, he also shouldn't consider him a threat. Caspen looked down on Leo in the same way the royals looked down on the basilisks. Leo was not important to Caspen—he never had been. But he was important to Tem.

She looked at Caspen, and he looked back at her.

In his gaze, she saw how deeply her absence had affected him. He *missed* her—she could see it in his eyes, in the way they drank in hers. And she missed him. She needed their mental connection back, needed that essential part of her. And in order to restore it, she needed to marry Leo.

Caspen spoke first. "It is up to Tem."

Leo nodded. "Of course." He looked at her. "It's up to you."

Tem opened her mouth, then closed it again. It was extraordinary—there was no other word for it. She couldn't believe she was standing here in this cave, between these two men, deciding the fate of a kingdom. It wasn't anything she ever expected for herself.

And yet it was everything she was meant to do.

There was no future for her on the chicken farm—no possibility of ever going back to the way things were. It was time to step into who she was always meant to be.

Tem was ready to speak her truth.

"I love you both."

There was a distinct change in the air when she said it, as if the universe had tilted on its axis. For some reason, she felt powerful. It was incredibly freeing to finally say it—to lay herself bare before both of them at the same time. They were all on the same page now. There was nothing left to hide, nothing to fight over. She loved Caspen, and she loved Leo, and she wasn't about to stop anytime soon. They would move forward together; they would forge their own path.

Tem wasn't sure what would happen next. There didn't seem to be much else to say after what had just been said. She found herself looking to Caspen, as she always had, for guidance.

He turned to Leo. "I still do not trust you."

Leo sighed. "Then allow me the chance to prove myself," he said calmly. "I will be crowned king at my wedding, at which time I will announce that we are entering a new era—one in which there will be no more bloodletting. If I don't keep my word, you are welcome to kill me then. That will be my fate if things continue as they have been anyway. Am I wrong?"

Leo was smart. He knew that the timing of this meeting was not accidental, that surely, the basilisks were planning to take down the royals. He didn't know about the crest—he had no clue that his father's free will was being used as a bargaining chip. But there was no need for him to know. Those were just details, scraps of information that would tangle a plan that needed to be perfect.

Finally, Caspen replied, "You are not wrong."

Leo nodded. And that was the end of it.

With one last lingering glance at Tem, Caspen turned and disappeared back into the passageway. Tem didn't go after him. There was no point. She would simply have to wait to see what the ripple effect of this conversation would be moving forward. She would have to hope for the best.

Leo broke the silence. "That went well."

Tem suppressed a bizarre urge to laugh. "You're still alive. So yes, it did."

Leo chuckled quietly. "Have you so little faith in his self-restraint?"

"I have faith in his self-restraint," Tem said. "But not in his temper. And if you knew him better, you'd feel the same."

Leo's smile faded. "I very much doubt he'll give me the opportunity."

"It doesn't matter, Leo," Tem said tiredly. "We just have to move forward."

Leo seemed to sense her exhaustion because his hand touched her waist tentatively, pulling her against him. It remained there as they made their way back to the carriage, moving to encircle her shoulders on the ride back to the castle. They exited the carriage together, and when they reached the landing before Leo's room, they turned to each other.

Tem opened her mouth to speak, but she was interrupted by the arrival of Vera, who flounced up the stairs with insistent glee. "I've been looking everywhere for you," she purred at Leo.

That much was apparent. It was nearly dawn; Vera had probably been roaming the castle all night in an attempt to bed him.

"Vera," Leo said dully. "Hello."

Her smile faltered at his tone. "You wanted to see me?" she said.

Leo raised an eyebrow, as if he'd just remembered something. "Ah." He nodded. "Yes, I did."

Vera flourished once more. "*Wonderful*. Because I was thinking we could—"

"I'm afraid we will not be continuing with our courtship."

Vera's mouth fell open. So did Tem's.

"*Excuse* me?" she scoffed, her hateful gaze flashing to Tem. "Are you telling me you're choosing *her*?"

"Yes," Leo said. "I am."

Tem sensed something new in his energy—something calm. He seemed to have discovered some sort of inner peace in the last day, an assuredness that sustained him from deep within. Nothing seemed to bother Leo anymore. He was a man with purpose now. It looked good on him.

But Vera wasn't done. "I hope you like the taste of chicken shit," she spat. "Because that's all you'll get with her."

Leo straightened. "I would ask that you not disparage my future wife in front of me. As of now, you are no longer a guest in my home. If you are unable to see yourself out, I shall find someone to escort you."

Vera's face went tight with shock. For all the times she'd publicly humiliated Tem, this was not how either of them expected their rivalry to pan out. Vera stepped forward, and for a moment, Tem thought she might smack her. Instead, she burst into violent, gulping tears before turning without another word and running sobbing down the stairs.

"Sorry, darling," Leo murmured, almost as an afterthought.

Tem was frozen in place, shocked by what she'd just seen. She barely noticed as Leo steered her back into his room, only snapping back to the present when he crossed to his nightstand, pulled out a small velvet box, and returned to her.

Leo knelt.

CHAPTER THIRTY-EIGHT

◦•✳•◦

T EM," HE WHISPERED.

The entire world went silent. Tem could hear nothing but her own heartbeat, which pounded like thunder in her chest.

"I know my time with you is somewhat borrowed," Leo said quietly. "And I know that I will never have all of you. But, Tem." He paused, looking her right in the eye. "It is without ego that I say your presence in my life has changed me immeasurably. You are headstrong. And stubborn. And infuriatingly difficult to please."

She smiled at that one.

Leo continued. "You are also courageous. And irresistible. And you invariably make me a better person, even when I struggle to return the favor. In short, you are too good for me. But I'm asking for you anyway."

Tears were coming. She didn't bother holding them back.

"I am greedy when it comes to you, Tem. I want every moment you're willing to give me. Even if our marriage offers me nothing but the opportunity to humble myself before you, it would be worth it to spend what's left of my life in your presence." He opened the box. "Would you do me the honor of being my queen?"

They were beautiful words. And they were all for her.

Tem had only one word for him in return: "Yes."

A wide smile split Leo's face, and he stood, drawing her into a deep kiss. Tem was floored by his vulnerability and deeply touched by his proposal. He was signing up for a compromise—agreeing to a lifetime of sharing her. The sacrifice was not lost on her. It was the highest compliment she could be given. She only hoped she was worthy of it.

Leo took her hand and slid on the ring. "It was my mother's," he offered. "We will get you a proper jewel if you wish. But I didn't want to propose with gold."

Tem looked at her finger. The ring was polished silver, not unlike the ring she used to wear for special occasions. It was not flashy or excessive or boisterous. And it was not made from the blood of her people.

It was perfect.

Leo kissed her again, and for a moment, Tem allowed herself to be happy.

But soon, fear set in. The only thing she could think about was how scared she was for Leo, how deeply she wanted to protect him, how even though she knew his proposal was exactly what was needed to keep him safe, she was slowly crumbling beneath the pressure to do so.

"When will the wedding be?" she asked when they drew apart.

"My family has already arrived," Leo answered. "And the ceremony has been planned for months. So whenever you wish."

Tem nodded. Adelaide had said she had less than a week before the consequences of Caspen's crest would take their toll. That meant they needed to get married in a matter of days. Tem wasn't sure how to suggest this without sounding insane.

Before she could truly spiral, Leo spoke. "The harvest moon is tomorrow."

The harvest moon was the official marker of autumn and would afford them ample moonlight in the early evening.

"You want to get married tomorrow?"

Leo only shrugged. "Every day we wait is a day your father continues to suffer."

Tem felt a sudden swell of tenderness for him. Leo had always known that the way to her heart was through the people she cared about. She thought of how willing he'd been to face Caspen, how immediately he'd considered her father's well-being. But Leo thought their only problem was the bloodletting, that their timeline was influenced solely by Kronos.

He had no idea what was to come.

"Tomorrow it is."

One glance at the sky told Tem it was nearly tomorrow already. They'd been at the caves for so long that the sun was already beginning to rise. Leo seemed to notice this at the same time as she did.

"I'll inform my father," he said.

"Should I come with you?"

"No."

Tem raised her eyebrows. He'd answered that awfully quickly.

At the look on her face, Leo softened. "He won't be pleased, Tem. I'd rather you not hear what he has to say."

Protecting her again.

Tem nodded, because it was just easier that way. She didn't particularly want to hear what Maximus had to say either. She could only imagine the criticism he would impart on his son. No doubt it would only be worse if the object of his vitriol was present.

"I'm going to tell my mother," she said.

Leo nodded. "I look forward to meeting her properly."

Tem smiled, remembering the time he'd kissed her on the porch while her mother was in the kitchen.

They parted ways in the foyer, and Tem said a silent prayer for the prince as he disappeared behind the parlor doors. Part of her actually did want to see Maximus's reaction when Leo told him he would be marrying Tem. But the other part of her was tired of the king's cruelty, and she figured the crest was revenge enough.

Tem spent the long carriage ride to the village watching the sun rise. When she reached her cottage, it felt like an eternity had passed since she'd last been there. And yet everything was just as she remembered it. The garden was slowly dying under the autumn chill. The front porch was still sloped. Everything was the way it had been for the past twenty years.

Everything except for Tem.

When she entered the kitchen, her mother looked up from the stove.

"The prince has proposed," Tem said simply.

Her mother's hand flew to her mouth. "Oh, *Tem*," she cried, crossing the kitchen and gathering Tem into a tight embrace.

Tem embraced her back. "I have accepted," she continued. "And the wedding is tonight."

Her mother pulled away. "Tonight? That's…quite soon."

"I know."

"I'm afraid I will have nothing to wear."

Tem waved her off. "We'll find you something."

Her mother tilted her head. "Is everything in order, my dear? You do not look… joyous."

Tem didn't feel joyous. She felt only deep-seated anxiety. There were too many balls in the air—too many things that could go wrong.

"I'm just…in shock," she said.

"But why? The prince has always favored you."

As soon as she said it, Tem knew it was true. But that didn't mean she was joyous. It only meant she felt guilty Leo had to share her.

"Tem." Her mother took her hands gently in hers. "Talk to me."

She sighed. Why lie anymore? "I love another," Tem said simply.

Her mother's eyebrows rose. "Who?"

"Caspen."

Her mother frowned. Tem knew she would recognize the distinctly basilisk name. She watched as the truth dawned in her eyes—as her mother realized that history had repeated itself. "Foolish girl," she whispered, looking down at Tem's hands and running her thumbs over her freckles. "Just like your mother."

You hold the stars in your hands. Just like your father.

Tem clasped their fingers together tightly. "It is *not* foolish to fall in love, Mother. I have been many things, but I'm not a fool. And neither were you."

Pain flashed in her mother's eyes. She dropped Tem's hands and crossed to the kitchen window. "Perhaps you are right," her mother sighed. It was a long moment before she turned back to Tem, asking, "Why are you marrying the prince if you love another?"

"I love the prince too."

Silence settled in the kitchen, broken only by the occasional crow of a rooster.

Tem broke it. "May I ask you something?"

"Of course, my dear."

"Do you still love my father?"

Her mother turned once more to the window. Morning sunshine dappled her face. "Love is complicated. It never goes away, only changes."

Tem had never heard her mother speak so vulnerably. She pictured her next to Kronos, wondering how they would look together. It seemed a simple thing for other children—to see their mother and father in the same room. For Tem, it would be a miracle.

"It is true that I left your father," her mother continued quietly. "But it was not what either of us wanted."

Tem nodded, thinking of how her father had belonged to the Senecas—how that quiver wasn't open-minded about courtships between humans and basilisks. Tem had never considered the ritual she'd endured a blessing. But now she realized she was lucky it had even been offered as an option. If Caspen's quiver hadn't allowed her to prove herself, their relationship would have suffered—maybe even ended—just like her mother's had.

She thought of how her mother had prepared her for her first night in the caves, how she'd rubbed the special oils on her thighs. At the time, Tem thought she'd need courage to have her first kiss. But perhaps her mother had wanted her to be brave in another way: brave enough to ask for what she wanted and to settle for nothing less. Brave enough to fight for those she loved. Brave enough to do what she hadn't.

Her mother continued quietly. "Your father said he would still visit me, but he did not. I assumed he had chosen another."

How wrong her mother was.

"Mother," Tem said, and she knew what came next would change her world forever. "I met him."

A curious expression passed over her mother's face—one of absolute hope. "How can that be?"

Tem had to remember that her mother wasn't connected to the basilisk world anymore. She had no concept of anything that had happened since she'd parted ways with Tem's father. She didn't know about the bloodletting, about Bastian's plan to seize power. Tem couldn't fathom explaining everything that had happened. Instead, she said, "He was captured and imprisoned by the royals. They're keeping him at the castle."

Her mother's face went slack with shock. "He's been imprisoned?"

"Yes. He's…weak. But alive. The prince plans on freeing him."

"So he…" Her mother didn't finish her sentence.

Tem finished it for her: "He did not choose another."

It was a curious thing to watch her mother experience joy. It wasn't something Tem saw often. They lived a hard life on the farm after all. Joy reared its head rarely—on holidays or when they exchanged gifts on birthdays. But it was fleeting, circumstantial. What she saw now was true, unencumbered happiness, mixed with deep relief. Tem couldn't help but smile.

Love is complicated. It never goes away, only changes.

"My dear, I…must know more."

They sat at the kitchen table. Tem told her more.

She told her what had happened since the first night in the caves, how serious things had gotten with Caspen and also with Leo. Her mother listened and told stories of her own. They sat in solidarity, mother and daughter, sharing pieces of their lives with each other.

Eventually, it was time for Tem to say goodbye to her childhood home.

She sat on her bed and looked up at the ceiling. She smelled the bottle of salt spray on her mother's dresser. And she walked through the chicken coop one last time, reveling in the fact that she may never hear a rooster crow again.

Then she and her mother stepped into the carriage and drove away.

By the time they reached the castle, wedding preparations were well underway. Even for a well-oiled machine like the royal staff, setting up a wedding in one day was a tall order. Tem and her mother dodged servant after servant on their way into the castle, finally managing to flag down a maid in the foyer.

"This is my mother," Tem said. "Can you find her a seamstress? She needs a dress for this evening."

"Of course," the maid said. "And when would you like to do your fitting?"

Tem paused. She'd completely forgotten that she needed a dress too. She was the bride after all. "Later," she said. "Have someone send for me."

She gave her mother's hand one final squeeze before ascending the steps to Leo's bedroom. He wasn't inside; perhaps his discussion with Maximus was still ongoing.

Tem walked around his bed, looking at his books the same way she had when she'd first come here. There was *The Raven and the Swan*. Tem smiled at the memory of Leo reading it to her.

Something occurred to her suddenly.

The wedding would be dangerous. Not just for Tem but for Leo. He was human, and he was the only son of the king. There was a target on his back. Rowe had tried to crest Tem. It was only a matter of time before he—or any of the other basilisks—did the same to Leo. Tem's bargain with Bastian had spared Leo's life, nothing more. She hadn't thought to add a stipulation that nobody could crest him. Tem would have to protect him the same way Caspen protected her. She would give him her venom—she would claim him. There was only one problem.

Tem had no idea how to produce venom.

She'd only watched Caspen do it once, and she'd been mid-orgasm, so she hadn't exactly been paying attention. Besides, she had no idea if her basilisk side was even strong enough to produce venom anymore.

It didn't matter. She would have to try.

Tem did her best to imitate what Caspen had done, focusing on her neck and tensing the muscles just below her ears where she assumed the venom glands were. At first, nothing happened, and doubt cut through her. Then a shooting heat erupted in her throat, and she lurched forward to spit into an empty whiskey glass.

Her venom was dark, practically black. Tem stared at it in bewilderment, wondering how she was going to get Leo to drink such a distinctive substance without him noticing. Even if he didn't see it, she was sure he would taste it. Caspen's had tasted like smoke; hers was distinctly woodsy in flavor.

But what if there was another way? What if she simply asked him to drink it? Caspen had given her his venom without asking. Was Tem really going to do the same thing to Leo?

At that exact moment, Leo walked in.

Tem looked up at him, still holding the glass. "How did it go?" she asked.

Leo gave her a tired smile. "How do you think it went?"

"Are we still getting married?"

His smile turned into a real one. "Tem." He crossed to her. "I'd have to be dead in order for us not to."

Tem smiled too. Then she handed him the glass. "Drink this."

Leo cocked an incredulous eyebrow at the black substance, holding it up to the light. "What is it?"

"It's my venom."

Leo blinked. "Your…venom."

"Yes."

"And what is it doing in my nicest whiskey glass?"

"I already told you. I need you to drink it."

"Yes, you mentioned that. But you didn't mention why."

"It will protect you."

"Protect me from what?"

"Oh, for Kora's *sake*, Leo. Will you just drink it, please? You wouldn't believe me anyway. I just need you to trust me."

The words came out harsher than she'd intended. Leo's eyebrows rose even more at her tone. He looked at her for a long moment, considering something. Then: "Very well," he said quietly.

Without another word, he drank. The moment her venom disappeared down his throat, Tem felt unmistakable relief. Leo was safe. Nobody could crest him. He would never be controlled by Bastian or any other basilisk.

Tem felt something else too. It was as if an invisible bridge had grown between them, a passage connecting her to him. It wasn't quite like the corridor she shared in her mind with Caspen, but it was an inarguable thread that was as real as a physical sensation. She wondered if Leo felt it too.

Tem stood on her tiptoes, pressing a kiss to his cheek. "Thank you."

Leo smiled beneath her lips. "Anything for you, Tem."

His arm wrapped around her waist, pulling her into a proper kiss. She could taste her venom on his tongue. A little smoky, like Caspen's, only sweeter and earthier. When the kiss deepened, she let it. But when Leo pulled her toward the bed, she stopped him.

"I need to get to my dress fitting, Leo."

"No, you don't. You need to kiss me."

"I'm the bride, remember?"

"We'll get married naked. It'll be delightful. The guests will love it."

"*Leo.*"

"*Tem*," he groaned, throwing his head back. "What's the point of marrying you if I can't fuck you whenever I want?"

"Some would say love."

"Ah, yes." He smiled. "That." The smile faded, and Leo became serious. He traced a finger up her neck, tilting her face to his. "You know I love you, don't you, Tem?"

He didn't need to tell her; Tem knew it from his actions. She saw Leo's love for her in every glance, felt it in every touch. Even when they were fighting, she knew he loved her. He always had. "I know, Leo."

Tem realized suddenly that the only time she'd said she loved Leo was in front of Caspen. *I love you both.* Even that, Leo had to share.

Tem whispered her next question, genuinely wondering the answer. "Do you know I love you too?"

If Leo looked happy before, he was positively euphoric now. "Yes, Tem." His arm tightened around her. "I know that. But I am certainly glad to hear it."

There was a sharp knock on the door.

Leo groaned again, and Tem laughed at his constant unwillingness to be interrupted. The door opened to reveal the same maid from before.

"Temperance?" she asked. "It's time for your dress fitting."

The rest of the day was a whirlwind.

A fleet of maids ushered Tem from one event to the next in a blur of pearls and tulle. There was not one but *three* dresses to be chosen, along with cake samples, champagne (which she gave to the maids to taste), and flower arrangements. A harpist sampled a song for their first dance as husband and wife.

Tem barely registered any of it.

Her mind was spinning with worry—with *fear*. She felt slightly better now that she'd claimed Leo. But beyond that, she had no guarantees that anything would go well. Soon the basilisks would be here, at the castle, and they would be angry. They were ready for war—a war that was completely up to Tem to prevent. Caspen was right; she was unprepared. At this point, she didn't even know if she *could* perform the crest. Perhaps too much of her basilisk side was already dead. Perhaps it was too late.

But there was nothing Tem could do about it now.

There was no time to prepare, no time to change course. She would simply have to do her best and pray that it was enough. She had always excelled under pressure, always risen to the occasion when the situation demanded it. Now she was demanding it of herself, and Tem refused to fall short of what she knew she was capable of.

At last, it was evening.

Tem donned the first of her three dresses—white, made of beaded silk—before joining Leo in the ballroom.

"Flawless," he said as he kissed her hand. "As always."

Tem smiled. "Finally, a real compliment," she said.

Leo grinned. He looked flawless too. He was wearing a dark green suit, his blond hair slicked back to accentuate his sharp cheekbones. For some reason, he seemed taller than usual, and Tem wondered if his newfound confidence was due to the fact that in a few short hours, Maximus would crown him king. Any son, especially one who had been through what Leo had, would feel triumphant.

"We will be married in the maze," Leo told her as they descended the patio steps together, joining the throngs of people on the grounds. "There is a clearing in the middle. My family uses it for all royal weddings."

Tem nodded, although she wasn't listening. She was observing the guests with hypervigilance, scanning them quickly to see if Caspen was here yet. Or Bastian.

Tem didn't know for sure whether the king would attend. She'd never been to a royal wedding after all. But she was positive that all the basilisks who'd been involved in the training would be in attendance, and that meant Rowe would be here. The thought made her exceedingly anxious, and her grip tightened on Leo's arm.

"I've got you, Tem," he murmured in her ear. She nodded but didn't reply. Leo could do nothing to save her if something went wrong. Tem was the one responsible for protecting Leo, not the other way around.

They rounded corner after corner as the sun began to set.

"There will be a cocktail hour," Leo said. "And then the ceremony. Afterward, dinner will be served."

Tem nodded again. They had arrived at the center of the maze, and for a moment, she forgot her worries. The clearing was impeccably decorated: candles twinkled on the tables, interspersed with the floral arrangements she'd approved mere hours ago. The harpist was playing a sweeping, melodic tune. At the far end of the clearing were rows of golden chairs, all facing a stage where an enormous arch was sheathed in white roses.

No basilisks yet.

As if Leo could read her mind, he leaned in and said, "They should arrive soon."

Suddenly, Gabriel appeared. He bounded over to them eagerly, grabbing Tem's hand and pressing a kiss to her cheek.

"My *blushing* bride," he crooned. "Congratulations to the happy couple."

Tem smiled, and Leo did too.

Gabriel winked at him. "Your Highness."

"How many times must I tell you to call me Leo?"

Gabriel shrugged. "I prefer Your Highness. I've got a thing for authority figures. Now"—he cocked his head at both of them—"I believe there was talk of me being the best man?"

Before they could reply, one of the kitchen staff waved him down, and Gabriel spun away.

"He's really something," Leo said.

"Something wonderful."

"He certainly is."

Tem felt a sudden rush of love for Gabriel. He was her greatest support system—her dearest friend. He never doubted her, and he reprimanded her when she doubted herself. He'd always encouraged her, long before Caspen ever did. It was because of people like him—the people she loved—that Tem would not fail tonight. She would protect the ones who had always protected her.

"Tem," Leo murmured, breaking her from her thoughts. He pointed to the far end of the clearing. "They're here."

Tem followed his gaze.

At last, the basilisks had arrived.

CHAPTER THIRTY-NINE

 ✦

T HEY WALKED IN A SOMBER LINE LED BY BASTIAN, WHOSE FACE BORE AN expression of utter disgust. Clearly, he was done hiding his disdain for the royals. Tem couldn't exactly blame him. Behind Bastian was Caspen, and Tem's heart jumped into her throat at the sight of him. He didn't look well. The part of Tem that was dying was obviously affecting him—his face was even more angular than the last time she saw him, his cheeks hollow. He was diminishing. And it was all her fault.

Beside her, Leo tightened his grip, nodding at Bastian. "That's their king."

"I know," Tem said.

Leo raised an eyebrow, and she remembered that he knew nothing of her time under the mountain.

"He's Caspen's father," she explained.

"I see," Leo said quietly. "Have you met him?"

The ritual flashed through her mind. "Yes." Tem didn't elaborate, and Leo didn't ask her to. Instead, she asked him something in return. "Have *you* met him?"

"My father has. They speak occasionally to ensure the truce is upheld."

Bastian's gaze fell onto Tem. A chill shot down her spine as he began to walk toward her.

"Leo," she said immediately. "Can you get me a drink?"

But Leo was watching Bastian too, his eyes narrowed. "No," he said simply.

This was not the time for Leo to be brave. Tem didn't want him anywhere near Bastian—especially when the king knew exactly how much the human prince meant to her.

"Leo," she said again, turning to face him. "Leave. Right now."

He opened his mouth to protest.

"*Go, Leo.* You're in danger if you stay."

Still, he hesitated. Bastian was getting closer.

Leo stood his ground. "If I'm in danger, so are you."

Tem shook her head. "I'll be fine. You have to trust me."

Leo's mouth was tight with worry. "That's not good enough."

"Caspen will protect me."

Sharp jealousy darkened Leo's face. Tem watched as it turned slowly to bitter resolve. They both knew he had signed up for this—that he had agreed to share her. Situations just like this were part of that agreement.

After an eternal moment, Leo bowed his head. "Very well." Then he turned and was gone.

A moment later, Bastian was in front of her.

"Temperance," he said smoothly, eyeing her up and down. "It would appear you have an entourage."

Tem's eyes slid to Caspen, who was standing at the edge of the clearing, watching them. Tem didn't need to turn around to know that Leo was watching them too. "I'm a lucky girl."

"Apparently."

There was a silence, and Tem dearly wished Leo had gotten her that drink. It was difficult not to feel nervous when Bastian was looking at her as if she were his next meal. It was not unlike the way he'd looked at her during the ritual.

"Congratulations on your nuptials," the king offered.

"Thanks."

A pause. The wedding guests milled around them. Then Bastian asked, "Are you ready to perform the crest?"

Tem didn't know how to answer him. She settled on "As ready as I can be."

Bastian nodded. "I hope you succeed." Somehow it sounded like a threat.

"Do you?"

A cruel smile slowly twisted Bastian's face. At the sight, Tem felt rather ill. "Of course," he said with feigned nonchalance. "Why would I not?"

"Because it wouldn't benefit you." The moment the words slipped out, Tem realized they were true.

To her surprise, Bastian let out a low chuckle. "I do not do anything that does not benefit me, Temperance."

Tem frowned, unable to stop her train of thought.

If she successfully performed the crest, it would give her an indescribable amount of power—far more power than Bastian possessed. It was not an ideal situation for someone who wanted to retain control over the quivers. Tem couldn't imagine a world in which the Serpent King would allow someone like her to surpass him. She voiced her realization out loud. "Once I perform the crest, I'll be more powerful than you," she said.

Bastian tilted his head. "Is that so?"

"Yes."

"How fascinating. I did not realize you coveted power so."

Something was brewing within Tem—an epiphany she didn't want to face. "I don't," she said slowly. "But you do."

The king raised a single, thick eyebrow. "Is that so?" he said again.

She crossed her arms, focusing on Bastian's face and blocking out the rest of the wedding. "Why would you let me become more powerful than you?"

Bastian's eyes narrowed. "Are you accusing me of something, Temperance?"

Malice bit into his voice, and the chill from earlier returned to Tem's spine. He was testing her, seeing whether she'd challenge him.

As it so happened, Tem was in a challenging mood. "You don't do anything that doesn't benefit you. You said so yourself. So why do this?"

The cool stone of Bastian's face hardened. "Those who have no experience with power do not deserve to wield it. Would you not agree?"

The words of her father came to her suddenly:

Power corrupts.

"No," Tem said, jutting her chin. "Those who deserve to wield power are the ones who will not be corrupted by it."

Bastian snorted. "That is the opinion of a child. Corruption is merely the other half of the coin. It is inevitable. *War* is inevitable."

"No. It isn't."

"Ah," the king said. "But it is."

Tem shook her head. She thought of the conversation she'd just witnessed between Caspen and Leo, how the two men had been willing to put aside their differences for the greater good. "It doesn't have to be that way," she said. "There can be peace."

"Perhaps," mused Bastian. "But why risk it?"

"What are you saying?" Tem whispered.

Bastian smiled at her—a cold, calculating smile. "I am saying that we cannot always get what we want, now can we?"

The same thing Caspen had said when she'd asked him to spare Jonathan's life.

Like father, like son.

In the following silence, Tem's heartbeat pounded in her chest.

Bastian stepped closer, and out of the corner of her eye, she saw Caspen step closer too. "So, Temperance," he said quietly. "Why don't *you* tell *me* why I would let you become so powerful."

Tem's palms were beginning to sweat.

Bastian wanted war. He *coveted* war. The Serpent King had held power for too long, and he was not willing to relinquish it. There was no scenario in which this wedding ended with peace. Tem saw that now. The council meeting was simply a way to get the Senecas to fall in line—to get *her* to fall in line.

It was crystal clear to her.

Tem realized finally what the crest really was: a ruse. A false promise—a lie. Of course it was too good to be true. Of course there would be no peace. The crest did benefit Bastian after all. It was true that it would make Tem more powerful than him. But that was exactly what the king wanted. She was merely a tool—a vessel through which Bastian could ultimately take that power for himself. Caspen's words came back to her suddenly: *He is the only basilisk with enough power to crest anyone he wants.*

The inevitable truth dawned.

"You plan to crest me," Tem whispered.

A slow, sick smile twisted Bastian's lips. "Clever girl," he said quietly.

Her eyes flicked to Caspen's. The question she'd asked him so long ago rushed suddenly through her mind.

What happens to a basilisk when they're crested?

They die.

Tem looked back at the king. "If you crest me, my basilisk side will die."

"Yes," the king replied calmly. "It will."

Little did Bastian know it was dying already. Tem grabbed the golden charm around her neck, brandishing it between them.

"My engagement to Caspen is bound by blood," she said. "His life is linked to mine."

"Yes," the king said again, just as calmly. "It is."

She stared at him in disbelieving epiphany. "You would sacrifice your own *son?*"

Bastian's nostrils flared. "My *son*," he hissed, and Tem recoiled at the vitriol in his voice, "makes irrational decisions. My *son* is ruled by his emotions. My *son*"—he leaned in, and the temperature between them rose—"is clearly not ready to be king. And you, Temperance, are certainly no queen."

The words were eerily similar to the ones Maximus had said about Leo. Two fathers. Two kings. Both with no faith in their sons. Tem had always known that Bastian was ruthless, that all basilisks were capable of cruelty. But this was despicable.

"And if I refuse?" Tem straightened. "If I don't perform the crest?"

It wasn't even an option. But she had to say it.

Bastian's cold smile returned. He pointed a single finger over her shoulder. Tem turned to see Leo, who was leaning against a statue, watching them.

"We had a deal, remember?" he murmured in her ear. "You perform the crest. I spare the human prince and his sister."

"I don't trust you anymore," she snapped. "How do I know you'll keep your word?"

Bastian's voice dropped even lower, sending a chill down her spine. "Because otherwise, his death is guaranteed. Are you willing to take that risk?"

Tem knew the answer, even if she didn't like it. She already had too many deaths on her hands; her fingers may as well have been dripping with blood. She would do anything for the chance to spare Leo. And Bastian knew it.

But Tem no longer believed that Bastian would keep Leo and Lilly safe. Their deal meant nothing; any promise of peace was a false one. It didn't matter that Tem was marrying Leo to bring their two worlds together; it didn't matter that Caspen and Leo wanted a different future for the kingdom. Nobody would be spared from the wrath of the Serpent King. The crest was supposed to save them all. And now? Bastian was forcing her to choose between Caspen and Leo. If she performed the crest, she lost Caspen. If she didn't, she lost Leo. It was an inconceivable choice and one that was pointless. No matter what she chose, Caspen's death was all but guaranteed.

Tem could see no way out, no solution to this terrifying problem.

"There has to be another way," she said desperately.

Bastian let out a humorless chuckle. "The time for negotiation has passed, Temperance." He took a step back, appraising her. "Crest the royals as soon as the ceremony is over," he said, his voice like silk. "Or accept the consequences."

Then he was gone.

Tem stood there, completely numb, her mind racing. Before she could even blink, a hand was on her back.

"Tem." Caspen's voice broke her from her trance. "What did my father say?"

What indeed.

Tem looked up into the golden pools of Caspen's eyes, wanting nothing more than to lose herself within them.

"Tem," he insisted. "Tell me."

Just when she opened her mouth to speak, Leo appeared.

"Tem," he said. "Is everything in order?"

Caspen's eyes flicked to Leo's before returning to Tem's. For a moment, nobody said anything. Tem was deeply aware of how odd they must look—the prince, his future wife, and the basilisk, standing at the edge of the maze.

She turned to Leo. "I'm fine." She turned to Caspen. It was time he learned the truth. "Your father means to crest me."

Caspen frowned. Leo frowned too, and Tem knew he was about to hear some things that he wouldn't understand and might deeply disturb him. But she could do nothing to prevent that now.

"Why would he do that?" Caspen asked.

"He knows I'll be a threat once I perform the crest. He won't let that happen." Caspen's frown deepened.

Leo held up his hand. "Please," he said. "I must know. What is a crest?"

To Tem's surprise, Caspen answered. "It is a way for a basilisk to gain power."

"By what means?" Leo asked.

But Caspen was done answering questions. He turned back to Tem. "You are the love of my life. My father would never crest you."

Beside her, Leo scoffed, and Tem prayed he'd stay calm. This was not the time for petty jealousy.

"I told you, that's exactly what he's going to do. He admitted it, Caspen."

"He would not—"

"Wouldn't he?" Tem cut him off sharply. "There is no end to what fathers would do to their sons."

A muscle twitched in Leo's jaw. A similar one twitched in Caspen's.

Caspen shook his head slowly. "He knows our engagement is bound by blood."

"*Engagement?*" Leo interjected.

Tem placed her hand on his arm. She needed him to stay calm for just one more minute.

"Yes." Tem nodded at Caspen. "He knows."

"That means he…"

Caspen trailed off, and Tem watched as the truth dawned on him. A myriad of emotions passed over his face. None of them were surprise.

"He values power more than he values anything else, Caspen," she said. "Including you."

Caspen's eyes met hers.

There was an incredible sadness in them, along with something resembling resolve. Perhaps Caspen had always known his father was capable of this. Bastian had asked him to crest another basilisk after all—an act that was forbidden. He cared nothing for the lives of others. He cared nothing for his family. He only cared for himself.

"There is a simple solution," Caspen said.

"Which is?"

"You will not perform the crest."

Tem sighed. They were coming to the heart of it now. She would not be able to conceal the truth any longer. "I have to," she said.

"And why is that?"

Tem paused. In the silence, both men stared at her, Caspen with anger and disbelief, Leo with restrained bewilderment. Caspen shifted closer. So did Leo.

It was time.

"I'm…hurt," Tem said.

"Who hurt you?" they asked at the exact same time.

Tem bit her lip. She looked at Caspen. "You did," she whispered.

Caspen's eyebrows shot up in surprise before knitting together with immediate concern. Beside her, Leo let out an enraged sound, and Tem tightened her grip on his arm.

"It's not what you think," she said quickly. "He didn't mean to."

"That *hardly* matters," Leo scoffed. He was already stepping forward.

Tem moved between them, still aware that they were at a wedding—her *own* wedding—and there were people watching. "*Stop* it, Leo. We don't have time for this."

It was true. The sun was setting, and the early moon would soon rise. People were beginning to find their seats. They had to resolve this before the ceremony commenced.

Tem turned to Caspen, her hand still firmly on Leo.

"When you crested me, it wounded my basilisk side. It's been dying ever since."

Caspen blinked. "How can that be? The crest did not work on you."

"It didn't work on the human side of me."

A moment passed as Caspen came to the inevitable conclusion. "If the basilisk side of you is dying, that means…"

Tem finished for him. "You're dying too."

Caspen was staring at her as if he were finally realizing something. "I suppose I have been feeling somewhat…off…lately," he murmured.

From the way he said it, Tem knew it was an understatement. She had no idea how he'd felt the last few days as their bond was slowly decaying. All she knew was how *she'd* felt—like she was losing the best part of her—and she figured Caspen had felt the same. Tem knew this was the last thing either of them wanted. The blood bond was supposed to tie them together for the rest of their lives. Neither of them thought it might cut their lives short.

"Tem," Caspen said. "I do not care if I am dying. You cannot do this. I will not allow it."

"There are limits," Tem said quietly back, "to what you can allow."

A moment of understanding passed between them. This was Tem's choice—no different from choosing between Caspen or Leo or choosing them both. It didn't matter what Caspen wanted. It never had.

Leo cleared his throat, breaking the moment. "Am I to understand that you are both injured?"

It was a gross oversimplification of their current situation. But it would have to do for now.

468

"Yes," Tem said.

"And that your lives are tied to each other?"

"Yes."

"And that you are engaged?"

She sighed. "*Yes*, Leo."

"Those would have been helpful details to know before our wedding day, Tem."

"Enough," Caspen said. They both fell silent. "What can be done?"

A beat passed before Tem began. "I can perform the—"

"No," Caspen said sharply. "You cannot."

"It will make me powerful, Caspen. I can resist your father's crest."

"He is ancient, Tem. He has had centuries of experience wielding his power. You stand no chance against him."

"You're the one who always told me I could do anything. Was that a lie?"

"Of course not. But this is not a matter of sheer will. He will overpower you."

"I have to try."

Caspen crossed his arms. "Crest just one person, Tem. Heal yourself, and then I will heal too."

She shook her head. "No. The deal was to crest the royals."

Tem said it without thinking. It was only when Leo drew away that she realized the effect her words would have.

"You plan to—" He paused, and she could see him struggling to say the word. "Crest my family?"

Tem felt the sudden urge to cry. "It doesn't hurt them," she insisted. "It's completely painless."

"But you would draw power from them? From me?"

Tem shook her head. "*No*," she said. "Not from you. Never from you."

Caspen watched their exchange in silence, his mouth set in an unhappy line. Despite his previous threat to reveal their plan to Leo, Tem knew he never would have actually done so. He was like Leo in that way—he refused to do anything to hurt her. Tem was the one who was always hurting them.

Tem stepped closer, taking Leo's hands in hers. "I only agreed to the crest because it would spare you."

"Spare me from what?"

Caspen took over. "From my father. He will kill you otherwise."

Leo nodded, although Tem had no idea how much of this was actually sinking in.

"Your sister will be spared too," Tem said. "And her children."

"And my father?"

Tem fell silent.

Caspen said it for her. "No."

Leo closed his eyes.

Tem wondered if now, finally, it would be too much for Leo. This was more than he'd bargained for. *She* was more than he'd bargained for.

"Leo," she whispered. "Say something."

The prince was silent for a long moment. He looked down at Tem's hands, his brow furrowed. Then he spoke. "If you are asking me to choose between you and my father, I choose you, Tem." He said the words so calmly that she briefly wondered if she had hallucinated them.

But then Caspen said, "I would choose the same."

This couldn't be real.

"Are you two serious?" Tem whispered.

"I am," Leo said.

"As am I."

She stared at them.

They couldn't be more different, but inside, they were cut from the same cloth. They had both been raised by power-hungry, cruel men—men who had marked their sons, physically and otherwise. It shouldn't come as a surprise that they would choose her over their fathers. They had already done so—multiple times, in fact. They had proven themselves to her more times than she could count.

It was time to return the favor.

"I can do this," Tem said.

Both men stared at her.

"You can do anything, Tem," Caspen said quietly. "Of that I am certain."

The gentle clinking of a glass broke the moment.

Maximus was standing on the edge of the stage, facing the aisle. "Ladies and gentlemen," he said, his voice floating over the crowd. "It is time."

Without another word, Caspen disappeared.

Tem looked at Leo.

She was immediately struck by the peaceful expression on his face. Was it possible that he felt freedom in this moment? For him, defying his father was his greatest wish. He was happy to be here with her—*marrying* her. For Leo, the limited time he had with Tem began today. And she knew he had no intention of wasting it.

Leo leaned in.

The rest of the world disappeared as he took her face in his hands and kissed her. Tem lost herself in their kiss, pretending that nothing was remotely wrong, pretending that this was simply her joyous wedding day. She focused on Leo's cologne, on the way he smelled like summer. She'd always loved that smell.

The crowd was filing into their seats.

Leo led Tem to the end of the aisle, where her mother was already waiting for her in a dress made of silk.

"You look beautiful," Tem told her.

"As do you, my dear."

Leo extended his hand. Tem's mother took it.

"It is a pleasure to meet you," he said graciously. "You raised an exceptional daughter."

Tem's mother blushed. It was her first time experiencing Leo's uncanny ability to say exactly the right thing, and it was something Tem was sure nobody had ever told her before. The words were even sweeter given the fact that her mother had raised her alone.

"Thank you," her mother said, her eyes wide. "You are too kind."

Leo smiled.

"Kindness is not my specialty, I'm afraid. But I intend to practice it every day with Tem." He released her mother's hand, leaning down to give Tem one more kiss. "See you up there," he whispered against her lips.

Tem didn't reply. She watched him walk down the aisle, his blond hair gleaming in the early moonlight.

Her mother touched her arm. "I can understand why you love them both."

For the first time that evening, Tem smiled.

Then her mother said, "Are you ready, my dear?"

Tem took a deep breath.

The time had come to do what she was always meant to do—to become who she was always meant to become.

"Yes."

The crowd turned to look at them as the harpist began to play. Nerves threatened to overtake her as her mother's arm linked in hers and they walked down the aisle together. Tem searched desperately for something to focus on, and her eyes found Leo. He was standing in the center of the stage, his hands clasped behind his back, watching her.

Tears gleamed in his eyes.

His sincerity touched her. There were far worse things, Tem realized, than to be loved by two people. She had no desire to live an ordinary life—a life devoid of passion and challenge and *truth*. She had always been destined for more. Her path may not have been a conventional one, but it was hers, and she wouldn't trade it for anyone else's.

Tem parted ways with her mother at the base of the stage, taking the steps up onto the platform alone. When Leo extended his hand, Tem took it, standing so they were facing each other. Maximus stood between them, and although she could feel him glaring at her, Tem ignored him. Instead, she looked out over the audience.

There was Gabriel, with the caterers. He winked at her when their eyes met. There was Vera, seated next to the other girls who had been eliminated. Her arms were crossed, her nose scrunched in displeasure. The basilisks stood at the edge of the clearing. There were fourteen total, one for each girl who had participated in the competition, and then Bastian. Rowe and Caspen stood beside each other, their shoulders six pointed inches apart.

Tem touched the golden claw around her neck. The moment she did so, Caspen's gaze flicked to hers. She saw an eternity in those eyes.

"Honored guests," Maximus said, drawing her attention back to the stage. "We are gathered here today to witness a union."

Leo's fingers wove into hers.

"My son has chosen his bride from a selection of the finest women this kingdom has to offer." Maximus turned to Leo. "I pray you may find happiness in each other, and it is my honor to wed you here today."

His speech was as bare as could be. There was no emotion behind it—no love. Maximus spoke as if he were reciting a list of ingredients. He turned to Tem.

She dearly hoped he wouldn't be the second king to betray her tonight.

"Temperance," he said, his cold eyes boring into hers. "Do you take my son to be your lawfully wedded husband, in sickness and in health, forsaking all others, until death do you part?"

Tem looked at Leo. Was it her imagination, or had he flinched at the "forsaking all others" part?

"I do," she said.

Maximus turned to Leo. "Thelonius. Do you take Temperance to be your lawfully wedded wife, in sickness and in health, forsaking all others, until death do you part?"

Leo smiled widely, looking at Tem as if she were a flower in a field of ashes. "I do."

"Very well," Maximus said. "I pronounce you husband and wife."

The words sounded bitter on his tongue. And why wouldn't they be? Maximus did not approve of Tem. He did not want Leo to be king. Nothing that was happening right now was even remotely in his favor, and Tem could relate to his disappointment. She felt the same toward Bastian.

"You may now kiss your bride."

Leo's lips were on hers before Maximus could finish his sentence.

The crowd cheered, although Tem barely heard them. She only felt Leo's hands pulling her closer, his entire body pressing against hers. Every ounce of longing he had harbored for her spilled into his kiss, enveloping Tem in an insistent rush. He kissed her deeply, for far longer than was appropriate. And she let him.

When they pulled apart, the crowd cheered. It was deafening.

"Kora," Tem whispered. She never would have expected such a response to her nuptials.

Leo only held her tighter. "See, Tem?" he murmured in her ear. "They love you as I do."

Tem smiled. The silence of the crowd when he'd kissed her in the town square had been humiliating for her. Now it seemed like a distant memory, another lifetime. Tem was struck suddenly by the enormity of what Leo had just done. Not only was he going against his own father, but he was forsaking the only world he'd ever known—a world that greatly benefited him. And he was doing it at great personal cost, on nothing but Tem's word.

For her.

Tem wrapped her arms around him, tucking her head into his shoulder so she could whisper right in his ear, "Thank you, Leo."

She felt him smile. "Anything for you, Tem," he whispered back.

Maximus clapped his hands together, and the crowd quieted. "Honored guests," he said, his gaze falling to Leo. "Now that my son has wed, he is ready for the responsibility of ruling this great kingdom with his wife by his side. To rule well means to take every citizen into consideration, to prioritize every human life."

Tem noticed how he emphasized only *human* life.

"It is a privilege to be king." Maximus turned to face Leo. "A privilege that I know my son will take as seriously as I have."

Father and son stared at each other. As if in slow motion, Maximus lifted the crown from his own head and placed it on Leo's. It was a mirror of the Passing of the Crown, only this time, it would remain on Leo's head.

"It is my honor to crown you king."

The audience erupted into cheers once more, continuing even as Leo stepped to the edge of the stage and held up his hands.

"My people," he cried. "I thank you."

Dread pricked Tem's stomach. The ceremony was over.

Bastian entered her mind: *It is time.*

Tem froze. His eyes bore into hers as Leo addressed the audience.

"With my rule, I intend to usher our kingdom into a new era of peace," he said. "The conflict between the humans and the basilisks has gone on far too long."

A murmur swept through the crowd. Nobody was used to hearing rhetoric in favor of the basilisks. They were considered the enemy; they were not worth the air the royals breathed.

The Serpent King was staring right at her—staring into her *soul.*

Crest them, Temperance.

But something was distracting her—a movement out of the corner of her eye. Several tall figures were entering the clearing, running along the edges of the maze. Tem squinted. Their smooth strides made it seem like they might be basilisks. But that couldn't be right. Only the teachers and the king attended the ceremony.

Leo was still talking. "There have been many cruelties on both sides. Those cruelties end today."

"Thelonius." Maximus grabbed his arm. "Cease this at once."

Leo ignored him, continuing on even louder. "It is my belief that we can coexist, learning from one another as we should have done from the beginning."

The figures were getting closer, encircling the crowd in an impenetrable line.

Now, Temperance.

Was she really about to do this?

A deep, animalistic urge swept through her. The basilisk side of her wanted to perform the crest. She could feel the need thrumming through her body like a pulse. But Tem was made up of two things, and she did not covet power the way Bastian and Maximus did. The desire to dominate wasn't something she identified with. Such hubris was reserved for kings. It was a useless thing to Tem—a facade of control that could break at any second, as it was breaking now. There had to be another way.

A shadow of an idea formed.

Perhaps Tem didn't need to crest the royals. It was a temporary solution anyway—an imperfect bandage for a wound that wouldn't stop bleeding. Even if she succeeded, Bastian would crest her immediately, and the power she gained from the royals might not be enough to resist him. There was only one source of unlimited power for her—a *renewable* source. Someone who wouldn't be hurt by the crest in any way, shape, or form.

Herself.

Tem was two things: human and basilisk. Her basilisk side was dying, but her human side was not. Why shouldn't she use one to feed the other? No harm would come to her at her own hand. An elegant solution. Bastian would be so proud.

Tem looked at Caspen, who had always protected her. Caspen, who had always called her perfect, who insisted from day one that she was flawless. Caspen, who had always told her that the traits she considered weaknesses were really her strengths.

For a moment, Tem dared to see herself as Caspen did: extraordinary. He'd been right all along.

She could do anything. And she would do this.

TEMPERANCE. NOW.

But Tem had made up her mind.

No.

A curious expression passed over Bastian's face. He looked almost happy. *So be it.*

"A new future begins today," Leo was saying. "Effective immediately, I will—"

His words were cut off by a scream.

CHAPTER FORTY

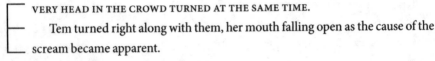

EVERY HEAD IN THE CROWD TURNED AT THE SAME TIME.

Tem turned right along with them, her mouth falling open as the cause of the scream became apparent.

One of the basilisks was transitioning.

Tem watched in horror as scales dappled his skin, his body elongating into a shape she'd seen many times before. Smoke plumed into the air, concealing the nearest row of chairs as people scrambled over one another in an attempt to get away. The basilisk opened its mouth, reared its great head, and sank its fangs into the neck of a stout man with a red beard. The man was so shocked he didn't even cry out. His mouth formed a surprised O right before his head was ripped from his shoulders.

Leo threw himself in front of Tem, pulling her back as more basilisks streamed into the clearing. Someone knocked into her, and she realized it was Maximus. He leaped from the stage, barreling down the steps without a backward glance.

"*Coward!*" Leo cried.

His voice was lost in the wind as the rest of the basilisks began to transition.

There was nowhere to go. Some people ran screaming into the maze, but without Leo's sense of direction, they were merely delaying the inevitable. Basilisks ran after them with all the glee of hunters stalking their prey. A woman ran hand in hand with her husband only to be yanked to a halt when he suddenly turned to stone. She shrieked in pain as his granite fingers crushed hers. Tem watched as another woman pulled her dress from her shoulders, trying to mount a basilisk that had crested her. He pushed her aside, already grabbing the throat of another.

Tem turned to Leo. "Go."

Despite all the chaos, his eyes were only focused on her. "Only if you come with me."

"I can't. I have to find—"

But she cut off as someone appeared beside them.

They both looked over to see Caspen. "Tem," he said. "Did you perform the crest?"

"No."

Relief, then immediate worry flashed across his face. He jerked his head at Leo. "He is vulnerable. If someone tries to—"

"I already claimed him."

There was the briefest of pauses. Then Caspen said, "Good."

He meant it: Tem could feel his approval, and she realized he liked the way she had thought like a basilisk.

He turned to Leo. "You must go."

Leo shook his head. "I'm not leaving her."

Caspen shook his head too.

"No harm shall come to her, Leo. You have my word."

It was the first time Caspen had called him by his name. Still, Leo hesitated. Caspen stepped forward so they were eye to eye, placing his hand on Leo's shoulder.

"I cannot protect you both at the same time, and I know she wants you to live. Go."

It was as close as Caspen would ever get to telling Leo that he mattered. For a moment, the two men simply stared at each other. Then Leo placed his own hand on Caspen's shoulder. Neither of them said a word, but Tem saw a mutual understanding pass between them; they both needed to stay alive for her. Nothing was more important than that.

They dropped their hands.

"Very well," Leo said. He turned to her. "Tem, I—"

"Tell me after, Leo."

He closed his mouth. Then he pressed a kiss to her temple and ran.

Tem watched Leo get halfway across the clearing before a basilisk grabbed him triumphantly by the throat. Before Tem could panic, the basilisk released him, looking down at his hand in confusion. A moment later, Leo was gone.

"Tem," Caspen said urgently. "We must get you somewhere safe."

She looked out over the chaos before her. Predators hunting prey. Strong killing the weak. The circle of life.

"No." She shook her head. "This is my fault. I have to fix it."

"You cannot fix this, Tem. My people are angry. You cannot stop what has already begun."

Before Tem could reply, someone joined them onstage.

Caspen immediately threw his arm in front of Tem as a basilisk in its human form advanced toward them. Blood dripped from the man's mouth, which was twisted in a horrible grin. He was already transitioning. Great claws formed where fingers had once been, spreading wide as Caspen pushed Tem behind him.

The basilisk lunged.

Caspen let out a grunt as the sharp claws found purchase. He stumbled backward, blood pouring from his bicep. The basilisk advanced again, its fangs thrashing together madly as the rest of his body caught up to his hands.

"*Caspen!*" Tem cried. "Transition!"

But Caspen only shook his head. "I cannot, Tem."

Understanding pierced Tem like an arrow.

Caspen was weak. He'd been dying for days, and it had progressed to the point where he could no longer embody his true form. Tem stood up straight, squaring her shoulders so air could reach her lungs.

It was time.

She closed her eyes, tuning out the sounds of conflict, focusing only on the way she felt inside. The void within her was glaringly large. Tem felt a primal ache at the loss, wishing dearly that she hadn't waited so long to address it. She quieted her mind, reaching for the remaining strands of her power.

It was there, but just barely. She drew from it, drinking from the endless well within herself, using one side to fix the other.

The moment she connected the two parts of her, every cell in her body lit on fire. Complete and utter clarity rushed through Tem's veins as her basilisk side immediately began to heal. The frayed edges of her mind knit together seamlessly, creating something that was even stronger than what was there before. Tem felt *buoyant*, as if she might float from the stage and into the endless sky. She was soaring into infinity, experiencing nothing and everything all at once. There was no greater feeling than this—no better way to understand herself. All the broken pieces of her identity came together in one perfect, limitless point. Her power was cosmic—as vast as the stars.

She was bound to no one. She was *free*.

Tem reached for Caspen, throwing open the corridor between their minds, gasping as their connection surged back into place.

Caspen. Transition.

Caspen didn't need telling twice. A great cloud of smoke billowed from his shoulders as his body snapped into something else entirely. He transitioned with a roar—one that was so deeply triumphant, Tem had to cover her ears. A split second later, the other basilisk was headless. It happened so fast, Tem didn't even blink. Without missing a beat, Caspen lunged at two more basilisks that were approaching from the back of the stage.

Out of the corner of her eye, Tem spotted Vera. Rowe was upon her. She watched as he wrapped his fingers around her throat, lifting her head to his. Vera's eyes rolled upward, and Tem knew he was cresting her. Beside them, two basilisks were having sex, their bodies thrashing together in the blood-soaked grass. Tem looked desperately around for Gabriel and her mother but didn't see either of them. She was about to step off the stage to find them when she felt a presence behind her.

Tem turned to see Bastian's black eyes searing straight into hers. Before she could speak, his hand wrapped around her throat.

Immediately, Tem felt her power seep in his direction. It was as if someone had begun to pour her into him, and the familiar euphoria from the crest started to swell over her. It would be so easy to give in. So simple. The king's pull was undeniable, his ancient presence so much stronger than hers—strong enough to override the protection of Caspen's venom. And yet Tem found she was able to resist him. Every time he pulled at her, she pushed back. The king grew impatient; she could sense his agitation.

Yield.

Tem would not yield—not her body and not her mind. Never.

She wanted to call for Caspen, but it took all her energy to hold off the king, and Caspen was occupied anyway. He was outnumbered, fighting two basilisks at once, trying to prevent them from ascending the stage. Tem didn't even know whether he'd noticed what his father was trying to do to her.

Do as I say, Temperance.

No.

The king let out a growl of frustration. His grip on her throat tightened.

Tem watched in horror as scales crept up the sides of his neck. She tried to pull away, but it was no use—he was holding her so tightly she could barely breathe. His mouth widened; his teeth became fangs. Tem knew, without a shadow of a doubt, what was about to happen. Still, nothing could prepare her for the way Bastian's jaw unhinged itself, opening to reveal the dark abyss of his throat. Tem didn't have time to think before his fangs crushed her shoulder with terrifying finality, the force of their bite nearly causing her to black out right then. She felt her collarbone break with a horrible *crunch.*

Then her shoulder blade.

Then her sternum.

Pain like she'd never known shot through her. It was worse than when her pelvis had broken during the ritual. Agony was all she could feel, overtaking her mind and forcing her body into a state of shock. Tem knew the bite had a purpose: to weaken the part of her she was drawing power from. Her basilisk side wouldn't be harmed by Bastian's venom, but her human side would. It was the exact opposite of the problem she'd just solved by cresting herself.

All that work for nothing, she thought vaguely.

Tem tried to fight back. But her power was stretched too thin—she couldn't free herself from Bastian's grip, much less heal her shoulder. The king's crest grew stronger, forcing her into submission. The well of power she drew from grew weaker. *She* grew weaker.

Tem screamed as her feet left the stage, stars clouding her vision as Bastian lifted her into the air. All her weight yanked against the injury, pulling on her with enormous, merciless pressure.

TEM!

Caspen's voice barely registered. Consciousness was fleeting. Bastian was mauling her, ripping her apart with monstrous glee. Her mind was numb; she couldn't resist his crest any longer.

Then, without warning, he released her.

Tem fell with such speed that she thought her kneecaps might split open on the stage. She heard Caspen behind her, recognizing his roar and the smell of his smoke as he attacked. Bastian fought back ferociously, matching his son with a roar of his own, landing blow after blow as they parried across the stage. But it was Caspen finally who landed a well-timed bite to the king's face. Bastian howled in pain, collapsing in a writhing pile of scales.

He was transitioning again, slipping into his human form as he weakened. As scales became skin, Tem felt the pull of his crest retreat, and with it, the last barrier between her and the insurmountable pain in her shoulder.

As soon as the Serpent King resembled a man once more, Caspen bent his head. Tem watched as his glorious fangs emerged from his mouth, curving down into Bastian's pale, exposed neck.

Bastian let out a tortured scream. The sound was so horrible it finally shattered Tem's daze, yanking her violently back into the present.

Caspen!

He didn't reply. There was no way he heard her over Bastian's cries.

Caspen—

She tried again, flinching at the horrific thing happening before her.

STOP.

But Caspen didn't stop. Instead, his fangs sank deeper into Bastian's body, ripping his skin and splattering blood everywhere. Bastian's ribs broke with a dull *crunch* as Caspen yanked the bones apart, forcing his way into his chest cavity, his mouth opening wider, his fangs slick with red. Tem saw Caspen's throat bulge, then swallow. Horror twisted her stomach as she realized what was happening.

Caspen wasn't killing Bastian quickly—that would have been a mercy, and he owed nobody his mercy. His father would be alive when he cannibalized him. Tem understood that it was Bastian's punishment. It was only fair. It was exactly what Caspen had just watched him do to Tem.

Tem couldn't save Bastian. She didn't want to anyway. But she wanted dearly to save Caspen from himself. It was a terrible thing to kill your own father. More terrible still to do it in such a violent way. But there was nothing she could do. Her head was clouded with smoke; the entire right side of her body had gone numb. More of her was covered in blood than not, and she knew it was all hers.

Finally, Tem blacked out.

When she came to, she didn't know how much time had passed. But Caspen was beside her in his human form once more.

Tem.

She could smell his rage.

Tem knew she would never get that image of Caspen out of her mind—bent over Bastian, eating chunks of flesh from his chest. She would see it in her nightmares.

Tem?

Caspen placed a tentative hand on her cheek.

He was soaked in blood and venom, bits of Bastian's organs sliding slowly down his torso in wet, gelatinous streaks. The smell was overpowering. She was going to pass out again.

"I—" Tem started.

But a searing pain cut off her words. Everything hit her all at once, the mangled remnants of her body screaming in sudden unison. She reached for her power, but it was barely there.

Caspen. I can't heal myself.

Caspen's hands were on her, trying to pull her upright.

Try harder, Tem.

Tem couldn't reply. The pain in her body was worsening. She was in agony as a crushing wave of sensation overtook her.

Fight it, Tem. You must fight it.

Tem tried. She harnessed her power, throwing up a shield against the pain. But her body was broken; both parts of her were weakened. No one could withstand what she had just gone through.

I'm not healing, Caspen.

She was using every drop of her power to stay conscious. She had nothing left over to fix the wound in her shoulder. Blood was pouring down her body, dripping onto the stage. Caspen immediately placed his hand on her shoulder, trying to heal her himself.

But she had crossed the threshold—she could feel it in her gut. No matter what Caspen did, she only bled more.

Hold on, Tem. Just a little longer.

Tem couldn't hold on any longer. Her injury was draining her, slowly but surely. Her shoulder was bleeding out, streams of her blood merging with Bastian's. There was some poetic irony there, but Tem was too tired to find it.

I can't fight it, Caspen. It's too much.

You need power.

Any ideas?

A long pause. And then: *Crest Leo.*

Tem shook her head. She didn't even have the energy to answer.

Yes, Tem. You must.

But Tem couldn't. She *wouldn't*. She'd just narrowly avoided performing the crest on the royals. She had no desire to force another human being to bond with her, to wield her power in such a brutal and unforgiving way.

I don't want to.

She'd claimed Leo to ensure that nobody would ever crest him. If she did it herself, it would defeat the purpose. Caspen was still talking.

Your human side is dying. You need to crest someone in order to heal it.

And that someone has to be Leo?

He would do anything for you. You know this.

It's not right.

He will feel only pleasure, Tem.

He'll be bound *to me, Caspen.*

He loves you. The two of you are bound together already.

Tem knew the words pained him. But she couldn't care about Caspen's feelings right now. She couldn't crest Leo. Not when he'd specifically told her how he craved agency, how the thing he wanted most was to be able to make his own choices, how he wanted to become the swan. There could be nothing crueler than taking that away from him.

Caspen was already turning away.

I will bring him to you.

He was gone before she could protest. Tem shut everything else out—the sounds of pain and death and anguish—focusing only on keeping herself whole. Every moment that passed, she became a fraction weaker. She knew Bastian had bitten her to punish her—one last way to keep her beneath him. Tem stared at his mangled, chewed-up body, barely recognizable under wet clots of organs and blood. A death worthy of a king, she supposed: vicious and brutal. Epic.

An eternity later, Caspen reappeared with both Leo and Lilly in tow. Tem looked up at Leo. His hand was scraped and bleeding. Lilly had a scratch on her face that was gently seeping blood. Her normally bright eyes were red with tears.

"Leo," Tem whispered. "You were supposed to leave."

"Tem." He knelt beside her. "I had to find Lilly first." His face tightened with concern when he saw the blood surrounding her. He glanced up at Caspen. "What happened to her?"

"My father bit her."

Leo removed his jacket, pressing it to her shoulder. He seemed short of breath, like he was on the verge of a panic attack. "Is she going to die?" he rasped.

"Not if you help her."

"Caspen," Tem said. "No."

Leo looked desperately between them. "How can I help her?" he asked.

"You must let her—"

"*Caspen*," Tem cried. "I already told you no."

It took *so* much effort to speak. Her lights were dimming, her blood flowing slower. She could no longer balance; she tilted backward, and Leo caught her.

"Tem." Leo's eyes were a wild mess. "What can I do? Just tell me." When Tem didn't answer, he turned to Caspen. "Can't she draw power from me?"

Caspen nodded. "Yes. But she refuses to do so."

Leo turned back to Tem. "Do it, Tem. I give you permission."

But Tem shook her head. Leo didn't know what he was signing up for, didn't know that the crest would bind him to her.

And yet Caspen was right. What was Leo's love for her if not another version of a bond? He had already pledged himself to her—already married her, for Kora's sake. She couldn't think of anyone who the crest would impact less. It was one thing to crest a stranger. It was quite another to crest Leo, who loved her.

"Please." He pressed his lips to her hand, and they came away bloody. "You know I would do anything for you, Tem. *Anything.*"

Caspen was watching them, his eyes dark.

Crest him, Tem. Do it now.

Tem looked up into Leo's eyes. He was terrified of losing her. It was written all over his face. "Do you trust me, Leo?"

She'd asked him that before. But this time, she wasn't asking to confide in him. She wasn't asking him to swallow her venom. This time, she was asking him to trust her with his life. His answer was the same as it always was.

"I trust you, Tem." His hands were shaking as they held her.

You are running out of time, Tem. I can barely feel you in my mind.

"It won't hurt," Tem said to Leo, continuing calmly as if everything that was happening wasn't happening at all. "I promise."

"I don't care if it hurts. Just do it."

The moment he said the words, Caspen knelt beside them, taking Tem's hand and wrapping it around Leo's throat. Tem was grateful for his help; she couldn't have done it alone.

It was the last thing Tem wanted. But she had no choice.

She pulled on the strings of her power, yanking with all her strength and aiming it at Leo. Energy thrummed in her hand. She sent the crest with everything she had left, feeling a bright beam of warmth shoot from her body to Leo's. His eyes slammed shut as it hit him.

Tem watched his face, recognizing his expression as the one he wore when he finished. She knew exactly how he was feeling right now—knew the utter euphoria the crest was giving him. What she didn't know was how it would feel for *her*.

It was different from when she had crested herself. That hadn't felt sexual, only powerful. This time, she felt an unequivocal sense of arousal, even stronger than anything she had felt for Leo before. It was as if someone were stimulating all the nerve endings in her body. Leo's face looked suddenly like an angel's—like every inch of him was made of diamonds. His skin shone in the moonlight, and before Tem knew what she was doing, she was leaning in.

When their lips touched, her whole body opened up to receive him. He was streaming into her, filling her with himself until the pain fell mercifully away and there was only lightness. Dimly, she felt Caspen's hand on the back of her head. He was holding them together, ensuring she drew as much power as possible from the human prince.

The wound on her shoulder was closing; she could feel the skin seaming back together as her body healed itself. Her bones clicked back into place; her ribs realigned. Clarity returned to her mind, bringing with it the focus she'd been unable to access just moments ago. Pure, unfiltered power shot through her.

Tem pulled away.

When Leo's eyes opened, he looked at her like she was the most beautiful creature he'd ever seen. It was the same way he'd always looked at her, she realized.

"What...just happened?" he whispered.

Caspen was still holding them an inch apart.

"You saved me," Tem whispered back.

Leo smiled. He looked so radiantly happy that Tem couldn't help but feel happy too.

Her gaze moved from his face to Caspen's. The two men she loved. This was all she needed: both of them, right here, beside her.

Eventually, Tem stood.

Caspen and Leo rose too, standing on either side of her as all three of them looked out over the clearing. The view was nothing short of carnage.

Some humans were killed, while others were crested. Still more were petrified; statue after statue filled the clearing, all cowering in various defensive positions, forever preserved in their final state of fear. The once-pristine grass was strewn with body parts that had been ripped from their sockets. Blood was everywhere. It stained the white tablecloths and dripped in great uneven splatters from white roses. Sobs and screams filled the air.

It was horrible. All of it.

Beside her, Caspen stepped forward. He leaned down, sinking his fists into Bastian's wet corpse before lifting what was left of his father high above his head. He let out a roar of anger and victory that echoed throughout the clearing with terrifying finality. All other sounds ceased immediately. Both basilisks and humans alike stared up at Caspen, the new Serpent King, wielding his dead father. As soon as everyone's eyes were on him, Caspen hurled Bastian's body off the stage. It landed in the middle of the aisle, crumpling into a bloody heap.

And just like that, it was over.

The remaining basilisks bolted for the maze, sprinting into the gaps in the hedges. Some of them wore their true forms, their giant bodies crushing straight through the walls. Caspen lowered his arms, watching them go. He would be merciful today.

Silence fell on the clearing.

Only then did the true cost of the evening become apparent. The grass was littered with bodies—some stone, some flesh, some halfway in between. Anyone who was still alive was huddled by the maze walls, their hands covering their eyes in case a basilisk wearing its true form was still nearby. Tem saw her mother in the distance, clinging to Gabriel. Pure relief passed through her.

"Caspen." She pointed. "My mother—"

He was already stepping forward. "I shall retrieve her," he said, touching her jaw gently. "Rest."

Tem didn't protest. She watched as he descended the steps, the humans on either side of him cowering as he passed. Lilly followed in his footsteps, extending her hand to the first person she saw.

Tem turned to Leo.

He looked back at her, his face still shining with love. "Tem," he began slowly. "That was...not how I thought our wedding would go."

Tem almost laughed. They were standing exactly where they'd gotten married earlier. It was dark now, the clearing lit only by the light of the harvest moon. Nothing was the same.

"Me neither," she said.

He brushed his fingertips along her shoulder. "Are you in pain?"

She shook her head. Not anymore. "Are you?"

Leo held up his hand. His palm was badly scraped, blood dripping down his wrist.

Tem took it in hers, pressing her own palm over the injury and closing her eyes. She'd never done this for someone else before, but she did it for Leo, using her power to fix the ripped skin, stitching it back together as Caspen had done so many times for her. When she lifted her hand, the wound was healed.

"That's...quite extraordinary," Leo whispered.

Tem nodded. It was.

For a moment, they simply looked at each other. Leo was covered in blood, but it was mostly Tem's. He extended his fingers, reaching for her face. Tem let him touch her, leaning into his warmth, remembering the way his lips had felt during the crest.

"I...have some regrets, you know," he said quietly.

"About what?"

He cupped her cheek with his palm.

"I'm afraid I wasn't what you deserved."

"You didn't need to be anything for me," Tem said.

"No, I didn't, did I? You already had everything you needed."

He brushed his thumb slowly over her bottom lip, just like he had when he'd told her about Evelyn. Then his fingers went lower, touching the little golden claw between her breasts. Tem remembered how Leo had tried to give her jewelry on their first date—*that could be special too*, he'd said—how she'd refused to accept it.

Now it was time to give him something in return.

Tem would not doom Leo to a life as her slave. That wasn't love. True love was doing what was best for the other person at the expense of yourself. True love was sacrificing your happiness for theirs. Leo deserved to be loved the same way Caspen loved Tem—unconditionally and without obligation. Leo deserved *more*. Their bond was permanent; there was nothing she could do to change that. But Tem would not take his agency away. She would bestow it instead.

"Leo," Tem whispered, knowing that her words would bind him, that he would have no choice but to obey. "I want you to find Evelyn. I want you to choose your future."

A slow, relaxed smile broke across Leo's face. It wasn't joyous exactly. Merely peaceful. "I don't know where she is, Tem."

"Your father knows. He'll tell you."

It was the least Maximus could do for his son.

Leo tilted his head, considering something. She knew he wouldn't protest—he *couldn't*. But it was almost as if he wanted to. Just when Tem was about to give him the order again, he said, "Then I suppose this is goodbye."

For some reason, Tem began to cry.

Leo lifted his finger, brushing the tear off her cheek. "I never thought I'd see you cry over me."

"I never thought we'd be saying goodbye."

"I'm not worth these tears, Tem. Trust me."

That only made Tem cry harder. Of course Leo was worth her tears. He was worth so much more than he thought he was—than *she* had thought he was. In another lifetime, there was a happy ending for them. But not in this one.

"Tell me this isn't the last time I'll see you," she whispered. She didn't care if it interfered with the order she'd just given him. Tem couldn't bear the thought of never looking into his gray eyes again—never seeing his tall, lanky shoulders angled in her direction.

It was torture to imagine it.

"This isn't the last time," Leo whispered back.

Tem couldn't talk anymore.

Instead, she kissed him gently, so different from most of the kisses they had shared. Leo was always raw energy, constantly in motion. Now he held her in his arms, sliding his tongue slowly against hers with all the care in the world.

"Tell me what we had was real," he murmured against her lips.

Her answer was the truth. "It was real."

When they pulled apart, they didn't speak again. Instead, Leo raised his hand, taking a single curl and twirling it around his long, slim fingers. He smiled, his gold incisors gleaming in the moonlight.

Then he walked away.

CHAPTER FORTY-ONE

T EM WAS STILL GETTING USED TO HER TITLE. BUT THE MORE CASPEN SAID IT, THE
more she believed it.

My queen.

They were in Bastian's bed. It was tradition for the new king to take over the former
king's chambers, and Tem saw no reason not to honor the custom. Such was the basilisk
way after all.

It was morning, or nearly so. They'd gotten in bed the day before and never gotten out.

My king.

Caspen's fingers brushed up her bare spine, tangling in her hair. He kissed along her
collarbone, pressing his lips to the vein in her neck. His cock was hard, but Tem didn't
touch it yet. Instead, she let him kiss her, knowing without a doubt that she was right
where she was supposed to be.

Tem pulled his face to hers and kissed him. *I love you.*

Caspen kissed her back. *And I you.*

There was nothing else to say.

Their bodies returned to each other, weaving a tapestry no one else could weave. It
was natural with Caspen, like breathing. The human side of her had always called to
him, and now the basilisk side did too. Tem savored every caress, every tender stroke of
his fingers, and eventually, his tongue. He gave to her; she gave to him. They did what
they were always meant to do, what they could do with no other. When the fractured
shards of Tem's soul split, Caspen's swallowed them whole.

Afterward, his fingers traced her spine once more.

"Tem," Caspen said quietly. "What did you say to the prince?"

Tem thought back to her conversation with Leo, both of them broken and bleeding
on the stage. "I said goodbye."

Caspen didn't reply, and she knew he was giving her space to elaborate.

After a moment, she did. "I told him to find the girl he loves."

Caspen frowned. "Was that not you?"

Tem shook her head. "He loved someone before me."

Caspen absorbed this information in silence. Tem didn't feel like explaining herself any further, so she didn't. Eventually, Caspen said, "You did him a kindness, Tem. I cannot think of a better way to utilize the bond of the crest."

At his words, Tem nearly cried.

Caspen cared nothing for Leo's happiness, but he cared deeply for hers, and no doubt he knew how much Tem needed to hear those words. Of course, his approval was also selfish. Now that Leo was tasked with finding Evelyn, Caspen would have Tem all to himself. But he would also have a happier version of her—a version that wasn't riddled with guilt.

They lay there together for as long as they pleased.

Eventually, Tem asked a question of her own. "Do basilisks have weddings?"

Caspen pulled her closer. "We do not."

"Then how do we get married?"

Caspen touched his fingertip gently to the golden claw around her neck. "You would give me a similar token."

"That's it?"

"Yes." He smiled. "That is it."

It was so simple. Tem thought about how much it had taken for them to be together. The ritual had been public—every part of her on display for his entire quiver to see. It was interesting to Tem that this next part would be completely private. But she found she liked the contrast. At the end of the day, sex was something that everyone did. But not everyone had a bond like her and Caspen.

Tem looked down at the little golden claw.

"Where do I find one of these?" she asked.

"You would have to make one yourself."

"*Make* one?"

"Yes."

"But how?"

Caspen shifted so he was looking at her. "Our engagement is bound by blood. You would need to complete the bond."

"So…by bloodletting?"

He shook his head. "Bloodletting is the name we give to what the royals did to us. It refers to an act of violence. This"—he touched the claw again—"is born of love."

"How will I know what to do?" she asked.

"Your instincts will tell you."

Tem sat up, touching the necklace. She remembered how the wires were fused to her father's hands, how the gold had seeped out of them.

Without another word, she concentrated. Caspen was right; her instincts took over, and she knew what to do. It didn't hurt. Rather, Tem felt a slight tingle just below her freckles, right at the base of her fingers. It was the easiest thing in the world to bleed for Caspen as he'd bled for her—to give him a physical token of her love. The claw formed in her palm, its golden curve resting on her freckles.

Caspen watched her in awe. Tem could appreciate how significant this was for him. He hadn't even done this with Adelaide. This was an act reserved only for Tem.

A single word flashed through her mind as she lifted the chain and placed it around Caspen's neck:

Mine.

It was the ultimate truth; nothing could be more certain. She was his, and he was hers, and they would be bound together forever. Caspen smiled up at her, his fingers wrapping around her waist as he pulled her on top of him once more.

Mine.

EPILOGUE

———•◦✳◦•———

LEO

I T WASN'T HOW LEO THOUGHT HIS WEDDING WOULD GO.

He hadn't thought that the happiest day of his life would end in bloodshed—in *death*. The image of Caspen holding his butchered father above his head would stay with him for a long time. Perhaps forever.

Leo had always known about the brutality of basilisks. He'd grown up hearing tales of violence and evil—animated retellings of the terrible battle that resulted in the truce. The stories were nothing compared to witnessing it firsthand. Leo had never seen such uncivilized, gruesome behavior. It was fucking appalling. He couldn't understand how his father had let this happen.

Or perhaps he could.

His father was a coward. That much was apparent. Leo stifled a wave of rage as he remembered the way his father had leaped from the stage to save his own skin. Disgusting. It had been an hour since the wedding, and he was still nowhere to be found. Leo, on the other hand, had immediately begun helping the injured guests until Lilly had forced him upstairs to his bedroom.

"The future king needs to rest," she'd said when he'd protested. What she'd meant was that he needed to stay alive. There were still basilisks roaming the maze, as evidenced by the sporadic screams peppering the autumn air.

The fireplace was lit, yet Leo was cold. The armchair next to him was empty, and he couldn't stop staring at it.

Tem should be here.

Leo barely grasped any part of the conversation that had occurred between her and Caspen right before the ceremony. The two of them were bound together somehow, although the details were unclear. They were engaged apparently as well. Leo tried not to let that bother him, but it was impossible. Perhaps basilisks did things differently; perhaps engagements did not mean the same thing to snakes as they did to humans. But it didn't matter ultimately what it meant. It was Leo who'd had the privilege of marrying Tem tonight.

She'd looked gloriously beautiful. There was no one more dazzling than her—of that

Leo had no doubt. Tem had always been stunning to him. But seeing her in a wedding dress—the one she wore to marry *him*—had been a wonder beyond his wildest dreams. She'd never quite felt like his. But for a moment, on that stage, she did.

And then it had all gone completely wrong.

Leo still didn't understand the crest. It was a way to transfer power; that was all he knew. Tem had told him it wouldn't hurt, and it hadn't. But it had felt…intense. Paralyzing even. The actual memory of it was fuzzy, as if he were viewing it through a fogged window. But he remembered how he'd felt after Tem drew power from him—how the only thing that mattered was *her*. That had always been the case. But there was something different about their connection now, something—for lack of a better word—*magical*.

The final moments of their wedding wouldn't stop playing over in his mind no matter how hard he tried to stop them. There were fleeting sensations: Tem's hands in his, the suffocating smell of smoke, the cries of innocent people. He'd almost been out of the clearing when Caspen had grabbed his shoulder.

"Tem needs you."

It was all he said, and it was all Leo needed.

So much blood. Most of it Tem's.

Nothing rattled Leo. Nothing made him fear for his life because he'd never cared all that much about living. But the sight of Tem broken and bleeding on the stage—her body crumpled in a motionless heap—made him want to die. He'd pictured, for a single moment, what life would be like without her. It was a terrible vision. Colorless and dull. Tem made everything better. He hadn't noticed the taste of whiskey until he'd drank it with her. He hadn't cared about the plight of the basilisks until he'd learned she was one. Tem had taught him how to live. And then she had left him.

I want you to find Evelyn. I want you to choose your future.

He would do anything for Tem. That had always been true, of course, but somehow it seemed even more so now. Even when leaving her felt completely wrong, he'd done it. Even if finding Evelyn meant losing Tem, he would do it.

But he wouldn't lose her. He couldn't. He'd never been happier than when his father had pronounced them married. But were they to remain married? Their marriage would have to be annulled. Leo couldn't be with Evelyn if he was still married to Tem.

Tell me this isn't the last time I'll see you.

This isn't the last time.

Leo would have to be dead in order for it to be the last time. He couldn't let their story end like that—in blood and chaos at their own wedding. Such an ending was unacceptable to him. Still, there were other problems to contend with.

Leo ran his tongue over his golden teeth. The metal felt cold in his mouth, as if it were no longer a part of him. The bloodletting could not continue. But Leo had no idea how to stop it. If it was true that the basilisks were the source of his family's wealth, without them, his family could suffer. The *kingdom* could suffer. He needed to find some other way to make money, and quickly. His father had always chastised him for acting like a child, yet the time for youth was over. There were real issues to deal with now—ones that could have devastating consequences. The thought of a future where the basilisks and the humans could coexist was a strange one to Leo. It would take time for the villagers to accept it, if they ever truly did. There would be difficulty—perhaps strife—moving forward. What came next would not be easy.

Leo sighed, swirling his whiskey.

He could still feel where Tem had healed the wound on his palm—how warmth had flowed from her body to his, mending the shredded skin. When he flexed his fingers, a shadow of the spark remained. Leo balled his hand into a fist.

He missed that warmth. He missed *her.*

Something had shifted between them after Tem crested him. The moment he'd kissed her, he'd felt…different. Broken somehow, yet also whole. As if a piece of his soul had walked out of his chest and into hers. But that was impossible. Leo had never troubled himself with magic. His father had raised him firmly in reality. There was no room for miracles in their world. No room for love either.

A gentle knock tore him from his thoughts.

"Your Highness?"

Leo recognized Lord Chamberlain's voice and briefly considered ignoring it. Then he remembered he was the king now. If there was an issue, it was his responsibility to solve it.

"Come in."

The door opened, and his uncle entered.

"Your father has been found."

"Where?"

"In the maze."

"Is he injured?"

"No."

The news should have cheered him. It did nothing of the sort.

"Do you wish to speak with him? He awaits you in the parlor."

Leo sighed. He had no desire to speak with his father. But he was the only one who knew where Evelyn was, and Tem had told him to find her.

"Shall I bring him to you?" his uncle asked when the silence lingered.

"No," said Leo. "Take him to the dungeon."

Lord Chamberlain frowned. "Are you sure, Your Highness?"

"Of course I'm sure. He belongs there."

"All the cells are currently filled."

"In that case, we had better empty them, hadn't we?"

His uncle shook his head. "Thelonius...your father will not support that."

Leo looked up at him. "My father is no longer king. I do not require his support."

"But if you—"

"Take him to the dungeon," Leo said again. "And if he resists, force him."

"How?"

"Summon the guards. Hold him at knifepoint. I don't care what you do. Just get it done."

A moment passed when Leo thought his uncle might protest again. But Lord Chamberlain was bound to the duties of his position. He could not defy Leo's order any more than he could have denied the former king's.

Eventually, he said:

"Very well. If that is what you wish."

"It is." Leo finished his whiskey, then stood. "I will meet you down there."

His uncle raised an eyebrow but didn't speak again. They parted ways on the landing, and Leo made his way slowly down the stairs. The castle was still in a state of complete pandemonium: wedding guests and staff were scattered in chaotic groups, all in distress. Most were covered in blood, and Leo winced at the sight. He felt a deep responsibility to keep his people safe, and he had failed to do so today. The guilt would no doubt haunt him for a long time.

Tem was nowhere to be found. It didn't surprise him; surely, the basilisk had whisked her away from the wedding to protect her from any lingering dangers. It was what Leo would have done had she let him. But now was not the time to think about Tem. For now, he had someone to find. She was standing at the edge of the maze, her head on Gabriel's shoulder.

Leo's heart jolted the moment saw her.

"Your Highness." Tem's mother bowed as he approached. Gabriel did the same.

"Please." He gestured awkwardly. "Call me Leo."

"Why are you here, Leo?"

Leo opened his mouth, then closed it. She looked *so similar* to Tem. How had he not noticed it when they'd been introduced earlier? They had the same soft eyes, the same determined jaw. The resemblance was so strong, he was tempted to reach for her but refrained when he remembered why he'd come. For some reason, he looked to Gabriel.

"Tem left. Caspen took her away." Gabriel said the second part gently.

"Of course." Leo nodded. "That's not why I'm here."

"Oh? Then what can we do for you, Your Highness?"

A pause bloomed, then settled. Leo flexed his hand again.

"Tem's father is in the dungeon," he said steadily. "I thought you might want to see him."

Tem's mother's eyes widened. "Yes," she whispered. "I would."

Leo nodded again. "In that case, please." He extended his arm, and she took it. "Come with me."

They left Gabriel by the maze. Neither of them spoke as they entered the castle, and Leo had no desire to anyway. He was content instead to guide them silently through the ballroom and down the stairwell. It was only when they stood before the door to the dungeon that Leo paused, turning to her.

"He is…not well. I don't want you to be alarmed."

Tem's mother lifted her chin. "I'll be fine."

The gesture was so familiar, Leo couldn't help but smile. *So that was where Tem got it from.*

"Very well."

He opened the door.

The dungeon was dark. His father wasn't here yet, but perhaps that was for the best. It would give them privacy for what came next. Without another word, Leo led them to the very last cell. When they reached it, Tem's mother gasped.

At the sound, Kronos opened his eyes.

"Daphne?" he whispered.

Tem's mother let out a strangled noise. "Yes." She pressed herself against the bars. "I'm here."

Leo immediately retrieved the keys from a hook on the wall and handed them to her. The lock slid open easily, and the moment the cell door opened, Daphne ran forward. She fell to her knees, cupping her palms around Kronos's face and lifting it to hers.

"I thought you left me," she whispered.

"I did not. I would never leave you."

She shook her head. "I thought that—"

"*Never*, Daphne."

Leo felt as if he were intruding on an extremely private moment. And yet he couldn't look away. Something burned in his chest at the sight of them together—something he knew he would have to face eventually.

"I never got to tell you about our daughter," Daphne whispered.

Leo straightened at the mention of Tem.

"I already knew," Kronos said.

"How?"

"I am not sure. I could…*feel* her. And you."

"And me?"

Kronos nodded. "Always you."

Leo turned away as they kissed.

The creature in his chest clawed at him, demanding his attention. He understood what Kronos meant—how he could *feel* Daphne, even when they were apart. Leo felt Tem now. It was as if they were tethered together, and when she moved, he yearned to move with her.

"Leo?" Daphne's voice broke him from his trance. "Would you help us?"

He turned to see Kronos attempting to stand. But the wires fused to his fingers held him back.

Leo stepped forward. "I'm sorry," he said. "I don't know how to remove those."

"They used a device to put them on," Kronos said.

Leo cast his gaze around the dungeon, searching for anything that looked like it could pry the wires from the basilisk's fingers. There was nothing. "I'm sorry—I—"

His father's voice cut him off. "Daphne?"

At the sound of her name, Tem's mother froze. She turned her head slowly, and Leo followed her gaze to see his father standing in the middle of the dungeon, flanked by two guards, his mouth twisted in surprise and disgust. His eyes flicked to Kronos. They narrowed.

"Him?"

Out of pure instinct, Leo placed his hand on Daphne's shoulder. But his father wasn't done.

"I should have known you left because of a *snake*."

Tem's mother didn't say a word, but her expression was response enough.

"It's no wonder your daughter acts the way she does," Maximus continued. "With you as an example, she clearly had no other choice."

Rage welled within Leo. "Father," he snapped. "Leave her alone."

His father turned to him. He let out a dark laugh. "Don't you understand, Thelonius? That *thing*"—he pointed at Kronos—"spawned your precious wife. You love a half breed. A *mutt*."

"Don't call her that."

"I'll call her whatever I wish."

Leo stepped forward. "You will call her by her *name*."

His father scoffed. "Hold your tongue, Thelonius."

But Leo was done taking orders. It was time to start giving them instead. "Hold *your* tongue, Father."

The dungeon was already freezing, yet somehow the temperature managed to drop.

Before his father could speak again, Leo snapped his fingers, and one of the guards stepped forward. "Bring me the device that will free the basilisks."

His father's eyes widened. "You would not dare."

Leo would dare. "Do as I say," he barked.

The guard disappeared. The one that remained stepped closer to his father, whose face darkened.

"Reckless," Maximus whispered. "Just like your mother."

Leo frowned. His father never spoke of his mother.

Before he could make sense of this, his father continued: "You will regret freeing them, Thelonius. Mark my words."

Leo shook his head. "The only thing I will regret is not doing it sooner."

"*Insolent boy.* I never should have crowned you king."

"Yet you did. Your reign is over, Father. I suggest you make peace with that now."

"You know nothing of *peace*, Thelonius. There will be no peace in this kingdom if you abolish this." He gestured at the imprisoned basilisks.

"There is no peace already," Leo said.

His father let out a bitter laugh. "Peace is an illusion. You will learn that one day."

But Leo shook his head. Peace may be an illusion, but so was power. His family hid behind their wealth—wealth they had stolen from creatures they deemed inferior. The cycle would end with him. He no longer cared what it cost him.

"Your reign is over," he said again, quietly this time.

The other guard returned, holding a metal device.

Leo pointed at Kronos. "Him first," Leo said. "And then the rest."

The guard hesitated for only a moment before obeying. As soon as the wires were removed, Kronos stood slowly, leaning on Daphne for support.

Leo made sure they were out of the cell before addressing the guard by his father. "Lock him up," he said coldly.

If his father hadn't been so shocked, he might have tried to run. Instead, his face went slack as the guard took him by his arms and steered him into the cell Kronos had just vacated. He was still silent as the bars clanked shut in front of him.

Leo turned to Tem's mother. "Go," he said. "Both of you."

Daphne looked at him for a long moment before slowly raising her hand and cupping his face with her palm the way she'd just done with Kronos. Leo stared into her eyes as she said, "Thank you."

His throat was suddenly tight. He thought she might walk away, but she didn't.

Instead, Tem's mother continued: "She left with him. But she loves you both." Her voice dropped to a whisper. "You will find your way back to each other."

It wasn't a prediction. It was a statement of fact.

Leo nodded. He could do nothing else.

Daphne dropped her hand and turned to Kronos. "Are you ready?"

In response, Kronos pulled her against him. They left the dungeon together, holding each other up.

Leo watched them go. As soon as they were gone, he turned to the cell. "Where is she?"

His father blinked. Leo noticed there was dried blood on his lips. Perhaps he had been injured after all. "Where is who?"

"You know exactly who I fucking mean."

His father smiled, and the blood cracked. "Now, now, Thelonius. Inquiring about a woman who is not your wife on your wedding night is in poor taste, even for you."

Leo's fingers tightened on the bars. "Answer. Me."

A heavy pause followed. Leo would not break it.

His father studied him in silence, his eyes roaming from head to toe. It felt as if he was appraising him, the way he had Leo's entire life. Only this time, Leo did not care to gain his approval. This time, nothing gave him greater pleasure than being the bane of his father's existence.

"She lives one village over," Maximus said quietly.

Leo frowned.

"Ah," his father murmured. "Not what you expected to hear."

Despite himself, Leo shook his head. One village over. All this time, she'd been just one village over. And she'd never—

"Aren't you going to ask why she left?"

Leo bristled. Of course he wanted to ask why Evelyn left. But a part of him—a larger part than he cared to admit—deeply feared the answer.

His father leaned closer. Leo saw the hate in his eyes—the sick satisfaction he got from tormenting his son. He answered the question Leo refused to ask: "I paid her."

Leo's stomach turned.

It was a lie. It had to be. Evelyn couldn't be bought. His father would say anything to hurt him, especially after being thrown in the dungeon by his own son.

"Don't you want to know how much it cost me?" his father whispered, holding Leo's stare. "Shall I tell you how much your love was worth to her?"

"You're lying. She wouldn't take a bribe."

His father let out a harsh laugh. "She *would*, my dear boy. And she did."

"I don't believe you."

"That is your mistake."

Leo shook his head. "Even if she did, I would understand. She had nothing. Her family was poor. Of course she—"

"Left you for the right price?"

Leo squared his shoulders. "You can hardly blame her considering what awaited her if she stayed. There was no future for us in our village. You made sure of that."

"And why would I want such a future for my son? She is a peasant, Thelonius. You are a prince."

"I am a *king*." He spat the words between the bars. "And you cannot tell me who to love."

A slow smile spread across his father's face. "That much is clear," he said quietly. "I should have learned long ago that you were incapable of rationality. But I, like you, chose to ignore what was in front of me."

"What do you mean by that?"

A vicious smile curled Maximus's lips. "Find her if you wish. Marry her if you must. But it will be harder than you think."

Leo's fingers tightened on the bars. "What will?"

"Knowing the truth."

With that, Leo left.

The castle was finally empty. Night had fully fallen, and any guests who were still alive or uninjured had long since gone home. Leo knew there would be a plethora of problems to solve in the morning. But there was only one thing he had to do tonight.

He flagged down the first carriage he saw and climbed inside numbly. His father's words beat rhythmically against his skull: *It will be harder than you think. Knowing the truth.*

But was it the truth? His father could be lying. He was *surely* lying. Leo refused to believe that Evelyn could be paid to leave him. Had the situation been reversed, no amount of money would have tempted him to leave. He had to believe she felt the same.

Leo rolled his shoulders. A pervasive ache was steadily penetrating his chest. The farther they traveled from the castle, the deeper the ache became. It was a physical pain, one that gripped his ribs and compressed his lungs, calling him back to Tem. But Tem had told him to find Evelyn.

Leo instructed the stable boy to drive through the night. He spent the hours wide awake, staring out the window, watching the stars in the sky. Was Tem watching the same ones? Or was she already deep beneath the mountain, sequestered in the caves with Caspen? It hurt Leo to picture her with him. He didn't want to imagine them together. He didn't want to think about the snake touching her the way he had, didn't want to imagine how she would cry Caspen's name instead of Leo's. But at least he knew she was safe. He knew, beyond doubt, that the only person who loved Tem as much as he did was Caspen.

It didn't make it any easier.

And what if she wasn't safe? What if the basic truth that Leo believed—that Caspen would protect Tem—wasn't true? Leo had seen Caspen's fury firsthand at the wedding. What if, one day, it was directed at her? The basilisk had ripped apart his own father. Kora knew what else he was capable of. Leo shuddered.

There was nothing to be done about it now. They had agreed to share her, but that agreement was void. Leo's future was one village over.

By the time the carriage finally slowed, the sun was rising. The village was small; Leo had visited it before on a royal tour. He made straight for the bakery, where he knew every villager must buy their bread. It took mere seconds to ask the baker about Evelyn. She usually spent the mornings down by the river, he informed Leo. Feeding the ducks.

Leo instructed the stable boy to pull over at the town square. As he exited the carriage, he rubbed his palms together, realizing they were sweating. He was still wearing his wedding suit. This was *insane*. Was he really about to see her?

At the thought, iron bars tightened around his chest.

So many mornings—he'd spent *so many mornings* sitting on the graveyard bench, waiting for Evelyn, hoping against hope that she would arrive. He'd never stopped loving her—never stopped praying she would show. Even as he fell for Tem, he'd still saved a piece of his heart for Evelyn. He couldn't help it; there was something inescapable about his first love. Even Tem had known that his heart was in two places. It was why she'd sent him to find Evelyn. She had known, better than him, what it was like to belong to two people at once.

Leo traversed the path to the river slowly, his legs heavy. A combination of sick anticipation and wild hope fought for dominance in his mind.

The rush of the river washed over him. He was nearly upon it.

Would she be happy to see him? What if she'd found someone new and he was too late? It had never occurred to Leo to court someone else after Evelyn. He'd only done so because the elimination process had forced him to. His love for Tem had been a happy accident, one that now—in light of what he was about to do—he didn't know how to contend with.

The river was loud; he'd reached the edge of the bank. Morning sunlight streamed into his eyes, framing the girl in front of him.

Evelyn.

Honey-blond hair. Just as he remembered it. The curve of her shoulder, the arch of her neck. She looked just as she did the last time he'd seen her. How long had it been? Months. A year nearly. He'd been robbed of a summer with her—robbed of the chance to see her skin tan, to see her hair lighten in the sun. They'd made plans to visit the sea together. Leo had never been, and neither had Evelyn. It was the first place they were going to go once they were free of the village—free of his father. *Sand between our toes, Leo*, Evelyn had said. *Don't you wonder what it would feel like?*

Yes. He'd wondered. Perhaps now he would find out.

And yet Leo couldn't move.

Something was holding him back, preventing him from taking even a half step in her direction. It was as if an invisible chain were wrapped around his ankles, bolting him to the ground. He needed to go forward. But going forward meant solidifying the gap between him and Tem. The moment he approached Evelyn, everything would change between them. The thought physically pained him. But Tem herself had told him to do this. So Leo stepped forward.

"Evelyn."

Evelyn looked up at him, her lips parting in surprise.

"Leo?"

CHALLENGERS

———•••✳••——

This scene is NOT CANON, meaning it does not occur within the plot of the book you just read. It is a scene inspired by the movie *Challengers* starring Zendaya, Josh O'Connor, and Mike Faist. It was written on a thirteen-hour plane ride back from Venice, Italy, after the author had consumed at least nine glasses of free cabernet sauvignon. If you were to place it somewhere in the book, it could serve as a different ending to the conversation that Caspen, Tem, and Leo have in the cave. In that scene, Leo says, "I just…want you while I can have you," after which Caspen would say the opening line below. The rest is history!

P LEASE," CASPEN SCOFFED. "YOU CANNOT TOUCH HER AS I DO."

"So teach me."

Tem's mouth fell open. To her surprise, Leo didn't retract his statement. He merely lifted his chin, looking at Caspen with stubborn resolve. The two men stared at each other, and Tem stared at them.

Tem broke the silence. "I don't think that's a good idea."

Leo's eyes moved to hers. They narrowed. "Why not? He taught *you*, didn't he?"

Leo had a point there. Caspen was nothing if not a good teacher. But this was unthinkable. Tem couldn't fathom a universe in which the men before her would get along, much less collaborate on something as paramount as this.

Caspen rolled his shoulders. "And how do you propose I teach you?"

A pause. Leo clenched his jaw. "Show me."

The basilisk scoffed. Tem held her breath.

"*Show* you?"

"You heard me," Leo snapped.

Caspen raised an eyebrow. A loaded silence followed.

Nothing about this conversation was even remotely normal. Had Leo really just asked Caspen to *show him how to touch her*? It seemed like something out of a dream. Tem had no idea what would happen next. She couldn't read Caspen's expression; he seemed to be considering something. He was regarding Leo with reluctant curiosity, almost as if he were intrigued by the proposition.

"Very well," Caspen said slowly. "I suppose you could watch us—"

"I'm not *fucking* interested in watching," Leo said sharply.

Caspen crossed his arms. "Neither am I."

Tem closed her eyes. This was absurd. She was tired. Tired of people fighting over her, tired of being defined and influenced and manipulated by *men*. She refused to let them control her anymore. Even the ones she loved.

Tem opened her eyes, training her gaze on Caspen. "Stop it."

Caspen blinked.

Before he could respond, she turned to Leo. "You too. Stop it."

They both stared at her.

Tem continued. "Considering this decision directly involves me, don't you think you should be asking *me* how to proceed?"

Caspen's eyebrows rose a fraction of an inch. His eyes flicked to Leo, whose face bore a similarly incredulous expression. Neither of them was used to taking orders from her—or anyone else for that matter.

But this was too important. If they were going to cross this line together, Tem needed to know that they would obey.

"*I'm* in charge," she said.

They were silent.

"Say it." Tem crossed her arms. "Both of you." She knew they would say it. She only wondered who would break first. To her surprise, it was Caspen.

"You are in charge, Tem," the basilisk said, bowing his head. "Of course."

Tem turned expectantly to Leo.

"Yes," he said just as quietly. "You're in charge."

"Good."

Now that they had established this basic rule, Tem had to figure out how to proceed. She glanced at Leo. This was never going to work if he remained this tense. At the thought, an idea occurred to Tem. She turned to Caspen. "Can you make him calm?"

He blinked slowly. "I could."

Leo's eyes flicked between them. "What does that mean?"

Caspen tilted his head. "I have the ability to influence your mood."

"You can make me feel calm?"

"Yes. With your consent."

Leo let out a harsh laugh. "Let me guess. You could do it without my consent too."

"I could," Caspen said again. "But I would not."

Tem knew it was the truth, even if Leo didn't.

"I don't want you in my mind," Leo said bluntly.

"I would not need to access your mind in order to make you calm. It is merely a sensation."

"How do I know you won't control me?" Leo insisted.

"That is not the nature of my power. Even if I wanted to control you, I could not. You are human. I can only access the minds of other basilisks."

Leo shook his head. "I don't trust you."

That was no surprise.

"In that case," Caspen said smoothly, turning to Tem, "I suggest you make him calm instead."

"Me?"

"Yes. You are part basilisk. You can do everything I can do."

It had never occurred to Tem that she could manipulate someone's emotions the way Caspen did. It was a fascinating thought and one she wished she could explore at a rather less pivotal moment. But as it stood, she would have to explore it now.

"How would I do that?"

"You must first feel calm yourself," Caspen said. "Then you can transfer that feeling to him. It will be easier if you touch him."

He gave instructions in the same reserved, factual manner he always did.

Tem turned to Leo. "Do you want me to do this?"

Now Leo hesitated. "Will I still be…me?"

Caspen answered before Tem could. "You will still be you. Only your mood will be influenced. It will not affect your judgment or your ability to make decisions."

Tem found that was an accurate description of the sensation. She thought back to the time when Caspen had taken away her desire—how she'd been angry with him but had been able to tell him to put it back.

Leo's eyes slid to Caspen's. Tem reminded herself that to the human prince, Caspen was a danger, an enemy. It wasn't natural for the two of them to interact like this. It wasn't natural for them to interact *at all*. Yet Leo was Leo. Tem recognized the flash of haughty determination that brightened his eyes as he turned to her.

"Do it," he said firmly.

Tem nodded, although the task seemed impossible. She was anything but calm right now. She felt agitated and eager and nervous, as if she were about to take an important test. It was not exactly a relaxing state of mind. So instead of focusing on herself, Tem focused on Leo. She thought about how much she cared about him, how deeply she wanted this experience to be a positive one for them both. She thought about how she would do anything to make sure he felt loved by her and how she knew he would do the same.

Finally, calm came.

When it did, she found she didn't need Caspen's instructions. She was able to feel for Leo's mind in the same way she felt for the basilisk's. It was not the same corridor she shared with Caspen; instead of a two-way street, the connection with Leo felt distinctly one-sided, as if she were viewing his consciousness through a window. She could not access his mind, and he could not access hers. But she found that she could send her calmness through the window, as if it were a basket of eggs from the farm.

The moment she did so, Leo's eyes closed. "*Oh*," he whispered. Then he smiled.

Tem glanced questioningly at Caspen, who nodded his approval. "Good, Tem."

Leo opened his eyes. "Is this how you feel when you're with him?" he asked her.

Even his voice was different. The sharp, teasing tone was gone, replaced by a languid, rugged murmur Tem had never heard him use before. It was sexy, she realized.

"Sometimes," she answered. "But only if I ask him to make me feel that way."

"It's a wonder you don't ask him all the time."

Tem wanted to laugh. "How do you feel?"

Leo smiled. "Calm. Just like you said I would." He pointed at Caspen. "And significantly more relaxed around him."

Tem nodded. "Good." She turned to Caspen. *Have you done this before?*

Tem wasn't even sure what she was asking. Had Caspen been with a man before? Or two people at once? His answer was all-encompassing *Yes.*

Tem didn't know why she'd bothered. Caspen had done everything before. He was a basilisk after all. There was nothing they considered taboo or off-limits. This situation probably didn't even rank in the grand scheme of his sexual experiences. In a way, Tem was glad for that. She herself had no idea what to expect and could feel herself getting anxious at the thought of what might happen. But then she remembered she had to stay calm for Leo, and she immediately recentered her thinking.

Was it so strange really to be with the men she loved? What exactly was Tem so afraid of? Caspen and Leo were deeply important to her. She loved them, and she knew they loved her. This was just an extension of that love.

But how to start?

Tem was in charge. So she did the only thing she could think to do.

She crossed to the mat, sitting on the edge and looking up at them expectantly. They sat too, Caspen to her left, Leo to her right. She turned first to Caspen, looking deep into his golden eyes, which were rapidly turning black.

Will you keep him safe? Tem asked.

Of course.

She needed to know that there was no danger of Caspen transitioning. It was one thing when it happened around Tem—she was used to it, and she would survive it—but it was quite another for it to happen around Leo. Tem had no idea whether Caspen could control his urges when faced with such an emotionally charged situation. The stakes were far too high for her to proceed without a guarantee. She wanted no harm to come to Leo; she would never forgive Caspen if anything bad happened to the human prince, and Caspen surely knew it.

Are you sure? If he gets hurt—

I will not hurt him, Tem. I understand he is precious to you.

Tem felt a rush of pure gratitude at his words.

You are precious to me too.

He smiled, and Tem was struck suddenly by the enormity of what Caspen was willing to do for her—what *both* of them were willing to do for her. Perhaps it was time to reward them for their loyalty.

Tem turned to Leo. She kissed him. He tasted like the sky before it rained; he tasted like summer, like *air*. His tongue immediately found hers. It was as if the calmness she was sending him made him even more self-assured than he usually was, as if it had removed his last shred of self-control. Tem was vaguely aware of Caspen's hands on her back. He was unlacing her dress.

She bit Leo's bottom lip. He did the same.

Tem unbuttoned his shirt, pulling it from his shoulders and letting it fall to the floor. His trousers followed shortly after. His cock was already hard, but she didn't touch him yet.

Instead, she turned to Caspen. She undressed him as she kissed him, sliding her palms down his torso and untying his trousers to free his cock.

Behind her, Leo finished what the basilisk had started, tugging her dress down so her back was exposed. He pressed his lips to her shoulder blades, and Tem shuddered. A moment later, her dress was on the ground. Only her underclothing remained, and Leo made sure that came off too. Tem pulled away from Caspen.

She sat there, naked between them, reveling in the way they were looking at her.

"Touch me."

It was an order for them both. But Caspen was the first to reach for her, brushing his fingers over her breast.

"She can come just from this," he said quietly, pinching her nipple with his knuckles.

"Is that right?" Leo said.

He mimicked the motion on her other breast, and Tem sighed. "More," she gasped. It was all she could manage.

Both men leaned in at the same time, and Tem closed her eyes as their mouths replaced their fingers. She could do nothing but surrender. It felt *so* unbelievably good. There could be no greater pleasure than this, no greater joy. Already, they were moving in tandem. Already, they were aligned.

Tem had never felt so stimulated, so *aroused*. She held them against her as they sucked her nipples, each of them doing it in their own perfect way. Caspen was sensual, his tongue more involved than his teeth. Leo was assertive, his golden fangs pressing into the soft tissue of her breast. Both felt good. Both felt right.

Tem was rapidly becoming wet. No sooner had she realized it than Caspen sat up straight. Leo sat up too, both of them watching as she let her legs tilt open.

Caspen's hiss immediately filled the cave, and Tem sent an extra soothing wave of calm toward Leo, who merely raised an eyebrow in mild curiosity at the sound. Then his attention returned to her, and both men stared at her center.

"After you," Caspen said softly.

Time slowed as Leo extended his hand. He didn't even touch her at first. His fingertips paused an inch away from her clitoris, and for a long moment, he simply looked at her. Then he slipped his fingers inside her, and the world fell away.

"She has the prettiest cunt I've ever fucking seen," Leo whispered.

Caspen's mouth twitched. "Yes," he said. "She does."

"This"—Leo rubbed her clitoris with two fingers—"I dream about it."

"As do I."

"And here." Leo's fingers dove deep into her wetness, and Tem let out a desperate moan. "If I could drown in it, I would."

Caspen's smile widened. "As would I."

There was no jealousy between them, no competition or ill will. There was only Tem and their dedication to her.

"Try this." Caspen took Leo's hand in his, pressing his palm flat against her clitoris. Tem immediately arched her back at the magnitude of the stimulation. Her hands went to her breasts. She needed more. She needed everything.

Leo's eyebrows shot up at her reaction. "Incredible," he said. He did the motion again and again, rubbing her with his palm, his long fingers flat against her stomach. Caspen merely watched, his eyes trained on her, making sure Leo gave her everything she needed.

Tem was close. But Caspen had other plans.

"Not yet," he said. "Make her wait."

Leo's lips quirked into a smirk. "Very well."

His motions halted, and Tem whimpered.

Leo flicked her clitoris lightly.

"Are you wet for us, Tem?" he murmured, a shadow of his usual smirk back on his face.

"Yes," she answered obediently.

Leo pressed his lips to her inner thigh. Caspen did the same on her other leg.

"Who do you want to taste you first?" Leo asked.

"You."

"Say my name."

"Leo," she said. "Please."

His smirk deepened. Leo's long fingers wrapped around her thighs, pulling them apart. He lowered his head, and Tem's eyes met Caspen's as Leo's tongue met her center.

Does it feel good?

Caspen's question barely registered. Of course it felt good. It felt *incredible*.

In response, Tem shut her eyes and moaned.

They took turns tasting her, sucking and licking her until she could barely take it any longer. Caspen would perform a motion—like stroking her clitoris with the length of his tongue—and Leo would do the same. Eventually, Tem couldn't tell them apart. She only knew the intense and searing ecstasy that came from having two people worship you at once.

They were attentive and caring. They belonged to her.

Every time she wanted something, Caspen said it aloud, and Leo did it. The three of them established a rhythm together, until finally Tem was falling apart beneath them.

It was Leo ultimately who reaped the reward.

"She is close," Caspen said as Leo's mouth dipped once more between her legs. "Bring her there."

His hand was at the nape of Leo's neck, holding his head down. Tem had a sudden flashback to when Caspen had held Rowe's head down in a similar manner. Only this time, his grip was gentle; he was merely guiding Leo, not forcing him, only using his strength to ensure Tem's pleasure and, by extension, Leo's.

There was no question that the human prince was enjoying himself. He was burying himself in her, his tongue eager and willing to taste every drop of wetness. Her first orgasm was sudden—an urgent push that whipped through her like lightning, leaving her breathless. When she finally rode it out, Tem opened her eyes to see them both staring at her, each of them wearing identical expressions of hunger on their faces. Leo licked her wetness from his lips before turning to Caspen.

"Well?" he asked.

Caspen raised an eyebrow.

"Well, what?"

"I'd say she liked that, wouldn't you?"

Caspen looked at Tem—who was sprawled blissfully on the mat—and laughed outright. "Yes. I would say so."

Leo's mouth widened in a haughty smile. He'd made her come after all. He deserved to feel victorious. But the night was not over yet.

"What do you want next, Tem?" Caspen asked.

Tem looked up at both of them, her knees wide open, her body on display. There was only one thing she wanted, and in the aftermath of her climax, she was just brave enough to ask for it. "I want to watch you kiss."

It was beyond the scope of what they'd agreed on. It had nothing to do with Caspen teaching Leo how to touch her. It was selfish and indulgent and entirely based on that fleeting night in her childhood bedroom, when she'd touched herself to the thought of them together.

Neither prince seemed shocked by her request.

Perhaps they expected this of her. Perhaps they knew she had fantasized about them both. Perhaps they had fantasized as well. Nobody could deny how good they looked together. Leo was blond; Caspen's hair was dark. Sun and moon. Day and night. Tem wanted to see them together—wanted opposites to attract. It seemed a natural thing to her. Surely, it would be natural for them.

"Very well." Caspen shrugged easily, his gaze sliding to Leo. "If the prince can handle it."

A slow, devilish smile twisted Leo's lips. Caspen had said the one thing that would guarantee Leo's participation: he'd presented the kiss as a challenge. Leo was competitive; he was prideful and headstrong, and he never backed down from a fight. Tem wondered if Caspen knew this about Leo—had sensed it somehow, as he'd sensed so many things about her. He had an intuitive understanding of humans after all; it was part of his nature to assess and to pursue.

There was an additional factor at play here: not even Leo was immune to the charm of the basilisk. Their job was to seduce anyone with a heartbeat. Caspen possessed a gravitational pull that would affect even those who were predisposed to resist him. Leo was one such person. Tem knew the fine line between love and hate better than anyone. The men in her life had always been on opposing sides, but why should that continue? Why shouldn't they come together, just this once, for her?

Leo's reply came just as easily as Caspen's had. "I can handle anything."

There was a pause in which they all seemed to realize what was about to happen.

To Tem's surprise, Caspen did not make the first move. Instead, it was Leo who leaned forward and wrapped his fingers around the back of Caspen's neck.

Tem watched as the prince kissed the basilisk.

It was an incredible view. If Tem hadn't been soaking wet already, she would have quickly become so just by watching their naked bodies together, knowing they could taste her on each other's tongues. Tem leaned back on the mat, propping herself up to watch them from the best angle possible. Her fingers found her clitoris, and she touched herself slowly to the sight of them.

Caspen's body curled forward. His tongue parted Leo's lips, coaxing him open to receive what he had to offer. Leo took him willingly, his neck arched, his shoulders relaxed. Tem's eyes traced his jawline, marveling at the way it mirrored Caspen's. She couldn't believe they were both here, that they were both *hers*. It was exactly as she'd imagined it.

When they pulled apart, Tem shook her head. "Again," she said.

Caspen didn't hesitate. He grabbed Leo's neck and kissed him again.

Tem sat up, driving her fingers deeper, watching them from mere inches away. She could smell Caspen's smoky scent, intermixed with Leo's cologne. They complemented each other, she realized. It only turned her on more.

Join us, Tem.

Tem tucked her hand under Leo's chin, pulling him away from Caspen and pressing her lips to his. Caspen's hands went to their necks, pushing their heads together, solidifying their union. A moment later, his mouth joined theirs.

All three of them kissed.

It was simple between them—like music. This was a language they all spoke, a dance they all knew how to do. Leo's cock was hard, and so was Caspen's, and Tem felt the sudden urge to touch them both.

And why shouldn't she? She had two hands, did she not? One for each of them.

Tem reached into their laps, her fingers first finding Leo's cock and then Caspen's, feeling how hard they both were for her. Neither reacted at first. It was only when she began to stroke them that Leo's eyelids fluttered and he let out a groan of surrender, his head falling back in ecstasy. Tem kissed his neck, and so did Caspen. The basilisk's hand joined hers, stroking Leo's cock at the same time she stroked his.

Leo moaned, "Fuck—*fuck*."

Caspen let out a gentle sound of amusement. *He is rather vocal.*

Tem smiled. *Yes. He is.*

You like that about him.

Yes.

Why?

It's nice to hear how he feels.

It was merely a fact about Leo—not a dig toward Caspen. Still, there was no mistaking the regret that tinged his response. *I am glad he fulfills you in that way.*

Tem didn't know what to say to that, so she said nothing.

She'd always known that they each provided her with different things, that Caspen was far more reserved than the human prince. Being with them together only reinforced those differences. It wasn't a bad thing—merely the truth. There were only so many similarities a basilisk and a human could have. It didn't matter to Tem; she loved them both.

Without thinking, Tem bent down to take Leo's cock into her mouth. Caspen accommodated the change, pulling her by her hips so she was stretched out between them. His hand was on the back of her neck, guiding her up and down Leo's length, ensuring she took every inch of him. Leo continued to moan, his own hands twisting into her hair, holding her between his legs. Tem was, as ever, a merciful ruler.

Pleasure. It was all that mattered to her—to *them*. There was no safer place in the world than here with the men she loved.

Caspen's knees slid under Tem's, opening her legs. She arched her back, lifting her ass, knowing what he was about to do. Still, she moaned as Caspen entered her, Leo's cock still in her mouth. And now Caspen's was inside her too. She couldn't believe how they *filled* her, how exhilarating it was to take them both.

Are two cocks not enough for you, Tem?

It was enough for her. It was.

But Tem couldn't answer him—couldn't even find the air to breathe. With Caspen behind her and Leo before her, she could do nothing but moan as they did everything she'd ever wanted them to do to her. They were the two most relentless men she knew. To have them both at the same time was nearly unbearable.

It was too much. And not enough.

It was everything Tem had ever needed—two men, both hers, two men who wanted her more than they wanted anyone else. Two men who would do anything for her.

With each thrust of Caspen's hips, Leo's cock went deeper and deeper down her throat.

"*Kora,*" she heard the human prince whisper. "This is—"

The rest of his sentence was lost in a moan as Caspen's hand gripped Tem's head and pushed her mouth all the way down Leo's shaft. Tem didn't have to see Leo to know the expression on his face. She knew how he looked when he was close, how his jaw tensed and his muscles flexed, how his chin tilted up in defiance. But Tem would not let him have it so easily. Just when he was about to finish, she straightened, pushing herself up so they were face-to-face.

"Such a fucking tease," Leo whispered. His hands grabbed her waist, holding her in place. He tilted his head to look at Caspen. "Does she tease you?"

Tem felt Caspen's breath on her shoulder. His hands were also on her, just below Leo's. "No," he said.

Leo raised his eyebrows. "No?"

Caspen's grip tightened on her hips. "I tease her."

"How?"

In reply, Caspen lifted Tem so only the tip of his cock remained inside her. She gasped at the sudden change, and Leo's pupils dilated at the sound. "Do you like that?" Caspen murmured against her ear.

Tem did like that, being teased. She liked it when she could barely hang on to any remaining shreds of dignity—when she was on the brink of being pushed to her limits. And she liked teasing in return, pushing someone *else* to their limits, wielding her power.

But for now, Caspen wielded his.

He thrust into her slowly, allowing Tem only an inch or two of his cock at a time.

"More," she moaned. "More...*please* more."

Caspen gave her more. But just barely.

His restraint was astonishing, as always. Tem should know by now that the basilisk's patience was endless, that he would not be swayed by her plea. He knew exactly how to tease her, how to take her to the edge without letting her finish—how to make her *ache*.

"Remarkable," Leo breathed as he watched.

Tem could do nothing but take it, nothing but surrender to the ungodly sensation that Caspen was giving her. It wasn't until Tem was a moment away that Caspen finally let her have it, pulling her all the way down so his cock filled her completely. Tem threw her head back, letting herself experience her climax without an ounce of shame. There was only Leo to see her, only Caspen to hear her. What could be better than unfolding in front of them?

The heel of Caspen's hand found the back of her neck, and a moment later, her head was once more between Leo's legs. They created a perfect circle, Caspen, Tem, and Leo. The time for restraint had passed; the time for gratification had arrived.

The three of them moved in tandem, Caspen behind her, Leo before her. Tem knew they would reach their apex together—that they would achieve the most perfect pinnacle imaginable. There was no point in resisting, no point in delaying. They had finally accepted the ultimate truth.

Tem felt them finish at the same time, Leo in her mouth and Caspen inside her, and with their climaxes inevitably came her own. They were moving, gasping, *breaking* together, falling apart into each other's bodies like waves on the shore. They experienced it as one—all of them—surging along a singular channel of ecstasy.

As soon as it was over, Caspen pulled Tem up by her hair so her shoulders were pressed against his chest. He settled back on his knees, Tem in his lap. She could feel his heartbeat, as steady as ever. As soon as she was upright, her eyes met Leo's. His eyes were hooded, his expression one of disbelieving bliss.

"Tem," he whispered.

Even now, she was his only focus. Even with another cock inside her, Leo still wanted her. "Leo," she whispered back.

Kiss him.

The command came from Caspen, and Tem was glad to follow it. She leaned forward, pulling Leo into a deep kiss, letting him know that even with another cock inside her, she still needed him. Tem wondered if the prince had ever tasted himself before, if any of the other girls had kissed him on the lips after he came in their mouths. He was tasting himself now, and she was sure he liked it.

Caspen was inside her—hard again, thrusting.

Tem gripped Leo's shoulders, holding herself steady.

"Leo," she whispered again, this time against his lips.

In response, Leo kissed her but only briefly. A moment later, he pulled away, his eyes raking hungrily over Tem's body, staring at the place where she took Caspen's cock. His nostrils flared.

Perhaps Leo *was* interested in watching after all.

Tem wondered if part of him liked seeing her with someone else, if his competitive streak secretly craved this—if he needed to know that the person he desired was desirable too. She half expected him to pull her off the basilisk. Instead, he leaned back to get an even better view.

If this was what he wanted, Tem would gladly give it to him.

Caspen's fingers wrapped around her throat, arching her back and displaying her to the prince. He thrust into her steadily, his pace unhurried, taking his time. Tem knew Leo was seeing everything: how her cheeks flushed as another man fucked her, how her body reacted to Caspen's penetration. The prince didn't seem to mind. Tem had stopped making him calm long ago—sometime when they were all kissing. Whatever emotions he felt now were completely his own. And it would appear that he felt good. Because eventually, Leo joined in.

Caspen fucked her while Leo touched her, his hands on her breasts, his lips on her neck. Tem gave herself over to it, to *them*. She yelped as Leo's head dipped down and he sucked her nipple between his teeth, pulling him even closer, savoring every second of this rapture.

If Leo's mouth hadn't been occupied, she knew he would have been talking. But he was torturing her in his own way, squeezing and biting her nipples until she squirmed against his grip. Every time she wanted to break, Caspen held her in place. They worked together, the two princes, to keep her in line.

Just when Tem couldn't take any more, Leo's fingers found her clitoris. He pressed against her, and she gasped. At her reaction, he bent down, using his mouth instead.

Caspen grunted, and Tem knew Leo's tongue was on the base of his shaft. He was pleasuring them both, sucking on Tem's clitoris while putting pressure on Caspen's cock. It was an assertion of his power, a way to remind them of his role in this. Tem welcomed it, threading her hands into his hair, holding him between her legs.

A moment later, she came. Caspen did too.

Their combined wetness coated his cock, and Tem knew Leo could taste it. When he raised his head, he kissed Tem once more. For a while, that was all they did. Then Caspen lifted her off his cock, setting her between them. It was then that Tem realized Leo was hard again. Before she could reach for him, Caspen did so instead.

She watched as his hand found Leo's cock, his fingers wrapping around the shaft and pumping in steady, even strokes. Leo let him do this, his eyes still hooded, his shoulders relaxed.

What are you doing?

Rewarding the prince.

Tem understood.

Leo had done well; he'd been a willing participant, and now it was his turn to receive his prize. Caspen's head dipped down, and Leo's eyebrows shot up.

"Fuck," he said hoarsely.

It was an amazing thing to see.

Tem touched herself as she watched them, bringing herself to orgasm long before they were even close to done. Leo alternated between staring at her and staring at Caspen, his long fingers grasping the back of the basilisk's head as he slid his mouth up and down the prince's cock.

"Tem," Leo whispered, his other hand reaching for her. "Come here."

Tem was happy to obey. She leaned in, kissing him softly, feeling the tension building in his body. Tem knew exactly how it felt to be pleasured by Caspen—how overwhelming and unrelenting the basilisk could be. For Leo to experience it for the first time, here with her, was an indulgence Tem hadn't known she needed.

Tem's hand joined Leo's. They held Caspen's head together.

The prince was close. His skin was slick with sweat, his breath coming in desperate gasps. Tem had seen him like this before, in the carriage. Only now it was Caspen bringing him to the brink, Caspen sending him into infinity.

"You can do it, Leo," Tem murmured. "Let go."

"Fuck," he whispered.

Tem savored the word, taking it from his lips and claiming it for herself. She pressed her mouth to his neck, nipping at his skin until it bruised. Leo's head fell back, and she knew he was finishing.

"*Fuck*," the prince cried as he came.

Caspen didn't swallow.

Instead, he straightened, reaching for Tem's face and coaxing her jaw open with his thumbs. Then he leaned down and released Leo's cum into her mouth. Tem swallowed as it slid down her throat, the act a perfect mirror of when Caspen had given her his venom.

It was so simple, so easy.

Tem loved tasting what the basilisk had brought forth from the human prince. There was nothing better than the fruits of Caspen's labor—better still when they were Leo's.

When she had downed every last drop, Tem turned to Leo, who was watching them in awe.

She pulled his face toward hers before slipping her tongue into his mouth. Leo accepted it willingly—*eagerly*. They kissed for a long time, and eventually, they were horizontal once more.

They lay together, all three of them, Tem in the middle, both of them facing her. Leo's hand rested on her stomach, Caspen's just below.

Caspen looked at Leo.

"You did well, Prince."

Leo propped himself up on his elbow. "My name is Leo. Anyone who's had my cock down their throat ought to call me that."

Tem had never seen Caspen roll his eyes. But he did so now, and the sight was so out of character she couldn't help but giggle.

"Your arrogance is unparalleled," the basilisk said. There was no bite to his words; he seemed just as amused as Tem was.

She felt Leo shrug. "I'm going to take that as a compliment."

"It is not one."

Tem grabbed Caspen's jaw, then Leo's. "Can you both shut up?"

Caspen's eyes returned to hers. With his mind, he asked, *Are you happy?*

She answered his question with her own. *Are you?*

Caspen's eyes traveled over her face with utter tenderness. *Endlessly.*

Tem didn't know when she fell asleep. The last thing she heard before she slipped into blackness were four simple words, spoken by Caspen and clearly meant for Leo:

"Take care of her."

When Tem woke, Caspen was gone.

ACKNOWLEDGMENTS

First and foremost, I wish to thank my parents. They showed me what it means to live an extraordinary life. Simply put: the best parts of me exist because of them.

I'd also like to thank my sister: my north star, my guiding light. It is an honor to walk through life with you. You are the pinnacle I aspire to—the lighthouse that always calls me home.

Anyone who knows me knows I have few close friends. But the few I have are exceedingly precious to me. Rather than name them, I'll impart a basic cliché: you know who you are. And you know I love you dearly.

Writing may be a solitary act, but publishing is not. I am forever grateful to my agent, Haley Heidemann, whose early advocacy landed my book on the desk of my exceptional editor, Christa Désir. That's when I knew my life was about to change. And change it has, thanks to the enthusiasm and support of the entire team at Bloom Books. Many hands have touched this project since, including the capable folks at WME Books, namely Suzannah Ball, who found *Kiss of the Basilisk* its UK home at Quercus. Many thanks to Anne Perry and everyone at Arcadia who worked so hard on the UK edition, and also to the talented designers at Sourcebooks, without whom the gorgeous cover would not exist.

I would be remiss not to acknowledge everyone who has supported my online journey. I started @oxfordlemon at an extremely low point in my life, when I felt I had nowhere else to turn. The love and support you guys have shown me has been, in a word, tremendous. I cannot thank you enough. Please know it is my greatest honor to make you proud. Trust me when I say this is only the beginning.

Lastly, I'd like to thank Chad. I owe my life to you. I will not waste it.

ABOUT THE AUTHOR

Lindsay Straube is a writer living in Portland, Oregon. She drinks tequila with lemon and watches TV with subtitles on. On any given Tuesday, you can find her at the movies. Come say hi:

Instagram: @oxfordlemon
Website: oxfordlemon.com